MISTS OF ELISTA

THE COMPLETE SERIES

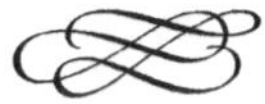

CLARA WILS

Gryphon's Gate Publishing

Gryphon's Gate Publishing
550 King St. N.
PO Box 42088 Conestoga
Waterloo, ON
N2L 6K5

Print ISBN: 978-1-990587-39-9

BONDS AND BLOOD

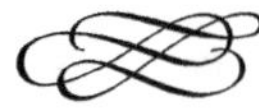

THE MISTS OF ELISTA TRILOGY, BOOK 1

CHAPTER 1

Where does my story start? Oh, it was quite some time ago. So much has happened, let me see what I can remember.

I suppose it starts in the year I had three names. Before that is... mostly prologue. But that year, everything changed. That year, my first name... was Sara. A normal name, a common name, and definitely not the name of a True-Bonded. Yet on that breezy spring day in the twenty-ninth year of the reign of Queen Whitewing, it was my dearest and deepest hope that I'd soon lose that name.

I prayed to the High Spirits that today I'd be Chosen.

At twenty years old, it was my last chance. I'd be too old next year. There were only a few others my age in the milling group of perhaps two hundred youths in the Miraline village square. The rest were younger, fifteen or sixteen, and being particularly tall, I stood a full head above most here. Few returned if they weren't Chosen in their first couple years. Yet I was determined. I had to be Chosen, because for me... there was nothing else.

I had no desire — nor skill — to be a tradesperson or a farmer. I definitely didn't want to be "some man's wife". When I married it would be for love, not to have a man support me because I lacked in skill or education.

To be fair, I didn't lack education. If anything, I far exceeded most in that department. I was the foster daughter of a pair of scholars who worked at the Library of Miraline, and had received the benefit of their vast learning. I wasn't bright, like my foster sister — the actual daughter of my foster parents — and hadn't picked things up quickly. But they'd been persistent in their attempts to teach me and eventually most of it had sunk in.

I wasn't pretty, or witty, or charming like some girls. I was educated but had no real-life skills. If I wasn't Chosen...

No.

I have to be Chosen.

The mayor of Miraline — a True-Bonded artist named Kestrel — mounted the platform at the far end of the square and a hush fell over the murmuring crowd of youths. Even the encircling ring of parents went quiet. My parents weren't there. My birth parents had died when I was young. My foster parents were... as usual... at the library, working. It's not that they didn't care, they did, but their studies were important and usually came first. I'd long ago accepted that.

The mayor was resplendent in a green dress, which set off her fiery red hair. Smiling, she raised her hands and the crowd knew she was about to speak.

"Families from Miraline and the villages of the North. You all know what today means, so I will not belabor the details. Instead, I welcome our wonderful companions from The Mistlands, the Lumani, to begin The Choosing!"

And there they were.

The Lumani floated over the crowd of youths, appearing as

glowing orbs, anywhere from the size of a small coin to that of a grapefruit. They were creatures of light and Anima, the mystical energy of The Mistlands. And I hoped and prayed that one of these Lumani would Choose me. My ticket out of this town and into a Noble House. It wasn't the most selfless and noble of goals, but supposedly that didn't matter. What mattered was a person's spirit. I hoped one of them would sense something in my spirit today.

However, of the almost two dozen or so Lumani floating over us, none headed in my direction. The Choosing could take some time. The Lumani might stop and consider several people, using their mind-voice to interview them, before finally settling on their Chosen.

Signaling, waving, jumping up and down, none of these things were permitted. We had to stand there as still as possible for the Lumani, as they hovered over us.

The time ticked by. The large clock, to one side of the city square, slowly marked the seconds... then minutes. Two hours were allotted for The Choosing, and I was sweating with anxiety after the first hour passed. By my count, thirteen children had been Chosen by then. That left — at a quick count — ten Lumani.

To take my mind off the minutes ticking down on my fate, I tried to observe and categorize the Lumani still floating around.

Three were rather large. We were told the size of a Lumani meant nothing, but most people still assumed the larger the Lumani the more powerful it was. Of these three, two were darker shades, a deep rose-maroon and a stunning purple. I'd love to be Chosen by that one, such a royal color! The last of the three was a pale yellow, near to white.

Five Lumani were of various middling sizes, like apples and plums. Of those, two stood out: bright red and sky-blue.

The last two were quite small, the size of cherries. One of those was a mottled red and blue, and the last a soft cream-yellow, and... it was heading my way!

I vibrated with excitement, but tried to be as still as possible as they floated closer, heading straight for me.

Then they stopped, hovering over the young girl in front of me. She blinked up at the tiny glowing orb. "Oh, hello!"

I caught one side of the strange conversation that then took place.

"I want to go on adventures! Perhaps be a sea captain or wilderness explorer!" the girl said. Then she paused as she listened to the Lumani speak into her mind.

"Because there's so much of this world to see. Wouldn't you want to see the world?"

Another pause.

"Ah... well... I'm quick to learn new things."

Ha! Everyone said that.

"And... I... uh... I have a heart for adventure and excitement. Yeah, I'm brave, that's it!" She seemed to be struggling now, reaching for the *right* answer.

Then suddenly the girl's shoulders fell. "Oh," she said a bit forlorn. "I... understand."

She'd been turned down. Perhaps another Lumani would Choose her, but not this little yellow one.

That Lumani began to float away. I panicked, my hope crumbling. I pictured myself reaching out to them, all my desires expressed in one imagined gesture.

The Lumani stopped, then circled back to me.

Oh Spirits! This is it! This was the first time one had even stopped to speak with me. I had to make a good impression I had to... but suddenly my mind drained of any useful and intelligent information and I was left a gibbering idiot.

"Hello?" I said pre-emptively.

Hello, child. The voice was calm, sedate, but resonating power.

Oh Spirits, oh Spirits, oh Spirits! They were actually talking to me!

Tell me, child, what do you want?

"I... ah..." Bloody bones! What did I want? "I..." Oh no, I was screwing this up, I'd never get this one to Bond with me!

Be calm, child. I got the sense of laughter, a faint chuckle. *Take a deep breath, and you'll remember. What do you want?*

I did as instructed, taking a long breath, and words came to me. "I want to be important." *Bloody bones! No! That wasn't the right answer.* I had to say something else. "I need to... I need..." Was this why none of the others had Chosen me in the past five years? Because I didn't have clear life goals? How was I supposed to know what I wanted? True, I was a full-grown woman, but still...

Perhaps I should ask a different question. If we were joined, what would you seek as your True Calling?

That I could answer. "I want to be a Noble. I want to join one of the Noble Houses and be a part of ruling Elista!" I'd finally managed a coherent sentence.

The small Lumani floated there for a long moment, saying nothing, and I began to wonder If I'd offended them somehow. I tried not to say anything. I feared I might offend them further.

Finally, they spoke again.

Why do you wish to be a Noble?

I hesitated. Closing my eyes, I drew a deep breath to steady myself, searching for the right words. "I do not seek power. I do not know yet, how best I might serve our nation, but that is what I truly wish to do, be of service and help to keep Elista as the peaceful and prosperous nation it is."

Again, there was a long pause.

I will not ask your name, child, for the name you held shall soon be a memory. I Choose you, child. The Lumani gave a weird chuckle-sigh. *I think you and I will do well together. You are driven and dedi-*

cated, even if you do not know what you are driven towards. But your spirit calls to me, child, and I hope we can be one. My name is Auwei.

I was too stunned to say anything.

I'd been Chosen!

This way, child, Auwei said serenely and began bobbing away. I followed, as if in a trance. This was it. I'd finally been Chosen.

Now... I just had to prove I was worthy.

CHAPTER 2

*D*o *you have anyone you need to tell?* A*uwei's* voice in my head snapped me out of my shocked reverie.

"Uh... yes, my parents... well foster parents."

Take what time you need. A carriage will be waiting for us when you're ready.

Yes, the carriages. A line of carriages had taken up one end of the town square, waiting to take the Chosen to Silverveil, the academy where Chosen worked to become True-Bonded. Only a few remained. One of them was for me.

Spirits and Sprites, this is happening!

I was still so agitated it took me a long moment to remember what had caused me to look for the carriages: leaving... and telling someone I was leaving! *Oh, right!*

This way, child. Auwei floated ahead of me to a long table with several sheets of parchment and sticks of charcoal. Sitting behind the table was Elder Madrin. The old man smiled at me.

"I'm glad you were Chosen, Sara." He laughed. "Though I suppose I won't be calling you that the next time I see you." He sighed. "Your parents will be so happy. Is there a message you want to write for them?"

"Yes, thank you," I said, taking one of the sheets and a stick of charcoal. The Elder was there for any children who didn't know how to write yet. He could scribe a note for them if their family wasn't here. Since young people came from all around Miraline for The Choosing, and most were uneducated farmers, that was a common occurrence.

I hesitated, my fingers fidgeting on the coal, getting dark and grimy. What would I say? The Clarks had taken me in at the age of six. I only had faint memories of my real parents. The Clarks had been there for my formative years... and yet not been there. Their primary concern for their children had been a solid education in various disciplines. Other than that, they'd been buried in their own work illuminating and scribing manuscripts.

My sister Ella — though now her name was Dove — and I had been left to ourselves for much of our youth. We'd grown up a bit free and wild. It hadn't been a bad life, but it hadn't been a truly warm one either. I was closer with Dove than I was with our parents. Still, they had done so much for me.

I put the charcoal to the parchment and quickly wrote, "Thank you for everything. I was Chosen. I'll write when I can. I love you."

Short, simple, and sweet, Auwei said.

I handed the parchment to Elder Madrin, who smiled. "I'll make sure it gets to them right away." He worked with them at the library, so he'd see them soon enough.

With that, I turned and headed for the line of carriages.

I had everything I needed with me in a satchel: my favorite book — hand-written by my foster parents of course — as well as a few dresses and some odds and ends.

"Sara?"

I turned at my name and was surprised to see my foster father,

Edrid Clark, hurrying up to me. I was so stunned I couldn't move until he swept me up in a hug.

"I'm so happy for you!" he said on the verge of tears.

"Where's mother?" I asked, but I knew she wouldn't be here.

"She couldn't bear to see you leave, or see you unchosen." As I'd suspected. "But I... I had to know and see you one last time if you were. Spirits Within! I'm so happy for you. I know you wanted this so much." He hugged me tighter, lifting me from the ground for a moment. When he set me down, he looked at Auwei.

"Thank you," he said to the Lumani. "She will do right by you. I've never seen a girl with more spirit!" He blushed a little, perhaps realizing what he'd just said. He looked at me. "Don't tell Dove I said that, but it's true. I love my daughters both, but you always had a bit more fire in you than she did. She was so bright of mind, and you of spirit."

I think that was the kindest thing he'd ever said to me. I slipped in to give him a long hug, tears in my eyes. "Thank you for everything. I love you, Papa."

"I know, Sara. And I'm happy you got what you wanted. Go and shine in your new life as much as you have brightened ours."

I squeezed him tighter, not able to say anything. It was a long moment before I could choke out the words, "Good-bye, Papa."

I released him and was just a bit surprised to see his cheeks as wet with tears as mine. He was usually such a stoic man.

He nodded. "Good-bye." Then he stepped back, holding me at arms-length as if to get one last look at me. I took the moment to do the same. He had ink smudges on his smooth cheeks, a smile on his wide mouth, and a softness to his brown eyes as his unkempt blond hair tousled about his brow.

"I'll return when I can," I said, though in truth I had no clue when that might be. Ella — now Dove — my sister, had been Chosen three years ago and had yet to return.

He nodded with a sad smile.

We stood there for a moment longer before he released me. I took that cue and turned, marching to a carriage. When I stepped up, half through the open door, I looked back.

He waved.

I waved.

Then I stepped into the coach and the driver closed the door.

This was it.

That was very sweet. I knew you were the right choice, Auwei said and glowed just a bit brighter. I hadn't thought that possible, but her cream-yellow color became just a bit more distinct and vivid. Then she giggled.

Giggled?

Were Lumani supposed to giggle?

Also... when had I started thinking of her as a "she"? The voice in my head did sound distinctly feminine, but the Lumani had no genders.

It is well, child, you can think of me as a "she" if you like. I have Chosen nearly all female Bonded in my many lives. And the two men I Chose were both, well... not like other men, let's say. So, I guess I've usually been a female once I'm Bonded. Another giggle. *And I guess I will be again soon enough.*

I was a little taken aback by this.

The carriage began to move.

"Auwei...?" I wasn't sure what to say. I thought the Lumani were a bit more composed and serene and majestic.

More giggling. *Once you've lived as many lifetimes Bonded to humans as I have, you pick up a few quirks. Sorry child, but you're gonna have to live with them if we're to be Bonded. I hope I didn't give you the wrong impression earlier. I like to be serious when Choosing. I* got the sense of a shrug. *But this is the real me.*

"The real you?"

Yup, the real me. And I think we'll work well together.

"You do?" I suppose I was a bit irreverent and wild.

Yup.

"Is that why you Chose me? Because I'm..." I didn't know how to say it.

Yes and no. That was one factor, the other, as your father pointed out, was your spirit. For a long time during The Choosing, you didn't stand out, but then there was a flash as I passed you, something bright and powerful. And as I spoke to you, I tried to draw that out. You keep it well hidden, but I know it's there. That's why I Chose you.

"Oh." That was a bit of a surprise. Before today I'd not thought of myself as anyone with a special spirit, but now... perhaps...

And that's what we'll work on when we get to Silverveil, your spirit. In order to make a True-Bond, we need to connect on that level. Also, we'll need to find what avatar you've Chosen for us.

I was excited to find my avatar, the animal form Auwei — and later myself — would take. The shape that would give me my true name. I hoped it was something as lovely as my sister, Dove, or as powerful as Skyfire — a wyvern — the leader of Wyvern House.

Auwei giggled again. *We'll just have to wait and see, won't we!*

Now, there are a few things you'll need to know before we get to Silverveil, Auwei said, becoming a bit more serious in tone. *Or perhaps you already know? What do you know of the process of True-Bonding?*

Time to bring out my extended education. I had learned a fair bit from my parents, but it had been my sister, who had gone through this process three years ago — and written to tell us all about it — from whom I'd learned the most about Bonding.

"All the newly Chosen will come together and live for a time at Silverveil. There is a girls' dorm and boys' dorm, and any fraternizing between them is frowned upon. We're supposed to be spending our time with our Lumani, not snogging behind the dining hall."

Auwei snorted and laughed a heavy guffaw at that. *That's an interesting way of putting it, but yes. Go on.*

Snorting? She'd actually snorted? This was going to be truly interesting.

"Once there, we'll work to bring out our avatar, our True Shape," I continued. "When we do, you'll assume that shape at first. Once you have, we will begin to work on Bonding. Unfortunately, no one, human or Lumani, truly understands how it works, it just does. We'll either Bond or we won't." But I didn't want to think of that option.

Still, Auwei brought it up.

Yes, that is perhaps the most important part of the time we'll spend at Silverveil. We must Bond during those three months. If we don't, it will never happen. She gave a heavy sounding sigh. *That has only happened to me once. It was... painful for both of us.* She perked up a little then. *I'm sure that won't happen with you!*

If it did, I'd have to return to Miraline, and I would never be Chosen again, even if I hadn't been too old. Some people were just not Bondable. If you failed out of the Bonding, even if you were young enough to try again the next year, you were banned from returning. Some people recovered from that and went on to lead productive lives. Others... didn't. I was certain I wouldn't recover. I knew if this didn't work out, I'd... well... it just had to work out.

I drew in a long breath, banishing those thoughts. "Right! I'm sure we'll be a good match!"

Exactly! What else do you know of Silverveil?

"Silverveil is more of a school than a village, though there is a village nearby, mostly to serve the needs of the school. Also, it's called Silverveil because it's so close to The Mistlands, your home."

The Mistlands may be where I come from, but I do not know if I consider them my home anymore. I have spent nine lifetimes in your world and much prefer it to The Mistlands now. Everything here is more... solid. I have come to like the tactile senses of you humans, they're so much more visceral and immediate.

"Oh...?" This was a bit of a surprise. The Mistlands were a mystical place and I couldn't imagine not wanting to be a part of them. "Do you think I could see The Mistlands?"

Yes, of course, we'll go at some point while we're at Silverveil. All Chosen need to see it to help them understand us.

That would be amazing! Being in the realm of The Spirits.

There wasn't that much more I knew about Silverveil. Dove had told us a lot, but not much on the details of how the Bonding actually worked, or the day-to-day activities. But there was one last thing she had mentioned.

On the bench of the carriage opposite me was an envelope. I picked it up and opened it to find three heavy cards within. "And I know what these are, my sister told me about them," I said.

The first card indicated my name during my time at Silverveil. Each Chosen was given an interim name while there. We were no longer who we'd been, our lives had changed and our names should reflect that. And, with luck, we'd have our True-Bonded name soon enough.

My card read: "Birch."

"While I'm at Silverveil, until I get my True Name, I'll be called Birch."

Ooh! It must be fate! Auwei said excitedly. *I've worked with two others who were Birch's as well! Hello, Birch!*

I smiled at that. It did seem somewhat lucky or fated.

The second card said "Forest" on it.

"This is the name of the group of other Chosen I'll be working with. We work in small groups to help each other out. I'm in the Forest group."

"And this last will be the name of my instructor." I picked it up and read: "Lady Kitsune." I shrugged. That meant nothing to me. She would be a True-Bonded, but I didn't know what type of animal a Kitsune was.

A flying, many-tailed, foxlike animal, Auwei said matter-of-factly.

There were far more animals in the world than I could name, but that one was a surprise. "Oh."

Now you're all set, just sit back relax and enjoy the ride to Silverveil. Auwei sounded chipper and calm, but I sensed her tension. She was worried.

Was she worried about me? About the possibility of not Bonding? If so, that's what I was concerned about as well, and her worry didn't help me feel any better about my prospects.

CHAPTER 3

SILVERVEIL WAS A WONDEROUS PLACE. PERCHED ON A PLATEAU, HIGH in the northern hills of Elista, next to the rushing waters of the Mist River, the walled compound captured the eye and the imagination. To the east was the famed Foggy Forest, where heavy mists clung to the lands at all times, the doorway to The Mistlands.

There was something mystical about this place. I could feel it as soon as the carriage passed through the gates. Perhaps it was all the Chosen and True-Bonded in one place. More than anywhere else in Elista, except during a conclave of the Noble Houses. I half-hung out the window of the carriage, eyes wide with wonder, gawking at the grounds and the many others milling around.

The Choosing in Miraline was one of several such events that happened all over Elista, which meant there were dozens of carriages arriving, disgorging passengers, and departing. It was chaos; beautiful, amazing chaos.

My carriage rolled to a stop and I was out the door before the coachman could open it.

I took a deep breath of the rarified air, catching the scent of the distant river and the pine forests. The same air so many before me had breathed. All True-Bonded came here to learn the ways of the Lumani and Bonding. Queen Whitewing and House Leader Skyfire may have stood in this very spot, or slept in the bed I'd be assigned.

My heart pounded so hard, I couldn't hear anything anyone was saying, even Auwei. I just spun in a slow circle taking everything in: the high walls, the many carriages, the Great Square in the middle of the grounds, the many low buildings. From Dove's letters, I thought I knew what each was. The closest, to the left of the gates, was an administration building. North of that would be the girls' dorm. Then a smaller building for the female instructors. The long building directly across campus from me would be the great hall and classrooms. And down the right side would be the male instructors building, the boys' dorm, and the stables and storage building, all perfectly symmetrically laid out.

Birch! Auwei's voice finally broke through my excitement. It took me another moment to realize she was speaking to me. I wasn't used to this new name yet. *There's someone just over there who's gathering the female Chosen.* Oddly, even though Auwei had no appendage with which to point, I knew exactly where she was indicating when she said "there."

I looked and saw a strict looking woman, to whom all the female Chosen seemed to be heading, and made my way toward her.

"What's your name?" I overheard a younger girl in a bright green dress say to another in a stunning blue dress.

"Cedar. Yours?"

"River!"

"At least yours sounds like a girl's name. I can't believe I got Cedar. And with my luck, I'll be stuck with a bunch of low-born dolts."

I hadn't really listened to anything past her name: Cedar,

which meant she was probably in my Forest group. I veered off to speak to her.

Birch, no— Auwei tried to warn me.

"Hello," I said introducing myself to the girl in blue. She looked to be fifteen and was pristinely attired with perfect bouncing blond curls and eyes as blue as her dress. "My name is Birch. I'm guessing we're both in the forest group."

She stared at me like I had two heads. "You're old!" she scoffed. Then with derision: "Let me guess, you're from Miraline?" I didn't even answer before she nodded to herself. "I thought so." She turned her nose up at me like I smelled of midden, and made a point of making a wide arc around me to get to the harsh-looking woman admitting people.

Sorry, Auwei apologized with a sigh. *I recognized her type. Some here will be... entitled. Their family has probably been True-Bonded or Noble or both for generations. Some don't like new-bloods joining their ranks. If it's a Noble you wish to become, you'll probably face more like her.* Auwei sighed heavily. *It's something that hasn't changed over my nine lifetimes, unfortunately.*

I was still just a little shocked at that reception. I hadn't been the most popular girl in Miraline. Dove and I had been a bit freer and wilder than most of the other girls. When they'd been playing with dolls or learning needlework, we'd been playing with boys by the river, getting dirty and having adventures. Still, the girls of town usually just thought I was a bit odd, not... trash.

And suddenly all my wonder and awe came crashing down upon me as Auwei's words sank in.

Some don't like new-bloods...

... you'll probably face more like her.

It's something that hasn't changed over my nine lifetimes...

I'd thought myself invincible now that I was Chosen, but I was starting to see this was still only the very beginning of a long journey. I blinked a few times as this realization settled on me. But then...

Oooohhhh! Auwei said as if shivering. *I felt that.*

I'd felt it too, a hardening in my stomach, a core of resolve and rededication to my goals: True-Bonded, then Noble, then... maybe even someday... queen? I gave a hard, grim smile.

That, that right there. That's why I Chose you, Birch. And... oh! She sounded surprised, almost pained.

Auwei had been hovering just above my right shoulder, but she descended to settle on me as tiny tendrils sprouted from her spherical form. Those tendrils formed into legs; eight legs. A tiny cream-yellow glowing ball, with eight legs. Two over-large eyes appeared on the orb as well, blinking.

Auwei laughed. *You have Chosen our avatar, Birch. We're—*

No, please don't say what I think you're about to say.

—A spider.

Bloody bones! A spider? Really? I was certain that wasn't going to go over well with the other girls.

Spirits of the Mists! This was going to be a long three months.

I squared my shoulders, drew in a long breath, then headed for the admitting woman.

"Name," she barked, voice level and cold, as I drew up before her. She hadn't even looked at me.

"Birch."

She flipped through her lists and used a wrapped piece of charcoal to check off a spot. "Primary dorm, room seventeen." She pointed, looking back toward the dorm. "You can go in that door there. Your room will be near the end of the hall on the left." Only then did her head swing back to look at me.

"Spirits Within! What is that?" She shrieked eyes going wide, pointing at Auwei.

She seemed to realize what she was seeing as I said the words: "That's my Lumani."

The woman blinked. "You've Chosen your avatar already?" She seemed an odd combination of astounded and disgusted, a shiver taking her.

I stood there a moment longer, wondering if there was more before she said, "Shoo, go! You know your room number, everything you need will be there." As I moved away, I caught her muttering, "Some young women these days! A spider? Truly?"

Ahead of me, Cedar and River had paused at the lady's outburst, then turned to each other and hurried ahead to the dorm. I had no desire to join them, so I made my way slowly, trying to savor and enjoy these first moments at Silverveil... and failing miserably.

I entered the dorm through a door at the end. Dove had mentioned that each Chosen got their own room. She'd been a bit stunned and surprised at that, seeing as she and I had shared a room for as long as I'd been with the Clark family. The doors down the left side of the hall had odd numbers starting with one, on the right side were even numbers starting with two. I looked ahead down the hall and caught Cedar and River giggling as they came out of a room, which — I couldn't quite tell from this distance — might be mine.

"Ooops!" Cedar called out to me. "Wrong room!" They were hiding something from me. Had they taken something from my room?

There isn't much to take, Auwei said. *But those two certainly seem like they're up to no good.*

I shook my head as they exited the far end of the dorm. If Dove's letters were any indication, there would be a girl's common room at that end of the dorm with doors from this dorm and the secondary dorm, as well as a door leading outside. I didn't want to chase the girls, so I just went into my room to see what they might have done.

I didn't see anything out of place and sighed.

Hmmm, Auwei hummed softly. *I think I know what those girls did.*

"Oh?" I moved in. The room was narrow with a good-sized window on the far side, sunlight streaming in. Next to the window was a bed, its head against the far wall and its side against the right wall. To my right stood a large cabinet and desk unit. A narrow door, the full height of the cupboard was probably a small closet. Two more, smaller cabinets were situated over the desk area.

On the bed.

I moved in and looked at what Auwei had indicated, a single folded dress in a dark-blue-grey color.

Yup, just as I thought. Auwei sighed. *Those pesky girls stole the other sets of clothes that should be here. Every Chosen is provided with three sets to account for different sizes, a small, a medium, and a large set. There should also be a note here with instructions for what to do next. They've taken that too. I don't know what they thought to achieve, their Lumani must know that your Lumani would be aware of what should be here.* A heavy sigh. *Some Lumani...*

"What did the note say?"

To get dressed and meet in the Great Square. Assemble with your group at your instructor, who should have a sign of some sort.

"Ah, yes, I would have just sat here all evening, clueless."

But they must have known I'd know that, so their intent wasn't to stop you, just...

"Humiliate me." I lifted the single garment they'd left. It would be a tight fit on me, almost scandalous. If there had been three dresses, this must have been the small one. Being rather tall, I guessed I'd have wanted the large dress. As it was, an intriguing set of buttons down the front of the dress looked like it allowed for varying builds.

I laughed.

What?

"I'll show them. I'll wear it proudly."

Or, just a thought, you could ask one of the other girls in the dorm to borrow one of their dresses if they're not using their large one.

"No, this'll be more fun." I shrugged. "I'm guessing there aren't many here with my height and, with you as a spider, I'm already going to stand out. I might as well play that up." I stripped off my clothes and squeezed into the dress.

There's a looking glass on the inside of that long closet door.

I opened the cabinet door and found the looking glass on the back... and burst out laughing.

I'd never been all that busty, more athletic and slender. Still, this dress made me look like some wanton lady-of-the-night. It was skin tight over my bust, waist, and hips, buttons bulging. Even as I stood there, a button popped off, exposing my belly-button. Then there was the length, it covered my thighs at least, but only barely, ending at the knee.

Oh yes, I'd make quite an impression in this.

Are you sure you want to do this? I'm certain one of the other girls would allow you to borrow one of their dresses.

"No, we're doing this! In fact... how much time do I have before the meeting?"

An hour perhaps, maybe two. They'll ring a bell when it's time.

"Then I know exactly what I'm going to do." My mind was working. If these girls wanted to humiliate me, I'd show them. I'd own this, make it mine, make them see there was nothing they could do to hurt me...

And all the young men out there were in for quite a treat!

CHAPTER 4

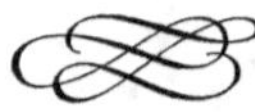

THE BELL RANG FOR ASSEMBLY AND I STRUTTED OUT IN MY NOW custom-made dress. I'd altered it with a needle and thread I'd brought with me, raising the hemline.

You're going to be in so much trouble— Auwei said with a giggle. *I love it!*

Despite my show of confidence, I felt horribly self-conscious. I'd never done anything like this before. I was near to busting out of a dress with a hem so high I was having to work really hard to keep myself from not pulling it down.

Cedar and River wanted me to be embarrassed, ashamed, but I was going to turn this back on them and... probably make a name for myself in the process. I'd never wanted to be noticed before, but something in me had gone all hard and determined. I was already the tallest girl here; I might as well stand out in other ways.

Outside, the spring breeze was chilly on my naked legs, but I soldiered on.

Cedar was already with the Forest Group. She caught sight of me and her mouth fell open, eyes going wide. The two boys in our group — they looked to be no more than sixteen — had the same look on their face, mixed with a heavy dose of shame-lust.

I flashed them a grin.

Lady Kitsune, my instructor, was a woman of middle years with dark brown hair pulled back tight in a bun and severe grey eyes in a sharp-featured face. She was nearly as tall as I was and rail thin. When she caught sight of me, she nearly dropped the large sign saying "Forest".

"Spirits, girl! What's the meaning of this?" Her shock and horror were clear on her expression and in her tone. Two other girls in the group giggled.

I blinked innocently. "Oh, sorry, I..." I looked at Cedar. "My new friend Cedar here strongly suggested I wear this dress. I thought we were going to make it a group thing. I guess I was wrong."

Lady Kitsune flashed a look at Cedar. "This was your idea?"

The girl sputtered for a moment, clearly not expecting any of this. She finally stammered out, "N-no!"

Lady Kitsune swung her gaze back to me. "Get changed at once!"

I feigned ignorance. "Changed? But I only had this one dress." I turned to Cedar again. "You said we only got one dress each and had to make do."

Cedar sputtered again, eyes going wide.

Kitsune looked from me to Cedar and sighed. "Ah..." She didn't even ask Cedar if this was true, the confused guilt was clear from the heady blush on the girl's face. Kitsune sighed and looked at me again. "We'll get you a larger dress once we're done here. We have many." Shaking her head, she went on. "I believe we're all here?" There were just the six of us. "Please state your new names," Lady Kitsune asked.

"Birch, tall and pale, that's me," I cut in before anyone else could. One of the other girls laughed at that, the boys were still having a bit of trouble tearing their gazes off my legs.

"I'm Ash," one of the other girls said.

"Maple." This from the slightly taller of the two boys, who finally managed to look me in the eye, after a slow drawing up of his gaze over everything else. "Hi."

I flashed him a grin. "Hi."

Lady Kitsune made an odd strangled noise, then said, "Next!"

"I'm Oak," the other boy said and seemed to hesitate for a moment before adding: "That's a *hardwood* tree." He winked at me. The way he'd said that had made his innuendo clear.

I nearly choked — as did Lady Kitsune — trying not to laugh. I probably didn't hide my surprise well, but I reassessed Oak. He may have been the shorter of the two boys, but he was quick and probably older, perhaps eighteen?

"Good to know," I said with a nod, finally getting myself under control.

Oak smiled. He seemed to have gotten over his fascination with my legs, his gaze solidly on mine. Oh yeah, he could be trouble, and not just for me. Those clear blue eyes of his and that pristine beautiful young face would go over very well with most young women.

"None of that!" Lady Kitsune said harshly. Her composure cracked just a little. We were going to be The Bloody Pits for her. I could tell.

"Cedar," Cedar said finally, pulling herself up and trying — and horribly failing now — to make herself stand out. She was curvy yes, and beautiful with that well-styled blond hair and those blue eyes, but I'd stolen all the attention away from her.

"Poplar," said the last girl, shy and giggly.

"Now!" Lady Kitsune snapped, trying to get focus back on her. "Please also share the names of your Lumani."

"Auwei," I said indicating with my thumb the odd cream-yellow glowing spider on my shoulder.

"You've already taken an avatar?" Oak said, nodding with surprise and admiration. "Truly you're a woman well advanced from the rest of us." Another wink from him.

"Hush boy!" Kitsune said.

"You mean she's old," Cedar said at the same time, though both she and Lady Kitsune were spoken over by Oak who continued:

"This is Oama." He indicated the large deep-blue ball floating nearby.

The others went around without incident. Cedar's Lumani was Eala, Maple's was Uesi, Poplar's was Aelo, and Ash's was Iana.

"Now, for the rules and procedures here at Silverveil," Kitsune said, trying to regain control. She succeeded for the most part, but Oak never took his eyes off me; neither did Cedar, though for a completely different reason and with a completely different look, full of contempt.

Lady Kitsune told us the times for the meals, and that missing them would mean we'd go without. She said we'd be working with her for the most part. Our mornings would be spent in specific activities meant to help us connect with our Lumani. There would be a few more classes in the afternoons, then some free time before the evening meals, during which we were expected to get to know our Lumani further in ways better suited to our pairings.

She finished with a hard look at me and Cedar — apparently still not sure with whom she was more upset — and said, "Tomorrow seamstresses and tailors from the village will come to take your measurements. You'll have a set of custom clothes before the end of the week." She emphasized the next part. "You *will* wear those clothes and *not* modify them in any way! Is that clear?"

I smiled and nodded. "Clear."

We were then herded into the great hall for the evening meal, though I was escorted by Lady Kitsune herself to get me a new dress and change. The largest of the pre-defined sets was just a little loose on me, though with the way the buttons could be used to help them conform to a woman's figure I made it work well. This one came to just above my ankles. If nothing else, it would be warmer.

I ate only a little, having taken time away from the meal to change, but it was enough.

Then we were told to retire to our rooms for the evening in contemplation with our Lumani.

My contemplation didn't last long.

There came a soft knock on my window. I rose from where I'd been sitting on my bed and opened the heavy curtains.

Outside was Oak. He smiled and winked.

Curious, I opened the window, latching it up and leaning out on the sill to speak to him. "Yes?"

"Hey Legs, wanna go for a walk?" Oama bobbed excitedly next to him.

"Legs?"

"Yeah, most of the boys have taken to calling you that." He shrugged. "You can take it however you want, but from me, it's a compliment. You have nice legs... as well as everything else, that is."

Oh, he was a charmer.

And he was handsome enough, his clothes falling perfectly from broad shoulders, blue eyes sparkling, reflecting the lamp-light from my room.

"How did you know this was my room?" I asked.

He laughed. "I had to knock on a few other windows first, but eventually one of the others pointed me in the right direction." He gave me the full force of his charming smile.

"Might we go for a walk?" He asked with courtly manners. His voice grew hushed. "Or I could come in."

Something about him didn't sit right with me and I didn't want to give the impression I was interested. Sure, he was nice to look at, but... not really my type. Yet, after my stunt with the dress, I'd probably need to do a bit of image-mending.

"Not tonight, Oak," I said. I didn't want to cut him off entirely though, just let him know I had standards. A walk with a handsome young man wouldn't be so bad, though I probably wouldn't want anything more with him. So, I quickly added: "Once you and Oama have come up with an avatar, *maybe* I'll consider it." I hoped he heard the emphasis on "maybe."

He nodded. "Of course. I'd expect nothing less than to be a match for you before we might *go walking*." He drew himself up to his full height and gave a single nod. "I'll return in a few days. I'm sure we'll have found our avatar by then." He turned and left.

I shook my head. He was handsome enough and confident, but... not my type. I liked my men just a bit less forward. Oak was too eager and almost arrogant in his approach. I'd always been a strong girl, now a strong woman, and I liked a man who let me know he was available, but let me do the pursuing.

Interesting. Auwei said, scurrying along the wall to the windowsill. *A rare man indeed, but I sense you've found such a man at least once, yes?*

"Yes," I confided as I closed the window. "There was a boy in Miraline, Kelen, who I grew up with. We were friends as children, then we became... more."

I sunk back onto the bed as memories returned like a flood. We had left the city on sunny afternoons and taken long walks in the fields around the town. At first, we'd talked. Then, as our bodies had matured, we'd explored each other, delving into our raging emotions. We'd bloomed together, learning and teaching, until our heated encounters were quite... rewarding. He'd been the first — and so far, the only — boy I'd been with.

But... then had come our first year of Choosing. We had

thought to be Chosen together that day, but... only he had been Chosen. When he'd left, he'd kissed me passionately and said he'd write, or return for me.

But I had received only one letter from him months later. His name was now Lynx. He'd joined the Panther House of Nobles. He could not return for me, he was too busy with his new duties, but he wished me happiness and hoped I might join him one day.

I spoke in hushed tones, telling Auwei all of this.

The Panthers rarely take non-cat avatars, Birch, Auwei advised with a note of care in her voice.

I nodded. I was a spider and unlikely to rejoin my first love. I smiled sadly. "I know." I hadn't expected to be reunited with Lynx, at least not in his Noble House. The truth was, after he'd left, my feelings for him had cooled. He'd been kind and giving, but we'd both been a bit too hot-blooded and young. I was tempered now. Perhaps, if we met again, the spark would reignite, or perhaps not.

I hope you find a man who is everything you wish, Auwei said. *Or a woman. Or several men, or some mixed group. I'm open to anything.* I was a bit shocked by this. Despite group relationships being a known thing in Miraline, they weren't common.

"Have you...?" I asked tentatively, not really knowing what I was asking.

Later, Auwei whispered and I felt a bit of hesitation from her.

I nodded.

Still, Auwei whispered. *I hope you find someone to love, who loves you.*

"I'll worry about that once I'm Bonded with you. Until then, you're my one and only," I joked.

If that's the case, let's get back to work, yes? She crawled over the bed and onto a hand I lowered for her.

I found it odd that now that she had an avatar form, she couldn't float. She was... limited. Such a strange process the Lumani must go through, going from free-floating energy, then taking the limiting shape of an animal, then combining souls with a human.

"Why do you do this?" I asked. "Why go through all this trouble of limiting yourself, taking the shape of animals, and joining with humans. What do you get out of it?" I sort of knew the general story of the Lumani, that they had sought the experience of a physical existence, but I wanted to know Auwei's reasons.

That... is a long story, Auwei said.

"We've got lots of time."

True. In that case, let's start with a history lesson. Long ago, The Mistlands and your world did not cross over as strongly as they do now. They were two different worlds. We knew of yours, as we could see it through the Mists, but you knew nothing of ours. Then... one day, the worlds meshed and merged and people began to wander into the Mists. That's when we first met your kind and it's fair to say... both sides were quite fascinated with each other.

CHAPTER 5

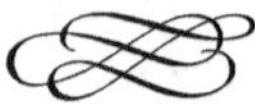

Those first few of your kind who stepped into The Mistlands, especially those who stayed there and survived long enough, became the world's first mistweavers, able to draw on the power of my world even after returning to yours.

I shuddered at the mention of mistweavers. Tales of those ancient and powerful beings were still told to frighten children into behaving. Humans altered by the Mists, imbued with great power and cursed with madness. Spending too much time in The Mistlands did things to a human's mind.

The mistweavers had reshaped the continent. Some had ruled nations, others had destroyed them. Hence the Shattered Lands to the north. Thankfully, there were no mistweavers in the world today.

Yes, that was... something no one foresaw. A terrible time for your world and mine.

"For yours?" None of the tales mentioned any harm to The Mistlands.

Yes, some of the mistweavers learned ways to gain more power by consuming the spirits of The Mistlands.

I shuddered at the thought. "That's horrible."

Indeed. Auwei was silent for a moment. *But that time eventually passed. And later, some of my kind were intrigued by your world and wished to see it. But... our experience of the physical world is limited. Everything is energy to us. We don't see or hear in the same way as humans, and we cannot touch, taste, or smell. So, the first bargains and Bondings were made. It was a difficult experience for both parties, but in the end, the Lumani obtained the experiences of your world that they sought. Yet... when those first True-Bonded hosts died, their Lumani, though powerful in their own right were limited once again. When they returned to tell of their experiences, many of my kind were fascinated and wished to Bond as well.*

Auwei was silent for a long time after that. She seemed agitated, crawling around my bed and up the wall, then across the ceiling. She even spun a strand of spider-silk and lowered herself from the ceiling back down to the bed.

This form is really quite fascinating, Birch. I think you'll like it once we Bond.

"You're stalling," I said. "Is this difficult to talk about?"

Auwei sighed. *Yes.*

"Then we can stop for now."

No... I just needed a moment. The small form scampered up my calf and snuggled behind the knee of my folded leg. I would not have thought I'd ever want a spider snuggling up to any part of me, but with Auwei it was different. She had the rough form of a spider, but still had her cream-yellow glow and was warm and comforting to have near me.

My first True-Bonded... in those days they didn't change their names, did you know that?

"No."

They didn't take on the name of their avatar form. Her name was Woleia. Again, silence for a long moment. *She will always hold a special place in my heart. She was... brave, a hunter, fearless when facing any beast of nature. She took the form of a wolf. And... she was my first experience of your world. I will always remember smelling my first rose, the sweetness of a ripe peach, and the soft press of a kiss upon her lips.*

I felt the heightened pleasure of these memories, transmitted from Auwei. I too smelled a summer's rose, tasted that peach, and felt the kiss. But there was more behind that kiss. Emotions spilled into me, the warmth of love and the wet heat of desire. For a moment, that overwhelmed me, and I felt a thrill of arousal at the phantasmal press upon my lips.

"Yes," I breathed softly as if responding to a lover's caress.

Birch? I'm sorry, I didn't mean to... That was too much.

It had been. I shuddered as I slowly came down from the rush of passion. I cleared my throat. "Ah... You were telling me about Woleia?"

Auwei hesitated for a moment before continuing. *Perhaps we can talk more about Woleia another time.*

I felt the depth of intimacy she was dealing with. There was a lot more to Woleia's story I guessed, but I wouldn't push. I let Auwei continue at her own pace and discretion. *You'd asked why I do this and what I get out of it.* A sigh. *Humans tend to think of us Lumani as being powerful mystical beings. And... I suppose we are when compared with humans, but our power is quite limited, in this world at least. In the Mists, everything is powerful, so... it's different. Our real power in this world comes from our ability to Bond with humans and make both sides stronger.*

She remained silent for a long time before continuing. When she did, her voice was hushed in my mind. *We... it hurts to lose a Bonded companion. Yet the joy we get from being with one far outweighs the loss we feel when they're gone. It's like... being in love. I know you've only had one experience with that, but I've had many. My previous True-Bonded have loved... and been broken hearted. It's amazing, the power love gives you, the height of joy and contentment.* Her voice soared for a moment before becoming sedate once again. *And when it's gone, it feels like the world has ended.*

A determined strength filled her. *Yet... I'd rather have loved and had my heart broken, then never have loved at all. And it's the same with Bonding. I am always devastated when my True-Bonded dies. Yet, the joy of Bonding with another will always draw me back to Choose someone like you, Birch.* Auwei giggled. *Or should I call you: Legs?*

"Spirits, no, please."

You brought it upon yourself.

"I know." I sighed. "But the fun and games are over. Tomorrow I need to focus on us, and Bonding."

I have faith.

I wished I did. I put on a smile and tried to feel strong and determined for Auwei, but doubt squirmed within me. If I wasn't able to Bond with Auwei I'd be sent back to my previous life.

That fear manifested in my dreams that night: living a life filled with a thousand mundane horrors, everything reminding me how worthless I was.

Suffice to say, I didn't sleep well.

CHAPTER 6

A knock on my door startled me awake.

I sat up. "Yes?" I said before I fully understood what was happening.

"Breakfast, m'lady," came a girl's voice I didn't recognize from the other side of my door.

"Thanks!" I called, then flopped back into bed. A faint rim of light silhouetted my curtains. It was easy enough, from the bed, to lift a corner of the curtain and see a sliver of the sky. It was overcast and only barely light out, grey and gloomy. What an auspicious start to my time at Silverveil.

You'll want to make sure you get a good breakfast, Auwei said. *There's a lot to do. These days will feel very long and full. I'm sorry, I didn't think to let you know I could wake you whenever you like in the mornings. If you want time before breakfast tomorrow, to get ready, I can give you that.*

"Get ready?" I asked. I groaned as I pushed myself up to sit once again, then slid my legs over the side of the bed. My new dress was a bit rumpled; I'd slept in it. I tried futilely, to smooth it out. "And do what?"

Some of my previous True-Bonded liked to take baths or showers in the mornings and do their hair or even put on some cosmetics.

Cosmetics? I'd never owned any. Also... "What's a shower?" I knew what a rain shower was, but I didn't know how a person could have one every morning.

There are facilities here where you can bathe, but also, you can have warm water pour over you in a consistent stream, called a shower. It's quite lovely.

"Perhaps I'll try one this evening. But no, I don't need to get ready, just wake me in time for breakfast." I rose and left my room. It seemed most of the other Chosen here had woken earlier as the great hall was full when I got there. I took some scraps of what food was left on the buffet and found an open spot at a table.

Still half asleep, I hadn't paid much attention to where I sat.

"Oh... hello," said a curious voice from beside me. "You're... ah... Legs... aren't you?" the young man's voice broke awkwardly.

With a mouth stuffed with warm bacon, I looked up to see I'd taken a seat amidst a group of boys. They stared at me with eyes full of... hunger, and not for the food in front of them. I'd never felt this *objectified*, and I was more than a little unnerved.

I blushed, suddenly wondering how I looked. I hadn't bothered with the looking glass in my closet. I usually had a rather frumpy tousle of hair in the mornings. *Spirits!*

Still, I tried to put on a winning smile. The boy next to me, the one who'd spoken, was small and slight with tanned skin and a tangled mess of light brown hair. Yet it was his eyes which caught my attention: soft brown eyes, so deep and curious and caring. His was a tender soul, I could tell instantly.

"Yeah... Legs, that's me," I said after finishing my bacon. "My actual name is Birch though."

"She's out of your league, Pebble!" one of the other boys called over. Instantly the one next to me — Pebble, an unfortunate name — blushed and shrunk into himself. "I'm Creek," the other boy said. He was across the table from me, head and shoulders taller than most of the boys here. A scruff of a beard grew on his chin, and his face was hard, eyes dark brown. I could tell instantly he was another charmer, like Oak, sure of himself and ready for action. All the boys at the table seemed to defer to him.

"I wish they'd let you keep that dress from yesterday," Creek said with a wink and a grin.

"Lady Kitsune had a conniption when she saw it," I said in response. "It's probably been burned by now. Hope you got a good look yesterday."

"I did," Creek said low and soft. "And if you ever want to show me... more..." He left the invitation hanging.

Yeah... no, sorry buddy.

Not your type? Auwei asked, but seemed to know the answer already.

Definitely not. I turned to Pebble, the smaller young man next to me. There was something about him, something in those eyes. *But him... maybe.*

Ah, yes, I see now.

I looked at Creek and decided to shut down any offers, from him or any other boys. "I'm not here to flirt or fulfill any boyish fantasies. I'm here to Bond with my Lumani, then test to become a Noble. Got it?" I stared down Creek, then each of the others in turn.

To be fair, you were the one strutting around like a peacock yesterday. Did your parents never teach you about the consequences of your actions? Despite her words, Auwei was giggling.

They did, yes. I just don't often think that far ahead. I wanted to have fun yesterday, make an... interesting first impression. I only realized after the fact that I hadn't vocalized those words. I usually spoke to Auwei out loud, but it seemed, when not thinking about it — or perhaps when knowing I might be overheard — I'd inherently used an "inside" voice.

You're learning. Good, Auwei said. *And you definitely made one Pits of an impression on these boys yesterday. Also, in case you hadn't noticed, I think you've made some enemies among the girls.*

Enemies? Other than Cedar?

Over there to your left, two tables down.

I looked. A group of girls was staring daggers at me.

Auwei said: *A lot of Noble Houses intermarry, and they would have told their children to be scouting possible mates at Silverveil. But right now, you're sort of hogging all the guys.*

Trust me, I'm more than willing to share.

That may be true, but currently half the guys in this room only have eyes for you. And those girls are seeing the same thing. You may be making that speech a lot over the next little while.

Oh.

I hurriedly finished my breakfast and excused myself, noting how many pairs of eyes, male and female, followed me. It seemed in my short time here I'd made a lot of sort-of-friends and definite-enemies.

I rushed back to my room, hoping to have a moment alone, but was surprised to find a small, elderly woman waiting for me.

"Take off the dress," she said with a sniff. "So's I can measure you."

Oh... right... seamstress. Still, I was a little taken aback by her forward manner. It took me a moment of standing there dumb before I began to unbutton the dress. I was then subjected to various indignities as the old woman poked and prodded and measured.

"Thank the Spirits you've already got a woman's figure. I hate making girls' dresses, especially at this age, when they're likely to grow out of them in a month. If'n you don't mind a bit of advice from an old woman, you're a little too straight and thin. Eat more lamb and pork, put a little meat on ya. It'll help with childbirth and..." She chuckled. "All the bits that get you with child to begin with."

I was fairly certain I blushed down to my toes at that.

She was finished soon enough and left. I dressed again and decided to get some air before morning classes. I went out behind the girl's dorm and climbed the stairs to a lookout tower to gaze out over the wall. Fog blanketed the rolling hills beyond and a chill breeze swept over the high plateau on which Silverveil was situated. Given the dark clouds sitting low over everything, I had a feeling it would rain soon.

Auwei perched on my shoulder, silent.

Prompted by the seamstress's comments I asked Auwei. "Have you ever had kids?" Here, with no one around I felt comfortable voicing my words again.

Yes. I've been a mother five times and a father once.

"What's the big deal?" I wasn't sure I wanted kids.

She sighed. *It's hard to explain. And just so we're clear, it is up to you, and I'll be well if you decide not to have any. I'll say this much. Raising children is the hardest, most grueling, and exhausting thing I've ever done, but also the most rewarding, the most joyful. Yet, you can have a very full life without them as well, I've done that three times and been quite happy.*

"Ah..." That hadn't really answered anything.

If you don't want kids, what do you want? Auwei asked.

"That again?" I said, deflecting. I still didn't have a good answer for the question she'd asked during The Choosing.

Auwei chuckled. *It wasn't a test. I'm just curious. I Chose you because I sensed a fire within you, a strength of spirit which seems to come and go. I think, once you know what it is you truly want in life, you'll have that fire within you all the time. I would love to help you find that.*

I sighed. She was right, but I still didn't know. "I'll figure it out," I murmured and promised myself I'd do some thinking on it.

A bell rang for first classes, and I hurried down from my perch to join my group.

Oak winked at me as I arrived. I'd need to tell him what I'd told Creek.

Cedar glared at me.

Lady Kitsune either didn't see any of this or ignored it.

The six of us and our instructor met where we had the day before, but once we were all there, Lady Kitsune moved us away from the other groups to one side of the main gates. "From now on, we'll meet here when doing our group work." Kitsune was all business.

The next bit she seemed to have memorized. "There is no one way to Bond with your Lumani," Lady Kitsune began. "But over the many years that the Bondings have been happening we've learned several things that help. Exercise clears the mind. Similarly, meditation, whether moving or still, can help you center yourself and connect with your Lumani."

She pursed her lips, as if somehow what she suggested so far should be enough, and any further options were less desirable. "Yet, it may not be a clear mind or still soul that one needs to Bond. What seems to hold true is that a True-Bonding often happens when one is doing an activity that speaks deeply to them and their Lumani. This could be swimming or solving complex problems. It could be writing a letter to a loved one or an act of creativity: painting or singing and such. It could even be doing something dangerous or exciting like engaging in combat, but I don't recommend that. There are many ways, and what you need to figure out is what will work best for you."

"*Many* ways?" Oak said with a grin. "Care to elaborate?" His sidelong look at me made it clear he hoped there was one way in particular which he and I might try.

"Ah, yes, well. Some Chosen in the past have engaged in various... activities, which are not recommended, but have been known to cause a True-Bond."

"Like sex?" Oak said plainly. Then he looked at me and smiled. Oh yes, we needed to have "the conversation" very soon indeed.

Lady Kitsune glared at him, tight lipped, but nodded. Her entire demeanor making it clear what she thought of that as an option.

"I've heard of Bonding happening while a person was playing pranks on another Chosen." This from Poplar. "Is that true?"

"It is." And again, Lady Kitsune did not elaborate. "You must find what works for you, BUT!" She raised a rigid finger. "Do not engage in such activities. We will follow a set course of classes and exercises which have been known to work in most cases. Only *if* that doesn't work *might* we consider other options."

"Got it," Oak said, but his grin was saying he was certain he knew what would work for him.

I shook my head.

And so began a morning of calisthenics and various other ways to work our bodies and minds and "open our souls" to the Bonding.

By lunch I was already tired and mentally drained. The food helped to pick me up a little, but I was still somewhat off for the afternoon. As Auwei had warned, I was quite exhausted by the end of my first full day at Silverveil.

It rained that afternoon, but then the clouds cleared. After dinner I was ready for a bath and my bed. Still, I lingered outside, climbing that lookout tower from earlier, to watch the sunset.

That's where Pebble found me.

CHAPTER 7

I SAW HIM COMING FROM THE CORNER OF MY EYE, TENTATIVE AND hesitant. He paused at the base of the stairs up to the tower, but then, after a moment, something seemed to solidify in him and he marched up the steps to me.

"Ah... Birch?" At least he wasn't calling me Legs. "I... I just wanted to apologize for how my table treated you at breakfast today."

He was apologizing? He hadn't done anything wrong. He'd been a gentleman. It was Creek and the other boys who'd been a little too forward. I looked over at Pebble. He was... well scrawny was the best word to describe his build. I doubted many girls here would look twice at him. Yet, once again something in his eyes caught my attention, a firm but tender determination. Something about it matched what I felt in my soul, my drive to become a Noble.

"Why are you apologizing for them?" I asked, curious.

He looked away, clearly self-conscious. "I just... don't think women should be treated that way."

I smiled. Yup, I liked this one. "How should they be treated?"

"With respect and honor, as an equal." Those soft brown eyes flashed up to look at me for the briefest of moments before looking away. "You are beautiful, yes, but I've learned that looks don't mean much. It's how a person treats another person that counts."

He was right. And he was being very respectful at the moment, which made me like him all the more. I pushed off from the railing and went to him. A finger under his chin lifted his face as I leaned down and gave him a soft, chaste kiss upon — what turned out to be — supple and pleasant lips. "Thank you," I breathed afterward. But I also felt the need to let him know that I still didn't want anything with any man right now. "When this is all done and we're both Bonded, come and find me."

He blushed a rather stunning shade of crimson, edging on violet, and nodded, seemingly unable to speak. I returned to the railing and Pebble left without another word.

When I heard steps on the stairs a moment later, I thought he'd returned, but I turned to see Oak approaching.

"Someone in the Rock class has already Bonded," he said, as he came to lean on the railing next to me, very close.

I'd noticed a bit of a hubbub and a carriage being prepared as I'd made my way to this spot.

"Truly?"

He nodded. "For some, it happens quickly." He turned, leaning his back against the low wall. "How are you feeling?"

"Tired, I just want a bath and a bed."

He quirked a grin at the mention of a bath, but since the girls' and boys' baths were nowhere near each other, the image in his mind wasn't going to happen.

I sighed. "I'm really not up for anything this evening, Oak; sorry."

He nodded. "Got it." There was a tightness to his voice. And with that, he left. Though, halfway down the stairs, he turned back. "And that walk, once I've found my avatar?"

I had said maybe to that earlier, but now...

You only live once, Auwei said. Then she giggled. *But I'll regret your mistakes for eternity.*

I laughed a little at that, but she was right. I couldn't help but feel that being with him would be a mistake. Though I couldn't say exactly why just yet.

"No, Oak, sorry," I said firmly.

His lips went tight and he gave a sharp nod. "Tease," he hissed. "You can go to The Pits for all I care!" Then he left in a huff.

And in that moment, I knew what it was about him that didn't sit right with me: he wouldn't take "no" for an answer. I had made no commitment to him, so it should have been a simple thing to accept, but he already thought I was his. No woman should be treated that way. I much preferred Pebble's approach to women.

Once the sun had set, I made my way down to the baths. A basement had been dug out beneath the common area and was accessible by a stairway from both wings of the dorm. The heavy fieldstone walls were dry and warm to the touch. There was some mystical power at work here. I didn't care to know the details, but Auwei informed me.

In some cases — in perhaps a quarter of True-Bonded? — the power that combines human and Lumani can produce powers beyond an avatar's abilities. For those with a particularly strong spirit, strange new powers can emerge. These are more like the powers the mistweavers held, though, generally far more limited in depth and variety. The baths of Silverveil were created by a True-Bonded with such gifts, about a hundred years ago. They possessed power over the elements. Her voice was hushed and reverent within me.

The ground was dug out from under the dorms without disturbing a soul, stones were gathered and fitted perfectly for the walls, then imbued with a pleasant warmth to keep the bathing area warm and dry. The baths and showers are fed from a large steel tank of water, which fills itself perpetually, gathering moisture from the air outside. The waters are warmed as they are piped to their location and once a bather is finished, their dirty water drains away to the soil outside of the building. It's really quite fascinating.

It did sound interesting, but I was too tired to care. I decided to try a shower since I got the feeling Auwei loved them. I stepped over to the small stall and opened the door to a narrow, segmented area. The outer area held towels and had hooks for clothes. I closed and locked the outer door, took off my dress, hung it up, and stepped into the second area.

The steam from the shower will help to get those wrinkles out of your dress. You probably shouldn't sleep in it again tonight.

"Yup, sure," I said, staring at the odd bits of metal protruding from the wall. "So...?"

The thing with the holes at the top is where the water comes from. Don't look directly at it or you'll get water in your eyes. The lever at the bottom has three settings: warm, hot, and very hot. If you turn it to the first...

I did, and pleasantly warm waters poured out onto me. "Ohhh-hhh," I sighed out heavily, leaning both arms against the stone wall, just letting the waters flow over me.

See? Auwei seemed to sigh with me.

"Yup, I get it now."

Curious, I flipped the bottom lever to its second setting and the water grew warmer, like a perfectly hot, but drinkable cup of tea, only... on the outside. I gave another heavy sigh.

"The only trouble is, I just want to sit right now. I'm not sure how long I can stand here."

Auwei's tiny legs tickled as she climbed onto my foot, working hard not to get washed down the drain, which she wouldn't, she was too large.

Here, she said tenderly.

An odd revitalizing warmth flowed into me from Auwei. It wasn't much, but it roused me enough that I no longer felt faint.

I can't give much. I'll be able to give more once we're Bonded, when my life energies will be one with yours.

I felt revived enough to wash myself. I found a bar of scented soap and began to clean my body. I was filthy. After the soap I took an abrasive scrubber to my skin, leaving it red and raw. I thought that was it, but Auwei pointed out a large bowl in an alcove of the shower. *That's a special soap for your hair; try it.*

I did, scooping some of the gooey liquid into my hand, then rubbing it through my hair. Seeing some of the dirt washing down the drain from that, I proceeded to do the rest of my long locks.

"Do you care about my hair, our hair?" I asked, curious. "Is there a length or style you like?"

I'm good with whatever you want. I've had all styles and lengths. I love the feel and weight of a long fall of hair and how it covers me, but I also like the weightless freedom and versatility of a short cut. One of the men to whom I was Bonded eventually went bald. That was a new experience, but not as much to my liking.

"That shouldn't be a problem," I said with a laugh. I'd have to figure out what I wanted. Dove had said she'd cut her hair back to just below her ears once she started taking more martial training at Pegasus House after she'd become a Noble. I couldn't quite imagine hair that short.

I finished with my hair and just stood under the hot water for a time, soaking it all in.

Finally, I turned the water off and grabbed a towel to dry myself. I'd seen some girls wearing the long towels — wrapped around them — back to their rooms. I didn't think I'd want to do that, but then... I looked at the dress I'd slept in the previous night.

Nodding to myself I wrapped the towel around me.

Almost as daring as your previous dress, Auwei teased.

It was wide enough that it covered me just a tad lower on my thighs. I laughed. "I think that's the most revealing I've ever been and probably ever will be."

Auwei chuckled. *We'll see.*

I didn't know what that meant, and didn't ask.

I turned the shower back on and washed the dress, giving it a good once over, then wrung it out and headed back to my room.

I hung the dress in the narrow closet, leaving the door open to help it dry. I was about to remove the towel, when I heard a commotion outside my window.

Curious, I snuffed out my candle lantern so my room matched the darkness outside, then pushed aside my curtain.

It took a moment for my mind to catch up with what my eyes were seeing. Pebble was running back and forth, trying to escape from three other, larger boys, one of whom was Oak. It looked like Oak had chased Pebble into the long alley between the dorm and the admin building, where two others had been waiting for them. Now the three larger boys were closing in on Pebble, backing him up against the admin building.

My fury rose. I couldn't abide a bully. Even back in Miraline, I'd often put myself in the way of those who'd tormented smaller kids. It had earned me a lot of bruises... before I'd learned how to hit back.

I opened my window and jumped out to help Pebble.

Even before I got there, the boys started throwing punches. Pebble looked terrified and clearly didn't know how to fight... but he was very adept at dodging, nimble and quick, evading their fists.

I reached the first young man, grabbed his shoulder and spun him around, landing a solid punch on his nose. My fist stung, but I followed up quickly with another hit to his jaw, turning his head and dropping him.

Now I had their attention.

And only then, as Oak, Pebble, and the other boy stared at me... did I remember I was only wearing a towel.

Bloody Pits! Too late to do anything about that now. Hopefully it distracted them, so I could end this.

Ah, yeah, they're boys, you're plenty distracting, Auwei noted.

"Legs?" Oak blinked in surprise, his gaze alternating between staring at my legs and the tops of my breasts showing above the towel.

I stepped over to the unknown boy and swept his feet out from under him. He fell.

"Run!" I hissed to Pebble, who now had a clear line of escape. He did, and he was fast.

"Bloody bones," Oak swore and looked at Pebble, then me, then his two friends on the ground, then back to me. "You love him that much, do you?"

What?

He must have seen you kiss Pebble earlier, Auwei said.

Oh... but...

To a rival boy, that would be enough to assume love.

Spirits! Why are boys so stupid?

I could see it now, Oak's jealousy. But he didn't go after Pebble, instead he reached for me... well, actually he reached for the towel.

Pervert.

Just as he got one hand on the spot where the towel was tucked in over my breasts, I punched him in the nose; stunning him.

He released me and stumbled back a step.

The guy on the ground near me grabbed for a leg, but I kicked him off, then kicked his face. Pebble was away, and now it was time for me to leave. I wasn't sure I could take on all three of these boys together.

Oak grabbed me again, his hand around my left wrist. He

pulled me close. Lust hazed his words as he whispered, "Maybe I'll just take—"

I kneed him in the groin, then elbowed his shoulder as he doubled over.

I tried to run, but the first boy I'd attacked was up by then and managed to grab my towel. I quickly undid it and let him have it.

"Spirits!" one of them breathed as I sprinted the short distance back to my window... completely naked. I was up and back in my room quickly, shutting the window, closing the curtains, and breathing heavily. I doubted they'd try to get in here. One shout from me and they'd be in deep trouble.

"Well," I said between huffs of breath. "That was fun."

Was it? You liked that? Auwei asked.

I had. There was a part of me that just loved putting brutes in their place. "Yup."

Interesting... Auwei said. *Very interesting.*

I just hoped Pebble had gotten away and would find some place to hide from the others.

I was too energized to sleep, so I paced my room for a moment.

I knew there was something truly audacious about you, Auwei said. There was a confidence in her voice, a resolute I-made-the-right-choice sort of tone. *You felt so... alive, when you were out there, your spirit shining bright, it was amazing!*

Was it?

Yes, Birch. I think I've figured out one thing you want, even if you haven't.

Oh?

You want to put bullies in their place.

Yeah, I did. *True.* I'd have to think on that a bit more.

Then, in my pacing, I caught a glimpse of myself in the long looking glass. Right... I was still naked. I'd blown out the candle earlier, so the only light in the room was Auwei's faint glow. Still, I didn't need to see my reflection to know what was there, I'd seen it enough times before.

Tumbling curls of brown hair framed an oval face with a weak chin, and russet brown eyes. Nothing special there, though I did like my cute button nose and full lips. My shoulders were just a little too square, not the elegant slope of a lady. My arms were thick and strong from all the physical play — and occasional fights — as a child. I was a bit straight through the body with not much of a curve at waist or hips. Legs were sturdy and strong as well, though a bit leaner looking since I'd shot up in height over the last two years or so.

Honestly, I didn't really know what boys saw in me. Yeah, I had long legs, but other girls my age had a lot more curves. I was far from the most beautiful woman out there.

What do you see in the mirror, I'm curious? Auwei asked.

"A girl who—" I cut myself off then sighed with a faint chuckle. "Yeah, that's the problem. I don't know whether I'm a girl or a woman. A part of me still wants to run and play and be free, but I also want to be... important and help this nation." Another sigh. "I can't decide if I'm a tall awkward girl, with too much of a figure, or an awkward woman with not enough of one."

Auwei gave the sense of a nod, bobbing a little bit. *Want to know what I see?* She went on, not waiting for my answer. *A beautiful and athletic young woman with so much potential in body, mind and spirit, to become whatever she wants to become.* My mother had said something like that the night before The Choosing. *I think you've just shown how much drive you have to follow your heart and your passions.*

"Thanks, Auwei." That meant a lot to me.

I slept fairly well that night, with pleasant dreams of knocking down arrogant bullies.

CHAPTER 8

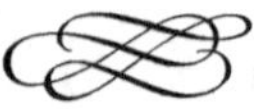

THE WEEKS WORE AWAY. THE CHOSEN BEGAN TO BOND AND LEAVE
Silverveil. By the end of the first month, roughly half of the sixty
or so Chosen had left.

Pebble was still around, though I hadn't seen much of him.
When I had, he'd been keeping close to a young woman, someone
from his group, I think. I didn't know much more than that.

Oak had avoided me after that night, though he'd taken to
glaring at me like Cedar did. I think he and Cedar eventually
hooked up, probably connecting over their mutual hatred of me.
But then they'd Bonded with their Lumani and left.

I still hadn't Bonded, and it worried me to no end.

Of my group, four remained: myself, the quiet Maple, the shy
and giggly Poplar, and the stoically determined Ash. We were all
working hard, but the feeling in the group was the same... a questioning: why not us? Why not yet?

Then finally the day came when I was to go into the Mists.
Generally, this was done either as a reward to those who Bonded
early or as a boost for those who hadn't Bonded yet. The five of us,
my group and Lady Kitsune, walked for most of the morning to get

there. First over a long ridge, then through rolling forested hills, then... to the thicker forests where the Mists hung heavy amidst the stout trunks of ancient trees.

"You will go in on your own, your guide will be your Lumani. Listen to them and heed their words. The Mistlands can be dangerous to unbonded humans." Lady Kitsune's tone gave no room for argument.

We spaced ourselves out, perhaps a dozen feet between us, then entered the Mists. One step into the heavy fog and I couldn't see the others, or much of anything. Occasionally, a thick tree trunk would appear, the Mists so dense I wouldn't see it until it was right next to me. Even then the trees seemed ephemeral. I tried touching one and had the oddest experience.

"I can reach into the tree," I whispered. This realm was made for whispers.

That's because it's not really there. It exists in your world, but you're in my world now and it's more a shadow of reality. You can walk right through that tree if you like.

I tried. It was unnerving, feeling it around me, but not stopping me. I didn't do that again.

"What did Lady Kitsune mean about The Mistlands being dangerous to humans? I thought all the spirits here were... friendly, like you."

Auwei sighed. *None of the beings here will hurt you... on purpose. But some of them are so anathema to physical life that they may... drain your essence. There are beings here, so foreign to your mind — and you so foreign to theirs — that they might feast on your life force and kill you, but think it nothing more than... as if you came upon a stream for a refreshing drink of water.*

"Oh." That was just a little terrifying.

But I'm with you, so I'll make sure that doesn't happen.

"Good." Slightly less terrified now.

What do you feel here? Auwei asked.

"Scared now," I said as a bit of a joke, though that was more truthful than I wanted to admit.

I mean physically.

"Oh... ah..." I stopped my wandering and closed my eyes to focus on my senses. It was odd. The fog against my skin felt like a breath of cool air. It didn't feel wet, like normal mist. "It feels cold but strangely dry." It only occurred to me then — and I couldn't help but blurt it out — that, "This isn't really mist!"

No.

"What is it?"

That defies explanation. It simply is. This is what my world is like. We never had a name for it until we met humans. You named it The Mists or The Mistlands, but we just think of it as home. This is our sky and earth, our water and plants. It is everything. Auwei giggled. *Want to know something truly astounding? You're not standing on anything.*

I opened my eyes and looked down. I could barely see my feet, so thick were the Mists. And below my feet, there were the faint hints of a forest floor, a few leaves, on which I was standing.

Just like that tree, the ground isn't real. Your mind is assuming you need to be on the ground because you always have been. But you can sink into the ground and be fine... or even fly.

"Fly?" That sounded fun. "I'd like to try that."

Auwei sighed. *Then do it. Though some of your kind find it hard to comprehend not being earthbound and are unable to fly. I can't tell you what to do or how to do it, since it's natural for me.*

I closed my eyes again and lifted my leg as if I was walking up a set of stairs. It was the easiest thing I could think of. It took a couple of tries before my foot stopped where I expected it to. Then I simply mounted that set of stairs, higher and higher. Some part of my mind knew there was nothing there, but as long as I assumed there was, it felt firm beneath me.

Well done, Auwei said with genuine praise in her voice. *You did that far quicker than any of my hosts before.*

I tried to picture a light and fluffy cloud of a bed before me. I reached out, making sure I could feel it, then fell forward onto it and... floated. I caused the made-up bed to float around, here and there, back and forth, as I lay upon it.

You have a vivid imagination, Birch. No one I've known has done that before.

"Now, if only I could do the mystical thing that would Bond us. I'm even in a mystical land, literally *The Mist-ical* land, and yet... oh..." I'd flown through something cold that sent a shiver down my spine. "What was that?"

You flew through a sprite. They were very confused. Luckily, they're not the dangerous ones.

Still, it had felt quite uncomfortable and awkward.

"I think I'm done flying for now." But then I wondered... "Where's the ground?"

There is no ground here, remember?

The image of falling forever flashed into my head and suddenly my "bed of clouds" dissipated.

I fell.

"Auwei!" I called, as I tumbled head over heels through the Mists.

Even though she couldn't float in spider form in my world, she had been floating beside me here in the Mists. Now she flashed down and under me and I slowed, then stopped. I didn't know what she was doing. She had no physical form with which to catch me, but I felt a sort of warm pressure on my back.

Relax, set your feet down, you can have ground beneath you whenever you like. Perhaps I should have phrased it that way.

"Perhaps," I said, righting myself and visualizing ground beneath my feet. And there it was, solid enough to stand on, though I saw nothing in truth. "How did you catch me?"

I have more power here in my world. I can... exude a sort of force, which has presence in the Mists... It's hard to explain.

I was just happy she'd done it.

"I... think I'm done in the Mists, if that's well with you?"

It is, yes. I'm glad you got to see my home. Just... imagine yourself walking out of the Mists back into your world. Take two or three steps and...

"Oh!" I gasped as I did indeed walk right out of the Mists. "I thought I was farther from the edge than that."

Distance is like the Mists themselves, ephemeral. You travel more by thought than physical motion. Now you can see why we were so fascinated with your world. It was so vast and... weighty.

"I guess it would seem that way, wouldn't it?"

"Perhaps," Lady Kitsune said in a scolding tone. "If you spoke to your Lumani in your head and through your spirit, you'd Bond with them sooner?"

I blinked at her. Poplar was also nearby, looking a little awed and terrified.

I spoke with Auwei in my head all the time when I wasn't alone. I just... preferred to use my voice, but... Kitsune was right. If we were supposed to be Bonded, two in one body, then I'd have to get used to speaking to Auwei internally.

"Thank you," I said with a solemn nod to Lady Kitsune. "You're right."

She seemed a bit taken aback at my formal and apologetic tone. Then she nodded and that was that.

When Ash came out of the Mists, she wore a beatific smile, eyes shining... and her Lumani was nowhere to be seen. It took me a second to understand, but Lady Kitsune knew immediately. "You Bonded? Good."

Ash nodded, still seeming a little stunned. "I feel... whole," she said, then her grin grew.

Maple took a while to return, but he hadn't Bonded.

We walked back to Silverveil in various moods. Ash seemed light as air. Poplar was still trembling. Maple just seemed confused, while I was disheartened. Yet another of my companions had Bonded, and even though I'd been to the most mystical place in the world, I had not.

Don't give up. You have two months left, Auwei said cheerily.

But by the end of the second month, we still hadn't Bonded.

CHAPTER 9

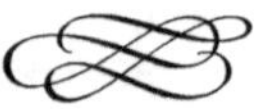

A CURIOUS THING HAPPENED AT THE START OF THE THIRD MONTH. Our existing groups were dissolved and remade with new instructors. Less than a dozen Chosen remained at Silverveil. Poplar and I were the only ones left in our original group.

They always do this, just to shake things up for those who remain, Auwei explained.

My new instructor was a dashing man in his prime, named Crown, with the avatar of a Crowned Eagle. I'd heard some of the girls talking excitedly about him in the past, and up close, I could see why. He was handsome, with an air of vitality about him.

Poplar and I were merged with the two remaining members of the Stone group: Pebble, and the young woman I'd seen him with, whose name turned out to be Hearth. She was plump and curvy, and the only other twenty-year-old in our entire class at Silverveil.

My anxiety was spiking, and not just because I hadn't Bonded yet. There was another, very important reason for my stress. The Noble-House Tests were in two weeks. But, given travel time, I'd need to be Bonded soon if I wanted to make it to the capital. They purposefully put them before the end of the Silverveil Bonding period. It was a motivator. If I wanted to join a Noble House, I'd have to go through those tests, and they were only held once a year. If I didn't Bond until after those tests, I'd have to wait a whole year to try, and even then, I might not get in. I had one week, maybe less, to get my act together and Bond, but the more I worried about it, the further and further that goal seemed to stretch before me. I was, at the same time, very close and impossibly far from achieving it.

Crown grinned at all of us as we gathered together. "You've probably been working your asses off trying to Bond, so here's a new strategy, take the day off. Wander the campus, even out on the hills, or sleep or lounge in a bath, I don't care. I'm here if you have any questions, but take all that pent-up frustration you're feeling and just... let it go. No one ever Bonded through frustration. Take today, get your energy back, and redouble your efforts tomorrow."

The four of us stood there, dumbfounded.

"What are you waiting for? Go!" He made a shooing motion with his hands, still beaming happily. "Have fun for a day!" he called after us as we began to disperse.

Poplar slunk back to the dorm.

Pebble came to me, followed by Hearth. "What were you going to do?" he asked me. He was still quite tentative and reserved in voice and posture.

Hearth spoke up. "Like we could *relax*!" she said, sounding as frustrated as I felt.

"We have to try," I said. "Crown's right. No one ever Bonded out of frustration. Maybe we *do* need to give ourselves a break. It scares The Pits out of me, but I'll try anything right now."

Hearth looked at me, then shrugged. "What do you plan to do? A bath sounded good."

I looked over at Pebble to see if he'd say anything and I caught the bright red blush on his cheeks before he quickly turned away.

Someone had just been thinking of Hearth and me in the baths. Poor awkward young man.

"I like walking, I think I'll go for a long walk... then maybe have that bath," I said. "You're both welcome to come with me." I was curious to hear how things had gone for Pebble... and to learn about Hearth.

They both nodded. Hearth said, "That sounds wonderful."

"But let's get out from behind these walls," I suggested and marched to the gates, then out onto the hills around Silverveil, the other two in my wake.

It was a gorgeous early summer's day. I took several long inhalations of the fresh, warm air and found the other two following suit. We walked in silence for a while before that started to feel awkward.

"How have you been, Pebble?" I asked.

"Good." His voice was soft. He didn't go on.

I sighed.

Hearth drew me aside a moment later. She spoke, voice hushed. "He probably wouldn't say it, but he's very grateful for what you did that night."

"You know?" I asked in a whisper.

She nodded. "I had been out for a walk and he nearly bowled me over as he'd run around our dorm. Then he... he just burst into tears and I held him. He cried in my arms for some time and then, once he could speak, asked if I knew of any place he could hide, he didn't want to go back to his dorm."

Spirits! That was awful. Would Oak and the others have tracked him back to his room? Probably. I hadn't even thought of that.

"So, I... ah... I sort of took him to my room," Hearth admitted.

I raised a brow at that.

"Oh, it was nothing like that, I was just giving him a place to hide. And, well... he never left. A couple nights later, we sneaked into his room and grabbed his things and his mattress. He's been sleeping on my floor ever since. We tuck his mattress away under my bed during the day and I... I have to sneak him down to the baths in the middle of the night. It's been awkward for him, for both of us." She looked me right in the eye as she said, "but we're just friends, that's it, nothing more."

"Oh?" It wasn't like I had some claim on the young man. "I would understand if you *were* more," I whispered.

She smiled. "No... I think he's got feelings for *you*. He's just never liked anyone like that before and he's confused. I've tried to talk him through it, but he gets all flushed and awkward and..." She sighed. "Poor boy."

I had to agree. "Thanks for letting me know," I said. Then, trying to include Pebble again, I raised my voice to ask both of them: "What did you two use to do before... all this?" I asked.

We waited, but Pebble remained silent.

Hearth went first.

"I was the daughter of a baker," she said with just a hint of longing in her voice. "I used to sit on a thick carpet to one side of the baking ovens and watch my father and mother work. I loved the smell of fresh breads and pastries." She gave a self-deprecating laugh, patting her slightly rounded belly. "I... may have had a few too many." She gave a pleasant sigh, then a heartier laugh. "I don't regret it. Everything they made was delicious. And when I was old enough, I joined them, helped them. My older brother worked too, and we were told early on that only one of us would be allowed to partake in The Choosing. My brother went for two years but wasn't Chosen. Then I went for three years and was Chosen in my last year."

She looked at the small green-brown mottled glowing bear that ambled along beside her. "Seioa Chose me, and I was so happy that day." She reached down to pet the oddly colored fur.

Auwei hadn't grown much when she'd taken the avatar form,

but she'd been a spider, so that wasn't too surprising. It seemed Seioa had grown considerably, now half as tall as Hearth. We'd be safe on these hills. Few things were likely to attack us with a bear as our companion.

"Still..." Hearth sighed again. "I do miss that warm oven and those tasty treats." She was silent for a long time after that.

I looked at Pebble, hoping Hearth's story would prompt him to open up. Yet, still, he took some time before he spoke. When he did, his voice was so soft I had trouble hearing him.

"My parents died when I was three."

Spirits! I knew what that was like, what that did to a child. Luckily the Clarks had taken me in.

"I went to live with my aunt, but... she died when I was seven."

Oh... Blessed Spirits! Wow.

"That's terrible, I'm so sorry Pebble," I said, heartfelt. I couldn't imagine how I'd feel if the Clarks had also passed while I'd still been young.

Hearth hummed an agreement. She even reached out and laid a hand on his shoulder. He looked at her, tears in his eyes. His Lumani's avatar was that of a tiny mouse, the white glowing form buried in pebble's tangled tousle of thick, light brown hair.

"After that, I was allowed to stay in my aunt's house, no one else claimed it. But I was young and didn't know how to take care of it. By the time I was ten, half the roof had caved in. I was hungry all the time." He looked at Hearth with these words, a bit of longing in his gaze. I guessed it wasn't for her so much as the warm and comfortable life she'd led.

"I had to beg or steal for food. When I was old enough to go to The Choosing, I did. Though I didn't know it was a thing until I was already seventeen." Only then did a hint of a smile find his lips. "That's where Haleia found me." He reached up and gently stroked the luminous fur of the mouse with one finger.

Wow, if he was seventeen, he was small for his age, but then, if he'd been living alone and starving, that might explain why he'd been so skinny. He'd been eating well for a couple months now, and was starting to fill out. There was a strength to his slight frame, and I had seen just how nimble he could be and how quickly he could run. He'd be a handsome man someday. Though, handsome or not, his eyes still drew me in. I could see in them his compassion and tenderness... and grit.

"I... I never thought I'd be Chosen." His brief elation fell into melancholy. "And now I may end up back on the streets." Haleia must have said something to him as he soon added, "I know, I know."

It was a bit odd to hear someone speaking out loud to their avatar.

My heart broke for the young man. "You'll Bond, I'm sure." Before he could comment with something negative, I kept going, "I know we're all feeling down right now, which is why Master Crown was right, we just need to enjoy today. We can worry about everything else tomorrow. Let's forget our worries, at least for the moment and—" I drew in a heady breath of the summer's air. "—just enjoy this beautiful day."

He smiled faintly and nodded. "What about you?" Pebble asked after a moment. I thought I heard just a hint more strength in his voice. "Who were you before?"

It was my turn for a sad, nostalgic smile. "My name was Sara, and I was the daughter of two scribes who worked at the Library of Miraline. Though, they weren't my parents in truth. My birth parents were merchants and... never returned from a trip east into Vauphan when I was four. We got word that their small caravan had been hit by bandits." I swallowed hard, a single tear in my eye. It had been so long ago, and yet still stung me.

"Friends of my family took me in. My best friend became my sister. She's now a Noble in House Pegasus. She's... frightfully smart. Her name is Dove."

"I've heard of her," Pebble said, sounding a bit surprised himself. "The grounds of House Pegasus weren't far from my aunt's house. They're pleasant and calm, and I used to sneak over the wall to sit on their lawns some days, when I needed a break from the city." Ah, so Pebble was from the capital, for which the nation was named: Elista. Most of the Noble Houses had their physical house there, including Pegasus. "They say she is going to remake the city, that she has plans to tear up the streets and add something called sewers."

That sounded like Dove, always with a project in her head.

"I hadn't heard that," I said. "But it sounds like her. Anyway, we grew up a bit wild and free, but well educated." I sighed. "I'd always wanted to be Chosen but had to wait for my last year before Auwei found me."

And I'm very lucky I did.

Thank you, Auwei.

"Everyone thought you'd be the first to Bond," Hearth said.

I looked at her, shocked, and she only then seemed to realize she'd said it out loud.

She blushed a little. "Well, you were the first to find your avatar. All the girls thought you'd be gone in a week."

Really?

I'd thought they'd all hated me. "I... didn't think anyone else thought much of me."

"You made quite an impression that first day," Hearth said.

Pebble nearly choked, coughing a bit to cover it up.

"Well, other than that," I said. "I'd thought everyone had forgotten about that quickly and just... avoided me."

"Well, yes, some did. But many others were intimidated by you."

"By me?"

"I'm not sure why you're surprised. You're older and towered over most of them. And you'd found your avatar on the first day.

All the boys seemed to have eyes for you. You were everything the girls wanted to be."

"Oh..." I said.

You never know what others think; hence, it's never that good to dwell on it. They don't matter in the end. Only you matter, as well as your friends and loved ones.

I nodded to that.

"It was all just a show, a joke," I said a bit softly. "A couple of the other girls, Cedar and River, had stolen my other dresses and—"

"Oh, I know, everyone knew. Everyone hated them for it. If they hadn't done that, then you'd never have stolen the attention of most of the boys. Those two weren't particularly popular either."

"Oh." There was so much I hadn't known about. "Was the attention of the boys really that much of a thing?"

Hearth stopped and stared up at me. I stopped too, and Pebble made a slow arc around to the other side of us, stopping. Hearth shook her head. "You... you have no clue, do you?"

Apparently, I didn't. "About what?"

I did tell you that many Noble Houses sent their boys and girls here to scout for a possible match, Auwei reminded me.

Oh, that.

"Silverveil is the place where young Nobles go to Bond, in more ways than one." Hearth seemed very shocked that I didn't know this. "Since people come from all over the nation, and any of them could be a Noble within a matter of months, everyone is on the prowl for who might be a good match. The boys are told to look for girls that are bright and beautiful and driven, and the girls are told to look for boys who are... well, pretty much the same."

She cleared her throat a little. "They're even told to dally a bit if they wish, but not to make any true commitments. The point is to pick out who they want to make alliances with later. You... you threw that whole process into chaos."

I smiled. Something about that appealed to me. I'd never known the Noble Houses were so... cutthroat and cunning, sending their youth out to make alliances for them. It seemed creepy to me. I was glad I'd messed up those plans.

"Suffice to say, if you become a Noble, you may receive several offers for marriage," Hearth said.

"Oh!" That shocked me.

What happens if someone from one Noble House marries someone from another Noble House? I asked Auwei. Have you ever done that?

Most marriages are within a Noble House. But when two Houses come together like that the couple gets to decide which House they would like to be a part of. They cannot remain in both.

Oh.

It is a way for some people to advance up into a more prestigious Noble House. Though I'll tell you now, more prestigious does not necessarily mean better or more generous, or anything of that sort.

That made sense.

I sighed. "I don't want any of that. I'm not here for a husband. I'm here to Bond, and yes I want to become a Noble, but... I..." Well, I didn't know if I'd want to "marry-up" or not. I guess it would depend on which Noble House I ended up in... and which man proposed.

I sighed again, running a hand through my hair, shaking my head.

"I need more fresh air," I said and turned, walking once more. With my long legs and swift stride, the others had to hurry to catch up. Once they did, I slowed a little to accommodate them.

"What do you two want to be?" Pebble asked, his voice so soft, I barely heard it. It took me a moment to register the question. By then Hearth was answering.

"I... I want to create a safe place. I want people to have a warm place to rest, and caring people around them, like I had growing up."

I nodded to that. Her bear avatar made more sense now. She'd do whatever it took to protect those in need, like a mother bear did for her young.

"That would be nice," Pebble said. "What about you, Birch?"

Oh, this question again. I felt like I needed an answer now, more than any other time I'd been asked. Hearth's answer had been so clear and concise. I could almost picture it. Shouldn't I want something that clearly?

I took a moment to ponder my avatar: a spider. If Hearth's bear was indicative of her desires, then perhaps a spider was indicative of mine. But what did a spider want? To spin webs and scare people?

No... so then what?

People talked about "a web of lies" so did I want to deceive people?

No.

There were other sayings about being caught in a web...

Caught...

Oh, I felt that. Did you think of something? Auwei asked.

Maybe... it feels sort of right...?

I tried to sound confident as I said, "I want to catch people, bad people, doing bad things. I want to bring them to justice." Something about that resonated deeply within me.

"People like me?" Pebble whispered.

"What?" Had he done something wrong? Oh... he'd mentioned stealing, being a thief. "No, not like that. You were stealing to survive, that's different. I'm talking about people who are really hurting others. Like Oak and those two who attacked you that night. I can't abide that."

Auwei had said, that night, that she'd figured out more about me. But it wasn't until now that it sank in for me. I'd run in to face those three without a second thought. I really did want to punish those who harmed or threatened others.

Even as a child I'd stood up to bullies and reported things that weren't right to my parents. I'd gotten my share of black eyes for my trouble, but they'd been worth it. I'd done what I'd known was right in the moment.

"Besides," I said to reassure Pebble. "I don't think a Lumani would Choose someone who was truly bad."

Ah... well... Auwei's hesitancy surprised me.

What?

Not all Lumani are as benevolent as you might think. Remember all those Noble parents who sent their kids off to scout matches. They're all True-Bonded with Lumani. And some Nobles I've met have been... ah... well even more corrupt.

Truly? I thought—

It's not something we share openly, but... we Lumani start to take on some of your human characteristics after a while. It's one reason I'm a bit girlish and giggly. Others have acquired less desirable traits over time. When they Bond now, they seek humans like them, which only perpetuates and builds upon their nature. I've met some surprisingly vile True-Bonded. I wouldn't say it's common, but you should be aware such True-Bonded are out there. I don't sense anything like that from Pebble or Haleia though.

I was too shocked to reply. What sort of world would I be getting into, if I was chosen for a Noble House?

Auwei tried to assuage me. *Some Nobles may be corrupt, but really, most of the Noble Houses are good places.*

Most?

Well, ah... yeah. I could sense her discomfort. She'd dug herself a hole, and I wouldn't let her out of it. *Your sister's House, Pegasus, is quite lovely. Some of their members are a bit full of themselves, but I wouldn't say they're bad people. And Pterolycus House is a bit wild and dangerous, but never to innocent people. They protect our border in the north and need to be a bit fiercer in nature. Panther House are insular and can be a bit superior. There may be a few not-so-nice members there. Wyvern... well I know you idolize their leader, and Skyfire is a true soul, but some of her members are a bit... bloodthirsty. They, like Pterolycus are fierce protectors of the nation, but some like battle and killing a little too much. The same is true of Grizzly House, they have a ferociousness to them, but few would ever dare to use it anywhere other than to protect Elista. Tanuki and Porcupine Houses are generally good and wholesome Houses, open and friendly, though looked down on a little by some of the other Houses for their charitable work.* She hesitated, pausing a moment. The only two she hadn't mentioned were the Royal House, Owl, and House Maverick.

What about the Royal House? I asked.

They are, strong and powerful...

What wasn't she saying? *But?*

But... they don't all want to use that power for the good of the nation. Some of them are a bit too power hungry. They'll stay in line as long as Queen Whitewing is in power, but I fear what may happen if she dies.

I was shocked.

I didn't know what to make of this. I'd thought the Royal House to be a strong and guiding influence over the nation, but if it was filled with selfish, power-hungry types, what would happen if the benevolent Whitewing stepped down? If she died, there would be a Council of Nobles, where the various House Leaders would choose a new Royal House and perhaps Owl might not be chosen. But if Whitewing stepped down then others from her House would rise to power. What then?

I asked Auwei.

I don't know.

Not what I wanted to hear.

And what about Maverick? I asked.

They're... odd. A House of misfits and outcasts. It began with a few

Nobles who left their Houses, seeking a place to fit in. They found that together and founded a new House. Maverick has made itself a safe haven for anyone, but I truly don't know what it's like there. Not a House I've ever been a part of.

Ah.

Wow.

That was a lot to take in. My thoughts whirled and I walked in silence, not even hearing the conversation between the other two for a while. When I finally did tune in to their words once more, I guessed I hadn't missed too much.

"What do you want?" Hearth asked Pebble.

Pebble sighed. "I just want to get off the streets... find a real home."

Maverick would probably take someone like him, Auwei said softly. *I don't think he's got what it takes to make it in any of the other Houses, though.*

Would I?

I no longer knew where I might want to be placed. I'd always wanted to be in House Owl but now... I wasn't so sure. Pegasus sounded nice and that's where my sister was. Perhaps Pterolycus or Wyvern? I'd need to be fierce to fit in there, but I was passionate about protecting the nation, so maybe?

You'll do fine, wherever you end up, Auwei said reassuringly.

I hoped so.

The day drew on and eventually we all grew hungry. We made our way back to Silverveil but had missed lunch. Hearth and Pebble waited in the shade of a tree, chatting, while I went looking for Crown. I hoped our instructor might be able to get us some food.

I found him in the great hall chatting with a few other instructors. He spotted me and nodded, breaking off his conversation and coming to me, a basket in hand. "I noticed you three weren't at lunch, so I put some things together for you," he said handing the basket over. "How was the walk?"

"Good. We learned a lot about each other."

His blue-eyed gaze caught mine for a long moment. "I think I'm going to let you take the lead with those two, if you're well with that."

"Oh? Why?"

"You took a natural leadership role with them. I'd like to nurture that." He shrugged. "We don't know much about how the Bonding happens so there isn't much I can really say, but I can help you to find out a bit more about yourself during this process."

"Oh, thank you," I said, a bit stunned.

He smiled and winked, turning away to return to the other instructors. I took the food out and we three had a quiet meal in the shade of the tree, while I pondered all the strange, scary, and surprising things I'd learned that morning.

Have faith, Auwei said to me. *Crown has faith in you. You should too.*

A leader?

That didn't seem like me at all, but... maybe?

CHAPTER 10

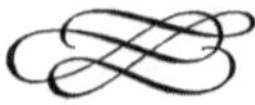

The attack came at night.

My only warning was Auwei screaming into my head: *Birch, wake up, move!*

I snapped my eyes open, already moving to sit up when I saw the shadowy form over my bed, and the flash of a knife.

I shifted at the last minute and the knife slid along my right arm, just below the shoulder, instead of hammering into my chest.

Pits! What was happening?

I reacted without thinking, kicking out. I caught the person on the side of their leg, hard enough to shift them. They stumbled to one side as I rose from my bed in a fury. My experience with those bullies meant I knew how to throw a punch and the attacker was caught off guard when I slammed my fist into their nose.

They reeled back, hitting the wall. I kicked up between their legs. Man or woman, that would hurt. They grunted, bending forward, and I brought my knee up into their face. Their head snapped back with a crack and they slumped lifeless to the ground.

Bloody Pits!

I stood frozen for a long moment, in shock, not knowing what to do. I should run, or light a lamp, or check this person, but I did nothing as my mind reeled.

They were dead. I don't know how I knew, but I knew.

I'd killed a person.

But they'd been trying to kill me.

It was all too much. I had to do something or I'd collapse into a heap, overwhelmed. I had to keep moving, and I certainly didn't want to be here. My mind latched onto the idea that if I had been attacked, perhaps others in the dorm were in trouble. So, I crept to my door, which was open, and peered carefully out into the hallway. I saw no other movement in the shadows.

I sneaked out, creeping to Hearth's room, which was three doors down from mine on the other side of the hall. As I reached it, the door opened cautiously and Hearth peered out. I could see Pebble further back in the room, looking frightened.

"What's going on?" she whispered. "I thought I heard something."

Yeah, she'd probably heard me, fighting for my life. But as to what was happening? I had no clue.

Remain calm and we'll figure this out. Though even Auwei sounded a bit stunned.

Before I could come up with any coherent response to her question, Hearth's gaze focused on my arm. "You're bleeding!"

I am? Oh right, the cut on my arm. I'd been so agitated, the pain hadn't fully registered. Even now, it didn't seem that bad, it was bleeding, but the cut was shallow. I'd be fine for a while.

I can help with that. Auwei was over the spot a moment later and spinning a thick web over the long slice, stopping the blood. It felt cool and slightly soothing.

"Ah, yeah, I know," I said finding my words again. "Someone attacked me. I don't know what's going on, but others might be in danger. I'm—" I'm going to do what? Go out and find trouble?

That was a stupid idea. Facing a few bullies was different than fighting armed killers. I'd only survived in my room because of desperation and flailing limbs.

So, what would I do?

"You two stay here and bar the door. I'm going to find out what's going on." That sounded more reasonable than going to fight. I'd just... take a peek, nothing more. Perhaps go find an instructor. Yes, that was a wise course.

Hearth nodded and closed her door. I heard furniture being moved. Good, they were safe.

Just remember, Auwei said. *You only live once, but I'll regret your mistakes for eternity.*

She'd said that before as a bit of fun, but now it was a warning.

I crept to the end of the hall. Reaching the door to the outside, I hesitated, terrified. I'd take a quick look out into the yard before going any farther.

The door creaked as it opened, just an inch.

"Is she dead?" a harsh female voice asked. A shadow next to the door began to turn my way.

She...? As in me? Just me?

Dead... as in...

What The Pits was going on!

My heart thundered. I stifled a yelp as time seemed to slow. I had to get out of the way, but where? I panicked as something seemed to shatter inside me. Everything became clearer, the dark hallway crisp in my vision. A great upwelling of energy and vitality sprung to life within me.

Jump! Auwei shouted. Her voice inside my mind had always sounded a bit distant, but in that instant, it became clear and close.

I leaped, but instead of launching myself back, I went up, and with far more ease and effect than expected. I put my hands out before I hit the ceiling with my head. When my hands touched the ceiling, they stuck. I didn't fully register this as I pulled my legs up after me. I was still in my nightdress with bare feet and I curled my body around to press my feet to the ceiling as well, crouching awkwardly. My feet stuck too.

Birch, we—

Not now! I hissed internally as a figure poked their head in through the door below.

"Arick?" the woman asked. She was masked, all in black, like the attacker in my room.

Another voice outside asked something, but their voice was low and I only heard "... happened?"

"I don't know. The door just opened on its own? Odd." The figure poking their head in looked carefully to either side, then slipped back out. I heard her say, "If he's not done soon, I'm going in."

Blackened bloody bones!

Not wanting to be here when they came in, I crawled away... on the ceiling.

Birch!

Not now, Auwei!

No, Birch, this is important, you're using my powers! We Bonded!

Some part of me was already quite aware that normal humans did not stick to ceilings. But I had more important things to think about. People were trying to kill me and I was freaking out. I had to get away.

Great... how does that help us? I asked.

Ah... I don't know yet, Auwei admitted.

Then be quiet and let me think!

I skittered to the far end of the hall and was about to open the door to the common room — from above — when all the hair on my body stood up and I felt the strangest sensation thrum through me. I was *hearing* people talk, very quietly, on the other side of the door. Only I wasn't hearing with my ears. The sound reverberated into my body through the thousands of standing hairs all over me.

At first, I couldn't decipher the noises I was taking in from this new sense, but I quickly adapted.

"...freaks me out."

"Yeah, I know. I can't believe we're working for her. She scares The Pits out of me."

"Hopefully this job will be over soon and we can..." I didn't need to hear any more to be both terrified and certain I couldn't go through *that* door.

I couldn't leave through the doors at either end of the halls. I probably should have gone back to my room and out the window, but that didn't occur to me in the moment. No, I could only think of the one other way out of this hall: the stairs down to the baths.

I crawled down the wall and back to the floor, slipping into the open archway to one side of the hall, and treading lightly down the stairs into the baths.

I don't know if you'll be able to get out this way, Auwei said sounding a bit desperate herself. *If they have guards on these doors, they're probably watching the other dorm as well.*

I gave a manic chuckle as an idea started forming in my mind. *I'm not going out. I'm going to stay down here.* Yup, I had a plan. It was a stupid plan and very crazy, but I couldn't think of anything else.

Oh? Auwei breathed, curious, then... *Oh!* As she found my thoughts on what I planned. *That's... interesting...*

You're being kind... My plan wasn't to run but to hide. And if they came looking for me. I'd be ready. I didn't know why I thought I could fight them, but I did.

The large, long bathing room was completely dark, but my body-hair, standing on end, seemed to catch every twitch of the air and I just knew where the walls were.

I moved with as much speed as I dared, first to a shower stall, grabbing the large bowl of liquid hair soap. I sneaked back out to the entrance, where the stairs ended, and dumped the bowl all over the last step and the area below that. It wasn't quite enough so I went to another stall and got its bowl, making that last step a slippery mess. I then did the same with the bottom step at the entrance from the other dorm. Then I went into each shower stall and turned them on to the highest heat setting, leaving all the doors open. Steam poured out, making the room very hot and humid as a thick fog clouded the area. In the last stall I grabbed the towel and the scrubbing brush from the stall before turning the hot water on. They weren't much as weapons, but they were something.

I moved into the far end of the room where the baths were located. There was a large common pool if girls wished to bathe together, and past that several smaller pools with half-walls around them for private bathing. I got more of the liquid hair soap and doused the area coming out from the showers, making a path straight to the large bath.

I wrapped the towel I'd taken around my left arm and tied it off as a bit of protection if I needed to deflect a blow. I held the body-scrubber like a knife, not knowing what I'd do with it, but I was ready.

I waited.

The room grew stifling hot, and the thick, wet heat began to steal my breath and sap my strength, but still I waited. My night-dress stuck to me like a second skin.

Then I heard it: soft voices approaching.

"...by surprise. Her window wasn't open so she's in here some-where." That's when it occurred to me to have slipped out my window, but it seemed they might have been watching that too... so perhaps this had been the best plan.

I heard a very faint squelch, then a clipped cry and the sound of someone falling hard.

There were murmurs for a moment, then a clipped curse. "The bitch killed Farin!"

Ha! Take that!

Another voice... the female one from earlier, said: "First Arick, now this. She's a clever little bitch, resourceful. Watch out for the last step and the area beyond, it's covered in something slick."

There were more murmurings for a moment, then finally a strong call: "Come out, girl! We know you're in here. Come on out and I promise to make it a quick death, painless. But make this any more difficult for us and I'll skin you alive!" This from that female voice. She must be in charge.

What have I ever done? Why do they want to kill me?

I'm not the one to ask.

Spirits of the Mists, save us.

Auwei gave a nervous laugh. *I am a spirit of the mist and I can save you. When they come, leave the fighting to me, I'll take control. You may have fought bullies, but I've fought far worse.*

Worked for me.

Two sets of footfalls crept closer. The light from a single lantern swayed and slowly illuminated more and more of the baths as they neared.

A foot appeared from the hall of showers about the same time as two hands, one with a lantern, the other with a knife.

The foot hit the floor and, as hoped, slid out from under the person. They slid forward just enough that when they placed their other foot down to steady themselves it was also in the shower hair-soap I'd put down. At the same time, I reached out and smacked the face I saw coming into view with the body-scrubber I'd acquired. The person fell back while sliding forward, crying out as they went over the edge into the large pool as hoped. The lantern fell from their hands and hit the floor to one side, rolling away, casting wild shadows around the room, but remaining lit.

"Bloody Pits!" the female voice cried out. She leaped around the corner, over the soapy floor and landed right in front of me, murder in her eyes. She held a long knife in one hand with her free hand open in front of her.

I felt Auwei take control, sensed her readiness. But even Auwei was fooled. We expected the woman to attack with the knife, but it was her open hand that snapped out. The base of her palm caught me in the nose. My head snapped back, then bounced off the stone wall behind me. Explosions of pain blossomed in the front and back of my head. Auwei raised my towel-wrapped left arm to block the knife attack I expected as a follow up, but instead the knife slid over my belly, cutting deep.

Pits! Auwei cursed, but then she moved with such speed and precision. Even with my eyes clamped shut, my new spider's sense gave me a good idea where the woman was and we kicked between her legs, hitting home.

She grunted.

Auwei swept my arm down and hit the woman's hand. I heard the knife clatter to the floor. That same hand of mine then surged up to punch the woman's face, my towel-wrapped fist barely hurting at all as it landed. At the same time my right hand was moving over my stomach. I didn't know what it was doing, but Auwei did. My body was producing great quantities of spider-silk... from... my belly-button? I gathered it quickly in my hand and pressed it over the wound on my stomach, helping to stop the blood flow.

I stepped forward, throwing myself bodily into the woman and knocking us both into the pool.

Warm water surged around me and far too much went in my mouth. I found the bottom of the pool with one foot and surged up, coughing out water, seeking air. I opened my eyes to see the woman righting herself in front of me, and the other man — who'd gone into the pool first — now wading over to me.

I've got this, Auwei said with a calm I certainly didn't feel.

My right hand reached down and pulled another quickly spun gob of spider-silk from me, splashing up to throw it in the man's face. It hit home, covering his eyes. He'd be occupied for a moment.

Then we ducked under the water, avoiding a punch from the woman. Going horizontal, my feet found the wall behind me and pushed off, launching me through the water to the woman. I hit her — head first — in the belly. She folded. Auwei quickly righted us, then dunked the woman's head under the water as we came up. The attacker had lost her footing and flailed, frantic, as I used every ounce of my weight to keep her under the water.

One of her fists caught my ribs hard enough that I'd probably bruise, but that was it. She struggled for a moment longer, then began to weaken and slow before going completely still.

Well... that was sickening. I'd killed three people tonight, and I hadn't liked any of it. My only solace was that they'd been trying to kill me. Yet it still made bile rise in my throat.

Releasing the woman's head, I turned. The man had managed to scratch some of the spider-silk off his face, enough to free one eye.

I needed to deal with him quickly. Even with the spider's silk — and my towel-wrapped left arm — over my gut, I was losing far too much blood, growing weak. The man saw it too, the growing dark-red cloud around me in the waters. He grinned, a nasty thing, and came at me slowly. He'd managed to find his knife, and the blade gleamed, flashing in the light of that remaining lantern.

"Hazra said you'd be trouble, but I don't think she foresaw any of this. You've killed Lyena there, and the others, but I think maybe all I need to do is wait and you'll be gone soon enough." That nasty grin grew.

My sight grew dim, blackness fading in around the edges. I didn't want to get close to him, not while he had that knife, but I'd have to do something.

That's when I saw the two shapes coming out from the shower hall behind him.

"No," I whispered, but there was no strength left in my voice.

The last thing I saw before I blacked out was Pebble and Hearth charging at the man in the pool.

CHAPTER 11

I WAS RATHER SURPRISED TO WAKE UP AT ALL, LET ALONE IN A comfortable bed.

I groaned as pain, more remembered than real, sank its teeth into my arm and stomach.

Don't worry, we survived and you're on the mend, Auwei said, sounding confident. *Now that we're Bonded, I'm only semi-aware while you're unconscious, but I know we've been healed a little and bandaged up.*

That sounded good, but I still felt like The Pits. I groaned again.

"Legs?" The voice was familiar.

I pulled my eyes open and rolled my head to the side, feeling groggy and exhausted.

Slowly my gaze focused on the woman sitting next to my bed. First, I saw a pristine white gown, hands folded neatly in her lap. I looked up the strong, slender figure to find features I knew better than my own: golden-blond hair, bright blue eyes, small mouth, slight nose, and a familiar head-tilt.

"Dove," I murmured, my voice sounding rough. My heart both leaped for joy and settled with ease.

"Hello, sister."

"When did you get here?"

"I flew from the capital as soon as I heard the news." The capital was hundreds of miles away. She must have seen my look of stunned awe. "Doves can fly great distances quickly when needed," she said with a smile. "And I had good reason to hurry."

I nodded, head moving against my pillow.

After a moment, as my mind slowly cleared, something... the first word she'd said returned to me. "You called me Legs." That seemed odd. "My name is Birch."

She shook her head slowly. "You're Bonded now. Your Silver-veil name no longer applies, and I'm afraid, in your case, you don't get a say in your True-Bonded name. It was what everyone here was calling you when I arrived. For better or worse, you're Legs now, Sister." She couldn't quite repress her tight-lipped chuckle.

Oh... great.

There are worse names.

Like what?

One of my Hosts was known as Tit for her True-Bonded name. To clarify, her Bonded form was that of a great tit, a bird.

Oh... yes, that would be awkward, wouldn't it?

She... we got used to it after a while. Just like you and that dress, we owned it.

"Legs," I sounded out the name. Auwei was right. It wasn't the worst.

"I sense there is a story behind that name," Dove said with a grin.

"Yup, but that's for later." I was curious. "How long...?"

"Five days since the attack."

Five days!

We were... very hurt. A Lumani can lend a little energy to help their host heal, but it's not much. It's a good thing there was a physician present at Silverveil to tend to you. If not for them... things may have been much worse.

And I am very grateful for your presence, I said and meant it.

You're going to have to live with me now, for a long while, or so I hope.

Me too.

"Who...?" I asked, still limited in my energy. Yet she seemed to understand what I was asking.

Dove shrugged. "They don't know who was behind the attack or why they seemed to be targeting you. Though..." She pressed her lips as if she'd said too much.

"What?" There was something in her look which scared me. "Tell me, Dove."

She sighed. "The attackers were assassins from the borderlands." That wasn't the bad part. No, given how she still looked shaken, I was sure there was more. "It's believed they were working with... a mistweaver."

I instantly went cold and heard Auwei's internal gasp of horror and fear.

"No," I whispered. "That's impossible."

She nodded. "So we all thought. But..." Again, she pressed her lips together for a long moment. I wasn't sure I wanted to know more, so I didn't prompt her, but she spoke after a few deep breaths. "There were five assassins taken alive, but before they could speak or tell us anything, *something* killed them. Some otherworldly force, taking the shape of mists, suffocated them. There was nothing we could do."

Well, wasn't that just horrible.

Also... why in The Pits did a mistweaver want me dead?

This is bad. Auwei sounded more terrified than anytime I'd known her.

Bad? Yeah, I know, but why are you worried? You're immortal.

Auwei hesitated within me, as if unwilling to go on, then she told me the truth. *Yes, we Lumani are immortal. We're energy, and when our host dies, we live on. But... it's possible... for a Lumani to be killed by a mistweaver with enough strength.*

Oh!

Exactly.

Auwei and I stewed in our fear and horror.

Dove, clearly sensing our confusion and dread, laid a comforting hand on the side of my head, stroking my hair. "You're safe now," she said softly.

Ah... no. I was being hunted by a mistweaver. I'd never be safe, ever again! But I didn't say anything. I let her have her comforting words; hopefully they comforted her.

We stayed that way for some time, and I managed to rest, even if I couldn't sleep or truly relax. After a while, Dove said: "I'm going to stretch my legs... maybe my wings. And it's time for you to have something to eat. Also, there are some others who would like to see you, I think. I'll be back." She leaned down to kiss my forehead, then rose and left the small room.

Then, in came a short procession of people. Master Crown came first with a tray of food, setting it on the chair Dove had just vacated. Behind him were Hearth and Pebble, neither had their avatars visible. Had they Bonded? I hoped so.

"How are you doing?" Crown asked softly as he sat on the edge of the bed. He pressed his lips together and I sensed a healthy dose of shame coming from him. "I'm sorry. I should have been able to stop this, or... something." Then he forced a smile. "I'm just glad you're well."

"I am, thank you." I tried to smile and failed.

"And you're Bonded! I would not recommend that method of Bonding to anyone, but I'm glad..." He trailed off. "I'm glad."

I nodded.

He rose, turned to the other two and nodded to them, then left.

Pebble took Crown's place on the edge of my bed, and Hearth took the tray of food and placed it on her lap as she took the chair.

"Can you sit?" Hearth asked.

"I think so?" I still felt achy and exhausted, but I wanted to show strength for these two. I started to rise, then fell back, my stomach spasming with sharp pain. That wound was still healing.

"Let me help," Hearth said, giving the tray to Pebble and helping to lift me and shift me so I was sitting sideways on the bed. She took my pillow and put it against the wall for me to lean on. "There."

My head spun a little now that I was upright, but it settled quickly enough. My stomach still stung, but Hearth had been careful and the pain faded as long as I wasn't moving too much. Just sitting here wasn't too bad.

Hearth took the chair again and Pebble handed me the tray of food. There were salted strips of dried pork, slices of plum, melon, and a few blackberries. There was also a thick slice of bread and a cup half-filled with water. I started with the bread, tearing off a few chunks to eat tentatively. They went down well and only made me realize how hungry I was.

The others spoke as I ate.

"We've Bonded," Hearth said with a sad, confused smile. "Like you." She forced a big grin. "Not the way I would have chosen, but it worked." A sigh. "I'm Blackclaw now. Not the most feminine name, but it fits. And Pebble is now Silence."

I smiled and nodded at each of them in turn.

"We... ah... well, we were terrified after you came around that night. We barricaded the door and hid, like you said, but then... so much time passed. We had no clue what was going on." She looked to Pebble — now Silence — and he nodded, taking up the telling from there.

His voice was still quiet, but now possessed a clear and resolute quality, which made it easier to hear and understand. "I... I was terrified and I just wanted to be as small as I could and hide." He looked away, clearly ashamed, but Hearth — now Blackclaw, what a name — leaned forward and put a reassuring hand on his knee.

He swung his gaze to her and something passed between them.

He drew a long breath and spoke again. "I felt the Bond happen, then... almost instantly I took my avatar form. I was a tiny mouse. Since we were so uncertain and curious, I sneaked out to the door and peered underneath to see what was happening. Two people were working their way slowly down the hall. When they got to your room, one of them cursed viciously and they mentioned someone was dead. From how upset they were I didn't think it was you. But then they went looking for you. They gathered someone from the far end of the hall then made their way down to the baths. I ran back to tell Hearth... ah... I mean Blackclaw this. She was the one who wanted to follow after them. She's far braver than I am."

I didn't know about that. He'd been there, right beside Blackclaw, charging in at my attacker, before I'd blacked out.

"It takes far more bravery to help when you're terrified, than it does when you're not," Blackclaw reassured him gently.

I agreed with that sentiment.

I had finished the bread and fruit and was moving on to the pork. I bit off a small chunk and sucked on it, savoring the salty, smokey goodness.

Blackclaw took up the telling. "I was terrified myself, but... I had to help. Something... shifted within me. I needed to protect, to defend, to help, and I think that's what caused my Bonding. When I heard what Silence said, we cleared away the barricade, as quietly as we could, and sneaked out." She drew in a long, steadying breath.

I could tell, even just retelling the events was frightening for her.

"We crept along slowly, keeping well behind them. We were just reaching the bottom of the stairs when we heard the fighting. Your trap there nearly got me too, if Silence hadn't caught me." She smiled at him. "He was sure-footed enough."

He smiled at that and blushed a little at the praise.

"Even then, we were both scared and cautious," continued Blackclaw. "So... we thought we'd arrived too late. You looked... horrible, just about to faint into the baths and drown. I rushed forward, throwing myself at that last man. I was very surprised to see Silence there next to me and between the two of us we managed to subdue him and rescue you." She chuckled. "I can apparently be... quite strong when I want to be."

"But she took a cut to her arm," Silence said, voice heavy with concern.

"Bears have tough hides," she said with a grin. "It wasn't that bad." She pulled up the short sleeve of her dress to show the long cut on her shoulder and upper arm, still an angry red, but scabbed over. She wore it like a badge of honor. She looked at the wound for a long moment then nodded to herself. "I hadn't been going to test for a Noble House before, but... I think I will now. I need to be out there, defending people."

"I'm going to test too," Silence said with quiet determination.

I'd lost track of time. "When is the test?" I asked around a mouthful of pork.

"A little over a week."

"A week? In the capital? We'll never get there in time." I didn't know the travel time exactly, but by carriage it would probably be a nine or ten day trip. A fast carriage could get us there quicker, but those specialty coaches were hard to come by.

Blackclaw smiled. "They've heard of what happened here and agreed to extend the tests over a few days if needed. They're also sending a fast carriage for us." That answered that. "The physician thinks you'll be fine by tomorrow and ready for the trip, and there'll be beds on the carriage to rest as well."

I nodded to that. Finished with my meal, I put the tray aside and gave each of these two a long look. "Thank you," I said from the depths of my heart. "You saved me. I will never be able to repay you for that."

Blackclaw grinned. "We're fast friends now. No need for repayment." She put a hand out and I took it. Silence reached out to put a hand on both of ours.

"Fast friends," he said stoically.

"Fast friends," I repeated.

You could have done far worse for your first friends as a True-Bonded, Auwei said with heartfelt joy.

Indeed.

They left after that, and Dove returned.

I rested again and found sleep, even as troubled as my mind was with visions of a mistweaver haunting me. I woke with a start several times during the night, and eventually found Dove curled up with me on the small bed. I slept well enough after that.

The next day I wore the finest dress that ancient seamstress had made for me, packing the others away; they were mine now. I said good-bye to Dove and kissed her on the cheek. She said she'd meet me in the capital — she'd be there long before we would — and a moment later, she veered into her Dove form and flew away.

"Your sister is beautiful," Blackclaw said staring after her.

Silence nodded, though his gaze seemed to shift from Dove to me and Blackclaw.

We boarded the specialty carriage and were soon off.

Experiencing a fast carriage first hand, I had to admit, they were quite a marvel. The passenger area was wide enough that the benches doubled as beds. Two additional beds could fold down above each bench as well, sleeping four passengers. The coach was also extra-long, with a small sleeping area in front of the passenger area for the second driver. The drivers would spell each other out, riding in turns. And special way-stations were set up at intervals to switch out the horses. This way the need to stop was much less frequent. The final amenity were special springs for the wheels, which minimized the bumps in the road, making the carriage seem to float along, soft and even.

We made it to the capital in six days, arriving the day before the tests were due to start.

And for the entire trip, I tried not to think about the mistweaver after me. Though... something had occurred to me during the passage. Something that last man had said as he'd come for me. My mind had hidden it away, buried in the trauma, but I recalled it in a dream one night, starting awake. He'd mentioned a name, probably the name of the mistweaver after me. It wasn't much, but it was something. I knew who my foe was, even if I didn't know why they were after me, nor how to defeat them.

Still, I knew their name, and that was something.

Their name was: Hazra.

CHAPTER 12

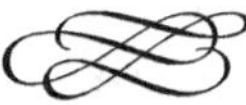

AND SO ENDED MY TIME AT SILVERVEIL. I WAS BONDED AND AT THE capital for the Noble House Tests, but I was still ill-prepared for the many trials to come. I thought myself tempered, but I was still so naïve.

I'LL NEVER FORGET SEEING THE CAPITAL FOR THE FIRST TIME. THE sight of the white marble buildings glistening in the summer sun took my breath away as I gazed out the carriage window. Descending from Elismount, a low ridge of hills north of the city, I could see nearly all of the sprawling, sparkling city, which nestled into a wide, long curve of the Elis River. And after we had passed through the gates on to the city streets — paved with flat, square stones, perfectly fitted, such that they gleamed as one smooth surface — I gawked at the height of the buildings, and the finery of those on the wide walkways on either side of the road.

Blackclaw and Silence laughed at my wide-eyed wonder.

I was feeling heartier and healthier after the restful trip. We'd eaten well, thanks to a purse of funds my sister had given to us for the journey.

I was feeling almost cheerful, though the thought of Hazra the Mistweaver, darkened everything. Still, for a moment, as I'd come into the city, I'd forgotten about my trials and simply marveled at the metropolis.

I kept the curtains of the window open but sat back on the bench. I couldn't help the great grin on my face, which made the other two snicker all the harder.

"You have to take me to all the amazing places in the city," I said, a little breathless. "After we all pass the Noble Tests, of course."

"Won't we be whisked away to our various Houses?" Blackclaw asked.

None of us knew.

"I hope we all get into the same House," Silence said, hopefully.

That wasn't likely.

Auwei had explained how the tests worked during the trip. After a True-Bonded had displayed their talents, one or more Noble Houses *might* offer to take them. Only then did a True-Bonded get to *choose* from those Houses offered. If only one House made an offer, that was their choice.

You *could* decline an offer, of course, then test again the next year, but few did. Declining an offer meant you were rarely given an offer again. Nobody liked being snubbed. Still, we had a small chance of ending up together. I secretly hoped for that as well, but mostly, I was just bubbling over with excitement at being in the city and being Bonded and being so very close to my goal of joining a Noble House.

If I was chosen.

But even the possibility of not being chosen, couldn't dampen my spirits that sunny day.

The carriage took us right up to the front of a massive building, a high-end lodging house called The Golden Rose, and stopped under a covered carriage porch, where I hopped out and ran to my sister, who was there to greet us.

"This city is amazing!" I said as I embraced her. She was shorter and a bit slighter of build than I was, and I nearly knocked her over with my enthusiasm. "I can see why you love it here so much and haven't gone back to Miraline."

She extricated herself from my aggressive hug and smiled, though her face quickly fell. "I should return home. I've been so busy. How are Mother and Father?"

"The same. Still spending all day at the library, and now that neither of us is at home to go get them, they'll probably spend all night there too."

She laughed at that.

"In all of my wildest dreams, I never thought I'd be staying here." Silence's voice, from behind me, was filled with awe.

"It's the finest place in the city," Dove said in return. "I wouldn't have anything less for my sister and her friends, those who saved her life."

I put my arm around my sister so I was facing the others and nodded. "Exactly. And we'll all be Nobles ourselves after tomorrow and be able to pay her back."

"There is no need for that," she said with a laugh. "It's my pleasure and my treat. Come, this way." She led us in through the massive wooden doors — which moved silently, light as a feather — to the sprawling lobby. It wasn't a common room like I was used to in other inns and taverns. The space was mostly empty. Though there was what looked to be a small wine-bar to one side, with a comfortable sitting area not far from there. The far wall had a desk with a pristinely attired young woman behind it. Dove approached her.

"These are my friends. What rooms were prepared for them?"

"Three-seventeen through to three-nineteen." The young woman handed over three keys to Dove with a smile.

Dove turned to us. "This way." She led us to a large space to the left and behind the girl at the desk. A wide stairway led up in a squared spiral, but what caught my eye — and I'm sure the others' — was the steel latticework column which the stairs were built around. A square area perhaps ten feet to a side was surrounded by this strong, yet somehow also delicate-looking steel latticework, which went farther up than we could see. At the base, there seemed to be a cage within that column of steel and a man within, also immaculately attired. He called out to us as we approached. "Would you like to use the lift? What floor?"

Dove winked at us. "Three." And she entered the contraption beside the man.

We all tentatively entered, and a steel lattice-work door was closed behind us. The man then pulled a cord next to him in three long, slow pulls. Nothing happened.

"We need to wait for the command to reach the operators," Dove said.

Then... we began to ascend through the column of steel.

Needless to say, the three of us who'd never seen or experienced anything like this, all gasped and suddenly clasped the brass bar which was conveniently placed at hip-height around three sides of the cage.

We passed one landing then slowly came to a stop at the third floor. The man in the cage opened the steel door with a smile and we exited, all a little breathless... except for Dove, who was grinning at the three of us.

"Marvelous invention, isn't it?" she said in breathless awe.

We were all a little speechless.

Dove laughed, a light and airy thing, and turned to lead us to our rooms.

"I'll let you rest for a bit, but if you'd like to meet me down in the lobby after the sixth bell, I know a place we can eat." She handed each of us our keys as we reached our rooms. I was the last and she clasped me in a quick hug. "Enjoy," she said before turning to leave.

I entered the room and gawked. This one room was half as large as the home I'd grown up in and many times larger than the small cell at Silverveil I'd known for the past few months.

A large sitting area dominated the center of the room: a low table surrounded by two long couches and four chairs. To the right of that was a bed that was easily twice the size of anything I'd ever slept in. To the left of the sitting area was a sunken portion of floor with a large porcelain tub that looked like it could easily fit two people. Massive closets occupied the inner wall to my right. Opposite that, along the far side of the room, was a massive bank of windows, the glass so clear I had to approach tentatively for fear I might fall through the openings. Two sets of curtains could be pulled across the wall of windows. One was sheer and gauzy, allowing for privacy while still letting in light. The other set was heavier, to block out the light.

And when I explored the room further, I found an indoor privy, complete with a cord you could pull which caused water to flow through it and wash everything away.

Amazing!

A knock sounded at my door, and I answered it to find Blackclaw and Silence standing there.

"It's too much space, we both felt a bit odd. Can we come in?" Blackclaw asked.

I nodded, still a bit overwhelmed myself. Blackclaw and Silence sat at one end of a long couch and I took the chair next to it, shifted to be a bit closer.

"I'm worried about tomorrow," Silence admitted. We hadn't talked a lot about the tests on our way here. Apparently, we were going to do so now.

CHAPTER 13

"So am I," I said. "In terms of my powers... I can sense things around me and walk on walls, that's not much to show off."

Don't forget your webbing, Auwei said

At the same time, Blackclaw asked, "Can't you also produce webbing?"

I grimaced. "From my belly-button, yes, but I'm not going to lift my skirts to do that. I suppose I could cut a slid in a dress, but..." I shrugged.

There are many different types of dresses and garments available here in the capital. I've seen some more daring designs with the midriff missing.

That was an option too. I wasn't sure how I felt about that. It seemed a bit risqué for me.

"I haven't even tried changing into my avatar yet," I added. "Not that a tiny spider would be that impressive."

"That is pretty much all I can do," Silence said, shaking his head. "And who will want a mouse in their Noble House?" He seemed to shrink in on himself. "I shouldn't have come."

"Pish-tosh!" Blackclaw said with a friendly slap to his shoulder.

"Of course you should have come. I think you two will do well enough. Remember that not every avatar's shape or abilities are flashy and impressive. Just think of the queen. She's an owl. She hunts well at night. I'm sure night vision wasn't something she could even show to the Nobles when she was testing. Buck-up, you'll be chosen, I'm sure of it."

I smiled. The stout young woman had a way of making everything seem... possible and easy. Even Silence perked up a bit.

"Now," she went on, "Seioa is telling me there is at least one problem we can solve right now. Apparently, there are dresses that have some of the stomach area missing. Why don't we use some of your sister's funds and get you something nice for the tests?"

See? I told you.

For someone who'd shown a lot of leg on my first day at Silverveil — and now had a name for the rest of my life because of it — I was feeling very anxious about showing my belly to anyone. Still... maybe it would make me feel as powerful as I'd felt that first day at Silverveil. Sure, I'd been terrified, but I'd been claiming my body, my power. Perhaps I could do that again.

"There's a shop not far from here," Blackclaw said. "Perhaps we can all pick up something special to wear." She rose decisively.

I couldn't help but be carried away by her excitement. I rose, and Silence followed.

We left my room and took the stairs down. The afternoon was waning when we left, though the midsummer sun was still high in the west.

We found the shop with ease — guided by Seioa — and entered. And so began a playful bit of shopping, looking for just the right thing for each of us to wear. The shop owners, an aging woman and her daughter, came to help us pick things out and fit them as needed.

Silence was the easiest to dress, a fine pair of black pants and a dark-blue linen shirt fit him well, and we purchased those.

Blackclaw struggled to find anything that would fit; she was an awkward size being a bit shorter but fuller of figure. Still, we found a dress that cinched under the bust and was easily hemmed up to fit her height. Silence blushed seeing her for the first time. The outfit certainly emphasized Blackclaw's bust, and she played that up, strutting around a bit.

Then came my turn. We found several dresses that met my criteria of missing a portion around the belly-button. Blackclaw made me try on all of them.

The first was an odd dress, hard to get into. It had a loop behind the neck, a front-piece over my bust, then two straps which went around the lower back and connected low on the hip for the skirt. It showed my stomach, yes, and the skirt was long, but it showed far too much of the rest of me, being backless and missing everything from below my bust to the tops of my hips in front. My face must have matched its flagrant red coloring, blushing furiously as I wore it to show to the other two. Silence's eyes went wide before he averted them.

Yeah, exactly.

You look beautiful. You have nothing to be ashamed of, Auwei said, supportive.

Thank you, but I won't be wearing this... ever... again.

That red dress was the most revealing of the three I'd chosen to try. The next had a small diamond-shaped cutout around the belly-button, and the top of the dress covered well, but the skirt was short, cut on a slant such that the left side came to mid-thigh, and the right to just below the knee. It also had a slit up the right side, and if I stood with my legs slightly apart, most of my right thigh was exposed. I couldn't decide if this was too much or not.

Blackclaw thought this one, a deep green, looked best on me and would serve to emphasize my name.

The last outfit was less of a dress and more a skirt and top. It was a lavish dark blue, with a long skirt, belted tight around my waist, just below my belly-button. That was fine. The top however, had a low-cut neckline and a high-cut under the bust. I kept wanting to pull it down to cover more, only to realize I'd still be showing so very much.

So the green dress it was.

My heart pounded just thinking of wearing it... and thinking of the tests tomorrow.

To get used to it, I wore the dress to dinner with my sister that night, who remarked on it with wide eyes; saying I looked amazing, but she was stunned I'd wear anything like it. I'd never been one for such things growing up.

I still wasn't.

But as the evening wore on, I began to get more comfortable with it. Perhaps I wouldn't turn beet red when I was presented before the Nobles tomorrow.

Spirits and Sprites, I was so nervous!

And when we returned to The Golden Rose, I found myself tossing and turning, unable to asleep. While I lay there, I recalled my words to Pebble — now Silence — from long ago: *When this is all done and we're both Bonded, come and find me.* I should talk to him. I didn't know how things would go after the tests tomorrow, but if we were chosen for different houses, we might not see each other much after that. If I was going to talk to him, I should do that now.

I didn't bother dressing, remaining in my nightdress as I padded along in bare feet, slipping from my room then down two doors to Silence's room. I knocked softly, hoping he was awake and would hear it.

I was about to knock again when he opened the door. Silence wore only a set of long, loose breeches, which made it easy to see the hard, flat muscle on his chest and stomach, no longer quite as scrawny as I'd once thought him.

His eyes went a bit wide. "Legs?"

"Can I come in? Can... we talk?"

He nodded and let me in, closing the door softly behind me. As I entered the room, I looked back. I couldn't hear him, but there he was, silent as a mouse. His new name suited him well. We curled up in two of the large padded chairs and he waited, while I tried to find words.

"After the tests tomorrow, we may be going our separate ways and... before that happened, I wanted to... I wanted to know how you felt... about me." Wow, I wasn't usually the one stumbling over my words, but that hadn't been easy to say.

He smiled softly and blushed, as he always seemed to do, but this time it wasn't as deep a red. He nodded. "I've been thinking about that too," he said. "I... your kiss was my first." I saw him look away for a moment a faint smile on his lips as he perhaps recalled the quick encounter.

"Back at Silverveil, Blackclaw talked to me about my feelings and... love." His voice grew quieter now, tighter. "Haleia tried to explain it to me too, but... I..." He sighed. "I don't know if I understand. I've lived such a secluded and sheltered life. Feelings like this are hard for me to express, hard to figure out. I don't know if I love you, but when I think about you, I feel... warm and happy and I... my body..."

"Yeah, I understand," I said to save him any awkward details.

As for how I felt about him?

How do I feel? What should I say?

Tell him the truth... about his eyes, Auwei said.

Yes, right.

"When I look into your eyes, I feel a connection with you, Silence."

"You do?"

I nodded. "Yes. I see all your tenderness and caring, but also a determination. I know you want to become more than you were and I'm determined to do the same. It's what I see in your eyes that drew me to you."

"Oh," he said, seeming surprised.

"If we are separated tomorrow... I will miss you, dearly," I said and meant it.

"I'll miss you too," he said, and his gaze finally found mine again. And there it was, that conviction in his soft brown eyes. "I don't know if any woman will ever find me... will ever look at me, like you do, Legs." He seemed to grow more confident in that moment, but trembled at the same time. He grew flushed again and nodded to himself then said, "I would... like to be with you, before we potentially go off to separate lives." The words came out in a rush. His face was beet red now. That couldn't have been easy to say, to ask for. He'd put himself out there and I admired his courage.

I smiled and reached across the space between us. He did the same and we clasped hot hands for a long moment before I whispered, "I'd like that too."

CHAPTER 14

I DIDN'T KNOW WHY I WAS SO NERVOUS. THIS WASN'T MY FIRST time... though I highly suspected, from everything he'd said, it would be Silence's.

This may not be your first love, but there is always a nervous excitement for... new love, Auwei said tenderly.

She was right. I was trembling and excited. My body felt warm and unsteady.

Don't worry about how you feel, just... feel it, enjoy it, Auwei said.

So I did. I opened myself up to this wild energy and suddenly sitting there felt so very wrong. I rose and, through our joined hands, brought Silence to his feet with me. He trembled, chest heaving with quick and heavy breaths.

We stepped in toward each other and he reached his free hand up to caress my cheek. I tilted my head slightly into that touch, resting my cheek in his hand. I closed my eyes, feeling the warm press of his palm.

He stepped closer, his chest brushing the silk of my nightdress, under which my nipples hardened, pressing back into him.

His hand on my cheek gave a slight pull. I let him draw my face closer, opening my eyes and seeing a turbulent fervor in his gaze, matching how I felt.

His lips were soft and tentative on mine. Our hot breath mingled as we tested and tasted with chaste kisses.

He released my other hand to slide that arm around me, pulling me closer, tight to him. Warmth pooled deep within me as I felt the hardness of his lean frame against mine, my entire body searingly sensitive. My breasts pressed to the flat plane of his chest through the sheer fabric of my gown. Every shift of our bodies sent thrills through me. I felt his arousal, the firm press of his erection low upon my abdomen, through two layers of cloth.

I put my arms around him, keeping him close. My mouth opened first, and I teased my tongue over his lips. When his mouth opened to mine, our floodgates released and we dove into each other with all the pent-up desire hammering through us.

My hands roamed his back, feeling his wiry muscle. His hot palms pressed over my nightdress, feeling every contour of my back, sides, and behind. One of his hands slipped down and began to bunch up my nightdress, pulling it up over calves and knees. And when he could slip a hand under, he stroked my thigh and cupped one firm cheek of my buttocks, pressing us closer still.

Our need became a bonfire, raging and unstoppable. I separated from him, grabbing one of his hands to pull him across the room to his bed. And there, I lifted off my shift and stood naked and unashamed before him. I wanted him to see all of me. And I wanted to see all of him.

He didn't blush; instead, his eyes were hungry as he took me in. He untied his breeches and let them fall away. His cock stood proud and tall before him, throbbing and firm. He was a beautiful man, covered in lean, firm muscle.

He stepped in again and kissed me, but this time one of his hands slid down between my legs. I moaned into his parted lips as he pressed upon my folds. I was already wet as his fingers explored me, thrilling me. With all the pent-up desire surging between us it wasn't long before I wanted more than just his fingers.

My lips moved to the side of his face and I whispered. "I want you, Silence." Then, I moved him, turning to push him down on the bed. He sat on the side of the bed and I straddled him. I was slow and careful, but also desperate with hurried need as I lowered myself upon him.

And when my loins ground down upon his, and I felt his fullness inside me, we both gasped with trembling pleasure.

His hands came up to cup my breasts as I began to move, hips swaying and grinding upon him.

We both overflowed with heated urgency. This was his first time and I knew he'd not last long. I could see his eyes and mouth go wide in the moment before he couldn't restrain himself any longer.

"Yes," I breathed, giving him permission, as I pulled myself closer to him. His lips touched my breast and I felt a moment of trembling pleasure as he gasped through his first release. He pulled me tight to him as he shuddered, his lips finding the tight bud of a nipple to suck and play as he surged within me. It was enough to send another thrill vibrating through me, mild but satisfying.

Then he released my breast as he gasped again. His eyes clenched shut, mouth open as he shook with convulsing bliss.

And when, finally, he'd finished and untensed, I pushed him back to lie on the bed and laid myself down, pressed atop him, kissing him gently.

"I... I'm not done, I can—" I hushed his lips with a kiss. I didn't care. I'd felt desired, hot and intimate, and had even experienced a thrill or two. I hadn't expected him to be a master of himself his first time out.

"Thank you, Silence," I whispered above him, my brown hair

falling around us like a veil. And I meant it. I was truly gratified at how he'd reacted to me. I felt sexy and wanted.

"Thank me later," he said and suddenly rolled us over.

I laughed at the playful turn of events. He drew himself out and we shifted, moving to lay fully upon the bed as he knelt between my legs. He reached down between us and I felt a spike of bliss as his fingers began to work. He grinned. "Haleia knows a thing or two about how to give you a bit more. I couldn't quite hear her over the pounding of my heart before, but now..."

And Haleia was a proficient instructor indeed, as Silence's deft fingers began sending thrill after thrill through me. I didn't care how I looked in that moment, though I must have been a sight, chest heaving with gasping breaths, eyes rolled back, then closed, lips whispering worshipful words.

I let out a cry of surprise when I felt more than just his fingers pressing against me. It seemed he was quickly ready for more. He lowered himself a little, pushing into me. His hands on my hips pulled me close, driving him deeper. Then his fingers were back to where they had been, now caught between us as he moved within me once again.

I'd been on the verge of an orgasm, and the welcome surprise of his fullness hard within me sent me headlong into a powerful release. My entire body tensed and flexed as I closed around him. He began to thrust, slow and steady, as his fingers continued to work wonders. The combination was driving me completely mad with bliss.

I grabbed the heavy blankets, balling them into my fists as tears of utter, amazed joy slipped from beneath my clenched shut eyes. I rode the waves of a perpetually building orgasm until his pace finally picked up. A second, body clenching orgasm pounded through me as Silence drove to his release. Clinging to each other, we merged in bliss, gasping and crying out.

We lay in a twitching pile for some time after that, sweaty, messy, and spent.

"Thank you, Haleia," I said, once I'd regained my breath enough to speak.

He laughed, and I joined him, feeling light and free and wonderful in that moment.

I stayed with Silence that night. I hadn't thought I'd sleep well the night before the tests, but in his arms, I found peace and slept far more soundly than I had in a long time.

In the morning, I slipped back to my room quickly to prepare, then the three of us made our way to the testing grounds along with about two dozen others.

This was it. My time to shine... hopefully.

CHAPTER 15

I SAT IN THE CIRCULAR THEATER, WATCHING THE TESTS BEFORE MINE.

The Royal Elis Theatre was three levels of steep seating formed in a circle, with no seats on the northern side of the theater; which was dominated by the stage. The stage and rings were covered, but the center was open to the skies above. The stone yard would be for the "masses" who wished to stand — there was no seating down there — and see a show. Today, it was in that open center where those being tested performed.

The Noble House representatives — the leaders of the nine Houses each with their second-in-command standing behind them — sat on the stage, evaluating those coming before them. There were few in the kingdom who could not name these powerful figures.

First among them was Queen Whitewing of Owl House; the Royal House. Her second was Merlin, a slight and small woman with a very intense look. The queen herself was relaxed and resplendent in a gorgeous white, flowing gown. Her long white-blond hair settled around her, icy-blue eyes intent on the tests.

Fang, leader of Pterolycus — or Winged-Wolf — House was a

large and broadly built man, powerful and dark of complexion with sweeping black hair and dark eyes. His second — and if rumors were true, his lover — was a tall and also strongly built woman named Retriever. She had beautiful black hair, cut short, and golden eyes. Together the duo looked both proud and dangerous. Lady Kitsune, who'd trained me at Silverveil, was a member of that House.

Next was one of my idols, Lady Skyfire of Wyvern House. She had flame-red hair and burning yellow-orange eyes. Behind her was Drake, her second. A rare duo were they, both with dragonesque forms, the rarest of avatars. He was tall with well-cropped brown hair and eyes which were constantly in motion. He seemed to be looking everywhere, on watch.

Another beauty, was Lady Silvermane of House Pegasus. She was the queen's daughter, but had chosen to start her own House instead of joining her mother's. She looked much like the queen, with silver-blond hair and cold blue eyes. She was young for a House leader, but already had a House which rivaled or exceeded the others. Dove was lucky to have been chosen by her. Behind Silvermane was Lord Horn, a massive man with grey in his dark hair and steely eyes. He'd been Silvermane's bodyguard for years and had become her second within the House. A dangerous fellow if the tales were true. Mild-mannered most of the time, until his charge was threatened, then a vicious and fearsome protector.

Jaguar was the leader of Panther House. A lithe and lean man with an easy smile, but an aura of impending danger, ready to pounce. His second was Tabby, a bookish woman, tall but willowy, with soft brown hair and spectacles before her orange eyes.

The last four Houses I didn't care as much for, but I still knew the names of the leaders, though, not their seconds. The enigmatic Lady Tanuki of Tanuki House, with dark eyes and fair hair. The massive Lord Grizzly of Grizzly House, a mop of dark brown hair on his large head. Everything about him was... oversized and dangerous. Then there was Lord Spike of Porcupine House, an odd-looking fellow, rake thin, with a wide grin. Last was Lord Maverick of Maverick House. He was a large fellow as well, a bit rounded of muscle and with an easy-going nature, often talking to his second, a severe-looking woman who never replied.

"Would Legs and Auwei, spider avatar, please come to the testing grounds!" the herald called out. My heart leaped with excitement while my stomach held a cold ball of fear.

Don't worry, do what we practiced and planned. You can do this, Legs. Auwei's words of encouragement helped to calm me, but only a little.

"You can do this!" Blackclaw said as I rose.

I'd sat in the top tier as I'd wanted to make a special entrance.

I kicked off my shoes and jumped up onto the half-wall at the inner edge of the tier.

"Here!" I called out. I quickly touched my belly-button, then the pillar next to me, then... I began walking down the wall.

I'd made sure to sit next to one of the massive pillars that supported the inside ring, so I could walk down that, without having to jump over the gaps of the tiers below mine.

The trouble was... I was heavy. This was far different from when I'd crawled along the ceiling back at Silverveil. I'd been on hands and feet then, supported. But walking down a wall without using my hands meant my upper body was sticking way out from the wall and it wanted to bend, pulled down. So, I walked — very carefully, making sure one foot was solidly placed before moving the other — down the wall, trembling not only with fear, but with the effort of my muscles straining to keep myself straight. When I finally reached the stone yard I was shaking violently from the effort, but I'd made it.

There were various strange objects around the testing yard, some large and awkward, some shaped like people, for the testees to use to demonstrate various abilities. I'd already demonstrated my primary ability: wall-walking. The only others I knew of so far were jumping and my spider silk. I had attached a piece of silk to the pillar up at the third level and grabbed that now, pulling myself up a little, demonstrating that I had the silk and how strong it was.

Letting myself down, I separated that strand, then put my hand over the small hole in my dress, quickly filling it with a ball of webbing. I threw the webbing at a human-shaped "dummy" in the yard. It hit low on the "man's" face, covering the mouth and nose and a bit of the neck.

"Bloody..." I whispered; eyes wide. It only occurred to me in that moment that such an attack could be fatal, if my opponent couldn't get the webbing off in time, they'd not be able to breathe. That is not what I had meant to show, only that I had the "web-throwing" attack.

Don't worry, you're doing very well, keep to the plan.

I shook violently, but I made my way back over to the edge of the inner ring and... leaped with all my might. I actually didn't know how far I could jump. I hadn't fully tested that. So I was just a little shocked — I may have let out a terrified scream — as I passed well up, out of the theater, to perhaps double or triple its height.

I flailed wildly as I then began to fall.

Don't worry, I'll catch us, Auwei said, sounding only slightly less terrified than I was.

We landed on the roof of the theater in a crouch, springing up to our feet.

"Oh!" I breathed. "I..." I hadn't thought I'd land so lightly.

It only makes sense that if we are able to jump that high we will be able to land from that height.

"Oh," I said again.

Or at least, that's what I was hoping. I caught Auwei's hint of relief. She hadn't been certain.

I'm glad you were right!

Me too.

As calmly as I could, I walked back down the inner pillar to my seat. Several people had risen, rushing to the edges of the inner ring to look up and seemed relieved to see I was well. I smiled and nodded to them. Returning to the half-wall where I'd started, I bowed to the Nobles.

Looking at the nine of them, most did not seem particularly impressed. But then... they hadn't for anyone else either.

I took my seat again and deflated into a puddle of anxiety induced tears.

"Are you well?" Blackclaw asked as her name was called.

I couldn't speak only nod weakly.

She smiled and rose, taking the stairs down to the yard.

Silence reached over and took one of my hands, squeezing it. "I think you did an amazing job," he said reassuringly.

I smiled at him too, but couldn't stop the shaking or the tears.

I missed Blackclaw and Silence's test as I slowly recovered from the anxiety of my own. The three of us were the last to be tested, since those who'd Bonded first were tested first.

Then... we were all called down to the yard. This was it, the moment the Nobles would pick their new House members. And again, it would go in order, so I would be close to last. I was so nervous I could barely stand; shaking and weak. Blackclaw supported me.

Cedar — now called Swan — was chosen for the Royal House. I was certain if we met again, I'd never hear the end of that. Oak — now Badger — was chosen for House Pterolycus. I hoped I wouldn't be anywhere near him. Creek — now Cougar — was selected by Panther House.

There were a few, perhaps five, who were not chosen. The silence after their name was called was deafening. And so... it came to me.

"Legs and Auwei, spider avatar!" the herald called out. The Heads of the Noble Houses, now all standing, were silent. No one rushed forward to claim me. I even saw Skyfire shake her head slowly. Lady Tanuki shuddered. Time stretched as the herald counted in his head the thirty seconds the Nobles would have to step forward and say... anything really.

"And—" the herald began. My heart constricted in that split second before... a voice cut him off.

"I'll take her!"

Maverick had stepped forward, that strapping body of his was apparently quick as well as strong. He grinned down at me. "The others may not want a spider in their House, but I think you've got potential."

Potential? I'd take that.

I had to reply and say whether or not I accepted his offer, but my heart was thundering and I couldn't speak. A part of me hoped that now that he'd stepped forward, others would as well... but that didn't happen.

"Say yes!" Blackclaw hissed at me.

"Yes!" I blurted.

And that was that. I'd committed myself now. I would be a Noble of the outcast and misfit House... Maverick.

Great.

Better than nothing, Auwei said, with the equivalent of a mental shrug.

And she was right, it was.

Maverick nodded and stepped back in line with a smile. I'd been his first pick of the day. I could practically hear Swan's derisive laughter.

I was so lost in my own world I didn't hear who chose Blackclaw, only that she said "Yes," and seemed excited. I blinked, turning to her.

"Who?" I asked.

"She's a bear," Silence said. "So, who do you think? Grizzly of course."

"Ah."

Then Silence himself was called. Again there was a long pause before Maverick stepped forward. "Come to my House, little mouse. We've a place for you!"

Silence blinked in surprise, then looked at me with a wide grin. "We're…"

"In the same House," I said, excited. "Say yes."

"Yes!"

Maverick stepped back.

That was it, the end of the Noble Tests… and all three of us had been chosen; Silence and I were even in the same House!

We three looked at each other and suddenly were whooping and hollering — among some others who were doing the same — hugging and jumping and celebrating.

Our House Leaders came to us, telling us to take a night in the city — to celebrate and say good-bye to friends — and meet them tomorrow.

Maverick took Silence and I aside and gave us each a small, but heavy bag of coin. "There's only the basics in Grovner's Green, the town near Hedgewild, where you'll be going. So, buy what you will today, there's a lot more here of whatever you may need."

Blackclaw had a similar chat with Grizzly, then the three of us were running out of the theater, arm in arm in arm, elated beyond reason.

We'd made it.

We'd actually made it!

CHAPTER 16

After a day of shopping and spending nearly all of what our new Lords had given us, we turned to celebration.

I drank more than I ever had that evening. Dove joined us for our party, temperate as ever, not drinking much, which was good, since none of the rest of us could remember how to get back to where we were staying.

I woke up the next morning with a splitting headache and a mouth that tasted like fuzzy dirt. Luckily Dove had stayed in my room, sleeping on a couch, and got me up and ready.

"You're a Noble now," she said once I was mostly returned to my senses. "You need to start acting like one." She grimaced. "There are some who take this charge lightly, spending their time gambling, drinking, or chasing men or women. I know you won't be like that. We are the leaders of this nation and need to be an example to others. Are you ready for this?"

I nodded. "No more drinking, ever... ever again."

She grinned. "I didn't say you had to stop drinking forever, just... maybe not that much all at once, yes?"

"Yes, definitely yes."

"Good."

She saw me to the lobby, where we waited for Blackclaw and Silence, who joined us shortly thereafter. Blackclaw looked little the worse for wear after the night of celebration. Silence looked as bad as I felt.

"Good-bye, sister. I love you, stay well," Dove said, embracing me.

"Love you too, sis," I said holding her for an extended moment. "Try to get home. They miss us... I think."

She nodded. "I'll try."

We held each other until it became awkward, then separated, nodding to each other, a few tears in our eyes. After that, the four of us went our separate ways. Well, Dove and Blackclaw went different ways, while Silence and I went another. The two of us paid a porter to carry our things. The man led a donkey with our bags and trunks — most of which had been purchased yesterday — on a cart behind it. Neither Silence nor I had had much before we'd come here, now we had... lots. Though I would eventually come to find out that what I thought of as lots was still a paltry amount compared to most Nobles.

"I wish I had a sister, or any family, like yours," Silence said softly.

"We have each other," I said with a wide smile. "And Maverick House will be our family now. Let's go meet them."

He beamed at that and we hurried to our meeting with Maverick.

The meeting place was to one side of the main carriage depot in Elista. We arrived to find Maverick leaning casually against the wall outside, thick arms crossed over his broad chest. He was a bull of a man — which shouldn't have been surprising given his avatar — with strong heavy shoulders and chest, arms packed with rounded muscle, a fit and slender waist, and strong legs. He wore a shirt with the sleeves ripped off, stained in a few spots. His breeches were sturdy leather, his knee-high boots, well worn. He had a mop of unkempt, thick brown hair, some of which threatened to cover his eyes, while most of the rest stood on end in cowlicks and curls. He didn't seem to care. His brown eyes and easy smile were welcoming on that broad and ruddy-red, leathery face of his.

Next to him, in complete antithesis of his appearance was his second, a woman of my height, slender and poised, standing straight. She wore a simple, long dress, belted at the waist, with full sleeves and a high neckline, conservative and respectable. Her pale silvery-blue hair was pulled back in a tight braid, which was then wrapped up in a bun behind her head. She was immaculate and clean, her grey-blue eyes sharp, small mouth pursed. It was she who spoke as we drew near.

"I am Lady Crane," she said with clipped, clearly enunciated words. "You know Lord Maverick."

He nodded and grinned.

"He will be staying in the city, while I escort you to your new home in the south. I will explain everything you need to know along the way, but we have a carriage to catch so, if you are ready to depart, then let us do so."

She turned, fully expecting us to follow and we did. She seemed a bit cold and harsh to me, very different from Maverick.

The large man spoke as we passed him. "I may not be home for a while, so I'll say it now. Welcome to House Maverick." He grinned. "Do what Crane says and you'll do well. She's in charge while I'm gone." Then he pushed off from the wall and ambled into the city.

"I don't think the two of them could be more different," Silence whispered to me.

I had to agree.

We were bustled into a regular carriage, with Crane sitting opposite the two of us, and she spoke again once we were underway. "The trip to Grovner's Green will take two days, and Hedgewild Manor — your new home — is another few hours out from the town. We will rest tonight in Elisford, then take a ferry across the river tomorrow and continue southward." She paused and looked intently at us, perhaps expecting questions, but we remained silent. She nodded. "You were given a small sum with which to purchase items while in the capital. I noticed you arrived with some bags and chests. Did you find what you needed?"

We nodded.

She smiled. "Quiet ones, are we? Good. I like the quiet ones. Listen to me and ignore the other gadabouts at the House, and you'll do well enough." Another pause, then, "Neither of you are the children of Nobles, are you?"

"No, miss," Silence said. "I... lived on the streets before I was Chosen."

Crane corrected him. "Please address me as 'Lady Crane.'"

"Yes, Lady Crane," Silence said.

She nodded to that. Oddly there wasn't any of the cynical repulsion other Nobles had had to Silence's low-born upbringing. If anything, I thought I saw just a hint of solace and sympathy in those cold blue eyes. Interesting. She was proper and stern, but not... superior.

She looked at me.

"I was the daughter of..." I trailed off. I shrugged. Might as well tell her everything. "Of merchants, but they died when I was young and I went to live with friends, scribes at the Library of Miraline, Lady Crane."

She raised her brows. "Are you educated then?"

I nodded. "Yes, Lady Crane."

"Good." She passed an assessing look over both of us again, then proceeded. "You will find those at House Maverick come from... a wide variety of backgrounds. All are accepted and welcome. Remember you are now Lord Silence and Lady Legs."

She pursed her lips after saying my name, I could almost read her thoughts: *Lady Legs? How vulgar a name.* Still, she forced a smile. "It will be up to you how formal you wish to be with your title. Some are less concerned with it than others."

"Like Maverick."

She grimaced. "Like *Lord* Maverick, yes." She shook her head. "The day I get him to fully accept his nobility and role as leader of our House will be the day I can finally rest." She seemed to realize she'd said too much and pursed her lips again, a habit.

"What questions do you have?" she asked.

"What... do we do... as Nobles?" Silence asked.

I could see the unasked questions on her lips: *You became a Noble without knowing what they did*? Still, she took the question in stride. "Nobles are the rulers and protectors of our fair nation of Elista." Her tone was that of a teacher. One I'd heard often from my parents.

"You will need to be educated, in case called upon to adjudicate civil disputes. You will also need to be able to fight in defense of the kingdom. House Maverick is tasked with protecting the south of the nation, which... is one of the easier assignments of all the Noble Houses since there are no southern neighbor nations, only the ocean. So, we fight off the occasional pirate, help towns hit by raiders, and otherwise keep the peace in the south. Occasionally the Royal House or the Council of Nobles will give us a special mission to complete. That... hasn't happened in a while."

Silence nodded.

For his benefit, I added, "The Council is made up of the leaders of all the Noble Houses, with the queen or king at their head."

"That is correct," Crane said. "Though some House Leaders defer their seat on the Council and rarely show up... like Lord Maverick."

My turn for a question. "What is it like at House Maverick?"

The name of the manor had been mentioned a couple of times, but it hadn't stuck in my mind yet. "Hedgemaze Keep, was it?"

"Hedgewild Manor." She drew in a long breath and actually seemed to relax a little. "The grounds are amazing. Rolling fields and hills in all directions, with scattered woods and the Greyling Forest to the west. To the east — about a day's walk — is Dyrens Bay, with glistening clear blue waters. There are tenant farmers who work the lands around the estate, so we have a variety of fresh fruits and vegetables depending on the season. And separating the fields from each other and the estate grounds are many hedges of varying heights, which give the manor its name."

She paused for a breath. "The house has two wings, a central hall, and five towers. It's... in a bit of disrepair at the moment, though I'm doing my best to keep it up. There is only a small staff who tends to the place, since our funds are somewhat... limited. We are not as important a House as those in the capital or guarding the north and west." She sighed at that. "But we do what we can. Life is... interesting. I am hoping you two will not be a burden on the House as some of the other Nobles are." Another heavy sigh. "Lord Maverick takes in... all sorts."

I was beginning to wonder what our new Noble family was going to be like. It sounded like they were a wild bunch, barely kept in check by our current hostess. Which led me to my next question. "Who are the other Nobles in the House?"

Lady Crane nodded. "You'll meet them all soon enough." Still, she listed them off: "There is Lord Ant, Lord Jack, Lords Fennec and Foggy, who are brothers, then Lord Fin, and of course Lord Maverick. For the ladies, there is Lady Amber, Lady Tusk, Lady Sparrow, and Lady Princess. Please note, 'Princess' is her name not her title. She is *not* actually a princess, as much as she acts like one. There is also Lady Midnight, but you won't meet her. She's on an extended mission, something even I don't know about."

I would like to have said I couldn't wait to meet them, but given how Lady Crane spoke, I didn't quite know what I thought of the eclectic-sounding group.

The rest of the day, as we traveled, Lady Crane informed us of the various duties we'd have around the manor and gave a bit of a summary of the usual missions we might be called out upon.

The road followed the Elis River for most of the day. That night we stayed at Elisford, a village near a spot on the river where it widened out into a small lake and was fairly calm most of the time. It was a fishing village for the most part, but being on the main road, it had a respectable inn, in which we stayed for the night. Silence and I went for a walk along the river, to stretch our legs after the long ride that day. We held hands and talked freely, a deep bond forming between us.

The next morning, we and the carriage were carefully loaded onto a wide barge and ferried across the river.

The second day, as we traveled, the lands grew hilly and at some of the higher peaks, I could start to see the distant strip of glistening blue: the ocean, specifically Dyrens Bay. We reached Grovner's Green just after noon and had a meal there, before continuing to Hedgewild Manor, arriving late in the afternoon.

We pulled off the main road onto a long driveway bordered by low hedges. At the end of the drive, it circled around a central fountain. There was no covered carriage porch. Instead, wide steps led up to massive double doors in the middle of the central part of the manor. Two long wings came out from the main building, flanking the drive-yard. At the front of each was a tower, several levels higher than the three stories of the regular building.

From what I'd seen descending into this pleasant valley, the back ends of those two wings — stretching out behind the building — also had towers of the same height. At the center, right above the entranceway, stood a fifth tower, taller than all the others, with a dome of glass atop it. Dozens of evenly spaced, dark windows peered out from walls of grey stone, which were almost completely covered in ivy.

As we pulled into the yard and around the circular drive, I could see what Lady Crane had meant by "disrepair." The fountain at the center of the front yard wasn't working, it was dry and missing bits of the stonework. The house itself — though the ivy hid many faults — seemed to be crumbling; this was evidenced mostly by the small piles of stone and mortar in places at the base of the walls. As the carriage came to a stop, I could see the wide steps up to the door were missing small chunks here and there, and the double doors seemed to be mismatched, perhaps one was older, or of a different type of wood?

I stepped out and was surprised to see a large, strapping man approaching the carriage. I hadn't noticed him as we'd come around the drive. I'd thought the yard empty, so he gave me a bit of a fright, especially given his size. He was well over six feet tall and if I'd thought Maverick was muscular, this man made him seem scrawny. Yet he had a twinkle in his clear dark-brown eyes and a friendly smile on his lips. He was also shirtless, showing off his dark skin and a massive expanse of chest, not to mention the chiseled muscles down his stomach, which were... distracting.

He greeted us with: "Hello all, I'll grab your things, you go on in." He reached the back of the carriage in two long strides and unstrapped our trunks. He curled my trunk and Silence's easily under one arm and Lady Crane's larger trunk under the other, like they were nothing!

"Lord Ant!" Crane said, scolding. "We have staff for that! And put on a shirt!"

Lord...?

Ant...?

For some reason, I'd pictured Lord Ant as being small and skittish.

Ant laughed, a full and easy sound. "Why make them do it

when it's so easy for me?" Another laugh. "And if you think my bare chest is bad, Jack's... in one of his moods."

I didn't understand that last bit, but it made Lady Crane pale. Then, she bristled, and the pallor disappeared.

"This way," she said and hurried us inside.

Silence opened the door for the two of us women, the vision of a gentleman. Inside was a long hallway, left to right, and another set of double doors across the hall from where we entered. Unlike the outside, this hall was immaculately clean and well preserved. I guessed this was Lady Crane's work, since the main entrance would need to make a good impression. She might not be able to patch every crumbling stone outside, but she could make this look good. Smooth tiles covered the floor in a patterned mosaic, and half-column stands held vases and other small items of note in even intervals down both sides of the hall. But that... was not what caught our attention as we entered.

"Hello ladies," said the fit and lean man who passed us in the hall. And I could tell he was fit and lean, with lithe, long muscles on that tall, slender frame... because he was stark naked. He winked a dark-brown eye at me — his hair a perfect fall of wavy, raven locks — and whispered, "Come see me later, and I'll give you a tour you'll not soon forget." Then his suave smile grew as he looked over at Crane. "And if you ever want to... unwind and let loose, I'll always be available, *Lady* Crane." The way he said *Lady* made it both an insult and a sexual invitation.

We all stood there blinking as he continued away from us down the long hall.

"That..." Lady Crane said, voice trembling with barely restrained rage. "Was Lord Jack."

I tore my gaze away from his tanned and perfect skin, blushing deeply as I turned back to the others.

"Let me guess," Silence said wryly. "His avatar is a jackass?"

Lady Crane made a noise I would have never thought to hear

from her, a sort of half-snorting-half-choking sound. I think it was a restrained laugh. She regained herself a moment later.

"His avatar is a jackrabbit actually, but... you aren't far off otherwise." She drew in a long breath. "He may be a rather good fighter, but he's impossible to live with. I still can't believe Lord Maverick chose him." Another steadying breath. "Now, if you'll follow me."

We crossed to the other set of double doors. Through them, a large hall spread before us, longer left to right than across, but... the view across was stunning. Many windows let in the light from the south and gave a view of the garden courtyard beyond. "This is the great hall where you'll take your meals. Breakfast service starts promptly at seven."

After that, we were given a quick tour of the estate. It was H-shaped with the great hall and entrance corridor forming the middle, connecting piece. Down the long wings were many other rooms of various sizes. I quickly lost count and forgot the specific names for most. Then we came to the library at Hedgewild, which occupied three stories at the south end of the west wing. So many shelves and so many books. I'd seen more in the Library at Miraline... but no other place. This was the second largest collection of books, tomes, and scrolls I'd ever seen.

Then we were shown to our rooms. Our trunks were already waiting for us, brought by Lord Ant, no doubt.

"Dinner service will be in one hour at six sharp." Crane left us with that and marched away.

And that was it.

We'd arrived at our new home.

CHAPTER 17

Silence and I arrived for dinner at six, dressed in our finest, and ate with Lady Crane. However, none of the others in the House showed up. Lady Crane ate with a rigid silence that we didn't want to break, so we returned to our rooms after that. Well, Silence came to my room and we sat together on a long couch and talked.

"What do you think of all this?" he motioned to everything around us. My room, like his, was large. A massive four-poster bed dominated one side of the room, with a small sitting area on the other. Closets lined the inside wall and a bank of windows stretched all along the opposite side of the room. It was a lot like our suites at The Golden Rose, only a bit smaller and without the bathing area, though there was still a small water-closet and privy. I couldn't believe this was mine now... all mine. I said as much to Silence.

He laughed. "Yeah, I'm... overwhelmed. I went from a run-down shack to *this*. I think I'll get used to it though." He sighed. "Mostly I'm just glad to have you here with me." He put a hand on my thigh and I liked the warmth and feel of it. I could feel his trepidation. I couldn't imagine what his life had been like before all this, nor how much of a change this must be for him.

I leaned over and kissed him lightly. "I'm happy I can be here for you. Just let me know if there is ever anything you need."

"I will, thank you, Legs." He grinned. "What did you think of Lord Ant and Lord Jack?" he asked.

"Ant is... big, and Jack is..." I shook my head I had no words. I laughed then. "Though, if they're indicative of the others, I think we'll be in for some more surprises."

"Yeah," Silence said, laughing with me.

We chatted idly about the house and a few other items before Silence kissed me lightly and rose. "I'm... heading to bed," he said.

I saw him out. I was glad he hadn't wanted to stay with me that night. Our encounter before the Noble's Test had been amazing, but... that had been when we thought we might not see each other again. Now, we knew we had time to get to know each other more, let our relationship grow and flourish. I honestly didn't know if I could say I loved him. I cared for him deeply and we shared a unique bond, but love...?

You'd know if I was in love, right Auwei? I asked.

Indeed I would, and you are right to think this is still... new. There is infatuation and connection, but true love, that usually takes time to blossom. I am happy you have found someone. Though I feel from you as if... you may want... more?

That was what I couldn't put my finger on. I liked Silence a lot, but some part of me didn't seem satisfied. And it wasn't that I wanted someone else, more like... one person just didn't seem like enough.

I've had hosts who entertained many lovers before. I think perhaps you may be like them. Something to think about, Auwei advised.

And think on it I did, as I fell asleep that night, though I reached no resolution.

Silence and I were in the great hall at seven sharp the next morning. Once again, it was only Lady Crane who we met there. But this time, after we'd eaten and she'd left, we stuck around and waited.

At half-past the eighth hour, a woman in a long, light robe entered the hall. Her head cocked to one side as she noticed us. She smiled and came over.

Silence averted his gaze. There were two things which probably caused his shamed blushing. The first was simply how the woman walked, a gliding, full-body movement which exuded grace and languid sexuality. The second was the robe itself, which, though opaque, was light enough that the morning light seemed to shine through it, silhouetting the woman's figure beneath. And from that shadow, I could tell she was wearing little to nothing beneath the sheer robe. She was also stunningly beautiful with perfect waves of shimmering brown hair, bronze skin, and large amber eyes.

"You must be the newbies?" The woman said sitting down beside Silence and sliding an arm around him. He went rigid with fluster-shock. "I'm Lady Amber, captain of the second squad. She began teasing a slender-fingered hand up into Silence's brown hair. "I'm going to get one of you on my team. Ant will get the other on his." She had been addressing me, teasing Silence without so much as a glance, but she looked at him then. "I think I'll ask for this one." She took her hand from his hair, sliding it around his neck to under his chin, forcing his face to look up at hers. "What's your name, boy?"

He couldn't speak, staring directly into her amber eyes... nowhere else... very focused. Her robe had fallen open just a little as she'd leaned toward him, and I was sure he'd get an eye-full if he looked down.

"Silence," I said for him. "His name is Silence." I didn't know how I felt about this. Mostly I felt sorry for my friend who didn't have a lot of experience with women and was being horribly teased.

A grin spread upon Amber's full, dark-red lips, then she laughed. "How very apt." She leaned closer, bringing her face alongside his, to nibble on his ear, then whispered. "A... *pleasure*... to meet you, Silence." Then she turned to me. "And you?"

"I'm... Legs."

She blinked at that. "And here I thought I'd always have the best legs in this strange family of ours. Well then, come on, stand up, let's get a look at them."

Now I was the one on the spot.

Lady Amber had said she was a squad captain, which meant she was definitely my superior — everyone here was my senior but she seemed to hold some additional authority — so I stood and moved to the side of the table, standing there awkwardly.

"Now, hike up that skirt and let me see these legs," Amber said. With this, she removed her hands from Silence who — once her attentions were on me — slumped in relief and slid away from her on the bench.

I'm fairly certain I turned beet red, feeling heat rise to my face... and every other part of me. "I... I..." I stammered incoherently for a long moment. It was my turn to be horribly teased, apparently. Amber was an equal opportunity teaser, it seemed.

"Here, I'll show you mine, if you like." She shifted off the bench and stood across from me. She pulled up her robe slowly, to mid-thigh, revealing a perfect leg. "Now your turn."

I figured I could do the same. It wouldn't be showing any more than the green dress I'd worn for my Nobles' Test. So, I pulled up my dress a little.

"Well damn, girl! Those are some bloody fine legs; long and lean. I think you've got me beat. It's that extra few inches of height you've got on me, all leg I bet." She didn't actually seem upset, more... playful.

"Stop bothering the new recruits!" The voice made me jump. It hadn't been loud, but it seemed to boom through the hall with resonant authority. I dropped the hem of my dress and spun, and there was Ant — appearing from nowhere once again — not far behind me. "Amber, you're insufferable some days!" He seemed more scolding than truly angry.

"You didn't think I was insufferable last night," Amber purred seductively. "I believe you whispered something about me being a 'sex goddess'?"

Ant blushed.

Oh... so she could get under *anybody's* skin; very interesting indeed.

I turned back to Amber, who was laughing lightly as she twirled around and headed for a screened passage at the end of the hall. "I'll grab something from the kitchens and leave the newbies be." Then she was gone, and the sexual tension in the room dropped from stifling to nothing.

I took a long breath.

"Excuse her," Ant said, coming to sit on a bench at a table across from where Silence and I had been. I sat again. Lord Ant was fully dressed, though the shirt didn't seem to do much to hide his massive frame and bulging muscles. He smiled kindly. "She's a tease, and... some... people like that." He cleared his throat and nodded. "And I'd say she's harmless, but she's not. You don't get to be squad captain by being harmless."

"Amber?" I said slowly. It was an interesting name, giving little clue to her avatar. "What's her avatar?"

"A butterfly," Ant said with a grin. "Specifically, an Amber-Phantom butterfly."

Amber-Phantom? That sounded beautiful and mysterious... yup, that worked.

And while we were asking questions: "How do you keep popping up out of nowhere?" I asked Ant directly.

He laughed. "Think about it for a moment and you'll get there."

Think about what?

What's his name, Legs? Auwei hinted.

Ant?

And that's when it hit me. He wasn't appearing out of nowhere, he was being an ant, tiny and virtually unseen, then veering back into his human form.

"Oh!"

"Yeah, I knew you were smart." He nodded. "That's why I've asked for you on my squad."

"Me?" My mind whirled. "Meaning Silence will be on Amber's?"

Ant nodded slowly. "Yeah. I'll have a talk with Fennec, see if he can't help the boy while keeping Amber from teasing him too much."

"Fennec?" I asked. I couldn't figure out from the name what the man's avatar might be.

"You'll meet everyone in time. Just stay in the hall and they'll all wander in eventually. As much as Crane makes sure her breakfast is served promptly at seven, the cooks make sure there's something around all morning. The rest of us work on our own schedules most of the time while we're here. If we're on a mission, things are different. Then you do as you're told, when you're told, no questions, no hesitations, got it?"

I nodded. "Yes, Lord Ant."

He cringed. "Ant is fine. I don't need the title. I was a farm boy before all this and became a Noble to help out and defend the nation. I'm no lord."

I understood that sentiment. "It does feel funny," I said with a grimace. "Lady Legs just doesn't sound right."

"Ha! Yeah, I see. Well, then just Legs it is. I haven't had a chance to talk to Crane yet. What's your avatar?"

"A spider."

Some manner of jumping spider I'd guess, Auwei said. I didn't feel the need to relay that to Ant.

He nodded with a smile. "Nice! I'll have to keep a wary eye out."

"Why?" He was three times my size and could easily—

"Spiders eat ants," Silence mumbled.

"Oh... right..." I shook my head. "I'm still getting used to this whole avatar thing. It's a bit disorienting."

He nodded. "I get it. Imagine me becoming accustomed to being an ant."

True.

"And you, what's your avatar?" Ant asked Silence. "With a name like Silence it could be any number of things."

"A mouse."

He nodded. "Ah, yes, that makes sense." Then he laughed, a full-throated and hearty thing. "Well then, since you'll be on Amber's squad, just remember... Mice eat butterflies."

I blinked, looking over at Silence, who was a bit wide-eyed with surprise as well.

"And Cranes eat all of the above!" This sharp-tongued voice came from above us. I looked up to see a gallery balcony along three sides of the great hall. Lady Crane leaned upon the railing glaring down at us. I didn't know what she was doing, and she didn't deign to explain before she turned and left.

Ant chuckled. "True... so watch out for her."

"Are there any in Maverick House that aren't tiny creatures?" I asked.

Ant smiled and gave a knowing wink. "Oh... yes. You just wait and see."

As the morning wore on, we met the other members of the House, all but two. We kept hearing about Lady Midnight and her secret mission, but nothing more. The other missing member was

Fin... whose avatar was a whale. He was out patrolling the ocean waters for pirates. But the rest we met that day.

Jack arrived for breakfast still completely naked, winking at me once again before heading into the kitchens.

"Ignore him," Ant said. "He's on my squad, and he likes to flirt and will probably make some advances on you, but if you tell him no, he'll listen."

That was good to know.

"That goes for you too," Ant said to Silence. "Jack... goes for all sorts."

Silence and I raised our brows at that, but same-sex pairings weren't uncommon in Elista. Silence nodded at the advice.

"Why is he..." I began.

"Naked?" Ant shrugged. "Just his thing. He only does it while he's here, out on missions he's fully dressed and a deadly fighter, quick and lethal."

Also good to know.

The next to arrive were two men who looked similar enough to each other I guessed they were brothers. What had Lady Crane called them? Fennec and Foggy? They came over and made introductions. Neither were large men, Fennec was only a bit taller than me, short for a man, and very lean; wiry was a good word to describe him. He had pale brown hair, almost dirty-blond and friendly hazel eyes. He had a way of twitching his head as if he was constantly hearing something distracting.

"A Fennec is a type of fox, very small, with large ears," he said, describing his avatar. He then went to talk to Silence after Ant told him to take the young man under his wing.

Foggy, on the other hand, was... just plain odd. He was even shorter than his brother, one of the few full-grown men I looked down at, yet he was a bit more filled out, though still lean of frame.

"Fog beetle," he said shaking my hand. Then... for no particular reason, released me and did a lithe half-flip, landing lightly on his arms and settling into a very relaxed hand-stand. "Nice to meet you." He had darker hair than his brother but the same hazel eyes. And he too moved his head in odd ways, but more extreme, tilting and moving around to seemingly look at everything from every angle all at once.

"He's on my squad," Ant said. "And you'll... get used to him in time. He may not be normal, but he has some very interesting ways of seeing things and perspectives on situations like no one else."

As the brothers were leaving, another pair entered, both women, and as different as two people could be. One was very large, heavy-set, and a head taller than me, which made her a unique woman indeed. The second was small, quite slight of build, and a bit fidgety.

"Tusk," the larger woman introduced herself. "A boar."

"She's the muscle on Amber's squad," Ant said.

The tall woman had wiry, unkempt dark-brown hair with a dark complexion, bright and clear yellow eyes, and a wide smile.

"It is a pleasure to meet you, Legs. I'm Sparrow," said the other woman. That name immediately made sense. She was small and a bit erratic of movement, like her namesake, with large green eyes and a small mouth. Her hair was a light red-brown. I liked her instantly, and she seemed to sense that, smiling at me.

"A scout, also on Amber's squad," Ant said.

"We're going to get some food and head to the library, would you like to join us?" Sparrow asked.

"I'd love that, thank you!" I said instantly. "I might stick around here until I've met the rest of the household, but I'll meet you there if I'm not needed elsewhere." This with a look at Ant.

"The first day is all yours. Your training begins tomorrow, bright and earlyish at eight. Be out in the back courtyard and ready to work." With that, he rose. "Feel free to stick around here or go with Tusk and Sparrow, but the last member of the

House may not be down for a while. Princess... likes to sleep *a lot*."

"There is often a sun-spot in the library where she curls up around this time of day, if you come with us, we can introduce you," Sparrow said.

So, after they'd gone to the kitchens for some food, Silence and I followed Tusk and Sparrow to the library.

And there, curled up in a sunspot, as promised, was a plump, ginger-coated cat.

"Princess!" Sparrow said going to her, then flinching back as Princess twitched awake. Right... birds would be afraid of cats. "We have a new member. This is Legs. She's a spider."

Princess rolled onto her back, presenting her belly to me. Odd as it was to think of this as my Housemate, I did as — I hoped — she intended, and went over to rub her belly. She purred.

When I sat back, she veered into her human form, sitting before me with a drowsy smile. "Nice to meet you, Legs."

"And this is Silence," Sparrow said. "A mouse."

Instantly Princess' attention snapped to Silence, eyes going wide. "*Very* nice to meet you!" she practically purred the words.

Silence flinched back.

Princess... was odd indeed. Very feline in her demeanor. She had bouncy pale ginger curls, with intent orange eyes. I couldn't rightly tell, since we were both sitting, but she did not seem tall, and was definitely a bit on the rounder side, reminding me of Blackclaw. She was certainly full-figured through bust and hips, but dressed in loose flowing clothes so it was hard to tell her exact form.

"Now, if you'll excuse me..." and she was back as a cat again, purring, curling back up in her sunspot.

"She stays like that, in her avatar form, most of the time while here at Hedgewild," Tusk said, shaking her head.

She was a cat; why wouldn't she?

I couldn't help but stroke her fine ginger fur, and she purred louder.

And that was that. I'd met all of the members of House Maverick, except the ones that weren't here.

It was an eclectic lot, but I sensed a bond between them. A bond I hoped Silence and I would merge with eventually. Right now, I still felt like an outsider. But that day Sparrow took the time to make Silence and I feel welcome. We chatted with her in the library for some time, learning all the ins and outs of this strange family, and the estate. By the end of the day, Silence and I were laughing easily with the witty young woman, instant friends. Sparrow even gave Silence the scoop on Amber and how to handle her, since they would be on the same squad together. The young man seemed far more at ease.

And just like that... this place began to feel like home.

The next day our training started... and the pain began.

CHAPTER 18

"Not bad!" Ant said nodding his approval. Meanwhile, I was shaking my aching, tingling fist, knuckles sore. I kept stretching my hand to stop the throbbing. Punching Ant was not something I wanted to do again. He was hard as rock!

That was how he'd started our martial training: "Punch me," he'd said. "Trust me I'll be well enough."

And I believed him now.

He was shirtless again and... just wow. All that rounded muscle looked a bit cushiony, but it wasn't. It was solid.

"Ants have a shell, remember," he said by way of explanation. "It takes a lot to hurt me."

Good to know.

"Your turn," Ant said turning to Silence, who blanched and shook his head.

Ant laughed. "A shy one, are we? Don't worry, we'll train that out of you. Nobles need to be able to face many different situations and protect the nation when called upon. Here, we mostly fight pirates, and that's not often. But still, you need to be ready. So go ahead, hit me as hard as you can."

Silence looked at me. I nodded for him to try. He shrugged, balled his fist, thumb tucked inside, and swung.

"Silen—" I tried to stop him. With how he'd made his fist, he'd break his thumb. But I didn't get there in time. He hit Ant.

Crack went his thumb and Silence shrieked in pain, retrieving his hand back to hold protectively, tears coming to his eyes.

Ant waved me off, kneeling before Silence. "Let me see," he said tenderly. It took a couple of tries before Silence let the large man look at his hand.

Ant took the hand and surrounded it with both of his — much larger — hands. Then he closed his eyes, took a deep breath, and seemed to concentrate. I watched, fascinated. So did Silence who sniffed back his tears as a look of blinking wonder came over him.

"There, better?" Ant said, releasing the hand.

Silence nodded. He wiggled his fingers and thumb, then smiled. "You can heal?"

Ant nodded. "I can heal."

"Is that an ant thing?" I asked, a bit stupefied.

"No," Ant said softly. "Has anyone ever told you about spirit-gifts?"

We shook our heads.

Ant sat, and even sitting was still taller than Silence, but not me. "Some True-Bonded, who have been with their Lumani for a while, and are strong in spirit, develop special abilities."

Oh… that sounded familiar.

I told you about them, not that long ago, at Silverveil. Though I didn't recall the name for them at the time. None of my Hosts has ever possessed such abilities. Ant must be a powerful True-Bonded if he has them.

I listened intently as he went on. "Several of us in Maverick's crew have them." He chuckled. "If you think I can sneak up on you, wait till you meet Midnight. She can be as silent as the space between thoughts, and be standing right next to you, and you'd never know."

She sounded powerful and mysterious. I sort of loved that everyone talked about her with such awe. It made me want to meet her all the more, and also... terrified of her.

"And Fin, our resident whale, he's developed the ability to instantly move between locations, but he can only go to a place he knows. I can heal, and Amber... she can take control of a person's mind."

"Control of their mind?" I blurted. "That's..."

"Yeah, she doesn't do it often, and doesn't like to do it." He hesitated. "Well, I don't know how much she likes to do it. She says she doesn't like it, but... these powers you see, they come from... something deeper within us, a fundamental part of our spirit manifesting itself. I heal because I have a drive to help people, do things for them, aid them. Fin loves to travel and see different places. Midnight loves to be hidden and secretive. Amber... my theory is... she loves to be noticed, the entire focus of a person's attention, so... mind control."

He smiled at both of us. "I wouldn't be surprised if you develop a spirit-gift someday. Maverick has a knack for picking people with strong spirits. Not everyone in the House has one, just us four and Maverick... so far. They often take some time to develop. I was in my early twenties before I began to sense... something, and it took years to harness it and use it effectively."

Fascinating.

Isn't it, though? Auwei was just a bit haughty sounding when she added, *I think of all my Hosts, you have the greatest potential to have such gifts.*

You think so?

I do. You're special, Legs. I know it.

Wow, thanks. I wish I felt that way.

That's part of what makes you special. You're modest about it. But that's also keeping your potential restrained, I think. Whenever you have your bold moments, like wearing that dress the first day at Silverveil, or your Nobles' Test, that's when I feel it. There is more to you. You'll see.

I smiled, sending Auwei a sense of gratitude.

Since Ant had mentioned it and not gone into detail, I had to ask, "What's Maverick's gift?"

Ant smiled. "He doesn't like me sharing. You'll have to ask him yourself someday."

Yeah, that wasn't going to happen any time soon. The well-built leader of our House still intimidated The Pits out of me. He also hadn't returned from the capital yet.

"Now!" Ant said rising. "Back to training. After those punches, I have a sense for your skill and natural ability. I'll work out a training program for each of you. Today, we'll just work on basics." He paused then, looking at me curiously. "Is it true you killed three assassins at Silverveil?"

Yup, that's me. "And nearly died in the process."

"Still..."

"Also, one of them was pure luck," I added. "A trap I'd set worked very well."

"But that means two weren't luck." He nodded. "I think you'll be moving on to the advanced course soon enough." He looked at both of us. "Until then, you're all mine. Pick up those practice swords, and we'll run through some forms."

The rest of the morning was spent learning three basic sword forms. We ended with some simple sparring, myself and Ant that was, Silence wasn't ready for that yet. I held my forms well enough, though I did get a solid slap on my hip with a practice sword when I over-extended on a shoulder strike. Ant didn't heal that minor injury. He said it would remind me not to make the same mistake again. By the end of the first week... I had a lot of reminders.

Mornings were martial training; afternoons were studies in a variety of other topics. I was already well educated so I moved on to more advanced subjects like state-craft and strategy, well before Silence did. The two of us also attended classes on how to develop our avatar abilities, which... was a slow process for me. Auwei was certain there was more I could accomplish, but nothing became apparent. I did get better, and more controlled at the few things I could do, though. And I was finally able to take my avatar form. I spent a day off exploring the house as a spider and found it terrifying. Everything was so much larger than I was... even a few other spiders.

Soon enough I graduated the basic combat class, no longer training with Silence. He was slow to pick up combat training. While I — as Ant had predicted — quickly moved on to the advanced classes. They were with Jack, and he was a completely different man during training, all business with quick and deadly precision. He also didn't take it easy on me, but that made me learn all the quicker and by the end of my first month at Hedgewild, I was sporting fewer bruises and feeling like I might actually be a productive Noble one day.

Silence and I saw less and less of each other, but still managed to grab a few moments together, sometimes alone, sometimes with Sparrow. But more and more, Silence was dedicating himself to study. He had a lot to learn and spent extra hours poring over books or practicing combat forms. Which meant much of my spare time was spent with Sparrow. I was surprised to learn she was three years older than me. She seemed so small and free-spirited: youthful.

A month passed. Maverick hadn't returned from the capital and Midnight was still on her "secret" mission. But I was getting to know all the other members of Maverick House.

Jack ended one of our practice sessions with an offer to join him in the baths. I declined, and he didn't bring it up again.

Amber didn't tease me... as much, and Ant was beginning to feel like a protective older brother, if a really handsome one. I still had no clue how to deal with Foggy, but then... neither did his brother, Fennec; no one did.

I got to know the feel of the place. How Tusk and Ant were usually up early and helping the farmers or gardeners around the estate. Where Princess would have her naps and that she did indeed spend virtually all of her time as a cat, except when eating or occasionally socializing. It became common to find Foggy in random parts of the house, doing head-stands or poking into dark corners. Fin came to visit a few times, a large man, even taller than Ant, but where Ant was all muscle, Fin was... not. He was brawny and sturdy and heavy, but still moved nimbly enough.

I got to know Amber's moods. She could be testy and stand-offish some days, but friendly and effervescent on others. No one talked about it, so it took me a while to figure out that she was always cheerier on days after she'd seduced Ant the night before. Fraternizing between Housemates wasn't forbidden, but I came to understand that it was generally frowned upon, mostly by Lady Crane. But since Amber could be a bit wild some days, Ant would "take one for the team" to keep her in high spirits. I don't think he minded, but part of him was still an innocent farm boy and, Spirits, how he could blush when it was mentioned.

Time passed, my twenty-first birthday came and went; there was a party. Despite my promises to my sister, I drank too much and woke up with another heady hangover. Silence had his eighteenth birthday; we'd both been born in the fall, apparently. That night, I offered to stay with him, but he declined. He looked exhausted all the time now, and yet, I'd never seen him happier. He laughed with Sparrow and me, even others from time to time, and seemed to love learning new things. I was happy for him, though I felt like we were drifting apart. I told myself he needed time to make up for all the learning he'd missed as a child. I hoped that was true.

I was also learning a lot, much more confident in my skills and martial prowess. I was anxious to prove myself.

Then, finally, came my first mission.

CHAPTER 19

FIN APPEARED IN THE GREAT HALL, INTERRUPTING THE EVENING MEAL. Since he'd transported himself directly here from the ocean, he was dripping wet, long pale-brown hair plastered to his round head. His slightly bulbous grey eyes blinked as they searched and found us. "Pirates," the heavy-set man said. "We need to go now, before we lose them."

Amber wasn't present, so Ant took control. With a quick look around, he nodded. "My squad, grab your gear, we head out as soon as you can make it back here." But his full squad wasn't there, Princess was off sleeping, most likely. But Fennec and Sparrow were there and he quickly turned to them. "You two are with us. Fennec, prep for a fight. Sparrow, you'll be on watch." She nodded, and a hardness that I hadn't seen before came over the small woman's eyes.

Jack, luckily, had just ended a session of small-scale combat theory with me, so he was fully dressed and had his weapons on him.

I turned to him. "Do I have weapons?" With a movement faster than I could see he'd tossed a dagger and it was sticking out of the table in front of me.

"Use that, stay out of the way, watch and learn. Stay in your avatar form once we're on the ship, no one will notice you. We don't expect you to fight your first time out." He stood and checked himself over quickly, slipping back on the heavy leather jerkin he'd taken off earlier. "You're good, Legs, and you've learned a lot quickly, but it's different being in the thick of a fight."

I nodded.

The others were soon ready.

Ant turned to me. "You ready for this? You don't have to come."

"I'm ready," I said, hoping I didn't sound terrified. In truth, I had no clue how I'd be in the thick of a real life-and-death fight. When I'd been attacked by those assassins, I'd reacted on instinct, then I'd Bonded and Auwei had helped a lot. This was different. I knew I was headed for something dangerous and I had time to think about it. Somehow that made it worse, all possible — mostly bad — scenarios playing through my mind.

I'll protect you, Auwei said and I knew she would. Though, even as I linked hands with the others, I recalled what Auwei had done, when she'd taken control of me during the fight with the assassins in the baths. I felt like I could do those things now, after months of training. I actually did feel... ready.

Then the world spun and I gasped as cold water splashed and surged around me. I slid under the waves, then came up sputtering.

The others were more prepared. They'd done this before. Fin went from being a large man to... a massive whale. That pushed us out from him a little. Ant caught me and pulled me up as everyone clambered on top of the huge form. Sparrow was up and away as a bird. Foggy veered into a beetle, wings out, also flying toward the ship...

The ship was close, moving toward us. It seemed Fin had anticipated where the ship would be and had returned us to a spot roughly in its path. Now it was barreling down on us. The rest of us held on tight as Fin submerged a little, keeping us above water, to move us into position.

It was evening, the sun just above the horizon in the west. Enough light to see by, but soon there wouldn't be.

"Left side," Ant said, leaning down over Fin, tapping the whale beneath him. I didn't think whales could hear, so the words had been for us. I guessed that the tapping of the large form beneath us had been indicating which way to go.

Fin shifted slightly and swam us toward the indicated side of the ship. Or more precisely, we didn't move much but Fin got us in a position so when the ship passed by, we'd be close enough to climb aboard.

Ant whispered to us. "We'll be coming up with the sun behind us. We'll be silhouetted and easy to see, but they'll have the sun in their eyes at least for a moment or two before it sets. Let's use that to our advantage." He looked around. "We're more than a match for a pirate crew, nasty and vicious as they may be. Keep together and stay sharp." He turned to Jack. "Carry me." Then he veered and was almost washed away as an ant, before Jack scooped him up and placed the small insect on his shoulder.

"The rest of us are good jumpers," Jack said, voice low, the ship close. "But ants can't jump."

I nodded.

Fin sank a little deeper, hiding us as much as possible. When the ship drew alongside us, Fin swept us closer and the remaining three of us jumped as one. I jumped the highest, intentionally this time, and landed on the spar holding up the mainsail. Then I instantly shifted into a spider to watch the fight below.

The crew was more than a little shocked when two men jumped up on deck and even more surprised when two more men

— Ant and Foggy — appeared in their midst a moment later. The pirates, at a quick count, looked to number perhaps close to twenty, though I quickly amended that count as more ran up on deck. There were thirty at least.

Thirty on four? Ant had seemed confident before, but I was suddenly worried for my companions below.

Then they began to fight. Jack used a slender-bladed rapier in one hand and a long parrying dagger in the other. Ant used a thick quarterstaff, spinning it in defense, while tripping up his foes and bashing them into oblivion. Fennec had knives, lots of knives; he'd throw one and another would appear in his hand. Foggy didn't so much fight as confound his foes, dancing and capering around the ship, narrowly avoiding so many lethal blows, while somehow managing to nudge, kick, or trip foes such that they often died on the weapons of their allies. Very quickly it was four on twenty; then four on fifteen and...

There came a sharp, high, trembling cry from nearby; a sparrow's call. I looked around quickly and saw what Sparrow was indicating. A woman, dressed in fine and flowing robes was standing on the stairs to the lower decks, watching the fight as I was. Then... she looked up at me and smiled.

How in The Pits did she know I was there?

I have a bad feeling about her, Auwei muttered. I had to agree.

With a wave of the woman's hand a fine spray of mist shot out from her fingers and shot across the deck, by the time it reached where the fighting was, it was a wall of mist which slammed into everyone — pirates and Nobles alike — knocking them off their feet, throwing them across the wooden boards.

A mistweaver! Auwei's terror flowed through me

Bloody Bones! I would have cursed out lout, if I could have.

The woman strode slowly, purposefully up onto the deck. She looked up at me again. "Time to come down, little spider." And with a grasping motion a ball of mist appeared around me and held me tight, pulling me from the yard, to float down to the deck.

Hazra! I knew it was her, even though I'd never seen her before. *But how?*

She knew...

A cold feeling filled me, settling first in my gut and spreading icy fingers into my very muscles and bones. Yes, she'd known where I was, that Maverick House fought the coastal pirates off the south of Elista. She'd known and set a trap for me.

But why me? I still couldn't answer that.

"I want to see your face when I kill you, slippery one," she said, and the fog surrounding me seemed to seep within me. I tried to hold my avatar form, even if only to confound her, but the mists ate at my very nature, eroded it until I was forced back into my human body. I sat on the deck, near the side of the ship, as she approached. The tiny ball of fog that had surrounded me as a spider was gone, so I tried to rise,

"No," she commanded with a grin and I was stopped, mists appeared over my feet and around my waist, neck, and wrists, keeping me in place.

"Why?" I called out to her, even as the mist — like iron bands — around my neck began to constrict and cut off my air.

She strode over to stand before me, slightly shorter, but seeming so very large and powerful, radiating an aura of intensity I couldn't ignore. I was terrified and so was Auwei.

With a subtle wave of her hands, fog surrounded her feet and lifted her so she looked down upon me. Her eyes burned with madness. "Why?" she whispered with a manic grin. "Because I like to kill," she said with a tilt of her head. "And you're in the way of our plans. Well, not yet, but you will be, and we can't have that, now can we?"

I flicked my gaze to where the men lay. Ant was rising, the others starting to regain themselves.

"They can't help you, child," the mistweaver said and with another casual wave of her hand, sent them all flying. "I made a mistake last time, hiring out your death. This time I'll do it myself and, just for fun, I'll make it slow and painful. Would you like that? No, probably not, but *I'll* like it."

She's insane, Auwei gasped in horror.

Yeah, I was getting that.

She stepped back as the bonds around the various parts of me began to tighten. I'd already been struggling to breathe, but now I was completely without air. My waist, wrists, and feet were being constricted and crushed as well. I would have screamed if I could. Then — because this wasn't bad enough — Hazra made a sort of sprinkling motion with her hand and pain, like a hundred needle-points pressed into me from every angle.

The pain was unlike anything I'd ever felt before, true agony. Tears leaked from my eyes, which bulged with my desperate need to breathe.

The mistweaver laughed. "I want to hear one scream before you die," she said, and the restraint on my neck eased just enough for a gulp of air. Then — as much as I didn't want to comply with her desires — I screamed in anguish. One long, clear cry, then the neck-binding tightened again, this time working faster, crushing my neck.

The world shrunk. Darkness threatened the edges of my vision and despite my desperation to live, I also craved that darkness and an end to this pain. All I could see was her, that pale face, blissful as she watched me die.

Then... a small white and brown shape attacked the woman's face. Sparrow.

Hazra screamed, waving her hands.

My bonds released, but I was too weak and too broken to do anything but crumple into a heap. I couldn't breathe, my throat still crushed. And with the next roll of the ship, I slid off the deck entirely.

The ocean swallowed me in cold oblivion, water pouring into my mouth. I couldn't stop it. I couldn't do anything. Darkness closed in again as I sank deeper and deeper.

Then... nothing.

CHAPTER 20

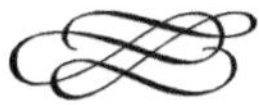

ccording to the others, I didn't actually die.

But it sure felt like it.

Air flowed into my lungs, and I gasped and sputtered out seawater. I was rolled onto my side as light stabbed into my eyes and waves of tremendous pain surged through my entire being. I had no energy to cry out, so I just whimpered.

"Amber!" I heard a voice shout.

Everything was hazy, my eyesight dim, but I saw a fall of auburn hair and intense amber eyes. "Sleep," came the soft but intense word and I had to obey it. I fell into unconsciousness again.

When next I woke from the black depths of a dreamless sleep, I blinked my eyes open to dim light, and a tremendous amount of pain. My hips ached and my feet throbbed. There still seemed to be a thousand points of fire across my skin, but they were fading, less urgent, more like a burning itch now. Though, my hands and throat were no longer sore. Curious.

Still, I groaned.

Sparrow came into view. "Legs?"

I groaned again. "Water?" I tried to say, but my voice was rough and raw. Sparrow seemed to understand and had a glass to my lips a moment later, lifting my head to help me drink. The water wasn't cold, but it felt so very soothing on its way down. While my head was lifted, I saw Ant, sitting slumped against the wall. He barely seemed to be breathing. I groaned again as Sparrow lifted the glass away, nodding my head toward him.

She looked, then looked back at me. "He's just resting. Your wounds are too severe. He can't heal them all at once, and it takes a lot out of him when he does.

Ah, that would be why my throat and hands weren't in pain anymore.

"You should rest, if you can," Sparrow urged, laying me back down.

I didn't see much point in remaining awake, so I slipped back into sleep once more. And that was how the next few days went. I woke, the pain present but diminished, and took some water or a bit of food. Silence or Sparrow was always there to spoon-feed me if needed. Ant was always there and always exhausted.

Then, finally, I woke feeling rested and refreshed, no pain at all. The room was dark, a single flickering lantern showing Sparrow curled up on a mattress on the floor. Ant was gone.

There was a noise, low and distant and it took me a moment to realize it was people talking somewhere close, but outside my room. I strained to hear what they were saying.

Don't listen with your ears, Auwei said. *You have another sense.*

Right! My spider's sense. I concentrated, feeling all my hairs prick up, gooseflesh covering me... then the voices became clearer.

"...attack her here?" someone said, it sounded like Crane.

"If they were going to, they would have, long before now. They had months before that pirate ship. No, they know she's well-guarded here." This was a firm baritone voice, one I hadn't heard in a while... Maverick? Was he here?

"She's a mistweaver for Spirits' sake!" This from Amber, I knew that voice well enough. "The lot of us are no match for a mistweaver. She could waltz in here and slay all of us with ease. No, there's another reason she hasn't attacked us here." She sounded afraid. I'd never heard her so frightened before.

Maverick grunted.

"Amber's right." This from Ant, another voice I knew well. "I saw her power, none of you did. She could have easily killed all of us, but went only for Legs. I think..." Ant trailed off.

"What?" Maverick asked, gruff. "I trust your instincts Ant. Say it."

"I think she doesn't want to or... or can't kill the rest of us? She only wants to kill Legs, a tactical strike."

"Oh! Yes, of course!" This from Crane. "I think I might know why, but perhaps here is not the best place for us to talk. Come with me." And I heard footfalls fading down the hall.

I wanted to hear what Crane had to say. I was feeling well enough to get out of bed, so I slipped from under the covers. I wore only a light shift. That would have to do since I didn't want to waste time dressing. I slipped, silent as a spider, across to the door, not waking Sparrow.

The door creaked something fierce when I opened it, but Sparrow must have been out cold as she didn't even flinch.

The others were just turning into the long cross hallway at the center of the estate as I peered out into the hall.

I hurried to catch up, stopping at the corner to spy around and see them step into the central stairwell. There was only one place they could be going: the dome at the top of the central tower of Hedgewild.

Once they were all out of sight, I crept along to the stairwell. But... I'd heard this door creak a lot when opened previously, so I went a different way. I backed up to the entrance to the great hall, on the second floor this took me onto the balcony around the hall.

From my explorations of Hedgewild, I knew that there was another access to the central stairs from here and no door, just an open archway to pass through. It was just to my left. So, I sneaked through that and slowly moved up the stairs. I got to the landing below the large domed room at the top of the tower and stopped there, keeping to the shadows. I could only just barely hear the whispers above, not able to make out the exact words, so I let my spider's sense do its thing once again.

My hair bristled, and the sounds came into focus.

"Out with it Crane, what's your theory?" This from Maverick.

Crane spoke, voice hushed. "Are we certain this room is warded? I've always wondered about that." She sounded uneasy, with a hint of awe in her voice.

"So Gander told me, when he passed leadership of the House to me. I've never had any reason to doubt the old man. Everything I've said in this room has stayed here. The only way anyone could hear is if they were actually here, not by any other means."

There was a long silence after that. My skin crawled. Did they know I was here, somehow, listening in?

I concentrated on hearing any movement with my enhanced senses and... there was something: a soft, almost imperceptible skittering of tiny feet. Curious about this, I focused, pin-pointing the sound. I heard two sets of tiny feet. One... a set of six skittering feet was *very* close.

Ant appeared right in front of me. "Hello, Legs. Glad to see you're up and about."

"I knew it! I knew someone was listening!" This from Amber up above.

"This concerns her, send her up," Maverick said, tone leaving no room for questions.

"You heard the boss," Ant said. "I'll stay down here and keep an eye out."

I nodded and went up the stairs to the top room. I'd only ever been in The Dome a few times. It was accessible to the House members, but it was held as a bit of a sacred space, so people went there sparingly. It was also Maverick's office, which made it awkward to stay for long periods. The tower itself was large, a twenty-five by twenty-five foot square. The stone walls continued up to around waist height as if this had once been an open turret. Perhaps the dome had been added later? The dome itself was clear glass, with a bit of a greenish tint. It began square at the base, following the line of the wall, then slowly morphed into the spherical covering.

Outside was dark, an overcast night. There were two large hearths in the room, on the east and west sides. In the middle of the room, close to one hearth, was a large desk and a couple free-standing book shelves. By the other hearth, was a large sitting area. The north side, where I was now, and the south side, were mostly open. In late fall, with no fires in either hearth, it was quite cool up here, especially for me in my nightdress.

As I looked around from the top of the stairs, I saw the source of the other set of tiny footprints I'd heard... a tiny grey and white mouse, keeping to the cracks in the stonework of the walls.

Hello Silence, I said internally and smiled. Apparently, he'd been listening in on all of this... probably from back at my room as well. He wanted to know what was going on as much as I did. I wouldn't expose him.

Crane fetched a heavy blanket, which had been folded over the back of a long couch in the seating area, then came to me, draping the warm cloth over me.

"You'll catch a chill, child," she said with motherly concern. Then she led me to the heavy rug which covered the floor under the sitting area, my feet on the cold stones had been uncomfortable indeed.

Maverick snapped his fingers and a fire leaped to life on the logs set in the hearth by the sitting area.

I started at that.

So *that* was his spirit-gift? I wondered what "fire" meant, what it was he "loved" to get that ability.

We all took seats.

Crane sat next to me, arm around me like a mother hen. She looked at me for a long time, lips pursed. "Do you know who wants to kill you? Or why?"

I *had* learned a bit. "I know the mistweaver's name is Hazra. She said..." I tried to recall more. My memory of the events on the ship were fuzzy, probably from my lack of air during the encounter. "She said... she liked to kill, but... it was more than that. She *needed* to kill me because I was... in the way?" No, that wasn't right.

She said, "You're in the way of our plans. Well, not yet, but you will be, and we can't have that, now can we?" You were a bit distracted, but I knew if we survived, we'd want to remember that.

Thank you, Auwei. I repeated the words for the others.

"You're not yet in the way, but you will be?" Amber muttered. "Then..."

"Yes, they have some means of seeing the future. Whoever *they* are," Maverick said, jaw set hard.

"That's where I have a theory," Crane said. She hugged me a little closer. "I think... other Nobles are behind this."

Amber started, eyes wide with disbelief. "No!" she gasped. "That's ridiculous. Nobles of Elista, trying to kill other Nobles? That's madness!"

I only nodded. I didn't understand yet, but I knew Crane would explain.

Oddly, Maverick didn't seem shocked at all.

He knows something. Perhaps that's why he remained in the capital for so long. Something's going on with the other Nobles.

"It makes sense," Maverick said, nodding. "It's why they don't want to kill the rest of us. Legs is in the way of their plans, whatever those plans may be, but to kill off an entire Noble House... that would bring attention they don't want. So, they need to kill one Noble very precisely and quietly without the rest of us being harmed... much." He shook his head. "Bloody-stinking-bones. Those bastards!"

"You sound like you know who it is?" I said, curious.

He shook his head. "No... I don't *know*. I *suspect*." He sighed heavily. "I think it's time I told you why I've been away so long." He took a long moment to collect his thoughts in silence.

I trembled with fear and anticipation.

Maverick ran a hand through his rough, spikey hair and heaved another sigh. "What I'm going to tell you doesn't leave this room. Understood?" He looked at me, hard, unyielding. "You're new. I wouldn't normally tell you this sort of thing, but it seems to involve you, so you're in. But that means you have to keep this secret as well. You tell no one. Not even the other members of our House, as it might unduly scare them. Definitely no one *outside* our House. We don't know who we can trust. Understood?"

We all nodded.

"I want to hear you say it," Maverick insisted.

"Understood," Lady Crane said seriously.

"Tell no one, got it," Amber said.

At this point, I knew I should divulge my little secret. "Ahhh..."

"What is it?" Maverick asked.

I called, raising my voice a little. "Silence, you should probably come out now."

"Silence?" Crane asked.

Shocked expressions appeared on all three of the other's faces. I turned to see the man standing in his usual sleeping attire: loose breeches and nothing else, standing near the wall by the stairwell.

I'd seen him off and on over the last half-year and he'd grown a lot in that time, not just physically, but in confidence. He was still quiet and reserved, but there was a surety to his stance now, a liveliness to his step. He'd also grown several inches and was roughly a match for me in height and build.

"Ah, hi," he said, blushing, looking like he'd been caught spying... which he had.

"Spirits, I didn't hear... that's amazing!" Maverick breathed. Then he looked at me. "How'd *you* know?"

"I have special super-hearing. I heard him when I was back on the stairs."

"He's literally quiet as a mouse, and you heard him?" Amber said, shocked. "His name is Bloody *Silence* for Spirit's sake!"

I shrugged.

"Sorry," Silence said, voice low. "I ah... I heard you talking about Legs in the halls downstairs and got curious."

Maverick sighed. "Well you know too much now, come and sit. But you and Legs need to swear you'll not tell anyone what I'm about to tell you."

Crane went and got a second blanket for Silence as he came to sit with me. We shared a smile then both turned to Maverick.

"I swear," Silence said.

"I won't tell a soul," I added. I was a little trepidatious about all of this. What was so important we couldn't even tell members of our own House?

Whatever it is, you can trust these people and you always have me. I'll take care of you, Auwei said.

That helped reassure me, a little.

Maverick drew a long breath. "Something's been happening to Nobles. Over the last two years or so, Nobles have been dying, some under mysterious circumstances, some not." He paused there, looking at each of us in turn. "That in itself isn't that odd, people die all the time. But some of these deaths have been *very* concerning. It's not something that's widely known — only the leaders of the Houses have been told the full details — but it seems that for some of these deaths... the Lumani within the Noble died as well."

Auwei gasped. I felt her shock, confusion, and horror.

Crane and Amber let out similar noises.

Silence looked confused, but I understood. Lumani were immortal, and shouldn't be able to die. Slowly, a look of understanding and horror came to Silence's face as Haleia must have informed him.

Exactly, Auwei said. *We are energy and when our host passes, we live on as energy. We're saddened by the loss, but we live. It shouldn't be possible for a Lumani to die with their host. Unless...*

"A mistweaver?" I said slowly, finishing Auwei's thought. I recalled that Auwei had said something about mistweavers being able to kill Lumani after the attack at Silverveil.

"Yes," Maverick answered. "Some of the leaders think it's possible a mistweaver has found a way to kill host and Lumani as one. Though others still think Mistweavers are legends and there has to be another explanation. Honestly, I was in that group... until I heard what happened on the pirate ship."

He blew out a long breath. "According to you, the mistweaver used the words 'we' and 'our.' And before I knew a mistweaver existed, I was beginning to suspect certain Nobles of these heinous deeds. I still suspect them."

He ground his teeth, jaw tense. I could tell he was struggling with this next bit. He didn't know if he should tell us or not. With another sigh, and a shake of his head I knew he'd decided to say it. "I think... it could even go as high as the queen herself."

"Spirits, no!" Lady Crane gasped.

I was too shocked to speak. I couldn't believe it either.

It was Amber, who was the most composed of all of us. "Why do you think that?" she asked softly.

He shook his head. "I don't know for certain, but... I can't imagine this sort of thing getting very far without someone pretty high up being in on it. Trouble is, if the queen or any of the other House Leaders are involved, I couldn't discern that when I was in the capital. I was there for months and saw no signs of deceit." He looked into the fire, frustration written on his rugged features. "And neither did Midnight."

"Midnight?" I asked. The mysterious member of our House, off on some secret mission. "Her mission was to spy on the other Nobles?" I guessed.

Maverick nodded. "But she's found nothing so far. The trouble is... there are a lot of Nobles, and she can't spy on all of them at once. So far, whoever is behind all of this is being *very* careful. I've kept her in the capital for now, hoping she'll find something, but..." He shrugged and didn't go on.

This is horrible, Auwei hissed, clearly still reeling from the news of the dead Lumani.

Ah, yeah. Our lives are in danger, both of us, so yeah, I'd say that's pretty horrible!

"So, just to get this straight," I said, voice trembling. "A mistweaver is trying to kill me, but not hurt the rest of you because that would alert too many people. That makes us think Nobles are behind this. And some Nobles are killing off other Nobles, maybe using a mistweaver... oh, and they can see the future. That's great..." Recapping things hadn't made me feel any better.

"Why? Why do any of this?" I asked.

Maverick shook his head. "I don't know," he growled softly. "There's something big going on here, but I have no clue what it is. I'm sorry, Legs."

"They must have some larger plan," Amber said. "Something that's potentially already in motion. And... and those they killed either were getting in the way or would get in the way in the future... like Legs."

Maverick nodded. "Sounds about right. Just wish I knew what it was."

This is wrong, Auwei said firmly. *If... if Nobles are behind this, that means their Lumani are complicit in the killing of other Lumani. That's unheard of. That's—*

Horrible? Yeah, I'm beginning to understand the full depths of the horribleness of all this.

Spirits! Auwei cursed.

Exactly.

CHAPTER 21

I BECAME A SHUT-IN. MORE THAN THAT, I WAS LIMITING WHAT OUR House could do, since one squad had to remain near me at all times. My training moved inside; they wouldn't even let me out into the gardens.

I'm afraid to say, I got a little morose and bitter, lashing out at people when I didn't mean it. Sparrow stayed by me, even though I didn't always treat her kindly. For that, I'll always love her. Silence saw me when he could, but he was still very busy with his work. I wanted his company more than ever, but I didn't ask for it. I was concerned that if this mistweaver found out about the two of us she'd use my feelings for him against us, perhaps capture him or... worse. So I stayed away from him as my heart broke just a little more.

When Ant's squad was away, taking both Ant and Jack, I'd train with Amber. I didn't think she'd have much to teach me.

I was wrong.

I landed hard on my back, my head bouncing off the special mats stuffed with straw. They were a bit of padding between my aching body and the hard floor, but didn't cushion that much. I groaned.

"What was that?" I asked, remaining flat on my back.

Amber hadn't even been using a weapon. I'd lunged at her with my practice sword, only to find myself laid out. We were in a long room in the east wing, which was specially designed for indoor combat practice. It was bare save for the mats on the floor and a few racks of weapons.

Nothing I have seen before, Auwei said, tone holding just a bit of awe. *I've heard of men from distant lands who fight open handed and can manipulate the energies within their own bodies, as well as the bodies of others, but... never seen it before, if that's what this is.*

Amber sighed. "As I thought. Those idiot men have been teaching you all wrong."

"Wrong?" I thought I'd been doing well. I was faster than Ant now and could even land a hit on Jack occasionally.

I sat up, rubbing the back of my head. "Go ahead, tell me how wrong I am, that everything I've learned so far is for naught because of... something." My bitterness was leaking out again. I didn't try to restrain it.

Amber sighed, crouching next to me. She'd tied her auburn hair back in a ponytail and was wearing a light set of buckskin leggings and a loose top. "If you think I'm going to take any lip from you, you're wrong. So what if you're a captive here? At least you're alive. The Boss and Crane will come up with some way to set you free."

I grumbled a little but nodded.

"Now stand up and I'll let you in on a secret."

You like secrets, Auwei said, trying to cheer me up.

I did like secrets.

I stood. "Go on then. What am I doing wrong?"

"You're trying to fight like a man."

Well, I had been trained by men, so that made sense.

"If you were as big and strong as Tusk, then maybe that would work for you, but you're not. You're strong and fast, yes, but in a straight fight against Ant you'd never beat him." That was probably also true. I didn't like hearing it, but I couldn't argue the point.

"Come on in!" Amber shouted, and a moment later Silence entered, dressed in practice leathers.

Having filled out a lot from the young man I'd first met, he was still lean, but there was a healthy roundness to his growing muscles. He was definitely all man now.

"You want me to fight Silence?" I asked a bit shocked. He still hadn't graduated to the advanced classes with Jack.

Silence smiled. "Don't worry, I can take it." The grin grew a little. "*If* you can hit me." He'd been more confident lately, but this was downright cocky.

"I saw how poorly little Silence here was doing with Ant and asked to train him myself," Amber said, putting a hand on his shoulder.

He didn't even flinch when she touched him these days. He also wasn't "little" anymore, taller than her by a couple inches, a match for my height.

"With his height and build, I thought it would be better if he learned a more womanly style of fighting. He's excelled at it." She beamed at him and he blushed a little then. Some of the old Silence still remained it seemed. "And we've been working on integrating his avatar abilities into his fighting as well. I think you'll find he's more than a match for you now, with your current style of fighting."

Really?

I was curious.

I picked up my practice sword and set myself.

Silence drew forth a single wooden practice dagger. He settled into an easy stance and nodded. "Whenever you're ready," he said.

I attacked. I'd thought to disarm him of his smaller weapon, then tap his shoulder to take out his primary arm. I didn't get that far.

I felt his blade run across the sleeve of my practice leathers. I'd blinked and missed his movement. And he wasn't done. The wrist of my sword arm was wrenched and suddenly weak. I dropped the blade as Silence, now somehow behind me, lifted his dagger to my throat.

"Hello Legs," he whispered in my ear.

At any other time, held by him like this, with his hot breath upon my ear, I probably would have felt a thrill, but I was too shocked to feel anything but confusion.

He released me and I stumbled forward.

"How'd you move so fast?" I gasped.

"Turns out, mice are quite fast," Amber said with a hint of a laugh. "Our little Silence has some rather amazing speed. I don't know if he can outrun Jack. We haven't tried yet, but I'm willing to bet it would be close."

Yeah, I had to agree. He'd simply vanished from in front of me.

"And what did you do to my wrist?" I said rubbing it. It ached a little, slightly numb, but feeling was quickly returning.

"That... is my style," Amber purred, a cat-like grin on her face. "Or more precisely, Midnight's style of fighting. She taught me when I was new. I taught Princess and Sparrow, then Silence. And now I'm going to teach you."

I nodded. I suddenly very much wanted to learn this style. If it had just been Amber's style I might not have been quite as impressed, but Midnight... she held a special place of awe in my heart for all her mysteriousness.

"I'm ready," I said, regaining myself. "Where do we start?"

"With no weapons," Amber said. "Toss that sword away. The first thing you need to learn is that your body is a weapon. More than that, if you know how to move in the right ways, you can make your opponent's weapon work for you."

I'd seen someone doing that... It took me a moment to recall Foggy capering around the pirate ship. More often than not, the pirates would hurt themselves or each other rather than him. "Is that what Foggy does?"

Amber laughed. "He knows some of this style, yes, though... he's just... odd to begin with. Never much liked weapons and is very good at avoiding them. Midnight trained him herself, before she went off on her mission. And even she was just a little baffled by his natural aptitude for... chaos."

That sounded right.

"So, my body is a weapon?" I still didn't fully grasp this.

"Well," Amber said with a grimace. "Not yet."

I spent that morning and all of that afternoon learning this strange fighting style. Amber taught me and Silence helped. I was happy to be spending time with him again.

Over the next week I learned more and even began to integrate my avatar abilities into my fighting. I could walk up walls or jump swiftly at or away from an opponent. My jumping also meant I could do strange kicks and leap attacks, which even Amber and Silence had trouble avoiding. I started to see how all my abilities linked together. I was actually anxious for Ant and Jack to return so I could try some of my new moves on them.

But when they did, they had bad news.

I was summoned up to the dome to meet with Ant, Maverick, Crane, and Amber.

"Tell her," Maverick said sounding grim.

Ant spoke. "We passed through Grovner's Green on our way home and heard tell of a strange woman seen around town. She matches the description of the mistweaver. She's close, Legs. We don't know what she's planning, but with you not going out, she may be getting desperate enough to come in."

Well blasted, bloody bones!

I nodded. "What does that mean?" I asked, surprised how steady my voice was. I didn't feel as calm as I'd sounded.

"Ant or Tusk will be by your side at all times, depending on who's around. Perhaps both if everyone's home. We'll be keeping a vigilant eye out for trouble," Maverick said in his no-questions tone. "I hear you've been doing well training with Amber. I want you to keep that up. You may not always have a weapon around to help you. Learn to use all your abilities. You may need them sooner than you'd like."

The next few weeks blurred together. I trained morning, afternoon, and evening, with every member of the House. Ant was still a wall of muscle. I could hit him now, but did little damage. With Jack, surprisingly, I came to see the laziness in his style. He was so quick that I don't think he'd trained as hard as he could. I began to hit him more often as well. Silence was still fast, but I was just about a match for him. Amber I hit occasionally, but still ended up on my back more often than I'd like. Tusk was a brawler and her punches hurt like the Bloody Pits, but I was faster and learned to avoid them quick enough. Fennec was about a match for me in speed and agility, with a hint of extra strength, but my avatar-based attacks worked on him nearly every time. Foggy... Foggy was infuriating. Amber was right, he was just naturally averse to being hit by anything. And he couldn't really teach me his style; it was so erratic it suited only him. Princess and Sparrow both surprised me. Neither liked to be in a fight, but both could defend themselves exceedingly well. I practiced a lot with Sparrow to learn her "flighty" defensive style. I couldn't mimic all of it, but I learned a few things. I didn't get the chance to fight with Maverick or Crane; they were too busy trying to figure out the larger picture of what was going on.

Most nights I was exhausted and went to bed, bruised but instantly asleep.

So went the winter.

Until... one late winter day, an unnatural fog billowed up around Hedgewild.

This was it: the mistweaver was coming.

I had to hope — had to pray — I was ready.

The entire crew was home and gathered around me. Gloomy day turned to blackest night and the Mists began to seep in through the tiniest cracks in the house and fill all the rooms and corridors.

She was here.

CHAPTER 22

THE NIGHT DREW ON. ALERT AND WARY, WE WAITED IN THE DOME room atop the central tower. The fog which seeped into the house billowed up the stairs, but stopped — a wall of billowing grey — at the entrance to the dome.

"Hunh," Maverick said bemused. "Apparently the dome is *actually* warded."

It seemed so, since the fog came no farther into the room.

Everyone surrounded me, ready.

But as the night lengthened, I could see the signs of fatigue start to show, after hours of taut alertness.

"Rest in shifts," Maverick commanded. He sat on the edge of his desk running a whetstone over the edge of his heavy-bladed arming sword, calm and serene, almost meditative.

Crane had a long straight cane she kept on her lap as she too sat calmly.

Ant, Fennec, Foggy, and Princess took the first rest.

The night stretched deeper.

I wore thick wool pants and a wool top that came to mid-torso, a heavy cloak over my shoulders. I'd come to accept that using my abilities meant leaving my midriff open. Also, to wall-walk I needed to keep my feet uncovered. I was glad for the thick carpeting, and the fires in the hearths which helped to keep us all warm.

Silence came to me, whispering, "can we talk?"

I nodded and the two of us moved to the far side of the dome, away from the stairs. There was no carpet here and we were far from the fire. My feet were a bit chilled on the cold stones.

When he spoke, I no longer had to strain to hear him, his voice was full and strong these days. He'd grown so much. "I know we haven't seen each other a lot these past few months. I've enjoyed training with you, though."

He sighed and smiled. "I just have so much to learn and the more I learn the more I see how much more I need to learn." He took my hands in his, held softly between us. "But I wanted you to know, Legs, that... I love you. I know what love is now and I know that's how I feel for you."

"And you're not just saying this because one or both of us might die tonight?" I asked. It was partly a dark joke, but partly not. Our previous moment together, before the Noble's Test had been a high-stress time as well.

He sighed. "I'm *saying* it now because of the danger. But I've felt it for some time and just not known how to say it... until now."

I nodded. I understood. The trouble was, I'd felt so disconnected from him recently. He'd obviously been thinking about me, while I'd thought we were drifting apart. That meant I didn't know how I felt in this moment.

He saved me the trouble, leaning in for a soft, quick kiss. Then he whispered, "You don't have to say anything. I know we've been apart a lot lately. I didn't say this to put you on the spot, only to let you know how I feel." He gave a faint smile. "Perhaps, if we both survive the night, then we can talk more, yes?"

That sounded great to me. "Yes, thank you."

We returned to the sitting area with the others. No one made any comment about our little escapade. Still, I was even more agitated after that, not only worried about the mistweaver at our doorstep, but my confused feelings for Silence as well. I sat, hands distractedly spinning out silk from my belly-button, forming it, then tossing it into the fire.

This tension is killing me, I admitted to Auwei.

Waiting can be an effective tactic of the enemy, Auwei quoted one of the texts I'd read on warfare. *Keeping a foe in a suspended state of tension wearies them. The attacker needs only wait for the right moment to strike.*

You're not helping.

Then get some sleep and—

Yeah, I don't think I could sleep.

Then find some way to relax. Or you'll be spent before the fight even starts.

She was right.

"Someone say something," I spoke into the silence. "I need a distraction." I rose and began pacing.

Maverick spoke, gruff but quiet in the stillness, trying not to disturb those who were resting. "Maverick House has only existed for eleven years. Before that, it was Gander House. I was a senior member of Gander House, so were Crane and Midnight." He gave a short breath of a laugh. "Midnight was the most senior of us. I don't know how old she is, but she's... well the rumor is she's half-Fey."

"Fey?" I said surprised. "The Fey are real?"

Yup. I don't know why you'd be surprised. You have a glowing being of energy inhabiting you. What's so surprising about an ancient race of long-lived beings?

Good point.

"Oh yes, they're real. They have secret towns and villages in the forest east of the Shattered Lands. Some say the Shattered Lands were created in a war between the first mistweavers and the

Fey. With the North destroyed, the Fey moved closer to human lands, and some are said to come south occasionally. Rarer still, sometimes they fall in love with a human. Given how old I know Midnight must be, yet how young she looks, and also the fact that she meets most known descriptions of the Fey: short, hair like night, eyes that glow, and skin pale as death." He shrugged. "Seems likely to me."

The rhythmic stroking of his whetstone over steel was almost soothing as he continued. "Anyway, she didn't want to lead the House, neither did Crane, so it fell to me." A long inhalation and sigh of a breath. "There were a few other members of House Gander who chose that time to disperse or retire. That's always an option when a House changes. So, it was just us. Then... Fin was the first, then Amber and Ant and so on." He rose and wiped down his blade, testing it. It was amazing how smoothly he wielded the heavy sword, with just one hand; mesmerizing.

"Before Gander, was Twitch, his was a cricket avatar. Before Twitch was Revel, some form of small dog if the stories are true. And before Revel was Mantis. This House has always been a haven for—"

An ear-splitting shriek split the night as a column of mist shot out from the stairwell to form into a woman in front of me. She held a dagger in her hand as she materialized, and it was at my throat a moment later, slashing.

My training saved me, evading without thinking. I tossed the webbing I'd had in my hands at her face as I flipped backward. As soon as I landed, I leaped again and this time caught myself high up on the dome, hands and feet attached firmly.

Spirits, the glass was cold!

But you're safe!

And the fight below was... intense. The woman had dissolved into mist as soon as I'd fled and was now weaving around the others, half-there half-not, trying to get to me. The others attacked when they could, but their blades and fists passed through the mist-woman. She materialize to strike at one or another, but the hits weren't meant to kill, only disable. And she was lightning fast. She had Fennec and Princess out of the fight quickly.

Ant's next attack passed right through her. She wasn't staying solid long enough to hit. And as mist, she could move with incredible speed to another spot amidst the group.

Tusk took a dagger-wound to her side, though seemed to shrug off the hit, bashing with her heavy mace, which passed through Hazra. The mist sped to Sparrow and solidified.

I screamed.

Sparrow wasn't there a moment later, quickly flitting away as a bird, as the mistweaver slashed through where Sparrow had been.

Silence could match the mistweaver for speed and, whenever she attacked him, he evaded her attacks with ease.

Mist and attack. Mist and attack, the woman was relentless. Then the mist launched up toward me. She materialized in mid-air, dagger slashing and taking my cue from Sparrow I shrunk to a spider in an instant. The blade passed harmlessly over where my neck had been.

She kicked at the glass to squash me, but I jumped away, leaving a strand of silk behind.

The mist followed.

I was nearly to the floor when she reached me and materialized. But Ant was there and caught her leg. With a vicious spin, he threw her across the room. She was mist before she hit the far wall.

"Go!" he shouted at me.

I turned human and leaped again, back to the dome.

She came at me again, but I'd learned a lot in the weeks since her last attacks and I was able to evade her. Also, it seemed that — perhaps because of the warding on the room — she wasn't able to use her mist to grab at me like she had on the pirate ship. She could turn to mist to move around, but had to attack physically with her dagger.

I jumped once again, landing on the warm stones of the hearth, seeing how the others had gathered near there.

The mistweaver materialized, but didn't attack me, she went for Crane.

Her mistake was assuming Crane was unarmed. She struck at Crane, who blocked with her cane. Then, with a twist and slide, Crane had a slim-bladed sword in her hand, pulled from the innards of the cane itself. She struck with amazing speed and the mistweaver shrieked again as blood blossomed on her leg.

"Stop!" Amber said, attracting the woman's attention... and that was it.

The mistweaver looked into Amber's eyes and the command sank in. Hazra froze and the dagger fell from her limp grip.

"The iron!" Maverick shouted and everyone was shocked into action once more. The only known way to bind and contain a mistweaver's power was with iron bands, which others quickly fastened around the mistweaver's neck, wrists, ankles, and waist.

Amber released the enchantment on Hazra and the mist-weaver fell to her knees with a keening cry. She was trying to shift into mist, but couldn't move beyond the confines of the irons around her.

I crawled down from the hearth, returning to the floor, but stayed away from the others. The cold stone beneath my feet, less of a concern now as my blood was pumping hard, my body hot from battle.

"Is that it?" I asked, wary.

I believe so, Auwei answered.

"Yes, she won't be able to escape now, or use most of her powers," Crane said. "Careful, though, she may still be able to affect herself." To evidence this, Hazra put a hand over the wound on her leg and mists seeped out of the hand to mend the injury.

"You may have caught me, but I'll tell you nothing!" she hissed.

"We'll see about that," Maverick growled, low and lethal. "Take her to the dungeons."

"We have dungeons?" I asked, blinking. In all my wanderings of Hedgewild, I'd not seen such a place.

Everyone looked at me like I had two heads.

"Yes, of course we have dungeons," I answered my own question. This estate was meant to be the center of peace and justice in the south. So, we'd need somewhere to put criminals.

Ant and Tusk hauled the mistweaver to her feet and took her away as the mists outside began to disperse. It was almost dawn, faint light in the east.

Maverick stopped me before I could leave.

"Legs," he said softly. He seemed concerned, jaw tight and tense. "I... that seemed a bit too easy."

Had it?

It had seemed like a bloody nightmare to me. But I trusted Maverick's judgment.

He continued, saying, "Just... watch yourself."

I nodded. "I will."

Silence came to me, throwing himself at me in a strong embrace. His words were a bit muffled from his head buried in my shoulder. "I'm so glad you're alive. I'm so glad *I'm* alive. I *feel* so alive! I love you, Legs!" I held him close, tight. I didn't know what to say in that moment. The only words I could find were,

"Thank you," I whispered them softly and he seemed to accept that.

As I left, I asked Auwei: *Maverick said that seemed easy. Did that seem easy to you? She almost had me at the start there. I was terrified and... the others were hurt and... and yet, we had caught a mistweaver, some of the nastiest known villains in history. Perhaps...*

I too am worried, Auwei said, hesitantly. *This isn't over, I can feel*

it. But... we did capture her, so that's something. Just remember, there may still be others out there who want you dead.

Right, yeah, thanks. Some Nobles of my own nation were trying to kill me.

Not the most encouraging thought.

CHAPTER 23

It was later that same day, that Raven, a member of the Royal
House, arrived with a message and a mission.

The woman, wearing a black cloak, with blue-black hair to
match her name, was taken to see Maverick directly. After she left,
flying away as her avatar, several of us were called up to the dome.

"I don't like this," Maverick started. He shook his head and
crumpled a piece of parchment. "This is all wrong, but... we have a
mission, and I can't think of any way to avoid a direct order from
the queen."

"The queen?" I said, at the same time Amber and Ant did.

Maverick nodded. "Yeah. They couldn't even trust it to a
courier or a pigeon." He kept shaking his head. "This feels wrong,"
he repeated, but then sighed. "Sit and listen."

We did. In the room, aside from myself, were Silence, Ant,
Amber, Foggy, and Sparrow.

Maverick paced. I'd never seen him this agitated. He'd been a
rock last night waiting for the mistweaver, but now...

Finally, he stopped and looked at each of us. "This mission is
dangerous, far more dangerous than stopping pirates or anything

else we've ever done... other than fight a mistweaver. I know why they've given it to me, but I don't like it at all." A sigh. "You're being sent to infiltrate the royal palace of Vauphan, and acquire intelligence on their war effort." He breathed out a heavy breath.

We all sat, stunned.

"War?" Sparrow said, confused. We all were. As far as I knew — as far as we all knew — Elista had a good relationship with its eastern neighbor. We didn't even share that much of a border. There was a bit of hilly forest in the north, not that far from Miraline actually, where the two nations met. Other than that, the nations were separated by Dyrens Bay.

"That was my thought as well," Maverick said. "This is the first I'd heard of it, but Raven was insistent that Vauphan has been threatening the border recently. So far, the attacks have been minor and mostly kept quiet by the queen. But she needs to know what they're up to, hence this mission. She feels they will attack in earnest soon, and needs to know when and how they plan to come at us. Their navy is far stronger than ours and if they cross the bay in force..." He sighed and ran his hand through that thick hair of his. "Like I said, this feels all wrong." He sat and put his head in his hands for a moment.

We all waited for him to continue.

"I'll summon Fin," Maverick said. "You six are the best at stealth, your avatars good at getting into small places. This is a spy mission, keep quiet and keep low. Get in, get the info, and get out." He swallowed hard. "And don't get caught." His jaw twitched. "Because if you are, we'll disavow that you went with our consent. We'll say you're rebels and leave you to their justice." He ground his teeth for a long moment. "I don't like it, but that's how it has to be." He turned away. "It's why they picked us. We have the best crew to do it and..." I could hear the distaste in his voice. "My crew is the most expendable, the least favored. We're perfect."

I could tell he was upset, even if only because the room was getting unbearably warm. Maverick's skin was a bright red, near to glowing with heat. His clothes were smoking. He got himself under control a moment later and the color faded. The room suddenly felt far too cold.

"I won't force any of you to go. I'll take volunteers only."

I had to speak up. "Should I be going?" I asked. I'd been locked down for weeks now.

Maverick gave a harsh laugh. "If anything, you're safer in Vauphan than you are in Elista."

I nodded; that was... confusingly true.

"And we have the mistweaver in custody," he said with a shrug. "We'll be questioning her while you're gone, trying to find out what we can, but I think you're... mostly safe now. And you've been cooped up for a while, so if you want to volunteer...?" He shrugged.

"I'm in," I said. I was terrified, but I was also desperate to get out. This mission, as much as it was dangerous, sounded like it was made for me. With my ability to be a spider and hear through walls and doors, I could easily overhear the right conversation.

"I'm in," Silence said, with far more confidence than I would have expected. Then he winked at me. "Someone has to keep an eye on you."

Ant and Amber spoke over each other. "I'm in."

Foggy laughed. "You're all crazy, I'm out, thanks." Coming from Foggy, that was an indictment indeed.

That left Sparrow. She looked terrified, but then looked at me and seemed to surprise herself when she said: "I'll go."

I had to smile. It would be good to have her along as a scout.

"Then it's set. We'll head to the coast first thing tomorrow and summon Fin. Get some rest. We were all up late last night."

We dispersed.

Silence followed me until we were outside of my room since his was just a little farther down the hall.

He put a hand on my shoulder, giving a reassuring squeeze, then wordless, moved on to his room.

"Silence," I said, voice hushed and uncertain. He turned back to me. "Would you... like to come in?" I asked, not really knowing what I was asking.

The faint smile on his lips grew and he nodded.

We entered my room and I closed the door, but there we stopped, standing in the entry hall for a moment.

"Legs?" Silence asked, probably curious why we were just standing here.

Why *were* we here? What had I wanted? Why had I invited him in? My feelings around him were still so confused.

Would you like some help? Auwei asked?

Spirits yes, please!

You may be confused, but you didn't want to be alone right now, did you?

No, you're right.

I guess the question is... how do you 'not want to be alone'? Do you want to talk to him? Just be held by him? Or, do you want more?

I wanted to be held, so I started there. "Hold me," I whispered, and he did, stepping in to enfold me in his arms. I put my arms around him too. I was glad he was my height now; I could rest my head on his shoulder without it being awkward.

"You're scared," he said.

"Spirits yes, aren't you?" I whispered. I couldn't recall, so I asked him, "have you been on a mission yet?"

He shook his head, I felt the movement. "No. My training is mostly done, but up till now, I'd always had too much to learn to go out. This will be my first. And yes, Legs, I'm scared."

I probably shouldn't have been. The mistweaver had been captured. This would just be a quick jaunt into Vauphan, a little light spying, nothing too dangerous.

A little light spying? Auwei laughed at that. *You have an interesting way of looking at things.*

"At least a mistweaver won't be trying to kill me on this mission," I said to Auwei and Silence.

He held me closer and I felt Auwei's soothing warmth. So far, every significant fight I'd had as a noble... had been with a mistweaver. That could shake a girl up.

And in that moment, I knew exactly what I wanted from Silence. "Make me forget about that," I asked, voice quiet. "I want to forget about everything for a while. Can you do that?"

"Yes, Legs," he said, then shifted to kiss my cheek.

I lifted my head and my lips found his. After that I let myself go, sinking into my senses, trying not to think.

Strong arms held me. Soft lips kissed me for some time before shifting to press all over my body. Our clothes were shed and we moved to the bed. Silence worked with deft fingers and soft lips between my legs until a powerful orgasm swept through me.

Then I rested in his arms as he simply caressed me, every touch seared into my sensitive skin. And when I wished for more, he kissed my breasts, bringing my nipples to hard peaks and teasing my clit with his fingers once again. Finally, I begged him to take me. He was hot and sure and thrusting deep as he drove me to the heights of a second release, then joined with me. And when I demanded more, he gave it, freely, finding new ways to thrill me and make the world wash away.

Silence stayed with me that afternoon and night. We lay in each other's arms, except for the times he rose to get us food.

Late that evening, a strange thought occurred to me as I drifted between waking and sleep.

"Have you been with Amber?" I asked, drowsy and content, but... curious.

He gave a light laugh. "No. She asked once if I wanted an... extended education. I declined. She didn't pursue it after that. She still teases me relentlessly, but that's it." Then, with a note of curiosity in his voice, he asked: "What about you, with Jack or Ant or..."

"No," I said before he named every other man in the estate. "Jack offered a *steamy* bath once, but I said no and he left it at that. Ant... he's different. He's a gorgeous man, but he's never approached me... in that way."

"Jack came to me once," Silence admitted. "Asked if I wanted to try something different." He paused for long enough that I opened my sleep-heavy eyes and looked at him.

"And?" I asked.

Silence whispered, "I think, if I didn't have you, I might have... tried... *something different*." He wore an odd grin.

I blinked, as the image of Silence and Jack, two slender and beautiful men pressed together, came into my mind. Suddenly I was getting quite hot. Curious about this, I said, "Oh?" And hoped he'd elaborate.

"When I lived on the streets, I got to know others who were... down on their luck. I met two men, a couple, who loved each other dearly. For most of my life, they were the only example of love I knew. Because of them, I've always been... curious."

That was interesting indeed. Spurred by some strange thought, I asked, "And if I wanted to invite someone to be with the two of us, a man or a woman, what would you say?" That feeling I'd had, that one person just wasn't enough, bubbled up within me.

His brows rose. "I... don't know. I'd have to think about that."

That wasn't a flat no. *Very* interesting. Somehow that thought helped me find the peace I needed to sleep warm and comforted in his arms that night.

The next morning, light flooded through my windows, waking us early. Silence dressed and hurried back to his room to get ready for the mission.

When I left my room, I saw Amber waiting, leaning against the wall in the hall. "He's always wanted you," she said with a half-grin. "Don't break his heart, Legs." Then she left.

I gaped, then let out a nervous laugh, not fully understanding that woman. I had so many questions. Not the least of which was... how had she known?

Not long later, after a quick breakfast, those of us going to Vauphan crammed into a carriage and headed for the coast. Maverick went with us.

A strange device awaited us on the beach: a large metal disk hanging from a frame, which could be moved down the rocky shore until mostly submerged in water. Maverick moved the frame until a little less than half of the disk was in the water. Then he took a heavy, cloth-headed mallet and struck the metal disk three times. We waited a few minutes, then he struck it again, three times.

A few moments later, Fin appeared on the beach with us.

"You called?"

Maverick explained the mission.

"I know the perfect beach for us, scouted it many times," Fin said, and we all — except Maverick, who would return to the House — took Fin's hands.

A moment later we were on a different beach far away.

Our mission had begun.

CHAPTER 24

I knew from my studies, that the capital of Vauphan was on the coast. I assumed Fin had brought us close, but all I could see was the expanse of beach before us, stretching away to the north and south. Inland, beyond the beach, were stark cliffs. To the south, there was a rise in the cliffs and a rocky prominence of land jutting out into the sea. The beach beneath that part of the cliff was a lot narrower and much rockier.

"The Vauphan capital is on the bay, just around that prominence there," Fin said pointing south. "The Palace is atop these cliffs. You'll see it above you once you're on the other side of that peninsula. From here, you can see some lookout posts atop the cliff." He pointed again. And now that he'd indicated them, I could see the small structures at the top of the cliff south of us.

"If there are lookout posts, should we be hiding?" Ant asked.

"Why? Mostly they're looking out to sea for pirates or ships that might be a threat. We're already on their shores. If they see us, they'd have no reason to think us anything other than Vauphan residents." Fin had a point.

After a moment with no more questions, he went on: "You'll want to get to the top of the cliffs, which, given this group, should be easy. From there, infiltrate the palace and find what you need. I won't be able to go with you, for... obvious reasons, but I'll be here, on the beach, when you're ready to leave."

It took me a moment to figure out those "obvious reasons." Fin was a large man, and his avatar was a whale. There would be no way for him to get up that cliff, but the rest of us, as he'd said, would find it much easier. Sparrow could ferry Ant and me, Amber could fly, and Silence...?

"How will you get up?" I asked him.

He smiled. "I'll climb. Mice are excellent climbers."

"Have you been practicing?" I asked, curious. There weren't many places to climb around Hedgewild, except for some much smaller cliffs of our own by the sea.

"He's been clambering all over the outside of Hedgewild," Amber said. "If he can climb that fitted stone covered in ivy, then he can climb a cliff well enough."

I nodded.

"Do we think it's better to go up the cliff here, and across to the palace?" Ant asked the group. "Or go up right under the palace. It would probably be easier to just get inside if we went in that way."

"I think you've answered your own question," Amber said, voice silken. She was practically purring, a sultry grin on her face. I guessed she and Ant had been together last night. Better happy Amber than catty Amber.

She wore a daring red dress, trimmed in gold and cut to show off her assets. We'd been told to dress up, but still be able to move around easily. The hope was to look like we fit in as courtiers inside the palace. Sparrow sported a lovely dark blue dress. Ant wore a dark green jerkin over a billowing white shirt. Which on him, made him look huge and imposing. His pants were a dark brown, and his boots black, and high, to below the knee. Silence had on a dark blue shirt and black pants. He'd acquired a new pair of boots, which matched Ant's. I was in my green Noble's Test dress. Amber had said I'd be more distracting in one of her gowns — she had a good selection which left the midriff uncovered — but I'd declined. I wasn't ready for that yet.

We walked down the beach to the base of the prominence.

"I'll wait here," Fin said. "Stay safe. If you get separated, return here."

We nodded and began to pick our way over the rocks at the base of the jutting cliffs. It took us a little time to move safely around the peninsula.

Once we had, we could see the city of Vauphan, from which our neighboring country took its name. It sprawled along the wide curve of a round cove further inland, where the land was more level with the sea. There were ships in the harbor, a fleet of large war ships and numerous small fishing boats, but all of that was far removed from where we were. The waters near us were scattered with jagged rocks jutting up from the surface, not safe to sail.

The only thing close to us was the palace and surrounding castle compound, rising from the cliffs above us. We could see it clearly now that we were on the south side of the prominence. Tall towers rose into the sky and stark white walls clung to the top of the cliffs, imposing while still being bright and cheery.

It was mid-morning by then. The sun bright on the brisk late-winter's day.

"Sparrow you're with me," Amber said. "We'll take a look around and see where we want to bring the rest of you." She turned to Silence. "You might as well start climbing. That's going to take a while."

He nodded, moved to the edge of the cliff, then surprisingly veered into his mouse form.

"I would have thought he'd stay as a human, the climb wouldn't seem as far," I said to no one in particular. Amber and Sparrow had already shifted and were flying away, so Ant was the only one with me.

"From what I hear," he said. "He climbs exceptionally well as himself, but far better as a mouse. So, it might be farther, but he'll move quicker and be safer."

That made sense.

Ant sat on a rock, looking out to sea. "Having a mistweaver after you can't have been easy. How are you faring?"

I sat next to him. "I'm still a bit... tense. Somehow, I can't believe it's over, even though we have her in the dungeon. Something..." My hairs all stood on end, my spider's senses perking up as I spoke. "Something doesn't feel right about all of this."

He nodded. "Yeah, I know what you mean. Capturing a mistweaver... should that even be possible?"

I didn't know and didn't answer.

Ant changed the subject. "I'm glad you've been doing well training with Amber."

I laughed, recalling how I'd managed to flip him onto his back the last time we'd sparred. "If I can get you on your back, I must be doing something right. I never thought I'd be able to best you after that first day of training."

He laughed, though the sound had an odd quality to it. He seemed about to say something, then didn't. Instead, he sighed and after a moment laughed again. "I hear you had Silence on his back last night?"

I instantly flushed a deep shade of things-I-don't-want-to-talk-about red, or so I assumed given the heat upon my cheeks.

"Amber told me," he said softly. "She has a way of knowing who's with who at Hedgewild. Some sixth sex sense." He laughed. "There's a tongue-twister."

I still didn't know what to say or why he'd brought it up.

"I just... you two are both young and I know things happen. I want to make sure it's not going to get in the way of the mission or affect you... adversely."

The words were out of my mouth before I could stop them: "Does sex with Amber affect you adversely?"

He didn't react other than to nod. "I suppose that's fair to ask." He looked back out to sea. My question hadn't thrown him at all.

He shrugged. "Some days it does." I hadn't been expecting this level of casual candor from him. "We don't... expect much from each other beyond our beds. She's alluring and sexy, and she thinks I am as well, but we're not really... together. It's mostly just a physical thing. That makes it easy to keep distant and not think about her when she's out on missions." He sighed. "But there are times when I worry about her." He shrugged. "To be fair, I worry about everyone when they're on a mission. Though I guess I have an extra helping of worry for her on occasion."

"It's the same for me and Silence," I said, though I didn't know if I meant it.

Pits! I didn't even know how I felt about the two of us yet!

Being with Silence yesterday had been... amazing, then relaxing and comfortable. I knew I wanted more of that, but my question to Silence about whether he'd be good with others joining us still hung over me.

If he said no... I wasn't sure what I'd do.

I had no words to express how I felt other than confused. I wanted Silence, but also wanted *more*. Worrying for Silence was distracting enough without trying to figure out the details of our relationship. Not knowing exactly what to say, I just echoed Ant's words back to him. "I have an extra helping of worry for him right now, that's all."

Ant nodded. "Good."

But that brought up a point I'd been wanting a bit of clarity on.

"What's the official policy on House members being together? Are there... boundaries I should know about?"

Ant nodded, still looking out to sea. "Yeah, we've always been a bit quiet on that," he said. "Officially, there's nothing against Nobles finding a spouse within their House. But each House has their own set of unwritten rules. Sometimes those rules are about who is right for who or when is right for a marriage. We at Maverick House don't regulate people like that, but at the same time, I think we have an unwritten rule that you can fool around a bit, but marriage is... different. Not that Maverick is against marriage. He just wants people to make sure they're right for each other and truly ready for it." Ant sighed. "You didn't hear this from me, but I think that's because he once asked Midnight to marry him and she turned him down."

What?

I didn't say anything, but my mouth hung open as I blinked loudly at Ant for a long moment, wanting more information.

He glanced at me and laughed at my expression.

"Yeah. I heard it from Crane. It was a while ago, when he was young and she was... well younger I guess, but who knows how old." He shook his head. "Midnight is truly fascinating. You'll see when you meet her. She looks like you or Amber, a youthful woman, but... there's something in her eyes that's... heavy. She's got the eyes of an old woman who's seen far too much." He digressed. "But yeah, the Boss was captivated by her and wanted to make it official. She... didn't. So now there's this undertone around relationships at the House. You can have some fun, as long as no one gets upset or hurt, but if you want more, you make sure you're fully ready. Boss won't allow it otherwise."

"Oh."

I'd just learned far more than I'd expected to, sitting on this rocky beach.

We sat in silence for a while after that.

Sparrow returned and let us know where Amber would be waiting. Then we all veered into our avatars and Sparrow carried Ant and I up, one in each small foot.

I watched the sea fall away as the craggy cliff sped by, higher and higher. I tried not to let the extreme height affect me. Though I found myself spinning out and knitting together a sort of sail with my silk. It was something I'd learned and been working on as an ability, which I couldn't yet do in human form, and had done a couple of times successfully in spider form. If I fell, the sail should flare out and catch me, slowing my descent.

As it turned out, we landed well enough inside an empty room, flying in through an open window. Amber was inside waiting for us. "Good, now that you're here, I'm going to go check on Silence and make sure he knows where to meet us. He may be a while." She veered into her butterfly form, and flitted away. This mission wasn't about time. We'd be able to fit in for a while before someone noticed we shouldn't be here. It was mostly about knowing where to be listening to hear what we needed to hear. That was far more uncertain and meant we might end up being here for a day or two. The hope was that if there was a war in the works — and it was well known — people would be talking about it openly in the palace, where they were safe.

But that remained to be seen.

It took a while before Amber returned and Silence joined us. It was mid-afternoon by then. Sparrow had flitted down to the kitchens and stolen us some bread and cheese.

Once we were all together, we went over the plan. Ant and I would search one wing of the palace, Amber and Silence another, while Sparrow kept to her bird form, flying around to hear what she could. We'd meet back in this empty room at midnight.

Then we were off.

My heart raced as Ant and I passed our first random person,

but we exchanged pleasantries and he went his way... that was it. The man hadn't suspected anything.

That helped to alleviate some of my tension.

This just might work.

CHAPTER 25

Everything went well… until dinner.

A functionary found us in the halls and asked if we'd be attending the dinner that evening in the Royal Hall. I hesitated, but Ant accepted the invitation easily.

"Yes, of course."

And when the functionary asked our names, Ant answered, "we are Lord and Lady Halvarion, in from Walthrick," he said with such confidence, even I believed him.

The functionary nodded and left.

Ant turned to me and shrugged. "Dinner could be a great place to get some information."

"Or get caught," I whispered, making sure no one was around.

He shrugged. "One or the other, I guess we'll see. You know where to meet up if we're separated. That room at midnight, or the beach where Fin left us. If things go badly change into your avatar form and find a crack to slip into. They don't have Lumani here, they won't be able to follow you. But I'm sure it won't come to that. You'll do well at dinner."

"As your wife?" I asked playfully?

"You could do worse."

"I could do better."

"How dare you talk to your husband that way!" He'd said it playfully, but given our discussion earlier on the beach, I was feeling just a little odd about playing the part of his wife.

And at dinner, things didn't improve.

I felt it as soon as I walked into the long hall, a humming tension in the room. Everyone here was on edge. Ant and I got a few curious, sidelong glances, but once again, Ant used that same name, Lord and Lady Halvarion, from Walthrick, and people seemed to accept it.

I pulled him aside. "Who are these people? Do I have a name? Why is everyone so accepting?"

He grinned. "Your name is Lady Ahlana Halvarion. I did some research before we left. The Halvarions are from the north of Vauphan, and fairly reclusive. People down here at the capital are unlikely to know them. We're also fairly insignificant, with a small holding. So, we're a curiosity at best. Oh, and my name is Viktor."

"Viktor, Ahlana, got it."

But then, once word got around who we were, people began coming up to us with a very similar question: "How are things in the north?" Or "Are you worried for your lands?" We answered with generalities and hedging vagueness, which people seemed to accept, but still. I began to wonder... what was happening in the north of Vauphan?

Then the dinner began.

We all sat, and the king and queen entered from the far end of the hall, a proud couple in their forties, but even from a distance I could see the lines of worry and weariness on their faces.

The first two courses were served, which was great, as I was famished, lunch having been a bit sparse. There was a break before the third course, during which the king stood. Everyone looked to the monarch.

The king sighed heavily. When he spoke, his voice was rich and full, filling the hall, yet his tone held a note of heavy fatigue and concern. "We have received word from the Fey of the Ne'er-wald Forest. They have agreed to help us in our cause. They can see the threat from Elista as well. They'll be sending several patrols of Haryagars to the front, along with some Kuznmeisters." The king sighed heavily, shaking his head. "I do not wish for what is to come. I did not start this war, but—"

He didn't get to finish as a building murmur turned to startled screams and cries of alarm.

"They're here!" someone shouted. "The Elistans are attacking! Protect the king!"

I tensed, ready for a fight... but no one was looking at me or Ant. They were looking at the unnatural, billowing mist, which was seeping into the hall.

Oh no! Auwei breathed.

Ant and I said it at the same time. "Mistweaver."

"There must have been another besides the one hunting you," Ant whispered urgently. "These people have no chance against one."

He was right. "Neither do we," I pointed out.

Ant nodded. "Things are going to get chaotic in a second. Use that to veer and find some crack in the wall. Get out of here. I'll meet you on the outside. We can't help these people." His voice was hard, it was clear he didn't like what he was saying, but it was the truth.

Guards rushed to the king, while courtiers tried to flee, but all the doors were sealed. We were trapped in here as the fog filled the room, as thick as could be.

"I'd hoped you'd be here," a voice whispered in my ear. A voice I knew *very* well.

I spun and saw Hazra right there beside me.

"How...?"

She laughed. "I'll kill the royals first, then I'll come for you." And she faded into the mists from which she'd come. The fog was all around us now, I couldn't see farther than a few inches.

Blackened bloody bones! My heart thundered in fear. I reached for Ant through the haze, wanting the comfort of his solid presence, but he must have already veered and fled, as he wasn't where I thought he should be.

I slid off my chair and turned into a spider. Finding a table leg, I crawled up that and onto the underside of the table. I felt safe here, at least for the moment.

Ant's words came back to me: *find some crack in the wall. Get out of here. I'll meet you on the outside.* But I didn't want to venture out into the chaos of running feet and swirling mists. I huddled where I was, terrified.

Somehow Hazra had escaped the bonds holding her at Hedgewild and gotten here... and she was going to kill...

Her words finally sank in.

...Kill the royals...

What in the Blackest Pits was going on here? My mind wasn't working. I didn't understand any of this.

I think I'm starting to understand at least part of what's going on here, Auwei said. *Though I still have no idea how Hazra got here. That woman terrifies me in a way I've never known.*

Me too. So, what's your theory? I'm all ears.

Technically you're all legs at the moment. Sorry, I'm nervous and I joke when I'm nervous. Anyway, I think Hazra's attack on Hedgewild was a feint, she let herself get caught so we'd feel safe and you could go on this mission. A mission that came that same day!

Spirits and Sprites, she was right!

The plan was to get you here so Hazra could kill you and the Vauphani royals all at once. I still don't know why we're killing our neighbors, though from what the king was saying it sure sounded like they were preparing for a war. Still, if anything, this will only provoke them more!

Which meant... *If we're discovered here, we'll be blamed for the assassination. We were set up. Someone back home WANTS this war. So... even if I get away from Hazra, I need to make sure I don't get caught... that none of us are caught!*

Agreed.

Horrible screams and the gurgling of the dying began to fill the hall. Spirits! I needed to get out of here. But my eight tiny legs were frozen in fear. I didn't know which way to go, where I might find some crack I could slip through. I'd already lost Ant and...

Something moved beside me and I shifted, skittering away a little.

It was an ant.

Oh, thank the Mists!

We couldn't communicate in these forms, one of us would have to transform back to speak. Ant did so, now crouched under the table.

"I'm going after her," he said, voice hard.

No! Get out of here, keep to your original plan. You can't defeat her alone! I couldn't say it, couldn't stop him. I was too terrified to shift back and speak. He rolled out from under the table and was gone into the mists.

Ant! No!

I was alone again. Alone in a foreign country, where everyone was trying to kill me.

I found a crack in the wood of the table and squished myself into it. Trembling, I waited for this horridness to be over, hoping Ant would succeed, but certain he wouldn't. As a spider, I couldn't cry, but internally I wept with terror and grief.

CHAPTER 26

"Legs?" The voice was low, a whisper, but near... and it wasn't Ant or Hazra, but...

Silence!

"We heard a commotion and came to check it out, I slipped under the door and could smell you in here, are you in spider form?" I saw him crawling along under the table, looking around. "You're close, but I can't see you."

Oh, Silence, go. Get out of here!

He can't hear you. You'll need to change back.

I know that!

He was right beneath me, sniffing around, which looked odd in his human form. "Legs?"

I dropped from my hiding spot onto his shoulder.

He started and looked, then smiled. "I'm so glad you're safe." He spun a tight circle and began crawling back the way he'd come. "This is the way out; I can smell Amber and..." He stopped moving and whispering, frozen in place. It took me a moment to sense what he had, all the little hairs on my spider-body were on end and not twitching at all.

There was no sound.

The fighting and dying that had been happening around me had stopped, and Silence had sensed the lull as well.

A moment later he veered into his mouse form and I fell off his now-much-smaller shoulder. I was too big to ride on him. We cowered, frozen, next to each other.

That's when it occurred to me. If I couldn't hear anything that meant one of two things: either Ant had killed the mistweaver... or she'd killed him. And given a thick fog still clung to the room, I feared the worst.

"Come out little spider," came the sing-song call.

My bones froze, icy claws of fear sinking into my soul.

Silence's red eyes looked at me. Even in mouse form I could see his fear.

And it was seeing that fear — matching my own — that shifted something within me.

Oh... I felt that. Auwei said.

My fear hadn't fled, it remained, but something deep within me had surged up to subsume it. Icy claws of terror still lingered in my flesh, but my soul and spirit were free, and I knew what I had to do.

I shifted back to human form and whispered to Silence. "Get out of here. Tell Maverick the Vauphani are bringing Fey from the north and planning for war. After this assassination of their royals, they'll be attacking us for sure. Also, someone back home set us up to die here, perhaps to blame all this on us! Now go!"

The tiny grey and white mouse skittered away, running swiftly across the stone floor.

I slid out from under the table, body trembling with... something. I didn't know what I was feeling. I was still terrified, but some unstoppable part of me had decided to run toward the danger, not away.

It's called bravery, Legs. Auwei said, proud but terrified. *Don't worry, I'll give you all the benefit of my nine lifetimes, all the things I've learned about combat. But I trust you too. You've trained relentlessly. You know what you need to do.*

I huffed a heavy breath and felt my skin tingle, muscles flexing as a thrill ran through me.

"I'm here, Hazra. Come and get me."

A laugh. "Oh, aren't we brash!"

I targeted that voice and threw a ball of webbing.

Another laugh. "Missed me."

I threw another, and another. Following the laughter as it danced around the room. I couldn't see a thing through the blasted fog, but if I could just hit her, hopefully that might distract her long enough for me to get to her.

"You'll never hit me," she chided, sounding distant.

I nearly leaped out of my skin when she spoke next, a whisper right next to my ear: "I am everywhere in this mist."

The combat training I'd been drilling for the last few weeks kicked in and without thinking I spun. My elbow connected with her ribs, even as a blade sliced across my side. It had probably been intended to sink into my back, but with how I'd turned, it caught me a glancing blow instead, across my ribs.

Laughter danced away as I grunted, putting a hand to the wound. It wasn't as bad as it could have been, but it was still bleeding freely. I spun some webbing to place over it, clotting the wound, but it still burned with searing pain.

This wasn't going to work. I couldn't keep still. If she could move freely in the mists, then I should already be dead. Unless she was playing with me. If she hadn't spoken the last time and just stabbed me, I wouldn't have known until I'd felt the pain, and not been able to react as quickly.

I didn't know why she hadn't just killed me, but the woman was insane, so perhaps she didn't know either.

I kicked off my slippers and hoped I remembered how high

the ceiling was in this hall. I jumped. If I leaped too hard, I'd crash against the stone above, but too lightly and I'd fall back down. Again, my practice paid off, and I was able to find the ceiling with my hands and stick, then brought my feet up and switched to walking upside down, keeping on the move, planting and placing silk-strands around the room. Perhaps, I could catch her in a web. Unless she actually *was* the fog, then I'd be damned to the Blackest Pits.

What saved me next was pure luck. I'd returned to the floor to place another strand when something slick under my foot — probably blood, but I didn't want to think about it — caused me to slip as she attacked. She'd been trying to slit my throat, but I fell and the blade instead cut my chin, then traced a line up my cheek, between my right eye and right ear, and up into my hair. I instantly veered into my avatar and skittered away, before returning to my natural form to leap back up to a wall. With each new strand of webbing I placed — quivering with the faint vibrations in the air — I was getting more and more of a sense for the room and her movements.

The failure of her last attack must have frustrated her. Her laughter turned to a growl. "You'll not catch me in a web, little spider. I'm done playing!"

The fog solidified around me, crushing me to the floor, then turned sharp, like the points of a thousand nails piercing into me.

I screamed, even as I veered into my spider form to get away from the constricting, piercing pain.

But that last attack had nearly done me in. Even in spider form I felt the wounds all over my body, the slow leak of blood. I'd be dead soon if I didn't find a way to turn the tides.

My hairs pricked up and warned me at the last moment as she materialized above me. I leaped away to avoid her stepping on me.

My hairs...

My spider sense! I hadn't been using it to the fullest. I'd been trusting to my web and my regular hearing to know where she was.

Yes, of course! Why didn't I think of that, Auwei said. *I guess terror got the better of both of us. You concentrate on finding her, I'll do the rest.*

I surged back to my normal form, eyes closed, concentrating on my spider's sense. I gathered as much webbing as I could in my hands and waited, still.

"I feel your life ebbing, spider. You've stopped running. Are you ready to die?"

I felt the voice around me. Each sentence from a different point in the room. She truly was everywhere, but I waited. I hoped my stillness meant she wouldn't use the solid fog on me. I gambled my life on her wanting to finish me on her own with that dagger of hers.

My hairs bristled. I felt the flow of fog as it swirled around me, felt her move within it, and I waited. I wouldn't hold out much longer. I was covered in my own blood, from the myriad of tiny punctures all over my body. I'd be too weak to stand in a moment, then dead not long after. She'd not even need to come for me. That meant I needed to get her attention.

"End this," I whispered, hoping my voice was filled with despair.

"As you wish," she hissed.

I felt — through my spider's sense — her materialize right in front of me and thrust with her dagger. I sensed her triumphant inhalation of breath...

And that's where I stuffed my handful of webbing, clamping it over her mouth. Auwei did her part, reacting far faster than I would have. She leaped back as the mistweaver's dagger pierced my chest over my heart. It sank an inch into my left breast before I managed to get away.

I heard the mumbled struggling as Hazra tried to breathe, the raking of her own nails over her face to remove the webbing. I surged back in while she was distracted. My spider's sense knew exactly where she was. I grabbed her arm, the one with the dagger, and forced it into her chest. Then I bashed the hilt with my palm to sink it in deep.

She must have freed part of her mouth as I heard a gasping scream. Then the fog whipped around me. I was tossed into a wall, hitting hard, sinking to the floor as the mists swirled in an agitated frenzy.

Her muffled cries lasted a moment longer as the mists whipped and thrashed and then... they were all sucked back to one spot, to her, as she fell to the floor, dead.

I laughed, a weak sound, surprised I'd actually won. But the laughter quickly faded as I saw the carnage in the hall. The freely flowing blood from dozens of bodies, the dead king and queen, the sliced-up courtiers. It was a testament to how weak I was, that I didn't even have the strength to be sick at the horrid sight.

Then I looked down at myself and saw my torn dress, bits of it falling away exposing far too much skin. But my modesty was a secondary concern, next to the wounds on my chest and side and face, not to mention the tiny bloody punctures, all over my body. I spun some silk to patch the larger wounds, but by that point I was getting dizzy, weak.

The many points of light in the room were fading to darkness. I slumped to the ground, as a large form drew close to me. I couldn't make out who it was as I fell into unconsciousness. My only thought was: if it's a guard, I'm dead.

CHAPTER 27

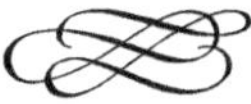

"You just refuse to die, don't you?"

I blinked awake, and grunted with pain, my body on fire with a thousand cuts.

Ant leaned over me. "I've healed you as much as I can, without blacking out myself. I think you'll live, but Spirits Within, you're a mess, a tough as nails mess."

"Don't mention nails," I groaned. It still felt like someone had stuck me with hundreds of those blasted things all over my body.

He grinned, but it was a faint thing. He looked incredibly drained and weary. Oddly, there wasn't a scratch on him.

"How...? You're..."

"I think she wanted me to take the blame for all this. I was trapped in solid fog, but left unharmed and alive." His weak grin widened. "So, you saved me." He held out a hand to help me stand. It took a couple of tries and when I finally got to my feet, I leaned heavily against the wall.

"I'm not gonna get far," I groaned. Just standing was a chore.

Amber appeared nearby, probably having inched under a door in her butterfly form, then rushed toward us. She took one look at me and her eyes went wide. "Girl, put on some clothes!" She scooped down and plucked up a cloak from one of the dead, it was slick with blood, but neither of us cared as she wrapped it around me.

"Thank you," I said. "Where's Silence?"

"I sent him back to Fin with your message. Hopefully he's long gone by now."

I nodded. *Good.*

"Let's get out of here," Ant said, picking me up like I was nothing. He even shifted me to one arm, as he easily lifted the heavy bar off the door with his other.

Sometimes I forgot how incredibly strong he was. Ants could lift many times their own weight.

Yet as soon as we were out of the great hall, my hairs pricked up as I caught the distant sounds of running feet... lots of them.

"Someone's coming," I said, voice so very weak.

"Yeah," Ant grunted as he an Amber both tilted their head in a very similar way. I'd learned it was an antenna thing, scenting and sensing the movement of the air.

"Too many," Amber added. "Except... from that direction." She pointed down an adjoining hall.

Ant and Amber shared a look, some unspoken communication passing between them. Then the big man sighed, gave a grim smile, and set me down. "I'll hold them off as long as I can."

"What?" A part of my spirit broke at the resigned look on his face. "No! You—"

"Hush, child," Amber whispered as she tucked an arm around me. "No use arguing when he gets like that. He's tough, he'll catch up. Come." I put an arm around her as she helped me limp down the corridor.

When I looked back, I saw Ant duck into the great hall and come out with a short broadsword. The weapon seemed tiny in his hands. How could he defend himself with something so small?

I turned to Amber, ready to tell her that I hadn't just killed a mistweaver to let my friends die like this, but the words died on my lips. There were tears on her cheeks. I'd never seen her shed a single tear before.

She must have caught my shocked look from the corner of her eye. With a slight shift of her head toward me, she gave that same grim smile I'd just seen on Ant's face. "Yes, I worry too. Now let's get going so his sacrifice isn't in vain."

I nodded.

Despite the healing Ant had given me, I could barely walk. He'd closed the larger wounds, but I was still bleeding — if only a little — from the dozens of small cuts all over me. I didn't move fast and Amber was half-carrying me. Finally, she laughed. "It's amazing what we forget when we're on edge." I didn't know what that meant until she said. "As much as I don't like the idea of a spider on me, could you shift? You'd be a lot lighter."

I laughed too, nodded, then veered into a spider, climbing up her arm as she rolled her shoulders.

"Much better," she said with a sigh. After that, she moved with greater haste through the corridors of the palace.

There were people everywhere: guards running this way and that, terrified courtiers huddled in groups. Nobody seemed to know what was going on, which was good, since that meant few had a moment to spare for a woman in a red dress hurrying through the halls.

It wasn't until she stopped suddenly, looking around, that two guards approached from down a short hallway to her left.

"Bones," she hissed. "I think I'm lost."

"Excuse me miss, you can't be in this part of the palace," one of the guards said. He approached with his halberd lowered just a little, not threatening yet, but ready.

"Yup, bloody bones, somehow I've ended up in the royal wing!" She hissed to herself, and probably for my benefit. She turned to the guards with a smile on her face. "Hello, boys." I saw her look intently into one set of eyes then the other, then she waved her hand saying, "Forget me." And she walked right between the two of them as they stood there, a bit stunned.

I turned around on Amber's shoulder as she casually walked down the short hall, so I could watch what happened to the two guards.

"I thought..." one of them said. "Did you just...? I...?"

The other one sniffed. "I don't know what you're talking about. We should get back to our post."

"Ah... yeah... right."

I thought, when they turned, they'd see us for sure, since we hadn't yet passed beyond the doors at the end of the hall, but their gazes seemed to look right through us.

Amber opened one of the large double doors and entered, and the guards seemed to see nothing. They returned to their places to either side of the door, facing out, as it closed behind us.

I hopped from her shoulder, shifted back to human, and slumped into a large cushioned chair. "What are we doing here?" I hissed a whisper. "We're in the royal chambers!"

She smiled and shrugged. "The king and queen are dead, it's not like we're going to be interrupted. Perhaps I can find more plans on their war effort. We're really going to need them now. Stay here, I'm going to snoop for a moment. Besides, the Royal wing is on the north side of the palace and opens up onto the top of that point of land. We can escape out there when we're done."

"But Ant... he won't know where to find us if we're not—"

"Don't!" she hissed, spinning back to me, lips tight and trembling, tears threatening. She lowered her voice when she continued. "Don't say his name, please." She drew in a deep breath and stilled her tears. "He'll know where to go if we're not in the room. He'll find Fin, and so shall we." She gave a valiant attempt at a smile. "We'll all meet there." And with that she spun and walked into one of the many rooms off this large main living area.

I didn't realize I'd fallen asleep until a voice woke me. "By the gods!" the voice was male, not Amber. At first, I thought it might be Silence, then I opened my eyes and was gazing up into two of the most beautiful blue eyes I'd ever seen. Well-kept raven black hair framed a face that still held a hint of youth upon firm, manly features.

I didn't know how much time had passed, but the room was dark, lit only by a lantern on a nearby table.

"Who are you?" the man asked me.

"Le—"

Not your real name he's not an ally! Auwei shouted at me.

"Lei—ana?" I hadn't meant to make it sound like a question but I wasn't fully awake yet and also... still only a few steps off from death.

"Leiana?" he said, then smiled. "What happened to you? How did you get here? What's that on your face? Do you know what happened in the palace? I haven't heard—" And a look of fearful uncertainty crossed his face.

My mind finally spun back to life and I realized who this young man must be. He looked like the recently dead king. This was the crown prince!

And I... I was a foreign agent, lying in his suite, dress torn to shreds with a borrowed, blood-soaked cloak not quite covering me. Then, there was the patch of spider-silk over the side of my face. Yeah, I must look a Pits-spawned sight indeed.

I blinked, feigning ignorance. "I... I don't know. I was attacked, then saved by some men who pulled me in here."

His face grew more concerned. It was clear he had no idea what was happening outside these rooms. He looked at the double doors. "I should call for the guards."

"No! Please. Just... stay with me for a moment?" If the guards came in, they'd not know how I got in here, given Amber's influence. And that would only create more questions, since I would have had to pass them to get here.

I started to rise, though that wasn't easy, and reached up to him. I put a hand behind his neck to help me up and to pull him down. I needed to distract him and the only thing that came to mind was a kiss.

He gave in, allowing me to draw him closer and even putting an arm around me to help me up.

Our lips touched. His were soft and full, and I pressed against their warmth for a long moment... until his entire body went oddly stiff, too tense.

I tried to pull back, but his arm behind me wouldn't budge. I could see confusion and panic in his eyes.

Something was wrong.

In order to slip out of his hold, I had to press my body against his in a most intimate manner as I shimmied to the side. Once I was out of his embrace it was clear he was frozen, completely immobilized, only a few muscles twitching.

Oh... Auwei breathed. *I... I think we've just found a new power.* Her tone was somewhere between bemused, confused, and horrified. *Some spider bites can cause paralysis, and your kiss is... sort of like a bite?*

I could tell she was trying not to laugh, though it was an I'm-sorry-for-you, pitying laugh.

"Bloody bones!" I hissed the curse. "Really?" *But then why didn't I do that to Silence when we...?*

I don't know, but my guess is that you felt something far different when kissing Silence and this was more of a survival instinct, so... yeah.

That made sense. The trouble was, I didn't know how toxic my poisoned kiss might be. I didn't want to accidentally kill the crown-prince. Oh wait... he was the king now. "Bloody bones!"

Yeah.

"Who's he?" I spun at the sound of Amber's voice. She had a satchel stuffed with something, probably important papers.

"The crown prince. I... I think I poisoned him... by accident. I kissed him... to distract him... and I think I have poison now...?"

"Isn't that just the topper?" She grimaced. "And it's new, so you have no idea how bad it is." She nodded to herself. "Blasted bloody bones!" She was thinking, her eyes shifting, probably trying to figure out what to do. I was still too weary to come up with any ideas.

"Pits... bring him with us," she hissed.

"What?" I didn't think I'd heard that right.

"We don't want to kill him, and if we leave him, we don't know what will happen. Yet, if we bring him back with us, we can hopefully find an antidote and give it to him. Either way, we need to go now."

"I can't carry him," I grumbled.

"I can, he's not that big. But I can't carry both of you, so can you shift?" She slung the satchel over her shoulder and came to us. I veered into my spider and hopped onto the prince who Amber picked up roughly and slung over her shoulder.

Amber left the lantern and moved slowly through darkened rooms out onto a balcony.

Stars twinkled in the night's sky above us as Amber navigated a set of stairs down to a long roughly triangular, walled garden, which I recognized as the top of the jutting peninsula. It was deserted as we made our way to the edge. There was an awkward moment, during which I had to shift back and help Amber get the body over a low wall at the top of the cliffs.

It was only when we stood upon the bit of land between the wall and the sheer drop, that we realized our problem. I could walk down the side if I needed to and Amber could fly... but the prince...

"Use your silk, it's strong enough to support a person, yes?" Amber said.

I nodded. We laid the prince on the ground, his eyes the only thing moving, and I wound him up in my silk, ensuring I had a good hold.

"Sorry about all this," I said to him. "We didn't mean for any of this to happen. We'll fix you up and send you right back. I promise."

"I'm not sure if your diplomacy means much after poisoning him," Amber said.

True. "Ready," I said. "Can you fly out there and make sure he doesn't hit anything too rough on the way down?"

She nodded.

I wove the many strands of my silk, which held the prince, into a heavy rope and looped that around one of the stone merlons atop the low wall. Then, I fed out my silk to lower the prince. I used my own weight as a counterbalance, my bare feet on the wall to ease the tension on me. Injured and exhausted, it took everything I had to hold the prince steady and lower him slowly. It seemed to take forever. My arms began to burn with fatigue, then turned soft, like jelly. Still, I held on. I didn't know how I was managing to do any of this in my condition, but didn't question it. Then....

A flapping of wings, and Sparrow appeared beside me. "Need help?"

"Oh, Spirits, yes, take this line!"

She did, bracing herself as I had, and taking over bearing the weight as I let out more and more silk. Then finally we felt the line go slack. We waited, resting, until Amber appeared next to us.

"Sparrow, good, carry Legs down." To me she said. "I made sure he went down smoothly and landed softly." Good. "Now let's get out of here!" She was back in her butterfly form in an instant.

I became a spider. Sparrow picked me up and we were all soon at the base of the cliff.

Sparrow helped Amber carry the prince off the rougher rocks, to a more level stretch of beach where it would be easier for one person to carry him.

And we didn't have to carry him far, as Fin moved out from the shadows of a shallow cave into the moonlight.

"Ready to go?" he asked. "Where are the others?"

"Ant will be coming," Amber said, stalwart. "And Silence should be here already, was he not?"

Fin shook his head. "You three are the first."

"Well Pits," Amber said vehemently.

My gaze shot up to the top of the dark cliffs above us.

Silence hadn't arrived? Where was he?

My heart lurched. Now we had two people missing.

CHAPTER 28

FIN RETURNED US TO THE GREAT HALL OF HEDGEWILD. NONE OF US liked leaving the others behind, but someone had to report what we'd found and the crown prince still needed help.

Fin vanished after returning us, going back to the beach to wait for Ant and Silence. I sat heavily on a bench and laid my head down on a table. The prince was laid out on another table and Amber and Sparrow then ran in different directions to get the others. Amber had mentioned that Crane knew something of medicines and there was an herbalist in Grovner's Green, but otherwise... the person who knew the most about poisons... was Midnight and she wasn't going to be of any help here. Ant might also be able to heal the prince, but...

I couldn't think about that.

I was in pain and overwrought with worry for Ant and Silence, yet still my exhaustion won out and I must have dozed, for I woke, sitting bolt upright when I heard a groan.

I looked over at the prince. Something seemed different.

His body is relaxed, not rigid anymore. I think maybe your poison is wearing off.

Auwei was right. He seemed less rigid and when he shifted, groaning again, I knew he was coming out of the effects of my toxin.

I should probably apologize.

You may want to wait for the others.

No, he's fine now, we don't need Crane. I rose, aching and weary, and made the short trip to the next table, slumping down on the bench.

"Prince?"

He rolled his head over to look at me. His face grew hard. "You're not going to kiss me again, are you?" His words were a little slurred, but understandable.

"No... and sorry about that. I didn't know that was going to happen."

He raised a single brow. I don't think he believed me. He rolled his head back to look straight up.

"I'm in Elista?"

"Yes."

"You've captured me?"

"No, well, I don't know. We brought you here to help you. I didn't know what my poison did to you and in case it was worse than just paralysis, we wanted to help you."

He nodded. "Why were you in the palace?" he asked.

Ah... what should I say?

Got me, I wouldn't have talked to him at all. Maverick should be handling this.

Oh... right, yes, that makes sense.

"I can't say right now." But... there was something he deserved to know.

Legs, wait, it may not be best to tell him about his parents.

He needs to know. And he needs to know it wasn't us.

But it was us, it was Elista. The mistweaver was from Elista!

Oh... right. But still...

It's up to you, my child.

Up to me.

I put my head down on my arms, which rested on the table, and groaned.

"Are you well?" he asked.

I looked up. "No. I was hurt, a lot... trying to save your parents." That wasn't entirely true. I'd just been trying to survive. But I'd killed the woman who killed his parents, that was worth something, wasn't it? Still, I glossed over the story a little. "A madwoman from... from Elista, she went to kill your parents, and probably you too. We... ah, we went to stop her. And we *did* stop her, but... not until it was too late. She was too strong. She... your parents..." I didn't know how to say it. I looked up to see him trembling.

"They're dead?"

"Yes."

A single tear left his eye, sliding down the side of his face into his ear. "But you fought one of your own, tried to stop her?"

Well, not exactly. "Yes."

"That's why you're all cut up?"

"Yes."

"Don't say anything else!" Maverick commanded as he strode into the room with Sparrow, Jack, Fennec, and Foggy. "Either of you. I'd prefer not to start an international incident over a casual conversation." He strode over to stand over me and the prince. His gaze lingered on me for some time. "You well?" he asked.

"Somehow, yes," I answered. Though I must have looked a mess in my shredded dress and bloody cloak, with spider-silk webbing over my face.

His mouth twitched a half-grin for the barest of moments. "Tough little one, aren't you?"

"I guess so."

He turned to the prince. "You're not dead?"

"It would seem I am not. I was just... immobilized for a while." He rolled his head to the side and looked at me with a clear we-know-whose-fault-that-was look.

Maverick drew in a long breath. "We can't return you right away. We're sorry for the trouble. Once our transporter returns, we'll—"

"I've been thinking about that." The prince's tone was weary and tentative.

"Oh?"

"It seems someone from Elista is trying to kill me." The prince lifted his head enough to look around at all of us. "But clearly none of you are. In fact, from what I've heard you've been trying to help? You may have saved me? I'm less certain about that, but I know this. If you wanted me dead, I'd be dead."

Maverick nodded, saying nothing.

"So... why *don't* you want me dead?" The prince sounded truly confused and curious.

"We have no quarrel with Vauphan." Maverick's tone was even.

"Then why have you been annexing our northern territories for the past three years?"

What?

I looked up at Maverick in shock, but it was clear he knew nothing of this. He seemed to be struggling with this news as well. Finally, he nodded to himself. "Your Highness, I knew nothing of such attacks. It would seem someone in Elista is doing this without the consent of the Council of Nobles."

The prince nodded. "We'd wondered about that. It did seem... odd." He sighed. "But with the attack on my parents, it certainly seems like Elista wishes to declare war on Vauphan." He grunted as he sat up. It seemed my poison wore off in stages and he was still weak, having trouble controlling his movements. "Or at least, *someone* in Elista wants war, if not the entire country. He looked directly at me, then Maverick. "What are your intentions, Lord Maverick?" So... the prince knew his Elistan Nobles. Interesting.

"I wish only peace between our countries, Your Highness."

The prince nodded. "Then I'm going to stay here," the prince said firmly. I'll need to coordinate a few things with whomever remains at the palace, and find some way to communicate with them, but... if there is indeed someone in your country trying to kill me, this is the last place they'd expect to find me, isn't it?"

Maverick nodded. "We'll have a room made up for you, Your Highness."

"And while I'm here, please don't call me 'your highness.' You can call me by my name: Alvere."

Maverick nodded. "Yes, Alvere." He turned to Sparrow behind him. "Have a room made up, please?"

She nodded and hurried off.

Maverick turned to Fennec and Jack, saying: "Please make sure nothing happens to the pri— to Alvere. I need to speak with Legs."

I stood.

"Legs? That's your name? You said it was Leiana," the prince said with a grin. His eyes dipped down to my — now mostly exposed — legs and he smiled. "Never mind, Legs suits you."

I'm fairly certain I blushed at that, then pulled the blood-soaked cloak about me and followed Maverick out of the room. He led me to a room stocked with supplies and grabbed several rolls of linen bandages. Then we went to my room, which I hadn't been expecting. Stopping at the door he nodded his head inside, holding out the bandages. "There should be some water in there, clean yourself up and get dressed. I'll wait."

I took the bandages and went in.

It took me a while to do as instructed. I removed the ruins of my dress and looked at myself in the long looking glass. I was a supreme mess.

Gently peeling away the web-bandages I found the larger

cuts mostly healed: Ant's work. There would be scars, but I didn't mind that. I was alive, that's what counted. Then I carefully used a rag to wash and clean the other small wounds... which were everywhere, it looked like a thousand nails had stabbed me. Some were healed, the rest weren't deep. Still, the cuts stung when cleaned, and some re-opened and bled a bit more. Then I began bandaging myself with the linen Maverick had provided. I did one leg, then the other, a bunch around my midsection and chest, then — the hardest parts — my arms. There weren't any cuts on my face that weren't already closed or healed by Ant.

I was incredibly stiff, so I found a loose dress, put it on, and went back out to Maverick.

He looked at me, shook his head, then motioned for us to go back in.

He sat heavily in a chair and I did the same, a bit more gingerly.

"Amber tells me you killed the mistweaver?" he said, right to the point.

"Yes, was anyone hurt here when she escaped?"

He tilted his head with a curious expression. "That's what you have to say? You kill a mistweaver and you're worried about *us*?" He grinned. "I knew I liked you. I made a good call selecting you. Yeah, we're good here. She didn't escape. Turns out we didn't have her at all, but a duplicate of some sort, a façade over someone else. That someone else is still in the dungeons, but they stopped looking like the mistweaver earlier today."

That was interesting.

"Back to you. How are you doing?" he asked.

Exhausted.

Achy and itchy.

Bleeding.

A soul-weary and emotional mess.

"Well enough. I'll survive these cuts and... well... mostly I'm worried for Ant and Silence."

He chuckled. "Yup, you're a keeper. Clearly in pain but worried about others." He shook his head slowly. "The mistweaver may be gone, but someone out there still wants you dead. We'll need to be careful." A sour grimace twisted his lips. "Though I think that goes without saying now that we have the prince visiting."

He rolled his eyes. "You have a way of bringing trouble to my House, little one. First a mistweaver, now the prince of an enemy nation. What next, the Emperor of Thraan and his host of dragons?" He grimaced. "Don't answer that. I don't want to know."

He leaned forward, running both hands through his thick, messy hair while blowing out a long breath. "I honestly don't know what's going on. Someone... someone high up in the Noble Houses is killing Lumani and invading Vauphan and somehow managing to keep it all quiet. There has to be some plan behind all of this, but damned if I know what it is."

He looked up at me then with a wry grin. "But I know one thing. Whatever their plans are, you're going to ruin them." He laughed. "All I have to do — and you're not making it easy — is keep you alive long enough to do so."

He rose and made his way out, stopping at the door, half turning back. "I'll let you know if Ant or Silence returns. For now, get some rest." He paused then shrugged. "Your standing orders are... stay alive at all costs. Got that?"

"Yes, Lord Maverick."

"Good."

He left, and I stumbled over to my bed, but as exhausted as I was, I couldn't sleep. This bed only reminded me of Silence.

So, bone-weary, I rose and made my way back to the great hall. Most of the members of the House were there. The Prince and Maverick were not, but Amber, Jack, Fennec, Foggy, and Sparrow were sitting around talking in hushed voices. And shortly after I arrived, Crane came in from the kitchens with warm soup and hot tea.

She gave me a cup and a smile.

Then we all waited.

It was hours later, near dawn, when Fin appeared. With him was Ant, who was a bloody mess and barely able to stand. The big man sat on a bench — a bit too heavily — and broke it, collapsing to the floor. Amber ran to him, tending to him. She peeled away his shirt, gasping and shaking her head as Sparrow came with bandages to help.

"Silence?" I asked.

Fin shook his head slowly. "Not yet. And..." He looked around. "Where's the Boss?"

"He's with the prince," Crane said, coming over to take a look at Ant. "Why?"

"Before Ant arrived, I saw two or three dozen ships setting sail across the bay. They'll be on our shores tomorrow." Fin's face was hard. "I think we're at war."

SHAPE AND SHADOWS

THE MISTS OF ELISTA TRILOGY, BOOK 2

CHAPTER 1

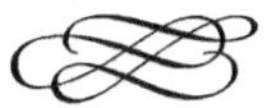

Late winter in the south of Elista could be quite mild, especially when a warm southeasterly wind swept up off Dyren's Bay. This morning, that pleasant breeze tousled my hair as I stood atop a low seaside cliff, gazing out at a small fleet of ships weighing anchor off the coast.

Fifteen ships, each teeming with hundreds of men, was not a comforting sight first thing in the morning.

"So many," I whispered.

No one around me replied. But I needed someone to say something, needed some reassurance.

"Someone tell me this is going to work," I pleaded with my companions. The sun, pulling higher into the sky, warmed me just a bit more than was comfortable, since I still wore a layer of bandages over most of my body under my clothes.

Maverick grunted, non-committal. I could tell he didn't like this sight at all. He could do little to stop such a force from walking over him and taking these lands.

"Yes, it will work," Alvere, Prince of Vauphan, said beside me. There was something in the quick look and the flash of a smile —

perhaps it was the clear depths of his blue eyes — that warmed me just a bit more than the sun did.

I returned his smile, just as the wind blew my brown hair across my face in a mess of wavy curls.

"It better," Amber said. She was still tense and uneasy — also probably exhausted — after tending to the extensive wounds on Ant, her sometimes lover. It was a miracle he was alive. He was a lot tougher than he looked, and he looked massively tough to begin with. He had the ability to heal himself and others, but he needed to be conscious, and he'd been delirious this past day, weak as a kitten.

Fin, the heavy-set yet surprisingly light-on-his-feet senior member of Maverick House was also with us. He'd be needed for his ability to transport himself — and anyone touching him — to any place he'd been before. If this all went well, he'd be going back with the Vauphani troops to set up a route to their palace so the prince could go back and forth with ease.

But first, the five of us had to convince thousands of enemy troops to go home peacefully.

The first ships were disgorging longboats, sending troops ashore.

"Shall we go down then?" the prince asked.

Maverick grunted again, nodding. He led the way down a steep path to the beach. The prince and I came next, with Amber behind us and Fin last.

"He doesn't say much, does he?" Alvere whispered to me, indicating Maverick.

"He can. I think he's just got other things on his mind right now, like surviving this morning."

The prince nodded at that and sighed. I hadn't known the man long, but his expressions and body language seemed easy to read. His current look: tight-lipped, back rigid, eyes a bit distant, seemed to say: *I didn't want any of this, but all of you forced my hand.* Then with a long inhalation, he stood a little taller, chest out, shoulder's back but relaxed, a hard smile on his lips. This look seemed to say: *time to take control.*

A part of me wanted to reach out and take his hand, tell him all would be well, but I didn't. And in truth, I should have been more worried for myself. To the army below, he was their prince, an ally. I was the enemy.

"This will work," he whispered. It seemed mostly to himself, so I didn't say anything.

The rough path down the bluff gave way to a sandy beach. My boots sunk into the shifting grains.

My emotions may have been turbulent and uncertain, but physically I felt surprisingly well. I should have been exhausted and in pain. Two days ago, I'd been shredded — and nearly killed — by The Mistweaver, Hazra. The same madwoman who'd killed Alvere's parents, the king and queen of Vauphan. Ant had healed me a little that night, before he'd gotten *himself* beaten to The Pits, but I'd been healing on my own since then. Also, I'd had trouble sleeping this past day. I'd dozed a little, sleeping for a few hours at a time through the past day and night. Yet, somehow, I wasn't particularly weary or sore.

I think it's your spirit-gift, Auwei said. Auwei was the Lumani spirit who dwelled within me. Our bond allowed me to shape-shift into a spider, my avatar form. I could also use other spider-based abilities in my human form, like walk on walls and spin silk... from my belly button of all places.

Oh? I was curious to hear more. A spirit-gift was a rare additional power that only some True-Bonded — the pairing of human and Lumani — possessed. Maverick could summon fire, Amber could instill simple commands in people's minds, Fin could teleport, Ant could heal.

I've had many hosts, Auwei said. I was her tenth True-Bonded. She'd lived nine lifetimes bonded to others before me. *And none have had your stamina and energy. I think you... I don't know how to put it exactly, but I think your sheer determination and drive has turned into a spirit-gift that allows you to keep going no matter what. I don't know what you'd call that, but Legs, you should be laid up, fatigued and healing, yet you're not. Something special is going on. I believe it is your spirit-gift.*

It would explain a lot. Remembering our escape from the palace of Vauphan, there seemed far too much I'd done that shouldn't have been possible. I'd been thoroughly thrashed by the mistweaver and near death. The only reason I'd survived at all was because Ant had healed me. But he'd only healed my major wounds. After that, I should have been a weak and quivering mess. Yet, I'd subdued the prince — that was when I'd discovered that kissing someone without passion in my heart meant I poisoned them — then managed to lower him carefully down the cliffs on my spider-silk, somehow supporting his weight. And since then, I hadn't slept much, even if I had been taking it easy. I should have been exhausted, but here I was.

You might be right.

We spread out on the beach, two of us to either side of the prince, but keeping our distance, hands out, making it clear we had no weapons.

The first men ashore looked us over, and luckily one of them recognized the prince.

"My prince?" the man said, rushing from the boat, drawing a slender rapier. He had a shock of blond hair and a rather prominent nose.

"It is well, Philipe, put your weapon away, these are not our enemies."

"But Your Highness! The palace, your parents. Have you seen what they did? They declared war upon us and—"

"That is enough, Philipe!" the prince said with stern clarity, though he did not raise his voice.

"Yes, Your Highness."

"Who commands this force?" the prince asked.

"General Hugo de Lanace, Your Highness."

"I know him. Spare these people their lives until I have spoken with him, will you do that? They have been nothing but kind to me." The prince glanced at me from the side of his eye with a faint look which said: *mostly*. The fact that that look had come my way meant he was still a little upset I'd accidentally paralyzed him.

That was fair.

I tried not to get too tense as more and more soldiers landed on the beach, forming up into a small army. The one Alvere had spoken to, Philipe, sent a messenger back to one of the ships, then left to organize some men. I guessed he was an officer.

Needless to say, Amber drew a lot of attention. She couldn't go out dressed in anything less than something spectacular. Today's choice was skin-tight, bright-red, silken pants, the sides of which were made of loose lace, which showed off her tanned skin beneath. On top she wore a white blouse, which I'd first thought was mostly unbuttoned but came to realize didn't have buttons at all on the top half, the plunging collar showing lots of skin.

She smiled and winked at the men on the beach.

I don't think I'd ever felt as confident and cool as Amber looked in that moment. I wore a simple dress with a long skirt and sleeves and no exposed mid-section. I didn't want people to see my bandages. And the point of this meeting wasn't to fight, so I wasn't worried about not having my spider-silk available.

Maverick was in tight buckskin pants and a green shirt, which brought out a little bit of green in his hazel-brown eyes.

Fin, big and imposing, but otherwise a jovial fellow, stood at ease. He wore a loose, long, white shirt and grey pants. I could see a few wary glances in his direction, but the soldiers needn't have worried. He wasn't much of a warrior.

A man in a navy-blue uniform — a shade or two darker than

the sapphire attire of the other soldiers — came ashore and went to Philipe. They spoke with haste, then the new man marched over to us, speaking to the prince.

"Your Highness, we feared the worst for you. I am glad to see you well." He eyed the rest of us. "Are these allies? Here to help us seize the lands of the traitorous Elistans?"

"There will be no seizing of lands, general."

The general was tall, with a rigid stance and significant grey at his temples and through most of his beard. This was a man who'd lived a long life and seen a lot of military action. He smiled a bit condescendingly at the prince. "Your Highness—"

"Majesty," Alvere said sharply.

The general blinked. "Sire?"

"My parents are dead, are they not? I have not been crowned, but I am king-to-be."

"Yes, of course Your High— Your Majesty. Now, as to matters of war—"

"You will do as I direct," Alvere finished. "And there will be no war in the *south* of Elista"

The general bristled a little but nodded. "As Your... Majesty commands. Shall we run home like whipped pups with no spoils then? After these Elistans murdered your mother and father in cold blood?"

"What we shall do, General, is sail north and re-enforce our troops massing for battle. That is where the fight shall be. We'll take back our lands and nothing more. And—" Alvere said, seeing another comment coming from the general. "As for the horrible atrocities done at the palace, the person responsible for that is dead." He then motioned to us. "These others believe in our cause, even though they are Elistans. They saved me from the murderess that night. They were trying to stop the woman. They will also be following up inquiries here, so that we can find out who was behind the attack and ensure they are punished."

Alvere then leaned in and put on a bit of a just-between-you-an-me tone. "These Elistans are divided and uncertain. They will be easy to defeat in the North, on our own land, but if we seized lands here in the south, they would be hard to keep. Our supply lines over water would be open to attacks, and their capital is only two days' march from here. We'd be overrun quick enough. We are not brutes and barbarians. We will take back what is ours and see that the right people are punished for the attacks on our soil, but nothing more. We are Vauphani, and we will stand proud on our morals."

The general nodded, chastised and yet somehow also emboldened. "You are right, of course, Your Majesty. I mistook your youth for inexperience, but I see now I was wrong. Forgive me."

"You're forgiven, general. Now please, get these men back on the ships. Myself and one of the Elistans will require passage back to the capital. These others—" again with a motion to us, "—are our allies and will be helping us by rooting out the traitor in their own government. We will need to keep in contact with them. I may be returning here frequently and for long periods to coordinate with them directly."

"I'll arrange for some men to accompany you, for your safety," the general said, and I didn't think he'd give on that point.

"I assure you I will be safe, but will allow a small guard, yes." He looked at Maverick who shrugged and nodded.

"Then it's settled. Let's board the ships and be on our way," Alvere finished.

"Back to the ships, men!" the general called out. Those who'd already come ashore began heading back to the boats.

"I'll return once I'm set at home," Alvere said to us. He took a step toward Maverick and whispered. "And I'll make sure your man is returned to you, if we have him."

Maverick gave a terse nod.

Instantly I felt like I'd been punched in the gut.

Silence!

I'd not thought of him since the mention of war, yet... the prince had. How could I have forgotten someone so dear to me? A friend and lover. The one I'd known the longest. The one who'd been with me back at Silverveil and helped to save my life! How could I have forgotten him, even if only for a moment?

"I'll see you all soon," Alvere said. He turned his jewel-blue eyes — like clear, dark beryl — to me. I can't say how I must have looked in that moment, but his brow furrowed, darkening. He nodded to me, then looked to Fin. The large man nodded and the two of them made their way down to the boats.

The rest of us retreated up the beach, to the path up the cliff.

As we reached the waving grasses at the top of the bluff, Amber put a comforting arm around me. "It happens to all of us."

I leaned into her for a moment. She was surprisingly strong, pulling me close to her side as we walked.

"How did you know?" I asked softly.

"It wasn't hard to guess. You looked like someone had crushed your heart when the prince mentioned 'our man.'"

I looked ahead at Maverick, walking stoically, still tall and strong. "How does he do it? It seems like he doesn't care, but I know he does."

"That, child, I have no clue. He's always been like that." She drew in a breath, squeezing me close, then releasing me to walk on my own. "Did anyone ever tell you where he got his spirit-gift from?"

"No." Ant had mentioned some theories on where our crew's spirit-gifts had come from. He'd told me Amber could control people's minds because she wished more than anything to be all anyone thought about.

But as for Maverick's fire...?

"Midnight told me once. She believes his powers come from

being hot and cold at the same time. Did you know he could summon cold too?"

I shook my head. That was news to me.

We reached the carriage which had brought us to the coast. Amber and I got in while Maverick joined the driver up front. Soon, we were headed back along the rough road to Hedgewild Manor.

Out the window I saw farmer's fields, newly tilled and waiting for spring crops.

Amber continued her explanation of Maverick's gift; voice hushed a little. "Sometimes, when he can't do anything about a situation, he gets cold. Also, if he's truly furious, a cold anger, then the temperature around him drops. That's the scariest thing I've ever experienced." She drew in a breath then let it out in a bit of a laugh. "I guess you could say he runs hot and cold? Anyway, Midnight thinks this strange ability comes from how much he cares for his family, us, his House. He's fiercely close and warm, but sometimes he cares so much that he also becomes distant. I know that sounds odd, but essentially, at times like this, he can't be thinking about what might have happened to Silence. He can't help the man, he can't be fire, so he's ice instead, unfeeling, except toward the rest of us, for whom he's warm. It's... an odd combination, but it works for him."

I think I understood the man a little better now. Amber was always a font of interesting information.

"I'm... I'm sure Silence will be well," she said a bit haltingly, not as reassuring as I think she'd hoped to be.

I nodded, but said nothing. I still felt a little hollow, and I'd continue to feel this way until I knew Silence was safe.

I wouldn't allow myself to forget him again.

CHAPTER 2

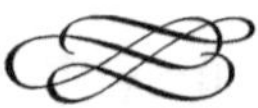

I FRETTED FOR ANOTHER DAY. ONCE AGAIN, I SLEPT PERIODICALLY, and generally not in my bed. I dozed off once in the library with a book — that I wasn't reading — in my lap. Later, I fell asleep with my head on my arms, slumped over a table in the great hall, an untouched cup of tea next to me.

The only thing of note I did that day was check my bandages. Well, Crane did. She removed the old ones and bathed me with a sponge, cleaning the wounds, but we were both a little shocked at what few injuries remained.

"I hate to doubt the word of Lord Maverick, but the wounds he described upon you... he must have been exaggerating."

I sighed. "No, he wasn't. Auwei thinks I'm developing a spirit-gift."

Crane blinked at that. "So young? Around healing?" She was a bit taken aback.

"Not healing so much as... keeping going. Doing whatever it takes to move past what's hurting me and do what I need to do. It's hard to put into words, but it's the only way to explain this." I motioned to my body. "I should be far more injured."

Crane nodded. "Auwei may be right. Now that I look closer, I can see the scars of the other wounds. By-The-Spirits there are a lot. And... nearly all healed up now. Amazing!"

I shrugged at the off-handed compliment.

We bandaged my right thigh, left calf, and left upper arm. Those were the only places with significant wounds still showing.

"You should tell Lord Maverick about your spirit-gift," Crane said as she left with the bundle of soiled bandages. "He has a way of discerning a person's gift, sometimes even before they do."

I nodded. "I will, thank you."

I went to see Maverick next, hoping that might take up some of this dreadful time waiting. He wasn't in the house. Sparrow, studiously reading in the library, told me he was probably out in the back pasture.

That shocked me a little.

I wandered out into the fields behind the estate as the day waned. The sun was dropping toward the west. It would be dinnertime soon.

I saw a large lone bull grazing in an open field. An actual bull would have been in an enclosure. Still, I didn't approach right away. I'd never seen Maverick in his avatar form before, and he was quite the sight. He was a bull of a man, but this was something else entirely. The heavy body, thickly muscled... everywhere, that heavy head with long horns. I'd thought him imposing as a man, even if he wasn't as big as Ant or Fin, he had a quiet power about him... and now I knew why. The thought of that massive bull charging me, sent chills through me.

He's impressive as man or beast, Auwei commented.

"Maverick?" I called out as I tentatively approached.

That large, heavy head swung in my direction and a moment later it was the man standing before me, latent power in his easy stance.

"Legs?" He crossed the distance between us with a few long

strides and gently enfolded me in his arms. "I know. I hate waiting too."

I tried not to cry, though I think a tear did escape one of my eyes. The earthy musk and latent heat of Maverick's body soothed me. I'd never felt such nurturing warmth from another person, even my foster parents. They'd hugged me, but never like this, never so intensely. After a moment, I sighed, feeling much better than I had when I'd come out here. I also remembered *why* I'd come.

"Auwei thinks I might have a spirit-gift," I confided. "And Crane said you're good at figuring out things like that."

A deep and rumbling chuckle emanated from that thick chest. "Yes, it is one of the few things I'm good at." He released me, stepping back, but keeping his hands on my shoulders. He looked me over, eyes narrowed. After a moment of this, he drew in a breath. "Yes, there is something there. It's new and budding still, but there's something. Tell me what effects you've been seeing, and I'll see if I can't divine your spirit-gift."

He motioned to a patch of grass, sitting himself down cross-legged. I did the same, hands resting in my lap. "Well..." I pushed one hand up the loose sleeve of my dress, revealing the unbandaged arm. "I seem to heal quickly. I... I don't know, but I suspect I can't heal others though, like Ant does."

Maverick nodded. "Go on."

"Well, I told you some of what happened when we were escaping the palace, but I didn't really tell you..." *Any idea how to describe this?* I asked Auwei.

You did things you shouldn't have been able to do. You pushed through and past exhaustion and pain and fear and showed strength far beyond what should have been possible.

You make me sound super-human when you say it that way.

You have a glowing ball of energy residing inside you and possess powers of a spider already. You were superhuman to begin with. This is even more.

Right...

I relayed what Auwei had said.

Maverick's brows rose.

"To be specific... well... you saw what state I was in when I got back, but still, somehow I managed to find the strength to lower the prince down a three-hundred-foot cliff on my spider silk. I kept thinking I couldn't do it, that I'd drop him, but... I didn't." I shrugged.

Maverick nodded.

He seemed to look within me again, and asked: "Auwei... why did you Choose Legs?"

This would be interesting. I stilled my body and let her take over, so she could respond. Her spirit bubbled up to fill me and I heard and felt her speaking through my lips. "At first... I saw just an ordinary girl, but then... there was a flash of something: a spirit and energy that called me back to her. I have sensed it on and off. She is... so determined and driven. She wanted to be a Noble, even though she didn't know quite why. But I think it's because she's driven to stop people from hurting others."

I smiled at that, as Auwei retreated within me.

Maverick drew in a long breath. "I'm guessing Ant told you where spirit-gifts come from?" he asked but didn't wait for an answer. "They come from what we love, what we need." He looked away. "Ant needs to ease the pain of others. Amber needs to be in control. Fin needs to see all the wonderous places of this world. I... I need... to kindle a fire in others, while remaining cool myself." He shrugged. "That's the best way I can describe it." He looked at me for a long moment. "What do you think you love, Legs? What do you need most in this world?"

I thought about that for a moment, considering Auwei's words.

"I can't abide bullies. I need to help those who can't help themselves?" I hadn't meant for it to be a question. "I love... helping?"

He laughed a little. "No Legs... it's a bit more than that."

He observed me intently as he went on. "Yes, you need to help, to defend, to stand up to those who would push others around, but I think what you love most isn't so much the helping part, as the feeling you get once you've helped, when you've put a bully in their place."

He nodded to himself as if he'd reached some conclusion. "You, Legs, need to be a hero." Another breath of a laugh. "And I should have seen it sooner, especially given what we heard from that mistweaver. They saw the future. We know you're going to disrupt the plans of the Nobles behind all of this. You couldn't *not* do it. It's in your blood. They're bullies, and you'll stop them at any cost." He sighed heavily. "You're going to be a handful for... anyone and everyone in your life. You're always going to be running toward danger, not away."

His words made my heart constrict a little, remembering how terrified I'd been in the King's Hall at Vauphan. I hadn't helped the king and queen. I'd been too afraid. "Then... why was I so afraid to help initially when the mistweaver attacked?" I asked, throat closing up, voice tight, as tears came to my eyes. "I... couldn't do anything but cower."

"And what made you stop cowering? What made you fight?" he asked softly.

My chest seized up even more at the thought. "Silence," I could barely say his name. I may have saved him from the mistweaver, but I was the one who'd told him to run off with the news of the war with Vauphan. If I hadn't, then he would have stayed with Amber and...

"You saved him." Maverick's tone was calming. I looked up through bleary eyes, blinking my tears away. They fled down my cheeks as I tried to get myself under control. "So, just to make sure

I'm hearing this right: you didn't want to take on one of the most powerful beings in the world at first? But then... you decided you would, to help a friend. For one friend, you'd take on a mistweaver. Legs, there is no shame in running or hiding from a superior foe. That's what most of us sane people would do."

He reached out to lay a hand on my knee. "But you couldn't flee with Silence, could you? You wanted to protect him and fight against that superior foe." Maverick nodded to himself. "If I had to make a guess, I'd say that's when your spirit-gift blossomed."

He lowered his voice a little, a conspiratorial tone. "Something tells me you won't be hiding or running away much anymore. I don't think you'll be able to." A heavy sigh. "And your gift is going to allow you to do that. It will heal you and give you strength to fight those fights." He shook his head slowly. "And it's only going to get stronger. Assuming you live long enough, you could become one of the most powerful True-Bonded ever."

I didn't feel strong right now.

Maverick rose and offered his hand to help me up. I took it and once again found myself in his arms, surrounded by his tender warmth. "Your life is probably going to be riddled with pain and loss, Legs, but it will also make you a force to be reckoned with." I felt his heavy sigh. "Come on, let's go in and wait for the prince to return."

He released me and we walked back to the house together.

"So..." he said conversationally. "What do you think of the prince?"

"He seems like a kind and proper man."

"He certainly is handsome, with those stunning blue eyes."

"Well, yes, I suppose so." I felt myself flush a little, remembering some of the private looks the prince had sent my way. "I certainly think—" I stopped myself, looking up at Maverick. "*You* think he's handsome?"

No Legs, he was goading you on a little. He's apparently seen the way you look at the prince.

Oh? And how do I look at the prince?

The same way he looks at you... with... interest.

I am not interested in him, I love Silence. But even as I thought those words, I questioned them. I didn't question my love for Silence, more... I questioned whether I wished to love *only* Silence. I'd felt for some time that I wanted more, but that I wouldn't risk what I had with Silence to get it. I wanted him to want more too. I'd asked him about that, the last night we were together and he'd not been able to answer me.

The prince was handsome and did seem interested. A part of me was curious too, according to Auwei. But I wouldn't betray Silence. I'd wait for his answer to me... and hope he wanted what I wanted.

Maverick laughed lightly, a friendly thing. "Someday you're going to figure yourself out, and when you do... oh, watch out world."

Figure myself out?

You are more than a little tied in knots at the moment, Auwei said.

True. Right now, I didn't really know what I wanted. My mind couldn't help but compare Prince Alvere with Silence, finding all manner of similarities and differences. They were both short, slight men, not large. The prince had a bit more of a plumpness to his face and features. Alvere had raven black hair and those piercing beryl-blue eyes, compared to Silence's mouse brown hair and soft brown eyes. The real difference was in their demeanor. The prince was strong and commanding. Silence was growing into his power but still mild mannered much of the time. They were both handsome, both good friends.

Well Silence was a good friend. I barely knew the prince.

But you want to know him... intimately, don't you? Auwei offered.

I flushed again at that, as Maverick and I entered the great hall through the outside door. I couldn't quite get the memory of my encounters with Silence out of my mind... and in my musings I kept switching out his face with the prince's.

"Oh... my!" Amber said.

That snapped me out of my reverie.

"You are a rather exquisite shade of crimson, my dear," she said to me. "Who are you thinking of?" And that, of course, only made me blush more.

We called for an early dinner, and I ate with my head down, hoping no one would notice my heated features. And while I ate, I thought of Maverick's words.

... you need to help, to defend, to stand up to those who would push others around...

... You... need to be a hero...

... We know you're going to disrupt the plans of the Nobles behind all of this. You couldn't not do it. It's in your blood. They're bullies, and you'll stop them at any cost...

... you're going to be a handful...

... always... running toward danger, not away...

Was that really true?

I couldn't deny that I'd stood up to a mistweaver, an impossible fight... and won.

Trust in yourself, Legs. Maverick is right. I can feel it. Auwei seemed certain. I wish I could have been.

Then Fin appeared in the great hall with the prince next to him and...

...Silence, laying bloody and limp in Fin's arms.

"He's alive," Fin said reassuringly, though his tone wasn't entirely confident. "Is Ant any better? Silence could use some healing."

Some healing? The man looked dead, covered in cuts and blood and bruises.

The sight was too much. I turned away and threw up everything I'd just eaten.

CHAPTER 3

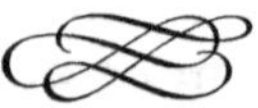

JACK WAS OFF LIKE A SHOT TO FETCH ANT, EVEN AS AMBER YELLED, "He's not ready yet!"

"I'll get bandages," Crane said as she too ran out of the hall.

I looked up, wiping my mouth, as Fin laid Silence on a table.

I stood, but couldn't draw closer. Even from here I could see the horrors done to the man I loved. He'd been tortured. His small, delicate hands were ruined, crushed and swollen. His face was covered in blood, shallow slashes on his lips, ears, nose, and cheeks. Most of his fine clothes had been torn away and what parts of his body I could see were covered in bruises and other injuries. My jaw trembled, clamped shut. I couldn't speak, only rage and weep.

"I'm... so sorry," Alvere breathed.

I couldn't look at him. His people had done this.

"How did they catch him?" Maverick asked, voice hard, stoic. I could hear his repressed rage.

"My people have some secrets—"

"Tell me!" The room suddenly grew deathly cold, frost rimed the insides of the windows.

Spirits Within! Was this Maverick's cold rage? It was terrifying!

Alvere started, and I could see true fear in his eyes. He swallowed hard. "I guess, since we're allies, I can let you know." He drew a heavy, shuddering breath. "My people have had some contact with the Fey, up north of our lands. They have equipped us with some intriguing items. One such is a trap meant for Elistans who can change shape. It attracts all manner of animals to a place and when they get there, forces them into their true shape. Most animals wouldn't be affected but one of your kind..."

Maverick nodded. "Clever." His jaw twitched. I was willing to bet he was as furious as I was, perhaps more.

And yet...

We had been at the palace to spy on the Vauphani. And their king and queen were dead along with a great number of nobles. They too must have been livid and desperate for information. And... finding Silence...

Would I have done this?

Could I do something like this?

If someone came into my house and killed the ones I loved... what would I do?

No, the real question was: What *wouldn't* I do?

Bloody bones, I hated every part of this. Mostly I raged at the corrupt Nobles of my own nation, who'd sent us on this death-mission. But they weren't here.

And Alvere didn't deserve my fury. I knew he hadn't done this to Silence. He'd probably stopped it the moment he'd found out. Still, I couldn't look at him, couldn't bear to see the pain in those clear blue eyes. He wasn't allowed to feel pain too, not now.

"You called?" croaked a weary voice from the doorway. Ant limped into the room, leaning heavily on Jack, who strained under the larger man's bulk.

"You shouldn't be up!" Amber chided. "Even for this." The concern in her voice real, but also torn. She wasn't truly fighting him. She wouldn't stop him from helping Silence, since she could see the massive damage done to the young man. Still, I sensed her concern for Ant. He might cause himself harm. I'd learned that if he went too far to heal another, he could die.

I felt compelled to add, "Please, help him, but... be careful."

Ant smiled at me. "Always."

That was a lie. He hadn't been careful when he'd faced those guards back at the palace, which had landed him in his current state. He'd been fearless, protecting myself and Amber, but not careful.

Jack helped him sit at the table where Silence lay. Ant reached out a trembling hand to the young man. He laid his other thick arm on the table and put his head upon it, clearly weary even before he began.

Amber stood beside him and laid a hand on his back as he worked. I didn't see much of a change in Silence. His hands seemed to mend a little and his face cleared of some of the cuts upon it.

Then two things happened at once. Ant groaned and his hand fell away from Silence, as Silence gasped, then screamed. It was a sound of pure agony, so heart-rending I fell to my knees in sympathetic suffering, covering my ears and weeping. I heard Amber's soft "sleep" command and the screaming stopped. When I looked up again Silence was still.

Crane returned with a heavy bundle of bandages and a pot of something, which she spread on some of the wounds as she went to work mending the young man.

Amber helped Ant to the floor, for he was close to dead-weight with exhaustion. There he lay and slept.

"Let's give these people some peace," Maverick commanded and the rest of us began to filter out of the great hall. "Silence will live," Maverick said, certainty in his voice. "Let's all give him the time he needs to recover."

I didn't realize I was trembling until Sparrow took my hand. "Let's get you to your room," she said softly and led me, like a witless child, to my bed. There she laid me under the covers, still fully dressed save for my boots, and tucked me in gently. But perhaps seeing my addled state she then curled up with me, one arm around me, hugging me close. Only then, did I begin to come down from the horrors I'd seen.

I woke with a scream. My dreams had been filled with blood and ruined bodies.

The purring form of Princess-as-a-cat lay next to me, not Sparrow. A moment later the pleasantly plump woman sat on the edge of my bed. "I'll tell Sparrow you're awake. We'll make you some tea, yes?"

I nodded, wordlessly, thankful.

Princess smiled and was off, back in cat form, running from the room.

I sat up in bed, bleary-eyed and feeling like I'd spent the previous night drinking heavily. Pulling my knees up, I hugged them and set my weary forehead upon them.

That's how Sparrow found me.

I turned my head, still laying upon my knees, to look at her as she put two steaming cups of tea on the bedstand and sat on the bed, one arm moving to stroke my back.

She spoke in a soft, reassuring voice. "Remember when you were hurt? Ant stayed by you, sleeping on the floor, resting until he could heal you again. He's doing that for Silence now. They're resting together, and Ant heals Silence when he can. With Ant being so injured and exhausted already, it's slow going, but Silence will recover fully in time. Fear not."

I lifted my head and nodded. "Thank you," I croaked, my voice raw, throat dry.

Sparrow winced, then rose and retrieved the jug of water from my sitting area, along with a cup. She returned and poured some out for me.

I drank as she placed the jug aside.

"Thank you again." I put the cup down on the bedstand next to my tea. Then I reached for Sparrow and embraced her. We held each other tightly for some time.

I was a little surprised when our lips met. Sparrow's were soft and warm as they pressed firmly to mine. But then she drew back quickly, a look of shock in her eyes. She looked down, head tilted away. "Sorry, I..."

I didn't know what to make of all this. What I did know... was how my heart had quickened, how my body had flushed with heat. Curious.

I put a finger under Sparrow's chin and lifted her face.

"It's well," I whispered. Her gaze met mine, and I could see shame mixed with desire in those shimmering dark-green depths. I brushed some of her wayward chestnut-brown hair aside and cupped her cheek, bringing her face back to mine.

I didn't know what I wanted in that moment except another kiss. She was first surprised, then quickly hungry, her lips hard on mine, opening as mine did, our tongues mingling. I felt the full body shudder which shivered through her as she tried to press closer. I didn't dissuade her. A part of me wanted this, needed this. I was exhausted with worry and horror for Silence and still couldn't dare to think of the prince. But I desperately needed someone, someone to hold tight and press close. I was confused and curious and thrilled all at once. Sparrow was a dear friend. Though it was quickly becoming clear that Sparrow wished for more. Silence had been a dear friend before we had...

Sparrow pulled away suddenly and rose, agitated. A heady blush colored her tanned cheeks.

"I'm sorry, Legs. Now isn't the time... I..." She turned away.

"Sparrow, no, please," I reached out to her as she turned back. "Stay with me."

She blinked.

"Are you sure?" she asked. Her hand clasped mine, so small, but so very warm.

In response I gently pulled her back to sit next to me. "Yes, I need someone to hold right now." I wrapped my arms around her again. Slowly her arms enfolded me as well.

"I'm sorry for the kiss," she breathed, trembling in my arms. "I shouldn't have—"

"Hush," I whispered. "I... liked it."

"You did?" She seemed shocked.

"I did." It was the truth. Kissing her was different, but no less enjoyable than Silence. There was something about the soft, pliable plumpness of her lips...

"I... I think..." I heard her swallow hard. "I think I love you, Legs." Her voice was so soft and tentative, yet her tone held a note of certainty. That hadn't been an idle admission. She didn't mean she loved me as a friend. *That* was a given. She was telling me she wanted more.

I didn't know what to say.

After a moment Sparrow pulled back. "Was that... too much?" Her eyes welled with tears, even as a fragile and uncertain hope blossomed in those deep green pools. "I... know it's not the time, but... I... I had to say something."

The longing in her gaze told me everything I needed to know, exactly how far beyond friendship her love extended. She wanted more than just to hold me.

And what did I want?

I couldn't say for certain how I felt for her, but I desperately needed the intimacy she was offering. My heart ached for a deep connection, a soothing of pain in mutual comfort.

I didn't know what to say, so instead of words, I leaned forward to give her a soft, chaste kiss. She tensed, surprised.

When I pulled back, I smiled. The words came easily now. "I love you too, Sparrow," I said tenderly. "You are my dearest friend —" I saw her fragile hope dwindle, "—and I *do* want this. I want *you.*"

Her breath caught, those already large eyes going wide as her lips trembled.

"Oh Legs, I... how much... do you want?" She was holding back, seeking permission. It was clear she wanted to give me everything, all of herself.

"I want you, Sparrow," I repeated. "All of you." And I kissed her again, with passion, holding nothing back, to show her how much I meant it.

We drank deeply of each other, our hands exploring hidden places until Sparrow was practically vibrating with desire.

She pulled away and slipped off the bed, quickly lifting off her dress. She wore a silken shift beneath and that too was quickly removed. It was perfectly normal to see her like this. It wasn't uncommon for us to bathe together. Yet this time, her body wasn't flushed red from the heat of warm water, but from desire... for me. Her small breasts heaved with heavy breaths, nipples tight with arousal.

She climbed back onto the bed as I threw back the sheets. Her hands trembled with anticipation as she helped me out of my dress. We knelt on the bed, poised but hesitant. Sparrow's gaze devoured me, her breath coming quicker.

Did she want me to make the first move?

No.

She reached out, tentative, her warm hand coming to my hip. From there, she caressed up along my ribs to the side of my chest. I lifted my arms out of her way, combing my hands into my hair. She bit her lip as her hand came to cup my right breast, heavier and fuller than hers. A trembling finger moved to the areola, tracing carefully around the nipple, watching as it rose and tightened before her eyes.

Her gaze rose to mine. "I never thought... I never dared to hope..."

I nodded. Same-sex pairings were common enough in Elista, but I understood how difficult it might be to ask another if they were interested.

She leaned in and kissed me again as her hand continued wonderfully working over my breast. Her other hand rose to do the same on the other side.

Curious myself, I lifted a single hand up between her arms to her chest. I felt the low swells of her breasts, the raised pucker of her areola, and the tight bud of her nipple. Her left breast was slightly larger than the right, but I caressed them both, wishing to return the sensations she was arousing within me.

One of her hands left my breast, moving slowly over my stomach, then between my thighs. She was insistent and firm, her fingers pressing and probing my folds with expert precision. And just like that, this experiment got far more interesting. Unlike a man, Sparrow knew exactly what pleased a woman and ensured I found such pleasure.

Her lips pressed firmer, her kisses growing deep and desperate as her fingers worked in my slick folds, furious and sure. Harder... seeking... Spirits Yes!

I tensed and shook with a sudden release, gasping into her mouth.

She eased off, caressing softly as we collapsed onto my bed, pressed close. It was my turn to slide a hand down between her thighs. Her folds were already wet as I traced the sensitive area. I too knew how to press and rub for maximum effect. I hadn't pleasured myself often, but I'd done enough to know what felt good.

She gasped, then bit her lip. "Oh Legs... I... you..."

I stopped her awkward words with a kiss as I quickened and intensified my massage upon her clit. I felt her legs open, one slim thigh slipping between mine as I leaned closer over her. I moved my lips to the gentle rise of one breast and sucked her hard nipple into my mouth, remembering how exquisite it felt when Silence had done it for me.

Her back arched, rising from the soft mattress as she moaned; needful and profound. She clamped her hand over mine, pressing me hard to her folds as she shuddered with her release.

Her brilliant green eyes flared wide with arousal, pupils dilated, as she gasped through her orgasm. Pulling my face up to hers, she devoured my lips as she took a long moment to finish her blissful convulsions.

I thought us done, but Sparrow took control and rolled me onto my back. I yelped with surprise at the playful turn as she kissed her way down my body, moving between my legs.

She was not as confident or proficient with her lips and tongue as she'd been with her hands, but that didn't make the sensations any less thrilling. Especially once she began using her fingers as well. Two slender fingers slid inside me as her lips sucked on my clit, tongue teasing. The combined pressure from within and without was too much, and I let out an involuntary series of moans as I clenched around her fingers.

She didn't stop, didn't let up, and I found my pleasure only mounting. My hands combed through her hair, gripping and pressing her closer as my hips rocked and rose. Tears of bliss escaped my clamped-shut eyes, tracing over my cheeks. I gasped and shuddered out heaving breaths, whispering "yes" over and over. Until finally she stopped with her lips on my folds and moved up again, her mouth finding my ever-so-sensitive-breasts. And feeling the gentle rake of her teeth on my nipples, as her fingers raged between my legs, I cried out with a final release so powerful it felt like my whole body rose from the bed.

Breathless and trembling with bliss, I could do nothing but ride out this pleasure as Sparrow settled beside me. Her lips teased up my neck to nibble on an ear as she breathed, "Thank you, Legs. I'd always wondered... Now I know."

And now I knew.

Have you ever been with a woman? I asked Auwei. As a woman?

This was a first for me too, she said, trembling with her own passion. *Thank Sparrow for me. This I shall not soon forget.*

"Auwei... wants me to... thank you," I gasped through heavy breaths.

"And you?" Sparrow asked tentatively.

"I thank you too," I said, turning to her, kissing those soft lips once again. I felt compelled to do more, however. She'd brought me to the heights of bliss, and I sensed that had been truly joyous for her, but she deserved more. I wasn't sure I'd be as certain in my work but I began to kiss my way down her body.

Sparrow stopped me. A hand on my chin moved my head up to look at her. "Legs, no. you don't have to. I am sated."

"And if I want to?"

I saw her lips press tight. A tear fell from one eye as her breathing grew heavy. She swallowed hard. "Do you? Truly?"

Did I?

In truth I wasn't certain whether I wished to kiss her as intimately as she'd done with me. But I wanted to do more. "I will do what I feel," I said, not really knowing what that meant.

Yet she nodded and let me go. I saw her eyes squeeze shut as she pushed her head back into the pillows, her hands moving to her breasts, stroking the taught nipples and raised areolae.

I kissed over her stomach, seeing it flex and tense, then down to her hips. There I stopped for the awkward moment of moving between her legs. She opened her thighs, pressing them to the sides as I slid my hands under her taut buttocks to lift her.

I was curious...

I pressed my lips to her folds as if they were her lips, in a long and lingering kiss, my tongue exploring her, before lifting away. Her body tensed and trembled before me and I returned to run my tongue over the taut nub of her clit. She gasped and shuddered.

I moved my lips to the inside of her thigh as I slid a finger within her. Her hips rocked forward and she gasped. The wet warmth of her canal gripped my finger as I stroked her ever-so-sensitive walls.

I kissed my way up her body as I slid a second finger into her folds, my thumb teasing her clit. Her thighs pressed tight around my hand, hips moving against me, her body trembling. When my lips touched hers, both her hands came up to my head, curling in my hair, drawing me breathlessly close. She was desperate and hungry, devouring me.

I found a rhythm, rocking my hand into her, finding the spots which most pleased her and stroking them with fervor. I felt her pleasure mount, body writhing, hips grinding against my hand. She went so tense and tight, like a stretched cord...

Then snapped.

Her body shuddered as a great moan welled up from within her. She tilted her head back, pressed into the bed as open-mouthed, wide-eyed bliss surged through her. I felt her pulsing around my fingers as she gasped and cried out. Her back arched, breasts thrust up at me. I kissed those soft swells as she rode the wave of this orgasm to its end.

After that, we lay in each other's arms for a long time.

Eventually, staring up at the canopy of my bed, Sparrow shook her head slowly. "I can't believe..." She let out a shuddering, "Ohh-hhh." Then she rolled her head to look at me, our noses brushing. "You're amazing," she whispered, then bit her lip, those deep green eyes searching mine. "I meant to comfort *you*—"

"And you did, thank you, Sparrow."

"Legs, please, let me finish. I..." She stammered for a moment lost for words. Then she swallowed, pursed her lips, and continued.

"What you've done for me... I... I don't know if this was just one moment of comfort for you. If so, then I will be forever grateful." She smiled, a shy thing. "Amber had offered, but... I'd never been certain this was what I wanted, to be with... another woman. I always felt it was, but I was never sure. And Amber always seemed... too much, if that makes sense?"

It did.

"But with you, I felt... safe. Now I know: this is what I want. And for that I thank you, from the deepest places in my heart." She kissed me lightly, then licked her lips. "You've given me a precious gift, and if this one time is all you wanted, I'll... I'll understand. I'm glad I could bring you some comfort when you needed it."

I placed a hand on her cheek as I smiled. "And I thank you, Sparrow. I... I will admit, I was uncertain of this, but... now..."

How *did* I feel?

Wonderful. I felt wonderful. This new and amazing experience had been so soft and caring, yet incredibly intense. I wanted more.

Did that change my desire for men? No... it didn't. Apparently, I wanted both men and women. I felt my heart open. This was the *more* I'd been looking for... at least in part. "I want more with you. I love you dearly, Sparrow."

She blushed, a deep and beautiful rose hue upon her soft brown cheeks.

And oddly, this hadn't felt like a betrayal of my love for Silence. I'm not sure I could say why, but I just knew in my soul that he'd understand this *experiment* to explore deeper intimacy with a dear friend. It was exactly what he and I had done. Yet, to go further without him knowing, that felt wrong. I knew now... I wanted more than just one intimate relationship, but everyone involved would need to accept this... amalgamated arrangement.

Exactly, Auwei said. *Though I have never been a part of one, group relationships are accepted in Elista. And from what I hear, as long as everyone knows what's going on and agrees to it, such groups can be quite fulfilling.*

That reminded me of something Ant had said about Jack. He'd warned Silence, saying Jack *goes for all sorts*. Which brought to mind the image of Jack and Silence and Ant all naked and kissing and...

"What are you thinking about?" Sparrow said, voice a little odd. "You're turning beet red."

I felt the heat upon my cheeks and probably wore some bemused look on my face. I shook that off. "Nothing, just... thinking that you've opened my horizons. I think I'd like to be with men *and* women."

"Together?" she asked, eyes wide.

Well... now that you mention it...

Naughty girl.

Yup, that's me.

"Maybe...?"

"Oh." Those beautiful green eyes grew larger still. "I suppose... I could *try* that?" Sparrow said tentatively.

"I won't force you to do anything. But I'll keep that in mind," I said with a mischievous grin.

After that, we lay dozing together for the rest of the morning before our stomachs started to rumble.

We dressed and headed down for — what would now be — lunch.

Once again, Amber was outside my room as the two of us came out. She smiled knowingly at us, then winked and nodded.

Putting an arm around both of us, as we moved down the hall, she whispered, "Now that you've figured yourselves out, you should come see *me* sometime."

I was curious... so I asked, "what about you and Ant?"

She nodded. "I care for him deeply," she said, but then her voice grew husky. "I care for all of you... deeply."

"Oh."

"Exactly."

I was learning more and more about my housemates.

CHAPTER 4

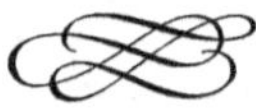

THE NEXT FEW DAYS PASSED WITH A HUSH OVER THE MANOR AS WE all waited and prayed for Silence and Ant to recover.

The prince came and went with Fin, but while he was with us, he was quiet and reserved. I could guess why. He may not have been a part of what had been done to Silence, but since it had been people under his command, he felt responsible. So he remained distant: solemn and quiet. We all avoided him. That was until the third day, when Amber grabbed his arm as he rose after breakfast in the great hall.

"Come with me, princey," she said pulling him to his feet.

He blinked, surprised. "I... ah... I'm not... please, what...?"

She turned her disarming smile on him as we all watched. "You're coming with me and we're going to work out some of your pent-up frustration."

His eyes grew wide, as did most of the rest of ours.

She grimaced. "No, not like that. I'm going to teach you some combat techniques."

"Combat...?" He was clearly confused. "I have been trained..."

"Not like this," she said low and secretive. "You've got a small frame, you're lithe and quick. I think you'll do well with my style."

Ah, so that's what she had in mind. Curious, I rose and followed as she dragged him out of the hall.

"Don't hurt him too much!" Maverick called after them. "He's royalty!"

Sparrow and Foggy trailed along with me as we went to the training room. But it was only once we got there that he turned and saw us. "We're to have an audience?"

Amber, ever on her toes, blinked. "Audience? No, they're here to help you train." She looked at me and tilted her head indicating I should step out. "Go ahead, see if you can get Legs on her back."

I blushed furiously.

"Ah... s-sorry, w-what?" Alvere stammered, also blushing. At least I wasn't the only one. "I'm not dressed for training," he said by way of excuse.

Neither was I, wearing a long, simple dress.

Amber wouldn't let him off that easily, though. "Neither is she. We'll sort out proper dress next time. If you're really worried about it, you could both just take off your clothes."

We both stared at her flatly.

Amber shrugged. "Or not. The point here is to see how good you are at hand-fighting. It doesn't require armor or special equipment, and frankly if this comes up in real life, you're likely to be wearing what you're wearing now. So just humor me. See if you can get Legs on her back on the mats."

The prince looked at me with an apologetic look and shrugged. "I'm sorry," he said as he stepped toward me. Only... it wasn't going to be him who was sorry.

He tried to be gentle, moving close then simply pushing me. It was almost comical how quickly and easily I bested him. His hands came for my shoulders, I reached across, grabbed the one while turning away from the other. Then I pushed his hand back, locking his wrist. I followed that up with my other arm locking the elbow of that same arm and forcing it up... which forced him down, and a moment later I was kneeling next to him, where he lay on his back. I released his arm and wrist, and he pulled them back quickly, massaging them.

"What was that?" he asked, confused and shocked.

"That," Amber said coming to stand over us both. "Was a very basic move. Would you like to learn it?"

The prince nodded. Then he looked at me as we both got up. "I should have known not to underestimate you." He shook his head, still staring at me, and I believe I blushed a little at his scrutiny. "A few days ago, you were cut up beyond reason, and now you're healed and hale as an ox, and it wasn't your healer who did it, was it?"

I shrugged, trying to be mysterious. "I'm just amazing," I said.

"You are." His voice was low and breathy, only for me. I *know* I blushed then.

For the rest of the morning Alvere practiced. It quickly became apparent that though he didn't know this style, he was well trained. He equated certain moves with others he knew from sword-practice or work with staves and pole-arms. That, and he was a quick learner. By the end of the first lesson, he'd learned the lock I'd used on him, plus a few other moves, and before we left for lunch, it was me who was on my back, with him holding my arm at a strange angle.

Sorry, he mouthed the word as he released me. His sweat-damp hair and flushed cheeks — from the morning's exertions — added to those stunning beryl-blue eyes, were making me sweat for a very different reason. Good thing I was already sweaty and messy and a little bit more wouldn't be noticed.

As he helped me up, I caught sight of Sparrow across the room. Her look toward the prince, along with a slight shrug and tilt of her head gave me all the information I needed: she might be ok with him joining us. I rolled my eyes in return, hopefully telling her we weren't going to be doing anything anytime soon. She smiled and nodded. The prince only caught the end of that.

"You have many close friends here, don't you?" He looked from Sparrow to me. "We don't really know a lot of how your Noble Houses work, given that you select Nobles instead of them being born to their title. Are you all close?"

Some of us were *very* close.

"Yes," I said with a smile. Then, to get the conversation away from that, I said, "I never understood your way. What if a noble isn't meant for rulership? He still gets his title and land when his father dies. And why does it always go through the male, not the female. Our way seems much more logical, based on skill and—"

He laughed. "I suppose so. But your way might have its flaws as well. Only people who *want* to rule are tested. Not all those who want to rule are good rulers. What if there were others who would be good rulers who don't decide to be tested, or aren't even Chosen by Lumani to begin with? What then? And Nobles choosing other Nobles also leads to the possibility of nepotism and favorites, or bribes. I'm not saying being born to it is better, but I don't think either option is perfect."

He had a point. And we'd gotten the conversation away from my personal life. I chatted with him about politics as we made our way back to the great hall for lunch. And we talked all through lunch. We probably would have kept going, if Maverick hadn't interrupted us.

"You two probably don't want to see this, but I think you should both come with me," he said heavily. From his expression, whatever *this* was, wasn't going to be fun. We looked at each other, then back to him.

"What is it?" I asked.

"We're going to question the fake mistweaver."

Oh...

"Fake mistweaver?" Alvere said with a note of horror.

Maverick nodded, then drew a long breath. "The one who... did what she did at your palace, also wanted our dear Legs dead as well. We thought we'd captured her, after she'd attacked us here at Hedgewild, but it was a decoy to make us think we were safe." His expression grew grim. "It's only a theory, but I think she wanted us to let Legs go on that mission, so that she could kill her along with... the others... and make it look like they'd all done it to each other. A convenient scapegoat."

The prince nodded, but there was a shadow over his features. "I thought your mission was to *stop* the mistweaver? But if you thought you had her here, why did you come to my palace?"

Maverick looked at me. "You told him we were sent to stop her?" Maverick nodded to himself. "Ah..." Then he turned and walked away. "This way," he called back to us without otherwise explaining anything. He was going to leave the truth to me.

Great.

I hoped the prince wouldn't ask, but as we rose to follow Maverick, Alvere looked at me. "What are you not telling me?"

I sighed. No use in denying it now. "Once we *knew* the mistweaver was there, it *became* our mission to stop her," I said.

That's still not the truth, Auwei said, and I got the impression of her shaking her head, even though she'd never had a head.

I know! But... it's close enough.

If you insist.

I do.

Still, I owed the prince more of an explanation, so I went on. "Our original mission was to find out if you were planning war against us."

His brow furrowed further. "So... wait... you were sent to find out if we were planning war? But you'd already invaded our lands."

"Not me, not us here. We didn't know anything about the war."

"But other Elistans..." He shook his head. "You really didn't know... and even the person who ordered you to go didn't know."

"Or they did know," I said with a grimace as Maverick led us down a set of stairs into the basement of the west wing. "And they were setting us up to fail and be scapegoats."

"That's horrible. Your own people...?"

"Yeah, exactly. That's why we trust you more than our own right now."

He nodded. "I see."

I was glad he'd taken the truth well. He could have been very upset with us, with me, but he actually seemed sympathetic. That was a load off my mind.

We reached the bottom of the stairs. The basement was quite dark. Early on in my time at Hedgewild, I had done a perfunctory exploration of the basements, but hadn't stayed long. There was no natural light and the narrow corridors, with cold stone walls, weren't the friendliest of places.

Maverick snapped his fingers and several torches lit themselves along the dark stretch.

The prince and I paused, looking down the eerily quiet hallway as torch light cast dancing shadows upon the gloomy walls.

Maverick led on and we followed, hushed to silence now. When we got to a heavy iron door, Maverick got out keys, but then tested the door, it was unlocked. I was curious about this until we entered and saw Amber and Jack within. They had a single lantern shedding light on the long room with barred cells along the far wall. With another snap of his fingers the lanterns were lit and the room grew brighter. I could clearly see the dungeons of Hedgewild now.

They weren't dank and gross, like I'd assumed. The cells looked to be roughly ten feet by ten feet with stone walls on three sides and a wall of iron bars along the front. All the cells contained a cot for a bed and a built-in basin, which I guessed could be filled with water for washing, as well as a not-so-private privy in the far corner. Two of the cells looked used, though only one was occupied. By "used" there were rushes on the floor and the bed was made up and water in the basin.

"We just moved her over," Jack said to Maverick. I didn't quite understand this, but I did then notice that there was a small metal door in the stone wall between every other cell, specifically there was one between the occupied cell and the other "used" cell.

Amber — intuitive as usual — slipped back to whisper to the prince and me. "We move any prisoners from one cell to another every other day to safely clean the now empty cell."

That made sense.

Maverick approached the bars, and I stepped forward to focus on what was to come. The woman inside looked... normal, a bit small of stature and plain of features with light brown hair and brown eyes. She sat neatly on the side of her bed in a long plain dress.

"You've finally come to question me?" she asked Maverick. "It will do you no good. I know nothing."

"We'll see about that," Maverick said, cold and hard. "You were gifted great powers. That is indisputable. Who gave you those powers?"

"The mistweaver," the woman said evenly. "I don't even know her name. She offered me enough gold to live happily for the rest of my life if I did as she asked."

"And what did she ask?"

"She said she would gift me with great power for a limited time. And during that time, my mission was simple: find and kill her." The woman pointed at me.

The cold way she said it sent a chill down my spine.

"Why?" Maverick's tone was as hard as the stone walls around us.

"I didn't ask. I did it for the gold, remember."

Maverick gave an odd sounding grunt-growl but nodded. "How did she indicate the person to be killed?"

I was curious about that as well. Had someone painted a portrait of me? I didn't recall sitting for one.

"She made an image in the mists. Looked exactly like that girl there. That's how I knew."

That made me shiver. It seemed the mistweaver could do almost anything. No one knew the extent of a mistweaver's powers, and that mystery sent a chill down my spine. At the same time, I felt just a little more bad-ass that I'd killed her.

"Who were you before?" Maverick asked.

The woman's demeanor shifted, becoming hard, shoulders set, jaw tight. It took her a moment to answer. "When I was six my parents sold me to a whorehouse. I cleaned and kept house for them until I was old enough to join those illustrious ranks. But I was not gifted with beauty, as you might see, and did not bring in much coin for my mistress. And, since she'd acquired a new cleaning girl by then, I was kicked out onto the streets to beg. I did what I had to, in order to survive, until that madwoman came along. Her offer was easy to accept. Kill one person for a wealth of coin?" The woman shrugged. "I'd not tried killing yet, but I'd been close. And to get away from that life, it seemed a fitting task."

"That's horrible," Alvere whispered to me.

I had to agree. Though I still didn't have a lot of pity for this woman who'd tried to kill me.

"Did you hear the mistweaver say anything about why she wanted this woman dead or who else might be involved?"

The woman smiled wide, with mock-innocence. "I didn't ask, and she didn't offer. I was a bit confused why a mistweaver would need the help of a wretch like me, but I see that clearly now. I was never meant to succeed. Only wear her face and be a decoy. Am I right?"

Maverick grunted a non-comital sound.

The woman nodded. "As I thought. What will you do with me?"

Maverick's tone was hard. "You will remain here and be well cared for until such time as you are needed to testify to what you have done before the Council of Nobles."

The woman shrugged at that. "At least it's mostly warm and mostly dry. More than I can say for my life beforehand." She lay back on the bed, though she left one leg over the side and as she put the other one on the bed, her dress rode up high on her legs. "And I'll be here if any of you men need my services."

Maverick turned away sharply and returned to us. "There is nothing here. I'm sorry."

"That's the reaction I usually got," the woman said with a sigh.

"No one is to touch her, is that understood?" Maverick said sternly.

Not that it needed saying, even Jack was shaking his head. "That goes without saying, Boss."

We left the dungeons, locking the door behind us, and Maverick bristled, seemingly shaking off the disgust of that experience. Then he sighed heavily. "I'd been putting that off and now I know why. I didn't suspect she knew much, and I knew I wouldn't like the experience."

"It had to be done," Amber said softly.

"What if she was lying?" the prince asked. "What if she made that all up?"

"She didn't," Amber said. "Before you arrived I... made her speak the truth."

"You can do that?"

Amber looked into his eyes for a long moment and stepped in close, whispering to him: "Tell me you love me."

"I love you," he said without hesitation.

"Forget that," she said. And he blinked and shook his head.

"What...?"

I took his hand. "I'll explain later," I said with a sour look at Amber. She shrugged. Maverick growled at her. That made her laugh.

We were an odd crew.

CHAPTER 5

Days turned to weeks. With Ant not at full strength, it took some time for him and Silence to heal.

I distracted myself, spending my time with Sparrow, or in training. I also talked with Prince Alvere, whenever he was with us. I loved to learn of his kingdom and he listened intently as I spoke of my home. We were becoming... friends. A part of me wanted more, he was handsome and intelligent and seemed interested in me.

But I'd do nothing more than get to know the man before talking to Silence. He was my first partner and I'd not explore my desires to expand my sphere of relationships without his consent. Yet Silence slept most of the time, still recovering.

So I had to wait.

I spoke to Sparrow about the prince. She thought him handsome as well, but wouldn't say much more than that. She wanted me to be happy, but she also knew how I felt for Silence.

The trouble was... some of my combat training with Alvere got quite intense. He was a good student and quickly became a match for me. If I didn't use my avatar abilities, he'd win as often as lose.

And we were both competitive, so we got a little... overzealous at times. Amber would watch us as we sparred, shaking her head, eyes wide.

I gulped in air, breathing hard, backed against the wall during one of our fights. He too huffed heavy breaths, sweat on his brow and soaking through his practice shirt. Something about him seemed harder now. I think he'd lost the last of the boyish round-ness in his features. Perhaps we'd been training him too hard.

He swept a kick to knock me off my feet, but I jumped. And for just an instant I used my abilities to plant my feet against the wall behind me and launch myself at him bodily. I hit him hard and we both tumbled to the mats, rolling over each other. He ended up on top and quickly pinned my right arm. I punched with my left, not as strong, but still hoping to stun him with a hit to the kidneys. But I only brushed his shirt as his hand clasped over my wrist stop-ping my strike. He smiled down at me.

"Now what?" he asked with a note of victory.

"Now you learn how to truly fight one of us," I said with a grin. Planting my feet, I used all my strength to buck him off me, though I may have been a little too zealous. He released me as he flew over my head, flipping forward.

I spun and rose to a ready-kneel, facing where he would land.

To his credit, he managed to land on his feet and did an awkward, off-balance spin back to face me. I swept his legs. He tried to jump, but I caught enough of his right foot to cause him to fall to his left. Then I was on him, straddling him, like he'd done with me a moment before. I pinned his left arm, his dominant hand.

I was unable to catch his right-handed strike and he hit me hard, just under the ribs. I grunted, but didn't release his arm. Still, that had hurt — I'd have a nasty bruise tomorrow — and I didn't want to leave myself open for another punch. So... I dropped low over him, pressing myself to him, faces inches apart, then I softly dipped in to kiss his cheek. I needed to end this fight and knew one way to do that.

"Surrender or you get the lips," I whispered.

He raised a single brow. "That's cheating," he huffed, breathless.

"Yeah, but I like fighting dirty."

He shook his head and tapped out with his free hand.

"Good boy," I said, kissing him again on the cheek. That second kiss hadn't been needed, but looking into those perfect blue eyes always got my blood pumping and I'd acted without thinking. That made me wonder if I'd have had poison on my lips if I *had* kissed him. I certainly wasn't feeling fear or animosity right now. No, mostly I wanted to keep pressing myself against him and kiss those beautiful full lips, while he kissed me back.

But... I couldn't, not yet.

I got one leg under me and did a back flip off him.

"Show off," he said, then did a flawless kip-up.

"Who's showing off now?"

He grinned and shrugged.

"Well," Amber said approaching us. "You know enough of the basics that you should have a much easier time defending yourself against attackers while unarmed." She looked back and forth between the two of us. To the prince, she said: "I think you'll be headed back to your own lands soon. I hear the war in the North is escalating."

He nodded slowly. "I'll be back here as often as I can, but I need to be there for my troops."

"Oh?" I said, surprised at the distress in my voice. "Leaving so soon?"

He smiled. "Not quite yet, but soon. And from what I hear, so too will you."

I was a bit surprised at that. I looked at Amber, who nodded.

Though she then gave the prince a scathing look. "That was not to be mentioned yet."

He shrugged. "She should know sooner rather than later."

Amber grimaced. "Fine." She turned to me. "Once Silence is well, which seems like it will be soon. A group of us will be heading to the capital."

Oh... From how Alvere had phrased it, I thought I might have been going with him. Now... I was conflicted. I wanted to be with him *and* Silence...

"Even me?" I said, a bit surprised. "Aren't there people in the capital who want to kill me? I thought I was to lay low?"

Amber's grimace quirked into a half-smile. "Boss seems to think we won't be able to stop you from going with us. He thinks you can handle it. Also, we've got a plan for you."

"A plan?" Why did I keep saying these inane two-word sentences?

"Yeah, you'll be going on the pretense of visiting your sister. She and her House should provide some protection for you. Also..." and with this she glanced at the prince with a slightly sour note. "Midnight will be keeping an eye on you."

"They didn't want to tell me about their secret weapon," the prince said with a laugh. "But I insisted there be no secrets. Though, to be fair, I don't know anything about this Midnight other than her name."

"In truth, I don't know much more than that," I said with a shrug.

I was a little overwhelmed. I'd be leaving soon? Going to see my sister? That would be fun... maybe... if I wasn't worried for my life the entire time. And seeing Midnight for the first time would be interesting. But oddly, it wasn't any of that which was foremost on my mind. No, I was mostly sorry the prince would be leaving, or more precisely that I'd be away from him.

Spirits woman, make up your mind! I shouted at myself.

Auwei laughed. *You're young and free. I've had hosts who were far more promiscuous than you. At least you've only been with those with whom you are truly close. I had one host who would sleep with any man who was remotely handsome. That was an... interesting lifetime, that one. I learned a lot.*

You'll have to share that with me sometime.

Maybe. Or maybe I'll let you learn it for yourself. It can be quite enjoyable to go through that particular learning process.

I bet.

The prince escorted me back to my room after practice. It was late afternoon and we'd need to be ready for supper soon, but we had a little time and I intended to have a bath.

"Legs?" Alvere said tentatively.

I looked over at him. The usually confident young man was hedging, lips pursed, looking at the floor. When he did look back at me, those bright blue eyes catching mine, something seemed to unlock within him. "I will dearly miss you, while I'm away, while we're both away."

"I will miss you too," I said and meant it.

"Might I have a kiss to remember you by?" he asked.

My heart was racing, now that those words had been spoken.

Though then he quirked his mouth. "A kiss that won't make me stiff all over that is."

No, just stiff in one place, Auwei said with a giggle.

Auwei, shame on you!

You were thinking it too.

Maybe.

"I think I could arrange that," I breathed, feeling heat rise within me, blood pumping, my entire body responding to this simple request.

He leaned over a bit, but I raised a hand. "Not now, please. We're both a little... ripe. I'd like to clean up first."

He smiled. "Yes, you're right, of course."

"After dinner, meet me in the reading alcove at the far back of the third level of the library," I said, laying a hand on his chest. I could feel his heart pounding.

He nodded. "I'll see you there."

And that was it. We had a date.

I slipped into my room and leaned with my back against the door for a long moment, waiting for my heart to settle. When it did, I stripped off my practice clothes and left them in the laundry hamper. Then I slipped on a bathrobe and headed to the first floor and a bath.

The upstairs hall was deserted, but as I came out of the stairwell, I saw the prince, in his own robe, heading for the bathing room. He was well ahead of me and there would be no chance of us running into each other if I stayed back. Also, there were separate bathing rooms for men and women. I reached the short hall, off the main hall, which had a door on either side at the end, leading to the two rooms and...

...the door to the men's baths was just a little open. The latch hadn't fully caught after the prince had gone in.

Auwei laughed. *Naughty girl.*

What? Why?

I know what you're thinking. You want to peek in there, don't you?

And the truth was, I'd been about to do just that, so I couldn't really deny it. *Well, then, I'm glad you're on board, I'll just take a quick look. I probably won't see anything anyway.*

I put my eye to the narrow crack between door and frame... just in time to see the prince's robe fall away.

There were four baths to a room. The stone of the foundation had been carved out to make the sunken baths quite large, easily big enough for two people to lounge comfortably. There was even a seat within the bath, the stone rounded and smooth to make it comfortable on one's skin. There were no showers here at Hedgewild, but the baths were maintained through some strange mechanism such that pulling a cord got hot water added to one of the baths. And once you were done, a separate cord would drain the water away.

At this particular angle, peering through the crack, I was only able to see one of the baths, but that had been the one the prince had chosen. He pulled the cord, then waited. The room grew warm as hot water poured into the bath. The prince leaned against a wall, sighed and... his penis twitched to life, rising slightly.

Oh! I flinched back from the crack and quickly took a look around.

No one there.

I debated leaving then. I should give the man some privacy, but I'd been just a little too curious about him. My heart raced and I was sure he'd be able to hear it from where he was. I'd only wanted to see him unclothed I hadn't meant to see... *that*. Apparently, he was thinking of something arousing. And now... so was I.

I dared to look back and found him stroking himself, eyes still closed, a soft, slow caress of his length. I watched, fascinated. His hand moved over his shaft, twisting and sliding along like he was his own lover, even stopping to squeeze the tip a moment, which caused a shuddering breath from him. Yet he remained hard and kept up his work, protracting his pleasure until finally the bell rang signaling the bath was full. He stepped in then, descending the steps into the hot waters, gasping a little. After that, I could see little but his head above the water. I sighed and turned away.

And there was Amber, leaning against the wall behind me, with a smirk on her face. Her bathrobe wasn't of the heavy, soft material like mine, but sheer and silken. She'd clearly caught me peeking and shook her head before silently going into the lady's bathing room.

I had been warm and flushed before, but got super-heated

with embarrassment as I stood there for a moment, then followed her in.

She disrobed as her bath filled.

"Wish to share?" she asked. She wasn't making any comment about my indiscretion.

I didn't want to share, but it would save water. I nodded, though I waited to disrobe until the bath was ready. I slipped in quickly as Amber sat on the cold stone rim and dangled her legs in the hot waters.

"I'm sure he'd welcome you, if you asked him," she said softly. "There are ways to bar these doors. It wouldn't be the first time a man and woman have shared a bath before."

Yup, there it was. Luckily now, with hot waters upon me, I had a reason to be flushed beet red.

I couldn't rightly deny anything so I just sighed. "I... don't know what I want with him yet. We're going to meet after supper to, ahh, kiss." That sounded so innocent yet so wrong at the same time.

"Just kiss?"

"I don't know yet."

"Do you want more? You may want to figure that out before you go tonight. If you don't want more, tell him first. Otherwise, it can be hard to stop things later, if you become... swayed."

That was good advice. The trouble was, I didn't know what I wanted with Alvere. Or rather, I *did* know, but couldn't allow it. I wanted to fully explore my feelings for the prince, but wouldn't do that until I'd spoken to Silence first.

It occurred to me, Amber might be a font of information on this.

"How does one keep... several lovers?" I asked a bit tentatively.

Carefully, Auwei said within me.

"With a great deal of care," Amber said echoing Auwei's thoughts. "It is often good to let all parties know that they are not the only ones. Otherwise, it can lead to confusion, anger, and heartbreak. Get that out in the open first, let them know you do not plan to be with just them. See if that's something they're willing to abide by. Some men and women will have no problem with that. Others will want you all to themselves. It's just who they are."

Exactly.

Sorry, I know I'd already talked to you about this, but...

No problem. Amber's information will be more... up to date. My particularly promiscuous host lived over a hundred years ago. Times were different then. Not to mention that my host didn't much care about what others thought, she was in it for the challenge of the chase and the thrill of conquest.

Amber smiled at me. "Are you finding the attentions too much?" she asked, with a tilt of her head. Her auburn hair fell to one side. It was an action meant to draw attention to her, and she knew it. She was playing with me now. She knew I'd been with Sparrow. Was this an invitation?

"Ah... no, not yet, just..." How could I say this? Well, I didn't have to mince words with Amber at least, she knew everyone I'd been with. "I love Silence. He's a kind man, caring and wonderful. And... I don't think he'd fault me getting some comfort from Sparrow, that's... different. But... from another man?"

Amber nodded. "Ah, yes I see."

As much as I wanted to explore a relationship with Alvere, I couldn't... yet. That much I knew. The question was: would a kiss, or a bit of play, still be betraying Silence? I also had to consider that it wouldn't just be the actions themselves, but who I was doing them with. Silence had been tortured by the Vauphani. Though it hadn't been the prince who'd done it, Silence wasn't likely to feel kindly toward anyone from Vauphan.

I sighed heavily.

"You have two options it seems," Amber said as she slid over the edge into the bath with a shuddering sigh of contentment. "Have your fun and check in with Silence later, or wait for Silence and then... have your fun." She shrugged.

The trouble was... "I don't know if the prince will still be around when Silence is done recovering."

Amber nodded. "I see the problem." Then with a silken smile and curious tilt of her head, she asked, "is there anyone else you're interested in?"

"No, of course not!" I said quickly.

Oh? Auwei said innocently. *I'm pretty sure you've had some inappropriate thoughts about Ant, Jack, and Amber herself. Not to mention how much of a hunk Maverick is.*

I... what? No. I... If I hadn't been beet red before, I was now. *You can be quiet now.*

Amber smiled. "I assume your Lumani is well experienced, but just in case Auwei is a prude, if you ever need any... lessons on things. Let me know," Amber purred. She made no move to draw closer to me. It wasn't an invitation, just an offer. She wasn't even looking at me. Her eyes were closed as she leaned her head back against the rim of the bath.

We were both silent after that.

I couldn't figure out what to do. Should I see the prince? Would a single kiss be anything for Silence to worry about? Would it be *a single* kiss? Should I just wait? These questions spun in my mind long after Amber had left the baths. The water was cool by the time I remembered to dunk under and give my hair a scrub. There were soaps around the bath and I quickly washed myself before retreating back to my room.

I'd missed the start of supper. Coming in late, I saw Maverick, Crane, Amber, and the prince huddled together at a far table. I sat alone and ate quietly, all the while anticipating — and now also dreading — my meeting with Alvere that evening.

CHAPTER 6

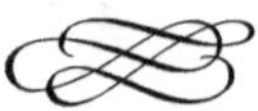

THESE HIDDEN ALCOVES WERE MY FAVORITE PLACES IN THE LIBRARY. Small reading nooks, laid with soft cushions, sat beneath tall windows for light. The shelves of books extended out from the walls creating a mostly private area. My heart pounded with excitement and fear as I waited, still unsure of what I wanted.

I should have talked to Silence. He was doing better, with only a few injuries remaining upon him, but he was still fragile and feverish. I didn't want to unsettle his rest with questions like this. But that meant I wasn't sure how I wanted this encounter to go.

A single kiss won't hurt, it's harmless, I told myself.

Then why did you wear your flirtiest outfit? Auwei asked.

That was an excellent question. I'd found this particular outfit before leaving Elista, a matching top and skirt in brilliant rose-gold. The top was actually fairly modest, with a high, round neck-line, tight across the shoulders and the tops of the arms, leaving the rest of the arm bare. The slightly scandalous part of the top was that it stopped mid stomach. It was loose and gave some shape to my breasts, but hung off of them, leaving a space between the sheer fabric and my skin.

The skirt was a matching color, sitting a little lower than most, exposing the tops of the hips and all of my lower back, not to mention a good swath below my navel. From there it flared out ending just below the knee. I hadn't had a real reason to wear it in all the time I'd been at Hedgewild. Now I didn't know if I loved it or regretted it.

Alvere peeked around a corner and smiled when he saw me. My earlier assessment of him hadn't been wrong, he'd toned up and lost the roundness on his face. The rest of him — as I'd seen earlier in the baths — had little roundness at all, with fine tight muscles over his slight frame. He was in a deep blue jerkin, white shirt beneath, and cream-colored pants.

He stopped, once he was fully around the corner, and I saw him swallow hard as his eyes grew wide, looking at me. I'm sure I imagined it — my mind still a little stuck on seeing him naked earlier — but I thought I saw a slight bulge in his pants.

Spirits, he looked good.

I was even more confused and torn. My body was clear in its desire for Alvere: racing heart, dry mouth, and a building wet heat between my legs. But my mind still whispered: *what of Silence?*

Alvere approached slowly. "You're... amazing," he whispered. There might be others in the library below. It was one of the reasons I'd suggested here instead of one of our rooms. In a room, we'd be alone, here we were... mostly alone with a constant unknown. "I have seen many beautiful women. As prince there is an endless parade of noble-women who wish to become princess and queen. Some of them were quite attractive, but... you... you outshine them all, Legs." He gave a breathy laugh. "Even your name... I... can't say it without thinking of that part of you." He swallowed hard once again as he stopped, standing over me.

He certainly had lots of flowery words that made me feel seen and loved and pretty.

I stood, heart pounding with a strange mix of uncertainty and desire. He'd been close, and once I was standing, less than a foot of space remained between us. We stood there, in silence, gazing at each other for a long moment. Then one of his hands rose and came to rest on the exposed skin at the top of my hip, then slid up to my waist. Just that soft touch, the brush of movement, sent a thrill through me. I was getting *very* hot and my body trembled with need.

Spirits!

I didn't know whether to flee from him or throw myself into his arms.

I gulped air and saw his eyes dip to watch my heaving chest.

"I... I don't know..." he began, gazing down at his hand and my hip. "Please tell me, Legs, what will happen here? I do not wish to presume. And... I should tell you: I probably can't be with you in a lasting way. I may have to marry one of those other noble-women someday. But until then I can... kiss who I like. And I would very much like to... kiss you. I would like... more too." His gaze rose to mine, beryl-blue eyes bright and intent. "What do *you* want?"

And there it was.

What did I want?

I wanted to move against his hand, feel his touch on my skin, over my hip and across my belly, or around back to pull me close. I wanted his lips on mine, his hands... everywhere, but... even that seemed like too much. Even if it didn't lead to more, I'd essentially be opening the door for Alvere and I didn't know if I could do that without talking to Silence first.

But all of this had come from him asking for a simple kiss. Perhaps... just that then? Lots of people kissed who weren't lovers.

That's a fine line, Auwei said, cautioning me. *What you say is true, but we both know he wants more, and you want more. So even a chaste kiss might become... more.*

She was right. But I had to tell him something.

"Just a kiss," I breathed the words, voice tremulous and weak. I might as well say what I knew we were both feeling, echoing Auwei's words. "I know I want more, and I know you want more, but we can't have it, not yet. I... I have some things I need to work out first. I hope you understand."

He nodded and gave a faint smile. "Yeah, I understand, my life is complicated too. I already mentioned that who I marry won't be up to me, most likely." He stepped in, close enough to feel the heat of his body, close enough that every one of my heaving breaths brushed my breasts across his tunic. He'd never feel it, but I did. The faint friction aroused my nipples, which stood against the sheer fabric of my blouse.

The pull between us was so strong I could barely breathe. I raised my hand to his shoulder, my touch light since I didn't know if I wanted to push him away or pull him closer.

His voice was just as hot and breathy and needful as mine when he said, "I want... all of you, Legs. But, if all I can have now, is a kiss, I'll take it."

Oh, be so very careful Legs, Auwei warned. *You two are both so hot right now, one kiss might start a fire you can't put out.*

Then I'll trust you to stop it for me... please. I already knew she was right and I didn't trust myself to stop at just a kiss anymore.

Understood, I'll stop you, if you need it.

Oh, I was going to need it. *Thank you,* I said sincerely.

I could trust Auwei to keep me safe from... myself.

Then Alvere tilted his head and I did the same. I don't know whether it was he who moved in or I, but our bodies pressed closer.

And then his lips met mine.

He didn't go stiff this time, well at least not all of him.

The kiss was soft and chaste as we tasted each other, savoring this moment of initial sweet contact. His hand remained on my hip. My hand remained on his shoulder. I thought I could feel his heart thundering in time with mine. Our bodies seemed to vibrate together, with the same intensity.

His hand slipped around behind me, and with the low-slung skirt, he pressed very low on my back, still flesh to flesh.

That simple movement caused a faint moan from me and I opened my lips to his. He responded in kind and our once modest kiss became hungry and deep. We'd moved from appetizers to the main course, and we were famished.

Legs! Auwei shouted at me.

It took all my effort to push away from him and break that contact. My eyes remained closed, lips still moving, remembering his taste and touch.

"Too much?" he breathed.

No.

"Yes," Auwei said through me.

Hey!

I'm only doing what you asked.

I shouldn't have been angry at her. I was angry at myself... but I was petty and redirected that anger at her.

It's your life, Legs. Make this mistake if you like.

But you'll regret it for eternity? It was a favorite saying of hers.

No, Legs. Not this one. This one you'll regret. She sounded sad, disappointed.

Well... Pits!

"I understand," Alvere breathed, but neither of us moved any farther apart. We stayed so very close: lips near but not touching, hot breath mingling. I wanted to taste him again, but I knew if I did... I'd not stop there.

For just a moment, I allowed that fantasy to play out in my mind. The rough, hard kiss as our mouths devoured each other. The needful press of his hands beneath my clothes: the grasp of a breast, the caress of my folds. He'd free his erection, barely even dropping his pants as I wrapped my legs around him, driving him deep within me. He'd take me, standing, pressed back to a book-shelf as we gasped and tried not to make too much noise, just in case anyone else was in the library. It would be so very intense, quick, and needful. We'd both reach a spike of heated passion as we released together, panting into each other's mouths.

The vision was so real to me I had to press my legs together to restrain my arousal.

I gasped and finally pushed away from him, backing off a half step.

"I really hope," I said between heavy breaths, "we can continue this... later." I brought a hand up to cup his cheek. "I *want* you, Alvere," I breathed.

"I want you too," he said, eyes sparkling like gems.

"But now is not the time." I pulled away from him and drew a long shuddering breath. "I hope we get... a time," I whispered.

"As do I," he breathed. He swallowed hard as his gaze traced over me, as if trying to capture this moment in his mind. "I don't think I'll ever feel for anyone what I feel for you. I don't care if I'm married or not, when you say you are ready, I will always be willing."

Wow... just... wow.

I nodded, not sure I trusted myself to say anything, as I was on the verge of throwing myself at him. Then I carefully moved around him and walked away.

I had to pleasure myself that night. I imagined a slight man with me, inside me, needing me... yet the face on that man kept shifting from Alvere to Silence and in the end, I was left only frustrated.

CHAPTER 7

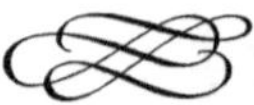

As you will see, for some of what is to come I was not there to witness it firsthand. I relied on accounts from others. So perhaps I should begin with some of those now...

Silence

Silence woke with a groan, sitting up slowly. It was the first time he'd felt comfortable doing so without help. He looked around and was a bit surprised to find his room empty. Before now, someone had always been there, tending to him. That and Ant had remained close, resting on the floor or a couch, but was gone now.

Strong, slanting beams of sunlight shone through the large windows. That made him smile. A beautiful, sunny day always lifted his spirits. But then, so did simply being in this bed, in this place. His smile widened just thinking about the impossibility of having been chosen for a Noble House. He thought he'd reached the limits of his smiling, but then he recalled who he was here with and his smile grew again.

Legs.

He fell back into his pillows with a sigh. Then felt a thrill at the memory of his encounters with her. He loved everything about her: those large, russet-brown eyes, that soft, wavy hair, her wide cheery grin, the slight up-turn of her nose, and so much more. He couldn't think about the rest without a specific part of him growing stiff and uncomfortable.

His smile faded at the thought that he wouldn't see her for a while. She'd left Hedgewild. Though, in all fairness... he was just happy she was alive.

She'd come to see him yesterday. He'd been a bit feverish, but lucid enough to recognize her and understand that she was truly alive. Before that, others had told him she'd not only survived the mistweaver but defeated her! He hadn't believed them. He'd thought their words the kind lies that you tell someone who's suffering so as not to worsen their condition. But then... there she was, alive and radiant!

She'd been happy to see him doing well and hugged him. That had been the delight of his day. She'd hedged a little and said there was something she needed to talk to him about, but he hadn't paid much attention to that, simply reveling in her aliveness, not to mention her body pressed to his. Later that day, she, Maverick, Amber, and Sparrow had left. They'd been waiting until they knew he would be well. And he was now, though his memory was fuzzy on everything that had happened since the palace. He remembered the terror of the mistweaver, and Legs' bravery, staying behind to aid his escape with information Elista would need. But... after that... things were a blur.

He heard the door to his room open, and someone came in, whistling. Jack appeared around the corner from the entrance hall, completely naked, of course. Not who Silence wished to see naked at that point, though he couldn't deny that the tall man had an exquisite physique with long, slender muscles. Jack was carrying a tray of food and sauntered in to set it on Silence's bedside table.

"You're up? And you look well. Good. Have something to eat and we'll talk."

Silence sat up again and carefully lifted the tray over to his lap as Jack sat on the side of the large bed.

"What do you remember?" Jack asked. "From... the palace?"

"Not much, everything's a bit fuzzy." Silence then bit into a thick, warm slice of bread and savored the soft texture.

"Good, very good."

"Amber did that, didn't she?" he said around his mouthful. "There's something you don't want me to remember?"

Jack nodded. "Exactly. And you don't want to remember it either. Trust me. But since you'll probably always be curious, I'll tell you what you need to know. You were caught by the Vauphani and tortured. But their prince, who is our ally now, stopped them and brought you home. You were in a bad way but you're better now, that's all that counts."

Silence nodded. Now he knew the facts without remembering the experience, and could see the benefit in that. Still... a chill ran through him. He recalled the pain and his long recovery well enough, even if he had been delirious. He'd make it a point never to be captured again.

"When do you think you'll be up for a trip?" Jack asked.

"A trip? Where are we going?"

"The capital."

Silence raised a brow. That's where Legs and the others had gone. He'd love to see her again. "Anytime, I'd love to catch up with... the others." He bit into a piece of bacon from the tray, crisp and smokey.

Jack grimaced and shrugged. "We'll see. We might see them, if things work out, but we've got a different mission, you, me, and Foggy. We're going to do some spying."

Silence shuddered, remembering — what he did recall — of the last secretive mission. "What about Vauphan?" he asked. Jack had mentioned something about their prince being an ally, but Silence wasn't sure how that could be possible.

Jack sighed. "Ah...yeah, the situation there has changed a little."

Silence raised his other brow at that. "Oh?"

"We're now friends with Vauphan. After Legs defeated the mistweaver, she subdued their prince and brought him back here."

She'd done that *after* having fought the mistweaver? "All by herself?" Silence asked around some dried fruit and hard cheese.

"No, Amber helped. Anyway, it turns out we had the whole thing backward. Vauphan was planning war, but only as a counter-attack. Apparently, someone in Elista has been taking their northern territories without telling the rest of Elista. We also figured out that our being sent to Vauphan was probably a ruse, to frame us for the death of the king and queen. Oh, and you probably don't know, but the mistweaver we captured here was a fake, probably to get us to drop our guard and send Legs on that mission to Vauphan, so she could be killed."

That was a lot of information to take in, and Silence sat for a long moment simply trying to absorb it.

"So... someone in Elista is behind all of this... even the war?"

Jack nodded. "Exactly. Which is why we're being sent to spy... on our own Nobles."

Silence had been in on Maverick's secret talk a while back, and heard that some Elistan Nobles had killed others, somehow killing their Lumani as well. He knew there was trouble here in Elista, and understood the need to uncover what was going on, but... "You're sure we can trust the Vauphani?" Silence didn't. He may not remember being tortured, but the pain had been real. He didn't much like how things had changed.

Jack shrugged. "Am I sure? No. But the Boss is. Maverick trusts the Vauphani prince, and I trust the Boss. That's good enough for me."

Silence nodded slowly at that. He trusted Maverick too. He'd have to come to terms with this on his own.

"What will you need me to do?" Silence asked.

Jack grinned. "We can get into the details later, but mostly, be your mousy self and get into all sorts of interesting places around the capital, then listen in on things. Foggy will be doing the same. I can't get into the same places you two can, so I'll be running things behind the scenes."

"Understood," Silence said. Then, "I do hope we get a chance to see the others."

"Missing Legs?"

Silence was a bit surprised the other man had gone straight there. He'd thought his relationship with Legs a secret... mostly.

Jack grimaced nodding. "Yeah, no need to say anything I can see it in your eyes." The other man then drew in a long breath and shook his head. "You're going to need to get in line, I think. She's becoming a sought-after woman." He looked off toward one of the windows. "I can't blame you. She's... something else."

Was Jack interested in her as well? And what did he mean by *a sought-after woman*?

But then Jack swung his deep brown-eyed gaze around to Silence and there was a certain appraising look in that glance. "But then... you're not so bad yourself."

Silence was suddenly aware that he was wearing very little, the bed sheets and the tray on his lap covering him to his hips, but nothing above that.

Jack smiled and winked. "My offer still stands. If you ever get tired of chasing that hen and would like to see what a cock is like, let me know."

Silence was flattered. He'd had always found both the male and female forms attractive and Jack was a handsome man. He had no memory of his parents and, for a while, when he'd been living on the streets, he'd stayed with a couple, two men. It was the only time he'd seen an example of true love. Right now though, he was a bit too consumed by thoughts of Legs to think of Jack.

Yet Legs had asked him if he'd mind a man or woman joining the two of them. It was clear she wanted to experiment.

And that worried him, a little, mostly because he wasn't sure what she really wanted. Did she want him *and* others, or just... others?

Silence was not an exemplar of manhood, being small and slight. He was as tall as Legs, but wasn't sure he'd get much taller. There were bigger, stronger, and more experienced men out there... or women... if that's what she desired. And if she wanted someone else instead of him... he'd be heartbroken, but he'd try to move on. And *if* that day came, he could do worse than the man before him.

But he wasn't there yet. He needed to talk to Legs first. He was — mostly — certain she loved him and wished to stay with him. If so, then he'd need to figure out if he was good with others joining them. Perhaps, if Jack wished to... Silence might be well with that. He'd have to see what Legs had in mind.

Perhaps he'd make an effort to find her, while he was in the capital. He was growing more and more impatient to be away and closer to her. He needed to speak to her, find out what she wanted, if it was indeed him or...

"When do we leave?" he asked.

"That's the spirit," Jack said rising and striking a bit of a pose. Silence suspected the way Jack was standing was meant to show him off in all his glory. And he was certainly a... taller and larger man than Silence. "We'll head out tomorrow late in the day and stop at Grovner's Green to rest." He grinned. "There, we'll pull a bit of a switch, just in case anyone happens to be watching us."

Silence raised a brow at that, putting his tray aside. Jack kindly picked it up to take with him.

"You'll see," Jack said with another flirtatious wink and turned to leave.

And Silence did see. The next evening Silence, Jack, and Foggy all went to a tavern in Grovner's Green. Jack encouraged Silence and Foggy to drink heartily, or at least look like they were doing so. They then all piled into their carriage and headed back toward Hedgewild in the wee hours of the next morning after having "partied" all night. However, the three of them departed the carriage outside the town and circled back to a farmer's barn, where a wagon had been stowed. Along with the wagon were some new clothes for them. Jack traded in his Noble's finery for home-spun rough cloth. Silence was a bit surprised to find himself in a simple dress. "I'm a farmer, you're my daughter or young wife, your choice. Depends if you want to share my bed or not," Jack said with a wink. Foggy became a beetle and stowed himself among the many bundles in the wagon. They headed out as dawn broke. To any who saw them, they'd be a couple instead of three men, on a wagon instead of a carriage.

Their clandestine mission had begun.

CHAPTER 8

ALVERE

THE CORONATION WAS DONE IN PRIVATE. PRINCE ALVERE BECAME King Alvere the Third. Publicly it was being put out that the prince was dead or missing, and the next in line, a cousin to the prince, named Pierre was being sought. Letters on pigeons had been dispatched already to Pierre, telling him he'd also be crowned in the coming days, as a decoy. Pierre had accepted the dangerous job as symbolic figurehead of the country, so the prince could rule in secret.

After the coronation the prince retired to his new rooms within the palace, a simple suite for a visiting noble and family. There he put the crown in a small, padded chest and locked it with a key, which would remain around his neck.

"I'm now Alain," he said to Fin, who'd waited in the rooms while he'd been crowned. "A simple young nobleman, who will counsel the new king on the war."

"Do you think the ruse will work?" Fin asked. The large man

paced, the constant activity seeming odd for a man of his bulk. Then Alvere remembered that in his other form, Fin was a whale, and they never stopped moving, despite their immense size.

"For a while at least." Alvere slumped into a padded chair. He needed to gather his things and be on his way to the warfront by the end of the day, but he could sit here for a moment.

He sighed. "Too many people know the truth for the secret to last more than a few weeks. I think the best we can hope for is to keep ahead of the news and be away from here quickly."

"And you're sure it's safe for you to go to the front?" Fin asked.

"I won't be that close, but I'll need to speak with the Fey. Their treaty is with myself and my family, not the kingdom." Still, Alvere was touched by the man's concern. In the short while they'd known each other, the two had become close. Fin went everywhere the prince did, always around in case the prince needed to make a quick escape... or return to Hedgewild, which was quickly becoming his second home.

Thoughts of Hedgewild were dangerous, though... they led to thoughts of Legs. He took a moment to close his eyes and picture her: wavy, golden-brown hair and large, russet-brown eyes. He recalled the softness and sweetness of her full lips and his imagined gaze traced down to her slender chin and that long neck.

Since he'd left, his mind always pictured her in that loose red-gold outfit. It was what he'd seen her in last. He loved the way it fell over her full breasts, like a silken waterfall, and how the skirt hugged her hips, low slung and sensual, dancing around those amazing, long legs of hers. He recalled the feel of her smooth skin, where he'd touched her hip and back.

He had to push the image away, lest he be overcome with desire for her. Shuddering a sigh, he drew his mind back to his immediate task.

Sitting straighter in his chair, he shifted positions to try to make his pants — which were suddenly very tight and constricting — a bit more comfortable. "From what I've been told, everything on our side is ready for a push to reclaim the lands taken by..." *your people*. That wasn't fair. Fin and House Maverick had no part in the war. "...the rogue Elistans. But the spring has been wet up there, and the conditions are not good at the moment. We'll wait and guard our borders, which will also give us time to reinforce our position. I want to walk among the troops and get a sense for their take on the coming battle. And, of course, talk to the Fey."

Fin stopped his pacing and turned, looking at the prince, with a grin. "You're part Fey, aren't you?"

Alvere had a moment of stunned shock, but now that his secret was out, saw no need to deny it. "Yes, though please do not make that common knowledge." He hung his head a little. "I loved my mother, the woman who raised me." He recalled her flowing blond hair and cheery blue eyes. He missed her and his father. "And I wouldn't want to bring any shame upon her or her family... because she wasn't the woman to whom I was born." He looked up at Fin. "How did you know?"

"I know a half-Fey," he said, tone a bit cautious and guarded. "She too wishes for her secret to remain unknown. But you look a lot like her: shorter than most, with that raven-black hair of yours. From what I understood your father was a large man, and your mother tall and blond, yet you are neither of those things." Fin smiled, a friendly grin. "No need to worry, your secret is safe with me."

Alvere nodded. He hoped everyone else wasn't as astute as this man. It had been a bargain struck by his father. Vauphan had watched the growth of the Lumani magics through Elista for the last several hundred years and feared that power. They had wanted something of their own. So, they'd made a pact with the Fey. He had lain with one of their women, and she had born him a child, the royal heir. The queen, his mother, had known of course and though she had not been fond of her husband being with another, had seen the practicality of the bargain. She'd gone into seclusion for her supposed pregnancy — in the North no less — and returned with him bundled in her arms. And to her credit, she had raised him like her own, loved him and cared for him as a mother should.

Yet, there was something Fin had said which stuck in Alvere's mind. "You know another half-Fey? In Elista?"

Fin laughed. "Just as I would for you, I will say little of her. I may have said too much already."

The prince nodded at that. He was intrigued that a half-Fey might have been born to an Elistan. The Fey lived in small, hard-to-find, communities in the northeastern hills and forest. That was no-where near the Elistan border. Perhaps there were some who roamed as far west as North Elista? He didn't know, yet it seemed odd and unlikely.

The Fey had been driven out of the Far North long ago by some mystical catastrophe, which had made the Shattered Lands. Those forsaken lands were close to the north of Elista and Alvere didn't think many Fey wished to be anywhere near the place. So, he was very intrigued by this mystery person Fin knew.

But he had other, much more important things to worry about. "Are you sure you'll be well, traveling by land for the next week or so?" he asked Fin. Fin was able to transport himself, and anyone with him, instantly from place to place, but only to places he knew, and he'd never been to the north of Vauphan. It would be a long journey in wagons and on foot, for one used to instant travel, or the deep sea.

Fin sighed and patted his full, round belly. "Maverick's been saying I could stand to lose a few pounds. I'm sure the journey will do me some good."

Alvere gave a breath of a laugh and nodded. "Do you have all your things?"

Fin shrugged. "Yes... and no? I don't travel with much. I can always slip back to Hedgewild to get anything I need."

"Does that mean you'll get me a warm breakfast every day?" Alvere joked.

"Sure, if you like," Fin said seriously.

Since he wasn't traveling as a prince — no, he was a king now — he'd have only a cold breakfast of hard trail rations like the rest of the men he'd be traveling with. The idea of a warm and savory breakfast was very appealing. Still, he shook his head.

"No Fin, don't worry about it, and if you can, pack what you'll need for the trip and bring it with you. I don't want us to attract too much attention from the men we'll be traveling with."

Fin nodded. "Understood, I'll pack some things now and return in a moment." And just like that he was gone.

Alvere laughed and rose. He had a little time to himself now and, since bathing would be a luxury during the trip, done in cold rivers most likely, he called for hot water to be brought for a bath.

When it was ready, he sank into the warm embrace of the waters, and closed his eyes again, imagining Legs once more, only this time without that flirty dress...

CHAPTER 9

"It's so good to see you!" Dove said, throwing her arms around me in a tight embrace. My sister — adopted sister in truth — hadn't changed much, still a picture of radiant beauty with her fair skin, pale blond hair, sparkling blue eyes and that stunning hour-glass figure.

While she was hugging me close, she whispered, "I've heard so many odd rumors about you recently."

That sent a shiver down my spine. Not so much her words, but the conspiratorial tone. What had she heard?

I drew back and forced a smile. "We'll have time to talk once I'm settled. Or perhaps we can spend a day shopping in the city. My House Leader gave me a small sum to spend."

Dove took the cue and nodded. "Let's get you settled, then we'll talk." She took my hand and motioned for a servant to grab my few bags, then hurried me up to her room, which was far more lavish than mine at Hedgewild. In fact, it was a small suite. The main room possessed a large sitting area and small dining area. Three doors led to: a small study, a private bathing room with attached privy, and a bedroom with a massive bed and several large wardrobes.

Once we were inside with the doors closed, she said, "The servants will take your things to your room, but come you must be tired from your journey, just relax and sit for a while." She'd been overly loud and the way she glanced at the door made me realize these words were not for me, but for anyone listening in.

Then in a hushed and concerned tone, she asked, "What in The Bloody Pits has been happening in the south?"

We sat, huddled close, on one of the large couches. "Can we talk here?" I whispered.

I was a bit surprised when she hesitated. She leaned in to whisper directly in my ear, voice barely audible even then. "There are those in my House very good at listening in on conversations." Leaning back a little she whispered. "I'd like to think we can talk here, but more and more I'm feeling..." She shivered. "...uncertain about a lot of things."

I nodded. This was interesting indeed. I hadn't been sure what had been happening in the capital, but it seemed there were undertones of mistrust here, which spoke volumes about the state of the nation.

"We're safe to talk here, at least for the moment."

The new voice startled us both, and we turned to see another woman with us in my sister's suite. She was short and slight of build. Her hair reminded me of Alvere's, raven-black and gleaming blue in the bright light coming in through the many windows. Her eyes were emerald green and the similarity of the jewel-toned eyes to the prince's beryl blue was also a bit shocking. She was pale with only a blush of pink on her slender lips. In build, she reminded me a lot of Sparrow. But where Sparrow's demeanor was open and bright, this woman was mysterious and dark. She smiled disarmingly at us.

"Hello Legs, I'm Midnight."

It took me a moment to register those words.

"Oh! Midnight!" I turned to my sister. "We can trust her." Though it occurred to me then, that I was just going off this woman's word that she was who she said she was and turned back to her. "How do we know you're you?"

"Maverick said I'd give you something, yes?"

Right!

That had been set up in advance: there would be a sign so I'd know Midnight was around and watching me. She would leave small green stones, smoothed to be perfectly round, in various places where I could see them to let me know she was there, even if I couldn't see her.

She extended a small hand, delicate fingers closed over the palm. She opened it to reveal a handful of such stones.

I nodded in relief. She put the stones away, somewhere under the all-encompassing black cloak she was wearing and drew in close to the back of the couch, leaning over it to be closer to us. "I am exceptionally good at determining if others are around and listening. But I hear you are too, Legs. You have a spider's sense?"

I did!

Why did I always forget these things?

It's been a long trip and you're tired. Also, Midnight just surprised you and I think you're a little off-kilter. Don't worry, I'll remind you of anything else you've forgotten.

Thanks, Auwei.

I drew in a breath and let my hairs prick up, to feel for any other noises or presences around me. I felt the disturbance in the air of the two women with me... but nothing else... no, wait. Someone passed by in the hall. But they walked past Dove's room without stopping. "Yes, I think we're alone."

"You two are a pair," Dove said, voice hushed. Then to Midnight. "How long have you been in my rooms?"

Midnight smiled a small, mysterious grin. "You don't want to know."

Dove's eyes widened at that, but she settled quickly. "Will one of you tell me what's going on?" she whispered.

I looked to Midnight. "I think you know more than I do."

Midnight came around the couch to sit beside me. I slid closer to Dove as the three of us all leaned in to speak quietly.

"I have been secretly working in the capital for over a year now, listening in on many conversations in many Noble Houses, and all I can say for certain is that... something odd is happening." She looked at me for a long moment, and I felt like I understood this intent gaze.

"Yes, you can tell her," I said.

Midnight nodded. "Someone or something is making it so that when certain Nobles die, their Lumani die with them."

Dove gasped. I'd known this for some time, and it was still a bit shocking. Lumani were immortal. They were not necessarily immune to harm, but it had been thought that the only things that could harm them were in the Mistlands, while they were in their energy form, not while they were True-Bonded to a human.

"Exactly," Midnight said. "We thought this the work of certain Nobles at first. Then, when we discovered the mistweaver, we—"

"Mistweaver!" Dove gasped again.

"Oh, yes," I said casually. "There was a mistweaver about. She was trying to kill me — in fact she's the one who sent those assassins after me at Silverveil — but don't worry, I killed her."

Dove just gaped at me, and I couldn't help a bit of an internal laugh. It did sound preposterous.

You're really loving this, aren't you?

Just a bit, yeah.

Auwei laughed.

It took Dove a long moment to say, "You're... serious?"

We both nodded.

Dove's wide-eyed shock remained as she looked away for a long moment. "So that's what happened in the South? We heard reports of an attack on your House, but not much more."

"There is a lot more, and I'll fill you in once Midnight has done her bit."

Dove nodded slowly, still stunned as Midnight went on. "I am certain the death of the Lumani is not the work of that mistweaver, since there were a couple deaths while she was rumored to be elsewhere and one confirmed Lumani death since the mistweaver's passing. This means one of two things, neither of which are good. Either there is a second mistweaver, or it is the Nobles themselves who have found a way to kill Lumani. Given the existence of spirit-gifts, that cannot be ruled out."

Dove blinked. "Is that how you remained unnoticed here?" she asked. "A spirit-gift? A couple members of my House possess such abilities."

"Indeed," Midnight said, though she did not elaborate. "What I know is this: first, this cannot be the work of one House. Those killed have been among nearly all the Houses, and given how far reaching these plots are, I can't imagine any one House doing all of this. Second, the Royal House must be involved. Perhaps this goes all the way to the queen, though I haven't confirmed that. But to cover everything up, they would have to be involved at some level. Third, there must be either some code these conspirators use when they speak, or they only talk of such things in the closest and most secret of confines, since I have not been able to determine any confirmed source of these deeds. I have several suspects, that I will not disclose just yet, mostly because I cannot confirm their involvement." She sighed. "It has been a trying year."

"What about the war?" I said.

"War?" Dove whispered. "So Vauphan *is* planning war? Perhaps *they* are behind this? That would make sense. They've sent agents to corrupt members of our Nobility, inciting this internal strife while they attack from without?"

Both of us looked at her.

"No, Dove," I said softly. "Vauphan is not involved. They are planning for war, but only because Elista has already annexed several of their northern provinces."

Dove blinked, shocked again. "What?"

Midnight nodded. "We believe whoever is behind these Lumani deaths is also quietly waging a war in the North. The two things are so grand in nature they couldn't both be happening in secret by *different* parties. It must be a single plot."

"*We* started the war?" Dove asked. "But then..." She seemed confused.

"What?" I asked, prompting her.

"Then why are we only hearing now that we're sending troops to the front? It's all the news around the capital. Most of the standing army and several members from Noble Houses are massing to go north, but that's in response to the threat of a Vauphan invasion, or so we were told."

That was interesting. I looked at Midnight, who nodded.

Dove went on. "But you're saying we started the war? If so... then we're just using Vauphan as an excuse to mass more troops, probably to take more land?"

"That seems likely," I said. "In truth, the war's been going on for three years now, from what we've heard."

"From who?" she asked.

"From Vauphan. I... we... happen to know the prince of Vauphan and believe his account of events. He is a good man just trying to protect his people."

Dove sat back heavily, shaking her head. "I never imagined..." I could understand her stunned dismay. It was a lot to learn. She turned back to me. "And you killed a mistweaver?"

"I nearly died doing it, but yes."

"You nearly died? I heard you were hurt fighting pirates, was that—?"

"That was the first time she tried to kill me. The second time was in the palace at Vauphan, when she succeeded in killing the king and queen. Probably to further destabilize their government so we could claim more lands."

Dove just stared at me, blinking slowly.

Midnight took that opportunity to speak to me. "I'll be close, watching over you. Watch for the signs. I should go now. I don't like to remain out in the open for too long."

I nodded and started a bit when she just vanished from next to me. For a moment, I wondered if she jumped from place to place, like Fin. But no, that's not what I'd been told about her spirit-gift. Hers was around stealth, which meant she was still here, just... imperceptible. I thanked her inwardly and turned back to Dove.

"Where did she go?" Dove asked.

"She's still here. She's keeping an eye on me, since someone out there still wants me dead."

"Dead?" Dove's voice rose an octave. She was having a harder and harder time with these realizations.

I nodded. "There was a prophesy or foretelling or future-seeing or something. Someone, maybe a mistweaver, saw that I'd get in the way of all these plans and potentially stop them. So, they're trying to kill me, whoever *they* are."

"Oh, sister! That's horrible. Why..." Her mouth worked for a moment with no words. Then she nodded. "Of course you couldn't tell me any of this. You probably suspected any correspondence would be spied upon or something." She leaned over and embraced me tightly. "Oh, Legs, I'm so sorry you had to go through all of this. It's just horrible! I'm here for anything you might need."

That was the best news I'd heard in a long time.

CHAPTER 10

THE NEXT DAY DOVE AND I WENT FOR A CARRIAGE RIDE, LEAVING THE city. Dove knew of some paths through light forest along the edge of the Elis River. We walked for some time, leaving the carriage far behind, before we spoke freely once again.

Dove sighed heavily. "I have to admit, all this talk of conspiracies and secret cabals within the Noble Houses is terrifying! And you... They're trying to kill you! How can you remain so calm? I hardly slept a wink last night."

I smiled, though it had a distinctly sad tinge to it. "I'm sorry to drag you into this, sis."

"You're sorry to drag me...?" She gaped at me. "I don't know how you've done this on your own for as long as you have."

"I'm not on my own," I said, sure and confident, if not happy about the situation. "I have Auwei and my Noble House. They've protected me, helping me through all of this."

"I'm glad you have them." She seemed to deflate a little. "I have a few friends in my House, but most of our members came from Noble parents. They're..."

"Distant, stuck-up, annoying bastards?" I supplied.

She laughed. "Not all at once no, but yeah. Some are distant, some treat me like I'm less than them because I came from 'normal folk,' some ignore me all together. There are forty-seven members of Pegasus House, and I can count on one hand those I'd consider a friend."

She shook her head. "And as for those I'd trust with my life... or your secret..." Her head just kept shaking to provide her thoughts on that matter. "It feels... cold, here in the capital," she said, voice trailing into melancholy. "The sad truth is, it wouldn't surprise me if members of my House were a part of this plot. I don't even know what half of the House is doing. A third of our members are generally not in the capital at any given time. And there are a few that I've still never met, after four years here." She looked at me and smiled. "You should count yourself lucky your House is small and close. It must feel more... like a family."

I grieved for the loss I heard in her voice. "I'm still your family. And you can come visit my new family any time you'd like. They'd welcome you with open arms."

She gave a tremulous smile at that, and I realized I'd only emphasized the comfort of my House compared to hers. "I'm sorry."

"No, don't be. I'm glad you found a home." She took my hand and held it tightly as we walked. She changed the topic: "Are there any boys you're seeing?"

Well, there was Silence...

...And a new lady friend...

...And the prince of Vauphan...

"That's... complicated."

Her eyes went wide, latching onto this diversion. "Oh! That sounds interesting. You have to tell me everything!"

So I did, remembering to keep my voice low and use my spider-sense to discern if there was anyone else around.

Oddly I did sense one other person around, and that... comforted me. Midnight was still nearby.

Dove gasped in all the right places as I told her of my lovers. There was wide-eyed, stunned silence when I spoke of the prince. And she gaped, all curious wonder, when I spoke of Sparrow.

"You *have* been busy and... adventurous, haven't you!" She elbowed me softly, shaking her head. "It shouldn't surprise me though. You were always more adventurous than I."

We walked in silence for a while and the mood slowly shifted from bright to gloomy once more. "Is there... anything I can do to help?" Dove asked after a while.

"You're doing it," I said and took up her hand again to squeeze it. "Just being here for me." Though... "And... if there is anything odd you hear from yours or other Noble Houses...?" I left that open.

She nodded.

After a moment, she asked, "I'm assuming you heard about the queen?"

"The queen? No. What happened?"

"Oh... well, she's gone into seclusion; shut herself away. Apparently, she needed some time to recuperate from... something? It's unclear whether she had an illness or just became overwhelmed from running the nation. Others in her House are handling the affairs of state. I assumed you would have heard."

I shook my head. "No. This is news to me." But did it mean anything? I had no clue. I looked around for Midnight, but she didn't make an appearance to add anything. "So, we're sending armies north, and the queen is indisposed. That certainly adds... something to all the oddities going on. I just wish we knew who was behind all this and what their ultimate plan was."

Dove nodded.

"The other thing I'm to do while I'm here, supposedly vacationing with you, is to be seen. I'm to go to balls and social events and keep my ears open for any strange rumors. Any thoughts for where to go?"

"There's a ball tonight at Lady Vicuna's estates. I don't know if anyone important is going to be there, or if there will be any talk of intrigue. It's supposed to be for the young eligible Nobles to go and meet and mingle."

"Well, we are both young and eligible," I said with a grin.

"Well, actually...?"

"No!" I gasped. "You're seeing someone?"

She flushed, grinned, then shrugged. "His name is Lord Hale. He's Lord Horn's son, but he's not in our House. He's actually in the Royal House."

It was my turn to gape. "You're dating a Royal? And from his name he certainly sounds buff and... healthy."

Her blush deepened. "He's a complete gentleman and... we haven't been... together yet, but—" A sensuous shiver ran through her. "He *is* big and so very strong. When he holds me close, I practically melt!"

"What's his avatar?"

She grinned. "A gorilla."

I nodded. "I'm happy for you. Will he be at this party tonight?"

"Only if I go and ask him to come."

"Will you?"

She nodded. "Sure, let's go and have some fun and forget about all this horridness, and you can meet Hale and size him up for yourself," she teased, then, with a mock scolding tone, added, "But don't you dare try to steal him!"

"From you? How? You've always outshined me!"

She grimaced. "You still can't see it, can you?"

"See what?" I asked. "Your amazing beauty and grace and poise. I've always seen that."

She laughed, then grew serious. "I may have all those things, but you've always had a... presence about you, Legs. People are drawn to you."

"Oh?" Though now that I thought about it, perhaps that had something to do with what Auwei was always going on about: my sometimes power of spirit.

It's nothing to mock. It's there, and your sister is right. You do have a presence. You may not be the most objectively beautiful woman in the room, but eyes are still drawn to you. I've noticed it, even if you haven't.

Oh...

"I'll keep my hands off him, don't you worry," I said. "He's all yours." I still couldn't believe it. "A Royal!"

"I know!"

And we giggled together as she told me more about him.

We returned to the city for lunch, and Dove sent a message to her guy saying she wished to meet him at this ball. Then, we spent the afternoon shopping for a gown for me. We settled on a flowing affair of crimson silk, which looked amazing on me. It even had an exposed mid-section, which was perfect. The top was form-fitting silk brocade with a golden-threaded pattern over the underlying crimson. It clung to my chest and arms, with long sleeves, showing off the needlework. A swath of material then ran down from below the chest, twisting around the left side to above the buttocks all along the back, leaving my belly and right side uncovered. The skirts were waves of silk, with trimmings of brocade at the hem and over the lower back of the dress, over my buttocks.

One of Dove's friends, a longtime member of Pegasus House named Lady Willow, helped me with my makeup and hair, which I was not used to doing, while Dove got ready. She, of course, was stunning in white, with her fair skin, hour-glass figure, blue eyes and pale-blond hair. As much as I thought I looked good in my dress, I still couldn't imagine anyone seeing anything but her at this party.

We took a carriage across town to a massive estate, the

sprawling four-story manor house seemed somehow small amidst the lavish gardens on the extensive plot of land at the edge of the capital.

I still cringed a little when the herald announced me as "Lady Legs."

And I was right, people did look my way, but far more looked when Dove was announced. I probably imagined it, but I even thought a hush fell over the crowd as they took in her beauty.

Then a massive form came out of the shadows, and I nearly jumped out of my skin. But he went to Dove, and she threw herself into his arms... and wow what arms they were. If this was Hale — and by Dove's reaction it certainly seemed to be — he was a sight indeed. He was taller than Ant by half a head, but just as massively built. The pale-blue silken fabric of his shirt strained over huge shoulders and thick arms. Though it was the massiveness of his forearms which stunned me, nearly as big as my head! He had to pick Dove up to kiss her, but that didn't seem a challenge at all. He had a bull neck, with a thick mane of blond hair and striking amethyst eyes.

"Legs, this is Hale!" Dove said, once she'd been set down. She was just a bit breathless from the passion of the kiss he'd laid upon her, and in public no less.

He turned to me, and those violet eyes looked me over. He extended a meaty hand, easily three times the size of mine and smiled. "A pleasure to meet you. Dove has told me so much about you." There was something in his dark gaze, a feral hunger. I suddenly felt like prey cornered by a predator.

"The pleasure is mine," I said with a bit of a curtsy... though I really had no idea how to curtsy. *I should learn.*

He raised my hand to his lips, but didn't actually kiss it. Just a motion of respect. Then his gaze was back on Dove, and I felt freed and lighter.

Wow, that is an intense man.

Agreed, Auwei said in awe.

He swept Dove easily into his arms, like she was weightless, and carried her the rest of the way into the large hall, as she laughed and playfully beat on his massive chest to be put down. He finally knelt and set her gently on the floor before asking for a dance. They swirled into the crowd of dancers and I was left alone. With Hale's size though, it was easy enough to keep tabs on him.

"I sense danger in him," Midnight whispered in my ear, and I nearly jumped to the high-vaulted ceiling. When I looked, she wasn't there, of course.

"Oh?" I whispered. "You don't say. Danger other than the fact that he could casually snap me like a twig?"

A soft chuckle. "There is that, but yes, something more."

And he was dating my sister. Great.

"I'm going to mingle and listen in. I'm assuming you'll do the same?"

"Yes, but I'll try to remain close."

Then she was gone. It only occurred to me at that point, that I'd sensed her presence — and been comforted by it — even if I hadn't seen her around. Apparently, I was getting the hang of using my avatar abilities all the time.

"Might I have this dance?"

I turned to the voice and was surprised to see Creek standing there. He'd been my height back at Silverveil but was now a half-head taller and had filled out rather splendidly. His golden hair was perfectly styled, those dark eyes sparkling as he smiled at me. He lowered his voice to say, "You look stunning, by the way. You're... one of my biggest regrets from Silverveil."

Regrets?

You turned him down.

Oh, right.

He is handsome though, and might be pleasant to dance with? Auwei suggested. *Perhaps he has news?*

Perhaps, I said to Auwei. The trouble was, I still hadn't had the conversation I'd wanted to have with Silence. He'd been conscious when I'd gone to see him before we left but in no state for that sort of talk. And that meant seeing anyone just felt a little wrong.

"Legs?" Creek asked again.

Spirits, I'd just been standing there like an idiot.

"Creek, it's good to see you."

"It's Cougar now, remember?"

"Right! Sorry."

"Would you like to dance?" he asked again, holding out a hand.

Right, he'd asked that already. I supposed a dance couldn't hurt. And he *was* part of Panther House. They were charged with protecting the North, our border with Vauphan. Perhaps he'd heard something about the war?

"Yes, that would be lovely, thank you." I took his hand and we walked out onto the floor.

It was only as he pressed me close that I remembered I didn't know how to dance.

Still, I moved with him and only stepped on his feet a few times. He didn't seem to mind. He was strong enough to sweep me around, so my feet barely touched the floor.

I declined a second dance, but asked him if he'd share a drink with me and catch up on things. I'd been a bit too dazed and dazzled by the swirling dance to ask him anything.

He brought me a tall glass of pale red wine. I sipped it as he spoke.

"I'm actually heading out tomorrow. I've finished my training and the remaining members of my House are being called to the front." His voice lowered, leaning close. "The Vauphani are threatening war, and I must go valiantly protect our nation." He leaned a little closer, putting an arm around me. "I would hate to be alone the night before I leave for war."

"And I'm sure you won't be," I said casually. "But you won't be with me."

He sighed, shifting away a little. "You've found someone at Maverick House?"

The easy answer was, "Yes." But I quickly changed the subject back to the war. "What do you know about the Vauphani and the war?" I asked, hoping the curiosity in my voice sounded genuine and innocent.

He grimaced. "I'm a junior member of the House, so not much." He shook his head. "But I've heard rumors that Vauphani soldiers, dressed as bandits, have been harrowing our towns along the border for some time, raping and pillaging with abandon."

I raised my brows with genuine surprise. "Truly?" I was certain this wasn't true, but then Auwei said:

Vilifying the enemy is a common tactic in war. Fighting just any other man is hard, but fighting someone you believe is a truly horrible person makes you a hero.

"As I said, it's a rumor, but the members of my House at the front are saying the situation is grim. Vauphan is a large nation and if they bring their full army to bear, we'll be sorely outnumbered. Luckily it will take time for them to do that. And our forces will get there first. Some have said we should hit them with a preemptive strike, while our armies are roughly even, cut down their numbers while they're still amassing their troops."

I nodded, listening in rapt engagement. I truly was astonished and curious about what people here had been told. I had little doubt now that those behind all of this were in positions of power. They had to be, to get armies moving and spread such misinformation so widely.

I thought I might try to seed a little doubt in Cougar's mind. "What if the other side is being told the same things, that we're horrible violent people? What if this is all just a misunderstanding or, a few warmongers who are seeking only glory and don't care about who dies on either side?"

Cougar frowned, then shook his head. "But why?" he asked, his own doubt showing through. "We've had peace with Vauphan for as long as we've both been nations. *We* have no reason to fight them, so *they* must have started this, trying to claim lands from a smaller nation, spreading their power. That must be it."

"But what if it isn't?" I urged again. "What if it was truly bandits preying on border towns and nothing more?" I didn't think that was the case, but since that's the rumor he'd heard I thought I'd play it up. "If they were doing that on both sides of the border, perhaps we're all up in arms against each other for no reason, and it's just a small group of rogue people we need to find and eliminate." I was proud of how I'd turned the bandits into a small group of rogue people. That might be easier for him to accept than them being members of our own Nobility."

He drew in a long breath. "I suppose." And I could see the doubt in his eyes before he looked away. "But what can I do, I'm just a new member to the House."

"Talk to your leader, perhaps—"

He scoffed. "I don't know how things work at Maverick House. You're small, right? You might be able to talk to your leader, but I've never even met Jaguar. He's been north, at the front while I've been training here. There are close to seventy members of Panther House."

"Don't you have a squad captain or something?"

"A sergeant, yes, but she doesn't have a lot of say in things either. She does what those above her tell her to do. Which, up until now, has been 'whip the newbies into shape.'"

Ah.

"Well, just keep that in mind when you get to the front. Maybe there'll be a chance to talk then." I could only hope I'd swayed him a little.

He nodded. "I will." He rose. "It was a pleasure to see you again, Legs." His eyes roamed over me, like he wanted to remember me like this. "But I do not intend to spend tonight alone and I must woo another it seems. Take care." He bowed and moved back toward the crowds near the dance floor.

That's when Dove and Hale found me.

"We're going for a walk in the gardens," Dove said, a bit breathless and glowing with a hint of perspiration from her dances. "Would you like to come along?"

I shook my head. "You two go, be all romantic. I'll just get in the way."

"No, I'd love to get the chance to know my beautiful Dove's sister," Hale said. He didn't look winded at all. "And the gardens will be quiet, easier to talk."

I shrugged. "Are you certain?" I would have thought he'd want to be alone with Dove.

He nodded. "Yes, please come along."

I rose. "As you wish." I linked arms with Dove. Hale enveloped Dove's other hand in his. And the three of us left the hall, stepping out into the night.

And that's when everything went to The Deepest, Blackest Pits.

IIT WAS A WARM SPRING NIGHT BUT COMPARED TO THE HEAT INSIDE, IT felt crisp and cool, refreshing. I took a long invigorating breath as we moved out from the dazzling, multi-colored light cast from the many windows of the manor.

Hale pulled Dove close, his arm going around her, which pulled her away from me. She leaned against him, head on his massive shoulder as they walked. I was happy she'd found someone.

There were pleasant little lanterns here and there among the sprawling gardens, which allowed passers to enjoy the streams, fountains, and greenery even at night. We walked in silence for some time before Hale spoke.

"I'm dying to know," Hale said with a certain eagerness in his voice. "How you survived a battle with a mistweaver and killed her!"

I was a bit surprised Dove had told him that. She hadn't known herself until the previous day. She must have mentioned it while they'd danced.

"It was harrowing indeed," I said, recalling the events, while not really wanting to recall them. Perhaps I'd just gloss over things. "She'd been sent to kill the king and queen of Vauphan, perhaps to enflame this war between our two nations. But she was also there to kill me."

It wasn't her first time trying either, but I didn't mention that.

"Another of my House was in danger, and there was information he needed to get back to those here in Elista. I had to give him time. In truth, I didn't know if I could fight the mistweaver. She came at me from all sides, using the mists themselves to attack me, but then I figured out how to sense her in the mists. I spun some of my webbing and when she appeared next — though I was half-dead — I managed to cover her mouth and nose with it. She couldn't breathe. Then, while she struggled, I used her own dagger against her." I shivered. Even saying that much was making me tremble and sweat in the night's breeze.

"That easy?" he said with a laugh.

"It wasn't easy at all," I replied. "I was on the brink of death. I only survived because one of my House has a spirit-gift of healing and was close by to help."

"Too bad," Hale said with a sigh.

I was a bit confused. "Too bad?"

He laughed. "Too bad she didn't kill you." He pulled Dove close, his arm having been around her, a meaty hand on her hip. "I was really looking forward to consoling my little Dove here when she got the news. Maybe *then* she'd finally spread her legs for me."

"Hale?" I could see Dove's confusion, trying to pull away from him. "What are you—" The rest was a muffled scream, which only I heard. We'd walked well away from the house, no one else was around as Hale pulled Dove close, one hand over her mouth, the other pinning her against him, her back to his chest. There was panic in her wide eyes as we both caught on too late to what was happening.

"Let her go, you—"

"You don't make the demands, girl," Hale growled. "I'm the one holding your sister's life by a thread. One wrong move or a shout from you and I'll snap her pretty little neck."

I froze, not quite believing what I was hearing, even as I felt something hard and powerful rise inside me.

Oh... I think that's your gift, whatever we're calling it, Auwei said. *But I don't know what to do. Though, why isn't Dove veering?*

I was thinking the same thing. As a bird, she'd have a moment of being much smaller, hopefully enough to fly away. "Dove, you need to—"

"Veer?" Hale sneered with a laugh. "She can't. And neither can you. That's my spirit-gift. I can even cut you off from your Lumani entirely."

That's not possible, is it? I asked Auwei.

Auwei?

Auwei?

But she wasn't there.

I tried veering, but couldn't.

Hale laughed. "I never thought my gift that useful, *until* I was assigned as an assassin. It makes things a lot easier." He grinned at me. "Now, keep quiet and follow me if you want your sister to live," he said, hurrying down the path toward the edges of the estate. We came to a wall with a small gate, meant for pedestrian traffic, not carriages. Perhaps it was a servants' entrance?

"Open that and step out," Hale said to me.

Everything was happening too fast. I needed to free Dove, but I didn't know what to do. I'd fought larger foes before. I could defeat Ant sometimes when sparring, but not every time. And this man was huge and still holding my sister. I couldn't do anything or he'd kill her.

Think! I demanded of my own mind.

I fumbled with the gate for a long moment, not really sure

what I was doing before realizing it needed a key and I didn't have one.

"Bash it open," Hale said.

I wanted to say: *you do it*! But instead, I just took all my anger and frustration and planted a nice hard side-kick on the latch area. With a screeching snap, it swung open.

I hoped someone had heard that.

Wait.

"Midnight?" I whispered.

No response.

"What was that?" Hale said. "Never mind. Move out into the lane, now!"

I did.

But I'd only taken half a step when I was grabbed from the side. A large man — though thankfully nowhere near as large as Hale — pulled me into a group of three brutes waiting in the alley. Huts and hovels crowded the lane, a shocking disparity from the riches we'd just left.

I struggled for a moment before Hale was through the gate. "Stop fighting or she dies!" he hissed.

Reluctantly, I did.

Blackened bloody bones in The Deepest Darkest Pits! What could I do?

"Midnight?" I whispered again. But again... nothing.

"No, it's not midnight," Hale hissed, confused. "It's not even— That doesn't matter. Listen up, as I'm only going to say this once. You've escaped death too many times already. You're going to submit and let these men kill you. If you do, you'll die quickly and I'll let Dove go. If you don't, you die painfully and I'll also take my time with my dear little Dove here. I'll do things you can't imagine before she finally dies screaming and alone. So, what will it be?"

Panic consumed me. I didn't want to die, and my spirit-gift

wasn't going to let that happen, but I couldn't let my sister die either!

"I submit!" I said, stilling my body. I wasn't submitting, but I needed a moment, needed Hale to think he'd won.

Now Think! I shouted at myself. *How do I get out of this?*

The brute holding my arm pulled me back, so my back was against the wall of the estate. Another brute grabbed my left arm and made sure I wasn't going anywhere as the third pulled out a long knife. My arms were pinned. I could kick that third man to keep him back, but if I did, bad things would happen to Dove. I looked around frantically, hoping Midnight would show up. Instead, what I saw, was not good. A carriage was parked a little way down this lane, dark in the night, but I could see at least two shadowy figures around it.

That's where Hale was heading, still holding Dove, who struggled in vain.

Hale looked away for just a moment as the man with the knife stabbed at my chest.

I reacted on instinct, kicking between my attacker's legs. He grunted and doubled over, but not before sliding the knife into my shoulder. I think he'd been aiming for my heart, but he'd shifted when I'd kicked him.

Pain exploded through my shoulder and, awkwardly, the knife had gone through the hand of one of the men holding me, pinning him to me. He screamed.

I screamed.

Hale turned, his muscles bunching as his grip shifted on Dove, getting a solid hold on her chin, so he could break her neck.

Then Hale screamed, blood flying as his hands came away from her. Dove fell to the ground limp with fear.

"I'm here now, fight!" I heard Midnight's voice.

Finally!

Pain became a distant thing, whether from my spirit-gift or just because of my fury.

I twisted, kneeing the man holding me — but not pinned to me — in the groin. He released me. With my now free hand, I plucked the knife out of my shoulder, then quickly slashed the throat of the man who had been pinned to me. He fell back, mouth open but no sound coming out as he died.

I grabbed a fistful of hair of the man kneeling in front of me, who'd had the knife initially. Pulling his head up, I sank the knife into his throat, not caring for the carnage I was wreaking. I saw only red, fury blinding me as I turned toward the third man, while Midnight fought Hale.

I would have thought she'd cut him up quickly, but it seemed he was quick for a man of his size and with his long arms he had significant reach over the much smaller Midnight. He had a dagger out and was easily keeping her short sword at bay as he backed toward the carriage. Even if she disappeared, he seemed able to track or predict her movements and though she was able to cut him, none were deep, nor hindering him much. He was truly a frightening foe. Luckily, he'd abandoned Dove, who still sat quivering in the laneway.

"Keep the last one alive!" Midnight called to me.

It took extreme willpower, but I stopped myself from gutting the third man. Instead, I kneed him in the face and he went slack. I tossed the knife away — over the wall into the gardens — and stalked toward Hale.

He saw me coming and bolted, jumping into the carriage as it took off down the alley.

"Let him go!" Midnight called. "Save your sister!"

No, he has to die, now!

No, Legs, stop. If Midnight couldn't take him, I don't think you can, not yet, not now. Tend to your sister, I don't doubt you'll have another chance with him.

Auwei was right. I ground my teeth, but my fury slowly subsided.

Also... *You're Back!*_Relief flooded me now that Auwei and I could communicate again. I had felt like I'd lost a part of me, a large part.

I'm guessing Hale's out of range to block us, she mused, sounding relieved herself.

Thank the Spirits for that.

Dove was not far away, stunned and weeping. I went and knelt next to her, holding her tightly. There was nothing I could say that would make this right. It was clear now that her beau had only been courting her to get to me, and he was very much not what he seemed.

This had all been my fault.

Spirits! When would this madness end?

CHAPTER 12

"WE NEED TO GET YOU AND YOUR SISTER OUT OF THE CITY," Midnight said, all business.

"What we need to do, is kill *that man*," I muttered, low and vicious, hugging Dove's head to my chest.

"No, we need him alive to lead us to whoever's behind all this." Midnight's tone held an edge of excitement. "Don't you see? They finally made a mistake. Our plan worked. Once we *capture* Hale, we can finally get some answers."

"I thought that's what he's for." I nodded my head to the one brute I'd left alive.

"No, he's to lead us to Hale. Then we question Hale."

"Then we kill Hale?"

She sighed, shaking her head. Motioning to my sister, she asked, "Can she walk?" Then as if a side note, she added, "You're bleeding."

Was I?

Yes, your shoulder, but the wound isn't as bad as it should be. I think your gift is already closing it up.

"I'll be fine. I'm a survivor." I rose, helping Dove up, but she was still a mess and not ready to stand. I scooped her into my arms. It was only once I was carrying her, with Midnight looking at me with a hint of surprise, that I realized, I shouldn't have had the strength to do this — especially wounded — and yet I hardly noticed her weight.

I thought we'd established that you were stronger with your spirit-gift. That's how you were able to lower the prince down the cliffs, remember?

Right! But that time I'd been struggling: wounded and exhausted. This... this felt easy.

"Where are we going?" I asked.

Midnight looked around. "I doubt we'll find a carriage in this part of town at this hour. Wait here, and keep an eye on him." She indicated the unconscious brute. Then she veered into a bat and flitted away into the night.

"I guess I can put you down," I said to Dove, though she didn't respond, still probably in shock. I couldn't blame her. Having the man you love — who you thought loved you — betray you in such a horrible way... I couldn't imagine what that must feel like. And it was all because of me. I wouldn't be surprised if, once she had recovered from all of this, she hated me.

I set her down, leaning her against the wall, and stood next to her, keeping an eye out for trouble.

Luckily, I didn't have to wait long before I heard the creaking axles and clopping hooves of a carriage approaching.

My *Hero* gift surged as I prepared for trouble, but it was Midnight in the driver's seat as the carriage drew close. She reined in the two-horse team and hopped down easily. "Get her inside," she said, heading for the brute.

"Where'd you get the carriage from?" I asked.

"Don't ask."

We loaded my sister and the brute into the carriage and were off.

Midnight took us out of the city, into the countryside. I didn't know how long we traveled, but the stars had not shifted much in the sky by the time we turned off the road onto a long laneway. We stopped in front of a low farmhouse and Midnight hopped down from the driver's seat.

"Stay inside. I need to confer with the locals."

She knocked on the door of the farmhouse. A woman answered, though I didn't get a good look at her, then Midnight returned. "Take your sister inside, we're preparing a bed for her. Once she's settled, meet me in the barn." She indicated a second large building. I picked up Dove and went inside, as Midnight dragged the brute toward the barn.

I was greeted at the door by a woman in her middle years with grey in her brown hair and a careworn look in her eyes. She led me to a small room with a simple bed and a chest of drawers, nothing else. I made sure Dove was resting, she'd passed out on the trip here, then went back out to the hallway with the woman.

"Thank you," I said softly. "For giving up your house so easily to us strangers."

She gave a little laugh. "You and I haven't met before, but Midnight is no stranger. I am Ana, Maverick's older sister."

I gaped. Maverick... well of course he could have family like anyone else. And now that I knew, I could see it. The same bronzed complexion and something similar around the eyes and nose. Even the hair, a bit wiry and unkempt. And she was built strong. I'd assumed that was from farm work, and it probably was, but she had a similar sturdiness to Maverick.

"What's your name?" Ana asked. "I'm always delighted to meet members of Maverick's House."

"Legs."

She grinned at that. Then her gaze was drawn to my shoulder. "I have some bandages, let me look at that." I sat at her kitchen table as she retrieved some cloth strips, then she tore away the shoulder and arm of my dress — it was ruined anyway — and bandaged up my shoulder. "It doesn't look that bad," she said. "You'll be able to use that arm again in a couple weeks."

Probably a couple days, knowing my accelerated healing, but I just nodded and thanked her. Then I made my way out to the barn.

Midnight had the brute trussed up, hands bound over his head, hanging on what looked like the stub of a branch protruding from one of the wooden support beams. A lantern was lit and she was just dousing him with a bucket of water as I arrived.

The man sputtered to life, squirming and opening his eyes. He quickly assessed the situation and turned hard. "I ain't tellin' you nothin'," he sneered. "You migh' as well kill me, 'cause those I work for surely will kill me if I tell you anythin'."

I could believe that.

I glanced at Midnight, hoping she'd have more experience with things like this. I surely didn't. She seemed to consider things for a long moment before saying: "What if I could guarantee that you'd live if you tell us just one little thing?"

He quirked a brow in question. "How's that?"

She smiled. "All we want to know is where to find Lord Hale. There are any number of common places he could be, but I'm willing to bet he went to ground, and that you know where that is." I saw him about to answer, but she spoke over him quickly. "And when we find him, we're going to make sure he talks." Her grin was a frightening and feral thing. "And then, no one will be looking for you. They'll be looking for him."

That sounded mostly logical to me.

The man considered for a long moment. "And you'd let me go?"

"Once we have Hale's location, yes." She raised a finger. "But... if you lie to us. I will track you to the ends of your days and make sure your death is slow and painful." And the way she said it, with little emotion and a cold smile, terrified me.

The man hung there, brooding for a long moment. Finally, he spoke: "There's a tavern called the Slippery Eel, down by the river. There're tunnels under there that take you to the Owl House estate, a whole warren of tunnels, easy to get lost, and down there are a few hidey-holes, places to lay low. That's where he'll be, if he hasn't already run home to..." The man seemed to realize he was about to say something he shouldn't and stopped himself. "He'll be down there, somewhere."

Midnight nodded. "Sounds reasonable. She made a movement with her hand and the thing I'd thought was a branch seemed to shrink back into the wooden beam. The brute fell, collapsing to his knees.

What was that? I asked Auwei. *She seemed to manipulate the wood of that beam?*

Fey Magic.

Oh... Right! Maverick had said something about Midnight being half-Fey.

But did that mean...? Prince Alvere looked so much like Midnight, the same dark hair and jewel toned eyes. *Is Alvere half-Fey too?*

It's possible. Those attributes are not always distinctly Fey, but it does suggest a Fey heritage.

Oh...

I returned to myself with a blink. If we were going to let this man go, I wanted to make sure he had something to remember me by. I went over to him and slapped him as hard as I could across the face. My *Hero* gift had faded, so I didn't break his neck, but his head turned and I left an angry red mark. "That's for trying to kill me."

The man shook it off and held out his hands and the bindings around them. I turned from him. "You do it," I said to Midnight. "If you put a knife in my hands, I can't say I won't kill him."

I walked out of the barn into the night. It had grown cooler, or perhaps I'd grown warmer, heated by my own anger at the night's events.

I heard footfalls scampering away out the other side of the barn, then Midnight appeared beside me. I'd known she was coming, using my spider-sense, even if I hadn't heard her footfalls. She was very quiet.

"What now?" I asked. "Searching a warren of tunnels sounds like an easy way to get trapped and killed."

"I'm glad you agree," she said. "For now, we wait. Tomorrow some help should arrive and we can make a plan."

"Help?" I knew Maverick, Amber, and Sparrow were in the city, though I didn't really know what they were doing.

She nodded and said, "Get some sleep, if you can." Then she vanished from beside me.

But... I had so many questions!

Midnight was certainly mysterious... and infuriating.

I went back inside and found Ana at her kitchen table, having made some tea. She offered a cup and I took it. She said nothing, but I needed to talk, so I asked: "How did you get involved in all this?" Though I felt I should clarify: "Other than being Maverick's sister?"

She smiled, looking into her tea, which she held in both hands, letting the steam warm her face. "We were always close, my brother and I, but very different. I had no desire to be Chosen, but it was all he wanted. After he was Chosen, he returned here. He didn't test for Noble right away. He helped out on the farm and discovered what he could do, but even before a year was up, I could tell he was growing restless. So, I told him to go and test; to be more. He grudgingly went and came back elated that he'd been selected. Even then, he returned as often as he could to help out here." She took a sip of her tea and sighed. "Even once he was master of the House, he'd make trips and introduce me to other members. Then he started making it a habit. After he'd selected new members, he'd bring them here, introduce us and make some silly threat that if they misbehaved, he'd send them to help on the farm." She laughed. Then she looked up at me. "He didn't do that with you. Odd."

I thought back and nodded. "He had business in the city. He stayed behind, and it was Lady Crane who took us to Hedgewild."

"Ah, that would explain it. She never liked me much. I'm too raw and blunt for her sensibilities. Anyway, my house has become a bit of a safe haven for his members. Midnight has been in a lot over the past few months. She can't reveal herself in the capital, and when she just needed someone to talk to, she'd come here."

That made sense. "Is it just you?"

She shook her head. "No, my husband Kal, and our newborn, Jacob, are sleeping. We have a four-year-old as well. I moved her in with her father and brother before we brought your sister in."

"I'm sorry to put you out like this."

"No trouble at all." Another sip of tea. "Midnight didn't say what happened, but with you being wounded and your sister looking all pale and weak, I assume it wasn't good. Don't feel compelled to tell me. I don't really want to know what trouble my brother is getting himself into." She grimaced. "And dragging young women like you into."

"I volunteered," I said with a tired smile. "I was bait and I got bitten, it was to be expected. I just wasn't expecting my sister to get so caught up in things."

Ana's gaze filled with concern and a curious fear when she looked at me next. "Is it bad... in the city? Midnight hasn't told me much, but I can figure out a thing or two. Something's happening amongst the Nobles, isn't it?"

I nodded. "Yeah, something is, and it's very bad." I tried to smile, but it was false. "And we're going to stop it."

She looked at me, tight-lipped for a long moment. "But your House is small and there are hundreds of Nobles...?"

"They aren't all against us." Though even as I said those words, I wondered. We were going after a member of the Royal House, the son of an upstanding Nobleman. If that got out... sentiment could very easily turn against us.

Whatever we were going to do next... we'd better be very careful doing it.

CHAPTER 13

I SLEPT ON THE SMALL BED WITH DOVE. WHEN SHE WOKE screaming, I comforted her and made sure she settled again. Neither of us slept well. When daylight came, I was bleary eyed and tired, but Dove still slept. I got up and went out for some fresh air. A thick fog hung heavy over the land, washing me with mist. It was refreshing, and I tried to find some sense of peace in this blanket of vapor.

"Sparrow came in the night."

I jumped at Midnight's voice next to me. I had been too tired and not using my spider-senses.

She chuckled softly. "Sorry."

What had she just said, before that?

Sparrow came last night. Auwei said.

Right, thanks.

"Sparrow?" I asked.

She nodded. "She's out there, scouting, keeping an eye out for the others. The master and Amber will be here around lunch, and hopefully... so will the new arrivals."

I raised a brow.

She smiled. "Jack, Silence, and Foggy are on their way to the capital, in disguise. The plan was for them to stop in here first. Once everyone's here, we'll discuss next steps." She half turned to indicate the nearby carriage. "I returned to the city last night and gathered a few things from your sister's rooms. I didn't know what she might want, but I was sure she wouldn't want to go back. I took what I could, including some of your things. It's all in the trunk on the back of the carriage."

"Thanks," I said, weary.

She put a reassuring hand on my shoulder and smiled. "We'll get this all sorted out, don't worry."

But I was so good at worrying.

"I'm going to keep an eye out," she said and then flew away as a bat.

Had she even slept?

She didn't look tired at all.

Probably a Fey thing. So is the fact that she's older than Maverick but looks your age.

Right. Fey.

I went to the carriage and lifted the trunk. It was heavy, but I lugged it inside. I tried to be quiet as I set it down in Dove's room, then rooted through it to find a simple blouse and skirt. I checked my bandage. The wound was still bleeding, but not in a stabbed-with-a-large-knife sort of way, more of an exceptionally-deep-scratch way. It also hurt like The Black Pits now that my *Hero* gift had worn off. I redid the bandages and changed, taking the bottom of the blouse and tying it up above my belly-button. I wanted to be prepared, just in case.

I went outside again as the sound of hooves drew closer. The fog was clearing, no longer the heavy mists around us, but still low overhead, billowing and ominous.

Maverick and Amber arrived on horseback. A small bird accompanying them quickly became Sparrow.

The small woman ran to me, throwing her arms around me in a tight embrace. "I'm so glad you're well," she said, voice muffled with her face in my shoulder; luckily not my injured one. She pulled back enough to be clear when she spoke next. "When Midnight said you'd been attacked, I was so worried." Her deep, forest-green eyes were filled with concern.

I found myself reaching up to smooth her dark hair as I held her close.

"She's harder to kill than that. A tough one is our Legs," Maverick said swinging down off his horse and grabbing the reins as he came to us. He winked at me, though he too looked concerned. So far, he was the only one who knew about the specifics of my spirit-gift.

I was a bit surprised in the next moment when Sparrow put her arms around my neck and pulled herself up for a kiss, even if a quick and chaste one.

"Do I get a kiss too?" Amber teased as she sauntered by. As always, she looked amazing, even after a ride out from the city.

"I missed you," Sparrow whispered once Amber was gone.

We'd only been apart for two days.

"I missed you too." I kissed her again, this time, lingering a little before leading her inside. "My sister's here, would you like to meet her?" I asked. Though, then I felt compelled to add, "Just... she went through a lot last night and she may be a bit fragile, so go easy on her."

Sparrow nodded, smiling.

I left her in the kitchen and returned to Dove's room. She was awake, sitting in bed, looking a bit stunned. When I closed the door, she flinched a little.

"Did... did that really happen?" she asked in a quavering voice. Then, as if only just noticing where she was: "Where are we?"

I sat next to her, arm around her to provide comfort. "I'm so sorry," I said with a sigh. "It did happen. And we're safe now at a farm outside the city. I promise I'll get you safely away from here and pay that horrible man back for what he did."

She blinked, confused. "Get me away? But my House... my home is here. I can't..." She trailed off as it sank in. Hale was the son of Lord Horn, who was the second in command of Pegasus House, *her* House. It was possible the older man had known of these machinations the whole time. Even if he didn't, that spoke to how unknowing and ineffectual the other high Nobles were. "Oh, Spirits," she breathed. Then she stood suddenly. "I have things I need to get... I can't just... How...?" she moved toward the door, but then flinched back as if it would attack her... no, not the door, but everything beyond it.

"My friend has already retrieved some of your things," I said. "They're in that trunk. If there is anything else dear to you, let me know and we'll make another trip to get it. But you're staying here."

"Yes, I..." She turned back to me, a lost and desperate look in her eyes. I'd never seen her this disoriented and fragile. "I'll stay." She looked directly at me then. "You'll take care of me, won't you Sara?" It was a testament to her unsteady state that she used my old name.

"I will, Ella. Now come and sit, tell me what you need." She moved listlessly and sat with me on the edge of the bed, listing off a few items she felt she couldn't live without. Yet there was little energy, little life left in her voice.

I searched through the chest and found most of what she'd listed. Then I laid her down to rest again. I brought her some food and helped her eat, and finally she settled down after that.

I left the room feeling drained. It was horrible to see her like this, she was usually so bright and full of life. I swore I'd personally tear out Hale's heart for what he'd done to her.

Midnight took Dove's short list of items to retrieve and was off as a bat once more.

I walked out into the yard. The fog was gone, but heavy clouds hung low, and a light rain had started. I didn't really notice. I was too distracted. I just needed to be out in the fresh air. My clothes soaked through quickly, but still, I just stood there.

"You'll catch a chill, you should come in," Sparrow said tugging on my arm.

I turned to her, then turned back as a wagon wheeled its way off the road onto the farm lane. From this distance it looked like a farmer and his daughter on the wagon. I was instantly on guard until they drew closer and I recognized Jack. For a long moment I wondered if the insatiable flirt had picked up some young woman in his travel here, but then... there was something familiar in that mousy brown hair and how the woman moved as she hopped off the wagon... then came running to me.

Silence?

He threw his arms around me and kissed me fully on the lips, and I was more than just a little confused by this, mostly because... he looked really good as a woman and I was just a little aroused at his disguise.

Foggy came tumbling out of the back of the cart and Jack got down slowly, ambling over to us.

"Do we all get a kiss?" he asked with a wink. Between him and Amber... I was always going to be a little off kilter, I think.

"I like the rain!" Foggy said capering around.

"Then feel free to stay out here, I'm going inside to warm up and dry off." Jack moved passed us.

Silence, still holding me tightly, whispered, "I can't wait for you to warm me up."

I smiled at him, but noticed Sparrow's heavy sigh from the corner of my eye. I reached out to her, pulling her into the embrace with us. "Let's all go in and warm up together." And suddenly the cloud hanging over me had lifted, just a little.

Once everyone was assembled and dried off — and Midnight

had returned, thankfully able to get the few things Dove had wanted — we all gathered around the not-large-enough table in Ana's kitchen to discuss our next moves.

Maverick spoke, steely and somber, "Things have happened, and I fear our enemies are moving too fast for us to stop." He sighed. "But we'll do what we can." Looking at Midnight, he nodded. "Midnight will remain here with Foggy, Silence, and Sparrow. They are to watch and learn. We finally have a lead, and—"

"I'm staying too," I said, soft but firm. "I have a certain lord to kill."

Maverick's heavy gaze swung to me. "No, Legs, you don't." And I felt his heat rise, warming the room before it dropped off suddenly and we were all left chilled. "I know you want revenge for your sister, but that's not going to come quickly. First, we need to wait and see who Hale leads us to. If we give him time—"

"If we give them time, they'll ruin this nation and kill even more people!" I blurted and instantly flinched back at the surge of annoyed fire in Maverick's eyes. His jaw twitched and bunched, as he stared me down. "Sorry," I mumbled. "Go on."

He nodded. "I don't like this either, just so we're clear. I have a suspicion Hale might be behind other deaths, even the Lumani deaths, and for that he'll need to pay, but for now we need more information." And only then did I realize that the fire in his eyes, the tense jaw, hadn't been for me. It had been for the necessity of this mission. He wanted Hale dead too. That was something at least.

"Legs, you'll be with me, Amber, and Jack. You've played bait long enough, and we have a lead, so we don't need you here anymore. I know you don't like it, but I think you'll like where we're heading."

He drew in a breath, and I could see he was half-expecting to be interrupted, but I remained quiet, listening. "We'll take your sister to Hedgewild and make sure she's safe, then... the next time the prince and Fin check in... the four of us are heading to the Vauphan war front." He blew out a breath. "It's a longshot, but we need to see if we can meet with the Elistan commanders and talk some sense into them. Stop this war before it starts. And if we can't... then we fight." He gave me a cold grin. "You can work out some of your aggressions and test your battle-readiness."

I felt a little cold at that. "Fighting our own people?"

He nodded. "That gives us all the more incentive to stop it before it comes to that. And make sure as few as possible are killed on either side if it does come to war. Trust me, Legs, we have the harder job here."

I believed him.

"Any questions?" Maverick asked.

"What do we do if we find the leader of these rogue Nobles?" Silence asked softly. "What if it is the queen herself?"

Maverick sighed. "Midnight has my orders around that." He shook his head. "I hope this conspiracy doesn't go that far up." He grimaced. "*Whoever* is involved, we can't just go after them. We'd need the support of other Nobles, other Houses or we'd seem like the betrayers, the criminals in all this. So, part of your mission is also to find out who's *not* involved so we can drum up some support."

Silence nodded.

There were no more questions after that.

"We head out tomorrow morning," Maverick said to me, Jack, and Amber. Then he rose and stepped out into the rain.

Both Sparrow and Silence were looking at me expectantly. I'd be leaving them tomorrow. That meant we had most of a day to kill, and I had a lot of pent-up energy to spend.

CHAPTER 14

MY heart thundered as Silence and Sparrow followed me out to the barn. The rain had stopped, but the clouds were still low and heavy, making the day gloomy and grey.

I'd asked the two of them out, away from the others, to clear the air and get things straight between us. And getting things straight would be great... if I actually knew what that looked like. My emotions were a tumbling mess of confused desire and friendship.

I was so distracted by my thoughts, I didn't even look for a ladder once inside the barn, I just jumped up to the hay loft and threw down the blanket I'd brought. Then I wondered why it was taking so long for the others to get up here.

Sparrow flew. Silence climbed, actually using the ladder.

I sat on the blanket, the soft hay a cushion beneath me. The others did the same, looking from each other back to me.

"Sooo...?" Silence said, clearly uncertain why we were all here.

Where to start?

Start with what you know. Tell them how you feel, even if it's confused.

I nodded.

"I love you both," I said, taking a moment to look into each of their eyes... soft brown and deep green. "You are dear friends to me and... more. Though I don't know how to quantify that more, or if I need to." I paused for a breath.

How do I tell them about Alvere?

Again, just tell them how you feel, Auwei advised. *They'll understand or they won't, but if you're going to be honest with them, you need to tell them. Then let them be however they're going to be: upset, or angry or accepting or whatever.*

You're so Wise.

I know.

"I am not ready to make a choice," I said softly, looking deeply at each of them. "And, I'll be honest, I hope I don't have to make a choice. I love you both... as well as... others."

"Others?" Sparrow breathed. Then, she seemed to make a connection and nodded. "The prince?"

I nodded in return. "Yes."

"The prince?" Silence said. But he had a quick mind. He must have been told the prince of Vauphan had been visiting, and our nation had no prince so... "The prince of Vauphan? You... love him too? Have you been with him?" There was a shocked — and slightly pained — curiosity in the man's soft voice.

"No... well, not like I've been with both of you. We kissed once, but I couldn't go any further in good conscience without speaking to both of you first." It had been a little more than just one kiss, but most of that "more" had been unrestrained feelings and not true actions.

Silence nodded to that, still seeming a bit distant. Then his brow furrowed and he looked at Sparrow. "You two have...?"

She nodded with a shy smile. When Sparrow spoke, her voice was a flighty thing, like her avatar form. "I'd always been curious about... women, and I love Legs dearly and..." She shrugged. "Now

I know how I feel." She looked away from Silence with the whispered addition of: "I still don't know how I feel about men."

"A lot of men can be jerks," Silence said with a grimace.

Sparrow giggled at that.

At first, I was a bit taken aback by the vehemence of Silence's comment, but then I recalled he'd been a thief and lived on the streets for most of his life. I guessed he'd learned a lot of hard lessons.

His voice softened when he said, "But some can be... loving and kind."

I smiled to see the two of them getting along. But then they both looked back to me expectantly. I didn't know what to say, or what they wanted, but finally Sparrow said, "You want to be with both of us... and the prince?"

"I do." That was the truth. I grimaced. "And *maybe* more? I don't know yet. I wouldn't want to be with anyone who doesn't love me like you two do. But if another did...?" I shrugged.

"But you love me? You want to be with me?" Silence asked directly.

"Yes," I said and reached over to take his hand. "I love you dearly, Silence and I will never give you up. You were my first, and if you say you don't want me to be with anyone else—" I looked at Sparrow and she nodded, a bit sorrowful, "—I'd accept that."

"Oh," Silence said and took a moment to consider this. Then he smiled faintly and whispered, "You love me." Then he looked at Sparrow. "And you love others." Then that soft, brown-eyed gaze came to me. "You have... too much love to give. You want to share it with everyone who loves you."

That was an interesting way of putting it. "Yes, I supposed that's it."

"And that includes... the prince of Vauphan?" His voice was just a bit hard.

"Yes, Silence. I... I know his countrymen did not... treat you well." That was a massive understatement. "But the prince is a good man. I hope, when you meet him, you'll see that."

Silence was quiet for a long moment before asking, "And what of us? What if we wanted to be with others, who love us?"

I smiled. "I'd be happy for you." Though I furrowed my brow in thought as I considered this fully. If they were getting all steamy with someone else, would I be well with that?

I think I would be, as long as they were just as steamy with me. Slowly, I smiled. "Yes, I think as long as we are all open with each other and our other lovers and everyone agrees, then... that should work, shouldn't it?"

"I'm not sure I wish to be with others," Sparrow confided. She seemed to think for a moment. "But I would be well with you being with others, as long as they are good to you."

"And as long as I return to you?" I asked. She smiled and nodded. "*And* return to you?" I asked Silence." He smiled.

Then Sparrow surprised me by turning to Silence. "I... would you... I am curious about being with a man, and I think... I would want someone like you; someone who will be gentle."

Silence seemed stunned. He looked at me, and I smiled.

I shrugged. "You're both dear to me. You have my blessing."

He blinked, perhaps surprised, then nodded. Turning back to Sparrow, he smiled. "You too are a dear friend. I can do this for you."

I began to rise. "I'll leave you two in peace, and—"

"No, stay, please," Sparrow whispered, reaching out a hand, even though she was too far away to touch me. "Stay." She looked to Silence, questioning.

He blushed deeply. "Are you... saying... you want me... with both...?" He swallowed hard, eyes going a bit wide.

Spirits of the Mists! He was adorable.

"I'll stay if that's what you both want," I said, a little uncertain about this myself.

They both nodded vigorously.

Ohhhh Boyyyyy.

I seek all manner of new experiences, and this would be new for me, Auwei said a bit excitedly. *I've never been with two others at the same time.*

We were all about to find out what that was like.

It was awkward, at first. Trembling, thick-fumbling fingers worked to undress ourselves and each other.

Sparrow gasped when she saw Silence's more-than-ready erection, swollen and red, twitching with barely restrained excitement. His entire body was flushed a beet-red as he looked between us, everyone exposed and uncertain.

I took control, the other two being a bit less sure of themselves. Also, with the level of arousal I was certain Silence must be feeling I didn't know if he'd be as soft and gentle as Sparrow wanted. So I went to him, laying him back on the blanket.

"Kiss him," I said to Sparrow and she leaned down over him, their hands reached and caressed as they drew close, lips touching. I took Silence's erection in my hand and knelt low, bringing it to my lips.

I heard his drawn-out gasp as he realized what I was doing. The trouble was, I didn't really know what I was doing, only that I'd heard men liked it. I used lips and tongue, bobbing slowly, taking him into my mouth as my hand slowly stroked his shaft.

And Silence did indeed like it. I didn't know if it was the use of my mouth, or this whole experience of being with two women, but his excitement quickly boiled over.

"Legs, yes!" he gasped again. "Sparrow I… oh!" and with that I felt his release hot in my mouth. I maintained my hold on him until he was finished, shuddering and breathing heavily.

Yet I didn't stop. I think he was surprised by that. Certainly, he was quickly aroused again, hardening as I encouraged him back to his full readiness.

Then I left off with him, encouraging them to shift, with Sparrow on her back, and Silence on his side, as they continued to kiss and caress.

It only seemed fair, after giving Silence the pleasure of my lips, to do the same with Sparrow. I kissed her slender thighs, moving inward to her folds. I wanted to make sure she was well aroused so her time with Silence was pleasurable.

I was rewarded, hearing her gasp amidst the other moans and breaths. With lips and tongue and fingers, I helped her grow wet and ready. When she finally gasped, "Yes, now..." I moved away.

Silence moved over her, entering her slowly, gently, and she responded with eyes going wide, chest heaving gulps of air as he pushed himself fully inside her. They moved together for some time until their pace began to quicken. Silence rose, kneeling, pulling Sparrow's hips back as he moved within her.

I laid next to Sparrow, reaching down to play my fingers over the aroused bud of her clit. I slid my other hand under her neck and drew her close, lips to mine.

She rewarded me with grasping, firm hands upon my breasts, kneading them with the urgency of a lover on the verge of release as she gasped into my mouth. Her body tensed, back arching, as she drew back from me to whisper, "Silence, yes, yes!"

His thrusts grew quicker.

I kept a steady caress on Sparrow's clit, watching her writhe and convulse through what seemed like an incredibly intense orgasm. Tremors like waves undulated up and down her body, as her eyes rolled up, head tilting back, mouth agape.

I leaned down to kiss her breasts, flicking an aroused nipple with my tongue. She cried out... far louder than I was used to her being. One of her hands clamped down on the back of my head as she called out again and again before finally going limp, body still trembling.

"Spirits and Sprites!" she gasped when she'd regained her breath. "That was... I never imagined..."

Silence beamed, but I caught how he was still rocking slightly inside her, still a bit tense. He'd not released.

I straddled Sparrow, pressing myself to her and our lips met in playful kisses. With my legs open, around Sparrow, I was presenting Silence with a good view of my sex. He got the hint. I felt his seeking fingers, then the press and pressure of his erection entering me. I simmered with arousal, more than ready after watching these two, especially seeing Sparrow reach such incredible heights of bliss.

I left Sparrow's lips long enough to glance back at Silence and say, "Hard."

I felt his hands on my hips, steadying me as he obliged, thrusting with abandon. He'd been so slow and gentle and caring with Sparrow. He deserved to let loose, and so did I.

Shaken by Silence's relentless thrusts, I could no longer kiss Sparrow without our faces jarring together. But she smiled, levering me up a little, supporting my weight on her hands as she grasped my breasts. That was until she pulled herself up and brought her lips to a nipple. The hand that had been upon that breast sought down between my legs as I'd done with her.

That was it for me. The combined pleasure of Silence's hard thrusts, mixed with Sparrow's grasping lips upon my breasts and her delicate caress of my clit, made me tense and cry out with my own hard orgasm. I felt myself clamp down on Silence's swollen shaft, needing him to release. And with a few more hard lunges I felt his explosion within me and heard his own cries of pleasure.

After that, for some time, we simply lay on the blanket, Silence behind me Sparrow in front, as we all came down from our respective highs.

"What did you think?" I asked Sparrow.

She blushed deeply, which only made her brown skin more

beautiful. "I... don't think I would have enjoyed it as much if you hadn't been here." Then softer, "It was perfect. Thank you." And finally, a little louder, "Thank you, Silence."

He laughed, then said, "It was literally my pleasure." Then, the two of them levered themselves up to kiss over me.

I couldn't help but join in, kissing their cheeks and then their lips, back and forth as we played once again. Something told me, we would be here for a while that afternoon.

CHAPTER 15

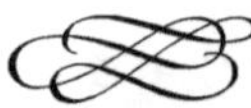

I left Silence and Sparrow the next morning amidst many mutual tears. The rains had stopped, and it promised to be a clear, sunny day. Yet a brisk wind from the north brought a chill, and I wrapped a cloak tight about myself as we left.

Sometime the previous day, Midnight had returned her stolen carriage and acquired a second wagon. It seemed best to travel incognito, so the five of us would become a family of merchants. Maverick and Amber up front, Jack, Dove and me with our legs dangling off the back.

The wagon had several trunks and chests on it, which could easily have been our "precious cargo" but was nothing more than our belongings.

I held Dove close. She'd recovered a bit more, glad to have the few things she'd truly treasured from her old residence, but I think everything that had happened still weighed on her.

I was a hot and cold confusion of emotions. There was sorrow for my sister, and sadness at leaving my dear friends, while I was also warmed by the memory of our precious time together. Then, there was my simmering rage for Lord Hale. I vowed revenge upon him, even if that wouldn't happen any time soon.

"You're shivering. Are you cold?" Dove asked, concerned.

I was cold, but I wasn't shivering because of that. I trembled in rage, recalling that devil of a man.

"No, I'm well." I hugged her closer and she leaned her head on my shoulder.

Jack shifted, leaning against the side of the wagon, one leg up, one leg over the back, looking at us. His tone was serious when he said, "Tonight, we're sparring. You're going to remind me how good you are with a sword before we head to a war zone."

"War zone?" Dove said, confused and frightened.

I glared at Jack and hushed her. "I'll tell you everything later, rest for now."

Luckily, she did. It was a testament to all she'd been through how easily she settled down. But Jack wasn't wrong. I'd fought the mistweaver one on one, but never been in a large-scale battle. I'd never been amidst the chaos of war. I nodded to him, and he nodded back. I'd need to be well prepared for what was to come.

That evening, when Jack and I began to spar, I was surprised that Dove wished to practice as well. Luckily, one of the trunks with us was a chest full of weapons. Jack selected twin dueling blades, I took a rapier and parrying dagger, and Dove took a longsword, one with a long grip, enough for two hands. We thought we'd be doing two on one against Jack, until Maverick stepped in as well. He joined with his thick-bladed arming sword and a large shield. He proposed a different "game." Each of us would attack one person while defending from another. One tap from the flat of the blade and you were out. I had Maverick attacking me while I attacked Jack. Dove attacked Maverick while defending against Jack. I didn't know which of us had it worse.

I quickly realized my little parrying dagger wouldn't be much use against that heavy arming sword Maverick wielded. So... I threw it at him, offhand and awkward. He blocked with his shield, though that left Dove an opening. She, however, was preoccupied simply defending against the onslaught of two smaller but no-less-deadly swords from Jack.

So... I changed the rules.

The best defense is a good offence, right?

Exactly, Auwei agreed.

So, I left off trying to attack Jack and attacked Maverick. "Smart girl," he said with a grin as he caught on.

I was quicker than Maverick, but not by much; his years of experience made him frighteningly quick with that massive blade of his. And with Dove not attacking — doing everything she could to defend against Jack — he could also defend with his shield. I was surprised when I landed a tap on his calf. Though even more surprised to feel a tap on my back. I spun to see Jack grinning and Dove grimacing and shaking her head.

"You left yourself open," Jack said. "You didn't think I'd attack, even though that's what you were doing yourself." He glanced at Dove. "Your sister is good, but once I didn't have to worry about you attacking, I quickly overwhelmed her with two blades, then turned my attention to you."

I sighed. I'd won and lost.

"Worse," Maverick added in. "Your strike to me would most likely have been debilitating, but not fatal. But Jack's strike to you would have been fatal. You sacrificed your life for a minor wound upon a foe."

I nodded, seeing it all now. "I need two weapons," I said looking at my empty left hand. "Or a shield. That parrying dagger is good against some weapons, but against anything heavy, it's useless."

"Agreed," Jack said. "I use it fighting pirates with cutlasses and sabers, but against a hardened warrior with an arming sword or halberd..." He shook his head. "He looked at his twin rapiers. "Even with these, I need to get out of the way often enough. I trust to the longer reach I have with these when fighting someone with a heavier weapon, unless it's a polearm or claymore."

"Then what would you do?"

Jack grinned. "Leave fighting them to Ant or Maverick and move on to someone else."

Maverick glared at him, clearing his throat. A clear indication that that hadn't been the right answer.

"I'd get in close," Jack said, amending his answer, "where their larger two-handed weapon isn't as useful."

Maverick nodded to that.

I had practiced mostly with the rapier, a little longsword and some staff work with Ant. I was curious. "What weapon am I the best with, when I spar with you?" I asked Jack.

He tilted his head and smiled. "I'm glad you finally asked that."

Yeah, I couldn't believe it had taken me that long to ask either. *What do you think I'm best with?* I asked Auwei.

"The staff," Jack said after a moment of thought.

The staff, Auwei confirmed.

And for a moment I had the two of them talking at me in unison:

"You're also exceptionally strong with your hand-fighting skills, your kicks being your strongest attack."

I think perhaps you are just a little afraid of bladed weapons.

"The staff can be used to augment those attacks, used to propel a kick farther, stronger."

Not that you'd hurt yourself, but the idea of actually cutting open another person... The staff is a devastating weapon, but less... overtly violent.

"You'd also have greater reach than most of the other weapons you've tried and it's good for defense."

It also seems more natural in your hands, it flows with you, where you're just a bit... hesitant and awkward still with a sword.

I stood there hearing both of them and trying to parse the words. Eventually I nodded. "So... a staff then?"

Jack shrugged. "Trouble is, you're not as strong as Ant. In an all-out battle it would be a good weapon for you, but you'd have trouble killing a foe with it outright and leaving live foes behind you is never a good idea."

"Not a staff then? What else would work?" I looked at Dove. She'd seem fairly natural with a longsword in her hands, but she also had three extra years of training on me. "Auwei says she thinks I'm hesitant to kill. That I'm more tentative with bladed weapons because they can cut and kill easier." I shrugged feeling a little disheartened. "Perhaps I shouldn't be going to war after all."

Dove came over to give me a hug. "I don't much like the idea of blades and killing either," she whispered, then she sighed heavily. "For Hale, I'd make an exception, but otherwise, I'm used to cutting up practice dummies and that's not the same thing." A shudder rippled through her. "I don't know how I'd do in a true battle."

She wouldn't have to find out. We'd be leaving her at Hedgewild. Which led to my next thought. "Perhaps you should just leave us both at Hedgewild," I said to the others.

"If that's what you want," Maverick said. He had a look in his eyes though, and I thought I could read it well enough. *I know you'll make a great warrior, if you apply yourself.*

I sighed, releasing Dove and turning to Amber, who was sitting nearby preparing the evening meal. "What weapons do you use?"

"Good-looks and guile," she said without hesitation.

"Those won't help you much in a war," I quipped.

She nodded. "True. So, I bring an assortment. My preferred weapons are dual short swords. They don't have the reach of longer blades, but they're sturdy and can take a hit from anything. It means I have to get in close, and that gets bloody and nasty." She gave a fierce grin. "But that's the way I like it." She shrugged. "I also carry some throwing knives, which can be used up close in a pinch as well. I've been known to use a spear also, if I think I want something with reach." She grimaced. "Trouble with a spear is, sometimes if you're really aggressive in running someone through, you can't get the weapon back. You have to give it up and move on to other weapons."

"She's so beautiful and yet so... nasty," Dove whispered.

I was very aware of that.

"Maybe I could try using a staff or two short swords?" I said with a shrug.

Maverick nodded. "Sure, we'll keep training you and see what you're comfortable with."

So, that evening, after we ate, Dove and I got a lesson in fighting with dual short swords from Amber and the two men. I think I took to it a bit more naturally, but with Dove's extra training she picked it up quickly as well.

Then lanterns were lit and hung off the wagon as the others bedded down, but Maverick and I stayed up to train with the staff. I wanted to see how the staff fared against his heavy arming sword. In the end, it was as I expected. I defended well but had trouble truly stopping him. I managed to swipe his legs out from under him at one point, but I had nothing to follow up with. He'd covered his head and upper torso with this shield. So, I could bash at his legs and such, but nothing that would truly hinder him and he was up again quickly.

When we finished, Maverick suggested, "Perhaps try training with a spear, like Amber. You can use it like a staff, so you'd not be relearning much, but it also has a pointed tip you can use to follow up once you've tripped someone." He shrugged. "Find what works for you, but find it fast, if you're coming with us. This war won't wait for you."

I fell asleep with Maverick's words in my head: *This war won't wait for you*, which led to dreams of battle and death.

Needless to say, I didn't sleep well.

CHAPTER 16

SPARROW

SPARROW SAT IN HER AVATAR FORM, HIDDEN AMIDST THE BRANCHES of a tall oak tree, watching the comings and goings of the members of the Royal House, Owl House. She had to be very careful. Many members of Owl House were birds, specifically birds of prey. If they caught sight of her, they might consider her a nice light snack. Hence, her hidden position. The oak tree was just outside the walled estate grounds of Owl House, the manor itself was massive, which it had to be for the nearly one hundred members of that House. Even if it hadn't been the Royal House, Owl would have been a powerful Noble House.

Yet she'd seen nothing untoward in the two days she'd been watching the manor, certainly no signs of Lord Hale in human or avatar form.

Sparrow had always been an odd mix of shy and timid with moments of unsuspecting boldness and bravery. She'd learned it early on. Fearing her father, a fisherman who plied the Austel

Ocean, she'd learned to keep quiet. The man had a temper and drunk far too much. Though not physically violent, he'd been prone to savage outbursts, shouting horrible things at his family. Her mother had been a rock, impassive against the storm of her father's emotions. She sat and mended nets and prepared their meals with stoic silence. She was distant, to everyone, including her children, which wasn't much better.

When Sparrow had been old enough, she'd gone for the Choosing and been surprised to find Ahena, her Lumani, the first year. She hadn't known what to do once she'd bonded at Silver-veil. She'd heard a few other students were testing for Noble and that sounded interesting, so she'd gone. Again, she'd been surprised to be selected by Maverick. He'd said he saw something in her, a core of something tougher than steel, another surprise.

Her time at Maverick House had brought her out of her shell in slow, small steps, and she'd been made a scout, rarely fighting, but useful by seeing what others couldn't from her high vantage point while flying.

Yet it hadn't been until the arrival of Legs, nearly six years later, that she'd found the courage to truly show herself to another person. And since then, she'd felt a new strength growing inside her, a surety, a confidence.

So, she wasn't too worried if any birds of prey came her way. She was fast and agile as a sparrow. And as a person, she was quick with her little knives. She'd only had to use them a few times in true fights with pirates, and her foes had always seemed just a little surprised when they found themselves stuck and bleeding.

As the day drew to a close, she took flight and returned to the small apartment she and the others shared in the city. She landed on the window, then flitted inside before resuming her human form. None of the others had returned from their day's scouting, so she quickly prepared a meal for them. Ahena was an excellent cook. She loved to bake but could work with nearly anything. The meal was warm and ready when the others returned.

Yet the news they shared as they ate wasn't good. Sparrow reported no interesting news from the Royal House. Silence and Foggy were working together to explore the warren of tunnels beneath the Slippery Eel that led to the Royal House. They reported seeing many people moving through the tunnels, but they hadn't found Hale yet, nor heard any other indicators of betrayal and subterfuge. Midnight had been within the Royal House, moving carefully. Specifically, she'd been trying to find out more about the queen and her supposed retreat away from society. Yet as much as she could go unseen, she could not get into some areas and had had no luck finding the queen. She wasn't in her royal rooms nor any of the easily accessible parts of the house. Two days, and they still had nothing.

"We need to be patient and persistent," Midnight said stoically. "We'll find something to help the others, I know it."

That night, Sparrow and Silence slept together, holding each other close for comfort, uncertain what the next day would bring.

They all went their separate ways the next day. A spring storm loomed over the capital. High winds and lashing rain meant Sparrow would not be doing much flying. So, she bundled herself up in a heavy oiled cloak and stood across from the Slippery Eel, in the shadows of a dark alley, watching the place.

Understandably, few people were out on the streets, so she stood there for some time, seeing no activity. Though her cloak kept her mostly dry, the shifting winds and driving rains managed to trickle some moisture down within the confines of the garment and she began to feel a chill.

As she was thinking of leaving, a large figure ducked out of the doorway of the Slippery Eel. The massive man looked quickly around before heading off at a quick pace into the rains.

Sparrow didn't know Lord Hale, but this man matched the

general description: larger than Ant with thick arms — especially the forearms — and blond hair. She'd caught sight of a few strands of pale hair peeking out from under the cowl of his cloak.

She hesitated only a moment before following him. She slipped from alley to alley, shadow to shadow, keeping the large man in sight through the sheets of rain inundating the city. He'd check behind him every now and then, but that large body of his telegraphed his movements, and when she saw his shoulder shift and twitch, she'd make sure she was safe in an alley or duck for cover.

Whoever this was, he was certain of his destination. He made his way through back streets and dark alleys, a circuitous route, but definitely heading across the city. Sparrow was half-certain of where he was going, and her suspicions were confirmed when he reached the walled compound of Pegasus House. He spoke quickly with a gate guard and was admitted.

Interesting.

She'd not be able to follow beyond this point... unless...

It was difficult but not impossible to fly in such downpours of rain. She'd have to make several trips most likely, but it was important enough to risk. She veered into her sparrow form and asked her Lumani Ahena to lend her strength, then flitted to the top of the wall around the Pegasus compound. She made it there in time to see the large man entering a small side door.

She wasn't certain, but she thought she might know where in the house he was heading. Before Legs had come here, only a few days ago — but seeming like a lifetime — Sparrow had scouted the house and knew where Lady Silvermane's rooms were, as well as Lord Horn's, Hale's father.

She made the quick trip up to a window of Silvermane's room to perch on the large stone sill. Peering within, she found Lord Horn there as well. This wasn't uncommon, since the large protector-knight was usually close by his charge.

And as suspected, the large man she'd been following was admitted a few moments later. This had to be Hale.

Her hearing wasn't as good as Midnight's and the three in the room gathered close, speaking in hushed voices. But Sparrow had learned a few tricks. Her eyes in bird form were keen and she'd learned to read a person's lips from a great distance. And as luck would have it, Hale was the one facing her as he spoke. Yet the other two occasionally got in the way, and she had trouble reading their lips from the sides, so she only got bits of the conversation.

Hale spoke, "...most dire... in danger... madwoman, Maverick has trained as an assassin. I don't *think* she'd hurt her sister, but she's quite crazy so I can't be sure. Even with all my skills I... protect my beloved and... away, killing three men. It's clear now Maverick House is working against Elista, though to what end I do not know."

Sparrow was more than a little shocked at this. The man was blatantly lying about the events of a few nights ago. Though, what was more worrying was that Silvermane and Horn seemed to believe him wholeheartedly.

"Maverick is... not think him a betrayer..." This from Silvermane. She shook her head. "This is dire news indeed. I am worried for young Dove."

Horn nodded at this.

"There is more," Hale said. "They are conspiring with Vauphan against us."

Well, that part was sort of true, but they only sought to stop the coming war, not betray Elista.

"That woman, Legs has seduced their prince and whispers in his ear encouraging their war."

Silvermane shook her head again. "To what end?"

Hale looked weary and sad, clearly an act. "That I do not know. The queen worries we may have a war on two fronts, that Maverick and his seductress will entice the Vauphani to come ashore in the South, while a smaller force, reinforced by the bedeviled Fey, holds the North. They will have us caught in the middle, fighting on two fronts. That is why..." Horn adjusted his position and blocked Hale for a moment. "... the north and overcome their forces now."

Silvermane was nodding. "What do you need?"

"Your most powerful spirit-gifted to bolster the forces in the North. Also, your portion of the army to march south and take Hedgewild."

A cold shudder ran through Sparrow. She hadn't thought it possible they would march on one of their own Noble Houses, but she'd clearly been wrong. Each of the top five Noble Houses controlled a portion of the army of Elista, a precaution from putting too much power in the hands of whatever House currently held the Royal name. Currently, that meant Panther protected the East, Pterolycus the North, Wyvern the West, Pegasus the South, and Owl the Central Capital Region. Though, Pegasus' army hadn't truly been in the south for some time, remaining close to the capital since there was no great threat upon the lands of Southern Elista. The only threat in the south was pirates, occasionally raiding the coast, and Maverick House dealt with them. But if Pegasus did march south... their army of five thousand men would easily overcome the few Nobles at Hedgewild; it would be a massacre. She wanted to run and tell the others now, but forced herself to remain and see what else she could learn.

"I'll do what I must to free Dove," Silvermane said, jaw firm, eyes cold.

"Finally," Hale said, rising. "Spread word to the other Houses of Maverick's betrayal. None in their House can be trusted." He sighed rolling his heavy shoulders. "And if your army or any other House manages to capture Legs... try to keep her alive. I want to make her pay for what she did."

There were grim faces all around.

Lord Horn said something Sparrow couldn't read, then he escorted his son out. Curious, Sparrow flitted over a few sets of windows to Lord Horn's suite and her suspicions were confirmed when the two entered. Again they spoke quietly, but Sparrow could read both their lips well at this angle.

"I don't like hiding things from my mistress," Horn said. He'd turned away from his son for a moment toward the window, and Sparrow saw his lips clearly. She also saw the pain on his aged and weathered face. "You're certain the queen does not wish her daughter to know?"

Hale was hard. "Yes. She must not know the truth. She believes this war to be just and we must keep up that façade."

Sparrow was stunned. So, the queen *was* behind the war in the North!

"For the sake of the Mists," Horn said.

"For the sake of the Mists, yes." Hale came and laid a hand on his father's shoulder. "No one likes this, but we're doing what we must." They were both facing the window now, Horn still unable to look at his son.

Horn nodded. "And Maverick?"

"Our plans went awry; we could not get ahold of Legs. As Merlin has seen, Legs will end all of this for us, she must be stopped. And if that means eliminating an entire Noble House." He sighed heavily. "We'll do what we must." Those massive shoulders shrugged. "They are small, some new Noble will easily be able to rebuild the South."

So, Lord Horn was fully aware of what was going on, and a part of the treachery, though, to be fair, he didn't seem to like it much.

And Hales mention of Merlin *seeing* that *Legs will end this* for them, was shocking, but confirmed what Legs had learned from the mistweaver, that one of the conspirators could see the future. That's why they'd been going after Legs to begin with. Merlin was the second-in-command of House Owl, the right hand to the queen. If she had some ability — perhaps a spirit-gift — to see the future, that was dangerous indeed.

Horn nodded again, stoic. "I do not like it..." Then he sighed heavily. "...but we'll do what we must," he repeated what his son had said a moment ago.

"For the Mists," Hale said. Sparrow found it interesting they kept repeating that phrase.

"For the Mists," Horn said with a heavy sigh.

They spoke only of familial matters after that, and Sparrow flew away once Hale had left.

Her heart raced. She needed to tell the others. This was far larger than they'd expected. The entire nation was turning against them.

They needed to get out of the capital and warn the others, now!

CHAPTER 17

Fin popped into the great hall, distracting Amber just at the right moment for me to slip past her guard with my spear. I tapped the long metal tip of the spear on her shoulder, a kill.

"Finally!" I gasped.

Amber eyed the weapon and smiled. "I'd say you only won because I was distracted, but distraction is no excuse. There are many distractions on the battlefield. Good for you. We'll practice more once we're in Vauphan." She carefully pushed the haft of the spear away from her, and I let her, drinking in the praise.

I'd excelled with the spear during the two days of relentless training. Dove had been practicing as well, but between the two of us, I'd been the only one to get past Amber's defenses, though not often. This was only the third time I'd been able to do so.

I put the spear aside and ran over to Fin, but the prince wasn't with him.

The large man looked like he'd lost a little weight, still barrel-chested and large, but with a little less of himself hanging over other parts.

"Looking good, Fin. Is everything set in the North?" I asked.

He nodded with a smile. "Eager to see your little prince?" he teased.

I think I blushed. I *was* excited. I hadn't seen him in a while. Also, now that I'd talked to Silence and Sparrow, I could do more than just kiss the man... if we got a moment alone.

Fin lowered his voice. "He's excited to see you too." He winked.

That shocked me just a little. I didn't think Alvere was one to share such things, but he and Fin had been together for some time, perhaps they'd formed a bond?

"Now, run and get your things, I'm having a bath and a good meal — I'm sick of trail rations — then we'll be off."

I nodded and ran back to Dove. She and I hurried to my room. She'd mostly recovered from her harrowing ordeal with Hale, but she still hadn't wanted to be too far from me. So she'd stayed in my rooms, sometimes sleeping on my large bed, sometimes on one of the comfortable couches. I had already gathered most of my things in a travel bag, but I quickly checked it.

"Well?" I asked Dove. "What's your decision? You coming?" I looked over at her, that flaxen-blond hair of hers, light and weightless, seemed to float about her as she sat heavily on one of the couches.

"So soon?" she whispered. "I... don't know." Her blue eyes clouded with uncertainty. "I want to be where you are, but the more I practice with you, the more I realize I never want to fight. I... don't think I'd do well in a war zone."

I smiled. "Don't worry, you don't have to come. Fin will be back often enough, and I'll visit." I closed up my bag and went over to sit with her. Putting an arm around her, I pulled her close and gave her a tight, side-long hug. "You'll be safe here."

It was ever-so-slight, but I felt a tremor pulse through her. "I don't know if I'll feel truly safe ever again." She gave me a tight smile, and I could see the pain in those blue eyes. "I don't know how you do it. You're so strong..."

I pulled her closer, both arms around her. I couldn't bear to leave her like this. Sometimes she seemed her old self, and others she seemed so delicate and fragile, like the softest touch would shatter her. "I love you, Dove," I said softly. "Don't worry about anything. Ant and the others will take care of you. Take the time you need to..." I didn't know how to end that sentence: *get back to your old self*? I was beginning to wonder if that was even possible. "You'll be well, I know it." I hugged her tighter and she returned the embrace.

I only knew she was crying when she sniffed and spoke, voice tremulous and valiantly trying to overcome her emotions. "You go be amazing out there. I know you'll change the world," she whispered.

Perhaps I was stronger than her, but I wouldn't have gone that far.

"I'll do my best," I said.

When I didn't move for a while, she pulled back and looked up. There were indeed tears on her cheeks, though they seemed all shed now, eyes clear. "Don't you need to go?"

"Fin said he was going to bathe and eat, and he doesn't eat quickly. I've got time."

She smiled and leaned back into me.

We held each other until it began to get dark. Then I finally released her.

She came down to the great hall with me and indeed Fin was only halfway through a large meal. The others who were going to Vauphan were already there, ready, waiting.

Maverick, Amber, Jack, and I would go. The rest of the House would remain here.

I went to where I'd left my spear and grabbed it. I also put on the sword-belt I'd removed while practicing. I felt comfortable with the spear now, as well as dual short swords. For ranged weapons, I'd been practicing with throwing knives. A bow had a much longer range, but the dozen or so small throwing knives were easier to keep on me and move around with.

As for my squeamishness about blades... that was still an uncertainty. We'd see how my first foray went.

My heart raced for so many reasons as Fin rose from his meal. I'd soon see Alvere again. I'd soon see battle for the first time. I was still a bit worried for Dove. And finally, I'd never been that far from home before.

I kissed Dove good-bye, joined hands with the others, then the world spun and we were in a small clearing at the edge of a forest. Through the sparse trees I could see a large camp in the fields beyond.

"Remember," Fin said. "The prince isn't a prince here. He's a minor noble in command of a small group of men. His name is Alain of Beauval."

We all nodded to this, and Fin led us out of the woods into the camp. We got a few interesting looks as we passed other men sitting around fires and eating in the growing dark of the evening, but no comments. They had no reason to suspect we were Elistan. Also, Fin had become well known to many of these men as a retainer to the young "Alain of Beauval."

Fin took us to a large pavilion and entered. No men guarded the tent. The prince was on his own here, trusting to secrecy to keep him safe.

There was a large front room to the tent with carpeting covering the grasses in several places creating areas for sitting and dining. Alvere was leaning over the long dining table, studying some papers. He looked up and a wide grin spread on his face as his gaze met mine. I saw his eyes go wide, his chest fill with a heavy breath.

"Welcome!" he said to us and motioned to several flaps leading to areas in the back of the tent. "Feel free to put your things in the rooms at the back. The one in the middle is mine." He was looking directly at me for that last bit. The suggestion was clear, if I wished to share his room, I was welcome to.

I didn't hesitate in taking my things through the central flap, ignoring some of the looks from the others. There were four other rooms, two on either side of Alvere's, so one for each of the others.

Once inside the "bedroom" I felt myself grow warm. I was really doing this. Committing to sharing a bed with him. It wasn't a large bed, but certainly large for a camp far from civilization. I put my stuff down and went to run my hand over the thick canvas wall. We'd have to be quiet so as not to disturb the others. I hoped I could manage that.

I returned to the living area as the prince poured some tea into five small metal cups.

"Now," he said sitting, as we all did the same. "Let me update you on the situation here at the front." He sighed. "At the moment, Vauphan has the advantage. We have six thousand warriors plus another roughly two hundred Fey, each of which is worth a dozen men."

This was news. I'd known the Fey were to be helping in the war effort, but I hadn't known they were *that* good. I wasn't sure if his comment was hyperbole or not. If not, that small group would be significant indeed. "On the Elistan side, nearly the full complement of Panther House is here, with their five thousand men. On that side, it is the Lumani which are the unknown factor for us. Panther has upwards of fifty members, all with the ability to become hunting cats or other predators. That is not insignificant." He didn't really need to tell us that. "Both sides are expecting reinforcements in the next few days. Vauphan will have two thousand more men by the end of the week and Elista roughly the same... part of the Pterolycus army has been diverted from what we've heard."

How he knew all of this was a mystery to me.

"And the more time passes, the more forces will arrive. I don't know how many more from Elista, but I'd suspect at least another five thousand or so army men and perhaps another fifty to a hundred Nobles?" He shrugged. "The Vauphan army is larger, but we have more terrain to cross to get them here. Another two thousand are expected next week, and after that, it may be a while before more arrive. Our eastern border with Fiore is... tentative right now. The Giulea River Valley has always been contested lands between our nations. Right now, we're ceding territory to them." He sighed heavily. "Some in my lands are very upset about that. They want us to strike at Elista now, and retake the lands they've claimed, then build forts to hold them, so we can regroup to the east and retake Giulea once more."

Things sounded complicated for the prince. I felt for him. He was in an impossible situation. He had to defend and maintain his lands, but with Elista pushing, that meant losing lands in the east.

"Are the Fey truly that powerful?" Maverick asked.

Alvere smiled. "They are one of our best kept secrets. Though, in truth, they are not of Vauphan at all. Yet, they have decided we are their allies, and we've tried to maintain that relationship. We had a brief war with them when we tried to move north and settle the forests and hills there. It didn't go well for us, even though we probably outnumbered the Fey ten to one. We quickly ceded the lands back to them and apologized, trying to make them allies. That was over two hundred years ago. It took some time, but they have become... friends of Vauphan."

It was only then I recalled all the features the prince shared with Midnight... who was half-Fey.

"Are you—" I blurted before stopping myself.

Alvere smiled and sighed. "It seems my secret is out," he said softly. "I am half-Fey, yes. My Mother was Fey. I've... never met her. She may even be among those fighting with us, but I wouldn't know, even if I saw her." He seemed a bit sad, and I couldn't blame him. To have never known his mother... Though my birth mother had died when I was very young. I only had fleeting memories of her.

Maverick cleared his throat. "Ah... yes, we suspected as much," he said with a sidelong glance at me. "We have a mutual friend who is also half-Fey and the resemblance to you is... fascinating."

"I said nothing to them," Fin said, hands up in defense.

"But you are all keen of eye and quick of intellect. I can see that now." Alvere sighed. "I hope I can trust you all with this secret. Not even my own people know. Only my family knew, my mother and father, and they're both gone now."

"We will tell no one." Maverick eyed everyone just to make sure the message was clear.

I nodded.

Maverick sighed in the way he had a habit of doing, like the world itself was weighing upon his shoulders. "So," he said slowly, summing up. "Currently the tides favor Vauphan, six thousand to five thousand regular army, with your Fey versus our True-Bonded."

Alvere nodded.

"Cavalry?" Maverick asked.

Alvere nodded more, sitting forward. "As you know, Elista has never favored cavalry. From what we can tell, the Panthers have about five-hundred light cavalry; more like mobile infantry." Maverick nodded to that. "Vauphan has found a good use for Cavalry, though it is hard to outfit and train them. We have a thousand heavy cavalry."

"That's another thing in your favor then," Maverick said. Those armored horses could trample five times their numbers. We could win this battle tomorrow, if we wanted."

Alvere gave a grim smile. "As has been our thought as well, the trouble is... we cannot be certain of our losses. Which means we'd be a diminished force, trying to fortify when the larger numbers of Elistans arrived fresh. There are just too many unknowns."

"What about those ships that sailed for Elista to save you?" Maverick asked. "You sent that army north, didn't you? If so, I would have thought you'd have more men here?"

Alvere sighed. "Some of them returned to the capital and some, roughly five hundred, are here, supporting our forces, but most are still out on ships patrolling our coast. We can't risk an invasion by sea across Dyren's Bay. If the Elistans managed to get a force on land behind us..."

Maverick nodded understanding. "Too bad, we could use those men here." He seemed to mull things over for a moment before nodding to himself. "Let's see if we can't clarify a few things for you," Maverick said. "Legs, Amber, tomorrow you're scouting. Get as deep as you can into the Elistan camp, find out who's there and what's going on. Are they preparing for an offensive or digging in to defend? My guess would be the latter, but let's get some solid information for the prince."

"That would be appreciated, thank you," Alvere said. "I will have some dinner brought, then we can all rest, yes?"

With nods all around, it was decided.

We ate in silence for the most part. Alvere and Maverick stayed up to talk, but with a potentially long day ahead of me, I wanted to get to bed early.

The next day I was up early and found that Alvere wasn't in bed with me. When I went out into the common area of his pavilion he was sleeping on a long divan. The others weren't awake yet, so I sat next to him and shook him softly to wake him.

He smiled drowsily up at me. "Legs?"

"You didn't come to bed last night," I said, concerned.

"We hadn't had a chance to talk. We left things a bit... uncertain last time and I didn't want to presume, even though you chose my room."

What a gentleman.

I leaned down and kissed his forehead. "Then let's talk—"

Though at that exact moment Maverick came out from his room. "—later before we sleep separately again, yes?"

He smiled, an eager liveliness coming to him as he seemed to realize what I was saying. "Yes," he breathed.

The others were up quickly and we all shared a warm breakfast before Amber and I were off to scout.

CHAPTER 18

AMBER COULDN'T CARRY ME AS A SPIDER; HER BUTTERFLY FORM wasn't strong enough. That meant I was walking... or flying. I made sure I had all my weapons, even some light armor: a breast-plate with grieves and bracers, then I walked out of the Vauphani camp to the north, into the forest. I moved carefully through the woods until I was close to where the Elistans might have scouts, north and east of their camp.

Finding the tallest tree I could, I climbed it, first as a human, then getting to the very top as a spider. I spun a sort-of sail from my webbing and caught a south-westerly breeze, which carried me right over the Elistan camp.

I set down lightly on the pinnacle of a tent, then scurried down and moved carefully around the camp. After a morning of looking, I still hadn't found a command tent, but I kept heading deeper into the camp and hoped. Finally, I found a large tent which looked promising and scurried under the canvas. Inside were a group of men around a large table.

Jackpot, a command meeting.

I got a little closer, hiding behind one of the support beams for the large tent, then let my hairs do the listening.

"They could easily overrun us," one man said. I recognized the voice, but I wasn't sure from where. Perhaps my spider-sense-hearing was distorting it a little? That wasn't important, so I kept listening. The same man continued, saying, "Why do they wait?"

Another man, with a much deeper and more commanding voice answered. "Our spies report that they are expecting another four thousand men in the next ten days or so."

"But why wait?" the first man asked. "We'll have received some reinforcement by that time as well and—"

"Shut up and let me finish, Lynx!" The second man cut off the first.

Lynx?

A shudder ran through me. Lynx was the True-Bonded name of my first love, Kelen. I felt both startled and relieved. I hadn't expected him to be here, a commander at the front, but then... he'd been Chosen three years before me, four years ago now. He could have risen in the ranks of Panther House in that time. If he was here, perhaps I could talk to him, perhaps he'd listen to reason. I had to hope.

That reminded me, Cougar would probably be reaching the front lines soon. I hoped he'd heeded my warning and listened to what I'd said. I didn't know if his queries and doubts would help shed any truth on what was going on, but it might.

I listened in again, having missed a bit of what the more commanding voice had said. "...may overrun us, yes, but after the four thousand soon to come, they aren't expecting any more rein-forcements for some time. Weeks away at best. And, in that time, if their spies are as good as ours, they'd know we're expecting a significant force as well. It's all in the math."

The same man put on a lecturing tone. "Let's say they wait until the four thousand new troops arrive. Their ten thousand against our seven thousand — since the Pterolycus troops will be here by then — would probably mean a victory, but at what cost? Let's say they lose two thousand men and we lose the same. That means when the remaining troops from Pterolycus, along with the reserves from the capital arrive, we'll have ten thousand men, half of whom are fresh. They'll have eight thousand, all of whom are weary from the first battle and a desperate attempt to build fortifications. We'd wipe them out, send them running. So, it's a stalemate for now. Though it may not seem it, the advantage lays with us. We have fortifications in place, not much, but enough to slow their advance and cause them some pain in their first strike. And the longer we wait, the more troops we'll have. We can sit behind our growing fortifications and wait for them, perhaps even raid their camp to demoralize them. We've already won this fight, it's just a matter of how. Unless they get some miraculous addition to their forces, they cannot win here."

Silence hung in the room for a moment.

"And..." I couldn't see the man, but with how he said that single word, I felt like he was smiling, pompous, arrogant. "Though I haven't received the latest command updates, last I heard, we were going to ask Pegasus' troops to head south to a fleet of ships being readied." The man laughed. "With all the Vauphani troops being funneled north, their southern coast will be ripe for the taking. We can't keep those lands, of course, but we can pillage and burn their coast with impunity while their forces mass in the north. That will show them who's superior, show them that it's our right to hold these lands."

A cheer went up, but I'd heard enough. I needed to leave before I was sick. It was clear now who the true warmongers were among these two sides. This show of aggression by my own people — or those I'd thought were my own people — nauseated me.

I forced myself to wait, to see if there was any other information I might glean here, but the meeting broke up after that.

I quickly crawled outside and waited where I could see the exit. I caught sight of Lynx and followed him as he went to a modest sized tent and entered.

I crept under the canvas again and found a two-part pavilion, like Alvere's, but with only one room in the back and a much smaller sitting area in the front.

Lynx was alone, facing away from me, so I transformed and cleared my throat.

He turned and was so surprised he fell on his ass. I must have been quite a sight, an armored warrior woman with spear in hand.

"Hello, lover," I said, hoping that might defuse the tension. "Remember me?"

"Sara?" he breathed.

"It's Legs now. House Maverick."

He blinked and got up slowly. "You're..." He gave me the usual once-over that most men do, but then did it again, slower, truly taking me in. "You've changed."

"I like to think so."

He didn't approach or try to embrace me, which I'd thought one of his possible reactions. Instead, I caught a quick glance toward the room at the back of the tent. "I... you shouldn't be here. How did you get here? When did you get here?"

I followed his gaze, purposefully looking at the separator between the two rooms. "You're not alone?"

"Ah..."

"No, he's not," came a voice from the back area. A moment later a woman appeared. She wore only boots and a loose robe, casually wrapped around her. She and I looked at each other for a long moment before she gave a breathy laugh and dismissed me. And I could see why. She was everything I was, but... more. My height but with far more curves, especially at her bust, the lazily applied robe showing an abundance of cleavage. Yet the belt tying the garment closed showed a slender waist. Her hair was a shade off of mine, brown and wavy, but tinged with golden-red. And her eyes were a brilliant gold.

"Aren't you going to introduce us?" She asked, languidly, going to Lynx and draping herself over him, pressing close while looking at me the entire time.

He hesitated before saying: "Lady Claw, meet Lady Legs."

As everyone did, she looked at my legs, then she shrugged. From what I could see of hers — and it was a lot — she had me beat there too. "Pleasure to meet you," she purred. Then turned to Lynx and licked his lips before giving him a wet, messy kiss.

It was a show, for me. We all knew it. She pressed herself against him and whispered, "I'm going to have a bath and return to my tent. You're welcome to join me, if this doesn't take long." With that she pulled away from him and slinked over to me.

With a sour look, she ducked a little to give me a good long sniff. Her lips pulled back, showing me her teeth as she hissed, "Hands off. He's mine." Then she veered into a small hunting cat with tan fur, roughly as large as a medium-sized dog and trotted out of the tent.

She'd done everything but pee on him to mark her territory.

I raised a brow. "She's... something."

"Sorry about that," Lynx said with a shrug. "She's a little possessive."

You don't say?

He sighed. "Why are you here, Legs?" He said it in an exasperated way. I had the feeling I'd gotten him in trouble with his lover and he knew he'd be paying for it later.

"I'm here about the war," I said, voice hushed. I didn't want anyone to overhear us.

It was his turn to raise a brow. "Maverick is sending us troops now? You're a long way from home. Why is Maverick House so concerned with what's happening up here?"

I grew grim. "Lynx, *everyone* should be concerned with what's happening 'up here,'" I said. "This isn't right. It needs to stop, and I was hoping I could talk to... an old friend who might have some pull here."

He scoffed. "Then you're in the wrong place. I have as much pull as a... mouse pulling a hay wagon. If you could hear the way Lord War was just putting me in my place, you'd know that."

"Lord War?" I said, curious. I'd assumed the other man talking in the meeting had been the leader of Panther House, Lord Jaguar. I had to wrack my memory for this new name.

"Oh yes. He's up from the capital. A *representative* of the Royal House here to *oversee* things." The way he said those two words made it clear the man wasn't overseeing so much as commanding. "Lord Jaguar is furious that he's not the one in control, but it seems there is more going on here than even we are privy to." He sighed heavily, shaking his head as he sought a chair and slumped into it.

I recalled the name now. It had been the mention of the Royal House. Lord War was the Field Marshal of the entire army of Elista, the highest-ranking officer. It was said he was a mean and vicious man who couldn't abide the ongoing peace Elista had with its neighbors. His presence here made perfect sense.

"We were doing well enough on our own the last three years," Lynx said. "Then he showed up and took control. I think he means to fully invade Vauphan. That's just crazy... isn't it?"

"Yes, it is." My tone was sour. But something else he'd said was curious. "You said something about 'the last three years'? That's how long you've been here?" I'd heard as much from Alvere, but wanted to hear confirmation from an Elistan source.

Lynx looked up at me blinking. "Yeah, doesn't everyone know how long we've been up here?"

"No, Lynx, *no one* knows. This war has been kept secret."

"Well... Maverick is in the South, so—"

"I was in Miraline just last year and I'd not heard anything about this." Miraline being the largest city in the North of Elista, and only three days or so from the boarder with Vauphan.

He cocked his head to one side. "Truly?"

It seems those here are doing a good job at keeping their own troops misinformed. Everyone here thinks the nation knows and those back home only found out recently as it's slowly coming out. This is... I can't fathom the work needed to keep all of this so... contained. Auwei seemed shocked and baffled.

I had to agree.

"No one knows what's going on here, Lynx." This was my chance. I sat myself in a chair next to Lynx, speaking quickly, whispering, hoping to get through to him. "This war, this invasion, whatever it is, it was kept a secret from the rest of the nation. No one knew. I don't know how that's possible, but someone on our side wanted to claim these lands in secret. It's the entire reason the Vauphani army is sitting out there. They have no clue why we took their lands and think we want more. Do we want more?" I asked, curious if he knew.

He shrugged. "I don't know. I'm still only a low-level Noble in Panther House. But I have a good head for tactics so I came here right after I was chosen for Panther." He too spoke quietly, perhaps a bit caught up in my tale of secrecy. "We were told Vauphan was planning an invasion." His volume dropped even more. "Not just of Elista, but... that they wanted to claim the Mists!"

That shocked me. "Truly?"

Oh, that's interesting indeed. That rumor would certainly worry many Nobles. I got the sense Auwei had hit on something, but if so, she wasn't sharing it yet.

"Yes. We were told their provinces near the border were crawling with spies and scouts and a large force was on its way, though it would take time for it to get here, and that the only way to confirm we held the Mists was to take the northern Vauphani provinces first, before they were swarming with troops. So... we did."

I blinked. I knew that wasn't true, but I couldn't say anything or I'd give away that I knew more about Vauphan than I should. But still the question remained... why? Why would Elista spin such a tale of impending invasion to prompt our own counter-invasion? I didn't think Lynx would know, but I had to ask.

"Why, Lynx?" I whispered. "It must be clear to you now, since it took the Vauphani army some time to get here, that that story was... just a story. So why would we want to invade their lands?"

He shook his head, and when he spoke his voice was hard to hear. It was clear he was afraid of speaking about this. "I don't know, and I don't want to ask. The ones who question things... Legs, they've disappeared."

"Nobles?" I said feeling a realization coming on.

Oh... do you think? Auwei asked.

Yes, I do.

"Yes! And some high-ranking ones."

I swallowed hard. I was willing to bet they hadn't disappeared. I was near-to-certain they were dead, and not just dead, but with their Lumani killed as well. That old rumor came back to me. Nobles and their Lumani dying. Before, I didn't know why, but I think I did now. Anyone who got too close to this massive secret — anyone who threatened it — died. And their Lumani were killed to keep the secret from passing on to their next host.

That's... I can't... Gah! I felt Auwei's anger as my own.

"Spirits!" I whispered and rose suddenly. "I have to go."

Lynx rose, looking a bit shaken by his own words. He seemed concerned for me. "If... what you're thinking is what I'm thinking and you're going to tell someone about all this... Legs, they'll disappear you too." He came close, hands on my shoulders. "Just... be careful."

I smiled. "I will. Don't worry." I stepped back and turned away.

Then turned back. I didn't want to shock him when I didn't leave the normal way. I smiled. "Now, if you don't mind, I'll go out the way I came in." I winked at him then veered into my spider form. He started, then laughed.

"Ah... farewell, Legs."

I crawled out from the canvas and began the very long walk back to the Vauphani camp. I had more than a few interesting things to report.

CHAPTER 19

I DIDN'T WANT TO RISK ANYONE MISTAKING ME FOR AN ENEMY, SO I remained in spider form as I crossed back across the barren would-be battlefield to the Vauphan camp. I didn't return to myself until I was safely within Alvere's pavilion, which meant it was well after dark by the time I finally reached it.

I returned to myself and immediately slumped into one of the camp chairs. Amber, Jack, and Maverick must have been in bed, but Fin and Alvere were still up, chatting quietly. They both looked at me, stunned. Then Fin rose, putting a meaty hand on Alvere's shoulder.

"Good night, friend," he said and made his way to his room.

Alvere came to me, kneeling beside the chair. "How...?" He shook his head. "No, your report can wait for tomorrow, you look exhausted. What can I do?"

"A bath would be lovely," I said, feeling filthy after crawling through mud all day.

"And... after that?" He asked, voice hushed. There were others around.

"After that, you're taking me to bed," I said, voice husky

partly from fatigue and partly with anticipation. "We can have that talk I promised while I bathe... while *you* bathe me." I grinned at him.

Alvere smiled so wide he looked a bit silly. He nodded, saying: "Most of the men and women in the army bathe in the river. It's mountain run-off, so it's cold all year and they don't stay long in those waters. I think I can get you something better. Wait here." He rose and left the pavilion.

I must have dozed. Alvere woke me with a soft touch to my shoulder. His kind beryl-blue eyes and sympathetic smile were exactly what I wanted to see waking up.

"I'm having a tub brought in and some hot water. It may take a bit of time. Rest for now." He leaned down and kissed my cheek, and I smiled, eyes drooping shut.

I woke again several times as servants came and went bringing and filling the tub.

Then Alvere woke me. "It's ready," he said, pointing to the large, roughly oval shaped metal tub. He helped me up, then scooped me into his arms — he was stronger than he looked — and carried me the few steps to the basin, setting me down next to it.

I was so tired, I stood there for a long moment staring at the water trying to remember what the next step was. I tried to step in, but Alvere stopped me.

"You're still dressed."

Yup, I was. "Fix that, please," I said with a weary grin.

He didn't need to be told twice and began removing my armor and clothes. The arousal and heat filling my body as his slender fingers brushed my flesh woke me further. After that, I made it easier for him, helping where I could, until I stood naked before him.

Those jewel-toned pools of eyes devoured me.

I couldn't get enough of him looking at me like that.

"Not right now," I said with a soft smile and a shake of my head. "I'm dirty."

He quirked a half-grin, raising one brow, then motioned to the tub. "You wanted to... talk?"

I stepped in gingerly, finding the water warm, but not hot. It must be hard to get the water warmed significantly. Still, I slid down, knees up, until I was reclining in the waters. It was wonderful.

"Yeah," I drew the word out. "Talk." And I knew I should, before these warm waters lulled me to sleep again.

"You... wanted me to bathe you?" he asked.

"Yup, please do."

"So, your... complications have... gone away?" He reached for some soap and a sponge.

"Yup." I needed to get this all out now. Hopefully I was awake enough to do it properly.

Alvere began to bathe me. His hands worked with soap and sponge to lather me up and scrub me all over. It felt delightful, sensuous and caring.

So, how to say this...? Silence and Sparrow were on board. They knew of the prince and I very much wanted to let him in, fully.

"The complications are gone," I began softly. I felt weightless, floating in a warm sea, which pleasantly washed over me. The words came with a sort of slow and sleepy, dream-like quality. "I am promised to know one, *but* there are others I love... Silence and Sparrow. I do not wish to limit myself to one lover. But... that means everyone I'm with needs to know how I feel, needs to know there are others I love and will be with." I smiled then as he paused in his ministrations, his gaze caught on mine. "I love you all, but when I am with you, I am with only you. There are no others on my mind. You are fully mine, and I am fully yours. If... if you are well with this, then I—"

His kiss stopped my words, impassioned and hard, soft lips pressing with a raging desire held in check for too long. Yet he pulled away quickly to say, "I am well with it." Then his lips were on mine again, his sponge forgotten as his hands dipped into the waters to roam my skin.

I came up for breath a moment later, loving how his hands knew exactly where to reach, how hard to touch, how to move and press. I moaned softly, but then said, "I'm still filthy. Give me a moment?"

He withdrew, hunger in those intense jewel-blue eyes.

I dunked my head under the water, finding the soap and scrubbing at my face and hair for a moment — coming up for air as needed — to cleanse myself.

When I came up for the last time, he had a towel ready. I accepted it as I stood, drying myself, and he watched with rapt focus, which made me blush.

I stepped out of the bath to dry my legs, and as soon as I was done, he scooped me up again and carried me to his bed. He placed me atop the fur-lined covers as he quickly stripped from his clothes. I gave a little gasp as he freed his erection and it leaped up to stand proud before him, thick and red and ready. I snuggled under the sheets and when he joined me, I put a finger to his lips.

"Please remember there are others close by and it's late," I whispered. "Let's try not to wake them." And with those words my fantasy from the library at Hedgewild returned, flashing in my mind. We were hot and needful, standing with me pressed to a bookshelf as we took our desire from each other with heated gasps, trying to remain quiet... just in case.

If I hadn't been aroused before, that steamy memory made sure I was now.

He nodded and when I removed my finger, his lips sought mine, desperate and needful. We pressed close, skin to skin, and I felt the rigid length of his shaft pressing against me. Between the sensuous bathing and my torrid fantasy, I was wet and ready for him, but he was in no hurry to enter me. His fingers found my folds first, pressing and playing, arousing me further. I opened my legs, inviting him in, but instead, when he shifted next, moving on top of me, it was to kiss his way down my body. He pressed his lips to my neck, then the soft curves of my breast and the hardened buds of my nipples. We both let out soft moans of pleasure as he worked upon those sensitive mounds for a prolonged moment, his hand hard upon my ever-more-slick folds.

Then... he kissed down my belly, disappearing under the sheets, bringing his lips to my ready entrance. He pressed the flat of his tongue against me, moving it slowly over the area, before flicking the tip across my clit in an amazing shock of pleasure. My hands dug through his hair, pressing him close, as his lips found me again, sucking and nibbling, his tongue darting inside me.

Sparrow's ministrations with her lips had been soft and tentative, slow to build and producing a gradual tidal wave of bliss. Alvere was intense and rough, hard and needful, and my ecstasy quickly overwhelmed me.

I reached a peak and gasped as my body stiffened and shuddered, back arching. My hands left his hair to grab my own breasts, pressing and tweaking my nipples to enhance my pleasure.

And just as I waned from that peak, Alvere stopped with his lips and moved up. I felt the press of his erection against me as his head and shoulders emerged from under the covers, gaze intent on mine... as if asking permission.

I nodded, wordless, and he smiled. He entered me slowly, watching my lip-biting reaction. He was thicker than Silence, and I could feel every inch of his hard flesh against all manner of wonderful places, filling me. His loins pressed to mine, grinding down hard. Spirits! He felt so big within me, even though he hadn't seemed that much larger than Silence.

His body trembled, and his eyes rolled up then closed for a moment as he pressed hard within and against me. He swallowed and his eyes opened, gaze meeting mine.

"You're too much for me," he whispered. "I don't know how long I can—"

I reached up, drawing his face down to mine, loving the feel of his body on mine, the press of his solid planes against my soft hills. I tasted myself upon his lips as we kissed and still drew him closer, deeper.

I pushed him back a moment to say, "I'm tired, Alvere, and you've already given me pleasure. Take yours."

That was all he needed. He gasp-grunted with each short, hard thrust, pressing his body to mine in amazing ways. The grinding of his pubic bone against my clit had me moaning and gasping as well soon after. He swelled within me as his pace grew frenzied. He was close. I too felt another orgasm building, ready to release.

With a final thrust and a quiet grunt, a full-body shudder took him and he exploded within me.

I was so close to my own release. I just needed him in the right place. So, I reached down to grab his buttocks, pulling him to me, pressing him where I needed him. He twitched and pressed closer, shifting over me, which made my bliss rise higher, but the release still eluded me.

"Oh, gods!" he whispered, "I can't... you're so..." Then another shudder took him as his release pulsed again and again, hot inside me.

"I just need—"

"I know," he whispered. One of his hands slid down between us, finding my clit. With a twitch of his fingers I felt a white-hot flash of ecstasy and bliss surged through me.

I bit my lip to keep from crying out. My sheath contracted, gripping his erection tight, squeezing. He gave a jaw-dropping, wide-eyed, silent shout as his release seemed to culminate into a single moment of ultimate bliss. His body tensed above me, he jerked and shifted for a long moment before he finally fell onto me, spent.

I was right there with him through that extended climax, feeling his pounding heart through his shaft inside me, matching my own as I shuddered and tensed with my own world-melting joy.

Then we lay, gasping and panting together for a long moment.

"I've never..." he whispered. "No woman... That was incredible." His head next to mine warmed my ear with his breathy praise. He nibbled my ear, sliding his tongue lightly along the ridges and hollows.

That sent a new thrill through me as I said, "For me too. I've never felt anything like that." It was the truth. Silence had always been intense and immediate; a spike of pleasure that I was quite happy with. But this had been a ridge-line of passion, rising higher and higher before it had finally, blessedly all come crashing down.

Alvere withdrew and slumped to one side of me. One of his arms remained over me, warm and comforting.

I floated in that strange place between wake and sleep when I heard his words, as if from a distance. "I may be required to marry and I may be with other women, but I don't think any of them will ever compare to you, Legs. I love you." I felt his soft kiss on my shoulder.

That warmed me as I sank into the depths of sleep... and my dreams of him and me... and Silence and Sparrow, warmed me even further still. I slept *very well* that night.

The next morning, once everyone was up, I gave my report, feeling an odd mix of elation and confused dismay. I longed to be in Alvere's arms again, feel him on me and in me and... ohhhhh! But I also had to keep to my duties and that meant telling everyone of what I'd found out from Lynx the previous day.

"They told him that Vauphan wanted the Mists?" Alvere asked, clearly confused. He sighed, raising a brow. "We've always been curious about that magical land, but haven't had any great desire to have it. Honestly, I think most of us believed it would somehow defend itself, or the Lumani would, keeping us from claiming it if we tried." He shrugged.

"I think your theory about why the Nobles and Lumani are being killed is a good one," Maverick said to me. "It makes a sick sort of sense." He shook his head. "And I think it's safe to assume Lord War is a part of the conspiracy. Which makes it more and more likely that the Royal House is behind all of this."

I couldn't believe the queen would do this, but I had to agree. With Hale and War both being a part of what was going on... the Royals were certainly heavily involved.

Amber reported on the state of their fortifications. Trenches and earthworks with palisades were going up on the far side of the battle-field, and were nearly complete. They spanned perhaps five miles, from the edge of the forest to the north, to the rushing waters of the Sacha River in the south. Yet it was only a front at the moment. A force would be able to easily skirt through the forest to go around it, or brave the frigid river waters on the other side. She also reported that the majority of the Panther Nobles she knew were already here, even a few from Pterolycus.

"They're not preparing for an advancement, not yet," she said, smooth alto voice like silk as she spoke. "From Legs' report, it sounds like they mean to hold here, at least until Vauphan cedes these lands and their army leaves."

"Though," Alvere said with bitter disgust. "As soon as we do, I fear they'll claim more. Their attacks in the south are just a feint, but we'll have to draw troops from somewhere to defend, in addition to constant patrols by our navy. And if we take troops from this front, I do not trust them to remain behind their walls."

No one countered that statement. We all knew it could very well be true.

Alvere sat forward, head in hands. "No matter my choice, my people die." His voice was heavy with sorrow. "What do I do?"

To that, none of us had an answer.

CHAPTER 20

SILENCE

SILENCE WAS RELIEVED WHEN HEDGEWILD FINALLY CAME INTO SIGHT as the day dawned.

Sparrow's dire news had gotten those from House Maverick in the capital moving quickly. They'd been away from the capital that day, heading south. And they hadn't stopped, traveling night and day, taking turns driving the cart Midnight had acquired. In Grovner's Green, they'd halted long enough to warn the small village that an army might soon be marching through. And when they'd left, Midnight and Sparrow had flown ahead to the manor, to get the others starting the preparations to leave.

By the time Silence and Foggy arrived, the house was in an uproar as everyone gathered their own things, along with items belonging to those who weren't present that they thought might be required or sentimental.

For those who'd been here the longest, it wasn't an easy process.

Silence didn't have a lot and gathered his things quickly. With that done, Ant ordered him up to the observatory to help Crane.

When he arrived, he found the usually staid and proper woman tearfully muttering to herself as she threw handfuls of paper into the roaring hearth fire behind Maverick's desk.

She looked up and gave him a sad smile. She'd always been so removed and emotionless. Her voice was trembling when she said, "How much can you carry?" Then shook her head. "No, I need Ant." She had several trunks out, packed with the books from the shelves to either side of the hearth. "We need to save as much of our history as we can."

"I'm stronger than I look," Silence said and, closing one of the trunks — which only just latched shut, stuffed as it was — he lifted it easily. "Everyone discounts a mouse," he said as he carried the chest toward the stairs. "But they can lift their own bodyweight easily. I'll be back for the rest in a moment." Mice also had exceptional balance and speed, so Silence was able to hurry down the many stairs from the tower to the front of the manor. He loaded the chest onto the wagon — which was quickly filling up and another was being brought around — before hurrying back up to get another chest.

The army wouldn't be here tomorrow or even the next day. The capital was a two-day ride in a carriage, and armies did not move that quickly. But still, everyone wanted to be away with all haste. Advanced scouts on fast horses — or True-Bonded with bird forms — could be here soon enough. So, the two wagons, loaded past capacity, were rolling out just before noon. Tusk drove one, with Princess beside her. A stone-faced Crane, matched with Midnight, led the other. Sparrow and Dove circled high above us as their avatars, keeping an eye out for trouble. Foggy, Fennec, Ant, and Silence himself, walked beside the slow-moving wagons.

It only occurred to Silence now to ask: "Where are we going?"

Ant answered. "Fin's family are fishermen from a small village not too far south of here, down the coast a little. He bought a cottage there a while ago, and Maverick liked the idea of a second home, a place where anyone could go for some privacy so he helped to ah... refurbish it."

A single cottage? How big was it? "Will we all fit?" Silence asked, looking at the group and the two wagons piled with chests and sacks.

Ant gave a low chuckle. "Maverick did a lot of... refurbishing."

Silence didn't know what that meant, but he supposed he'd find out soon enough.

They reached the Sea Road — one of the few true stone roads in the south, which ran the entire length of the southern shores — and turned south. By late afternoon, the seaside cliffs began to slope down, and Silence saw a village up ahead.

Surprisingly, they didn't go there. Even before they got to the village a small cottage at the side of the road came into view. And that's where they stopped.

Ant knocked on the door instead of just entering. Silence was curious who lived here, if the cottage belonged to Fin. A spry man in his later years with a wiry body, large eyes, and mostly grey hair answered. He looked around quickly then nodded.

"Silence, meet Clam. He's the one who did the refurbishments on the cottage, so as a reward we let him live here." The way Ant kept saying "refurbishment" gave Silence the impression it was far more than just new thatching on the roof. Also, this cottage looked large enough for a small family, no more. If Clam lived here... where were the rest of them going to fit?

"You all unload, I'll get the home-fires burning!" Clam said with a grin missing several teeth, before ducking back inside. Silence helped to unload the wagons, though when he went inside the old man was nowhere to be seen in the one-room house. Odd.

When the wagons were unloaded Fennec and Foggy drove them away, toward the village.

"They'll sell the wagons to a teamster," Ant said in response to Silence's curious look. "We'll probably be here for a while, and hopefully Fin will have returned by the time this is all over and can help with transporting things back to Hedgewild." Ant smiled reassuringly. "This will all be resolved soon enough, you'll see." He put a thick hand on Silence's shoulder and led him inside.

Silence decided to ignore the contradiction of: *we'll probably be here for a while* and *this will all be resolved soon*. Ant was trying to make him feel better, but he doubted anything could truly allay his concerns in that moment.

It was cramped inside with all the people and the cargo from the wagons. One end of the house was a living and sleeping area with a bed and a few comfortable looking chairs. There was a hearth at that end, already warm. The other side was a kitchen area with a long table, shelves well stocked with all manner of provisions and another hearth for cooking. And still no sign of Clam.

Crane went to the far end on the bedroom side and slid her finger into a knothole in the wall, silently pulling open a hidden door. Princess and Tusk moved the two chairs out of the way, onto the bed, making a cleared area to move things to the door... and beyond.

Eager and curious, Silence picked up a small chest and carried it to the door behind Ant. The space beyond the door was narrow, perhaps two feet wide? Since it was the corner of the house there was a small landing, then stairs descended steeply down to the right, into darkness. Ant went slowly, having to move sideways because of his bulk, the chest he was carrying now lengthwise under one arm.

Silence was skinny, but even so, he and the chest he was carrying could — just barely — fit if he walked sideways as well.

Several steep steps led down to another small landing. The outer wall of the cabin, beside Silence, transitioned from wood, to fieldstone foundation, to solid stone carved smooth. Then came another right-hand turn with a low ceiling here, probably the floor of the house above as they moved underneath it. Ant had to duck awkwardly, but Silence made it under with only a bit of a nod of his head. After that, the stairs weren't quite as steep and the stone-carved hall broadened. After about a dozen steps, they made another right turn. Another set of stairs descended for a long stretch. Small torches on the walls barely lit the long downward hall. They came to a landing and a switchback, then down more stairs to an open area... a cave, but with the walls carved smooth and straight.

"Silence! You're holding things up!" Princess said behind him. He hadn't realized he'd stopped to gawk and moved to one side, setting the chest down. Then he truly took in the large room. It was roughly as wide as the length of the house above, with heavy carpets covering most of the smooth stone floor. There were two hearths, on either side of the room. Silence tried to re-imagine things in his head and could see how the chimneys for these hearths might go up right under the hearths in the house's bedroom and kitchen. The smoke from those chimneys would seem to be coming from the house... ingenious! Yet the room was long and spacious. There was a sitting area before the hearth on one side, and a kitchen with a long table with benches, probably able to sit ten to a side, close to the other hearth. On the far side were a number of tunnel-like windows, with long shafts through the stone between the glass on this side and the edge of the cliff on the far side. They would let in some light, but only have direct sun first thing in the morning when the sun was close to the horizon.

"The bedrooms are down here," Ant said. He pointed to another set of stairs heading down, back behind Silence. Leaving off with the lugging of supplies for the moment, Silence followed Ant down, deeper into the stone of the cliffs. Another long set of stairs led down to a landing, then a switchback and more stairs down. At the bottom was a hallway, perpendicular to the stairway. Smooth stone archways — hung with heavy cloth curtains instead of doors — dotted one side of the hall at even intervals.

Silence peeked past the curtains into the closest room. It contained a bed and a small chest next to it, which could double as a nightstand. That was it. There was a window, like the ones up above, glass on this end of a long tunnel out.

"How...?" Silence whispered. This place was amazing, and someone had painstakingly carved these perfect tunnels and rooms. "Who...?" but then he remembered who. He turned to Ant. "Clam did all of this?"

Ant nodded. "Bet you didn't know clams were good at digging through stone."

"I didn't, no." He looked down the long hall. There had to be at least twenty doors. "Still, this must have taken him his entire life."

"Only about seven years, actually."

Silence marveled at that, shaking his head.

"It's not the most comfortable place. It can get very cool down here, but the beds have lots of covers and we have lots of wood for the hearths upstairs." Ant rested a strong hand on Silence's slender shoulder. "Come on, let's help the others unload."

Silence nodded and followed Ant up the many stairs once more.

Seven years to make all of this... Amazing!

Clam had prepared a dinner for them in the main hall by the time they had everything unloaded down into the caverns. It was also about that time that Fennec and Foggy returned from the village, and Dove and Sparrow returned from keeping an eye on things above.

The news wasn't good.

"We got out just in time," Sparrow said with a note of sorrow in her voice. "Advanced scouts reached Hedgewild this evening. It will be crawling with men soon. She shuddered at that thought. Silence couldn't blame her.

They ate in silence that evening. They'd lost their home, Their true home. And these caves were beginning to feel more like a prison than a cozy hideaway.

Silence hoped that this madness would not continue much longer, but he could see no end in sight, and from the silence of the others... neither could they.

CHAPTER 21

WE WERE A SOMBER GROUP THAT DAY AS WE TRIED TO COME UP WITH ideas to stop what Elista planned for Vauphan. But no resolutions were forthcoming. After supper, when Alvere asked me if I wished to walk in the woods, I accepted happily. We strolled, hand in hand, through the camp and then into the woods to the north.

The edge of the woods was mostly open, with large swaths of mostly flat ground and little underbrush between the sparsely placed trees. But very quickly, heading deeper, the trees grew closer together, and the bushes and brush thicker.

Yet Alvere moved with purpose and seemed to know a path. So, I followed, still holding his hand as we began the climb up a heavily forested hill.

I could feel his tension, the weight of the coming war upon him. He didn't want his men to die, and I believed he didn't want the mostly innocent men who'd be on the front lines for Elista to die either. It was all so senseless. He sighed repeatedly as we walked, then the forest suddenly gave way to a clearing at the top of the hill. A single tree stood at the peak of the knoll, tall with a wide tangle of sprawling branches and a thick trunk. Alvere took me straight to it.

When we drew close, I noticed something odd. Small, low branches, which seemed to have been carved flat on top, progressed up around the tree... like steps! We mounted those, circling tightly upward — we had to release hands for this part — until we came to a wide platform in the high branches of the tree. From the bottom, this had looked like a tangled web of branches, but from the top... they were perfectly smooth, a lattice of merged branches with only tiny holes between. The trunk continued up and there were branches above us, but this entire level was open and flat, all the way around the tree.

Oh, this is wonderful! Auwei said in awe.

I had to agree.

Alvere stood there, ignoring the wonder of this strange tree and instead looking out over the forest and the plains beyond. Admittedly, it was a spectacular sight, sun setting behind a bank of clouds, turning the sky turquoise and the clouds to yellow and orange flame.

I grasped his hand again and squeezed it. "Thank you for bringing me here, it's wonderous!"

He smiled faintly. "I found it not long after coming here. I felt... drawn to this place. I think it's a Fey lookout." Those beryl-blue eyes twinkled at me, but only for a moment before growing dark and dim, and he looked away. "What are we going to do Legs?" he asked, sounding a bit hopeless.

I didn't know and couldn't answer.

But perhaps I could take his mind off his troubles, even if only for a moment... just not here. It was a bit too exposed and open at the top of this tree. It was my turn to pull him. I tugged his arm and got him moving. We descended out from the branches and once back on solid ground, feeling less exposed, I turned to him and threw my arms around him for a surprise kiss.

His eyes widened. He was stunned only for a moment before I could feel some of his tension drain away as he held me.

I lingered in the kiss for some time, allowing it to develop organically until our mouths were wide: desperate and deep. Then I drew back with a mischievous grin. "I want to give you something," I said softly. "Help you forget about everything and think only of me, even if only for a time."

He smiled and raised a brow in question. I don't think he was expecting me to slip down to my knees and undo the tie on his breeches.

"Oh, Legs, no. Prince or King or whatever, you will never have to kneel before me. I—" he gasped as I ignored what he'd said and, pulling out his stiffening erection, ran the tip of my tongue along the underside of his shaft.

"Legs... Oh!"

My mouth enveloped him and I drew him deep, moving my hand down to his heavy sack and testing its weight in my palm. His length went rigid as I worked my tongue and teeth over him. His objections stopped, turning to shuddering, gasping breaths. When I stole a glance up at him, his head was tilted back, looking at the branches above us.

My intent was not to work him to release as I had with Silence. No, I wanted him hard and ready for the next bit.

I withdrew my lips but grasped him hard with my hand, squeezing a little. He looked down at me as I ran my tongue around his tip. "Are you thinking only of me now?" I asked playfully.

"Gods, yes!" he breathed.

"Good, because I want you concentrating fully on me for this next part." I rose and went to untie the belt of my skirt.

"Allow me," he breathed.

Curious, I moved my hands away, waiting for his touch... but instead he simply waved a hand and the belt undid itself and my skirt fell away. With another wave the tie at the bottom of my blouse — to keep it up over my belly-button, just in case — undid and the loose shirt lifted off.

I blinked.

He winked. "I'll tell you later," he said as he came for me hungrily, his erection throbbing from my previous ministrations.

I always seemed to forget how strong those slender arms of his were. He lifted me easily, and I threw my arms around his neck, legs around his waist as he lowered me upon his solid flesh.

It was my turn to gasp at his sudden thrusting, but I quickly progressed from tight and pained to receptive and eager. He turned, pressing my back to the rough bark of the tree, but I didn't care. It was the price of sex in nature, rocks and bark and roughness.

Raised as I was upon him, his lips found my breasts, kissing around their fullness as he picked up his pace, hard and needful inside me.

With my hands behind his head, I hugged him to me, encouraging his work upon my bosom as I tilted my head back. "Yes, my love!" I urged him.

His release came quickly, as I had suspected it would. He kissed his way up my neck and I tilted my head down to kiss him as he tensed and throbbed and trembled through his orgasm.

He gave me a pained look. I hushed the apology I felt coming with another kiss to his lips, then the soft words, "This was for you."

Something shifted in his look then, his clear blue eyes twinkling. He grinned. "Then the next will be for you... and I'm certain I'll remain distracted."

I smiled, liking the sound of that.

He withdrew and I was carefully set down. Then he removed his shirt and, with another wave of his hand, it wrapped itself around the rough bark of the tree. "Sorry if that hurt," he whispered. If it had, I hadn't noticed, though I'd probably have a scrape or two. He pulled me close and we kissed for a long moment again, as I felt his erection revivify between us.

When he released my lips, he turned me around slowly. I was a bit confused by this until I felt him pull me close again, his firm chest against my back. His arms around me seeking, stroking, caressing. He had much more ease of access in this position to touch me. His lips were soft upon my shoulders and neck, as I pulled my hair up and away for him. His one hand was firm upon my breasts as his other stroked softly over my folds. He had all the control, all the power, but I was the benefactor of everything. I leaned my head back upon his shoulder, looking up at the branches once more as his hands worked my arousal up to body-trembling heights.

I felt him shift and move. His erection slid between my legs then up to my opening. I was far more ready for him this time as his fingers, slick with my wetness, helped to guide him in. And though he could not go deep, this angle felt amazing!

I moaned and moved against him, letting him hear my appreciation. And he whispered in my ear: "I love you, Legs. I need you. You are my world."

Good, that was the point of this exercise. It was also pleasing to hear, and with his slow thrusting and miracle fingering, I merged those hot words into the whirlwind of passion swirling within me. He did not pick up his pace, but simply kept up all his precious teasing touches upon my now trembling flesh. For a moment his one hand left my loins to rise to my other breast and both hands grasped me hard, pressing me to him. I gasped and felt a mini-peak of bliss, body tensing. Then he moved those strong but agile fingers out to tease my hardened nipples and that peak rose and built.

"Yes," I gasped. "I'm so close!" I needed to let him know. If he was going to let loose, now was the time.

He tugged at an earlobe with his lips as his hands, hard-pressing, slid down my body to the front of my hips, one slipping a little lower still to press against the raging nub of my clit as he did indeed pick up his pace.

The first orgasm bucked me forward. I pressed my hips back against him, needing him deeper as I put my hands against the tree — now covered by his shirt — and used that as leverage to roll my hips back with each of his thrusts. I could hear his heavy breaths, but only barely over my own rough gasps as he slipped his fingers over my clit again and roused a second and more powerful wave of full-body bliss. I froze, tense and trembling as he thrusted harder still until his release. And feeling that heart-pounding surge inside me sent me spinning into an oblivion of ecstasy, my body going weak.

But his strong hands were there to guide me, help me up, as we trembled together for a long moment. Eventually he helped me to lay with my back upon him as he reclined on the ground. It was his turn for the rocks and roughness.

It was a long time before I could speak, asking, "What are you thinking about now?"

"You," he said kissing my shoulder. "And right now, I couldn't imagine thinking of anything else." His hips bucked with an aftershock of bliss as he gasped. Then I gasped. Then we laughed together. "I love you, Legs, thank you. You are the most amazing woman."

"You're pretty amazing yourself. Don't forget it. When you're troubled by anything else, just remember me and how amazing we are together and know you can do anything."

Awkwardly, we shifted so we could touch lips. The kiss was deep but brief.

"I will," he whispered. "I will."

We lay together for a while longer, as the evening grew dark, before finally separating and dressing.

"What was that thing you did, with my clothes and your shirt?" I asked, remembering now.

Oh yes, that was fascinating! I'm so curious! Auwei was near to giddy. This was what Lumani lived for, the many new and interesting experiences of this world.

He laughed. "I don't tend to show that to anyone, even my own people. It's a Fey thing."

I raised a brow. "Oh?"

"Yes, Fey magic comes through the working of material. Some are good with wood, others with metal, some with clay and earth, others with living beings, and some... with cloth." He flipped his hand and put his arms up and his shirt slid itself over him. He grinned.

I recalled how Midnight had made that branch appear then disappear from the wooden support in the barn, when interrogating that brute.

Oh yes, you're right; fascinating!

"It's actually very useful. I don't need armor, I can make my own clothes as hard as steel. It takes little concentration now, I've been practicing it most of my life. I can unravel threads, and make them reach across a room to get a cup or pour a kettle. Again, I don't do it often, only when I'm alone, and I'm sure I'm not nearly as proficient as a full Fey would be, but..." He shrugged. "It can come in handy from time to time."

I imagined so. "That is amazing," I said and meant it.

"I wouldn't say it's any more or less amazing than you becoming a spider or having powers of such an animal."

I nodded. "True."

I am pretty amazing, aren't I? Auwei said with mock modesty.

You are. I laughed inwardly with her.

Alvere and I chatted, comparing our powers as we made our way back down the hill and into the forest. Apparently, he also had exceptional night vision. While I had to trust to my spider-sense in the dark.

And perhaps it was because it was dark and I was already concentrating on my spider sense that I sensed something. I stopped us both with an outstretched arm and a quick, quiet, "Hush."

He looked at me inquiring as my hairs prickled and listened. There were people around... many people... creeping through the forest. It took me a moment longer to sense the number and direction. A force of perhaps five hundred, moving west to east through the forest.

I pulled Alvere close, hot breath on his ear in the barest of whispers. "It's an Elistan raid on your camp!"

I felt his body tense.

Neither of us had brought weapons.

We were trapped, behind the enemy, with no way to warn the Vauphan of the impending raid.

CHAPTER 22

WE HID IN SOME BRUSH, HUDDLED TOGETHER AS THE NIGHT GREW
chill. The force in the woods was moving slowly and hadn't turned
south toward the camp yet. I was confused by this, until I thought
of something. I whispered my suspicions to Alvere, so close my
lips brushed his ear as I breathed the words. "I think they're trying
to get *behind* the camp."

He made a face. My night-sight wasn't as good as his, but I
could still see him by the faint, few speckles of moonlight filtering
down through the branches above. Shifting, he breathed in my ear
and the hot breath and soft voice made me shiver just a little...
even if it wasn't sweet-nothings he was whispering.

"Why? Five hundred men could do some damage if they
surprised us, but... where will they retreat to when finished?"

I couldn't answer. But they must have some plan.

Luckily, if this troop passed us by, we'd be able to run back to
camp and warn them, hopefully before the attack occurred.

So, as soon as I sensed that the five hundred were far enough
away that it would be safe to move, we rose and began our dash for
the edge of the woods.

But we only made it a few feet.

Once again, I stopped Alvere and we ducked into bushes. "More!" I whispered. Another group sneaked through the woods from the west. My spider sense had picked them up, and I could see distant shadows moving among the trees.

"How many?" Alvere whispered to me.

"Another five hundred is my guess," I breathed in return.

But these troops found spots to hide and hunkered down.

"An attack from all sides?" Alvere whispered to me.

I nodded, it seemed likely. We needed to warn the Vauphani camp.

You could float like you did to get into the Elistan camp, Auwei suggested.

Yeah, if the breeze is right. I sighed. It might be our only option. The trouble was, I wouldn't be able to bring Alvere with me, he'd be stuck here, alone, with enemies virtually all around him.

I didn't want to leave him, but someone had to warn the Vauphani. I put my lips to his ear once more, to fill him in. "If I get high enough in one of these trees, I can float on spider silk and probably fly over this group to warn your men, but... you can't come." I felt his hesitation. He wanted to turn his head and speak, but I continued. "You need to flee, go back to that tree or find some Fey, get to safety. I'll warn the camp."

I felt his jaw tense.

He drew in several deep breaths, before finally nodding. Turning to me, he whispered, "Good luck, my love." Then he kissed my cheek.

"And to you, my love," I whispered. Then with a final kiss, we parted. He rose and padded away as silent as the night, back up the hill.

I veered to spider form and scampered up a tree to the very top. I did as I'd done before, weaving a sail of spider-silk and catching a breeze.

But the breeze was strong and from the east. It pushed me in the wrong direction until I caught on another tree.

There was another option though...

I scampered down the tree to a branch which would support me as a human, then transformed back.

I launched myself, with my powerful legs, up and angled out of the forest to the south. This worked, though I did tear through the upper branches of a few trees, acquiring a few scrapes and ripping my clothes.

Once I'd hit my apex and began to fall, I transformed back to a spider and quickly wove another small sail of silk, to slow me a bit before I landed. This way I wouldn't scare any of the Vauphani sentries, nor would I alert the Elistans in the woods.

I floated to the ground at the edge of the camp, then ran for all my little eight legs would carry me for Alvere's tent. Once I reached it, I returned to my form and called out for the others.

Only Maverick was still in the front part of the pavilion. "Attack! Surprise attack from all sides!" I hissed at him as I ran for my armor and weapons.

He was up in an instant and roused the others.

"I'll get help!" Fin said and disappeared.

We all hurried to get into our armor. Each second that ticked by felt like an hour.

Once we were ready, Maverick commanded us, "Get out there and make as much noise as you can. If we're lucky we'll wake the camp, if we're luckier still the enemy will hear us and call off their attack, but I doubt that will happen."

Just before we left, Fin returned with most of the rest of our House: Ant, Midnight, Tusk, Fennec, Foggy, Princess, Sparrow, and Silence. The last two I didn't want to be here, not in the middle of a fight like this, but I couldn't fault them for coming, the people they loved were in danger.

Maverick told them what to do and we ran in all directions calling out, shouting as loud as we could.

"Alarm!"

"Men in the woods."

"Men behind the camp."

"Watch from all sides."

"Sneak attack!"

That got the camp moving... but it also must have spooked the enemy, or we were just a little too late, as we began to hear the sounds of combat, shouts and cries from all sides; all sides except the direction the enemy should have come, across the battlefield.

The battle had begun.

CHAPTER 23

she could, while Silence stuck close. He had a longsword and small shield but no armor.

"We had to flee the manor," he said as we moved carefully through the night toward the sounds of fighting. "And we couldn't bring everything. Some brought armor, but I... didn't think I'd need it. I feel a bit stupid about that now." His voice was quavering as we drew closer to the battle-line.

Sparrow returned, flashing back to herself, shaking her head. "My night vision isn't great and the enemies carry no torches, I saw only a shadowy mob of men moving from the forest in to the edges of the camp. Sorry," she said, and I heard the fear in her voice too. She had armor like mine, a breastplate, grieves and bracers, with the addition of a chain skirt to protect her hips and upper legs. She carried a bow and quiver, a short sword at her hip.

What were we doing? I was barely trained for this. Silence was little better. Sparrow was the most experienced but still had never seen true battle like this. She'd always been a scout.

"We... could go back," I said hesitantly. Yet, my *Hero* gift was rising within me, and I needed to be out there. I couldn't run away. I was less concerned about my own death and more about theirs.

You must fight, but you can't bear to see those dearest to you hurt, it's natural. All warriors feel some mix of fear for themselves and their allies. It is what you do now, in this critical moment that counts. Auwei was right.

I saw the momentary relief on Silence's face at my suggestion, but quickly that turned hard. Sparrow's jaw twitched, clenched, determined.

"We stay," Silence said, stalwart and firm.

"We fight," Sparrow echoed his tone.

"We fight to protect this army and... each other," I said. "Stay close if you can."

They nodded to that, then we were moving out, faster now, hurrying to the front.

Had we gone south or east, things might have been different. I'll never know. But the North was where the fiercest fighting was that fateful night... and where my true enemies waited.

The three of us reached the battle lines and supported the Vauphani troops already fighting, most without armor, some in nothing but nightshirts, fighting without weapons. They'd been caught mostly unawares, sleeping, but they fought fiercely, knowing their lives were on the line.

Silence, Sparrow, and I fought as a unit. Sparrow stayed behind Silence and me, using her bow to pick off targets coming from the sides. I was quick. Silence was quicker, darting in and out, avoiding the slashes of axes and swords. My spear worked well, I had a longer reach than most of the enemy and dealt with them before they were a threat. But then some strong man caught the haft of the weapon as it was thrust at him. A quick jerk and he pulled it from my hands. Sparrow put an arrow through him a moment later, but I didn't have time to pick up the weapon with others rushing in. I had to switch to swords.

I was surprised to find out how good I was in the chaos of a melee. I would have assumed these dedicated soldiers were well trained, and it isn't that they weren't, but my training seemed to have been... better.

The fighting drew close, the enemy on all sides. Sparrow had thrown down her bow and was using her sword now, the three of us fighting in a tight circle. We may have been better trained, but the sheer number of the enemy wore us down. We all bled from various nicks and cuts, nothing serious... yet.

"I love you... both!" Silence called out.

What was he doing?

I couldn't see him beside me and couldn't spare a glance for fear of an enemy taking advantage of my lapse in attention. But when I heard him grunt in pain, I couldn't help myself.

I looked quickly to see him holding his stomach, shield lost, but he was fighting still. I returned to fighting my foes, but my concern spiked.

He'll not last long with a wound like that, I whimpered internally.

It's a gut wound. He'll last long enough.

Long enough for what? I asked Auwei.

But she had no answer.

Yet it turned out she was right.

A moment later fresh Vauphan troops found us, these ones well-armed and armored. They had probably been at the center of the camp and had time to prepare for the fight. They swept past us, pushing the Elistans back. The three of us were left alone in their wake.

Silence fell to his knees, and Sparrow and I both dropped our weapons to turn and try to catch him as he swayed.

We helped him lay back. His gaze flicked back and forth between us. "I love you," he kept saying.

Spirits no! Don't die you wonderful, innocent man!

I pulled up the light padding under my armor to get a handful of my webbing. "Show me the wound!" I said urgently. He didn't seem to understand, but Sparrow was able to pry his hand away from his belly. I could tell instantly, it had been a stab, not a slash. A small opening, not a long one, but that meant it might also be deep, which seemed likely given how it was gushing blood. I pressed the webbing over the wound, hoping to close and clot it, pressing hard. "Tear up his shirt," I commanded Sparrow. "We need bandages."

"It's filthy."

"It's better than nothing!"

She nodded and began ripping off this shirt and tearing it into strips, tying them together so we could wind it around his midsection. He lost consciousness, but was still breathing, if shallowly.

I couldn't lose him.

Turning to Sparrow, tears in my eyes and hoarse desperation in my voice I said, "Find Ant, please!"

She nodded and flitted away as a bird a moment later. Her night sight might not be good, but Ant was massive and hopefully easy to find.

The sounds of battle receded. I hoped that meant the enemy was retreating. I wasn't paying attention, consumed with trying to keep Silence alive as if by force of will alone. He just needed to survive long enough for Ant to get here and heal him, just that long. But time seemed to pull and stretch. Every instant with Silence felt like an eternity. My vision became blurred with tears. The *Hero* gift inside me hardened into a terrible thing fused to revenge. If Silence died, so help the Elistan army. I'd slay them all myself!

Legs! Auwei tried to warn me, but I wasn't listening.

"There she is."

At first, I thought the female voice was Sparrow, leading Ant to me. It was a testament to how addled I was, that it took me far longer than it should to realize two things:

First: that wasn't Sparrow's voice, but I'd heard it before...

Second: there were more than two people drawing close to me. My hairs pricked up and my spider sense detected a group of five, three of them in the forms of large cats.

Pits!

Legs! Move! I listened to Auwei this time.

I ducked and rolled to the side as a clawed hand swept through where I had been. But I couldn't go far, I was surrounded.

Looking up, I saw Lady Claw sneering down at me. Her armor was well fitted showing off her curves, while still remaining practical. She held no weapon, but her hands were gleaming with long claw-like nails. It had been her who'd just tried to kill me.

"I'll gut you and eat your entrails," she said with a feral grin.

How very unpleasant.

The other one in human form was Lynx. His face was hard. I could see a hint of remorse, but far more hatred and fury. He spat out his words when he spoke.

"We got the news of your betrayal just after you left our camp." He clenched his jaw, showing his teeth in a mockery of a grin. "You played me for a fool, trying to sway me while gathering intelligence." He shook his head. "Your House is a menace, and you are the rot at its core!" He held two long curved knives, both nearly the length of a short sword.

I scooped up one of my swords — only one was within arm's reach — and rose, terrified. I may have been able to take Lady

Claw and Lynx, but they were not alone. With them was a massive tiger, a powerful lion, and the slinking, deadly form of a jaguar.

I could leap away, out of reach of all of them but Silence would surely die. I knew I wouldn't have time to bend and scoop him up; they were too close. I should have picked him up instead of my sword, but I'd made my choice and now I was stuck. If I left, Silence died. If I stayed, we both died.

My *Hero* gift decided for me. I couldn't leave. Power surged into me, strengthening me as I settled into a fighting stance.

Lady Claw laughed, then lunged at me.

CHAPTER 24

IT WAS A FEINT. CLAW DODGED AWAY AS I SWIPED AT HER. I HAD hoped to remove one of those deadly, clawed hands of hers, but she was too quick.

The real attack came from Lynx, behind Claw, and Lion behind me. I'd sensed the movement of both of them. I lunged forward, getting in close with Lynx, hoping to avoid Lion. Yet, I only managed to block one of Lynx's long knives, the other blade skittered along the front of my armor, hard enough to leave a gouge, but not hurt me. And I only partially avoided Lion's attack, one of his claws raked over my left calf. I'd shifted enough that the cuts weren't deep, but they were deep enough to bleed and that would cost me strength eventually.

As they retreated, Tiger and Jaguar surged in. Tiger leaped high, while Jaguar kept low. I waited for the perfect instant, then leaped a little while veering into my spider form, with the effect of suspending myself in the air, over Jaguar's slashing claws and under tiger's flashing teeth. They passed by and I returned to my form, lashing out as I did, a glancing blow on Jaguar's hip. The large cat yowled.

I laughed with elation and victory. Five on one and I'd still managed to land a hit. Not a deep one, but enough to celebrate.

Lynx and Claw came at me from different angles, and I spun, going up on one leg to put myself near to sideways, lunging at Lynx, blocking his attack while moving the rest of my body out of his reach, and at the same time kicking Claw's arm.

I then threw myself at Claw, following up with a second, spinning kick and caught her shoulder, sending her to the ground. But I'd ignored the others for just a little too long. I sensed Lion leaping at me while in the middle of my spin kick, I couldn't get out of the way and tried to veer into a spider, but Lion was too quick and caught me mid transition. One set of claws raked along my side, then slammed me — now a spider — down to the ground. I hit hard and three of my spider's legs crumpled under me. Lion leaped away, but the damage was done.

I shifted back to human, feeling the pain in my left leg. I'd not be moving quickly from now on. And his claws had hit behind my armor, my exposed back above my hip, and I felt the burning sting of the four marks upon me.

I tried to move out of the way of Tiger rushing in but put too much weight upon my left leg and fell, crumpling. Tiger hovered over me — massive maw open and heading for my throat — as time seemed to slow.

This was it.

Then a sparrow — shifting into a small woman — hit the side of Tiger's head in full flight and knocked the beast off course, the two of them tumbling to one side.

A charging bull tore through the scene, scoring a glancing blow on Lynx, while Claw nimbly slipped out of his way. She managed a raking claw attack on Maverick's flank. Then my Housemates flooded in to surround me as Ant appeared, kneeling next to Silence. The large man looked at me and my wounds.

"Him first!" I said through gritted teeth and Ant nodded.

I tried to rise, but my leg gave out beneath me, and I cried out despite myself.

Shouldn't I be stronger than this? Shouldn't my gift be helping?

Your gift let you survive five on one for long enough for your friends to arrive. Now let them do some work for a bit.

I conceded that point to Auwei.

Ant gasped, finishing with Silence. I could see the weariness on his features as he turned to me. I wanted to tell him I was fine, to save his strength for fighting, but I couldn't, I was aching and stinging and needed help.

His healing energies flowed through me, my leg strengthening as my cuts shrank, not completely healed, but enough not to bother me too much.

Then Ant winked and drew forth his staff. Yet I saw how he stumbled when he rose. I wondered how many others he'd already healed this night.

I got up, trying to take in everything around me, but in the dark my eyes couldn't catch the movement. It was all too fast. So, I closed my eyes and let my spider-sense take over.

Maverick and Amber were managing to get Tiger to retreat. Jack was attacking Lady Claw, and keeping her at bay. Ant headed for Lion, who was attacking Sparrow. Sparrow herself was a dervish of speed, flitting around the battle even in her human form, dodging the large cat's attacks. I couldn't sense Jaguar, perhaps he'd fled when the reinforcements arrived?

Fennec fought Lynx. Though even as I sensed them, Fennec grunted and went down, Lynx stalking in toward me. That was it for reinforcements from my House, the others must have been elsewhere in the battle and Sparrow had not been able to round them up.

I had one sword in hand and my other was close by. Diving at it, I rolled and came up with both swords before sinking into a fighting stance to face Lynx.

"You've learned a lot of tricks in the short while you've been Bonded," he said, voice heavy with loathing and a hint of weariness. "But I've been Bonded longer, and I know more."

We'd see.

He roared and charged. For a moment, it was all I could do to block his furious attacks, barely able to see his blades in the dark of night. I even closed my eyes, focusing just on what I could feel and centering myself as I defended.

Then I dug in, my gift rising, and I stopped giving ground, holding firm. He roared with frustration as I began to counterattack, seeing the patterns in his swift-bladed style of fighting.

I sensed it, something from him, some intent, before it happened and even as he veered to his avatar, I did the same, doing my leap-evasion from earlier, managing to land on his back as he dove through where I had been. I bit his back, letting all my venom sink into him, but it seemed to do little and he spun his head around raking a tooth over where I was. I jumped away before he hit me. Shifting back to human I slashed at his flank, but he was too quick. He ran a short distance, then turned and roared again, though as a Lynx it came out as a shrieking squeal, not the most intimidating thing, but certainly jarring.

He charged back in and I braced. This time I wouldn't evade. My gift surged, my legs strengthened, arms swelling with power. Again, my senses picked up his intent before it happened. He shifted back to human as he leaped at me, both knives out before him. I saw the opening instantly. Time slowed as I brought my swords together, tight, then as his blades passed to either side of mine, I drove my arms out, causing his blades to go wide of me. But he was still headed straight for me, and seeing his predicament he was veering back into a cat, fangs ready.

But I was inside his guard and just had to time myself right...

...bringing my swords together with all my strength, crossing before me, and severing his head.

The body still hit me with all the force of a leaping, large cat, and knocked me to the ground.

I rolled it off me, blinking blood out of my eyes, as the body twitched and spasmed in the throes of death.

Far too much hot blood covered me. That was a consequence I hadn't entirely been prepared for, but should have expected, cutting a man's head off at close range.

Sparrow appeared next to me.

"You look like The Pits," she gasped, breathing hard.

"I'm aware." I was still trying to get blood out of my eyes. I concentrated on my other sense while I did, but still asked. "How are the others doing?"

"Ant's got Lion under control. Jack's still battling that crazy woman, and Amber and the Boss—"

I heard the cry of pain and felt through my senses the large shape falling to the ground.

Maverick. Though I couldn't tell what had taken him down.

"No!" Sparrow cried out.

I turned, squinting through the blood and tried to peer into the night, but I couldn't see. All I knew was that Amber was now fighting Tiger alone, and he was a big bruiser with speed to boot.

"See if you can do anything for Fennec," I said to Sparrow, remembering how he'd been taken down by Lynx. "I'll help Amber." And I launched myself in her direction.

My vault was more horizontal than vertical, rushing over the ground. I was on track to plunge my swords into Tiger's side... when everything went to The Pits.

I sensed the form only as I drew near. A tiny form, a flying bug of some sort. It moved fast, flying into my path then shifting into a large man, whose fist came up into my gut. Lord War's punch hit me so hard it threw me backwards and my swords were tossed from limp hands.

I landed heavily on my back, skidding in the dirt a few feet, the breath knocked out of me. I gasped but couldn't seem to draw a breath as the massive form of Lord War stalked toward me.

It was only then I recalled his avatar was a warrior wasp.

I was still stunned, frantic for air and unable to move. I couldn't get out of the way as he knelt and slammed his fist into my face.

The bottom of my face crunched, crushed: nose broken, teeth knocked in, my jaw twisted to the side, dislocated. I blacked out—

—and was instantly brought back as pain, unlike anything I'd ever felt before, surged through me and I would have screamed if my broken mouth had been capable. My body convulsed and writhed, out of my control, as my face exploded with pain far beyond the damage already done. Some distant part of me — perhaps Auwei — knew this to be the warrior wasp's sting, one of the most painful things imaginable. But as a man, War's stinger was his fist.

I was distantly aware of Lord War laughing as he slipped a hand under the collar of my armor to lift me, his fist rearing back for another strike. I'd not survive a second hit.

Then the massive form of a bull hit Lord War, knocking him aside, throwing him. The bull snorted then became a man.

"Spirits," Maverick breathed, kneeling over me. "Ant, we need you now!"

Maverick looked pretty rough himself, bleeding from several wounds, one of his arms held close as if he didn't want to move it much.

"That sting packs quite the wallop, doesn't it? Took me out for a moment." His voice was panicked. "Legs? You in there? Spirits of the... Ant! Hold on, Legs." He smiled as if trying to reassure me, but there were tears in his eyes. "Of all of us, you need to live.

You're the one the mistweaver said would ruin all their plans. So you live, you hear me? That's an order!" He looked away. "Bloody bones, War is up again. I gotta go, Ant will be here soon, I promise! You keep fighting!" Then he rose and squared his shoulders. "You want her? You'll have to go through me!"

CHAPTER 25

MY WORLD SPUN, TILTING WILDLY AS THE SHOCK-INDUCING PAIN slowly faded. That left only the broken face pain, which was still enough to make everything hazy.

I'd probably black out again, but I couldn't. I couldn't let Maverick face Lord War alone. Yet all I could do was watch — my spider sense setting the scene — as War charged in. He and Maverick were weaponless, but one hit from those powerful fists of Lord War and he'd sting Maverick, stunning him. That was all he'd need. But Maverick was far from being a hapless bumpkin. His unarmed technique was different from what Amber had taught me, but he was no less skilled and kept batting away War's fists before they could reach him, even managing to land a couple hits of his own on his massive opponent.

Something's happening! Even Auwei's voice seemed far away. She must also be using my spider sense, but was able to sense farther than I could, since I was only barely conscious.

I couldn't talk, but I could still communicate with my True-Bonded. *What?* I asked.

Auwei's voice surged with hope. *Lady Claw is fleeing from Jack.*

But just as quickly I felt Auwei's hope turn to despair. *Oh no! It was a feint.*

What?

Jaguar is back! He caught Jack unawares and... Sparrow is trying to stop him, but... he's thrown her off, she's down... and oh! Spirits Alive! Jack's... not moving.

Is Panther going for Sparrow? My heart lurched.

No... Spirits! He's going for Amber. She's having a tough enough time fighting Tiger alone. She's held her own this long, but she won't see Jaguar coming!

Through the haze and the pain, I tried to call out, tried to warn Amber, but all I did was croak a pathetic sound and cause myself more pain. I nearly blacked out. I lost contact with Auwei for a moment, and when I regained enough of myself to speak to her again, I felt her anguish.

Amber?

She's...

No!

Yes.

I heard a roar, a sound so terrifying, so full of primal rage and pain my entire being sought to flee this place.

And I knew who had made that sound.

Ant?

Yes. He's dealt with Lion and is now taking on Jaguar and Tiger alone. Spirits, he's... terrifying...

Wait... someone is arriving... it's... Midnight! She's hurt Lord War. He's fleeing!

Distantly I heard Maverick's weary voice. "I don't know if you can get in there without being hurt yourself, but if you can help Ant, or get him away from those two, Legs needs help!" Then he was kneeling over me again. "One more moment, Legs, Ant is coming." I saw the strained look on Maverick's face. His forced smile and pained eyes were saying: *by all the Spirits you're a mess.*

Auwei continued her narration of events. *Midnight has joined the other fight. I... yes! Tiger is down, Jaguar is fleeing. He's too fast for Ant to catch. Ant... I think he wants to give chase, but Midnight has stopped him. He's... coming this way. Midnight is flying off, perhaps to make sure Jaguar doesn't circle back once again for a final run at us?*

I saw Ant, face hard, but streaked with tears kneeling over me. I faintly heard him mutter, "At least I can save you." Then I felt his healing pour into me once again, my face mended, the pain faded, but I could see how much it took out of Ant. He'd pushed himself too far. Maverick caught him, laying him down as he passed out. But I was healed.

Take it slow, I can feel how exhausted your body is, all this healing has taken a lot out of you.

Not to mention fighting for my life... and the lives of my friends and family in House Maverick. I sat up slowly, feeling so very weak. My head spun for a long moment, and I breathed a long "ohhh..."

Maverick looked over at me. "You're quite the sight. Who's blood are you covered in?"

After what had happened to my face, probably a lot of my own, but mostly... "Lynx," I groaned.

Maverick smiled. "Good." He got into a crouch and offered a hand to help me up. I took it.

I looked away only for a moment, to get my feet under me, and in that instant the hand holding mine went limp and for the second time that night a hot spray of blood poured over me.

I hadn't been paying attention, hadn't had my senses up. I'd been too tired. I fell back as Maverick released me.

When I looked back, I saw Lady Claw standing behind Maverick. In one hand she gripped his hair, pulling his head back. Her other hand, claws extended, was a mess of gore from ripping out his throat. She looked a fright, bloody and bruised, eyes filled with madness.

Maverick... was dead, his eyes vacant and unseeing.

It had happened so fast, and I was so weak, I just lay on the ground trembling. My *Hero* gift fled, my spirit shattered at the sight of Maverick's dead eyes and blood-covered body.

"I've killed the head of the House," Claw sneered, voice pained. I could tell she wasn't doing well either. "Now for its heart." She tossed Maverick's corpse to the side as her eyes went hungry with bloodlust.

An arrow caught her a glancing blow on the shoulder and she cried out in shock, looking toward the woods in the distance. She snarled and a moment later was in cat form, bolting away at full speed.

Uncertain what was happening, I knew only that I had to help Maverick. I crawled toward him. Maybe, if I could wake Ant...

But no, Maverick was well dead, far too much blood staining the ground around him. I couldn't believe it. I lost myself, weeping hot bitter tears.

This was my fault. Those Nobles had come to kill me and... and my Housemates had died, protecting me.

Maverick's words came to me, replaying over and over in my mind:

Of all of us, you need to live. You're the one the mistweaver said would ruin all their plans. So you live, you hear me! That's an order!

I needed to live, and for that — for me — how many of my new family had died? Maverick, like a father to me, would never again smile that warm smile of his. Fennec was probably dead. Foggy would never forgive me. Jack had been like an older brother, well more like a stepbrother who thought you were hot and wanted to sleep with you. Ant was alive, but I'd seen the pain written clearly on his face. His words made sense to me now: *At least I can save you*, which meant he hadn't been able to save Amber. She'd been like an older sister to me, more experienced in... everything and always seemingly knowing what I was doing and who I was with. Always there to help. Now she was dead too, and her death had nearly killed Ant.

Spirits! What had I done?

"Legs? What happened?" I recognized the voice, but it took me a long moment to register it.

Alvere knelt, holding me close. "Gods above, this is a mess. What in The Deepest Pits happened here?"

I couldn't answer. If I tried to speak only sobs came out as I cried upon his shoulder.

"Hush. We're here now," he said, stroking my hair. "I found some Fey in the woods. They repaid the fleeing Elistans for their treachery tonight. Then I went looking for you. I saw that woman kill Maverick and come for you. I..." He sighed heavily. "I'm sorry I missed her, but that shot was taken from nearly five hundred yards." I cried harder. "Yes, I know, just..." He held me tighter. "Gods, what a mess," he whispered.

And I couldn't agree more.

A mess that *I* had caused.

<h1 style="text-align:center">CHAPTER 26</h1>

IT WAS A LONG TIME BEFORE I COULD DO ANYTHING OTHER THAN cling to Alvere in desperation and defeat. Wordlessly, he helped me to my feet. I looked around slowly, but there weren't any bodies around me.

"The Fey moved them," Alvere said softly. "Come, you should rest."

"No," I croaked, voice hoarse and raw. "I... I need to see them. I need to know who's..." *still alive and who's dead... who I killed.*

You didn't kill any of them, Auwei said, trying to reason with me, but I wasn't in any mood to listen.

They died for me. That's the same thing. I may not have killed them with my own hands, but I got them killed.

Auwei sighed deeply. She kept trying to send me warmth and love, but I was hollow and cold right now, a void sucking in her emotions without feeling them.

"This way," Alvere said.

I walked, leaning heavily upon him, my legs faltering often, weak as water. Eventually he lifted me into his arms and carried me.

We came to an open area and laid out before us were some of the dead. Of the foes were Lynx, Lion, and Tiger. There were other mundane soldiers, but I gave them little attention.

I sought out those from my House. I found Maverick, Amber, Jack, Fennec, and Tusk. The last must have died elsewhere that night. I stared at them cold and unfeeling for a long moment, as I thanked the Spirits that Sparrow and Silence weren't among the dead.

"Have you seen enough?" Alvere asked, and I could hear the pain and sympathy in his voice.

I took another long moment to paint this picture in my mind. I needed to remember each of these faces. My friends, no my family, who had died for me. Finally, I turned away. Alvere scooped me into his arms once again and carried me to his pavilion. The common area in front had been filled with extra beds and on them lay wounded men.

Alvere set me down at my request as I sought my friends. Silence looked healthy but hadn't yet returned to consciousness. Princess was sleeping, her hands and head were bandaged. Fin looked rough, covered in a lot of bandages, many of which were soaked with blood.

If Fin died, we'd have no way to return home quickly.

"Will he live?" I asked Alvere, knowing the prince had no more information than I did. But a nearby woman, small and pale with dark hair — a Fey — replied to me.

"He will live, though he may be some time in recovering." The small woman seemed to be tending the many wounded in here.

Sparrow looked rough, a bandage on her head, covering one side of her face, and many others on various parts of her. Yet she smiled when she saw me. "I... didn't know what happened to you. I lost consciousness and woke to the Fey tending me." Her smile grew. "I'm so happy you're alive." A tear traced her cheek on the one side of her face not covered by bandages.

I couldn't share her joy. I was happy she was alive, but I was consumed by sorrow over the others who weren't. "Too many died," was my reply to her.

And saying that, I broke down again, falling to my knees and sobbing through my tirade. "They died because of me, died for me. I got them all killed. I'm a curse upon this House. I killed Maverick! He died... I... saw the life go out of him. He was so full of life and now it's gone. How can I ever...?" I babbled some more, incoherent words through my tears. I was lifted to sit up on Sparrow's bed and felt her and Alvere both embracing me, holding me as I blubbered and wept. Yet the pain wouldn't leave me. It was a thorn in my soul, no a thorn was too small, it was a mountain of agony, made of razor-sharp stone, tearing through me.

At some point, I lost consciousness.

I woke in Alvere's bed, but he wasn't with me.

Faint light filtered through the thick canvas. The night had passed.

I rose, still feeling weak.

You should rest, Auwei said.

I ignored her and stumbled out into the common area. Alvere was there, looking tired, speaking to the small Fey woman from the night before. It was she who noticed me first and hushed their conversation, ending it. Alvere came to me.

"You shouldn't be up. Rest."

"I'll rest when I'm dead," I said, voice bitter and harsh.

"There is nothing more to do now," he said.

"There *is* something to do," I spat back. "I'm going to the Elistan camp. I'll kill them all. You and your army can come with me, or not, I don't care."

Alvere sighed. "My army is in no shape to fight. I have all able-bodied men digging in, building fortifications. We cannot advance and cannot allow them to advance. We must hold here, but we have far too few men." He sighed. "Their attack was a success.

Nearly twelve hundred of my men died last night and almost two thousand others are wounded."

He sat me on a nearby cot. I wondered if the person who had occupied this bed had healed or died. In my current mood, and given what Alvere had just said, I presumed they were dead. "The enemy lost roughly six hundred by our count, perhaps more if they took some of their dead with them. And we don't know their wounded. Your Midnight is trying to do some scouting to find out more." He looked down at the thick rug over the earthen floor. Our numbers are roughly even now, and they'll end up with more once all reinforcements arrive. We need to be fortified by then." His voice broke a little. "I don't know what to do, Legs, I..."

I had an answer. "Let me go and kill them all."

"You can't!" he shouted at me. He was at his wits' end too. I knew it, but I had no sympathy for him. I had no feelings at all, only the hollow need for revenge. I needed to hurt something, kill something. "You can't," he said again softly, the bluster having left him. "Please, I can't lose you."

Too late, I was already lost.

No, Legs, you can have your revenge later, when you are healthier and have friends and allies to help you. You have so much to live for! There is love, for Silence and Sparrow and Alvere, and all the others still living of your House! There is the future. You are the one who is going to tear down the corruption within Elista. It won't be today, but you will. It's already been seen. Believe in that. Believe in something. Spirits, you feel so empty. This isn't you!

Yet all I heard of that was: *you feel so empty.*

I am empty, I said to Auwei.

No, you're not, her voice was stern. *You have me inside you at the very least, and I won't let you give up and die!*

I don't want to die. I want to kill. Kill them all. Kill everyone who did this!

No, Legs. Auwei was stern. *I can feel your true emotions. You say you want to kill, but in truth, you want to go into the enemy and thrash about taking some of them with you as you die. You think dying will ease the pain, but all it does is move your pain onto others. And you don't want that. You don't want Silence and Sparrow and the prince to feel what you're feeling now, do you?*

I felt something go hard inside me as I realized the truth of Auwei's words. I *did* want to die. I wanted my death to have meaning, because then *my life* would have meaning. Those who had died would have died for something. And no, I wouldn't wish my current state upon anyone.

But just because I saw the truth, didn't mean I liked it. If I couldn't die, then what could I do? All of what Auwei said earlier was true, there were things that could be done, but not now, perhaps not for some time. And that gaping chasm of time was the emptiness in my soul. An unending abyss into which I fell and fell and fell.

I rose stiffly. "I'll go back to bed then," I said to Alvere, and he smiled. Perhaps he'd thought his words — his love — had swayed me, but they hadn't. I felt hollower than ever. I returned to his room and fell onto the bed. I lay there, unsleeping, unable to rest, staring into the dark void that was my soul.

Days passed.

I was fed and tended to, but otherwise dead to the world. Alvere and Silence visited me, tried to help with words of encouragement, but I didn't hear them.

Even Auwei tried to lift my spirits. *I never told you the story of Woleia, my first True-Bonded, did I?* she asked, trying to rouse my interest. When I didn't respond, she continued. *I don't like to think of it. There was so much of interest we did together, but all of it was overshadowed by the one great loss in Woleia's life.*

I didn't want to hear about loss right now, so I didn't know why Auwei was telling me this, but I didn't stop her.

There were two men, Andus and Breem, both of whom loved her with all their heart. Auwei hesitated and I could feel her sorrow adding to mine. *But... both wanted her for himself, alone. They weren't willing to share and it tore all three of them apart.*

Again, I didn't want to hear this, but I couldn't block Auwei out.

Please stop, I growled at her.

She ignored me.

Eventually it came to blows. The two of them fought for her. I don't think they would have killed each other, they'd been friends before all of this... but Breem did die in that fight, an accident. He fell and hit his head on a rock. Andus won, but could never forgive himself, and neither could Woleia. They were never together after that.

Great story. I'm feeling so much better. Now be quiet, I grumbled.

You're missing the point, Legs. Auwei gave the sense of a heavy sigh. *You have people who love you, who are willing to share and even work together to give you all the love you deserve. That is the greatest gift in the world and something worth living for. Something to get out of this bed for!*

She was right, but still, I didn't want to hear it. And when I didn't get up and didn't deign to respond to Auwei she gave up, letting me wallow in peace.

Eventually, Lady Crane came to me, sitting on the edge of my bed.

"You've been sulking long enough," she said sternly, though with a motherly care and concern in her voice. "It is time to get up and rejoin the world. You have duties to attend to."

When I didn't respond, she went on. "The House has met. We talked and decided a few things. Firstly, you should know we've accepted Dove as a member of our House."

Dove... another loved one I'd endangered and who would probably die because of me. I remained stoic, unmoved and unmoving.

"Second, we needed a new head of our House and we've chosen one."

I felt the faintest sliver of curiosity, the only emotion I'd felt in a long time. Still, I lay there, staring at the canvas above me.

"We discussed it for a long time. Neither Midnight nor myself wanted it when..." She sighed heavily. "...when Maverick was chosen, and we still don't."

The man's name sunk like a knife into my heart. I winced.

"Fin is the next most senior member, but he doesn't want the position. He likes being off on his own. He knows he's not a leader. Next would have been Ant." I caught the twitch in her jaw. "He has a good tactical mind, but not a strategic one. He has trouble seeing the big picture at times. And... he... well..." Another sigh. She moved on without finishing her thought. "Foggy's too erratic. Princess too sedate. Dove is too new. Sparrow... well, she agreed with the rest of us on who our leader should be."

By this point, I knew what was coming. A sour sneer crept onto my face.

"We chose you, Legs."

I couldn't help myself, I let out a bitter, harsh laugh. A single "Ha!"

Crane sighed. She let me have my moment of incredulity before she went on. "I don't know how you did it in such a short time, but somehow you've become more to the rest of us than just a Housemate." She laid a hand on my shoulder, giving me a soft squeeze. "Legs, you've become the heart of this House, and now we want you to be its head as well."

Those words — echoing what Lady Claw had said after ripping out Maverick's throat — drove a spike of pain and fury into my heart. I sat up as an indignant rage flared to life within me.

"You're all bleeding mad!" I yelled at Crane, and she flinched back at the vehemence of my vicious words.

At that, the flap to my room was pushed aside and Silence and

Sparrow entered. Sparrow limped, leaning on Silence, still covered in bandages and looking weak. Wordlessly they came to me sitting to either side of me, hugging me without shame or pity, just the purity of their love.

Behind them, the rest of the House filed into the small room. Next was Dove, beautiful and resplendent in white, as usual. She sat on the bed close to me. Then Fin, still in bandages and looking like he could barely walk. Ant, looking like he'd lost some of his massive muscle, drawn and fatigued. I wondered how much he'd been helping with the healing. Midnight, grim but stalwart and sure, green eyes blazing with intensity, drilling deep into my soul and shining a light in the darkness there. Foggy, drawn and sad — he'd lost his brother and they'd been so very close — but with a determined quirk of a smile on his face. Princess, with the ferocity of a hunting cat in her golden eyes.

Behind them all, peering in without entering, was Alvere. He wasn't a part of the House, but I saw the immensity of his love for me in those brilliant blue eyes. He smiled and nodded as my family of Housemates drew close around me.

"I believe in you," Crane said with certainty in her voice.

"I believe in you." The words were echoed by the others:

Ant's deep baritone...

Foggy's high tenor...

Princess' soft silken tones...

Fin's full base...

Midnight whispered the words, but her tone was sure. "We believe in you."

Dove smiled. "I've always believed in you and known you'd do great things."

Sparrow kissed my left cheek and breathed close to my ear. "I love you, and I believe in you."

Silence kissed my right cheek and whispered, "I *need* you, Legs. I believe in you and need you to believe in yourself."

I believe in you, Auwei said firmly within me.

And the outpouring of love and esteem from my family finally broke the armored dam I'd built around my soul. All the emotions I'd been repressing flowed out. I felt an immensity of grief for those I'd lost, as well as my wonderous love for Silence, Sparrow, Alvere, and my family. So much pain and sorrow, but also a heartfelt joy. I was alive and so many I loved were still here with me.

I broke down and wept for a long time as my family drew closer around me, hands outstretched to touch me if they couldn't get close enough to hold me.

I let out all the pent-up filth I'd been clinging to. I'd wanted to wallow in the agony of loss, the pain of what I felt I'd caused. I couldn't quite let it all go. I still blamed myself for far too much of what had happened, and rightfully so. If I'd never joined Maverick House, most of what they had gone through would not have happened. If I'd died in that first attack by the mistweaver the nation would have left Maverick alone.

But I couldn't deny that what we had done was right, was just, was good. And if Elista was to see the error of its ways it would need Maverick House to show it.

No, not Maverick House anymore.

Legs House?

Spirits, that sounded silly. I actually laughed in the middle of my heavy tears and several of the group moved back a bit. I managed to get ahold of myself long enough to mutter through my tears, "You all win. But by the Spirits, we can't call it Legs House."

Others chuckled a little as well.

"What would you suggest?" Crane asked.

We would be the House that crawled, unexpected, under the feet of the nation of Elista. We'd bring them down, even though we were small, and almost broken.

We were: "House Spider," I said firmly.

And with that I accepted my position... and my fate.

FORM AND FURY

THE MISTS OF ELISTA TRILOGY, BOOK 3

CHAPTER 1

PRINCE ALVERE OF VAUPHAN AND I STOOD ATOP A NEWLY constructed watch tower, his arm around my shoulder. I leaned into him, sliding my arm around his waist. We could see the distant ramparts of the Elistan camp. Closer to home were the earthwork and palisade the Vauphani were constructing. After the raid on the Vauphan camp twelve days ago, the Vauphani didn't have the numbers for any sort of offensive action. They had to dig in and defend. And the hope was, after this coming night, the Elistans wouldn't be able to form another assault either.

"You should be telling me I'm crazy," I said softly. "Railing against me going out there. Telling me it's futile and that I just want revenge for the death of Maverick."

Alvere shrugged. "Would it do any good?"

"No."

"I didn't think so."

"Am I crazy?" I asked, a hint of uncertainty creeping into my voice.

The plan we'd devised had two parts. First, a small group of us from Maverick House would sneak into the Elistan Camp —

shape-shifted into our small avatars — and take out the Elistan leadership. In particular, I'd vowed to kill Lord War and Lady Claw. The hope was that, without leadership, the Elistans wouldn't be able to mount any sort of assault. The forces here would be stuck in a stalemate. Second, a group of Fey in the Vauphani camp — those whose magic pertained to metal — were already performing a lengthy ritual. When they unleashed their power at dawn tomorrow, it would hex most, if not all, of the metal in the Elistan camp. Armor would burn when worn, weapons would sear the hands that held them. Between our attack and the curse, we hoped that would keep the Elistan forces at bay.

After that, House Maverick — no we were House Spider now — would return to our nation, to cut out the rot of corruption within Elista. I had no clue how we were going to do that... but one step at a time.

"You'd have to be crazy to do what you're planning," Alvere whispered, "but I've accepted it. Crazy or not, I love you." He turned to kiss me on the cheek. I shifted so I could meet his lips in a quick, chaste kiss. I knew he was a prince — technically a king now — and who he married would be out of his hands. It certainly wouldn't be me. But we'd have some time together before that happened, maybe even after, depending on how possessive his future wife was. I was certainly willing to share.

And that thought made me think of Silence and Sparrow, my other lovers. I longed for them as much as I ached to be with Alvere. I hadn't been with any of them these last few nights as we'd planned our counter-attack upon Panther House and its forces. But I'd seen Alvere and Silence and Sparrow together from time to time. Given Silence had had some reservations about the prince, I asked Alvere, "Has Silence spoken to you... about... us?"

He nodded. "Yes." Alvere smiled. "While you were laid up Silence and I had a long talk. Silence even... kissed me." He touched his lips. Alvere seemed confused yet pleasantly surprised.

I raised a brow. That was a turn-around indeed.

"I had a chance to speak a little with Sparrow as she healed as well. They are wonderful and kind people and I see how much they love you," Alvere continued. "We may come from different places and different backgrounds but we all agree on one thing: our love for you." He sighed; voice tinged with shame when he said, "Despite the atrocities my people committed upon him, Silence seems to have forgiven me. I... I don't know how or why. He is truly a kind and generous soul."

"That he is. I'm glad you two are getting along. I'm very much looking forward to being with... both of you."

Alvere raised a brow and the curious intensity in his jewel-blue eyes let me know what he thought of that idea.

But that wouldn't happen tonight. Tonight would be for a different kind of action and excitement. Yet once this mission was done and we could take a well-needed break from things, I planned on getting all three of them together and *celebrating*.

I might even see if Ant wished to join our strange group of communal love. The large man was still devastated by Amber's death. It was clear, he loved her, even if he'd never admitted his love. She'd known, we all knew it, but I could see now how much it weighed on Ant that he'd never fully expressed himself to her. I vowed not to make that same mistake. Those I loved would know it.

And those I loved now included an entire Noble House. I was in charge and would need to care for all of them. It may have been a small house, so few members now, but that made it all the easier to know each one of them deeply. I didn't know half of them as well as I should, something else I vowed to change.

They had come together to help me escape the devastating dread and depression I'd fallen into after the death of Maverick, Amber, Jack, Tusk and Fennec. I still blamed myself for their deaths, just a little. But I also blamed the Elistan Nobles who'd actually killed them. And in the end, I knew they'd gone into that fight willingly, knowing they might need to lay down their lives for myself, for their House, and for peace between these two nations.

It was such an odd concept that for peace, some people had to die. I had hoped that wouldn't be the case, I had tried to talk to the Elistans — my own people — to get them to stop this madness, but to no avail. Those who led this army were part of a shadowy group of Nobles. They were the true enemy. They'd started this war, though we still didn't know why, and they'd also been killing off any Nobles — and their True-Bonded Lumani — who opposed them.

Tonight, I'd stop this war before those vicious Nobles could do more damage. The warmonger: Lord War, Field Marshal of the Elistan armies, would die so he couldn't retaliate. And Lady Claw would die for killing Maverick, that I had vowed. I hoped those who died tonight would be the last of this war... but I feared they wouldn't be.

The sun began to set.

"I need to get to my people and organize them," I said breaking away from Alvere.

"There's something I'd like to show you first, a bit of a surprise, if you'll allow it."

"What is it?"

"A surprise," he said with a mischievous grin. "Come on, I'll show you."

Curious, I followed him down the ladder of the watch tower. He walked fast, knowing I was needed elsewhere. I kept pace easily, as tall as him but with a bit more leg on me. His black hair shimmered with raven-blue highlights in the evening's dim light; his brilliant jewel-blue eyes dancing with life. I'd learned that these — along with his pale skin — were traits of the Fey. They were small and pale with dark hair and jewel-tone eyes. Alvere was half-Fey, but that was not widely known.

"Where are we going?" I asked, curiosity growing as we passed farther and farther to the back of our camp.

"You'll see." He grinned and winked at me. "Here," he said a moment later as we came around some tents to the makeshift smithy that had been set up by one of the Fey. I hadn't seen it done, but people said stones had been summoned from the earth to form the large forge-hearth and chimney, then a tent had been put up around it.

When we entered no one was there, and the forge was cold. The Fey smith who worked here would be helping the others who had affinity with metal perform the ritual to curse Elistan weapons and armor.

Alvere went to a long table on one side of the tent and picked up something before turning to me.

"What do you think?" he asked, holding up a beautiful breastplate. "I had Eorthan make a whole set of armor for you."

I moved in and ran my hands over the odd-looking metal. If it was steel, it had a strange golden burnish to it. "What is it made from?" I asked in awe, feeling the smooth curves of the armor. He handed it over to me and it felt light as air.

"It's steel, but Fey-forged, with their own unique magic." He grinned wildly. "Go ahead, put it on."

"There are no straps," I said, looking at the formed metal. "How do I put it on?"

He smiled and took the breastplate from me, then simply held it to my front. I felt an odd sensation, as if it was sucking itself against me, molding to my form. When Alvere released it, the armor stayed in place perfectly. What was more... it seemed to move with me, bend and flex as if it were cloth.

"Amazing," I breathed in awe. "I could get used to this." I looked up at him with excitement. "You said there was more?"

He helped me into the full suit: a breastplate and backplate, pauldrons and coverings for the upper arm, then bracers. A solid metal "skirt" in two halves, which fused together when put on the front and back of me, then it relaxed and moved like silk, even though it was hard as steel. Finally, there were grieves and even a pair of metal boots, which fit better than any leather set I'd ever had, comfortable and snug.

"This is incredible!" I gushed.

Have you seen anything like this before? I asked Auwei, the Lumani spirit who dwelled within me.

No, it's so light and comfortable. I've only worn armor for a couple of my previous lives and never much liked the feel of it, but this... this is a miracle!

And it was, truly.

"Thank you!" I said, overwhelmed with gratitude, throwing my arms around Alvere in a tight embrace.

"Thank Eorthan," Alvere said. "He's the one who made it. I'll introduce you tomorrow, once he's done with his ritual and you're... safely back here with me."

"I will," I said, growing solemn again, releasing him from the embrace to look him in the eye. Time was short, and I'd soon be away. I knew he was concerned for me. He'd given me this gift to protect me. "And I will return safely as well. I promise."

He nodded, but I could see the worry in his beryl-blue eyes.

As we made our way back to his pavilion he said: "There is another surprise I have waiting for you."

I was curious but patient. The first surprise had been amazing, so I hoped the next was just as good.

When we entered his pavilion five Fey in black cloaks stood off to one side. Also present were those going on the mission tonight: Midnight, Ant, Foggy, and Sparrow. The rest of my House: Fin, Princess, Dove, and Silence would be staying behind, but they were all here for this final briefing.

"Before you begin," Alvere said, raising his voice so all could hear, "I wish to aid you in tonight's mission. So, I have arranged for a few Fey to accompany you." He raised a hand at my stunned look and the questions he knew must be coming. "Surprise," he said with a just-try-and-stop-me grin. Then, "They have their own way of moving unseen and unhindered by walls and obstructions." He nodded to the group.

One of them stepped forward. Their cloak began to flap about them and they lifted from the ground slowly. At the same time, they seemed to fade into the darkness at the fringes of the tent. After a moment I had trouble seeing them and had to keep blinking to see their barely-there silhouette. In deeper darkness, they'd have been invisible.

"Thank you," Alvere said and the Fey landed, becoming visible again. That one continued forward, pushing back the hood of their cloak. It was a woman, small and slight with the Fey's pale skin, raven hair, and sharp features.

"I am Ahmaia, and I serve at The Uniter's will." She bowed to Alvere.

"Uniter?" I whispered to Alvere.

"Long story," he said. And now wasn't the time for it. I'd ask him again later.

Ahmaia rose and looked up at me. "We will aid as we can, but we will not kill. Life is most sacred to our kind." Her rose-gold eyes were hard, firm. In their depths I felt a weight of wisdom and age, though she seemed no older than myself. But then, Midnight was half Fey and seemed young, even though she was undoubtedly the oldest member of our — no, *my* — House. I didn't know how old she was, but I got the feeling she was past her fiftieth year at least. Ahmaia seemed older still.

"Understood," I said. "I appreciate your help."

Ahmaia nodded and returned to the other Fey.

I took command from there. "The plan is simple," I said, looking at each of my people in turn. Alvere leaned against a support post for the tent and smiled, watching me be all boss-like.

"Midnight will go in just after full dark and scout the locations of the leaders in the camp." I turned to Ahmaia. "Is that something you or one of yours could do as well?"

She nodded. "We will all go, that will expedite things, yes?"

"Yes, very much so. Just be back before the moon is at its zenith. That's when we'll regroup and set out. If the leaders are all close, we'll go as one team, if they're not, we'll divide up as needed. Our three primary targets are Lord War, Lady Claw, and Lord Jaguar."

"Jaguar's mine," Ant growled and the raw hatred and vehemence in the usually jovial man's voice made me flinch.

"Understood. Lady Claw is mine," I said, hopefully a bit less frighteningly. "Our secondary targets are any other high-ranking members of Panther House who would be able to take charge of their forces in the absence of the others. We want to leave no potential leaders alive."

"Might they be captured?" Ahmaia asked.

"We have no way of bringing them back here," I said.

"We do," the enigmatic Fey woman said with understated efficacy.

"Then yes, capture them and return them here. I'd prefer not to kill if necessary." Which then begged the question: did we *need* to kill War and Claw and Jaguar?

Perhaps not, but I didn't think I could stop Ant... and I wasn't sure I wanted to stop myself from dealing with Claw. I hated her with a fire in my soul which burned night and day and threatened to eat me up if I didn't do something about it.

I guess we'd see how the night went.

"Any questions?"

Foggy, standing on his head, as usual, said, "You already killed the one who killed my brother, didn't you?"

"Yes." Lynx, my old flame from long ago had killed Fennec, Foggy's brother. I'd then killed Lynx when he'd come for me next.

"Then I think we should try to capture as many as we can. We don't know who on their side knows the real reasons for this war. We shouldn't punish them all for something they may not know about."

Fair. "I'm fairly certain War, Claw, and Jaguar know," I said. "But you're right, outside of that we don't know and should not punish them for following orders. Capture if you can, work with the Fey." I turned to Ahmaia. "How many can you capture and bring back?" I assumed the answer was one each, but I'd learned not to underestimate the Fey.

Ahmaia considered for a moment. "Perhaps six or seven each?"

I blinked. "How?"

Ahmaia smiled. "Our cloaks and clothes are enchanted, there are pockets within where we might store... more than usually would be possible."

I didn't bother asking how. It was Fey magic. Giant-super-pockets, sure, I'd accept that. I had a glowing ball of spirit inside of me, granting me powers, so who was I to question strange things.

I am far more than a glowing ball of spirit, Auwei said indignant.

Yes, you are, apologies.

I nodded to the others. "It's nearly sunset. Let's all get something to eat and a bit of rest... Tonight we end this war.

CHAPTER 2

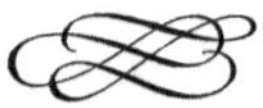

fly on their own, as could the Fey. I heard the faint fluttering of the
fabric of their black cloaks but couldn't see them in the night. One
Fey would accompany each of us. Our scouts had told us the
leaders were scattered throughout the camp, though there was a
concentration of a few near the center of the camp. Perhaps they
thought themselves safe there.

They were wrong.

I'd woven a small sail for myself, and when Sparrow let me go,
I floated down slowly. Ant wouldn't be coming with me. Jaguar
was elsewhere, and he'd promised his revenge on the man.

I was going after Lord War and Lady Claw. It seemed they
shared a bed now. It hadn't taken that long after Lynx's death for
Claw to move on. I didn't really mind. It made my job that much
easier.

I landed lightly and, through my spider-sense, I knew three
allies were nearby. One was Midnight, the other two were the Fey
accompanying each of us. Still in spider form, I crawled under the
tent flap to the dimly lit interior of the large pavilion. There were a

few guards within, dicing. When the two Fey moved through the tent-flap, the guards looked but saw nothing of course. A moment later, the four men let out muffled screams as cloth reached out to cover their mouths. I couldn't quite make sense of how the Fey 'pockets' worked, but the four men were swept into the cloaks and simply vanished. The two Fey, one of them being Ahmaia then shimmered to become more visible. I transformed and Midnight stepped out of the shadows. She put a finger to her lips. Not that the signal for quiet was really needed.

She motioned to the central room and held up two fingers and pointed to me. So... War and Claw were in there. And from the grunts and moans escaping through the canvas, I thought I knew what they were doing.

Ahmaia drew close and whispered in my ear. "I sense your desire to kill. Is this truly needed?"

Yes, Legs, is this truly what you want? I sensed Auwei's reservations. One of the reasons the Lumani Bonded with us was to have new and interesting physical experiences of the world. But killing wasn't one that Auwei wished to participate in. She felt my grief as her own. Even though their Lumani would have survived and returned to the Mists, those in my House who'd been killed had been to her as they had been to me, like family. Still, she did not wish for death as a revenge.

For a moment I hesitated. Was death what I wanted?

But then I remembered the hot blood pouring down onto me as Maverick died, the look of mad glee in Claw's eyes as she'd torn out the man's throat.

"The man can live," I whispered back. It might prove useful to have Lord War as a hostage. "The woman dies."

I felt Auwei's sigh of resignation. She didn't like this, didn't approve, but she'd allow me to do what I felt was necessary.

Ahmaia's eyes were hard, gazing at me for a long moment, but she eventually nodded. "I will take the man."

We moved to the tent flap. I veered into my spider to scuttle under the cloth. Ahmaia would know when to enter. She'd told me as much before we'd left.

I tried to ignore the sounds of passion from the bed and scampered along the ground to the far bed leg then up that to peer over the top.

The two were in the throes of passion, the large man kneeling as he drove himself into her. Claw's legs were wide, pushed to the side so he could get in close. He loomed over her, one hand rough on a breast, the other on her throat. Claw gasped and writhed, and somehow still seemed thrilled by this violent sex.

Even though my spider form was small, I didn't want to risk getting any closer than this. Despite their distraction I was sure I'd be noticeable against the pale sheets in the dim light.

So, I simply transformed where I was and stabbed at Claw with my short sword. She had no clue, eyes rolled back in blissful delirium, but War was quick to notice my transformation and lurched them both to one side, such that my blade only nicked Claw's shoulder. War leaped off and away from Claw to land on the other side of the bed. I was just a little distracted by the immensity of his glistening erection, and it was that moment of hesitation which cost me a quick victory.

Claw was up quickly and spun to kick the sword from my hand with a hissed, "Bitch!" My sword went flying. Even as I tried to draw my other, she lunged, claws out. I had to use both hands to block her. One of my hands caught her wrist, the other only adjusted her clawed strike slightly such that instead of it tearing out my neck the claws raked down the side of my face, not deeply, but enough to sting and bleed.

Ahmaia was in the room, I noticed through my periphery, even though I hadn't seen the tent flap move. War turned toward her as lengths of cloth reached out from her. But then he vanished... no, veered.

Claw tried to use her free hand the strike again, but as she reared back, I landed a quick stunning punch to her jaw. I then grasped her neck, squeezing, hoping she hadn't caught enough breath yet and I'd be able to weaken her, but I should have recalled how she'd found such things exciting.

She smiled, eyes flaring with pleasure. Her claws raked over my arm, skidding off my bracer before finding a small, unprotected area on the inside of my elbow. She tore at my flesh and kicked at the same time. I blocked with my own raised leg. I wouldn't be able to maintain my grip on her neck with my forearm torn open, so I simply threw her to the ground with all my strength, releasing her.

She hit hard, but rolled and sprang to her feet, facing off against me.

Ahmaia cried out in pain her hand going to her neck. That distracted me for the moment it took for Claw to sweep my legs out from under me.

I hit the ground hard, on my back.

She pounced.

I reacted on instinct, drawing my legs up and kicking her as she jumped upon me. She went flying, up and back, with a grunt. I spun to my feet as she landed — on her feet, like the cat she was — then she turned and tore a hole in the canvas wall of the tent, fleeing out into the night.

I followed, drawing my sword.

The pain of my arm and face had faded. My *Hero* spirit-gift had risen, even though I would be no hero tonight. Tonight, I was a spirit of vengeance.

Claw launched herself at me, and with a swipe of my sword, impassive and quick. I removed one of her hands.

She screeched a yowl of pain as the claws on her other hand skittered off my armor. She lashed out with her leg, another sweep, and I leaped just high enough to avoid it, landing close to her, my injured arm grasping her hair and yanking her head back.

"This is for Maverick," I hissed and ran my sword across her throat. I lifted her head up and back to let the blood flow faster, freer, and the fight went out of her quickly.

She went limp,

Dead.

Good. Something hard inside me hardened even more. It was done, I had my vengeance.

I tossed her body to the ground.

And only then became aware of the dozen or so men who'd come out from their tents, probably having heard Claw's scream. They'd seen me slay her. I whipped my sword down to shed the thick blood upon it and slowly spun my gaze to look at each of them in turn.

I can't imagine what I must have looked like in that moment, the look in my eyes, but every man around me cringed and fled.

Good.

I turned back to the tent... and Lord War's fist hit me solidly in the gut.

But unlike the time he'd punched me out of the air, and I'd gone flying, this time I was only knocked back a step as my armor seemed to disperse the hit, rippling like water when a stone is dropped into a still pond.

Lord War blinked, stunned. That had not been the reaction he'd expected.

I snapped a kick up to his face, which knocked him back... into Ahmaia's writhing cloth-arms. A moment later he was sucked into her magic pockets.

"You're bleeding," Ahmaia said, stoically.

I looked at my arm and shrugged. My *Hero* gift meant I was feeling little pain. I reached for my belly to gather some webbing to place over the wound. Even as I realized I was wearing armor over my belly-button and wouldn't be able to access my webbing, the metal of the armor... moved. It parted like flowing water once again, and I was able to gather some webbing into my hand. The armor closed up as I moved my hand away. I could definitely get used to this. I spread the webbing over my injured arm, stopping the blood for now. "I'll be well enough. There are more."

Ahmaia blinked then nodded. Midnight and the other Fey were finishing up with the two other Nobles who'd been asleep in the pavilion, and we spread out into the camp.

Claw's scream had woken others.

A man raced toward me, spear leveled, as another — in the form of a large cat — leaped at me.

Ahmaia's writhing cloth grabbed the leaping one out of the air, shunting him into her cloak as I deflected the spear thrust with my sword, driving it to one side of me before I lunged in and landed a strike on the man's leg, cutting deep. He fell screaming... for a moment... before he too was scooped into Ahmaia's cloak.

"That is five," Ahmaia said calmly. "I could take perhaps one or two more."

Just then, two younger Nobles ran at us. I recognized one from my time at Silverveil and the Noble's Test, though I couldn't recall her name.

One veered into a tressym and flew at me, claws extended. Ahmaia sucked that one into her cloak as I engaged with the other. She used a whip, and it was clear she'd been trained in combat, but... not as relentlessly as I had. She struck and the whip wrapped itself around my sword arm. I released the blade to grab the leather whip, then pulled the woman in close. I caught her by the neck, then tossed her to Ahmaia, who gobbled her up. The woman hadn't even screamed, she'd been so surprised.

Midnight and the other Fey joined us after that.

"There are no more Nobles left here," Midnight said stoically. "We're done."

I nodded, feeling the fury of battle begin to ebb, my gift starting to fade. Pain would return soon.

"Let's go," I said and veered in mid-hop, caught by Ahmaia, who then tucked me away in her magical cloak.

Even having known this was my escape plan, I still wasn't prepared for the absolute darkness and the press of heavy, grainy fabric on all sides as I was held, unable to move.

Luckily, I had no reason to leave this place and relaxed as much as I could for the trip back to our camp.

Still, I was relieved to be released once back in Alvere's pavilion. We were the last to return.

Sparrow flew into my arms and embraced me. I could sense and feel her excitement and relief, the pounding of her heart. She held me for a long moment before releasing me. She then turned to Ant.

I saw the man, covered in blood, looking at his large hands, still dripping with gore.

"He tore Jaguar apart," Sparrow said with frightened awe. "I knew he was strong, but..." her voice died. "He's still... not himself."

I could see that plainly.

"I'll talk with him, but not tonight." I raised my voice to say, "We have done what we needed to do. The war is over." Still, I felt no victory. "Get some rest. We still have lots to do." And perhaps that was why I didn't register the win. The battle here was over, but the war raging within the heart of Elista still needed to be dealt with...

...and I had no clue how I was going to do that.

CHAPTER 3

Fin let out a painful grunt as the last of us were transported to the caves which were now my House's residence in Elista. Silence had told me all about them. They'd been dug out over a period of years by a man named Clam, forming an upper communal living area and a lower level with bedrooms. Above us, on the cliffs overlooking Dyren's Bay, was a cottage which Fin owned. Clam stayed there now, a reward for his hard work.

Speaking of Fin, the large man shouldn't have been exerting himself, but he'd insisted he was well enough to bring us all home. Fin was still wounded from the fight that had killed Maverick and the others, even though that had been nearly two weeks ago. Ant hadn't been able to heal him, he'd been tending to others who were more gravely wounded throughout the camp and was also exhausted. Though now, Ant was just... distant. He'd been consumed with revenge, but now that he had it, I think he felt hollow.

Like me.

Fin sat heavily in a comfortable looking chair and smiled. "See, I'm fine." Then he winced and shifted in the chair. "Almost."

After a moment he added, "I'll just rest here until dinner. Once I've eaten, I'll limp down to my bed and sleep for a week."

"This is a strange yet amazing place," Alvere commented, looking around the large cave-like common area in awe. I had to agree. This was the first time I'd seen the underground hideout. It was impressive in its scale and the precision with which it had been carved from the bedrock here.

I was glad Alvere had been able to come with us. Leaving the command of his forces in the hands of his trusted generals and the Fey, he'd thought it safe to leave the front for a while, at least for one night... to be with me.

There was little left for us to do back in Vauphan. We'd tried to question the prisoners, but we weren't brutal like they were, wouldn't use violence to get our answers, which meant most of them weren't talking. We'd learned a little bit about what forces they were expecting for reinforcements over the coming weeks, but that was it. Lord War had, since being captured, remained as a wasp, we'd gotten nothing from him. Of all of them, he was the one I'd have been most willing to... hurt... a little, for information. I knew he wouldn't hesitate to do the same. But Ahmaia had stopped me. These people were under her care now and wouldn't be harmed. So, we had little to go on, which was frustrating.

I didn't want to think about that now. Today was meant to be a break from all that.

Crane, who'd been sent ahead to prepare for our arrival, walked briskly into view from the shadowy stairwell to one side of the large room.

She came directly to me. "It went well?" I could hear the concern in her voice, even as I caught her gaze moving around, counting us.

"Yes, Crane, we're all here." I sighed heavily. "The war in Vauphan is done for now." Lowering my voice so only she could hear, I added, "I have no clue what to do next."

She smiled sympathetically. "You'd be surprised how often Maverick said that."

I *was* surprised, and my shock must have shown, as her smile widened and she put an arm around me, comforting, motherly.

Drawing me aside from the others for a moment, she spoke softly. "He made certain he was always calm and sure in front of the rest of you, but I spent many sleepless nights with him while he paced, frantic and uncertain. He always found the right thing to do, the right things to say, as I'm sure you will too. And if you need me to stay up and watch you pace while we consider ideas, I'm here for you."

"I appreciate that, thank you," I said and hugged her close. "I'll probably take you up on that... tomorrow. Today, what remains of it, is for mending and celebration."

She nodded to that. "I'll have a feast prepared."

I hugged her again then moved away, going to Alvere. Kissing him lightly on the cheek, I whispered, "I have a few things I need to do. Make yourself at home. I'll find you later."

He smiled at that thought and I directed him into Sparrow's custody to be shown around.

Which left the largest item on my to do list: Ant.

I'd caught him heading down the stairs as soon as we'd arrived. I asked where his room was and went to it. There was no door to knock upon, only a heavy curtain, so I just entered.

I caught him mostly naked, perhaps readying for sleep, even though it was mid-afternoon. He saw me, paused with his pants halfway down his legs, then with a lifeless look in his eyes simply shrugged and continued.

"What?" he asked heavily, not seeming to care that he stood nude before me.

Wow, what a body. He was muscular and large, I'd seen him without a shirt before: his dark skin bulging with muscles, thick across his shoulders, chest, and arms. Now I saw his tight round butt, thick powerful legs and a long, swinging shaft that made my mouth dry up and my legs grow a little weak.

He sat heavily on his bed and I heard it creak.

"What?" he repeated, and I realized I'd been staring at him.

I sighed and — trying not to ogle him — went to sit on the bed, staying at the far end.

"You're hurting," I said, not really knowing how to have this conversation. "I can see it. Everyone can see it."

His head fell, his gaze upon the thick carpet over the stone floor. He leaned forward elbows on knees to hold his head as if the world itself weighed upon his shoulders. "She's gone," he said, voice hollow and pained. "I thought killing Jaguar would help, but... it didn't. There was a moment of satisfaction at making him suffer, but then..."

"I know," I confided, shifting just a bit closer to reach out my arm and stroke his back: his Oh-My-Spirits massive, V-shaped back. "I thought killing Lady Claw would make me feel better, and it did, for the briefest of moments, but now... I still feel hollow. Her death didn't bring Maverick back."

Ant nodded slowly. "What do I do?" He sounded so small and uncertain, so unlike himself.

I had no clue. "What do you need?" I asked.

"I... I..." He swallowed hard, voice becoming husky. "I never got to tell her how I felt. I... I think she knew, but I... I just wanted to say it, to say that I loved her and to say good-bye and... Spirits, I just want to hold her again."

I shifted closer still, though I couldn't reach across that broad back of his to hold him, hug him.

I had an idea.

"Close your eyes," I said softly. I didn't know if he complied or not, I couldn't see his face hidden behind his hands. "Now... hold me. Imagine I'm her. Tell me what you need to say."

He shifted, his face turning toward me. But he hadn't closed his eyes, and those dark orbs gazed at me for a long moment, tears on his cheeks.

I shifted close, brushing against him, feeling the heat and latent power of his form looming next to me. I lowered my voice, made it breathy and soft. I'd never fully sound like Amber, but this would be close.

"Close your eyes," I said again in that voice.

He winced, then sighed and shut his eyes.

He turned, reaching out, awkward but tender, to put a large, strong hand on my leg. I flushed a little at his touch, how he slid his hand up to my hip, then onto my waist and up, slowly, to my shoulder then my face, gently cupping my cheek.

"Amber?" He said, hopefully imagining her.

"I'm here," I said huskily, putting one of my hands on his cheek as he had with me.

He gave a shiver and I saw his face contort in pain and grief. "Oh, Spirits, I love you Amber!" He suddenly pulled me close, his other arm going around me. It was amazing how gentle he could be, how warm and loved I felt while held by those massive, muscled arms.

He wept as he poured his heart out to me. "I know you said we would always be casual, that it meant nothing, that you like my body and I liked yours and we should do something about that. You always had the right words, that casual caring grace and wonderful softness I needed. But... Oh Spirits, Amber." He sobbed for a moment before he continued, half choking on his words. "After our first time I was hooked. I needed you, I loved you. I should have said something, I should have told you. My heart is... I... You were everything to me."

"I know," I whispered. "I love you too." I was being her, but in that moment, I was also caught up in his words to me, even if they weren't to me.

"I was always a healer, but only of physical wounds. You were a balm on my soul, the caring and comfort I needed when the world got confused and torn. I love you so much!" He was blubbering now, holding me close. I held him as best I could, given his hugeness.

"I love you too," I whispered again.

Then, suddenly his lips were on mine, hard and needful, pushing and opening. I responded, caught up in his passion, surprised by how much I liked it. No man had ever been this rough with me, this hard and forward and...

He pulled back suddenly, eyes opening.

"I'm sorry," he said. "Legs, I..."

"You want to hold her one last time, be with her?"

"Yes, but—"

"Then do it. Be with me, like you would with her."

"But you can't—"

"It's my choice," I said, voice hushed but firm. Perhaps I was too caught up in his professions of love, but I was feeling desired and needed. From the corner of my eye, I caught his growing erection, so very tall and thick. A part of me was *very* curious what that would feel like. I'd never been with a man *that* big before.

I put a hand to his face, fingers tracing down over his eye-lids, encouraging his eyes to close. "Close your eyes," I said, voice trembling, mouth dry, swallowing hard. "And hold me, take me, one last time, my love."

"Yes," he breathed, voice choked with all his love and loss pouring out of him.

Then he moved in and I lost my breath in a savage kiss. He pushed me down to the bed, half over me. I felt the press of his weight upon me. His one hand sought the curve of my breast, over my dress, and gripped it hard. I gasped, or would have if I'd had any breath to give. My body responded to his need, aching, heating, throbbing with desire to have him close.

Then his lips left mine and I sucked in a long breath, only to have it gasped out again as his hand moved from my breast to my thigh, pushing up the skirt of my dress.

"Yes, take me," I whispered.

He gave a low chuckle. "You know I won't fit, not yet," he said as he shifted his body down, kneeling beside the bed, opening my legs to kiss my thighs, then... I gave another gasp as his tongue flicked over my clit. His lips pressed hard to my opening, as aggressive and driving with need as he'd been before. And it was exactly what I wanted. I pressed my hands to the tight curls of his dark hair, urging him closer. I felt my folds grow slick, my body flushed, heat pooling deep within me.

He worked with a probing tongue and biting teeth. I gasped and moaned when he slid a thick finger inside me, knowing just where to press and caress. He ravished me with a vigor the likes of which I had never known. I responded with groans and yelps, whispered words of encouragement and breathless gasps as he worked me up and up and up through the soft peak of one orgasm to the body-clenching, aching, screaming bliss of another.

I lay gasping in bewildered bliss, floating on a cloud of ecstasy. He moved over me and removed my dress with astonishing care. I hardly noticed. Then he rolled me onto my stomach, pulling me close. I tucked my knees up under me, against the edge of the bed as I felt his fingers slip into my folds, first one, then another, then a third, pushing inside me. That was *a lot*, almost too much. Yet as he probed and played inside me, I felt myself build to a new and — hopefully — even more amazing orgasm.

Then he removed his fingers, and I ached for the loss, whispering a plaintive, "No, please!"

But then I felt something large — the tip of his erection — press against me and I gasped. And as he pushed inside me, I breathed, "yes." My hands curled into the sheets, grabbing and kneading as he filled me. He was so big, just... wow! I now knew why he'd needed to work with three fingers for so long. Even with just his tip inside me I felt stretched and tight.

His massive hands grabbed my hips and I trembled with the anticipation of what would come next. He gave a series of slow, shallow thrusts, working a bit deeper each time as he grunted with pleasure. I let out a series of muffled screams into the sheets, biting them, eyes wide and body shaking as every slow and powerful inch of his erection pressed deeper and deeper inside me. Given how much he stretched me, I couldn't imagine the pressure and squeeze he must have felt.

And when he was as deep as he could be within me, there was a moment of pain, then an amazing spike of bliss. I jerked and shook for what seemed like an eternity as he simply sat fully within me. I couldn't tell — with my head pressing into his bed — but I didn't even think his entire length was inside me. I couldn't feel the press of his body to mine. He was just too long and large. And as a powerful wave of ecstasy rocked through me, I found myself going limp and relaxed. This extreme, yet serene plateau of pleasure was something I'd never felt before. I trembled faintly, waiting, desperately wanting to feel his aggressive thrusts. Spirits, I was overcome with bliss and he hadn't even really begun yet.

He stayed there, deep and large, as his hands moved up my sides, lifting me. I was pudding, melting in his grip as he easily raised me up to lean against him, hands under my breasts, feeling their weight for a moment before pressing and caressing them.

I let out a shuddering sigh of a moan and felt his body respond to the sound as he grunted and finally began slow, deep thrusts.

One hand moved down from my breasts to press to my clit as he moved within me and suddenly, I was on fire once again, stiff and stimulated beyond reason.

"I love you, Amber," Ant groaned as I felt a massive release shudder through me. I cried out a long, "yes!" and tried to move against him, shifting my hips to help with his thrusting as he began to pick up his pace.

I leaned my head back against the wide plateau of his shoulder and whispered, breathless: "Take what you need."

"Yes," he whispered in response. Then his hands were on my hips again, as we rocked and moved together, harder, faster.

Then...

With a cry of passion, he let loose upon me, thrusting with abandon.

Spirits Above!

Each slam of his massiveness inside me caused a tidal wave of pleasure to wash through me. I fell forward, landing on weak arms as I felt his immense strength pounding to infinite depths within me. My mouth and eyes opened wide in a silent scream of unimaginable bliss.

His pace quickened as he swelled inside me, stretching me to my limits. He was close.

My arms gave way and I fell forward onto my face. I reached one arm down to furiously rub my clit. I wanted to come with him.

With a roar and a final thrust, he planted himself deep within me and exploded in his bliss. As his hot surge rushed into me, I couldn't help but come with him, my body shuddering, hands pounding the softness of the bed over and over as I was rocked by his profound release.

I felt him slowly curl over me, arms wrapping around me as he wept against my back. This had been the release he'd needed, in more ways than one. He could finally begin to let Amber go and heal himself.

Eventually we slumped onto the bed together and he quieted. "Thank you," he whispered with a soft kiss on my shoulder. Then with a heavy sigh he said, "Good-bye, Amber."

CHAPTER 4

I staggered, walking funny when I left Ant's rooms. I'd be sore down there for a little while, I suspected. I hoped for a bit of a rest before dinner, but alas, that was not to be. Sparrow stood outside my room. As the leader of the House, I got a slightly larger room than the rest, or so I'd been told. I hadn't actually seen it yet.

She spoke softly to me with a faint smile. "Silence and the prince are inside... ah... getting to know each other."

I raised my brow at that.

Sparrow, ever-perceptive, then cocked her head in a slightly bird-like manner. "You seem... different."

I had nothing to hide from her, or the others. I'd tell them the truth about where I'd been. "I spent some time with Ant. He needed to let go of Amber, and now he has. But to do that I told him to imagine I was her, to give her what he needed to give her. And he gave it to me... hard. I'm going to be sore for a while."

Sparrow blinked, those large forest-green eyes going wider still as she gave a shy-shocked smile. "Oh." She looked away, blushing. "I have to admit, I've always been curious about him."

"I can tell you all about it, or you can be his next paramour if you like." Though she was even smaller than I was. "*If* you like your pleasure to be on the verge of punishment."

She blushed deeper. "I... don't think so."

I shrugged and stepped in close to whisper, "You should try it at least once before you make up your mind." Then I kissed her cheek. "Now, I'm curious what Silence and Alvere are up to."

What I saw when I entered was the last thing I expected: Silence and Alvere kissing softly, arms around each other, sitting on my bed.

Despite my soreness, this scene caused a rather instant arousal to rush through me. "Oh!" I breathed.

They stopped kissing to turn to me, but kept their arms around each other.

"Silence was... initiating me into your little harem," Alvere said, a bit flushed.

"Given your desire for Sparrow and willingness to be with her..." Silence shrugged. "I was curious what this might be like." That made sense, since I knew that Silence's only true example of love growing up, had been two men.

"And?" I asked, also curious.

They looked at each other and I saw something kindle there, even if it was uncertain and undefined as of yet. I couldn't blame them: they were both attractive men with a healthy dose of curiosity and an abundance of love.

Alvere responded, still looking longingly into Silence's eyes. "We... think we'd like to find out more?"

Silence nodded to that.

Alvere turned to me, "But for now we can focus on you."

"No," I said quickly raising my hands. "Actually, please continue." I could get behind just watching this.

Both raised their brows in question.

"I'm a little tired and sore right now," I said, fully meaning to explain, but Sparrow jumped in first.

"She got Ant through his grief for Amber by allowing him to imagine Legs was Amber, and giving him one last release with his beloved."

Silence's and Alvere's brows rose even higher. "But he's huge," Silence said in awe.

Alvere nodded, "Ah, hence... tired and sore. Understood." He turned back to Silence. "What do you think? Would you like more... with me?"

Silence considered for a moment, then nodded and they rose, hand in hand, making to leave.

"No, stay!" I said quickly. I hadn't told them my intention to watch. "I... want to..."

"Watch?" Alvere said with a grin.

I nodded, growing more heated and excited at the thought.

Alvere turned to Silence, a question in his glance, and Silence shrugged and nodded. The two then came together again, embracing and kissing.

Spirits Within! That is so hot!

I skirted around them to my — quite large — bed. That seemed appropriate since I had a lot of people I wanted to share it with. Sparrow came with me, sitting next to me as I reclined on some pillows, holding me close.

I could get used to this.

I watched the gradual kindling of passion between the two men, soft kisses slowly deepening to tongue-play, then hungry, open mouths. It was one of the most sensuous and stimulating things I'd ever seen.

I shivered with a surge of bliss when Sparrow suddenly kissed my neck, her hand reaching up over my dress to gently cup one of my breasts.

She whispered: "I'll be gentle." And her kisses moved over my cheek and into my hair.

Turning my head, I captured her lips with mine, savoring their plump sweetness as the heat within me bubbled up to a strong simmer. When I drew back, our hot breath mingled between us.

"Just relax," Sparrow whispered, and I did. I turned back to watch the boys as Sparrow spent her time with slow soft kisses over my neck and ear, into my hair and down over my cheek.

Silence had his shirt off now, Alvere's was in the process of being removed. Once it was off, their lips met again, their hands roaming the exposed expanse of nearly twin bodies. Silence was leaner, muscles long and wiry on his limbs. His chest was flat, just beginning to swell with muscle. Across his abdomen were a series of well-defined and squarish abs.

Ant's abs were like... fresh, plump buns, hot from the oven.

Where had that thought come from?

Auwei giggled. *I've had a man like Ant before, only once, and I may have thought of him like that: one big sweet dessert, too rich to have often, but nice to have once in a while, when you want to be filled up more than usual.*

Wow, really?

Oh yes. He was... something else, but I must admit, your Ant is even more. I very much enjoyed that experience, thank you.

You're welcome, you don't have to live with the soreness afterward.

I do feel what you feel.

Oh... right.

Now, Auwei said, and I could hear the breathy eagerness in her voice, *back to the steamy buffet in front of us. This, just watching, is new for me too.*

And for me. Aren't they just beautiful together?

Indeed. Now let me watch in peace.

So, I went back to gazing longingly at my men. Compared to Silence Alvere was a bit larger, his chest and arms and shoulders more rounded, though is abdomen was the same flat, chiseled perfection.

Silence removed Alvere's breeches and I gasped as his erection was freed, leaping up before him. Silence kissed down Alvere's perfect abbs, then knelt, stroking that perfect shaft, kissing the tip softly.

Blessed Spirits! I hadn't expected them to go this far!

Alvere gasped as his erection visibly swelled. Yeah, Ant's massive manhood was a sinful and slightly painful pleasure, but Alvere's was perfection. Just the right size and length.

Sparrow softly bit my earlobe, and I gasped with a surge of pleasure. I suddenly wanted more from the woman and shifted away and to my knees so I could lift off my dress.

I caught Sparrow doing the same from the corner of my eye and heard Alvere's new gasp. His erection seemed to grow larger still as he gazed over at me... just before Silence took him full into his mouth and Alvere's eyes rolled back. He put a hand to the wall to steady himself.

Sparrow pushed herself against my back, her soft breasts, nipples hardened with her own arousal, pressed to me as her hands moved around me, slowly and softly caressing my abdomen, then up to my breasts to gently cup and knead. My own nipples were rigid and standing proud and needed little in the way of further stimulation.

The men had shifted, Alvere's back against the wall, head back, hands softly sliding through Silence's mouse-brown hair as Silence's head began to move quicker, his one hand on Alvere's thigh, the other gently cupping and stroking his sack.

"Enough," Alvere breathed and urged Silence's head away. Alvere's hands motioned and helped Silence stand and their lips met feverishly again for a moment before Alvere spun them and pinned Silence to the wall. "Your turn," he breathed and was quickly kneeling, removing Silence's breeches.

Alvere greedily plunged his mouth over Silence's throbbing erection, his grip hard and stroking. It was Silence's turn to gasp.

Then his gaze rose and saw me and he gasped again, mouth hanging open in awed desire.

"I won't... I can't... Oh!" Silence groaned as his hands curled into Alvere's black hair and his eyes rolled back with what I guessed was an unexpected release. Yet Alvere continued his work, moving over Silence's twitching length with rapid intensity. "Yes." Silence drew the word out as his gaze caught mine. "Yes," he repeated, and I was just a bit surprised to have Sparrow's fingers lightly trace over my folds in that moment.

I'd lost track of her caresses while watching Silence's bliss, but now I was keenly aware of her subtle movement.

"Gently," I reminded her.

"I know," she whispered, hot breath on my ear. She was being so very tender, so much so that her featherlike brushes made me want more. Her other hand joined the first and stroked the insides of my thighs with urgent, but careful caresses.

Silence, in the meantime, had gone a little slack, now taking long, deep breaths, moving his gaze from Alvere to me. "By all the Spirits! That was... oh!" Silence breathed as Alvere moved away. Silence was still semi-erect but clearly spent.

Alvere himself looked flushed, ready for his own release, his erection still straining before him. He stepped away from Silence and breathed his own "oh." He laughed a little, clearly giddy. "Well, that was... new."

Silence let out a bit of a laugh as well. "Yes. I was... very excited. Can you blame me?" He motioned to me. Alvere turned to me and bit his lip.

"No, I can't."

"Shall I return the favor?" Silence said as the two of them came together for another series of deep kisses. Silence's hand sought and stroked Alvere's erection, which looked ready to burst.

"No, I have another idea, if you're up for it," Alvere said when they separated. "Something that will allow us to both watch our beloved Legs being pleasured."

Silence raised a brow, then his eyes widened and he nodded. He'd figured out what Alvere was saying, even though I hadn't.

Alvere's going to enter him from behind, Auwei filled me in.

"Do you have oil?" Alvere asked me as he quickly went to the single drawer in the nightstand next to the bed. I'd never been in this room before, so I had no clue. He opened the drawer and breathed a sigh — mixed with relief and anticipation — as he pulled out a small glass container filled with golden liquid. He removed the stopper and smelled it nodding. "Great!"

Apparently, this room came well stocked.

Silence had moved to the edge of the bed and Alvere returned to him, pouring a little of the liquid onto his fingers, reaching around behind Silence. Alvere handed over the small container and Silence also doled out a bit, stroking it onto Alvere's swollen erection. Both men were flushed and breathing heavily, gasping just a bit as they worked upon each other in preparation.

I hadn't known how much I wanted to see this, until now.

Anal sex can be very stimulating for men... women as well, if you're ever interested, Auwei said.

I hadn't been interested before, but with my heart racing, I was suddenly curious.

When they finally shifted, Alvere moving behind the other man, I could barely breathe, throat tight with thrilled anticipation. Silence gasped in what looked like a mix of pain and pleasure as I guessed Alvere carefully inserted himself.

Silence moaned and leaned forward onto the bed, as Alvere, hands on Silence's hips, moved slowly, pushing deeper. The prince's eyelids fluttered, mouth agape, body shuddering: lost to bliss.

And Sparrow, prescient as ever, chose that moment to *finally* brush my clit. I let out a surprised cry as my body tensed, suddenly very ready for more.

"You can be just a little harder," I breathed between gasps, and she applied just a bit more pressure as her fingers slid around my folds and stroked my ragingly sensitive nub.

I raised my hands to my breasts, kneading and tweaking to add to my pleasure.

Poor Sparrow, the remaining three of us were all about to orgasm, and she was content to passively pleasure me. I'd have to reward her for that later. But then my mind wasn't on her anymore. The beautiful men before me were both gasping and grunting as Alvere picked up his pace, thrusting hard and needful into Silence, who was also near to another peak it seemed. He fell to his elbows, arms weak, and one arm disappeared, probably to stroke himself as the three of us shook and shuddered toward an ultimate release.

I was more than ready. Sparrow's hands worked miracles, pressing hard enough to get me ragingly hot and bothered, while not so hard as to cause any pain to my aching entrance.

Alvere came first, crying out with a final desperate lunge into Silence. Silence also cried out, but it wasn't until a moment later when Silence's eyes rolled back and he jerked and tensed with another cry.

And I couldn't help myself. My beautiful men were so hot in their mutual pleasuring and Sparrows fingers were so nimble and quick, that I too cried out, body tensing and convulsing as I squeezed my own breasts in the throes of one of the most pleasurable orgasms I'd ever had. So very different than what I'd had with Ant, and yet just as powerful and intense.

I even heard Sparrow moan a little as she withdrew her fingers.

When Sparrow released me, I collapsed onto the bed. She

remained kneeling, hungry eyes devouring me as she pleasured herself. It wasn't long before she too was crying out in bliss.

Alvere collapsed over Silence, kissing his back between heavy breaths. After a moment he looked up at me and Sparrow and softly stroked Silence's hair as he said, "I think I could get used to this."

CHAPTER 5

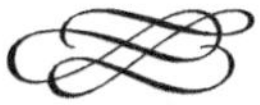

I FELT ENERGIZED.

After that stunningly sexy encounter in my room, our little troop had joined the rest of the house for a wonderful and filling meal. Alvere, Sparrow, Silence, and I had shared furtive glances and secret smiles as we ate.

After dinner, everyone gathered in the common area, a fire raging in the large hearth. It was time to talk about next steps.

"I have a crazy idea," I said as I paced back and forth in front of the fire.

"Why do I get the feeling all our briefings are going to start with that phrase," Princess mock-whispered to Foggy. He gave a snort of a laugh. I couldn't help but laugh as well, and others followed suit.

"Perhaps they will," I said in a playfully threatening sort of way. "We'll find out. But for now, I have probably the craziest idea of them all." I stopped pacing. "I want to kidnap the queen."

I stood there, waiting for the expected shocked gasps and protests. Instead, I saw my house slowly nodding and grudgingly accepting this idea.

"We need to know what's going on, and the Royal House is clearly involved," Crane said. "Either she must know what's happening, or we'll find out if she's completely unaware, which seems unlikely. Yes, this seems a logical course of action, though I have no clue how we'd pull it off."

"I might have an idea," Dove said, voice hesitant. My sister still hadn't fully recovered from the betrayal of her former lover, Lord Hale. It seemed he'd only been seeing her to get to me, and when he'd turned on us both, it had devastated my sister. She was better now than she had been, but still a little deferential in her new House... My House. As my older sister, it must be odd to have me as her House Leader.

"I'm all ears," I said. "I had no set plan in mind, just a knowledge that, as Lady Crane said, we need to know what the queen knows."

"The Spring Festival will be in a few days," Dove said. If it happens as usual, then the queen will lead a parade of Nobles through the capital, from her House to the Great Square."

"So, she'll be out in the open," I said.

"And surrounded by Nobles," Lady Crane added sourly. "How will we ever take her unnoticed?

Dove nodded. "That would be the downside." She sighed. "Perhaps that wasn't the best idea."

"No, I think we can work with this," I said, beginning to pace again. "The trouble with the queen has been her seclusion these past few weeks. In order to get to her, we'd have to search the Owl Estate. The chances of getting in and getting out without encountering some of her Nobles would be highly unlikely anyway. This way, at least we know where she'll be and when."

"If we wait until after the parade and her speech in the square, she may retire back to her House with only a few guards." Dove shrugged.

"I wish..." I silenced myself. I'd been about to say I wished that Amber was still here. Her power to influence the minds of others would have been handy. But despite Ant's turning the corner and starting to let her go, I didn't think he'd want to hear that right now. So, I threw the question out to the group. "How do we get her away from a few Nobles and guards without harming anyone?" We didn't really know who was a part of this intrigue and who wasn't, and the idea was to kidnap the queen without casualties.

"Fin could pop in and grab her and pop out?" Silence said looking over at the large man. Fin had lost some of his girth these last few days, and he was still covered in bandages. He didn't look like he'd be up for much, not right away at least.

Fin grunted and shrugged. He was half asleep as it was. If we were going to use Fin at all we'd need to make sure he was well recovered.

"Good idea... though we also need to account for Lord Hale. If he's with the queen that could mess things up for us. I know he can stop people from veering and cut them off from their Lumani, what I don't know is if he can stop a person's spirit-gift. I'm guessing he can't, since Midnight and I were able to use ours while close to him, but... there is a slim chance he can, but has to concentrate or somehow activate that power and he didn't at that time because he just didn't know we had spirit gifts." I shrugged. "For the moment, let's assume he can. If so, we need some way to neutralize him and any others safely."

"There has to be a way," Crane said, looking into the fire in thought. "Perhaps if we each share what we can do, that might spark something?" She looked around. "I know we've done this many times, but I think it might help to do it again."

Alvere shrugged. "You all may have done it many times before, but I haven't been here. So, I'll go first. I can control cloth," he said, then blinked, head slowly tilting to one side. He was clearly stuck on some thought. For those of the House who hadn't known that

Alvere was half-Fey and had some of their abilities, this statement had opened some eyes.

Alvere turned to me. "You know, if you asked for some help from the Fey, they might be able to take some others out of the picture. Those like me could potentially stop anyone in regular clothes. And if there were guards in armor, a few of those who control metal could help as well." He shrugged. "I can ask them if you like."

That might be very useful. I had hoped to do this with just the members of my House, but a little outside help might go a long way. Certainly, it would be something the Nobles wouldn't be used to fighting against. I'd seen how powerful and useful the Fey could be during our raid on the Elistan camp. The way Ahmaia had scooped people up and hidden them somehow, in the "pockets" of her cloak, was amazing.

"That's a great idea, thank you Alvere."

"If that fails you could just kiss everyone," Foggy said with a wide grin.

I didn't understand what he meant for a long moment... then remembered my toxic lips, my ability to stun people. I laughed. "We'll save that as a backup option."

"And what do we do with the queen once we have her?" Midnight asked softly. "Do you truly expect her to spill all her secrets?"

"No, not really, but—"

"Then what's the point of kidnapping her?" Trust Midnight to get right to the heart of things.

I thought for a moment before answering. "My hope is that once we start questioning her, it will become apparent whether she knows nothing of the events happening around her, or she does know and isn't doing anything about them. I think those will be two very different responses, even if she isn't all that talkative.

That alone will tell us a lot. And if she does know something and is willing to talk, then... that's even more."

Midnight sighed. "That's fair." She shook her head slowly. "I don't know why, but I suspect she's not the one behind all of this. It's just a hunch. I guess we'll see."

Time for specifics. "The mission team will be Alvere, myself, Fin, and the Fey, if they're willing. If not, we'll re-evaluate. The rest of you, make a room ready for the queen, we're about to have guests."

"Do we know if the queen has a spirit-gift?" Silence asked looking around.

A good question. I surely didn't.

"The trouble with most spirit-gifts is that they are personal. Most people don't share that they have them, except perhaps to those in their own House." Crane's tone was hard. "She may have one, but the public, even the other Noble Houses, haven't been told of it. We have to plan for... anything."

"Do that," I said.

"I'd like to come along on the mission," Midnight said. "I can stay behind, see what trouble we stir up, who reacts and how."

"A good idea. You're in." I looked around. "Anything else?"

No one said anything.

I sought out Ant after the meeting as people went to prepare. He hadn't said anything and had been avoiding eye contact. "How are you feeling?" I asked tentatively. The dark skin of his cheeks flushed as he looked at me, then quickly away. "I'm doing a lot better, thank you. I... just... You..." He cleared his throat. "Are you well? I was... rough."

I didn't laugh, even though I wanted to. I did flush a little myself as I smiled. "I'm tough, I can take a beating," I said remembering all the moments of my time with him. "I'm a bit sore, but I'll heal." I put a hand on his massive shoulder. "And if you ever need me, I'm here for you." I didn't really know what I was saying. Did I want more rough, powerful sex with this amazing man?

I can answer that, Auwei said with a chuckle. *Yes, yes you do. Just not often.*

Ant looked at me then. "You want more?" And the interest, the desire that kindled in his eyes sent a thrill through me, heat pooled low in my abdomen, making my sore parts tingle.

"Do you?" I asked, curious. No one else was around, so I was open with him. "I'm not a one-man woman, I think you know that. I seem to have a growing harem of those who I'm with. That's just who I am, and I'm not going to change that. But if you're well with that, then..." I lowered my voice to a sensuous, heavy whisper. "I could submit myself for a little punishment every now and then."

He grinned, while still looking a bit concerned. "Is that what it felt like? Punishment?"

"The most pleasurable pain I've ever felt," I breathed. I slipped my hand behind his neck and urged him down to me. He let me move him and leaned down for a quick nip of a kiss, his lips hard and hungry.

"I'd like to be with you again," he whispered.

"And I you. It's set. I'll let the others know there's a new member of the Loving Legs Club." I just made that name up on the spot and frowned at how silly it sounded.

"I'm not sure I'm up for others being with us," Ant said, honestly. "But... perhaps... I could try it. Once."

"It's good to be open to new experiences." I pulled him down for another kiss.

We drew apart after that. The heat within me lasted as I went back to my room. Alvere, Silence, and Sparrow were waiting for me there.

"What's this?" I asked, blinking in mock innocence.

"We just wanted to make sure you slept well," Alvere said.

"So, you're going to tire me out?" I shrugged. "Works for me." I drew into their loving arms, adding, "Oh, and I had a chat with Ant. He wants to be with me too, occasionally. How does everyone feel about that?"

"You know we only want you to be happy," Sparrow said, before her soft lips touched mine. The two men murmured their agreement as they pressed close... and began to show me just how happy they wished me to be.

As I slipped into a pleasantly contented sleep that night... I casually wondered if anyone else in my House might eventually join my little — but ever-growing — harem.

CHAPTER 6

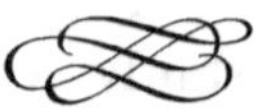

AHMAIA AGREED TO HELP US. WITH HER CAME ELVI, A TINY FEY woman who could work with stone, and Eorthan, a stocky Fey man who controlled metal. Eorthan was the one who'd made my special armor, and I took a moment to thank him profusely for his amazing work. As for Elvi, it was thought that since the streets of the capital were made of stone she might be able to literally stop people in their tracks if needed.

Ahmaia insisted that Alvere not come. He was upset, but conceded to her argument that he was too significant to risk on a mission. As the king of Vauphan, fighting for his own country was one thing, but this was another. There was a vehemence and sternness in Ahmaia's insistence, and before we left, I took her aside for a quick chat.

"You're his mother, aren't you? Or a relative?" I asked, straight to the point. She didn't look old enough to be his mother, but I'd learned that Fey aged differently than humans.

She stared intently at me with her rose-gold eyes. "Yes," she said simply. "You are very astute."

"He doesn't know, does he?" From how he talked about his Fey parentage I'd gotten the feeling he'd never met his real mother.

"No." Her gaze never wavered when she asked, "Will you tell him?"

I smiled slightly. "It's not my place." Though I was curious. "Why... haven't you?"

I saw the slight twitch of her blue-pale skin at her jaw. I'd hit a nerve. "It will not help him. He had his parents. They raised him, I did not. He is a king and the Uniter. He will bring Fey back to the world. I... would only hinder him."

"I don't think so," I said. "I think having a parent, even one he's never known until now would only help him. But that's your choice to make. I will say nothing."

She nodded stiffly. "Thank you." She seemed about to leave but hesitated and said, "Our sages have seen things about you." She smiled. "I cannot tell you what. For that might influence your decisions. But... I know from what I have witnessed that you love my son. Thank you for that," she said softly. "Take care of him."

"I will," I said, curious as The Deepest Pits what those sages had seen. First the mistweaver had seen things about me and now this. What was a girl to think? I could get a complex, thinking I was someone important. Luckily, I knew better. Important or not, I was me, and I always would be. I'd do what I always did, and if that fulfilled someone's prophecy, good for them.

I met up with Fin, Midnight, and the Fey. We were all dressed as commoners, in concealing apparel which wouldn't seem out of place. Fin transported us to Ana's farm. Ana, being Maverick's sister, had to be told what had happened to her brother. Midnight offered, but I knew I had to do it.

When I did, Ana's features hardened, taking the news stoically.

"I always knew his life would be dangerous, or at least more dangerous than mine. I'm... glad he passed fighting for what was right, for his country... even if it was against his country." She shed a few tears and embraced me while I felt awful. I hadn't told her Maverick had died helping me, nor the gory specifics of his death, but both of those things still haunted me.

We walked from Ana's farm into the city, taking a room in a rundown tavern in the slums on the other side of the river. The Festival began tomorrow, and we'd be in place when it happened.

Midnight scouted during the night. We were all up before dawn to catch a ferry across the river and claim our spot near the square, a flat roofed building which would give us a good vantage point to watch the queen's speech. The building was behind the stage which had been erected for that purpose. We'd only see the back of the queen. But then... we weren't there for the speech. The building did have a good view of all of the exits the queen might take from that stage, assuming she left off the back and wanted to remain out of sight as she returned to her House. As the morning wore on, it even became clear exactly which route she'd take. We were in luck. We watched guards clear people out of the alley right next to the building we'd claimed. We'd have a perfect view of the queen — and whoever was with her — as they left. The guards stationed men along the alley and at both ends, so no one would use the road.

Our first problem came when three guards climbed up to our rooftop and found us. Luckily, they didn't know who we were, just thought we were peasants there to claim our spot early.

"This roof is off limits, find somewhere else to view the queen's speech," the one guard growled. We could take these three easily, the trouble was... if we did, someone might notice that they'd gone missing.

Fin stepped forward and spoke in a voice I'd never heard from him before, a full-on, back-woods peasant drawl. "Sorry, mas'ers," he said holding up his hands. "We's jus' trying to get a peep at the queen. We don't think no'un woul' want dis place. We won't be no bother. If'n you're gonna watch the queen from up here, we coul' jus' watch with you."

The guard blinked, and I could see him trying to parse Fin's words. "Sorry lad, but no one can be up here. Now if you hurry, perhaps you can find some other rooftop. Just, go on now."

That hadn't worked.

For a moment I considered trying to subdue the guards and take their clothes. That way anyone down below would only see guards, but... I was the only one who *might* possibly fit into one of their uniforms. Fin was too big and the others were all too small.

We all stood there, awkwardly — guards and us both — for a long moment. My *Hero* gift rose within me. It wanted to fight, to remove these impediments to my plan. But I resisted that pull.

Any thoughts? I asked Auwei. *I'm desperate.*

Just one, but I'm not sure if you'll like it.

I'm all ears. Anything goes.

It'll be easier for me to show you.

Do it!

Auwei swept through me, taking control. The next moment, I walked forward in a sexy swagger. All three guards watched me. I wasn't even dressed in anything particularly provocative, but that was the trick to Auwei's walk. I'd never quite learned to move like this. I'd always been a bit of a rough-and-tumble girl, not the flirty type, but Auwei had been all sorts of people and this walk, though it felt extremely odd, was doing the trick. The guards seemed mesmerized by my swaying hips and long legs and shifting shoulders.

Trust me it's not your shoulders they're looking at.

I reached the first guard, pressed myself against him, wrapped my arms around his neck and laid a kiss upon his lips. I could tell he enjoyed it. I felt his body respond, his mouth open... then... he went stiff.

Oh, right!

I moved away from him, leaving him seemingly stunned, to kiss the second guard. Apparently, Midnight caught the first one as he fell forward, lowering him gently to the ground. The third guard had the benefit of seeing the other two go stiff and fall. He backed a step away from me before I reached him. Still, somehow, he melted at my kiss, responding before going stiff himself.

I stepped back, catching the last guard as he fell.

Too easy, especially with your body. Auwei was purring with glee.

Thanks?

It's the legs, they make all the difference in that walk.

Oh...

She giggled as she receded from controlling me.

"And what did that get us?" Ahmaia asked coming over to us.

Yes, what did that gain us? I asked Auwei

Then I repeated her answer verbatim to Ahmaia. "Now those guards are going to be seen up here, guarding things and no one should bother us. Just lean the men up against the side walls so others can see them, and from below, they may seem a bit stiff, but hopefully no one will notice."

Ahmaia cocked her head to one side. "That might work. How long will they remain like this?"

"About an hour."

"Will that be enough time?"

It was just past dawn and the queen's speech was to be mid-morning. "No, I'll have to kiss them again from time to time to keep it up."

"You have a... stunning kiss?"

I laughed. "Yeah... some time remind me to tell you how Alvere and I met."

She raised a brow at that. "I have time now, it seems."

So we did.

I told her.

The shocked-strangled sound she made when I spoke of kissing and abducting Alvere was one of the oddest sounds I'd ever heard.

As the morning drew on, crowds gathered, the square below filled, and others could be seen on rooftops. We had to keep low, as there was a contingent of guards on the roof on the other side of the alley. They called over to our guards every now and then and Fin and Eorthan did a decent job of mimicking the guard's voices to call back. Luckily no one else came up to the roof to check on these three.

Then it was time.

We spotted the queen and her escorts moving down the cleared path, which had been made for the parade toward the platform. The queen's white-blond hair was easy to spot, flowing free, waving slightly behind her as she walked. With her was her second, Lady Merlin, a small woman with an intensity of nervous energy. But my eyes were drawn to the massive form of Lord Hale, even larger than Ant. I suddenly seethed with rage, remembering what he'd done to me, but more importantly, what he'd done to Dove.

"I'm going to kill you," I whispered.

Ahmaia looked at me askance. "The queen?" she whispered.

"No, the large man behind her. He... hurt my sister and tried to have me killed. He's marked."

"Ah... it seems you've marked many people."

No, only him and Lady Claw, who I'd already dealt with.

What I found even more interesting was the woman Lord Hale had on his arm. I knew her. Her name was Lady Swan, but I'd known her as Cedar at Silverveil. She'd never liked me. It didn't surprise me at all that she and Hale had hooked up. Also in the procession were a few more from the Royal House as well as other Nobles. Of note were Lady Silvermane of Pegasus House, the queen's daughter. We knew she was involved somehow, though

perhaps not entirely willingly. It was her second, Lord Horn —
Hale's father — who was much more involved and probably influ-
encing her to help. Yet, I had trouble believing that she knew nothing. If her mother, the queen, was involved, Silvermane would
have to know something.

Another spike through my heart was seeing Lady Skyfire, of
House Wyvern, marching with the queen. I'd always admired her
and didn't want to believe she would be involved with any of this.
In truth, she might not be, but might just be a pawn, supporting
the queen here, but not knowing what was truly happening. I
wanted to believe that, but I had to assume everyone was against
me right now.

The queen took the stage and began her speech. Someone
used magic to enhance her voice so everyone could hear; perhaps
that was her spirit-gift?

My heart thundered in my ears — anxious for what was to
come — and I hardly heard the speech. The queen finished far too
quickly — though that was probably just my perception — then
she was moving down the stairs at the back of the stage and
heading for our laneway.

My heart pounded all the harder. I was going to do this. I was
going to kidnap the queen.

I looked to the others, wondering if they were as scared as I
was. Yet they all looked at me with certainty. They believed I could
do this.

I smiled to reassure them, then we joined hands with Fin,
ready to jump down.

This was it.

CHAPTER 7

WE APPEARED BEHIND THE QUEEN'S PARTY. THE ONLY NOBLES WITH her now were her second Lady Merlin, Lord Hale, and Lady Swan. They, along with half a dozen guards, were moving quickly down the laneway. Eorthan made a motion sweeping outwards to the side with both of his hands. Anyone in armor was suddenly flying to one side, which included Lord Hale. That left the queen, Merlin, and Swan.

Elvi, the stone wielder, made a motion pushing down with her hands. Merlin and Swan were suddenly trapped calf-deep in the stone street.

Fin Jumped to the queen and vanished with her.

The guards lining the street were only now beginning to react. My *Hero* gift surged. I'd hidden a short-sword under my commoner's clothes and already had it in hand. I reacted faster than they did, moving to protect our group. Midnight did the same, but unseen. Ahmaia was throwing about guards with her cloth-arms.

We only had to last a moment or two before...

Fin returned.

We rushed to him and a moment later were back in our cliff-side hideout.

"We did—" My words cut off when I saw Alvere catch the queen as she collapsed. She had both hands at her throat. "What...?"

I rushed to kneel next to Alvere, who cradled the queen in his arms.

"You've killed me!" the queen hissed, as she strained to gasp in a breath.

"It started as soon as Fin arrived with her," Alvere said, just as shocked as I was.

The queen's desperate, wild-eyed gaze found me and she let out a sort of coughing laugh. "Of course," she croaked. She reached up to grasp my arm, her nails digging into my flesh. "You can't save me, but... you need... to..." She struggled more and more to get air. Her words became quieter and more frantic. "Merlin..." a long gasp, as her eyes rolled back. "...is..." I couldn't even tell if she was breathing now, her body convulsing as if trying to breathe, but getting no air. "M—ahhh..." The last of her air escaped with that last attempt at speech and she went limp. Her hand fell away from my arm, slapping the floor. Then, the faintest bit of mist slipped out from her lips.

"What in The Blackest Pits!" I hissed.

What had just happened?

"A mistweaver did this," Crane said crouching next to me.

"Sorry, what?" I hadn't heard that right. I couldn't have heard that right.

"A mistweaver," Crane repeated.

"We killed the mistweaver. *I* killed the mistweaver."

Crane shrugged. "That last puff of mist leaving her, that's what seals it. A mistweaver did this, some sort of curse. Perhaps something to the effect of: if she left the capital she'd die? It may have been something lingering from the one you killed, but we can't discount the option that another is out there."

"Another mistweaver?" I'd nearly died fighting the first one. I would have died if Ant hadn't been there to patch me up afterward.

My mind spun out of control. None of this made sense. I'd tried to kidnap the queen and instead I'd killed her, because of some mistweaver's curse?

"What was it she said at the end?" Alvere said laying the body down gently. "Merlin is Ma...?" He looked at me. "Merlin was her second, yes?"

I nodded, though I wasn't really paying attention to what he was saying. My heart swarmed with guilt and fear. I sat back heavily on my rump, putting a hand to my head.

"Perhaps Merlin is a mistweaver?" Crane suggested.

"Or Merlin is the master? Perhaps she's the one behind all of this?" Alvere offered.

"Either way, it would suggest Merlin is the person we need to watch," Crane agreed.

Their words faded, growing distant. I didn't want to be here. I couldn't be here. I couldn't believe another choice I'd made had killed another potentially innocent person, though we didn't know that. We didn't know anything. My whole plan had hinged on getting some information from the queen. What did we have now?

No information and a dead body.

I got up and walked away, then ran. I was in my bed, face-down in a pillow before I knew it, hot and bitter tears wetting the softness against my face.

I felt a gentle hand on my back, moving in slow circles and knew who it was instantly. Sparrow. She asked nothing, said nothing, she simply sat there, softly rubbing my back until I'd cried myself out and was ready to do something other than weep.

My thoughts were still a mess of confusion and swirling uncertainty. My emotions were bunched into a tight ball of frustration, regret, and dismay.

I rolled onto my side and looked up at Sparrow's kind face. Her forest-green eyes were shaded with concern. She smiled softly, her soft cheeks rising. Her hand came to my face and swept some hair from my brow.

"What do you need?" she asked softly.

My voice warbled and broke as I said, "I don't know how to be strong right now. I need to be strong for the House, but..."

She nodded. "We understand," she whispered. "No one was expecting this. It's a shock. We're all trying to come to terms with it. We know it's not your fault."

But it *was* my fault. One of my first plans as leader of his House and I'd gotten a woman killed. I'd gotten *the queen* killed.

"I don't know how to do it," I said, sniffing as tears threatened again.

"Do what?"

"Live with all these lives, these deaths. I... I can't. What if..." I couldn't go on as tears flooded back. I'd been thinking *what if you had died, or Silence, or Alvere, or Ant?*

And then it occurred to me that I was favoring certain members of my House over others. I'd feel doubly guilty if Princess or Foggy or Midnight or anyone else died, because I hadn't been as concerned for them as I had for some others. That prompted tears of shame, to add to my tears of grief.

Sparrow laid herself down gently upon me, embracing me awkwardly.

"I don't think it gets easier," she said softly.

Not what I wanted to hear.

"But I'll always be here to comfort you, and if not me, one of the others. That's the point of having a House. We're family."

Family... Dove! I'd completely forgotten about my sister! That spurred another wave of heaving sobs. And Sparrow held me through all of it. Eventually we shifted and ended up with her laying on her back, taking the place of my pillow as I lay with my head upon her chest. She held me close, stroking my hair.

It was a while before my tears stopped again. By then I was getting quite hungry. My stomach rumbled. I hadn't eaten since early that morning.

Sparrow gave a few breaths of a laugh. "Hungry?"

"Yes."

"Silence?" she called out and the young man was in my room a moment later.

"Yes?" he said, brown eyes filled with concern.

"Food?"

He nodded and left.

"Was he just waiting outside?" I asked, shocked at how quickly he'd entered after being called.

"Yes," Sparrow whispered. "He wanted to come in with me, but I thought that might be a bit overwhelming, that one would be best. So, he stayed outside in case we needed anything."

"Oh."

Your family loves you, Legs. They'll do anything for you. I'd do anything for you.

But you can't die for me, I replied to Auwei, *they can. And I don't want that. But there will be other missions... and I'll have to put these people I love so dearly in harm's way. Some of them may die, and that will definitely be my fault. How can I do that? How can I send them out? How can I live with that?*

I don't know, Legs. Perhaps talk to Crane. Maverick must have dealt with feelings like this too. Perhaps she knows how he dealt with it.

He was a rock. I...

I'd been about to say I can't imagine him suffering over the deaths of others... but instantly I knew that was wrong. He'd cared deeply for everyone in his House. Just because I'd never seen him suffering, didn't mean it didn't happen.

Perhaps you're right.

"Sparrow, can you fetch Crane for me? I'd like to talk to her."

"Of course, my love." She kissed the top of my head, then extricated herself from under me.

I sat up on my bed as she left.

Silence returned with food as Sparrow returned with Crane.

I ate from the plate of cold meats and soft breads, hard cheese and dried fruit. Crane sat in the hard chair at the small table in my room and waited patiently.

"We'll be just outside," Sparrow said and exited, shooing out Silence.

"You want to talk about failed missions?" Crane asked. "About the people in your House who'll die? About... all the pressures you're feeling. Am I right?"

I nodded. "Are you sure your spirit-gift isn't mind-reading."

She smiled softly. "No, but I've been through this before."

"With Maverick?"

"Yes."

"I can't picture him crying in his room," I murmured. "Even though I know he cared deeply for all of us."

"He did. And he did cry... sometimes. More often he'd turn into a bull and go ruin a few fences out in our farmers' fields." The side of her mouth quirked into a sad smile. A tear passed over her cheek. "But you're right, he wouldn't let it show. I was the only one who knew. Our House budget went to mending a lot of fences."

I let out a hoarse laugh at that, before sniffing back a few tears of my own. "So... what do I do?"

Crane's sad smile shifted as her face fell a little. She sighed. "That I can't really answer. You'll know how best to grieve and deal with loss, but I think there are a few things you need to know which may help... or may not, I don't know."

That seemed ambiguous. I raised a brow in question.

"First... know that, if we disagree with one of your plans, if we think it's too dangerous or too... something, whatever, we'll let you know. We all agreed that as crazy as this plan to kidnap the queen was, it was the best plan. And to be fair, it worked. Everything we planned for worked. We just weren't prepared for the queen herself being cursed. No one could have known that. You can't blame yourself." She sighed. "Well, you can, but it wasn't you who killed her. It was the mistweaver who cursed her."

I nodded to that. I still blamed myself, but her words made sense.

"So yes, some of us might die, but it will never be just your call if that happens. We will all agree on the plan and go willingly, knowing the dangers."

"Did knowing that help Maverick?"

"Ah... well... no."

"That's what I thought. Go on." I nibbled on some cheese as she continued her list of *things I should know*.

"Second, we know that you're willing to die for us."

I blinked at that, brow furrowing. I hadn't been expecting that. Was I willing to die for my House? The answer came quickly: yes, I was.

"And none of us want to lose you, just as you don't want to lose any of us."

Interesting. I hadn't thought of things in reverse. How others would feel if I died. I supposed they'd feel how I'd feel if *they* died.

"And *because* we don't want you to die, we'd die for you, Legs. We know, you'd die for us just as easily. It's a give and take. I know that doesn't make dealing with any of our deaths any easier, just as your death wouldn't be any easier for us. But you have to understand... we're all in this together. We'll all stand up for every other member of this House. And that means putting our lives on the line occasionally. Just as we know you'd put your life on the line for us."

It was certainly a different perspective. I nodded. "Thank you."

"Finally — and this is something that never came up with Maverick — we know that right now is a very difficult time for all of us." She gave a harsh little laugh. "Legs, we all know that what we're facing is next to impossible. We're a small house, ten people, going up against the entirety of the rest of our nation. That's... madness, but we're doing it because it's right, because we know it needs to be done. And we're doing it because we know *you* can do it."

"Can I?" I asked, voice quiet. I put my plate aside and gazed hard at Crane. "Do you really think that?"

She stared back just as hard. Her voice didn't waver when she said: "I do." She gave a grim smile. "Because our enemies have already foreseen it. They know you'll defeat them and it scares The Pits out of them!"

Oh... right.

"What's more," she added, "I don't think Maverick could have done it."

I raised a brow at that. "Truly? I thought he could do anything!"

"Almost anything, perhaps, but he tackled problems head on. He knew tactics and strategies, but often ignored the devious way of doing things in favor of the direct. And this isn't a problem we can attack head on. But you, Legs, you think in all manner of weird and wonderful ways. And it's that kind of thinking that's going to get us through this. I know we have the help of Alvere and Vauphan, but I also know they won't be able to divert many resources to help us. Your plan to use the Fey on the mission to get the queen was inspired."

"That was Alvere's idea, not mine."

"But you picked it up and ran with it, making it work." Crane rose and came to sit on the bed next to me, she took up one of my hands and held it gently between both of hers. "Legs, the world has turned to madness and we're the only ones who know it. We all know that it might mean our deaths to do this, but we all believe that you are our best chance of getting through this alive."

That was something I was still curious about. I shook my head, brow furrowed. "Why?" I asked, perhaps a bit too harshly. "You all made me your leader, but... why? Why do you think I can do this? Just because I don't think in a straightforward way? That can't be it." Even before she could answer I rushed on. "I'm the second youngest member of the House, others have more experience or are stronger, others are more conniving or devious, I'm sure. Why me?"

She squeezed my hand. "You're right, of course," she began softly. "Others are more devious, or stronger, or experienced, but..." She paused and made sure she had my gaze upon hers before she went on, holding me in suspense. "None of them have all of those qualities in as great a quantity as you do, Legs." She smiled. "Your spirit-gift is bloody *Heroism* for Pit's sake!" I'd never heard Crane swear like that, twice in one sentence.

I blinked, still not quite understanding.

She went on. "Legs, you may not be as strong as Ant, or as curious and odd as Foggy, or as experienced as Midnight, but you're more of all of those qualities combined than any of those others.

"Even Midnight?" I asked, a bit disbelieving. "She's pretty bloody strong and experienced and—"

"And her spirit-gift is going unseen, Legs. Don't you see? What leader can lead from the shadows? She knows that. You're out there, first into the fray and fighting just as hard as anyone else. So yes, she might be stronger and more experienced, but she doesn't have the one other quality that makes a good leader: the will to lead." Crane smiled once again. "Legs... she's terrified of leading. If you think you're scared, she's ten times as worried as you are. Why do you think she never even became a squad leader? She hates giving orders. She doesn't want to be in charge of people. She works best alone and she knows it."

"Oh." I hadn't known any of that. "Everyone really sees me that way? As a leader?" I tried to think of what I'd done to inspire such thoughts.

"You should hear Silence tell the story of how you saved him from the mistweaver, valiantly fighting the impossible foe yourself, keeping her at bay so he could get away with the information from the Vauphani raid."

I suppose I had done that.

"More than that," she whispered softly. "People... love you, Legs. Even more than those you share your bed with. There is just something about you that draws people to you. We all feel it."

"You're not interested in sharing my bed, are you?" I wasn't attracted to Crane. I saw her more as a mother figure.

She laughed. "No, Legs, I'm not. And I believe not everyone will be, but still... you're just... easy to know. You're open about how you feel and people are drawn to that sort of openness I think." She smiled. "*That* was something Maverick didn't do well. He kept his feelings hidden for the most part. People were still drawn to him, but more... as a curiosity, I think. They wanted to know more about him because he was so closed off." She shrugged. "I don't know if that's it or not, but I know people love you, Legs."

"Oh."

"And don't worry, the ones who aren't in your little harem don't feel left out. From what I've seen, Princess and Foggy are becoming quite close." She cocked her head to one side. "And I could be wrong, but there's been something in how your sister has been looking at Fin."

That surprised me. "Truly?"

She shrugged. "Perhaps it's nothing."

"And for you?" I asked.

"Alas, I've always pined for people I couldn't have." I did notice how she didn't say men. "And I'm an old woman now. I fear there won't be anyone for me."

"You're not that old." I figured her to be in her forties, no older.

She smiled. "I hope you're right."

Some strange little part of me made it my mission to find someone for Crane... and Midnight... if they wanted someone. After this whole war thing was done, I'd focus on that.

For now... I had other things to worry about.

And something Crane had said had gotten me thinking. "We need help," I stated.

"Yes," she said.

I pulled my hand out from hers as I smiled and rose, ready to get back to work. "And I think I know where to get it."

CHAPTER 8

SILENCE SQUIRMED. HE WANTED TO HELP, KNEW HE COULD HELP, BUT he didn't like this plan at all. Even though he had volunteered for this mission.

Legs' plan was to talk to Blackclaw. Hopefully their old friend wouldn't think Legs was a horrible traitor. Then Blackclaw would convince Grizzly House of that same fact. As soon as he'd heard Blackclaw's name, Silence knew he had to come along. He hadn't known exactly how he could help, but he was the only other person who knew Blackclaw well, so him making contact made sense.

He just hadn't known how to do that. He'd had the entirety of the trip to Cragmount to think but hadn't come up with anything.

Fin hadn't been able to take them. The Grizzly House Manor — Stonehold — was in the badlands in the north-west of Elista. Since Fin had never been inland in the west, the closest he could get the team was to a small coastal village in the southwest of Elista called Bell Cove.

There had been some debate over who would go. Silence had made his case, Midnight would come for her stealth, Fin for his transport — even if he couldn't get them in quick, he could get them out quick — and finally Ant as muscle if needed.

It had taken them a little more than two weeks to travel by carriage from that small coastal village to the town of Cragmount in the north. The ride hadn't been comfortable. Fin and Ant in the same carriage left little room for others, and since Fin's other form wasn't smaller, he remained as he was, while Silence and the others took turns in their avatar forms.

Once at Cragmount, Midnight procured the team two rooms at an inn, one with two beds for sleeping in shifts, the other for meeting and planning.

After one day of scouting, mostly by Midnight, they'd discovered that Blackclaw was at Stonehold and wasn't part of the Grizzly forces that had been sent east to help with the "war" with Vauphan.

And now, it was Silence's turn. He was the one going in... but he didn't like any of his options.

"I know, I know!" he said, holding up his hands to stall any more comments from the others. Fin was sleeping, as was Midnight. Ant and Legs were both staring him down. "I know I'm the best choice to go in and I know why... I just don't know how!" He squared his shoulders and straightened to his full height, which was just ever-so-slightly taller than Legs. "I can't walk up to their front door like this." He motioned to himself. "Which means I'd have to go in as a mouse, and there are a lot of things in that house — some of the avatars of the Nobles included — that would love to eat me."

He'd seen Stonehold from a distance, up on a higher hill than the aptly named Cragmount. This whole area was badlands, craggy, rocky hills, best for grazing sheep and mining the many minerals beneath the ground. Stonehold was a fortress and probably had any number of holes through which a mouse might sneak in. However, those dark places within the walls housed other denizens, many of which preyed on mice. And it wasn't a small fortress either. He'd have to go quite a long way as a small creature to reach Blackclaw's rooms.

Legs sighed. "I know you're scared, we're all—"

"I'm not scared!" he said, and instantly realized he sounded like a frightened child saying he wasn't scared. He calmed himself. "What I mean is. I'm not scared of dying for our cause or doing something dangerous... but... I may be just a bit scared of dying for no reason other than I was a tasty morsel. And if I do, you'll never even know what happened to me!" He sighed. "That seems... just so... sad."

"You want me to go with you?" Ant asked. "My avatar's even smaller."

Silence grimaced. "Then we'd both get eaten, a main course and dessert."

Legs laughed her unique I'm-thinking-something-dirty laugh then coughed and was serious again. "You've convinced me. We'll all go. My venom should stop most things in those walls. I'll make sure you get where you're going, and Ant and I will be there, just in case."

Silence nodded. It was settled.

They waited a full day to make sure they were rested then snuck out of the town and up to the manor in the darkness before dawn. They did indeed find a nice hole to slip in through and made their way up inside the walls of the ancient fortress.

As predicted, there were many interesting creatures living in those old walls, though the only one they found which posed any real threat, was a large rat, which Legs paralyzed. Silence felt a bit ashamed of his fear after that.

They made it to Blackclaw's rooms and found a small hole in the stone of the windowsill where the wooden frame had been worn away by rot over many years. Silence managed to squeeze through; the other two made it through the tiny hole easily.

Silence stayed on the sill for a moment taking in the room. There was a door in the far wall, probably leading to the rest of the keep. Not far from that, on the same wall, was a small nightstand, then a large bed. On the other side of the bed was an open area with a couple of chairs before a large hearth. In the close right-hand corner was a built-out area of wooden walls with a door. Probably a small privy. On the left-hand wall were a large wardrobe and a tall chest of drawers. The room was empty.

Silence waited for a while, just to make sure Blackclaw wasn't in the privy. Then he scampered down the wall and was halfway across the room when the door to the hall opened. He rushed under the bed, out of sight, and watched as two booted feet stepped into the room. He heard a heavy sigh. It sounded like Blackclaw was frustrated or perhaps tired?

She moved around the bed to the fireplace and threw some more wood on the embers of the fire, waiting for it to catch. It was spring, but this high up, in this drafty castle, it was chilly. She moved to one of the chairs before the fire and sat heavily with another sigh.

He ran out from under the bed on the far side before returning to himself, crouching low behind the large piece of furniture.

He drew in a long breath to steady himself, then rose.

"Hello Blackclaw, it's me, Silence, don't be afraid. I'm—" His words cut off as he caught site of her. She'd shot to her feet upon hearing his voice. She'd changed a lot in the nearly a year since he'd seen her last. Gone was the bulk from her figure, but remaining were all her curves. She was a stunning woman now, not slender, but fit and strong and much fuller of figure than Legs or Sparrow. Her black hair had been cut short, framing a narrower face, which seemed to enhance and enlarge her brown eyes.

She had claws out on her hands, but quickly put them away. "Silence?" She blinked. "What are you doing here?"

"I... ah..." He blinked his confused-attraction away. He had a group he loved very much, and who loved him. "I've come to ask for your help."

It was only then that she stiffened and her claws returned. "No, wait, you're... with the traitor." She looked around quickly. "Is she here?"

Silence held out his empty hands. "Please, Blackclaw, I'm here in peace. Don't call out, don't be alarmed. I just want to talk. Please?" He inched a bit closer to her, moving around to the end of the bed.

She settled again with a sigh, and he noticed then the darkness under her eyes, the fatigue upon her. "What am I doing?" she muttered to herself. Her claws vanished again, and she rushed to him, hugging him. "It's so good to see you." Her words were soft and low, but her hug was tight and strong, perhaps just a little too strong, too desperate.

Her ample body, pressed to his, distracted him, but he quelled his startled arousal and returned her embrace. "It's good to see you too. Can we talk?"

She drew back and nodded. "Of course, come, sit." She motioned to the chairs, and they sat before the fire. Even before he began, she spoke, and the words came out in a rambling mess. "Spirits, Silence, what's been happening? I've heard so many things. I don't want them to be true, but, with the war and... she killed the queen for Spirits' sake! I... I don't know what to believe anymore. Are you here to flee from Legs? Has she harmed you? We'll take you in, I'm sure. I... Spirits, what am I saying? I don't even know. I'm sorry, what did you need to say? Why are you here?"

He smiled softly. "It may be a long story. Is there any chance we'll be interrupted?"

She shook her head. "No, I... well... ah... oh..."

"What is it?" Silence noted the flush of her cheeks.

She rose and went to the door, sliding a bolt to hold it closed. "I have a... friend who might stop by."

Silence had the distinct impression this *friend* was the sort that joins you in bed, given how flushed she'd become.

"She sometimes stops by in the afternoons if she's free. I'll tell her I'm not feeling well if she does." Blackclaw returned to her chair. "Go on."

Silence gathered his thoughts, then began with a measured pace. "What you've been hearing are just rumors, they are unfounded and mostly lies." He sighed. "The trouble is that they are coming from high up, so other Nobles tend to believe them. If you'll let me, I'd like to tell you a story. It... may be a bit hard to believe from your perspective, but I hope you'll keep an open mind."

She nodded, so he went on, telling her everything he and Legs and the once Maverick House had been through. He didn't quite tell it in order, jumping around a bit to add in the pieces he and his House had learned later, but which were earlier parts of this story. "And, she didn't kill the queen, though, the queen *is* dead. Whitewing had a mistweaver's curse upon her, and when she was taken from the capital, it was enacted. That is what killed her, not Legs. We were only trying to find out more of this plot and who was behind it. So no, I'm not here to flee from her or join with you. We're here to get your help, to try to convince you and your House that we're not evil, because we need help to take out those who are."

He could see the skepticism written clearly on Blackclaw's face. She'd listened without comment to his entire story, but now sighed. "Mistweavers?" It was clear she didn't believe in such things. "Silence, do you know how crazy that sounds?" She looked away into the now-dwindling flames of the fire. "But then... all of this is hard to believe." She shook her head. "But the Royal House being behind everything?" A grimace twisted her face. "Your story is just as outrageous as theirs. You're casting them as evil, while they do the same to you. How... how can I trust you... or them?" She threw her arms into the air and rose, pacing the room. "Spirits, what a mess." Then she stopped suddenly. She turned to him slowly. "You swear by the Spirits your story is true?" she asked slowly and there was something about how she asked, which made him shiver.

"Yes," he said with a confident nod.

"Then... there may be a way to convince not only me, but this entire house of that truth and get us on your side." She looked at the door to the hall for a long moment. "Will you come with me?" she ventured, tentative. "My *friend*... has a spirit-gift. She can determine the truth of anything. If you tell her your story...?" Yet Blackclaw seemed hesitant. She looked back to Silence. "Are you sure you want to do this?"

He nodded again, rising.

"Take me to her," he said with confidence.

"No," Legs said, appearing on the other side of Blackclaw, leaning against the wall. She must have been listening in. "Take *me* to her."

CHAPTER 9

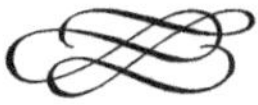

BLACKCLAW NEARLY JUMPED OUT OF HER SKIN, SPINNING WITH HER claws out and ready. Then she saw me, saw I was relaxed and unarmed, and she settled, claws vanishing.

"Legs?" She laughed. "I should have known you'd not be far away." She hesitated only for a moment before coming to embrace me. I returned the gesture. She had certainly become quite the beautiful woman, though it seemed her time here had worn heavily upon her.

"I don't want any of this to be true," she whispered. "But I'd rather know the truth than keep believing a lie."

"I know," I said and we drew apart. "So, let's see this friend of yours."

Blackclaw nodded. "Just to be safe, both of you better return to your avatar forms, I'll carry you to her unseen."

Silence and I did as instructed and were put in a pouch, the draw-string pulled not completely closed so we'd have an escape if needed.

Then we trusted ourselves to the care of this old friend, not knowing where we were going, feeling only the jostling of the pouch at her hip. We heard a bit of muffled discussion then the bag was carefully being moved and opened. Silence and I clambered out and returned to our human forms.

We were in a larger room and Blackclaw's "friend" turned out to be Ursa, the second of House Grizzly. I didn't know all the members, but I knew her; she was hard to miss. One of the few women taller than me, over six feet of powerful physique, with cropped blond hair and stunning, deep blue eyes.

She started when she saw me... just as I was shocked to see her.

"They are my friends," Blackclaw said quickly. "Please don't hurt them. Just... listen with your gift, and we'll all know what the truth is."

Ursa calmed quickly, though I felt the latent power in those strong limbs. She was a full-figured woman like Blackclaw, just a little bigger and taller in all aspects. Strong and powerful and beautiful. She nodded. "I'll listen." But there was a threat in her voice. It was clear she didn't expect to believe our story.

We were in a sitting room, heavy carpets over the cold stone floor, and comfortable chairs surrounding a low table. A low fire burned in a nearby hearth but gave little heat. I paced to keep warm.

Ursa sat in a large chair and watched us keenly. She didn't seem to mind the cold.

Blackclaw nodded for me to begin, and I told them my tale.

The way Ursa twitched her nose from time to time made me believe she wasn't so much reading my mind as... smelling the truth of my words on me. Perhaps it was both?

Either way, when I finished, she looked a bit stunned, shaking her head slowly. "I can't believe it," she said slowly. "But I *must* believe it. Not a word of it was a lie. Still... how could our own Royal family be betraying us like this?"

Only then did I relax. I saw Blackclaw do the same, finally knowing we weren't lying to her.

Ursa looked at me for a long moment. "I need to take this to Grizzly. And I'll need to do some internal housecleaning to see if we have any traitors working for the Royals in our midst. That will take some time, but we are with you, Legs of House Spider. Anything you need that we can provide we will."

"Can you recall your troops from the front?" I asked quickly.

Ursa frowned. "No. That would let the Royals know we were against them instantly. Perhaps it would be best if we played along for a bit to see what we can find out. But I'll let the commanders of our troops know they are not to fight or support those at the front in any way. We don't want to make things worse."

She sighed heavily. "How could we have come to this?" Shaking her head, she asked, "And you have no idea why the Royals are doing all of this?"

"That piece of the puzzle has eluded us. We do know they've been killing Nobles and their Lumani — somehow — because they knew too much. So, be very careful in how you move."

Ursa nodded to that. "It will take us a bit of time to get our house in order. How can we contact you?"

"Send a pigeon for mundane things, but they can be intercepted, so... for most things, we have a member of our House, Fin, who will come and go regularly to keep you up to date on events and carry messages back and forth. We'll need to bring him up from the village to someplace safe in your keep so he knows where to transport himself. That's his spirit-gift."

"Very useful."

"So is yours."

Ursa smiled. "Indeed." But her grin quickly faded. "It would be best if you were not seen here. We'll arrange to have your Fin brought up, but otherwise, you should go for now. I am not certain of everyone in my house yet. Some of the newer members from Blackclaw's cohort, have always been a bit... odd. I wouldn't want to give anything away." She sighed. "I do not like using my gift on members of my own House. I like to think I can trust them, but now... I will do what I must."

I nodded to that.

We were bundled into Blackclaw's pouch again and carried back to her room. It was only once we were there, and the door latched shut, that we returned to ourselves and spoke freely with Blackclaw.

We summoned Ant out from the hole in the wall, and Blackclaw tried not to drool over him, though I could see the instant attraction in her eyes. He remained to one side, while the three of us sat on her large bed and caught up.

"So..." I asked after enough other talk that I thought it safe. "You and Ursa are... together?" I smiled. "I'm happy for you. She seems like a wonderful woman."

Blackclaw blushed. "Yes, but... that's not the entire truth."

"Oh? Do tell," I said, leaning forward intently.

Her blush deepened. "I, ah... well, I worked very hard when I got here, trained relentlessly, and I began to lose a little weight and..." She laughed. "I never thought I'd catch anyone's eye, but—"

"I always thought you were beautiful," Silence admitted, no hint of hesitation in his voice.

She blushed. "I know, but... I... didn't really allow myself to believe it, I guess." She sighed. "Anyway, it wasn't just Ursa's eye I caught. You see, she and Grizzly have been together for some time and... they wanted me to join... *them*." She went from a blushing red, to a deep maroon, lips pressed tight for a moment.

Yet I only smiled. "Sounds lovely to me."

She blinked. "Oh?"

I reached out to touch her shoulder. "Yes. Perhaps I should mention — since I didn't talk much about my personal life during my retelling of the past year — that I'm now with a whole group of people."

"Oh?" Her eyes grew a little wide. She looked back and forth from me to Silence to Ant.

"Yes. Silence and I have been together, so have Ant and I. I'm also seeing Sparrow, a woman from my House, and... ah... the Prince — no, I guess he's King now — of Vauphan."

Blackclaw's jaw dropped. "Truly? A prince? And... all at once, or...?"

I took a bit of time to explain how the odd relationship worked, how we all loved each other... except for Ant, he'd only been with me so far, but... who knew what might happen. "And I'd be open to others if they were agreeable to the whole situation," I said with a grin.

Blackclaw looked a little stunned, then her eyes went a little wider. "Oh... wait, you don't mean... me? Do you?"

I laughed. "I wasn't thinking of you, no, but now that you mention it, you'd be welcome." I slid Silence a sidelong look. "I think Silence wouldn't mind warming your bed sometime."

I caught their combined blush at that. "I... ah.... appreciate the offer," she said... and I waited, but she didn't go on to explicitly deny it. Interesting.

We talked for the rest of the afternoon until it began to get dark. Then Ant, Silence, and myself took our avatar forms and crawled away through the walls. We didn't get back to the inn until well after dark. Midnight had food waiting, which we were all thankful for, not having eaten since breakfast.

"How did it go?" Midnight asked.

"We have an ally," I said between bites of warm bread and hearty stew. "Finally, things are starting to turn our way."

Now I just had to figure out what I was going to do with this newfound help.

CHAPTER 10

ALVERE STOOD JUST INSIDE THE CAVE, WATCHING THE TIDE SLOWLY recede off the rocky beach before him. Somewhere, out across the expanse of Dyren's Bay was his home. Odd though, how he felt just as home here as he did there. In fact, he felt more at home here, amidst friends and lovers, not subjects and people who depended on him. Here he could be himself, there... he was *King* Alvere.

It would be known soon. With things calming in the North, he'd sent word that it would be well to do away with the charade of his cousin, Pierre being crowned. The country could know its true leader and true king had survived and would be leading them. But that also meant, his time here would be limited.

This vacation, away from his responsibilities, would soon end. He'd be a king in truth and have far too much on his plate to go galivanting off to see these dear people whom he loved. He'd grown close to all of them. With Legs and Silence away, he'd spent time with Sparrow, gotten to know her better. They'd slept next to each other a couple of times, but only that, lying together for comfort and warmth in these chilly stone halls. They loved each other, but knew their hearts were given to another, the same other. It was Legs who truly made this group... work.

His half-Fey heritage did give him rather good hearing, and he caught the sounds of someone's footfalls crunching on the stones behind him, coming out from deep within the cave, where a rope ladder had been lowered down a long shaft, the "back door" of the house in the cliffs above.

Arms wrapped around him and warm soft lips kissed the back of his neck. "Hello my king," Legs whispered. "I'm back."

"How did it go?" he asked, putting his hands on her arms crossed over his stomach as he savored the feel of her lithe body pressed against his back.

"Very well. Grizzly House is on board." She sighed and slumped a little. "Now... I have no clue what to do." Another soft kiss on his neck. "I was hoping you might join me... join us... for some... inspiration?"

He smiled. "There is nothing I'd want more." He turned in her arms and swept her up in a passionate kiss, his heart thundering now that he held her, his home, his heart, his core. He curled a hand up into the waves of her brown hair, pressing her lips close, as his other hand found the small of her back and urged their bodies together. She slid a leg up his thigh, which pulled her skirt back to her hip. He ran a hand along that exposed skin as his arousal surged. His cock was hard and ready, yearning to be inside her. For just a moment, he wanted to be alone with her, selfish, wanting her just for him, not sharing... so he reveled in this passionate embrace for as long as she'd allow.

Finally, she drew back. Breathless, she said, "That was an excellent start. Shall we reconvene with the others?"

He nodded. He knew he had to share her... and he loved the

others as well, if not... quite as much as he loved her. He smiled as
he let his soul sink into those russet brown eyes. "Yes, lets."

She took his hand and led him back into the cave and to the
ladder. They climbed up — it was a not-insignificant drop — and
found the ledge and entrance back into the cliff-house. He could
sense her excitement as she nearly dragged him to her room.

Inside, he was surprised to see Ant standing off to one side.
The large man looked like he felt just a bit awkward and out of
place. "He's just going to watch this time," Legs explained. "See
what he likes."

If any more joined this already large group, things were going
to start getting awkward quickly. Still Alvere smiled and nodded to
Ant. "Glad to have you." The man was certainly much larger than
anyone else in this group. It sent a shiver running down Alvere's
spine to think of just how "large" Ant might be. Would he want
such a massive erection inside him? From the sounds of Legs'
encounter with the man, it was... painful but pleasurable.

He put those thoughts aside as his arousal grew. Legs was
clearly eager, stripping off her clothes. Sparrow and Silence were
already on the bed, mostly naked and gently caressing each other.
He quickly disrobed as well, wishing to join them all.

Legs came to him and whispered in his ear, "Go get the oil
from the bedstand, I want you inside me like you were with
Silence last time."

Alvere's eye's widened in shock. "Truly?"

"Oh, yes. I know exactly what I want." She stepped back and
finished disrobing, and he took just a moment to marvel at her
form: that perfect fall of brown hair, the soft wide lips, and those
red-brown eyes. Some men might be put off by her strong shoulders and arms, not delicate and lady-like, but he loved every part
of her. Her breasts were not large but full, ample pear-shaped
swells with those small but sensitive nipples. Her waist and belly
were taut and tight, her hips, curved but not rounded. It was her

namesake legs, which truly sealed his desire for her, long and lean, allowing her to move so swiftly and gracefully as she mounted the bed and whispered to Sparrow and Silence.

They would all give her whatever she desired. She was their goddess, their truest love, their center. She didn't know it. She thought them all in this together, but in truth, they were all in this for her. Alvere had discussed it with Silence and Sparrow at varying times and they'd all agreed they'd not tell her. She wouldn't believe it. She was too humble to think she could be the center of so many people's worlds. So, they'd continue to love her and love each other and do whatever she asked of them. If it pleased her, they rejoiced in it.

Alvere got the oil from the drawer, noting Ant's awkward fumbling as he got out his oh-dear-gods massive shaft, stroking it slowly as he watched the naked bodies positioning themselves on the bed.

When he turned back to the bed, his arousal spiked. This was... new.

Silence lay on his back, and Sparrow was kneeling, hovering over his face. Alvere couldn't see, but he assumed Silence would be pleasuring the woman with his mouth. Sparrow faced Legs, who was currently straddling Silence's hips, still high, man-handling Silence's erection — and using her own fingers — on her folds to tease her arousal. She leaned back a little on Silence's upraised legs as she slowly teased him into her, sinking down to straddle him, leaning forward to kiss Sparrow, forming a triangle of sorts with the three bodies. Silence then spread his legs, his thighs on top of Legs' calves behind her, and Legs looked to Alvere with longing in her eyes. "Your turn," she said, voice already hitching with rising bliss as she rocked herself on Silence.

Alvere took the hint, moving behind her. First, he doled out some oil onto his hands, liberally spreading it around Legs' rear opening, massaging the tight and puckered hole before inserting a finger to help massage the oil into her.

Legs gasped and moaned, even with just Alvere's finger inside her. Though, in truth she was also fully enjoying Silence's erection, not to mention Sparrow's hands on her breasts and lips on her mouth. Just seeing her passion mount, her pleasure rise, was nearly too much for Alvere. His urgency grew as he oiled her more, slipping another finger inside her, then a third, working them around until she began to loosen. He hoped she was ready. He was more than ready himself, and he knew she'd be tight and the pressure upon him exquisitely hard and needful.

He couldn't wait any longer and moved in closer, liberally oiling himself before pushing the flared tip of his erection into her.

"Oh, Spirits!" she cried out, going still, then shuddering, a tremble which seemed to run from her head to her toes, then back. "Oh, yes, more," she gasped, clearly already quite over-taken with ecstasy.

He grabbed her hips and thrust himself fully inside her in one hard plunge, and she stiffened again. "Oh, Spirits, it's... oh!" She was having trouble speaking, so Sparrow stopped her lips with a kiss. Alvere, Silence, and Sparrow all threw themselves into pleasuring this amazing woman.

As Alvere had expected she was so very tight, clamping down upon him with delicious intensity. It was only the oil which allowed him to continue to thrust into her. Despite his earlier urgency and the pressure squeezing him, he found himself not finishing as quickly as he'd expected. He wanted this to last for Legs, and it seemed he was able to delay his gratification, riding his own pleasure, building and building, intensifying and focusing until he was as engorged and ready as he'd ever been, but still holding his release.

Legs was gasping, murmuring words as she shook through

the throes of, what seemed like, one prolonged orgasm. She leaned back against Alvere, and he held her, moving his hands up to her breasts, cupping them, holding and caressing them, feeling their weight and the tight towers of her nipples. He flicked one of those nubs and she seemed to half-collapse with another surge of bliss. Over her shoulder he saw Sparrow, clasping her own small breasts, eyes clenched shut as Silence brought her to release.

Alvere heard Silence's grunt and saw the man's hands grasp Legs thigh's tighter as he bucked up from under them in a final thrust. Alvere slid one of his hands down Legs' sweaty body to her opening, feeling the pulse of Silence's erection as the other man came. Then Alvere slowly circled Legs' clit.

She trembled and gasped.

He flicked that sensitive nub, then began rubbing it furiously.

"Oh, Spirits! Yes!" Legs cried out and she clamped down hard upon him, shuddering through a powerful release. With that Alvere allowed himself to join the others in a jolting, body-shaking mutual orgasm, holding Legs tight to him, feeling her body thrum in time with his as they came together.

Legs leaned her head back on his shoulder and they kissed, if a bit awkwardly, before her gaze caught on something and she sat up a little.

"What did you think?" she said to Ant, her breath still catching as she shuddered with the aftershocks of their joining.

Alvere turned his head and saw Ant, stroking a raging erection, with a look of semi-pained restraint on his face.

"Want to join us?" Legs asked him.

He nodded quickly, no words. He moved to the bed as everyone else slowly disengaged from each other. Legs slid off the bed, and sank down before Ant. "Let's give you a little release first, yes?" she said as she grasped his erection and moved it into her mouth. With his size, she couldn't take much of him, but it didn't seem like that would be needed. Almost as soon as he was in her mouth he grunted, his shaft twitching as he came.

Alvere wondered what it would be like to have a man that large in *his* mouth. The thought aroused him far more than he'd expected. He'd have never thought to be with a man before he met Legs, but with her, anything and everything was possible; not just possible, but arousing and exciting and enticing.

Once Ant was spent, Legs remained where she was, bringing him back to arousal with her mouth. Alvere caught movement from the corner of his eye to see Sparrow doing the same with Silence. And once the other man was ready, Sparrow turned to Alvere with a questioning glance. He shook his head, watching these two women arouse these two men had him almost fully engorged once again. Though, now with the extra member in their group he had no clue how they'd come together.

It was Ant who initiated the next position. Once he was ready, he told Legs, "Enough!" and she rose. He laid her back on the bed, kneeling at the side, between her legs, heartily pleasuring her with mouth and hands. Legs then reached out toward Silence and Alvere's erections. They moved to either side of her so she could stroke the two of them, moving her head from side to side to take them into her mouth in turn.

Sparrow moved over Legs, giving Ant a second set of folds to pleasure with hands and lips. She alternated between kissing Legs and taking Silence and Alvere in her mouth as well. Those two sets of lips and grasping hands were quickly bringing Alvere to a peak of arousal, just as Ant's earnest ministrations were making both women moan with pleasure.

Ant rose partially, erection in hand, moving it back and forth between the two sets of wet folds, teasing and testing.

"Too big for me," Sparrow breathed, and shifted off Legs. Ant then focused his attentions on Legs, slowly working his massiveness into her. They began a tentative rhythm which forced the others away. Legs focused entirely on Ant.

Legs wrapped her legs around Ant and drew herself up to cling to him as he supported her with his hands under her thighs. He stood, holding her easily in his arms as he rocked his hips to push that huge erection into her, then pull it out in slow thrusts.

The remaining three on the bed were distracted, watching Ant's massive length slowly pushing in then pulling out of Legs.

Silence moved behind Sparrow, his hands on her body, working her to another shuddering release.

Alvere was left a little uncertain, until Ant seemed to sense his desires.

Ant knelt at the side of the bed, spreading his legs out to lower him and Legs to the right level. Alvere didn't need quite as much oil to get her rear opening ready again and was soon inside her. The feel of her pulsing canal gripping him — and the shifting of Ant's erection inside her as well — surged his bliss to a sublime instance of purest pleasure.

Legs was already in her murmuring-incoherent-words-while-trembling stage of mid-orgasmic bliss and Ant had his eyes rolled back, breathing through his teeth, clearly ready to release, but holding himself from it. Alvere himself maintained long, slow strokes, feeling his own release building, the exquisite intensity of pressure swelling his erection to near painful extremes as he too waited for just the moment...

Then Legs convulsed with a powerful orgasm, clamping down upon him and he could hold it no longer. He joined with the other two in a massive release. Something clicked into place in Alvere's soul as he shivered through that epitome of bliss, tears of ecstatic joy and fulfillment on his cheeks.

He may be a king, but this was where he belonged, giving everything he had to the woman he loved.

It took a long time for them to finish their chain of pleasure before staggering apart. They fell to the floor or the bed, weak and smiling, like this had been their first time.

Legs laughed, a thing of purest joy and relief. "Spirits Above and Below!" she breathed. "That was amazing. I'm ready to take on the world!"

Alvere smiled. That was what he — what they all — had been hoping for.

CHAPTER 11

"Okay, so, what do we know so far?" I asked, once again pacing the front of the common area. "The queen didn't give us any information, unfortunately, other than Merlin is... something, perhaps the mastermind behind all of this? But we don't know that for certain. So, let's start from the beginning, what do we know?"

Crane began the brainstorming session: "Some Nobles are seizing lands in the North, why, we're not quite sure, but even most of the Nobles in the northern army don't seem to know why either."

"Lynx said it was something about the Mists?" I recalled that from my conversation with him, before he'd been told I was a traitor, when he'd still been a friend. "He said that they were told Vauphan wanted to invade and claim the lands with the Mists."

"Which we don't, just to be clear," Alvere said.

"I know," I said with a smile, rolling my eyes. "They were told they needed to claim the northern provinces of Vauphan preemptively to stop the invasion, which makes little sense to me, but apparently made sense to them."

"Or perhaps it didn't make sense," Silence suggested. "Didn't Lynx also say something about those who questioned the orders were the ones who vanished?"

"Yes." I nodded. "That's right. So maybe it didn't make sense to them either, but it was do or disappear. That's an interesting thought." I pondered that for a moment. "I can't imagine Jaguar wasn't in on it though, either that or he was just extremely loyal to the nation and wasn't questioning things, which seems a bit... well... extreme." And we'd not be able to ask him now. He was dead, Ant's revenge for killing Amber. "So, three years ago, they invade Vauphan and anyone who seems overly concerned or questioned this... disappeared, which meant everyone remaining went along with it, whether it made sense or not," I summed up. "And we still don't know why."

"Yeah," Ant drawled. "That excuse about the Mists seems a bit flimsy to me."

I agreed.

Crane said, "And we know Merlin, Hale, and Horn are in on it." It was a testament to how disgusted she must be with them to not say their titles.

"Perhaps Lady Swan," I added, having seen her on Hale's arm. "But that's less certain."

"And it has to be more than just them for all of this to be kept hidden and to disappear those in the north who needed disappearing," Foggy said. "I can believe some people followed them just because they were important, but... disappearing someone... that would require some extreme loyalty or knowledge of what's going on."

"Which lends more credence to Jaguar being in on it." I finished that thought. "And yes, probably many others as well."

"But we don't know who," Princess added.

"We know we can trust Grizzly house though," Silence piped up.

I hated to disagree with him but... "Well, not yet."

That raised a few brows.

I wasn't sure we could trust Grizzly entirely, not yet. We could trust Blackclaw, but as for Ursa? We had proven ourselves to her... but she had done nothing to prove herself to us. It was something that had occurred to me when my mind had cleared after that mind-bending, body-breaking, world-shattering sex. I usually had my best ideas after sex.

It's all those wonderful chemicals surging through you, Auwei said analytically.

Among other things 'surging' inside me.

Do I have to scrub out that filthy mind of yours?

Oh, you know you love it.

Auwei giggled.

"Blackclaw we can trust," I stated. "But it occurred to me earlier that Ursa and the others haven't really done anything to prove they're on our side. They didn't kill us and they did listen to us... but that might be a long-con."

"But then Blackclaw might be in danger!" Silence said, worried.

"Yes, that occurred to me too. Unfortunately, we'll have to wait and see what happens with them. Either we can trust them or they'll betray us. We'll need to be ready for anything, until they've proven they're on our side, all of them."

Silence was still worried but nodded. "Perhaps..." He seemed to be thinking as he spoke. "We could ask for Blackclaw as a sort of liaison, keeping her here?"

That was an excellent idea, except... "We already have a liaison, pigeons and Fin. It would be odd to ask for her to stay with us... but I can try it, feel out their reactions." Silence nodded. I'd do it for him, even if it did cause some questions on Grizzly's end of things.

"Perhaps," Crane began slowly. "Perhaps there is a way they

can prove themselves, though it would be dangerous and potentially an opportunity for them to betray us as well."

"What are you thinking?" I asked, curious.

I felt Auwei's curiosity too.

Crane rose and began pacing, which was odd for her, usually so stoic and calm. "What if we use Grizzly as a way into the thick of things?" she asked, clearly a rhetorical question. "What if Ursa approaches Merlin and the others, saying she knows what's going on and wants in. With her ability to read minds or sniff out the truth, whatever it is, it wouldn't be out of the realm of reason for her to have gleaned the conspiratorial information off someone. So, she goes in and joins them. She could work on the inside for us, find out everything we need to know to prove these people are traitors." She stopped her pacing. "And perhaps she could even get some of us in close as well? That would be the risky part. If she *is* in on it, we'd be walking into a trap with her leading us along."

It was an interesting idea, and I agreed, potentially dangerous for Ursa and potentially very dangerous for us if we went in with her and she was a traitor. But we had to start somewhere. A plan began to form in my mind and a smile spread on my lips as I figured out exactly how we could make it work... and keep anyone who went in with Ursa as safe as possible.

CHAPTER 12

SPARROW WAS SCARED AND UNCOMFORTABLE, BUT SHE'D PROMISED Legs she could do this, and she'd follow through, even if it meant she might die.

Ursa had agreed to their plan. She'd go in, supposedly alone, to join up with Merlin, Hale, and the others. The hope was to find out the true reason for all the machinations. Yet Ursa wouldn't be alone. The trouble was Hale's ability to revert any True-Bonded back to their original form. It meant hiding as an avatar wouldn't work, but there was something Hale couldn't affect.

Which was how Sparrow found herself in a strange dark place, hiding with Ahmaia, who'd used her cloth ability to hide them both in one of her 'pockets' which was in turn hidden inside a small pouch on Ursa's belt. Neither Sparrow nor Ahmaia would be able to see what was happening. Sparrow could only see a spot of light above her — the opening of the pouch — which seemed, at the same time, both close and incredibly distant.

Yet, they'd be able to hear events beyond the pouch to get a sense for how things progressed.

"We are in a large hall," Ahmaia said.

Sparrow could hear the echoing footfalls of Ursa as she moved into the chamber.

Then a deep, hard voice cut over the dying echoes of those footfalls. "Welcome Lady Ursa, it is our honor to have you here with us."

"Lord Hale, Lady Swan, Lady Merlin," Ursa said. "It is an honor to be here."

Sparrow silently thanked Lady Ursa. Now they knew who was in the hall with them.

"With the traitors of Maverick House having killed our beloved queen, I would ask that you address Merlin as My Queen or Your Majesty." This from Hale as well.

"Indeed, that news was horrible, I still can't quite believe it," Ursa said sounding shocked. "How did they do it?"

"Right in the very streets of this great city!" Hale said, voice raised in rage. "The used some fire magic to incinerate her where she stood! It was horrible to see."

Wow, that was — at the same time — so very far from the truth but vaguely believable.

"It must have been. I'm so sorry you had to witness that, and I'm sorry that we have all lost such a great woman." Ursa went on to say, "But surely, Lady Merlin, you will abide by the Council of Nobles when they meet to select a new Royal. They haven't selected you yet."

"They most certainly will." Hale's voice was low, lethal, threatening, but also with a hint of glee.

"Indeed," Ursa said, and nothing more on that topic.

Sparrow was just a bit shaken. The implication that the Council of Nobles would be so easily swayed to select Merlin was preposterous. There were many other more experienced leaders.

Skyfire was the most likely candidate. Even Silvermane — the previous queen's daughter — had a shot at the throne.

A new voice joined the conversation. It was a powerful alto, a woman's voice, commanding and sure, but with just a hint of something Sparrow couldn't place, something just a little bit... off. "Check her for any True-Bonded avatars," the voice commanded.

"As you wish, My Queen," Hale said, indicating the previous speaker had been Merlin herself.

Heavy footfalls echoed in the chamber, growing louder, closer: Hale was coming.

This was the true test of how well Ahmaia's hidden pocket would work. They hadn't been sure if Hale could sense Lumani in addition to his other powers, but if so, and he sensed Sparrow and the presence of her Lumani: Ahena, this would all be over soon.

Sparrow's heart thundered in her chest. She clenched her eyes shut, not that it would do her any good in the event of discovery, but she needed to do something. She needed to be able to move some part of her, have some agency over what was happening, and shutting her eyes was virtually the only thing she could do.

"I recall Hale from the day of the queen's speech, a large and powerful man," Ahmaia said. "Does he scare you that much?"

Short answer: yes. Sparrow was well trained in a style of fighting which made her small size a strength, not a weakness, but she had never been comfortable in a true fight. She might be able to defeat Hale, she'd bested Ant a few times in her practices, but not every time, not by a longshot. If a large man could simply grapple her, pin her arms and keep her off the ground, all she could do then was flail her legs and hope to hit something vital. Also, with Hale's powers, she'd not be able to veer into her avatar form to escape.

Sparrow tried to calm her rapid breathing, taking long deep breaths before she replied. "I'll do what I must, if I must," she breathed; she couldn't help but keep her voice low. Ahmaia had said no one outside the pouch would hear them, but still...

Moments passed with no word or sound other than shuffling feet. Sparrow couldn't help but feel like any moment she'd be discovered and then...

"No, there are no other True-Bonded here," Hale said, almost sounding a bit disappointed. "They'd have reverted to their true form by now. She is alone."

Sparrow allowed herself to begin breathing normally again and was surprised to hear Ahmaia's sigh of relief accompanying her own.

They'd made it past the test.

"Come forward," Merlin said, cold and commanding.

There came several sets of echoing footfalls, the sounds mixing, making it hard to determine exactly who was moving.

"Hale follows closely behind us," Ahmaia said.

Sparrow nodded her thanks for that clarification.

"Why have you come?" Merlin said, suspicion plainly evident in the woman's voice.

Ursa responded, sure and confident. "I was concerned for those of my house going to the front. I wished to go myself and see what was happening there."

"Oh?" Merlin cut in quickly.

"Yes, My Queen, I took a fast carriage to the front." Ursa sighed heavily. "I was discouraged to hear of the loss of the Nobles there. I surveyed the front and... I must admit I was surprised. What I saw did not match with what I'd been hearing about the war. Both sides are dug in and the Vauphan forces do not seem that extensive. So, I tracked down one of the few remaining Nobles of House Panther. He said the previous orders had come from Lord War himself, who'd been there recently, but was now missing. I... I just want to know more about what my men are walking into. Something doesn't feel right."

"You dare question the queen!" Hale's voice was vicious.

"Unhand me!" Ursa's voice was equally as hard. There was some movement, as the pouch bounced a little, and Sparrow could hear grunts, then a hard thump and gasp.

Ahmaia gave a low chuckle. "I think Ursa just put Hale in his place."

Good. Sparrow would have loved to have seen that.

"Hale, calm yourself. We should not assault our Nobles. Ursa, if you wouldn't mind releasing him?"

"Yes, My Queen." More rustling of clothes.

"Good."

For a moment no one spoke, but Sparrow could hear Hale rising, grunting, and moving away. A softer feminine voice then cooed over him quietly. Lady Swan no doubt.

"Tell me, Lady Ursa," Merlin began softly. That odd quality to her voice was back. "What is more important: maintaining Elista and her powers at all costs, or maintaining peace?"

Ursa took a long moment before answering: "Elista must remain strong, even if that means war."

"Good, I'm glad you agree."

Sparrow wondered how much of Ursa's responses were lies and what was truth. Legs hadn't been entirely sure they could trust Ursa, which was why it was only Sparrow on this mission with Ahmaia. If things went badly, she could try to fly away, and if that didn't work, at least it would be only her which was lost. She didn't like that option, but she'd agreed to do this for Legs; she'd do anything for Legs. The thought of the other woman, her truest love, sent a thrill through Sparrow. Thinking of Legs always made her smile, gave her strength and courage, and made her so desperately wish to be back in the arms of her lover. She pulled her mind away from that to listen. She needed to know if Ursa would betray them. She hadn't yet, but...

"And what do you think of the traitor Maverick and his House of filthy betrayers?" Merlin's voice rose just a little, not in volume, but intensity, that odd quality more pronounced now.

Ursa's reply was quick: "I do not know what happened with that once Noble House. I've heard that Maverick betrayed us and went over to Vauphan, and that his House is now in hiding. Obviously, they found a way to come here to the capital to kill the queen, which I cannot comprehend at all, but I do not know much more than that."

"And what does that tell you? What do you think of their actions?"

"They have betrayed us all."

"And…?"

"And for that, they should be hunted down and slain. And for the one who murdered the queen, the death should not be quick but torturous and slow."

Wow. Sparrow desperately hoped Ursa was just telling Merlin what she wished to hear. The other option was not pleasant to contemplate.

Merlin sighed. "I'm glad you agree, Lady Ursa." Something in Merlin's voice suggested she relaxed a little.

Ahmaia said, "Despite her words, I sense no duplicity from Ursa, I do not think she will betray us." She reached out to touch Sparrow's shoulder, a strong and firm hold. "I have not sensed anything in her tone which would indicate she is doing anything other than playing along, telling Merlin what she wishes to hear. I think we will be well, little one."

Little one? Sparrow wasn't tall by any means, but Ahmaia was a half head shorter still. Though Ahmaia was probably something like two hundred years old — even though she looked Sparrow's age — or something like that; no one knew how long Fey actually lived.

"And tell me, Lady Ursa, will you do *anything* for Elista?"

Merlin's tone became twisted, a hint of sadistic glee sneaking into it. Sparrow then realized what the odd quality to Merlin's voice had been and still was: the woman was insane. "If it was for the good of the entire country, would you kill some of our own citizens?"

"I... ah..." Sparrow could hear the moment's hesitation in Ursa's voice. Yet it quickly resolved. "Yes. Though I would never wish for the deaths of any Elistans. If it were necessary, for the greater good of Elista and must be done, then I would sorrow in the act, but I would do what was required."

"Do not sorrow to kill traitors, Ursa. Never that." Merlin seemed pleased. A long silence stretched after this. Sparrow wondered what was happening. It frustrated her to just listen, not able to do anything. Yet she was ever so curious what would come next.

"Come with me," Merlin said, and there was the rustle of fabric and soft footfalls. "Hale, you are dismissed." Then in a more confidential tone, closer and quieter: "We need to speak in private."

Two sets of footfalls padded along for some time before a door could be heard opening then closing.

"Sit," Merlin said. And again, fabrics shifted and the pouch jostled.

Sparrow hadn't known she was holding her breath until she had to let it out suddenly, starting to feel strained, struggling to breathe.

"Would you agree that the Mists are at the core of Elista's identity as a nation?" Merlin probed, voice manic.

"Yes," Ursa said quickly.

"And what if we no longer possessed the Mists?"

Ursa didn't answer right away. When she did, she spoke slowly, "You believe Vauphan will try to take them from us?"

Merlin chuckled. "No, that is only the tale we have told

everyone else, the truth… is far more infuriating as there is little we can do about it."

Silence.

Merlin continued: "The truth is that the Mists are moving. In fact, they've always been moving, but so slowly we hadn't noticed it until recently. They shift perhaps a quarter of a mile a year, but they are shifting *toward* Vauphan, you see. They've always been close to our border, but in twenty years, they'll be on the border, and in a hundred years they'll be mostly in Vauphan. The Mists will no longer be ours… unless we conquer the north of Vauphan first."

Ursa released a heavy breath. "That's horrible. No wonder you've acted as you have. We must protect the Mists at all costs!"

"Indeed."

Sparrow understood. All of this, the deaths and war… were to protect the Mists. But… Sparrow knew Vauphan didn't want the Mists, didn't care about them. They probably would have been happy to have Elistans make the pilgrimage into their lands to visit them. And… that wouldn't be for a hundred years or more.

"What can I do to help?" Ursa asked, intent and sounding eager.

"I'm glad you ask." Merlin practically purred. "With your ability to seek out the truth, I have a special mission for you: seek out and find that bitch Legs and the remainder of Maverick House. Kill them, kill them all!" Merlin's voice had risen to a fanatical, maniacal, semi-laugh. "If you can do that, you can ask anything from me once I am crowned as the new queen, and it shall be granted."

"Thank you, My Queen. I see now why you must be queen. You are the only one who truly understands what's at stake."

"Yes, indeed. The others will understand and fall in line."

"I'm sure they will. And I will not fail you in this mission. I swear House Maverick shall be no more soon enough." Those words made Sparrow feel a chill... but then... perhaps Ursa's words were an inside joke. Maverick house was already gone. In its place was Spider House.

"Thank you, Lady Ursa, that is all. You may go."

"Thank you, My Queen."

Fabric shifted, feet scuffed, then came footfalls and the sound of a door opening and closing. Then only the single footfalls for some time before Ursa dared to speak again. "Well... that was informative," she whispered.

Yet still she walked for some time. Only once it sounded like she was in some private room, far away, did she say, "You can come out now."

Sparrow gasped as the world spun into light and largeness. She staggered, falling to the floor and sitting there for a long moment.

"Did you hear all of that?" Ursa asked in a whisper as she pulled closed the curtains over the one window in the room. They were back in the inn they'd stayed in the previous night.

"We did," Ahmaia responded before Sparrow was recovered enough to speak.

Ursa turned back to them. "She's completely mad." The tall and sturdy woman seemed to let her guard down, and Sparrow could see the fear in her eyes. "I... can't imagine what she'll do to this nation, to us all. Whatever it is you and Legs are planning, I think you need to do it soon. I'm behind you fully, and I'll see if I can't get some others on our side. Now that we know what's happening... they'll have to listen."

"Let us hope so," Ahmaia said earnestly.

"I'll fly to Legs, let her know," Sparrow said. "Open that window for me?" She veered into her avatar and hopped up onto the sill as Ursa parted the curtains just a little and opened the window. Sparrow was out like a shot. She wasn't the fastest bird, but this news was dire. She'd not stop until she reached Cliffside, not for rest or food.

Sparrow agreed with Ursa. They must act soon, or it would be too late...

...for their House, for the nation, for everyone.

CHAPTER 13

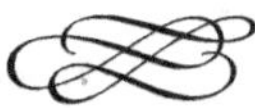

I sat heavily on one side of the long couch. "The Mists? All this for the Mists?" I understood the importance of the Mists and how closely linked Elistan culture was with them, but still. "We invaded a nation, started a war, to claim where the Mists *will be...* in a hundred years?" Something occurred to me then, something Lynx had said about how they'd been sent to claim lands in fear that Vauphan was planning on invading to claim the Mists. The reasoning was very close to the truth, just... that it wasn't Vauphan that planned on moving, but the Mists themselves.

Now it all makes sense, Auwei said. *And I can't believe I didn't know. Shouldn't I have known the Mists were moving?* She sighed. *I guess when I'm within them, I don't really know or care where we are in your realm and when I'm Bonded, I'm usually not close enough to them to tell if they are exactly where they were dozens of years ago. Though...*

What?

Now that I think of it, when showing some of my previous True-Bonded to the Mists, I think that the part of the forest where we entered the Mists was different for some of my earliest hosts than it is now. They are ever-so-slightly further away than they used to be. Fascinating. I've sort of known this entire time, but not really thought anything of it.

Well, someone did think of it and it's causing madness!

Sparrow continued: "Also, Ursa has been tasked with killing all of us and eliminating 'House Maverick.'" She quirked a smile. "Too bad that house doesn't exist anymore."

"How did she seem?" I asked. "Ursa, that is. Is she with us?"

Sparrow shrugged. "She had plenty of opportunity to give me up but didn't. It's possible she's playing a much longer game, but Ahmaia seems to trust her."

I nodded.

I think we can trust her, Auwei chimed in.

Yeah, me too. Thank the Spirits!

"And Merlin is insane," Sparrow added as an afterthought. "I think... she's been behind this all along. I can't be certain, but given how the others deferred to her and the way she was talking, how she acted like she was already the queen—" Sparrow shuddered. "I think if the queen hadn't died, Merlin would have found a way to kill her."

"Great, so we just gave her more power while giving the nation more reason to hate and fear us," I said bitterly. The trouble was, even now, knowing the why behind everything that had been happening, I had no clue what to do. But looking up at Sparrow, small and hopeful, those forest-green eyes seeking some form of acceptance and validation, I smiled. "I'm sorry." I rose and hugged her close. "Thank you. You risked so much, and I can see you're tired. Get some rest. I... I just need to take this all in and think on it."

Her arms went around me, and she held me close. Her voice was a tremulous whisper when she said, "I was so scared, even though we were hidden. I'm glad I could help."

"You have, so much, thank you."

We held each other close for a long time before drawing back to kiss softly. Then she smiled and retreated to get some rest.

I felt restless. It was already quite dark in the caves, but outside it was early evening, and light enough for a walk. So, I made my way down to the lowest level of the stairs to the rope room. The hooded lantern in the room was lit providing a little light, and the rope ladder was already down, someone was on the beach. Two bright-white scarfs hung on the wall, indicating two people were out. I grabbed another and hung it on a hook. This way if they returned before I did, they wouldn't pull up the ladder. Then I climbed down and walked out of the cave.

I saw the two on the beach, they weren't far away, both sitting on a large rock, looking out over the ocean: Alvere and Silence. Silence had his arm around the other man, as if comforting him.

A part of me wanted to sneak up on them, hear what they were talking about, but I wouldn't betray their trust.

"Hey guys!" I called as I got closer.

They both started and turned their heads back to me. Silence's brown eyes were hard to read, but Alvere's ever-so-clear blue eyes were a bit shocked and... was that ashamed? What had they been talking about? I was curious but wouldn't ask. They'd come to me if they needed me.

They love you, don't worry what they might speak of. Auwei's voice was soft, comforting.

I know, I know.

"I was just going to take a walk down the beach, either or both of you want to join me?"

Alvere smiled, his demeanor changing instantly to bright and cheerful. "I'd love to!" He turned to Silence.

The other man nodded. "As would I."

They rose and came to either side of me, and we clasped hands as we walked.

Silence asked. "Have you heard from Sparrow yet?"

"Yes, she just got back. She's resting. It's because of her news I needed to walk and think." So as to not leave the men in suspense, I told them what Sparrow had told me. Part of me hoped the retelling would spark some ideas for me, but alas, it didn't.

"Vauphan would never think to claim the Mists," Alvere said, bewildered.

"Well, *you* wouldn't, but who knows what some king a hundred years from now might do. I don't approve of any of this, but I can see the twisted logic they used to get to where they are."

Alvere shrugged. "I suppose that's true." He sighed. "All this for... magic, is that it?"

"It's a significant commodity," I said. "Isn't magic the reason your people reached out to the Fey?"

He nodded. "Yes, you're right."

"We have our Mists, you have the Fey, Thraan has dragons, and who knows what other mysterious and wonderful things are out there in the world. Certainly, Thraan has used their dragons to good effect, expanding their empire and dominating the West."

The two men walked in silence. They couldn't dispute what I'd said.

"The Mists are a part of our identity as a nation," I said. "If we didn't have them, we... well we wouldn't be the *same* Elistans we are now."

You wouldn't have me, Auwei whispered.

And that would be a great loss. Have I told you how much I appreciate you?

No, but I can feel it.

Well, I'm telling you anyway, I appreciate The Pits out of you. Without you I'd be...

Normal?

... so very much less than I am now. And not able to help Elista as only I can.

True.

Alvere sighed. "You're right. And given our work with the Fey, they will probably become a part of Vauphan's identity in another few decades." He shook his head. "We're all so driven by power... Why can't we just live in peace?"

"That would be nice," Silence said with a sigh.

"We can live in peace, when we have leaders who make that a priority, and we don't fear our neighbors." I sighed. "There are rumors from the West that Thraan will invade Basia, and if they do, Elista would be next. Which means we always have that in the back of our mind. We need to be prepared for war. I just never thought our war would be with Vauphan." None of this was helping me form a plan of action. "Enough talk of what is," I said. "What can I do? What can *we* do about this?"

More silence.

We watched the shadow of the cliffs to our left spread farther and farther out into the waters. The tide was going out, which was good, since at high tide the waters of the bay would be crashing against those cliffs and we'd not want to be stuck out here. We had at least another hour or so until low tide, which gave us two or three hours until we'd need to be off the beach. I didn't know if it was the news from the capital or the deepening shadows of evening or something else, but I felt my mood slip into darkness. I think Silence and Alvere felt the same.

What could we do?

Obviously, we had to stop Merlin, but she had the entire nation on her side. We had ourselves, few of us that there were, and one other — small — Noble House. And the real trouble was, if we exposed what Merlin was doing, made it public, I honestly wasn't sure how people would feel. They might just support her decisions.

"Even if we tell people what Merlin is doing," Silence said, sounding disheartened, "the nation still might rally around her, not us." He seemed to have read my thoughts.

"I think," Alvere said, pensive, "if you're going to do this right, you need to make less of a deal about the Mists and more about the war. Tell your people Vauphan — the current Vauphan at least — doesn't want war and would be happy to share the Mists. And if we can make peace now, perhaps we can make it last. It isn't that Merlin's *intentions* were wrong, but that her *actions* have cost so many their lives. People need to know that she's killing Elistans and forcing a war which isn't necessary." He gave a breathy laugh. "We thought the why would be important and change everything, but it doesn't. The war and all the deaths are the problem and no matter the reason, they need to stop. Isn't that right?"

Alvere's words had snagged on something in my brain. I was forming an idea, but it was still fuzzy.

"We need to stop the war," I said, trying to form my thoughts into words.

"We need peace," Silence said and that's when it hit me.

Peace.

We needed peace and there was an easy way to do that.

"I know what you need to do," I said, even as my mind was working through this new idea.

"You mean what *we* need to do?" Alvere asked.

"No, what *you* need to do, as The King of Vauphan." And even as I said the next words, as my idea formed, I saw just how truly horrible this solution might be. "You need to show your people and mine that you want peace, that you will do anything for peace, that our countries can come together as allies and share the Mists. You—"

"Legs, no, don't say what I think you're going to say."

But I had to, even if I didn't like it. "You're a king without a queen and we have a queen without a king. Now for us, that's never been an issue, but if you—"

"I'm not marrying that mad woman!" Alvere was adamant. "And I don't know how you could even suggest it!"

"I don't like it either, but don't you see?" I insisted.

"See what? How easily you can throw me away?" Alvere released my hand and turned to me, furious. I couldn't blame him.

"Alvere, no, I love you, but—"

"You love me... but? But what? But you need me to marry an insane megalomaniac to bring peace to our countries?"

"Well maybe you won't have to. Maybe just the proposing of the idea will show Elista that we have nothing to fear from Vauphan."

"Why can't I marry you?" The words flew out of his mouth, and he blinked, surprised.

So was I.

"Is that what you want?" I desperately wanted to know. Because if it was, that would change everything about our relationship. I loved our free and open love, but marriage... how would that work? Would we have a bunch of mutual lovers we shared in our marriage bed?

"I... I..." he stammered and looked at me and Silence. Then the bluster blew out of him and he shrank down on himself. "I do want that, more than anything. I want to marry you and not have to marry any other. I want to be with you always, even if that means sharing you. But once I'm married, that's it. I can't be with anyone else after that... and neither can the woman I marry."

He turned away. "It's what Silence and I were talking about before you came out." He walked down toward the waterline. "I... I can't stay here forever. This feels like home to me, but I have a country which needs a king. And that king will need a queen and an heir and... By all the gods, I want you to be my queen, but if you were... I don't know if you'd be able to keep these others, whom I know you love as much as you love me. I don't want you to have to give them up, but you would have to change if you were my queen. Otherwise, the line of succession would always be in question."

Damned line of succession. I was so very glad Elista had done away with that many, many years ago.

"I love you, Legs, but…" He gave a self-deprecating, harsh laugh. "Now I'm the one saying 'but.'"

And I saw all of this from his perspective for just a moment: his love for me, but his duty to his country. I couldn't be his queen, no matter how much either of us wanted it. I could be his mistress, his lover, perhaps, but nothing more than that.

What was more, "If you married me, especially now, that would only solidify me and my House as traitors," I said softly, seeing how horrid this truly was. "That wouldn't bring our countries together at all, but divide them all the more."

Yet my plan was sound. "Alvere, I love you and I don't want to lose you, but don't you see? You have it in your power to start the peace process. Even just suggesting the idea will show your people and mine how much you want peace, which means if Merlin turns you down, it will show them how much she wants war."

"And what if she accepts?" Alvere said sourly.

Spirits, I couldn't imagine what he'd go through if he actually married that woman.

He went on, tone still bitter. "Legs, I can see where you're going, but there is one flaw. If Merlin accepts my proposal, she could very easily turn that to her benefit. She becomes the benevolent peacemaker. She could blame the war on you or the previous queen and say this is what she wants. That wouldn't achieve what we want at all. There would be peace, but the maniacs in power would still be in power. And…" He shuddered. "Once I'd given her an heir, I wouldn't be needed. She could easily do away with me and control both countries. I'd be dead and nothing would have changed except we'd have handed Vauphan to Merlin!"

I nodded. "You're right."

"But…" Silence drew out the word. Alvere and I both turned to him. "What if it became known that Maverick House didn't betray Elista? What if everyone was told that we were the ones who began the peace talks?"

He didn't seem entirely sure of his idea, but continued. "I don't know how we'd spread the rumors, but... we could suggest that our House went to make peace with the Vauphani and were betrayed by our own... who didn't want peace?" He was still questioning his own idea.

Then suddenly Silence blinked and lit up. "Yes! Something like... Vauphan is suing for peace, at the behest of Maverik House, now Spider House, and the prince wants to come in person to seal the alliance. A Royal marriage isn't out of the question, *but* only after the question of how the war started is put to all the Nobles of Elista... because... someone in Elista tried to sabotage our house from pursuing peace. We act like we don't know who that was, and we just want to come before all the Nobles to work out what's going on. That way, Alvere could bring us into the peace talks with him, not as traitors, but as peacemakers. And yes, Merlin could spread rumors about us being traitors, but that would make her seem like the warmonger. Wouldn't that work?"

I thought about it. There was something in that idea. It was close, it had something to do with putting Merlin in a corner. If she wanted peace, she'd have to acknowledge us as peacemakers, not traitors, and if she didn't want peace, she'd be seen as the warmonger. Yet...

"There is still a lot that could go wrong with that," I said slowly. "It all depends on who is on her side and loyal to her. She could have one of her allies, Fang or whoever is the new leader of Panther House, call for war and claim we're traitors, that way she stays clean and untouchable." I sighed. "And there really isn't anything stopping the other Nobles from thinking we *were* traitors, who saw that we'd lose the war so we changed our tactics to peace. That *is*, sort of what we're doing. How do we prove we've always wanted the best for Elista?"

"What about Ursa?" Silence said.

"Ursa," I said, repeating the name. I sighed heavily. We'd trusted her so far. Could we continue to do so? I'd rather not put all our eggs into that one basket, but...

A smile spread slowly on my face. "Yes, Ursa."

Auwei giggled. *I sense a crazy plan coming on!*

"You have an idea?" Alvere said. I could hear the hope in his voice, he didn't want our time together to end, even though we both knew it would have to, someday.

"Yes..." I spoke slowly as the plan clarified in my mind. "You send a letter to Merlin and tell her you want peace, that a political alliance, perhaps a marriage of some sort is on the table, *but* you won't make any decisions until the new queen or king of Elista is elected."

"Right!" Alvere breathed.

"Oh, yes!" Silence said at the same time.

It seemed we'd all forgotten that Merlin wasn't officially queen yet. She had to be elected first.

"Tell Merlin you would like to come to peace talks, but only if all the Nobles are gathered and have a say on the outcome, that you want to see the election process."

"But wait, what if the Nobles actually do elect Merlin?" Alvere asked.

"That's where Ursa comes in. *Before* those talks, a small group of us go with Ursa to several Nobles whom she thinks we can trust. You go with her, tell your story. I don't know yet if it would be wise to have me there or not, but we can figure that out. If we can sway four Noble Houses, then that would create a stalemate at least. That's assuming the Nobles *don't* let me vote, which I'd expect."

But in the case of a stalemate the current Royal House is the tie-breaker, Auwei added in.

So my plan's not perfect, but it's close. Perhaps we can flip more than four houses? Who knows. Or perhaps they'll let me vote.

That's unlikely.

Still... do you have a better plan?

... No.

Well then?

I'm just trying to temper your expectations.

Consider them tempered.

"I think the best outcome we can expect is that with so many Houses voting against her, Merlin gets angry and exposes her true nature," I said. "That might sway things further in our favor."

If she is truly mad that may not be too hard. That might actually work.

Thank you.

I turned to Alvere, taking the few steps to close the distance between us. "Well, what do you think?"

He sighed. "I think I still love you and I'm still going to have to marry another and that breaks my heart."

It broke mine too.

But that was a battle for another day.

I embraced him and felt his strong arms around me. "We'll figure something out," I said.

Alvere said nothing, just held me all the tighter.

CHAPTER 14

My plan had a lot of moving parts, and we used Fin a lot.

First Alvere went home to the capital of Vauphan and drafted his letter to Merlin, but he was delayed there as several matters of state had to be addressed. In the meantime, Ursa and I went to see Lord War in his makeshift prison behind the Vauphani battle lines up north.

"I won't tell you anything, you filthy bitch!" War spat at me, before turning back into a wasp and buzzing angrily around his enclosure, pushing against the fine mesh netting which had been put in place around the dual cage.

Eorthan, the metal wielding Fey had outdone himself on this structure, an internal cage with fine, yet strong bars in a lattice which had square holes no larger than a couple inches across. No part of Lord War could reach through gaps that small except his fingers. Then there was a second, outer cage — perhaps six inches out from the first — of the same material and lattice, and around that was the mesh netting. If War changed into his avatar and slipped through the inner cage he'd be stopped by the netting, but he didn't have enough room to return to himself between the two cages, so he'd not be able to rip a hole in the netting to escape through.

"You don't have to say anything to me," I said with a grin, "But the Nobles will want to hear your side of the story when we choose a new monarch. So, we're taking you with us. As a peace offering."

He transformed back and smiled, a devilish thing. "Oh?" I could see the gears turning in his head. If we let him out, he could escape, and even if he didn't, we were taking him back to his mad master, she'd free him.

I moved away from the cage with Ursa.

"He radiates deceit," she whispered. "Even without my abilities, I'd probably be able to tell when he was lying. I can see how you intend to use him, but how will you keep him in line and restrained for that long?"

I grinned. "Follow me."

We went to another section of the camp, to Eorthan's forge. I recalled when Alvere gave me my unique Fey armor, which I was currently wearing. I ran my hands over the moving metal and smiled.

"How's it going?" I asked Eorthan.

The small man shrugged. "I don't have willing subjects to test them on, so I'm glad you're here. There are three sets over there, I'm hoping one of them works." He pointed to the side table. Ursa and I looked to see three sets of manacles.

"I'll try them on!" I said excited.

Ursa looked at me. "You want to be chained up?"

I laughed. "I want to make sure these will work. Eorthan has been using Fey magic to see if he can make manacles that can stop a True-Bonded from veering into their avatar."

"That's horrible!" Ursa gasped.

I have to agree, Auwei said, disturbed. *They may also cut off our connection.*

I guess we'll see. Sorry if they do, but this is necessary.

I know, but I don't have to like it.

To Ursa I said, "These will be necessary if we want to get Lord War from here to wherever without him escaping."

She nodded reluctantly to that.

Ursa and Eorthan helped me into the first set.

Are you there Auwei?

Yes.

So... not cut off. Then I wonder if I can veer?

I veered into my spider form and the manacles fell away, thumping to the ground. That was an interesting start. Usually everything I had on me would shift with me, which might have included the manacles but they'd remained autonomous. Still, they hadn't stopped me.

With the second set, I felt an indescribable resistance to shifting, but it was still possible. I told Eorthan as much. Also speaking to Auwei was possible, but our communication was sort of slurred and difficult, as if we were two drunken people trying to shout at each other.

He nodded. "I used different aspects of the nature of steel to imbue them, this one focused on steel's resilience. The last set might work. I focused my crafting into the steel's generally unchangeable nature."

"But steel is changeable," Ursa said. "You made it into manacles, isn't that changeable?"

"Only at high temperatures. So, you'd have to heat the manacles to a very uncomfortable heat to overcome their magic."

"Ah." She nodded.

I tried on the last set.

Auwei?

No response. Curious.

When I tried to veer, nothing happened. "It worked!" I said, excited. "Here, Ursa, try them on, I want to make sure they'll work on anyone."

Once I removed them Auwei gasped. *That was horrible, like being in a cold dark place. I couldn't sense anything from you at all!*

Was it different from when Hale cut off our connection?

Yes, very. Then I was still a part of you, I just couldn't reach you. This was like being torn away from you entirely.

I'm sorry you had to go through that.

I know it was necessary, but let's not do that again, shall we?

Agreed.

Ursa was hesitant, but saw the need to test the manacles and did as asked. She too, couldn't change with them on. She tried to use her extreme strength to break the manacles, but only succeeded in wearing herself out and hurting her wrists.

"They work," she admitted, then grunted a sour, "Ow."

That was another part of my plan in place. The next bit would be the hardest yet.

Fin returned Ursa and me to Cliffside and then was off to wait for Alvere to be done to return him here as well. I met with Dove and Ursa in my room.

The plan was for Fin to take Alvere, Ursa, and Dove to some of the Nobles we thought we could trust. Already Grizzly himself had talked to Tanuki, and she seemed on board with the plan, but we'd stop in to see her, just to verify. We also would speak with Spike, the leader of Porcupine house. Fin could get us close to that one, since it was further up the eastern coast of Elista. After that... we'd try with Wyvern and possibly Pegasus. Those were the two risky ones.

"I'll be there, every step of the way with you," I said to my sister. I would go along too, but in avatar form, hidden among their clothes. As long as Hale didn't make an appearance, I'd be fine.

"Are you sure we should be visiting Lady Silvermane?" Dove asked, worried. "We know Lord Horn sides with his son and it would be nearly impossible to get a meeting with Silvermane without Horn there." Even though these were members of the House she'd once been a part of, I could see the fear in her eyes. She was a strong woman, but the betrayal she'd endured when Hale had accosted her... had left deep scars. It was hard for her to trust anyone outside of myself and my House.

"I could do that one with just King Alvere," Ursa said.

"No, I think Silvermane needs to hear Dove's story. From what Sparrow told us, Silvermane never believed Dove to be a traitor. Hale convinced her I'd stolen my sister away. She's always hoped to free Dove and bring her back home."

Dove nodded. "I'll go." I could see her strength, her bravery in the face of her fear, putting herself potentially in harm's way.

I nodded. "Once Fin is back, we'll visit Tanuki first and confirm her allegiance. Then to Porcupine House and Spike. I don't think he'll be in Merlin's sway, so hopefully he'll be easier to bring to our side. After that to the capital and Skyfire and Silvermane." I sighed. "I just don't know which one to do first. If the first goes badly, we'll have to flee and won't be able to do the second."

We all considered for a moment. I spoke my thoughts aloud: "Both Skyfire and Silvermane were with the queen the day of her speech. That doesn't mean anything per-se, but..." I shrugged.

"Silvermane might be willing to listen to Dove, but she may also think you killed her mother," Ursa advised. "That might not go well."

"So Silvermane could be good or bad, depending on which way she leans. She might believe Dove but still not trust me." I sighed. "That doesn't help us. Skyfire is a complete enigma. So, I guess the question is, do we do the complete mystery first, or the one where we have some intel, but it could go either way?"

"Do Silvermane first," Dove said resolutely. "I'll convince her."

"Are you sure?" I asked.

Dove nodded.

That was it. We were set.

CHAPTER 15

Our meetings with Tanuki and Spike went well. They were on board, on our side. I allowed myself to feel just a little confident that everything would work out. Three Houses had sided with us. That alone was a significant triumph. But now came the hard ones: Pegasus and Wyvern. We needed one of the two with us if we wanted to be sure of a stalemate, both if we wanted a victory. These meetings would make or break my plans.

As such, we wanted to be ready and rested before we went in, staying for a day — hidden away in a small inn — in the capital before we went to see Silvermane.

I spent the day with Alvere. I wouldn't see him much after this, so we sat together and talked the hours away. Dove and Fin did much the same in the next room. I'd happily noted how they'd been spending more time together. I was glad my sister had found someone. Fin was a big man, but gentle and caring. I wished them well.

Ursa, being the only one of us who could move freely around the capital, went out to gather what information she could. She didn't discover anything of note.

The next day, we went to see Silvermane.

I was hidden underneath Alvere's cloak as our group was escorted into Silvermane's sitting room. The cloak hampered my spider's ability to sense things around me, but I knew Lord Horn was in the room when he spoke first.

"Lady Ursa, we were expecting only you, not such a group as this and cloaked against the world. Who are these others?" His tone was accusing.

I heard a gasp, then Silvermane's soft voice. "Dove!"

"Yes, Lady, and this is the King of Vauphan. He comes to talk of peace."

"Hello, my Lady." I heard Alvere's voice, felt the rumble of it in his chest, and the motion of his arms as he removed his hood.

"This last is a guard for the King," Ursa said, indicating Fin. That was his cover. The large man was wearing heavy armor including a helm to hide his identity. He hated the armor, saying it chafed something fierce, but he'd agreed to it.

"The King of Vauphan?" Lady Silvermane's voice sounded shocked. "This I had not expected when you'd asked for a private meeting, Lady Ursa."

I crawled up Alvere's back, high enough so I could be free of his cloak. I felt his shiver — I'm sure having a spider walk up his back had been... interesting — but he settled quickly. I didn't need to peer over his shoulder, just be free of the cloak, then my senses were free to take in the room. The four from my delegation were still just inside the door. Lady Silvermane sat behind a large desk with Horn standing behind her. A large bank of windows occupied the wall behind them.

Silvermane rose and came around the desk to embrace Dove. "I was so worried about you. Your sister... what we've heard..."

Dove embraced her former leader. "Thank you for your concern, Lady. However, what you have heard is mostly rumor and lies, but we'll get to that shortly. The King should speak first."

"Yes, of course," Silvermane said, and I sensed her going to Alvere. She curtseyed, offering her hand, which he took and bowed his head, though his lips didn't quite touch her knuckles. "Your Majesty."

"Lady, thank you for seeing us. I apologize for the subterfuge in Lady Ursa's message, but it was necessary. Unfortunately, we do not know who we can trust here in Elista. As Lady Dove has said, there are far too many rumors and lies about. I am here to hopefully clear up some of those and to tell you of my proposal for peace." With his hand still holding hers, she guided him to a chair and he sat. Silvermane returned to her chair behind the desk. Dove sat next to the King, and Ursa stood behind her. Fin stood behind the king, a looming presence. I felt a perilous tension from everyone in the room, but most of all Lord Horn. He would be the wildcard in this meeting.

"Say your piece," Silvermane said, voice just a little cool. That wasn't a good start, but at least she was willing to listen.

"What do you know of the war in the North?" Alvere began.

I heard Silvermane's heavy breath. "I have heard many things," she said, enigmatically. "Mostly I heard how a force from Vauphan somehow crossed into our camp and slew or captured all of the high Nobles of House Panther. I've also heard of mysterious magics which hinder our men from wearing or wielding steel. Do you deny this?"

"No, I do not," Alvere said evenly. "But I ask, did you hear of the attack on the Vauphani camp which prompted our counterattack?"

"No," she said, hesitant and curious.

"As I suspected." Alvere's tone was even, not accusing. "Lady, please understand I do not wish for this war, I—"

"Then why did you start it?" Horn said, hard and cold.

I felt Alvere's calming breath. "Lord Horn, I hope you will

listen to my full story. If you do, you will see, not only did I not wish for this war, but Vauphan did not start it either."

"That's a lie," Horn said, voice growing heated.

"Horn, let him speak." This from Silvermane, who didn't sound convinced, but again seemed willing to listen.

"Thank you, Lady. From what we have gathered, most of those in Elista have heard the following about the war: That Vauphan was either planning an invasion or had already attacked. Your Panther House responded to these actions or expected actions by pre-emptively seizing Vauphan lands, or defending themselves then claiming those lands to stop any further attacks. Does that sound right to you?"

"It does," Silvermane said.

"And when did this start?"

"About a year ago, if I recall correctly," Silvermane replied.

"What if I told you the war began almost *three* years ago?" Alvere said cautiously.

"That seems a bit preposterous." Lady Silvermane laughed. "I would have heard something in such a case."

"Indeed. Then let me begin my tale a bit more recently. Were you aware that a mistweaver, sent by your government, attacked and killed my mother and father?"

"Legs is a mistweaver?" Silvermane gasped. "Your sister... I..."

"Lady, no, that is not the case," Dove said firmly. "You believe my sister killed the king and queen of Vauphan?"

"Why yes," she said, as if it were the obvious truth. "She was sent to spy and went rogue, killing the royals."

"And in this matter, would you admit that I may know more than you, as to the events?" Alvere asked. "I was there that night. I saw it with my own eyes." That was a bit of an exaggeration, but close enough to the truth.

"Yes, of course," Silvermane acquiesced. "You say it was a mistweaver? And... not Legs-the-traitor?"

"That is indeed the case," Alvere said evenly.

"I find that hard to believe," Horn said with a scoff. "A mistweaver? You speak of fairy tales."

"My Lord, respectfully, a mistweaver did indeed attack my parents, and she was not sent by Maverick House, as you may believe. No, in fact, it was Lady Legs who stopped the mistweaver, saving my life."

A silence hung in the room.

"I find that even harder to believe," Horn said after a moment. "Mistweavers are legends for a reason. They were nigh unstoppable. And you want us to believe a novice Noble stopped this mistweaver?"

It *was* hard to believe. Even I had trouble believing it some days, and I'd been the one to do it!

"Legs had help." Another small lie. "Others from her House were there and together they defeated the mistweaver. As you say, they were at the palace to spy, of that I am aware. I was not impressed by that, but I was willing to forgive, given they saved my life from that same mistweaver. If we can start with this as fact, does that change anything of what you might believe?"

"What you say is hard to believe, Your Majesty." Silvermane sighed. "But for now, we shall take your word on this. Assuming this to be true, what followed?"

Alvere's shoulder's fell in a heavy sigh. He'd cleared the first hurdle, if only just. "Follow my logic for a moment if you will," he said. Then he launched into an impassioned argument. "If indeed it wasn't House Maverick who sent the mistweaver, but who stopped it, then..." He let that hang for a moment. "Then, who sent the mistweaver?"

"Perhaps they were acting alone?" Horn's voice was hard. He still didn't believe any of this. "Your nation began a war and perhaps they sought to end it in one go."

A sudden shift in Alvere told me he felt his tenuous hold on the two before him slipping away. "This is silly," Ursa said finally. "Lady Silvermane, are you aware of my spirit-gift?"

Oh, thank the Spirits.

"Your spirit-gift? No."

"I have the ability to discern truth from lies. To prove it, I ask you to tell me five things. Make some truths and some lies, and I shall tell you which is which."

I sensed Silvermane's hesitation. A stifling silence hung heavy in the room, but finally Silvermane broke it. "As you wish." She drew in a long breath. "First, Lord Horn and I are lovers. Second, I have a daughter, which I have hidden from the world. Third, I am currently pregnant. Fourth I hate my mother for pushing me so hard as a child. And finally, I want to kill Legs for killing my mother. How's that?" The hotness of her voice was evident, along with a tremulous nervousness. I got the sense she never would have said half these things otherwise.

"Oh..." Ursa sounded stunned and apologetic. "My Lady, I am sorry for making you go through this. That couldn't have been easy for you. The first three things you said are all true, the last two are lies.

Wait... Lord Horn — a man who was well more than twice her age — was Silvermane's lover? No wonder she'd never taken a husband. And Horn had gotten her with child twice? Fascinating. But that also meant she didn't hate her mother and didn't want to kill me. Odd, I would have thought killing me would have been a priority if she thought I killed her mother.

Silvermane sighed heavily. "Indeed, that is correct." She cleared her throat quickly. "And I do not wish to discuss any of that, and I hope you will all keep it in the strictest confidence."

"Of course, Lady," Alvere said quickly.

That oppressive silence dominated the room once again, before Ursa remembered to speak. "I trust I have proven myself?"

"Yes. Go on."

"Do you trust me to evaluate the truth of what the King is saying?"

"How do we know you're not in league with him?" Horn said skeptically. There was no convincing him. Though perhaps he was angry at what the woman he loved had just been put through.

Ursa sighed heavily. "Do you want this war?" she asked directly. "Our people are dying. Some of your Nobles are at the front now. Do you want them to die if this continues?" Before he could answer she pushed on. "Then you'll need to trust someone at some point, and if you can't trust me, another second from another Noble House, then whom can you trust?"

The trouble was, I knew who he trusted. He trusted his son and his lover and that was probably it. Still, I waited for his reply and hoped.

Horn let out a grunt then said, "Perhaps I will trust you, but first, tell me this. How did you come to know the King? How did Dove come to be in your care? All of this rings a little too much of the work of someone else."

"I presume you mean the work of the traitor Noble House once known as Maverick?" Ursa said easily. I didn't like that phrasing, but I was in no position to argue.

"Yes."

Ursa sighed. "You want the full and honest truth, then fine. Know that we are not here to hurt you, only to talk, so please don't be alarmed. Legs, please come out."

I hoped she knew what she was doing. I hopped off Alvere's shoulder and returned to myself in mid-jump, landing lightly and bowing to Lady Silvermane and Lord Horn.

"Your Ladyship, Your Lordship."

The room froze in a tense tableau. Silvermane and Horn wore expressions which were both surprised and not surprised at the same time. As if my appearance confirmed their suspicions about this meeting, but they were still shocked that I'd dared to show my face.

"Trust us or not," Ursa said softly, but sternly. "We only ask that you listen, then let us go. Will you abide by those terms?"

Silvermane nodded, looking a bit dumbfounded.

"Your Ladyship, no!" Horn hissed. "We can't let her go! She must pay for what she did to your mother!"

"I did not kill the queen," I said quickly.

"The truth," Ursa confirmed.

"How can we trust you? Any of you?" Horn bit out.

"Again, Lord Horn, you don't have to, just listen. Then we'll be gone." Ursa's tone was hard. "Do you agree."

"Yes," Silvermane whispered. "I have to know..." Her voice barely a breath. "If you didn't kill my mother, who did?"

"A mistweaver," Dove said for me. "A curse had been placed on the queen. She died as soon as she left the capital."

"And yes, taking her from the capital was my doing," I said. "But I had no clue that would kill her. I just needed to speak to her. I am so very sorry."

"All truths," Ursa said.

"A mistweaver? They're real?" Silvermane looked terrified.

"Yes." The word came from myself, Alvere, and Dove at once.

Silvermane blinked for a moment. She looked like she didn't believe any of this, but she nodded. "Go on, say your piece, then leave." Her tone, though quiet, was hard. She didn't like any of this, that was obvious.

I took up the telling from there. "The mistweaver sent to kill the Vauphani king and queen, had also been tasked with killing me. It seemed I would get in the way of someone's plans. At the time I didn't know what those plans were, I was only trying to survive. I did indeed kill the mistweaver, though I nearly died myself. That is how I came to know the prince, now King of Vauphan. We have only ever wanted peace between our two nations, but someone else is behind this war." I couldn't go into specifics, not yet.

I hoped Silvermane would see it for herself when the time came for the Council of Nobles. So, I left things vague. "Someone on our side, someone in Elista, started this war. They know the Mists are moving and will eventually migrate into Vauphan, and they wished to take the lands in the North of Vauphan to protect our Mists, a noble but misguided goal. Vauphan would never have cut us off from our heritage. The King is here to say exactly that and to offer a political alliance. He will come to the Council of Nobles, and whoever is chosen as the new king or queen will be bound to him, either to marry or for their children to marry, thus bringing our nations together and ending all this needless bloodshed. I have never betrayed Elista, but someone high up in the Royal house must be involved in this plot and has been spreading foul rumors about me. I stole my sister away from the capital as I feared she might be in danger." That was true, I just wouldn't mention Lord Hale specifically.

"Yes, we fought against our own kind, fighting for Vauphan at the front lines, but I'm willing to bet you didn't know Lord War was there, and it was him and Jaguar who attacked us first, killing Maverick and several Nobles of his House. Our attack on their camp was only to stop the fighting, end the hostilities, which were initiated by the Elistan side. Believe me or not, but you'll see the truth of things at the Council of Nobles." I paused, a bit out of breath. I looked at Alvere and Dove. "Did I miss anything?"

"How did Ursa get involved?" Horn asked.

I nodded. "I had a friend from Silverveil who is now a member of Grizzly House. I went to her to ask for help. She brought me to Ursa, who used her abilities to determine I was truthful and agreed to help me."

Silvermane looked a little confused. "So... you killed the mistweaver that cast a curse on my mother?"

"I hope I am being honest when I say: yes. I cannot be certain. I killed *a* mistweaver. There may be another one, but I hope to the Spirits there isn't." I shrugged. "So... it seems likely that I killed the one who cast the curse upon your mother."

Silvermane nodded.

"That is a fanciful tale," Horn said, clearly not believing it.

"We shall consider what you have told us," Silvermane said. "Now, please leave."

That was not how I had hoped this would go, but we weren't being apprehended or chased out, so it definitely could have gone worse.

"Thank you for your time," I said, then we all linked to Fin and were gone from Silvermane's office.

We returned to the room we'd rented in the city.

"Do we go to Skyfire?" Ursa asked. "Horn may be warning others even as we speak."

"Then we go quickly," I said.

Ursa nodded.

CHAPTER 16

It seemed Wyvern House had not been warned, at least not yet. We were admitted to Lady Skyfire's study.

Yet even as Fin closed the door behind us and Ursa was about to speak, Lord Drake, Skyfire's second, hissed: "Legs is with them, on the back of the short male. It's a trick, a trap!" How he knew, I had no clue, but it threw everything into chaos.

Hidden under Alvere's cloak, I didn't see what happened next. I felt the cloak being ripped off Alvere as he was pushed to one side...

...By Lady Skyfire herself.

Faster than I could see, she plucked me off the man's back, holding me by one of my tiny legs, careful not to crush it, but precise enough to hold just the one small limb.

"Show yourself!" she commanded.

I couldn't believe *this* was how I'd finally meet my childhood idle.

I shifted back to myself and Skyfire had one of my hands grasped in hers, bound in a grip like iron.

"I have you now, traitor!" she hissed.

"Wait!" Ursa's strong voice stopped everyone. The tall woman stalked over to Skyfire. "This is no trap."

For a long moment the two powerful women squared off. Ursa was taller, but Skyfire had an intensity about her, which made up for the difference. Both were powerfully built and strong. Steel-blue eyes met fiery-orange eyes.

"Who do you serve?" Ursa asked quickly. "Merlin or Elista?"

"Merlin?" Skyfire scoffed. "Never. She's a wimp who's inherited her power. She'll be out after the next Council. I serve Elista. Who do *you* serve?"

"I serve Elista," Ursa said. Then she looked to me and added, "She's telling the truth."

Skyfire looked back and forth between us, flame-red hair bouncing around as she did so. "Of course I'm telling the truth." To Ursa she countered, "What is the meaning of this? Bringing a traitor into my House?"

"I do apologize for the subterfuge, but she couldn't walk in here on her own, now could she? She and The King of Vauphan have something they'd like to say to you."

"The King of... what? Where?" She looked at Fin in his armor. "Are you—?"

"No, my Lady," Drake said cutting her off. "The small one. I can see it now."

Still holding my arm Skyfire turned to Alvere. "You're the King of Vauphan?" I could tell she was off balance now.

"Yes, Lady Skyfire. It's a pleasure to meet you," Alver said, calm and genial.

She glared at him. "What's going on here?" she said, her temper — which was notoriously short — clearly rising. I felt her hand leave my wrist, but at the same time she became a blur, moving around the room so fast I couldn't follow her. Even before my arm had fallen an inch, she had it again. Then both my arms were wrenched behind my back and I was moved — so fast I couldn't see a thing — to the other side of the room. I found myself in Drake's hands as he pulled a dagger, putting it to my throat. Somehow, during that flash of movement, Skyfire had bound my wrists together.

Wow.

"There!" Skyfire said with a huff. "Now I feel better. Someone better explain things quickly or you'll all end up like Legs here." She sat behind her desk and leaned back in her chair, clearly in control.

Even in my very precarious position I admired her power and authority. She dominated this room, even though she was outnumbered. She smiled with easy confidence as she stared down Ursa — a powerful Noble, in both position and physique — and the King of Vauphan. A part of me — the part not freaking out about being captured and having a knife at my throat, nor the part that was still a little sick from being moved so quickly — was giddy at being so close to this amazing woman!

You really admire her, don't you? Auwei asked.

I have all my life. If there was one person I wanted to be... it was her.

I'm sorry you didn't meet under better circumstances.

Yeah... me to.

Ursa recovered quickly. "May I sit?" she asked, motioning to a chair.

"Whatever," Skyfire said with a wave of her hand. "Just get talking!"

Ursa took a chair. Alvere sat in another. Dove and Fin stayed close behind the other two. I could see the concern in Dove's eyes, but some part of me hoped this would all work out, and I gave her a reassuring wink. I wasn't worried... yet. Ursa had said Skyfire was telling the truth about not serving Merlin, which meant we had a chance.

"I know we don't know each other well," Ursa began. "But I'd like to think we know each other well enough to trust each other?"

"I did, until you brought a traitor into my study," Skyfire countered.

"And who said she was a traitor? Merlin?"

"Yes, as well as half the nation. Why do you keep mentioning Merlin?"

"I'll get to that. First, why I'm here. To introduce you to the King of Vauphan. He wishes to discuss terms of peace. He is hoping to be at the Council of Nobles to propose that Vauphan and Elista be joined in marriage, either through him or his children. That way there is no need for war. What do you think of this?"

"Sure, peace is good. As long as I don't have to marry him." Skyfire surveyed the king. "He's a little scrawny, not my type."

"Do you wish to be the next queen?" Ursa asked.

"Not really your business, but no. I'll take it, if I'm the only choice, but I'd rather not. I like my life as it is."

"Would you support Merlin as queen?"

"Pits no!" Skyfire seemed disgusted by the idea. "I'd like to think we have other options than her. She hasn't done much to impress me." All of this was sounding positive. Skyfire definitely wasn't on Merlin's side. Now we just had to convince her to join our side. "Why all the talk of who's going to be queen?"

"That would be very important to me," Alvere said.

Skyfire grunted. "Yeah, I suppose it would. So, if a queen is chosen for Elista you'll marry her, and if not, your kids and the chosen king's kids will hook up?"

"That is the plan, yes." Alvere remained calm, though I caught his furtive glances in my direction.

"The King's in love with Legs," Drake said behind me.

How in The Pits did he know these things? Did he have a spirit-gift like Ursa's?

"Really? The traitor? I heard she went over to your side. Now I know why."

Alvere sighed. "I do love her, but I'll do what I must for my country." He spoke up a little more. "And while we're on the topic, one of the reasons why I love her is that she saved my life from a mistweaver who killed my father and mother, the king and queen." He then stared directly at Drake when he said: "Is that a lie?"

Skyfire looked at Drake.

I couldn't see the man who was holding me, so I waited, curious what was taking him so long to answer.

"I do not believe you are lying, no. But something about this whole meeting is out of place." He paused for a moment. "You, the woman behind Ursa, you're Lady Dove are you not?"

Spirits this man was keen. He seemed to know everything.

"Truly?" Skyfire turned and looked at Dove. "Is that who you are?"

"Yes," Dove said with a bow. "We just came from telling Silver-mane what we're telling you, that Legs isn't a traitor. We believe Merlin to be the one who is destroying our country."

"She is earnest," Drake said.

"Well Bloody Pits!" Skyfire leaned back again. "Who do I believe?"

"Lady," Drake said firmly, and I felt the dagger at my throat pull away a little. "I believe them to be honest. I do not think Legs will harm us, nor any of the rest of them, and... my apologies for not mentioning it sooner, but I fear Lady Merlin is quite insane. I have not seen her enough to know for certain. She hides it well, but I've suspected as much for some time."

"And you didn't tell me because...?"

"I wanted to be sure."

"That our *queen* is off her rocker? I think we could have gone with a hunch on that one." Skyfire threw her arms into the air. "Fine! Let her go."

Drake removed the dagger and used it to cut my bonds.

"Thank you," I said to him with a smile. He nodded to me. It was only then, as his pale brown eyes met mine, that I saw how keenly he looked at me. Was that his gift? He could "see" things? His eyes did seem to take in everything, keen and alert.

Curious.

I made my way around to rejoin my friends as Skyfire said, "So, you think Merlin is the traitor? What has she done?"

We told her everything we knew about the mistweaver and the war and Ursa's meeting with Merlin... and the Mists.

Then we stood back and waited.

"You sure these aren't the crazy ones?" she asked Drake.

"I see no betrayal, even if their words are hard to believe," he said reluctantly.

Ha! So, it *was* something with his sight!

"Well, Pits!" Skyfire said. "Isn't this just fantastic!" She rose and began pacing.

I also paced! We were so alike!

She's a bit erratic, and you're not. You may have some similarities, but you are also very different. I like you a lot better.

You would say that, you're my Lumani. You're stuck with me... also, thanks.

"You've given me a lot to think about," Skyfire said, not looking at us. "I'm assuming I'll see you again at the Council of Nobles?"

"Yes," I said.

"Well, I'm not sure I'm with you, but I'm definitely not with Merlin. Personally, I think you're both crazy. You'll have my answer then," she said.

And that was that.

Before we left, I couldn't help myself, I went to Skyfire. "I just wanted to say, I've always admired you and looked up to you."

"Well yeah, of course you did." Skyfire sniffed.

You also don't have an outrageously large ego, Auwei said.

Yeah... wow.

I turned away, a bit put out by this, but Skyfire called me back. "Hey, kid."

I turned around.

She smiled. "Your House may be tiny, but you're the youngest House leader ever. That ain't nothing." She gave me a wink.

I smiled and nodded at the compliment, my giddiness at meeting her returning.

We left and returned to Cliffside.

That was it. We didn't know how Silvermane or Skyfire would vote, but at least they knew the facts, even if they might not believe them. I had to hope that would be enough.

The Council was called a few days later. It would be in Miraline in two weeks.

Two weeks and everything would come to a head.

I couldn't wait, anxious and fidgety.

Luckily, I had several people willing to distract me.

CHAPTER 17

IT STARTED INNOCENTLY ENOUGH. I WAS A TENSE WRECK — PACING around the common area — so Ant offered to give me a massage. I lay on the long couch, and he dug those thick, strong fingers into my shoulders, neck, and back until I'd turned to mush with contentment.

It was only once he'd finished and risen from straddling my legs, that I turned my head to see the heavy bulge in his breeches.

"It looks like you could use a massage too," I purred.

"I wouldn't turn one down." His voice was husky, deep and needful.

I rose, but he quickly swept me off my feet, cradling me high in his arms. I wrapped my hands around his neck to pull my face to his for a long and probing kiss. Then he carefully carried me down to my room.

As we reached the lower landing, Silence was coming up from the beach-exit. Alvere was back home in Vauphan, ruling his nation and planning for the upcoming summit. Sparrow was off scouting, as she and Dove often did, to ensure our secret base remained a secret.

Silence raised a brow. Ant nodded, so Silence followed us to my room.

Apparently, my guys could communicate with only their expressions now.

Once inside, Ant set me down and the two men slowly undressed me. Their hands — one set hard, thick, and strong, the other soft, nimble, and quick — moved over fabric, then under, as my blouse and skirt were removed. Then I went from one to the other, kissing and caressing one while the other quickly stripped. And when they were naked, they sandwiched me between them, skin pressing to skin.

Silence had spent our time in exile improving his combat skills and it had made his muscles fuller and harder, but still nothing compared to Ant. Yet with the two hard bodies pressed against me I was already in heaven.

"What do you need?" Silence asked in a whisper, kissing around my ear from behind.

"Ant needs a release first, then I want to forget about everything for a while." I hadn't forgotten the reason for coming down here. Ant had already given me a wonderful massage and now he needed something in return.

"Allow me," Silence said and gently moved me out of the way, going to his knees in front of Ant, taking that Oh-My-Spirits sized erection in his hand and bringing it to his lips.

Ant's eyes never left me as I moved to the bed and lay down. I opened my legs so he could watch me stroke myself. My other hand traced over my body, coming to a breast, pleasuring myself, feeling the tight bud of a nipple and flicking it playfully.

Ant, it seemed, didn't need much encouragement and was soon having full body contractions, bending him slightly as he found his release. His gaze never left me.

When Silence went to the pitcher of water on the small table in my room for a drink, Ant came to me, kneeling beside the bed and pulling me close to press his lips to my wet folds. Hard hands grabbed my hips to push his face in closer as he sated his hunger and spiked my desire. I ran my hands through the tight black curls on his head, raising my hips to welcome him deeper. My body moved to the rhythm of his lips and tongue, my back arching, eyelids fluttering, and eyes rolled back as Ant's incessant hunger nearly drove me mad.

The bed shifted. I glanced over to see Silence next to me. He lay propped up on an arm, leaning over so his free hand and lips could find my breasts. The delicate and delicious suction of his mouth upon the already aroused bud of my nipple was all I needed to find a body-shivering orgasm, tensing with tremors of delight. I let go and rode the waves of pleasure these two glorious men were inciting.

Silence's lips found mine, playing and pulling, sucking and sliding. I reached out with a hand, fumbling and finding his erection, rigid and ready. I gripped it tight and heard his corresponding grunt of pained pleasure.

At the same time Ant's amazing lips left my folds, and a moment later I felt the probing tip of his erection, aroused once again. The heavy press of his length slid over my more-than-ready opening and though I couldn't see, I assumed he was directing it, playing. It slapped down hard upon my engorged clit a couple of times prompting convulsions, spikes of pleasure.

Then I finally felt his push, slow and careful, as my folds enveloped him, opening ever so wide to accommodate his massiveness. He took his time, remaining with just his tip inside me, giving slow shallow thrusts. A heavy hand ran up one leg to lay low on my abdomen, his thick thumb slipping down to press and caress my clit.

When Silence's lips next left mine, I whispered to him, "I want to suck on you, the way you did to Ant."

Surprise and a swell of desire flickered in his eyes as he shifted, kneeling beside me. My hand, already on his shaft, brought it to my mouth, and I created a seal with my lips, sucking gently upon him. His eyes rolled back, his hips rocking ever so slightly, thrusting into my mouth. One of his hands, on my breast, squeezed that soft, sensitive flesh, just as Ant pushed deeper within me. These two certainly knew how to work together — even though they couldn't have been doing it consciously — to bring me the most bliss. I rocked and shuddered with another orgasm, removing Silence's erection to gasp and moan before sucking upon him all the harder, as his moaning joined with mine.

With a slow, persistent push, Ant buried his monster erection deep inside me. He maintained his shallow thrusts, easy and slow, but still, the fullness of him, pressed so wonderfully tight inside my wet and sensitive sheath, was making me mad with pleasure, especially since his thumb was still stroking my clit.

"Silence, I'm going to shift," Ant said, his voice husky and low.

I let Silence withdraw from my lips, admiring the glistening tip of his manhood as he slid back a bit.

Ant put his hands under my sides and lifted me. I got the hint, wrapping my legs around him to help pull myself up. We met in a wet and hungry kiss as he turned around.

Then he was sitting on the bed. I unwrapped my legs and straddled him as he lay back, keeping his legs together. Silence got the hint and made a detour to my side-table — for a refilled bottle of oil — before moving around behind me, also straddling Ant's legs.

I was in control now, at least where Ant was concerned. With all my weight upon him I keenly felt him pressing upon the deepest parts of me. His shaft pulsed and twitched in time with the beating of his heart. One of his hands reached down between us, his thumb once again pressing to my clit. He wasn't fully inside me, he was too big, a couple inches remaining outside. But I could lean forward a bit to press his thumb between us and put more pressure on my ragingly sensitive clit. Ant's other hand reached up to grasp a breast, massaging it with all the skill and power he'd used on my back earlier. Spirits, I loved how hard he was, insistent and grasping, just teasing the edges of pain.

I felt the cold touch of oil on my other opening, the press of Silence's fingers for a different type of massage. But I must have been quite ready for him as he didn't need to tease me open for very long before his slickened erection was pushing inside me. He grabbed my hips to pull me close, sinking deep into me.

I began a slow rocking motion, forward onto Ant, back onto Silence and the two of them joined the rhythm. Silence kissed my back and neck, one of his hands around me, low, slipping down to press on my clit, replacing Ant's. Ant brought his freed hand up to my other breast and now both were being gloriously, savagely, kneaded. I added more pressure still when I leaned forward, all my weight upon his hands.

I lost my breath as pleasure swept through me and spiraled up to wrap around my heart, squeezing every last drop of passion from me. I raised my hands up into my hair, playing and piling it, swaying and growing more frenzied in my movements upon the two hardened men. I was so ready, but wanted them to join me when I came.

"Please," I whispered. "Now!"

I shuddered with a full body wave of bliss, clenching tightly around both men, milking their lengths. I heard their corresponding grunts and moans. Ant swelled impossibly within me, and I knew his release was imminent as Silence found a new frenzied pace. For a moment, my orgasm jacked up to mind-blowing heights at the vigorous movement.

Then both men froze with final grunts and cries. There came an incredible pulsing flood, as both men exploded within me at once, sending me into a delirium of bliss as micro-orgasm after micro-orgasm built then blossomed into a massive tidal wave of pleasure surging through me. All we could do was twitch and groan for a long time, before we finally collapsed together in a sweaty heap of divinely satisfied bodies.

I was so loose from Ant's earlier massage and so extremely satisfied, that I dozed. I did indeed forget about my worries and the coming culmination of our plans, and when I woke to find both men cuddled close to me, somehow under the covers of my bed, I smiled and allowed myself to sleep again, relaxed and relieved. Hopefully I'd be ready for what was to come.

CHAPTER 18

THE VAUPHANI DELEGATION TO THE PEACE TALKS AND MONARCHICAL Vote was led by Alvere. With him were Ahmaia, Eorthan, and Elvi of the Fey, a small honor guard of twelve of Vauphan's elite soldiers, and a contingent from Spider House.

Fin came, just in case we needed a quick exit. Other than that, I'd agonized over how many of my so-very-few people — my family — to bring.

Dove came, she'd insisted, even though I'd been unsure. She said her presence might help sway Silvermane, so I allowed it. Just in case though, I had Eorthan make her a set of armor like mine, only in gleaming silver over a gambeson of purest white. As with all things between us two sisters, she outshone me, seeming like some warrior goddess with her streaming blond hair and perfect poise. I wore my Fey armor as well, not taking any chances.

Sparrow stayed behind, since she was the only flying scout left at Cliffside with Dove gone. Silence and Ant insisted on coming to protect me. But to keep our party looking small, they remained in their avatar forms in a special pouch at my belt, ready to pop out at a moment's notice. Midnight was around somewhere, unseen as usual.

The final member of our party was my "special guest" Lord War, currently travelling in one of Ahmaia's pouches.

Ursa wasn't with us, she'd returned to Grizzly house as their second and would arrive with that delegation.

As I marched down the main avenue of Miraline I saw my parents waving from the side of the street. They looked concerned. If they'd heard any of the rumors floating around about me or Dove, I didn't blame them. I waved back, as did Dove, but we couldn't speak to them, not yet. We were part of a formal delegation and stayed with our host, the King of Vauphan. Alvere looked truly Royal that day, in a cloak of deepest purple lined in ermine. His clothes beneath were of navy and gold. His Black hair was free, flowing down to his shoulders, glistening blue-white in the late spring sun. Those beryl-blue eyes were focused ahead, on The Great Hall of Miraline, one of the three largest buildings in the city. The other two were the mayor's manor and the library, all of which were on the grounds of the mayor's estate. Those buildings had all been emptied, which was why my parents weren't at their books today.

We entered through the large double-doors and were shown to our section of the hall. There was but a single chair, for Alvere, the rest of us were meant to stand near or behind him.

We were not the first to arrive. Merlin was there, Hale at her side as her new second. Swan stood amongst the Owl House delegation, along with over a score of others. She glared at me.

I smiled back easily. And when I caught Hale's eye, my smile only grew, though it wasn't with mirth. I was thinking about squashing him like a bug.

Others already in attendance included Fang and Retriever of House Pterolycus, with a score of their Nobles. Fang looked just as menacing as usual, big and dark and powerful, glaring at everyone, not just me. Retriever's golden eyes scanned over everyone present. I couldn't read that hard look. She didn't seem impressed with me, but then... she didn't seem impressed with anyone else either.

The only other Noble present I didn't recognize. They were seated beside Merlin with only a very small contingent behind them of two others, that was it. By process of elimination I figured this had to be the representative of House Panther. The woman seemed small and fidgety, as if she wanted to run from this meeting. I got the feeling it was fear and awe of Merlin that kept her here.

The others arrived in short order. Spike and his second Quill of house Porcupine. Quill was Spike's brother, and his avatar was actually a hedgehog, but the two men looked so similar most people just assumed they shared the same avatar.

Skyfire and Silvermane arrived together, talking quietly. I found that intensely intriguing but couldn't do much about it. I couldn't quite hear them either. My spider senses were on high alert, but there was too much other chatter in the hall and the two women were speaking far too softly. Behind them Drake and Horn entered, both tall, but otherwise vastly different, Horn was large and fair with greying hair. Drake was thin and dark, but still exuded presence and power. The two men didn't talk to each other. It was as if there were some unseen barrier between them, that's how 'cold' they seemed to each other.

Lady Tanuki and her second Red arrived next, both willowy and tall, genuinely happy to see everyone. Their House seemed so... happy. I envied them just a little.

Last to arrive was Grizzly and Ursa with a small contingent, which made sense since they'd have come the farthest to get here. Grizzly didn't look at anyone really, just seemed vaguely dangerous as he took his seat. Ursa stood next to him. She didn't acknowledge me. We had to keep our association a secret, for now.

And then... we began.

"We call this Council of Nobles to order," Merlin called out in a clear voice. I couldn't help but grimace at her usage of the royal "we." Queen Whitewing had never used it. "Our beloved queen was slain by a betrayer, and a new king or queen must be selected. We also have, as our special guest, the King of Vauphan, who has seen the might of Elista and wishes to sue for peace."

That was interesting wording. It definitely made it sound like Elista had the upper hand, when in truth the war was a stalemate at the moment.

"The King offers his hand in marriage should we choose a queen. And if we should choose a king, his daughter shall marry our king's first son."

Wait what? Daughter...? Why had she not said 'children?' Why so specific?

Do you think she knows? Auwei asked.

How could she? Unless... she's the one who's seen the future?

That sent just a bit of a chill through me.

Less than a week ago, Auwei, with her intimate connection to my body, had informed me I was pregnant... with a girl... Alvere's child. This child wouldn't be recognized by Vauphan as a legal offspring of the King of course, but still...

I couldn't help but put a hand to my stomach. The inadvertent reaction of my armor was to peel away, allowing me access to my spider-silk. Many eyes in the room caught the movement, and I quickly put my hand at my side once more. That had been a mistake.

Merlin continued, "Since this is a time of war, we wish to invoke the seventh codex, which states that the current ruling house will remain in power during times of war, even if the king or queen is killed. Their second shall take their place until such time as the war is concluded."

"And the war is concluded," Skyfire said quickly. "The king's presence here is indication enough of that. I do not accept your invocation."

That caused a few murmurs around the room. Still the new head of House Panther seconded the motion and a vote was held, but no other Nobles voted in favor.

I was a little surprised by this.

Auwei, as always, was there to help me understand. *This doesn't mean the others don't want Merlin to be queen, it only means they are agreeing with Skyfire that the war is concluded and the seventh codex won't be a factor. It means they want to hear arguments for and against certain members first, before they make their choice for monarch. Even if there are those who are already on Merlin's side it behooves them to vote against this, so as to look impartial when they vote for the next monarch.*

That made sense.

"Then we shall hear nominations and arguments," Merlin said, smiling just a little too contentedly. She thought this was all going according to her plan. I certainly hoped that wouldn't be the case.

Almost before Merlin had stopped speaking, the new House Panther leader spoke up in a tremulous voice. "I nominate Merlin of House Owl!"

There were a few chuckles in the room.

Auwei assisted me again. *She spoke out of turn. The first step in any meeting like this is always for each House Leader to re-introduce themselves and THEN state any nominations. As a new House Leader, she would undoubtedly go last. Merlin should speak first.*

Merlin smiled. "Thank you, Lady Margay," Merlin said as she rose. "I am Lady Merlin of House Owl. First, with the leader of my house recently deceased comes the choice of a new name for my House. I choose to respect our previous and illustrious queen and keep House Owl."

A bold move, not claiming the House title for herself. It makes her look modest, though perhaps weak as well. Interesting. Auwei was quite caught up in all this intrigue. I just wanted to survive today and come out of this with a new king or queen, I didn't much care who, just not Merlin.

"As the new leader of House Owl, we formally denounce house Maverick and the so-called successor House Spider. We seek to remove them from the lists of Nobles. We also nominate ourselves for the next queen. House Owl has ruled well for thirty years and we know We can continue that noble tradition." She looked over at Alvere, her gaze sliding over me. She smiled, but her expression bore no kindness, just... possession and greed. "We will happily marry King Alvere and produce for him an heir who would rule our combined kingdoms." She sat again slowly, gracefully. She didn't even offer arguments for why she should be queen. That's how confident she was that she'd already won this battle.

We'd see.

Skyfire rose next. "I am Lady Skyfire of House Wyvern." She stepped forward into the roughly circular open space in the middle of the room and took a long moment to look around at each Noble. What I found most interesting was how she included me in that group. Her gaze held mine for a long moment, not Alvere's, mine. That was a quiet nod to my right to be a House Leader, very interesting indeed. When she spoke, her voice was hot and impassioned, as usual. "I see no solid proof of the betrayal of House Maverick and its successor House Spider," she said, voice carrying. "I have heard rumors and hearsay, but no proof has been presented to me. So, upon the question of removing House Spider from the lists I delay my vote. If any here has evidence to present. Do so."

Well, that wasn't a huge vote of confidence, just a delay. But it was something.

"On the question of the new monarch..." Skyfire paused,

holding the room's attention in her palm and milking every moment of silence. "I nominate Lady Silvermane of House Pegasus."

The room murmured for a long moment at this. Silvermane, despite having a powerful house, was still one of the younger and newer leaders. She wasn't even thirty, and her house was only eight years old. Compared to some of the others that made her very inexperienced.

That's a surprise, I was sure she'd vote for herself. Auwei was a little aghast.

When we asked, she said she didn't want to be queen. She's a powerful woman, but she likes her position.

True.

The murmuring died down, and Skyfire continued, "Silvermane may be one of the younger leaders, and of a newer House, but—" She drove her finger up into the air to emphasize her coming point. "In the short time that Pegasus House has existed, Lady Silvermane has made it a powerful and indomitable force in Elista. If nothing else, this proves her worthiness to rule. I believe she will be a fair and equitable queen and a handsome bride for King Alvere."

I looked at Lord Horn. He wasn't happy. I didn't blame him. I was in his same position, lover to someone who might potentially soon marry another.

Interesting. Auwei said drawing the word out.

What? I asked.

I... don't know yet. And I don't want to say anything until I'm more certain.

Fine, be all mysterious and stubborn like that.

Fine... I will.

"That is all I have to say," Skyfire said, bowing to the assembly with a flourish. She then returned to her chair. Spirits, she was always so dynamic in everything she did. I couldn't help but admire her. I was ready to vote for Silvermane, even if that meant handing Alvere over to the woman. Though, we'd see if I'd even have a vote at all in any of this.

Fang rose.

I didn't know much of the man, but everything I'd heard was that he had some odd affectations and was generally a man of few words.

"Fang votes to remove House Spider. Fang votes for Merlin." He sat again.

"I'm curious Fangy," Skyfire said, out of turn, but not caring at all. "Do you have any evidence against House Spider?"

Fang looked to Retriever who stepped forward. She looked at me directly. "We have it on good authority that Legs kidnapped and killed the queen. Do you deny this?" she asked me directly.

"For the charge of kidnapping, I do not deny it," I said, loud and proud. I'd done it and I'd face any consequences for it. "For the charge of killing the queen, yes, I deny it." I said no more. That was as it should be. If asked, I could go on, but otherwise I should keep any out-of-turn speaking to a minimum.

A murmur rose in the hall and quickly died down as Retriever held up her hand. "And do you deny killing Lady Claw of House Panther, or that members of your house killed Jaguar, Tiger, Lynx, and Lion of House Panther? Do you deny working with the Vauphani against us in the war?"

That was a bit harder to answer. I tried not to smile, thinking about my revenge upon Lady Claw. In truth, that hadn't brought me the satisfaction I'd hoped.

Oddly, before I could answer, it was Skyfire who came to my rescue, sort of. "That was war, Puppy." Retriever glared at Skyfire, clearly not liking that nickname. "And yes, Legs may have been on the other side, but who's to say she wasn't trying to make peace? Things get confusing in war."

"Members of House Panther saw Legs kill Lady Claw at night, during a sneak attack!" Retriever growled, growing angrier.

"After we attacked the Vauphani at night, in a sneak attack, isn't that right?" Skyfire asked easily.

Several people gasped and low murmurs filled the hall. That was clearly not common knowledge.

"It was, yes," Retriever said sourly.

"Then, like I said. War is war. The girl has admitted to kidnapping the queen, and that's going to have consequences. but we can't know for certain how the queen died or by whose hand, *unless*... anyone has a way to be certain?" Skyfire looked around. It was a testament to her guile that she didn't look in Ursa's direction at all.

"If I may!" Ursa spoke up stepping forward. "I have a spirit-gift which allows me to know a person's mind, I can sense truth. Shall I use it?"

As far as I knew, no one other than Silvermane and Skyfire knew Ursa and I had been working together. The murmurs around the hall died down as Retriever smiled. "Yes, that would be wonderful, thank you Lady Ursa." She motioned to me.

Ursa crossed the floor to stand before me. She addressed me harshly, directly.

"Lady Legs, did you or did you not kidnap the queen?"

"I did."

"Truth!" Ursa looked around before going on. "Did you kill the queen?"

"I did not."

"Truth!" That got a wave of chatter. Merlin's brow furrowed, her face dark with rage. Ursa waited for the hubbub to die down then asked. "Did anyone in your House kill the queen?"

"No."

"Truth!" More chatter. Again, Ursa waited then asked, "How did the queen die?"

"After we took her to our home, simply to ask her a few questions, she began to have trouble breathing. She did not seem to be able to get air. She suffocated and after she died a puff of mist came from her mouth. I cannot be certain, but I believe she was under the curse of a mistweaver."

That got the place into a full-on uproar. Shouts of "liar" and "mistweavers aren't real" dominated the calls.

Ursa waited. "Lady Legs' description of the queen's death is truth. And though it is truth that Legs *believes* the death was caused by a mistweaver, that is conjecture only." She turned to me with a vague wave of dismissal. "Unless you have proof a mistweaver exists?"

"I do, or rather, one did, before I killed her."

Ursa gave a masterfully shocked reaction, then shouted, "This is truth! A mistweaver did exist, and Lady Legs killed her!"

That sent the hall into a shocked silence.

Going on quickly, Ursa asked, "Sometimes, before a person dies, they implicate who they think caused their death. Did the queen give you any name before she died?"

Oh... another masterfully asked question. Ursa knew as well as I did that the queen's mention of Merlin was vague and unfinished, but by asking only if a name was mentioned it was easy for me to say:

"Yes, she said one name: Merlin."

CHAPTER 19

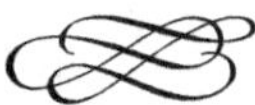

MERLIN FLEW FROM HER CHAIR AND SHOUTED. "THAT'S A LIE!"
Spittle flew from her lips. She was so vehement everyone in the
room jerked back with alarm, including me.

Ursa turned slowly. "No, it is truth. The queen spoke your
name." Ursa, living dangerously, approached Lady Merlin. "Tell
me, Lady Merlin, were you aware that a mistweaver existed?"

Merlin was barely holding on. "No!"

"That..." Ursa said slowly, with masterfully acted confusion
and shock, "is a lie."

Merlin glared daggers at Ursa. Hale stepped in and restrained
the small woman before she threw herself bodily at Ursa, which
seemed likely to be her next move. "How could you? I trusted
you," Merlin spat.

The rest of the hall, recovered from Merlin's outburst, was in
an uproar once again. And happily, for the first time, it wasn't my
fault.

With momentum moving in my favor, I decided now was the
best time to spring my little surprise.

"Lady Ursa!" I called out over the raised voices of concern and confusion in the hall. "Would you mind questioning another I've brought along?" I turned and nodded to Ahmaia.

A moment later Lord War was standing in the hall, not far from me and looking very angry.

I couldn't help a smile as more voices around the hall joined the confused cacophony.

"I believe he knows more about this war then most here have been told," I shouted over the tumult of voices.

Ursa nodded and approached the seething warlord. Lord War glared at her. The best part of all of this was that he wouldn't know she could tell truth and lies. He'd not known anything which had happened up until now. Ahmaia had made sure he could hear none of what had gone on.

Ursa asked simply: "Lord War, before the gathered Nobles here, would you tell us how the war began?"

War scoffed and grinned. "Gladly. The war began when Vauphan threatened our northern borders. Our spies informed us they intended to invade and capture our Mists!" He'd raised his voice, even though the gathered Nobles had begun to hush to hear him.

"That is a lie," Ursa said evenly and sounding just a bit curious.

"It is not!" Lord War, even though shackled, bunched his muscles as if he intended to strike her.

A roar rocked the hall, which silenced everyone and froze them in place. It hadn't been Ursa, but Grizzly himself, who'd veered into his massive, fearsome bear form. He shifted back quickly. "Lord War! Perhaps you are unaware, but my second has the ability to discern truth from lies. If she says you lie, then you are questioning the veracity and loyalty of Ursa, myself, and my House!" The challenge was implicit, but Lord Grizzly made it very clear. "If you deny the truth once more, you'll face me in a Noble's Duel!"

Lord War did not look afraid in the least, almost... interested.

He was certain of his abilities and his strength. He grinned, even let out a laugh. "I might like that, Lord Grizzly. Don't tempt me."

"I think it's time the truth was made known." This, surprisingly came from Lord Horn. The large man in silvery armor, with grey dominating his beard and hair, stepped forward.

Silvermane looked surprised.

I glanced over at Hale, who looked just a little panicked.

Horn stepped forward to the center of the circle, glaring at Lord War. It was clear those two didn't much like each other. "I have kept this secret from even my own mistress." He turned to Silvermane. "I'm sorry," he said, ashamed. "My son convinced me it was for the best of the nation, for all of Elista, but if it is, then all of Elista should know it."

A hush fell over the hall. Everyone listened intently.

"The war was no contrivance of Vauphan." Horn's voice was clear and carried. "We invaded, quietly at first, slowly taking farmers' lands. This began over three years ago. *We* began this war."

That caused a hubbub, and it was interesting to see who the chatter was coming from. Mostly it was lesser Nobles. It was clear Lord Fang knew the truth. He didn't seem surprised at all. Grizzly and Skyfire didn't seem shocked either, but we'd already told them the truth. Tanuki and Spike were clearly surprised. Silvermane was shocked, though it was hard to tell from what: the news of the war, or her lover having betrayed her.

"And the reason we did so was to protect our Mists," Horn said slowly. "It was discovered not long ago, that the Mists are moving, and within a few generations they won't even be in Elista any longer. We sought only to protect our heritage." He turned to Alvere. "I am sorry for our treachery, Your Majesty."

Alvere nodded. "Thank you for your honesty, Lord Horn."

No one even looked to Ursa to verify if this was the truth. By this point, we all knew it.

"We have to remain strong!" Merlin shouted, drawing everyone's attention to her. She had regained herself *a little* from her earlier outburst, seeming to vibrate with a barely restrained, trembling intensity. She turned to Alvere. "Would you have let us cross your borders to visit our Mists?"

"Perhaps," Alvere said evenly. "We have had peace for many years before this. The Vauphani do not want your Mists. It is clear that they are a part of your cultural heritage and you would have been welcome to continue your traditions."

Merlin seemed a bit shocked at that. But she quickly countered with, "Ah! But you would not be King forever, and by the time the Mists are within your lands, the King of that time may not allow us in!"

"And that justified war and death?" Alvere countered evenly.

"Yes!" Merlin shouted before she realized what she'd said. She calmed quickly. She twisted her face to a strained-looking, odd, contorted semblance of peace. "I call for the vote now! Let's settle this and make the peace this King has promised! Who votes for me?" she shouted. "Raise your hands!"

This was breaking all sorts of protocol, but given all the other disruptions to the meeting people seemed to go with it. Merlin herself raised her hand, as did Fang; it was clear he was in her pocket. Not surprisingly Margay, the puppet leader of House Panther, also raised her hand. That was it.

Merlin's eyes bulged with rage. "Traitors!" she shouted.

"Who votes for Lady Silvermane?" Skyfire shouted, raising her hand. Grizzly and Spike joined her. Oddly that was it. I found it odd Lady Silvermane didn't vote for herself. Everyone looked at her.

"I am curious who Lady Tanuki votes for?" Silvermane said softly.

Tanuki accepted the looks from everyone in the room with a cool smile. "This is a momentous occasion, and I do not believe this choice should be made lightly." She looked over at me. "Also, we have not determined the validity of Lady Legs' House and whether she has a vote. So, I abstain for now. Too much remains uncertain."

"Legs is a traitor!" Merlin seethed. "She gets no vote!"

"That has not been definitively determined," Tanuki countered.

Merlin glared at the Noblewoman. "You're a traitor too!"

"Because I will not vote for you?"

"Yes!" Merlin's tenuous façade was breaking down, her madness starting to show through.

Time for me to push her over the edge.

I stepped forward. The space in the center of the hall was getting a little crowded with the large Lord Horn, the dangerous Lord War, and the powerful presence of Lady Ursa, and now me.

I felt my *Hero* gift rise within me as I spoke. "Let Lady Ursa vouch for the truth of my words!" And whether it was my gift or the power alone in my voice, the hall hushed.

"Lady Silvermane, though it would pain both of us, I believe you would make a far better queen than Lady Merlin. I urge you to vote for yourself, bring stability and peace back to our torn nation!" With Tanuki abstaining, it fell only to Lady Silvermane to vote. If she voted for herself this would all be over. "I will submit to whatever punishment you deem necessary for my actions against your mother, the queen. Though it has been attested that I did not kill her. I believe that to be the work of the mistweaver, whom I have already dealt with. So, in a way I have already killed your mother's killer."

Something caught my eye then, it was subtle and only there for a moment, but I was certain I saw two quick emotions flash over Merlin's face at my words. She'd seemed furious at the mention of my killing the mistweaver, then... oddly satisfied and relieved at the mention of the queen's killer being brought to justice. Very odd indeed.

I addressed the hall next. "We have become a divided nation, at war with ourselves and our neighbors. We need to be united and strong. If that means the dissolution of my House, I am willing to do that. But I ask you to look around and ask yourselves. Would you be so willing? If it was for the best of our beloved Elista, would you give away your power and dissolve your House? If we are not willing to do that, then we have lost our way. We should be servants of the people, not despots addicted to power. So punish me if you will, remove my House from the lists, but do so only in a nation that is united in peace and only when you have taken a long look at your own House!"

"Wise words," Ursa said. Her words carried to all corners of the hall. She turned to Silvermane. "Lady? How do you vote?"

Silvermane looked pensive, sturdier than she had before, when she'd learned Horn had been lying to her, but still undecided.

"My Lady?" Dove stepped forward and all eyes turned to her. She was a picture of strength and beauty in her silver armor, those blue eyes flashing with courage. I was certain no one in the hall would be able to look away from her. "I was once of your House, and would return, if you will have me. I fled because Lord Hale attacked me." She looked briefly at the large man. He didn't even try to deny it, glaring at Dove with lustful superiority on his face. He didn't think his house would fall.

"This is truth," Ursa said, resolute.

"Indeed," Dove continued. "He got close to me, only to attack and try to kill my sister. It was that which drove her into hiding and also when she began to suspect there was rot within the Royal House. I will not say anymore as to whom I suspect is behind Lord Hale's actions. I say only this: you, Lady Silvermane would make a far better replacement for your mother than any other here. I urge you to vote for yourself and end this madness."

Lady Silvermane took a long look at Dove, nodding, then

slowly looked around the room. "Indeed," she said to herself, then drew herself up and spoke. "I vote for myse—"

Time seemed to slow.

I caught movement from the corner of my eye: Merlin raising her arms. Mists spilled out from her palms forming two massive blades in front of her outstretched hands. One she unleased toward Lady Silvermane. The second came for me.

I knew, from my encounter with her, that Lady Skyfire could move with incredible speed and she did so then, sprinting like a blur to block the blow meant for Silvermane. The massive mist-blade severed her left arm mid-bicep and bit deeply into the left side of her chest. Even with that sacrifice she didn't block it fully and the blade took Silvermane low on her torso, throwing her back against the wall behind her, and pinning her there, blood gushing out of her from the hole in her abdomen.

My mind whirled with the realization that Merlin was a mist-weaver, even as I tried to throw myself out of the way of the mist-blade meant for me. I was too slow.

Someone pushed me down. The blade only just clipped my right arm, but it hit my savior — Dove, my beloved sister — on the left side of her chest, spinning her around with a wild spray of blood as she screamed and fell to the floor, limp.

Time resumed.

Chaos erupted. People screamed and ran.

"Ant!" I shouted, though my voice didn't seem to be making a dent in the uproar. "Come out. Save..." He was there, standing next to me, but words had stalled on my tongue. Dove was closer and probably not as badly injured as Silvermane. And if Silvermane was to be the next queen. Spirits, it was a horrible choice. I felt hot tears on my cheek as I said. "Silvermane. Save Silvermane!"

He nodded and began pushing through the chaos of Nobles.

I spun out a glob of spider-silk into my hand and slapped it onto my arm as I crawled over to Dove.

Merlin, floating high above the commotion, on a cushion of mist, laughed maniacally, throwing more razor-sharp bolts of mist toward the Nobles who had voted against her.

"Pits Below! She's a mistweaver?" Silence said next to me, having come out of his avatar form.

Ah... yeah!

And suddenly I understood those strange looks of hers from a moment before. I'd said I'd killed the queen's killer, but I hadn't. I was certain now...

...Merlin had cursed the queen.

CHAPTER 20

My arm stung like an over-sized paper-cut, but I'd stopped the bleeding with my spider-silk.

Silence tried to help me up, but I pushed him away as I reached Dove.

"I'm not the one that needs help, can you do anything for her?" There was so much blood around my sister, staining that white gambeson a garish red. I clamped a wad of spider-silk over her wound, but it wasn't enough. She kept bleeding.

"I'll do what I can," Silence said kneeling next to her as I doled out more spider silk. He tore off his shirt and pressed it to her wound. That seemed to help... a little.

I rose and took in the scene. My eye caught Ahmaia's. She'd been headed for Alvere, but, seeing my desperate look, she glanced at Dove and nodded. I wasn't sure what she could do, but she hurried over and a moment later long strands of cloth were tightly binding the deep wound.

Good.

The hall was in complete chaos. Hale and the Nobles of Owl

House were openly fighting other Nobles. Fang was on their side, despite being across the hall from them. The battle was hindering Ant from getting to Silvermane, but Horn and Skyfire were already at the woman. I didn't know what they could do, and Skyfire herself was in bad shape, but they seemed to be trying to help her. So I turned my attention to Merlin, still hovering high enough to be out of reach of anyone in the hall, laughing as she sowed destruction around her.

My *Hero* gift surged, and suddenly the pain in my arm wasn't as intense. I hadn't thought I'd be able to wield a weapon, but now...

Drawing my sword, I leaped, easily reaching her and slashing with my blade. I needed to end this now. I'd done what I'd come to do, expose Merlin for the villain she was... though now I could see how devastating that discovery had been for the others present. This madness was — as usual — my fault, and I needed to end it. I'd killed one mistweaver, so why not two?

With an easy laugh, Merlin waved a hand and a shield of mist blocked my blow. Then, that same shield, hard as steel, slammed into me, throwing me back, pressed to a wall, constricting around me. The binding mists compressed my chest, my arms held tight at my side. Without my Fey armor, I'd have several broken ribs right now. As it was, I couldn't quite catch my breath.

Merlin flashed from where she was in a puff of Mist and appeared next to me.

"I don't think I'll kill you now," she said, in a low venomous tone, madness and vengeance in her eyes. "But you need to pay for killing my sister, Hazra."

Her sister? The other mistweaver had been her sister? Now the pained look on her face when I'd mentioned killing the mistweaver made sense.

Spikes slowly speared into me from the mist clamping me to the wall. My armor stopped most of them, but where my armor didn't cover, my neck, and hands and the small gaps between the plates, pain burned through my skin. I gritted my teeth, not wishing to give her the pleasure of hearing me scream. But she could clearly see I was in pain.

"Oh, yes, that is delicious, but not the sort of pain I wish you to feel. No, you need to feel the pain of loss, of losing someone you care for deeply." She swung her head around looking at those in my party. "Your sister perhaps?" she said. "That is fitting, yes. But she is already dying." She swung her gaze back to me. "But you need to suffer so much more than I did. Twice as much perhaps? Shall I take another from you?" Her head swung around again and locked on Alvere. "The King perhaps? You love him, do you not?"

"No!" I couldn't help it. The word escaped my lips before I could stop it.

She chuckled. "Yes, that would be perfect. A sister and a lover." Her gaze returned to me. "I'll cripple your body so you'll no longer be a threat and take those you love from you." She laughed. "That is what you get for working against me, little one."

The mists around me crushed harder, spikes digging deeper. I felt the bones in my arms crack, heard the hollow popping sounds. My ribs would give way next. Even my armor, strong as it was, couldn't stop this force.

Merlin laughed as she flashed away in a swirl of mist to arrive next to Alvere, who was up and had his sword out, his honor-guard creating a circle around him. But they were facing out and never saw Merlin grasp his neck and lift him from the ground. She looked back at me as she choked him, his sword falling from his spasming hand as he flailed against her. She circled slowly so she could keep eye-contact with me as she brought Alvere's face to hers in a mock kiss. Mist flowed from her mouth into his and the spasming stopped suddenly.

She grinned, then vanished, disappearing with Alvere, both gone.

No! I tried to scream, but I had no air. I struggled to breathe as pain surged through me. Ribs fractured and cracked with a new surge of pain. As hard as I struggled to hold on, to hold out, to fight against this magic, I couldn't. My breath wouldn't come. The world faded away to darkness, an inky nothingness filled with pain and loss.

I'd enraged Merlin, and it had backfired horribly.

I knew I wouldn't die, not yet, she'd promised that. But as I succumbed to unconsciousness, I also knew... I'd lost this fight.

I woke with a gasp. My eyes snapped open to see the haggard and exhausted face of Ant above me.

"Oh, thank the Spirits," he breathed.

I still felt a burning agony over so much of me, but my breathing came easier, my ribs no longer pained. He must have thought me dead, but I knew better. That had not been Merlin's plan. Though I doubt Merlin's plan had included Ant healing me either.

Still, even though my body was mending, my soul was shattered.

"Alvere," I breathed the name, voice hoarse. "Dove."

"I stabilized Dove, but she'd lost a lot of blood. I don't know if she'll pull through. I'm sorry Legs. The same is true of Lady Silvermane. She's been taken to other healers as we speak, alive for now." He swallowed hard. "But... Alvere is missing."

No! My soul clenched in a new agony.

I could do so little in that moment, lying on my back in the hall. The fighting seemed to have stopped, but I didn't really care about that. My heart burned with an indomitable ache for my sister and Alvere, so I simply wept.

"I'm sorry," Ant said softly. "I... I need to go, others are hurt." I heard him rise and the heavy footfalls moving away.

But a moment later, lighter ones drew near. "Oh, Blessed Spirits! Legs!" Silence's voice. A soft hand touched my cheek, one of the few spots that didn't still hurt. I opened my eyes, but couldn't speak, voice choked with the sobs I couldn't stop.

Silence leaned down, careful not to touch certain parts of me — I guess I looked as bad as I felt — and pressed my face to his chest in an awkward embrace.

"They'll survive," he said softly. "And we'll get Alvere back, don't you worry."

If he wasn't already dead. He'd been hanging so limp and lifeless in Merlin's grip. And even if he wasn't dead, perhaps the mists she'd forced into him were a curse like the queen's? If we rescued him, it might just mean his death.

"Just rest for now," Silence said. "The fighting's over. We need to regroup and recover. Then we can make Merlin pay for what she's done."

He was right.

I felt my *Hero* gift surge within me, helping to numb the agony as I rose. My tears stopped as my jaw tightened.

Silence held me closer, a bit easier now that I was sitting.

And in that moment, even though I still couldn't speak, I vowed to all the Spirits and any gods that might listen, that I would kill Merlin and make her pay for what had happened here. She'd made a mistake, leaving me alive, a dire one, and I intended to make her realize the full and vicious depths of that mistake before she died.

CHAPTER 21

Despite my vow of vengeance, nothing happened right away. We remained in Miraline for nearly another week as people recovered. With my gift, I was well by the third day. Even though I told him not to, Ant visited often to give me what little energy he had, looking more and more worn out. Dove healed, but remained in a prolonged sleep of recovery, still and pale. My parents took Dove to their residence to rest, in their care. I told them both I was so sorry for what had happened. They didn't blame me, but I did. Fin visited her often and got to know my parents. They were overjoyed that Dove had met a good man.

We got word that Lady Silvermane would live, though it would take her a long time to fully recover.

A few other Nobles had been seriously hurt, but not any of the House Leaders, except Lady Skyfire. She was a tough one though, up and about soon enough, despite orders to rest.

That left Grizzly as well as Lady Tanuki and Lord Spike as the full Noble's Council for the moment.

As for our foes? Unfortunately, Lord Hale and Lady Swan escaped. Though much of the rest of House Owl had been captured or killed in the fight. Lord Fang was dead and Lady Retriever was being held in custody, as was most of the Pterolycus House. Lady Margay of House Panther had survived and surrendered. She was cooperating now, telling the others everything she knew, which unfortunately wasn't much.

On the fourth day after the event, I was called before the reduced Noble's Council.

Lord Drake was there, to represent House Wyvern, even though he'd have no vote. A woman I didn't recognize represented House Pegasus. They were arranged in a line across one side of the hall, the three heads of Houses sitting, while everyone else stood. I was happy to see Lady Ursa alive and well, though also bandaged, her left arm in a sling.

"Lady Legs," Grizzly said, then shook his head. "That name of yours is... interesting." The large man was still covered in bandages, but they didn't seem to hamper him.

"I know, and I have to live with it," I said with a grimace.

He nodded. "You have been called before *what's left* of the Noble's Council for a reckoning."

I nodded. "I accept that the events of the peace talks were my doing," I said stoically. "I was the one who arranged it and who, in many ways, urged Merlin to madness. I am deeply sorry for—"

"Shut up and let me talk, woman!" Grizzly growled.

So... I did.

"No one here blames you for those events." He sighed heavily. "I can see how you might blame yourself, but you'll need to stop that if you're to lead your House effectively."

Did you hear that? Auwei said, enthusiastically. She was trying to lift my spirits after everything that had happened.

But what does that mean? Lead my House? Have they accepted me?

I think so.

I didn't ask Grizzly though. He'd told me to shut up. So I remained silent, for now.

Grizzly continued. "Through *various* means, we have ascertained the events of the past few months. We even have a clearer picture of what happened over the past three years, since the war began. The war is definitely *not* your fault, and if it hadn't been for you, none of us would know the truth of what Merlin had been doing. We know you are no traitor to the Crown, so your standing as head of House Spider is affirmed. Welcome to the Council of Nobles."

See, I knew you'd be exonerated!

They're not done yet. I still have to account for kidnapping the queen.

"Thank you, my Lord," I said with a bow. Even though I was technically his equal as a House Head, I was still of a junior House and owed him respect for his seniority and experience.

"Now," he said, gruff and stern.

And here it comes...

"You killed a mistweaver once, any idea how to deal with Merlin?"

That was not what I'd expected. Apparently, we were going to skip over the queen-napping for now and move on to other matters.

I must have been shocked for a moment too long as Grizzly then prompted me with: "You can speak now."

I found my words. "I will personally kill Merlin and Lord Hale," I said with a vicious grin. "She's plagued this nation long enough and she..." I swallowed hard. I could say it. "She killed—"

"The King of Vauphan is alive," Ursa said firmly.

The force of those words nearly knocked me over.

"What?"

"King Alvere is alive. We got word from the capital that Merlin is holding him for ransom. She'll return him to Vauphan once we and the Vauphani recognize her as queen... of both countries."

"Bloody Pits!" I couldn't help myself.

Grizzly gave a significant look to Ursa. Ursa's look was just as cool. "She needed to know."

"You weren't going to tell me?" I blurted.

"We didn't want you running off before we'd had a chance to determine our course of action."

"And if it were your wife, someone you loved, would *you* wait?" I shot back.

Grizzly grumbled. It was clear he'd not want to wait either. "From what I hear you have many 'loves.'"

Really? That was his argument. You have others...?

I didn't want to shout at him, so I took a moment to calm myself. I answered with, "Don't we all have many people we love, who we'd die for, who we'd want to rescue from madmen or madwomen?" I knew he was sleeping with not only Ursa, but also Blackclaw. I was sure he loved more than one person himself.

He grumbled again. "And what do you plan to do, knowing this?"

I very much wanted to run off and save Alvere immediately. But... "I will wait and see what this Council decides," I said diplomatically.

"And if you don't like it, you'll do your own thing?" Lady Tanuki said with a faint grin.

I looked at the calm visage of the astute woman and nodded. "Pretty much, yes."

She sighed. "Oh, to be young again."

"There is more," Ursa said with a heavy sigh. "From what we've heard, the Vauphani nobles are strongly considering ignoring Merlin and... raising a new king from their own ranks. Apparently, they were not happy with Alvere's short reign as king. He'd talked about doing away with the nobility. This way they can keep their titles and get rid of a nuisance."

"But..." Wow, just wow. "That will infuriate Merlin. She'll kill Alvere!"

"Exactly." Grizzly grumbled. "That way the blood isn't on the hands of those sniveling *hereditary* nobles."

This wasn't good at all. "So, what's your plan?" I asked.

The assembled Nobles looked at each other. It was clear they had all been thinking about this but not decided anything.

"We were waiting for you," Grizzly said stoically.

And in that moment, it became clear to me that despite the many years of experience of the lords and ladies gathered in this room, they had no clue how to deal with a situation like this. All they'd ever done was debate minor changes to government and protect their lands.

But I'd been battling mistweavers and dealing with internal intrigue for nearly all of my — admittedly short — Noble career.

In this matter, I had far more experience than they did.

But before we got any further there was one thing — a curiosity that had been driving me mad — I wanted to know. I turned to Lord Drake and asked him directly, "You have a spirit-gift, yes? What is it?"

Everyone looked at him.

"Apparently my secret is out." He grimaced, his dark eyes drilling into me. Then he sighed. "But yes, perhaps it is wise for us to share our various gifts if they might be of use in what is to come. I, as Lady Legs knows, can see things others cannot. I see people's auras and can often determine how they feel by seeing even the slightest change in their expressions and carriage."

So that was it.

Grizzly shared that he had a gift of strength, making him far stronger than he should be. But none of the others had any gifts. I told them of my *Hero* gift, and we moved on to planning how to defeat Merlin.

"Can I get a chair?" I asked. "I think we're going to be here for a while."

And at that, several of the others visibly relaxed. For all of their seniority over me, I'd just taken control of this meeting... and that had been exactly what they'd wanted.

Didn't I say you were destined for great things? Auwei said with pride.

I don't know if you ever used those words exactly, but... thank you for your faith in me.

As you can see now, it was well deserved.

Indeed.

By the end of the afternoon, we had a plan, if a rough one. And even though every fiber of my being was yelling at me to run and save Alvere, I knew I had to stay here and oversee this new, small coalition. They all deferred to me, even Grizzly. He was big and tough and in a one-on-one fight I'd not want to face him, but strategizing an internal coup... was not his forte.

Apparently, it was mine.

Merlin held the capital and had the considerable might of the Owl House army protecting her, not to mention the city's defenses. A frontal assault would only harm citizens and weaken our armies as a whole. So, the plan was to assemble the rest of the combined armies and march on the capital in a show of force, but go no further than Elismount, a wide hill overlooking the city from the north. We'd stop and dig in there and see if Merlin sent her forces out to meet us. That way there would be no fighting inside the city.

But the hope was to avoid that fight with subterfuge. From my House's scouting, we knew of a secret way into the Owl House residence by means of a tavern called The Slippery Eel. And, from questioning one of the House Owl captives, we now knew the exact route through the warren of tunnels to get into the estate.

The plan was simple, a small group would sneak into the city and through those tunnels into the residence. We'd free Alvere first, making sure he was safe, then face Merlin.

As much as Merlin and Hale were on my list and I'd sworn to

kill both of them, the other Nobles convinced me that they should be captured, if possible, to be tried for treason.

I doubted Merlin would let herself be captured and said as much to the others. They conceded that her death was a likely outcome, but still hoped she could be brought to justice.

We'd see how things turned out.

My emotions were all over the place when I went to my parents' house that evening for a quiet dinner. Exhausted and soul-weary, I ate in silence. Fin ate with us, having been at the house, tending to Dove. After dinner, I went to see my sister. She'd always been fair-skinned, but her current pallor was just a little too close to that of a corpse for my liking. I brushed back some of her golden hair as I sat on the bed next to her.

"I'm so sorry, sister," I whispered. "I know I didn't get you into this. You wanted to come along to appeal to Silvermane." I sighed. "Though I guess I did get you into this, way back at the beginning of things with... Lord Hale and..." I couldn't speak, jaw clenched, infuriated. "He'll get what's coming to him I promise." I sighed again after that. I had hoped something I said would rouse her somehow. But she remained still. After a time, I lay down next to her and held her. "I'm here, sister. Take my strength if you need it. You need to survive." I couldn't live with myself if she died having protected me.

It was late when I left, even more fatigued. Fin and I returned to the inn where Silence and Ant were staying. I checked in on Ant, sleeping like a log, good. Silence wasn't in his room. I suspected I knew where he was and I was right. He lay curled up on the bed, waiting for me. He rose when I entered and wordless, came to me, holding me. My strength gave out and I cried into his shoulder.

He helped me into my nightdress and settled in bed with me, simply holding me, helping me to find the peace I needed to rest.

The next day was the same. More meetings and an evening with Dove, then crying myself to sleep in Silence's arms.

The sixth day after that fateful Noble's Council, we concluded our preparations and dispersed to arrange our various parts of the plan.

Dove remained unconscious, though some of her color had started to return. She'd live now, we all knew that, but the question became, would she ever wake?

I couldn't stay any longer. I had things to do, so I left her in the care of our parents and returned with Fin, Ant, Silence, Midnight, and the Fey to Cliffside. That night I spent curled up with Silence, Sparrow, and Ant, though we did nothing more than hold each other.

I wanted to go in now, face Merlin and get Alvere back, but I needed to wait for the others to move armies, which was never quick.

So I waited, day after day, growing ever more restless and distressed.

CHAPTER 22

ALVERE

Weak and bloody, Alvere hung by his wrists, which were manacled above his head and now numb from lack of circulation. He wasn't sure if he wanted to feel them, given how bloody and torn-up they were after his various struggles to escape. The rest of his body wasn't much better. His legs ached, strained from standing on his toes to try to take as much pressure as he could off his wrists. These restraints weren't made for someone of his height. He'd made the mistake of using his Fey ability of manipulating cloth to escape. He'd almost made it. He would have, if Merlin hadn't been on her way to see him just as he'd picked the lock on his cell door with a stiffened strip of cloth. She'd taken all this clothes after that. Now he had nothing but the stinging lash marks Merlin liked to leave on him, and the bruises from when she brought Hale to rough him up. He was near to delirious with lack of sleep and lack of food. He got only a small portion of water and a moldy lump of bread every day, force-fed to him in no kind way by the jailer.

His keen ears picked up the soft padding of footfalls outside his cell. He knew those steps and had learned to dread them. Merlin was coming.

The key clanked in the lock and the door swung open, the light of the torch held by the jailer stung his eyes and he winced as Merlin strode in. At first, she'd come to him as a torturer, delighting in hurting him, healing him with her mists between sessions so she could continue her work. But now... she came as a seductress, in a wrap, made only of translucent mists.

She pressed her lips to his in a kiss which he didn't return. As she did, he felt more mists slip down his throat. He'd learned not to resist them, that only led to long, exceedingly painful choking sessions.

"You are mine," she whispered when she stepped back. "You might as well accept it, King Alvere. I've received word from the nobles of Vauphan. They don't care about you, don't want you back. *But*, they *would* be willing to take your heir to mold as their own. It solves all their problems, a new king without breaking the line of succession. And I, of course, would be a trusted advisor to the young king, being his mother and all." Her dark eyes gleamed with her lust for power. "So why don't you give me your child, a true heir of Vauphan for your people." She fondled his manhood, trying to bring it to arousal. He remained unstimulated, horrified by this woman and her insane plans.

"No," he croaked, voice dry and cracked. "I'd rather die."

She smiled but there was no mirth in it. "That is also an option." She raised a finger as mist formed a long blade at the end of it. She dragged that down over his cheek, biting deep, drawing blood. Then she ran it over his chest and stomach in a slow waving pattern.

And where she cut him, pain lanced into him, far more than

such a cut should elicit. Her mists somehow amplified pain, shocking through him in throbbing agony.

He didn't know by what force of will he was able to resist screaming, but he did.

She leaned in and licked the blood off his cheek. "You can end this pain with pleasure. Give me an heir." She stepped back, and the gauzy mists around her vanished. "Am I not an attractive woman?" She reached down for his cock again, pulling hard on the limp flesh. "What will it take to get you to be with me?" She pressed her body to his, which only caused pain where she hadn't yet healed the long cut down his torso.

"Perhaps," she whispered. "If I looked like this?" Her form shimmered as mists covered her, then... in her place was Legs. She leaned in to kiss him again and this time, in a moment of weakness, delirious, Alvere returned the gesture, longing for his lost love, seeing her there with him. And now the stroking of her hand was indeed bringing him to the fullness of an erection.

"Yes, my king, I need you inside me," she begged, and though the voice was one he knew so well, it was then that he snapped back to reality.

"No!" he hissed again. "You're not her. You could never be her!"

The form shimmered and Merlin returned, growling in fury. "You are a stubborn man. You could have been free long ago, endured much less pain, if you'd only agreed to sleep with me. But no! You insist on pain! Well, then pain you shall have!"

With mist-claws on all five fingers of one hand, she slashed it down over his body, gouging flesh, cutting deep. This time, he did scream, as she raked her claws over him again and again, lost to rage. Then, finally, she returned to herself, blinking, breathing hard.

She waved a hand and mists covered him to mend much, but not all, of his shredded torso.

"I am a benevolent host," she said, words belied by the insane fury in her eyes. "I'll give you one more chance. When I come next, if you don't pleasure me and give me your seed willingly, I'll just take it from you, then I'll make you suffer ten times what you just felt before I kill you. But, if you comply, you live. The choice is yours."

She released him and spun, leaving the cell.

Alvere was broken. He knew it now. For all his protests, he didn't want to die. He wanted to live to see Legs again. His will wavered. One moment he'd be strong, willing to hold out, hoping he'd be rescued, hoping he'd not have to face Merlin again. Yet, in the next moment his resolve wavered and he feared he'd submit to Merlin if she returned, especially if she disguised herself as Legs again. Would it be so bad to give her what she wanted, to end his pain with pleasure as she put it?

No! He couldn't allow himself to be weak. He had to hold on.

But his will kept failing him.

"Please, Legs, anyone, get me out of here," he whispered. It was his prayer; and he repeated it over and over until he had no more voice. Then he repeated it in his head. He didn't know what he'd do if Merlin returned before he was freed, and he hoped, he wouldn't have to find out.

CHAPTER 23

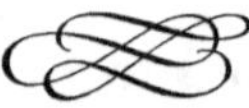

A*S THE ARMIES OF THE ASSEMBLED* N*OBLES GATHERED TO THE NORTH* of the capital, those who would be going in, in secret, met on a farm that belonged to Maverick's sister, to the south.

It was a cool and rainy day with thick dark clouds overhead, which seemed to reflect the mood of those gathered in the barn.

Sparrow looked around at the grim faces of those who'd volunteered for this dangerous mission.

Legs, stalwart and brave, gave a curt smile as their gazes met.

Ant looked tired. He'd had a few days to recover after healing so many in Miraline, but still seemed fatigued.

Silence had turned hard, face set in a vicious glower. Sparrow didn't envy him his part in today's events, but he seemed ready for the gruesome task ahead of him.

Midnight was stoic and calm, as always.

Ahmaia, the Fey woman, stood a bit apart, ageless face unreadable.

"We may not be able to leave with the King," Legs said to Lady Ursa. The large woman wore armor which made her seem even more imposing than she already was. "If Merlin has cursed him the way she cursed the queen, we won't be able to take him too far from her, I'm guessing."

"Do we know any way to remove such a curse?" Ursa asked.

"Kill Merlin," Legs said bluntly. It was clear that was her preferred option.

Ursa grimaced. "I'd ask if there was any other way, but I think you're right."

Here, away from the Council of Nobles, it was becoming clear that capturing Merlin wasn't going to happen.

"A mistweaver is too erratic and too powerful to detain," Legs said. "The others of her House, perhaps, but Merlin..."

Ursa nodded sagely.

Spike, the leader of House Porcupine, spoke up. "There is no way to take her alive?" he asked. As the only other house leader here, he tried to be a voice of reason.

"Can *you* think of any way to disable a woman who can become mist at will and just float away?" Legs said, voice cool.

"Couldn't we knock her unconscious?" Spike asked.

"Have you ever tried that? It's a lot harder than you think," Ursa said.

"And how many people will die while we're attempting to beat her into submission?" Legs added. She shrugged. "Bring the manacles if you like and if a chance presents itself, by all means capture her, but I won't sacrifice any more lives if killing her ends this sooner."

Spike nodded. "Agreed."

We were set.

From outside the barn came the flapping of great leathery wings and the heavy thump of something large hitting the ground.

Everyone turned. Through the open barn doors, Sparrow

gawked at the dragon-like figure. She'd never seen a Wyvern before. They were much larger than she'd thought. Standing on its powerful hind legs, it was probably the height of the barn, or so Sparrow assumed, only seeing the bottom half of it. The beast had no forelegs or arms, the wings took their place. Folding those massive leathery limbs back, it settled on the large knuckles at the joint of the wing. A long serpentine neck angled down to look into the barn. Thick scales — dark red with traces of gold — covered the being, a permanent armor over the massive form.

A moment later the form shrank to become Skyfire in battle armor, who marched into the barn.

"I'm coming with you," she said, her tone leaving no room for argument.

"As you wish," Ursa said, sounding dubious. "But at least let Lord Ant heal you. You look pained."

Sparrow had to agree. Skyfire looked rough. She'd lost most of her left arm and seemed to be favoring her left side. Sparrow hadn't been at the Council of Nobles, but she'd heard many versions of the fight, and in all of them Skyfire had not fared well.

Skyfire held up her remaining arm to stop Ant. "No. I am well enough to fight and the pain is mine to bear, a memory of my failure." She quirked a determined grin. "I may have lost an arm and a tit, but I still have one of each and that's enough." To demonstrate, she drew her sword and flourished it. "I wear my wounds with honor, as a memory of the day I couldn't protect those I loved."

The people she loved? From what Sparrow had heard, she'd been protecting Lady Silvermane.

"How is Lady Silvermane?" Ursa asked, as if Skyfire hadn't just admitted her love for another House leader.

"Still recovering. Her wound was grave, and she'll be on the mend for some time still. Healers are helping her regain... some... of what she lost." Skyfire's tone was grim.

It had become known that Silvermane had been pregnant when attacked. She'd lost the child. Sparrow could only guess at the torment the woman must be going through.

Sparrow leaned over to Silence. "Did you know Skyfire loved Silvermane?"

"Nope. That's news to me."

Sparrow nodded. At least she hadn't missed anything the others already knew.

"We're happy to have your battle expertise with us," Ursa said.

Skyfire grinned, a vicious and deadly thing. "You certainly will be." She passed Legs and nodded to her. "Drake tells me you're a House Leader in truth, now? Good." She slapped Legs' shoulder hard in camaraderie, nearly knocking Legs over. "Glad to have you." Then to the rest of the group she said, "Let's go kill a mistweaver."

"Our mission is to apprehend her, if possible," Spike said.

"Yeah, right, of course," Skyfire said, clearly ignoring the man.

Sparrow had to laugh at that, despite the dire times.

Legs turned to Sparrow. "You know what to do."

Sparrow veered into her bird form and flew out of the barn. The rain was light and the winds calm, so it was easy enough to fly to the capital. The first part of the plan was hers to undertake.

Sparrow landed in a dark alley and shifted back to herself, pulling up the hood of her cloak and stepping out into the street. It was quiet. A tense stillness hung over the city. By now, they'd know a large army waited to the north. Streets that should have been busy and bustling were empty. Those who were out, moved with haste, glancing about.

Sparrow turned a corner and headed for the Eel. The first thing she noted were the two large men standing outside in the rain. So, the Royals were being very careful. She approached and tried to simply walk up to the door, but a meaty arm reached out to block her way.

"Sorry, little miss," The one man said. "The Eel's closed to everyone but a private party."

Sparrow didn't doubt she could take both these men. They were hired goons, not Nobles, but subduing them wasn't the plan.

Instead she huddled into her cloak a little more and answered in a soft, scared voice.

"I'm here for Lord Jird."

"Another one?" one of the men said. "That old man's got some stamina. Wasn't there another girl here this morning?"

"Yeah, that's what you get when you're a Noble," the other man said. "Whores all day every day." Then he opened the door for her. Sparrow hurried in out of the rain.

Her gamble had worked. Lord Jird — a rather unsavory member of the Royal House — was a known lech, who lusted for particularly young women.

She tried to still her thundering heart as she approached the bar. There were other brutes inside the tavern as well, a full dozen tough-looking men. They weren't eating or drinking, clearly there to guard the place.

"Who're you now?" the barman said, suspicion thick in his voice. Several of the men in the room shifted, paying attention.

It didn't take much to make her voice soft and meek, a bit scared. "I'm sorry, good man. I... I was requested by Lord Jird. Told to wait for him in a room upstairs?"

The barman scoffed a laugh. "How old are you girl?"

"Seventeen," she lied. The one perk to being smaller and less developed than some other women was passing as younger.

"Twice in one day?" The man shook his head then shrugged. "Top of the stairs, third door on the left. Wait there and I'll let the good Lord know where you are when he comes through."

She nodded and left, slinking up the stairs.

She got to the room and closed the door behind her. That was the first part done. Now she had to wait for a while.

She opened the shutters of her window and lit a single candle, placing it on the sill. Luckily the rain was falling straight down and wouldn't put out the flame.

It was sometime later when a little brown mouse scurried in through the window. A moment later Silence was standing before her. She rose to embrace him, glad to see a friendly face.

"How'd it go?" he asked.

"Icky and nerve wracking, but no one suspected a thing."

He nodded. "My turn then." And he veered back into a mouse.

Sparrow's part was done for now. Others would arrive via this window shortly, but the next bit was all Silence.

CHAPTER 24

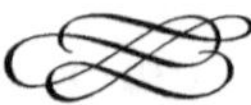

SILENCE SCURRIED DOWN THROUGH THE CRACKS AND CRANNIES OF the tavern into the tunnels below. He'd been here before and knew the way well enough. Long ago, what seemed like a lifetime, when they'd been searching for Lord Hale after his attack on Legs, he and Foggy had scouted these tunnels extensively, but he'd never found the entrance into the Royal Estates. Now he was armed with the correct path through the warren of tunnels.

His mission was twofold. First to scout the tunnels and find out who or what might be guarding them. Second, to scout the estate itself and see if he could find Alvere.

The back room of the tavern had a trap door in the floor: the entrance to the tunnels, which was guarded by two large men. Neither were paying much attention, probably expecting people to actually open doors, which they'd notice. Silence easily slipped under the door to the room, and through one of the wider cracks in the floorboards down into the tunnel. He was just a bit surprised to find several more guards not far from the bottom of the ladder. They were down the tunnel a short distance, behind a barricade, facing the ladder. The make-shift fortification was mostly made of wood, with a bit of earth to help keep the planks in place. The men behind it would be mostly protected from anyone attacking from the ladder. And they had small slits through which they could fire their crossbows. Once on the other side of the barrier — no one paying much heed to the small mouse — he took a long moment to study the layout of the men and equipment. Of particular note was an area just behind the fortification where several thick, wooden poles propped up a wooden door in the ceiling. This hadn't been here before. Curious, he climbed one of the poles and slipped between the wooden boards above to see what he could. It was dim here, but sensing through his whiskers, he felt stones all around him. A chill swept through him. This was to block the tunnel. If people were coming down the ladder and it seemed like the forces down here wouldn't be able to kill them all, they'd retreat and pull down the wooden supports to drop these rocks down into the tunnel and block it. Which meant... Silence himself would have to deal with this, before people started coming down into the tunnels. But he'd wait for now. He'd do it on his way back from scouting.

He quickly navigated the maze of tunnels to the estate entrance. Here, two men guarded the ladder up. They were not on high alert, they would most likely be warned by hearing combat from the other end or from fleeing comrades. So, Silence snuck past them and up into the estate. He peaked up through the wooden floorboards just a bit to see the room beyond.

It was a stone room with a heavy metal door to one side. Two men manned this room as well, looking more alert than most of the other guards, but still bored.

There was another blocking mechanism in this room. What looked like a heavy metal plate, perhaps five feet to a side, and two inches thick. It was propped up against one wall by two planks. If those planks were removed and the plate knocked over, it would cover the trap-door and be very hard to move. So, these men would need to be dealt with before he left as well.

Now came the hard part... waiting. If it came to it and he was going to have to deal with the guards down here, he'd been told to wait — for as long as he could — to see if the guards switched at all. If at all possible, he'd want to eliminate the guards after a shift change, so that their deaths wouldn't be discovered quickly.

But he knew time was precious. It might mean the difference between Alvere being alive and dead. And that ate at him as he sat there, hoping and praying to all the Spirits that the guards would change soon.

He didn't know if it was seconds, minutes, or hours that he sat there, but finally, the door to the small room opened and men came in.

"Go grab some grub," one of the men coming in said.

Silence took the moment while the group was milling around in the room, to rush out from the trapdoor. He dodged boots as he scurried out the open door. From the size of the group in the hall, it was clear all of the guard stations here and below were being switched out.

Good.

Now he just had to find Alvere and get back here to deal with these guards as quickly as possible. He ran off to explore the lower levels of the estate.

It took some time, in this small form, to check the various doors and tunnels in this sub-basement. But then, finally he slid under one door into a dark room, letting his eyes adjust to the darkness from the barely-lit hall behind him. Mice didn't have particularly good sight, but he caught a familiar scent in this cell. He sniffed around until he was sure, then transformed back to himself.

"Alvere?" he whispered.

"Silence?" The voice was hoarse and so very desperate. It made Silence's heart break. Especially given what Silence knew was coming. "Are you here to free me?"

"No," Silence said, his heart shattering a bit more. "But!" he added quickly. "We are on our way. If I took you now, we'd not be able to get past all the guards." That wasn't entirely true. Silence was fairly confident he could deal with the guards and would have to on his way out, but the truth was they suspected Alvere had been cursed like the queen and couldn't leave without dying. But he didn't want to say that to the sorrowing man. So, as much as it tore at his heart, he lied. "I just needed to know where you were so we can come and rescue you. Don't worry Alvere, I'll be back soon with others."

"Silence? No, please, don't go, not yet." And Silence knew he couldn't. With no light in the room Silence felt his way around until he touched flesh. Alvere gasped, then wept. Silence's hand swept over naked skin, feeling the roughness of what he assumed was dried blood, and the raised flesh of long cuts. "Don't. Please!" Alvere begged, pain in his voice.

But Silence drew closer and raised his hand to find Alvere's face; it helped that they were roughly the same height.

"Don't worry, my love, we're coming, I'll be back soon." He kissed the man's forehead softly.

Alvere sobbed. "I... had hoped... so much..."

"And we're here. Can you wait just a little longer?"

More sniffs and sobs. "Yes, I can... but please hurry." The pure agony and desolation in the once-strong man's voice tore at Silence. He tensed his jaw.

"Yes, we will. I need to go now, to bring the others all the quicker."

"Yes, go," Alvere said, still weeping.

Silence, though it wounded his soul to do so, veered into his mouse form and ran from the cell, retracing his steps back to the room with the trap door. He pressed himself as flat as he could to squeeze under the well fitted metal door and before he entered the room, he glanced within. One guard stood, the other sat beside the trapdoor.

Silence had no desire to kill these men, but it had to be done. So, he hardened himself for what was to come. It was easy, knowing how his friend and lover had been treated. He cut out any sympathy for the guards and told himself they deserved what they got, that they'd kill him given half a chance.

There would be no mercy tonight.

He scurried out, between the legs of the man standing, then veered, returning to his normal form even as he drew forth a dagger and drove it up under the man's jaw, into his skull.

Without hesitation, he hurled a second knife, made for throwing, at the man sitting. The guard let out a clipped cry before the knife found his eye and sank into his brain. Then he was silent as he fell back, limp.

But he'd made a bit of noise...

Silence stood stock still, listening.

Had the men below heard that?

"Everything well up there?" One man from below shouted.

Bloody bones!

Silence whipped opened the trap door and dropped down, landing lightly to slash out quickly, again taking one of the guards before he knew what was happening. The other didn't have his sword out, but he tried to draw it. Silence was there before the sword cleared the scabbard, plunging his blade into the man's eye. The guard went down like a board, falling flat.

Like death coming quietly in the night, Silence stalked down the maze of passages to the five guards behind the barricade at the far end. They were all facing away from him. Two died before they knew he was there. The third fell before he could draw a weapon.

The last two tried to fight him, but they had neither his training nor his cold rage and didn't take long to deal with. The fight made some noise, but not much. Silence was certain the guards in the tavern wouldn't have heard anything.

His job here done, he slipped back through the tavern as a mouse, past the guards in the back room back to Sparrow's room. It was quite crowded now.

He shifted back, grim and stoic. The others all gasped, eyes wide. He was covered in blood and must have looked quite the site.

"I know where Alvere is. They... haven't treated him well. We need to hurry."

Legs' face darkened, growing grim. She nodded, signaling out the window to those waiting outside, then they were off.

CHAPTER 25

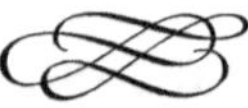

I RUSHED DOWN THE STAIRS, BUT THE FORCE FROM OUTSIDE HAD beaten us to the common room. Dead men lay sprawled over the room and the barman was trembling in Ursa's iron grip. A gore covered Skyfire flicked the blood off her sword and grinned at me.

"I haven't had a good fight in a while," she said. It seemed losing an arm hadn't slowed her down much.

"This way," Silence said, still stone-faced and scary as The Blackest Pits, covered in blood and not even noticing. I had to run to catch up with him, even though I had the longer legs.

Silence kicked open the door to the back room.

The two men within lashed out at once, ready for a fight. My *Hero* gift rose, but Silence was done with them before I'd moved in. One man went down with his own sword in his gut, the other with Silence's dagger in his neck. Spirits, sometimes I forgot how quick he could be.

The rest of us hurried along behind Silence, following where he led us, past the scenes of carnage in the tunnels and up out the other side.

As we came up into the Owl House estate, Skyfire caught me by the arm. "The little man did all of that?" she whispered.

"He did."

"Amazing." She watched Silence stalking like death itself down the hall away from us. "You've got a good team."

"I do." We nodded to each other.

Skyfire and a small group would remain here, guarding our exit, while I led a second group to find Alvere. Once we'd returned with him and he was safe, then we'd all move into face Merlin.

I hurried to catch up to Silence. We found him stepping out of the jailer's office, keys in hand. I peered inside to see the jailer trembling but alive. Though, long shallow cuts had been traced over his torso, cutting open his shirt. The large, heavy-set man should have been able to crush Silence, but instead was a quivering mess.

Spirits!

This side of Silence was terrifying.

We paused as Silence reached a heavy metal door farther down the hall and unlocked it. As he did, he said: "Ant, he'll need you."

The large man, holding a lantern to shed light in these dark tunnels, nodded.

I steeled myself for what I might see on the other side.

Legs... Auwei was concerned. I knew she wanted to say more, wanted to console me before I even laid eyes upon my lover, but she had no words. Even with nine lifetimes of insight, there was nothing she could say in this situation.

Silence opened the door and we rushed in. Ant stepped to one side, shedding light on the scene and I stopped dead, sickened by what I saw. Alvere hung by his wrists. Blood — fresh and dried — covered his arms, dripping down from above. Cuts and bruises, old and new covered his naked body. He winced at the light, a limp and dejected form, hair sodden, his own waste around him.

The stench of blood and worse hit me like a brick wall, but I forced myself forward to him.

Ant reached him first, laying a hand on the man to heal him as Silence unlocked his manacles. I caught Alvere as he fell, weak as a baby bird, his arms slammed down onto him, dead weight.

"Spirits of..." Ant breathed, and I saw the man's jaw go tense. "I never..."

"Legs," Alvere breathed looking up at me through hooded eyes, with heavy bags beneath them. "Is it you? I prayed." His voice was raspy and weak.

"Let's get back to the others," I said as we moved as a unit. I carried Alvere, but Ant stayed close, hands on the man, healing him even as we made our way out of the dungeons.

Once we'd reached the area the others had secured, I laid Alvere down on the floor, kissing his forehead, kneeling close as Ant continued his work. Sparrow had found a blanket and laid it over Alvere's naked form.

"He lost blood flow to his arms," Ant said, concerned. "They're... Spirits, I don't know if I can save them. The rest of the damage is mostly superficial, though his dehydration and exhaustion aren't things I can heal. He needs water."

"Here." Ahmaia was at my side a moment later, producing a heavy water-skin, seemingly from nowhere, probably from one of her many 'pockets.' She handed it over to Ant who dribbled some onto Alvere's cracked lips, wetting them. He licked the moisture away and Ant continued in the same fashion, giving him a bit at a time. The poor man drank heartily.

"Thank you," Alvere said, head lolling to one side, gazing at me. "I... knew you'd come. I wasn't going to give her what she wanted... I promise." He was still delirious, that was clear.

Ahmaia produced bread and slices of dried fruit. I fed my love slowly as he rested, helping him regain his strength.

"I'll stay with him," Ant said as those around us fidgeted,

wishing to be away. We'd been here too long already, the chances of someone finding us grew with each passing moment. "He'll be safe and I can tend to him."

As much as I wanted Ant with me for the fight to come, I agreed that Alvere needed him more.

Remembering that he might be cursed and probably couldn't go far, I said, "Take him down into the tunnels and guard him there. Hopefully he'll be safe."

"I'll guard him with my life," Ant said.

Ahmaia used her cloth "arms" to lower Alvere down into the tunnels and Ant went down, continuing to tend to him.

Good. Alvere was safe and I could focus on the fight to come.

Time to face Merlin and make her pay for everyone she'd hurt.

We made our way up out of the basements of the estate to what we believed to be the main floor. Moving carefully, Ursa led us to the great hall.

Anyone we came upon was scooped into one of Ahmaia's pockets before they could raise an alarm.

We reached the closed double doors and I let my spider-sense do its thing, listening for any voices on the other side.

I caught a distant conversation.

"... matter of time before they send a force in against us. The city walls won't stop most of the Nobles out there. Legs in particular is a sneaky bitch!" This was Hales voice and I smiled at his compliment.

Yes I am, And we're already here, surprise!

"So, do your thing," Hale continued, "Look into the future, tell us how we get out of this!"

"I already told you, I can't!" Merlin shouted. Her voice consumed with rage and madness. "I can't see my own future. I saw only that legs would thwart the war and bits of that damned Council of Nobles, nothing after that!"

Now that was interesting to learn, and a Spirits-sent bit of good news.

"Perhaps you should try," Hale snarled.

"Perhaps you should die!" Merlin raged and I heard a heavy grunt, then what sounded like a body hitting the floor and sliding... for a while.

"Darling!" I heard Swan's panicked voice and running footfalls. So... Hale was down?

I didn't think we'd have a better opportunity than this.

"Now!" I hissed softly, then veered into my spider to slip under the door.

A moment later, Silence, as a mouse, followed beside me.

I instantly got a sense for the large room. We were in luck, other than Swan and Hale, Merlin was alone, no guards. Hale seemed injured but alive, groaning as he struggled to sit up. I knew Swan wouldn't be an issue. The only remaining threat was Merlin.

I sensed Silence's soft padding feet as he scurried behind a pillar. I followed and once he was out of sight, he shifted back to human and whispered, "I told the others outside to wait till they heard the sound of combat, then rush in. I'm going to distract her. You stay hidden and wait for your time to strike." The smile he gave was half-crazed, half cock sure. "Don't transform and try to talk me out of it. I know what I'm doing. You saved me from the last mistweaver, I'm not afraid anymore. I trust you to kill her before she kills me."

Wow.

The look in his eyes told me I'd not be able to talk him out of this wild plan. I just hoped I could hold up my end of the bargain. I bobbed my entire spider form in a sort-of nod.

Silence smiled, then veered back to a mouse.

We kept to the edges of the hall. Silence broke off at one point, but must have waited to act, allowing me time to get closer to Merlin, behind her.

I was almost in position when Hale hissed. "An avatar! Merlin, watchout!"

Across the room I saw Silence revert back to himself, but he was still some distance from Merlin. Hale must have used his ability to transform Silence back before he was prepared.

"Pits," Silence hissed.

"You!" Merlin called, then instantly she seemed to catch onto our plan. "Legs is here!"

Well, so much for surprise.

Silence let out a terrible, feral roar and charged at Merlin.

CHAPTER 26

Not wanting to waist his distraction, I returned to myself and rushed in, swords drawn and ready.

Mist blasted out from Merlin. A tendril caught Silence's leg and smashed him to the floor so hard he bounced. I heard his grunt of pain, his bones breaking.

I couldn't help it, I shrieked in horror-filled rage as I stabbed at Merlin, but mists formed a solid wall behind her, stopping my blades.

The others threw open the doors and rushed in as Merlin turned toward me with an obscenely maniacal grin. "Did you see what I did to your little king?" she taunted me. "I'd heard he liked it rough, and yes, he did." Then she laughed.

A red haze of rage filtered over my vision.

She's goading you. She wants you to face her head on. If you do, you'll die! Auwei's warning stopped me. Furious, I jumped away as tendrils of mist reached for me.

I landed on the side of a pillar, then quickly bounced away, moving around the hall, trying to keep ahead of the mists lashing out at me. Finally, I threw myself over the railing into the second level balcony and out of Merlin's sight, hoping that would give me a moment to regroup.

"Come out little spider," Merlin called gleefully. She enjoyed this, playing with me.

"Continue to keep her busy, I'll get behind her." The voice was Midnight's and it was close. I looked around, but of course couldn't see her.

"Will do." I whispered.

It seems we're to be the distraction now, Auwei said. I heard the fear in her voice.

It makes sense, Merlin is already focused on us. Let's do this!

I whipped myself back out into the hall. As I sailed through the air, I caught sight of everything below me.

Merlin's mists had spread out, covering the floor of the hall. I couldn't see Silence and feared he was too hurt to get up.

Skyfire, moving faster than I could see, only a blur, dodged the mists grasping for her.

Ursa dragged Hale to one side. The man couldn't stand. Whatever Merlin had done had injured him greatly. Swan was nowhere to be seen.

Ahmaia flew on fluttering cloth wings, batting away Merlin's misty arms with cloth ones of her own, a stalemate for now.

Sparrow fluttered about in bird form, weaving through the tentacles of mist reaching for her. Spike was dragged down into the mists as I watched, his scream clipped off as he fell below the rolling waves of fog.

Merlin floated, raising herself on a pillar of mist in the center of the room, cackling, head thrown back, in a fit of ecstasy.

It only occurred to me then, that Merlin might be *more* powerful than her sister, Hazra. If so... we were in for one Pits of a fight.

I landed on the side of another pillar.

"Over here!" I called, though I needn't have bothered, Merlin had already spotted me.

"Yes! Let's play," she giggled and with a wave of her hand, the mists on the floor spilled out farther around her. Skyfire tried to escape, but the mists caught her before she could use her incredible speed and sucked her down into their depths.

No!

Ursa wisely stayed back, but that put her out of the fight, too far away to do anything but watch. Ahmaia backed off as well, unable to get any closer with the mists rising to meet her.

It seemed it would be up to me.

And Midnight, wherever she was.

"Come on Legs, let's see what you've got. I'm slowly killing those I've trapped in the mists below, including that pretty young man. Let's see if you can save him before I kill him."

She was trying to split my focus, make me worry for Silence instead of concentrating on her. It almost worked. But I blocked out the trembling rage building within me — my *Hero* gift straining to be released — and closed my eyes to focus on my other senses. I could feel the billowing mists and the bodies trapped within it, Silence, Spike, and Skyfire, all twitching desperately. I also felt Merlin and her literal attachment to the mists. She wasn't floating on a cloud so much as her feet and legs had become mist. She was a part of all the mists in the room.

I didn't know how Midnight planned to sneak up on her, but that wasn't for me to know. I was just the distraction. Time to be distracting.

"You want me, come get me," I shouted, then launched myself away, leaping around the great hall as Merlin lashed out with her mists.

"Oooh! You are quick aren't you! This is going to be so fun!" she cackled.

When I leaped next, she vanished in a puff of smoke and

appeared in my path. Her hand moved and a larger hand of mist appeared to slap me out of the air. "Swat the little spider!" She giggled as I fell to the floor, hitting hard and rolling. I tried to leap away, but the swirling mists, as high as my waist, held me fast.

Pits!

"Is that all you have?" Merlin appeared next to me with a smug smile of superiority. Then her face contorted slipping through pain to rage. "How did you ever beat my sister?" she spat at me.

A fist of mist slammed into my stomach, doubling me over, and blasting out my breath. Without my armor, I was sure that hit would have crushed organs and scrambled my insides.

How *had* I defeated Hazra? I'd used all my tricks: my senses telling me where she'd materialize next, then I'd used my webbing to suffocate her.

I already had a hand on my stomach, doubled over from her hit. I spun out a ball of webbing into my palm. Then, as I righted myself, threw it at Merlin.

But she'd already puffed away to a spot closer to the middle of the room, laughing with glee. "That won't work on me. I saw how you defeated my sister. I know all your tricks. You can't defeat me!"

We'd see about that.

This time... I had help. My senses picked up the small flurry of movement as a sparrow landed on my back. I flashed into my spider form and Sparrow sped me away, high into the hall.

Only then, while I had the briefest of moments to take everything in, did I notice: the wooden railing at the edge of the balcony had a branch growing out of it.

Midnight could manipulate wood! That must be her.

Sparrow released me over the second level and I landed as myself, but didn't stay long, jumping away — in a different direction from Sparrow — on the move once again, keeping Merlin's attention.

.   .   .

I DESPERATELY EVADED HER SPIKES AND FISTS OF MIST, JUMPING around the hall in a frenzy, keeping Merlin's focus away from that branch. I just needed to keep her occupied a moment longer and...

Midnight appeared as she plunged down, knife in hand, but Merlin must have sensed something as she flinched at the last minute, the blade meant to sink into her neck tore down her back instead.

It didn't kill her, but by the screech of pain she let out, it had hurt like The Pits!

The mists in the hall suddenly contracted back into Merlin. Perhaps it was some defense mechanism? I didn't know, but I was thankful for it. Skyfire and Spike gasped for air. Silence, however, was a little too still.

I needed to help him.

But I also needed to help Midnight defeat Merlin.

My hesitation didn't help either of them.

Midnight cried out as Merlin caught her in a fist of mist, then slammed her into a wall. Merlin screamed with rage crushing Midnight, who'd die if I didn't help now!

I launched myself at Merlin, just as Skyfire — as a wyvern — also chose that moment to attack.

Neither of us hit the madwoman.

CHAPTER 27

MERLIN SHRIEKED AN UNENDING SCREAM AS SHE SPUN, FLINGING OUT her hand. A circular blade of mist expanded out from her. It caught Skyfire and me mid-leap. Skyfire managed to get mostly out of the way with a flap of her large wings. I shot silk at the ceiling and tried to pull myself up as well. I pulled up one leg in time, but the mist-blade caught my other ankle. If not for my armored boots, it would have severed my foot, but still the cut was deep and bled profusely.

My *Hero* gift kicked in hard, blocking the pain even as I paused on the domed ceiling to pull more silk and clot the wound. It would be hard to walk or leap or do much of anything with that one lame foot.

Skyfire breathed fire at Merlin, who blocked with a wall of mist.

I had no clue how to stop Midnight from being crushed. Though... Merlin held out one hand toward Midnight as if controlling the mist upon the woman. So, I shot silk at her hand and tagged it. Then I yanked the silk and managed to pull the hand away. Midnight cried out and fell to the floor as Merlin's mists vanished, but it was clear Midnight had taken extreme damage and wouldn't be participating anymore in this fight.

"I've done what I can," she gasped. "Kill that bitch!"

I would be more than happy to oblige, but... how?

Merlin, with her arm now roughly extended in my direction, opened her palm and a wall of mist rushed at me. I leaped off the ceiling, though with my lame foot, it was more of an awkward fall. The mist-wall caught my shoulder, sending me somersaulting through the air. An uncontrolled fall from this height was going to hurt, a lot.

I braced myself.

Then Skyfire swooped in to pluck me out of the air. She too had a wounded leg. I guessed her tough hide had protected her from that attack the same way my armor had. Still the wound was deep and she'd quickly lose a lot of blood from it. I reached down and put some silk over it to help her.

An idea was forming in my mind. I'd gotten my silk on Merlin once. Perhaps, if I did it again, I could pull her to me, get in close where I could finally attack her. Skyfire and I were physically stronger than Merlin, so perhaps if we could get in close...?

But I doubted she'd let me get a solid strand of silk on her again.

And before I could act, Skyfire didn't quite dodge a slam of mist and we both went tumbling to the floor. I hit so hard, the bones in my right arm shattered on impact. Neither my armor nor *Hero* gift could prevent it. I rolled like a ragdoll and came to a stop abruptly when I hit a pillar.

All I could do was lay there and groan, even as my gift surged to reduce my pain. I got up slowly, it felt like forever. I couldn't quite clear my head and get back into the fight. A part of me wondered why Merling hadn't crushed me.

But when I finally looked up, I saw why.

Merlin — still floating, and seemingly fully recovered from

Midnight's attack earlier — had captured Skyfire, who'd returned to her human form. Mists formed a noose around Skyfire's neck, lifting her as she flailed and gasped for air. Merlin cackled with glee as she turned toward me.

"You can watch her die, knowing you're next," Merlin said holding the other woman out in front of her, turning Skyfire to face me, so I could watch her die. Then Merlin formed a blade of mist extending out from her free hand and slashed it toward Skyfire's mid-section.

I screamed reaching out with my good hand, but could do nothing. The blade flashed in...

...but stopped, trembling, cutting no more than an inch into Skyfire's side. Merlin screeched with rage, eyes wide.

I didn't know what had happened and frantically looked around for an explanation. I saw Ahmaia. She stood next to Silence, who was now tightly bandaged in ribbons of her cloth. I hoped that meant the man was still alive. Ahmaia had her hand out toward Merlin, but hadn't used any of her cloth strips to reach the woman, so how...?

It was a testament to how dazed I must have been from that last attack, that it took me this long to figure out... Merlin was wearing clothes and Ahmaia was controlling that cloth, keeping Merlin from moving, even slowly pulling the mist-blade away from Skyfire.

Merlin's mists tossed Skyfire to one side. The woman hit the floor hard, gasping desperately for air and out of commission for the moment.

Even though Merlin couldn't move, the mists rotated her to see her attacker. Her shrill screech hit a new maddening pitch seeing Ahmaia. Mists lashed out at the Fey woman, who parried with the cloth "arms" floating around her, even as Merlin was pulled down to the floor.

"We have her trapped for a moment, what should we do?" I

flinched, surprised at the voice next to me, but it was only Sparrow. "You well enough to fight?"

"I'm hurt pretty bad," I admitted, even if my gift was blocking most of the pain.

As for what to do. My plan to get in close to Merlin was the only one I had, even with a wounded foot and a broken arm. "I just need to get close to her. Can you distract her for a moment?"

"Me?" Sparrow whispered, terrified.

I smiled at her. "You're quick and agile. I know you'll be fine. I need you Sparrow. Spirits, we all need you!"

The fear in her eyes turned to a hard determination. "Then I'll do what I can."

She veered into her bird form, but even as she flew toward Merlin, mists were tearing away Merlin's clothes so Ahmaia wouldn't have control over her. Sparrow did a quick pass at Merlin's head, pecking with her small beak and the madwoman flailed at the attack with one freed arm but missed.

I had to act fast. My *Hero* gift ebbed, strained by the extent of my injuries, but all I needed was one good punch on Merlin.

Ahmaia had moved in, trying to capture Merlin with tendrils of her own robe. Merlin deflected the cloth arms with her mists. Sparrow flitted about with speed and grace, weaving to avoid the strands of mist trying to capture her. Another peck at Merlin's head and the mistweaver roared in rage. A large box of mist appeared around Sparrow, then quickly crushed in.

"No!" I cried out.

Merlin spun to face me.

But that gave Ahmaia the opening she needed to grasp Merlin with her tendrils of cloth.

"Now!" the Fey woman screamed.

I launched myself off my one good foot and slammed my fist into Merlin's face. The mistweaver reeled back, even as I kneed her in the stomach.

A bubble of mist — some instinctual defense — pushed myself and Ahmaia away, freeing Merlin.

But... I'd landed a single strand of silk on her face when I'd punched her. I pulled myself back in before Merlin fully recovered.

I grasped her neck and pulled her close. "This ends now!" I whispered, then pressed my lips to hers. She jerked and I could sense her trying to summon her mists, but my toxin had already affected her. She went stiff, paralyzed.

I slammed her to the ground, straddling her, and spun webbing over her mouth. Her eyes went wide with fear and rage.

A sword skittered over the floor to me. I looked up to see it had been pushed my way by Ahmaia of all people. The message was clear: even the Fey — who revered life — wanted the mistweaver to die.

I plucked up the sword in my good hand. "For all your crimes against Elista and Vauphan, for all those you've killed, for all the pain and suffering you've caused, I Legs, Head of Spider House and High Noble of the Realm sentence you to death." I slammed the blade down into Merlin's heart so hard the sword shattered when it hit the floor on the other side of her. I took the jagged bit still attached to the hilt and ran it across the woman's throat, for good measure.

Merlin twitched once, then stilled, vacant eyes staring at me: dead.

I collapsed off Merlin, the fight going out of me. Ahmaia caught me in tendrils of cloth before I hit the floor and lowered me to the stones.

I could hear the distant groans and whimpers of the others in the hall.

"Get Ant," I whispered to Ahmaia before I passed out.

CHAPTER 28

I woke, days later, still in a lot of pain and slightly feverish. My body was slowly healing itself, which begged the question: why hadn't Ant healed me? So many questions raced through my delirium-addled mind. I needed to know if the others had survived.

Auwei?

Yes, I'm here, but I don't know much. I've only been peripherally aware of what's been going on. Ant never came to see you. I don't know why.

Startled by my pained groan as I tried to sit up — and failed — Princess, who'd been laying on my bed in cat form rose and shifted to human.

"You're awake? Good. We were worried for a while there."

"Ant..." I said, barely able to form words, struggling to remain awake.

"Ah... well... about that. He can't help you, not anymore."

What?

Princess then gave the full report on what had happened after the fight.

The good news was, everyone had survived, but it had come at a cost. Apparently, Sparrow, Midnight, and Silence had all been so badly hurt that Ant had had to pull them back from the brink of death... but he'd nearly killed himself, burning out his spirit-gift, doing it. He could no longer heal. Luckily, he'd already healed Alvere before that, and none of the others had needed too much mending... except for me and Skyfire.

Skyfire had stubbornly refused healing. She wished to keep the scar around her neck and her now raspy, damaged voice as another reminder of her failure.

And even despite Ant's monumental effort, the other three still needed time to recover fully. So that's what we did: rest and mend.

Knowing everyone was alive, I let myself succumb to sleep once more.

It was about two weeks later when I woke finally feeling healthy and rested, my *Hero* gift having healed me far faster than normal.

Sunlight flooded the room, making me smile, even if it hurt my eyes a little. I blinked, pulling myself up to a sitting position.

It was then I noticed Lady Crane sitting quietly on a chair pulled up next to the bed.

"Good morning, Lady Legs," Crane said with a respectful tilt of her head. "I thought you'd want to know, your sister is awake. We got the news by pigeon late yesterday."

I smiled, breathing a heavy sigh of relief. I hadn't known how much that had been weighing on me until now. "Is she well?"

Crane nodded. "From the report, she is doing quite well, and will soon be on her way here to see you and Lady Silvermane."

"That's a relief, thank you." I smiled, feeling refreshed by this news and the sunny day. I wanted to get up and move around. But before I could slip out of the large bed Crane spoke again. "There is more news... of a mixed nature." Her tone was odd, and when I turned to her, I couldn't read her expression.

She continued, "Lord Hale's trial concluded two days ago. He was sentenced to hard labor in the quarries of the north-west."

"Oh?" I'd really hoped I'd get the chance to face him, maybe kick him in the balls as part of his punishment. He certainly deserved it, but... I supposed hard labor wasn't *too* bad.

Crane grimaced. "But there was an attempt to free him. Lady Swan, who'd fled the capital after Merlin died, hired a group of mercenaries to attack the caravan." Crane tilted her head to one side. "I suppose I shouldn't call her Lady Swan anymore. Her title has been stripped from her, so I suppose she's just Swan now."

"An attempt?" I didn't like where this was going.

"Yes, the fighting was fierce and the mercenaries killed, but Hale was freed. He fled but was pursued by one of the Nobles escorting him... Lord Horn."

"They let his father escort him?" I blurted. I was certain Hale had escaped now.

"Indeed, and..." Crane sighed heavily. "Lord Horn was forced to kill his son to keep him from escaping."

I stared at Crane, wide-eyed. "Truly?"

"Yes. Hale is dead, and Lord Horn has gone into seclusion." She grimaced. "Swan escaped again, however. The search for her continues."

Wow. That was... mixed news indeed. I didn't fear Swan. She would be a pest at most, and probably soon captured as well. But the loss of Lord Horn... "That must have affected Lady Silvermane deeply."

"Indeed. She has stepped down as head of her House. As to who will replace her, that is still in question. Some in the House would like Lady Dove to take the leadership. But that will be decided internally."

Dove? That could be fun? Us two sisters as House Leaders.

I finally slipped from the bed and went to my wardrobe. Not

caring if Crane saw me naked, I removed my night-dress and began dressing.

"Going somewhere?" she asked. Her tone suggested I should still be resting.

"I've been in that bed for how long?"

"Almost two weeks."

"Exactly. I'm fully healed now and I need to get out and see the world, see people."

Crane laughed. "You're more like Maverick than you know, young one. He never could stay still for long. Would you like an escort?"

I smiled at being compared to Maverick. I was a bit surprised the mention of his name didn't fill me with melancholy. Perhaps now that those behind his death had finally been brought to justice, I could remember him with peace in my heart.

"No, thank you Lady Crane. But... is Lady Skyfire up?"

"Yes," Crane said with a hint of disapproval. "She, like you, can't remain in bed for long. She's been up for a couple days now, despite her injuries." Crane huffed. "I don't understand her insistence on remaining injured."

I pulled on a loose white blouse. "Have you ever been in such a pitched fight?" I asked Crane. I honestly didn't know. She usually stayed away from the fighting.

"I... have been in a few skirmishes in my time, but... probably nothing like what you or she went through, no."

I nodded. "We all carry scars from those fights, Lady Crane. Even if you can't see them, they're there, marks in your soul you have to live with the rest of your life." I gave a heavy sigh, feeling my own internal scars. "Perhaps, for Skyfire, wearing her wounds on the outside is a way to cleanse her soul of the marks on the inside." I looked up at Crane and smiled softly. "Or maybe she's just a stubborn and highly-irrational woman. I don't really know."

Crane laughed. "Did you want me to deliver a message to her for you?"

I nodded. "Yes, if you will. I'd like to have lunch with her."

"I'm sure that can be arranged." Crane rose and, to my surprise, stepped in to embrace me.

"What's this for?" I asked softly, returning the gesture.

"For everything you've done and I'm sure will continue to do for all of us, for our House and this nation of ours." She chuckled softly. "And for staying alive so I wouldn't be forced to lead this House." She squeezed me just a little tighter. "The shoes I'd have to fill would be far too large for me."

I found a tear on my cheek at her praise and kind words. I held her tightly too. "Thank you."

She was back to her usual dignified self when she released me. She walked with me from my room into the hall, explaining that we'd all been put up in Wyvern House's estate in the capital, Skyfire wouldn't have had it any other way. The others were in nearby rooms and Crane pointed out who was where before bidding me good day and going to deliver my message to Lady Skyfire.

I stood in the hall for a moment, deciding who I'd visit first. I knocked then entered the next room, not waiting for anyone to tell me to come in.

I interrupted Ahmaia speaking softly to Alvere. She rose sharply and nodded at me. "Lady Legs."

Alvere sat up in bed, looking far better than he had in the dungeons. I smiled at him, and he returned the gesture. "I'm sorry to interrupt, I can come back."

"No, stay," Ahmaia said, and I caught her glance moving between me and Alvere. "I've had many days to speak to my... my son. It feels so odd to say that." She smiled and her face seemed to light up with it. "I'll stretch my legs and let you two catch up." With another nod of her head, she began to make her way out.

"Thank you, ah... do the Fey have titles or should I just call you Ahmaia?"

She paused next to me, laying a pale hand on my arm. "You could call me Mother, if you like?" Her words were light, her meaning heavy. She seemed to see how that hit me and chuckled softly. "Or Ona, if that is more... comfortable."

"Ona Ahmaia? What does that mean?"

"For the Fey, any woman who is related to you, but not a mother, or sister, or daughter, is Ona."

"Oh... so not a political title, then?"

"We have been blessed to have little politics among the Fey."

I chuckled. "Yeah, that would be a blessing." I nodded to her. "Ona Ahmaia."

She nodded and left.

Once I heard the door shut, I looked at Alvere and mouthed the word *mother*?

He smiled. "I think that just means she likes you." His smile faded. "I've been trying to explain to her how I'd have to marry for my kingdom, not for love." His smile returned quickly. "But I think she'll always see you as my wife, no matter who I marry."

I sat on the bed next to him, putting my arms around him. He did the same as we leaned on each other. "I will always love you, no matter who you're with," I said softly but firmly. "I don't think I can give you up."

"I can't give you up either. Whoever I marry will have to learn to live with you."

That was the best news I'd heard all day.

When he lifted his head from my shoulder and turned to me, I kissed him softly. That led to a very long time of kissing and caressing.

He pulled back and we paused in our enjoyment of each other. "How are *you* feeling?" he asked softly. "I... I've only heard what happened, but some of what I heard..." he trailed off. He looked down and withdrew his hand from where it had crept under my blouse, becoming somber. "I'm glad you killed her." His voice was hard.

I pulled him close and held him for a long moment as his temper turned to tears and he wept. "I felt so helpless!" he sobbed. "And... I... I began to doubt you'd come. I didn't want to, but... it felt like I'd been there for ages, in the dark."

"I'm here now," I said. "And I'll never let you go again, if that's what you want."

He gave a sobbing laugh. "That might make it hard for me to be king."

"I'm sure your people wouldn't mind me sitting on your lap, holding you, while you held court and met with foreign nobles."

He nearly choked on his laughter and tears. "That would be a sight." He drew in a long breath and pulled back. "But... I'll need to stand on my own, Legs." He sniffed a laugh. I joined him. Sometimes my name was just a bit... confusing. He tried again. "I'll need to stand on my own legs... Legs. And I'll never give you up."

I didn't know how it was going to work between us, but I was very happy he'd said that. I added, "With Fin around, I'll never be that far away."

He nodded.

Something in his beryl-blue eyes shifted then, his expression intense and heated. "Take off your clothes, before I tear them off," he said suddenly impassioned.

I did, and he pleasured me repeatedly as our desire spilled over after so long apart.

As such I was a little giddy when I slipped into the next room, which belonged to Sparrow.

From what I'd heard, that last attack from Merlin, crushing her avatar, had nearly killed Sparrow. Ant had brought her back from the brink of death, but not been able to mend all her shattered bones. She was still on the mend, wrapped in heavy bandages.

She smiled when she saw me.

"How are you?" she asked, as if I were the one still in casts and slings.

"I'm doing well enough. How are you?" I moved around the bed, standing next to it. She sat propped up by many pillows and I reached out to stroke her soft, brown hair.

Despite the pain she must have been feeling she smiled, a bright and cheery thing. "I'm doing a lot better now that you're here." The smile faded a little. "There's still a lot of pain and it's hard to sleep. A healer, one with a spirit-gift, but not as strong as Ant's, took a look at my left foot. She said it may never heal properly. She did what she could, but..." Her smile returned and she shrugged. "We'll see."

I couldn't understand how she was so lighthearted about all this.

"I'm so sorry I... I asked you to..." I couldn't quite finish.

Oddly Sparrow only smiled broader. "No, Legs, never apologize, not for that. My body may be broken, but my spirit has never felt better."

I cocked my head to one side, curious what she meant by that, as I came to sit on the side of the bed next to her.

She reached out to me with one arm — only a few bandages on it — and I took her hand in both of mine. "Legs, I... I was always so terrified to fight, terrified of... of being hurt... like this." I opened my mouth for another apology, but she went on quickly. "And when you asked me to help you, I was so afraid." Her smile seemed to brighten even more. "But I did it, Legs. I fought against a mistweaver. I distracted her long enough for you and Ahmaia to finish her. *I* did that!"

"And it—"

"And it was *glorious*," she said, cutting me off. "I've never felt so alive and brave and... and..." She sighed, her smile fading only a little. "And now I know the pain is worth it."

I motioned to her bandaged body. "All of this... was worth it?" I couldn't help but ask.

"Yes, Legs. Don't you see? I lived!" Her mood darkened just a little. "True, I only lived because Ant was around and he can't heal anymore, but still... I lived." Her green-eyed gaze met mine. "Yes, I'm in pain, but most of this will heal. I may limp, or ache a little on stormy days, but that doesn't matter." She beamed once again. "Now I understand what you and the others feel, what you go through, when you throw yourselves into battle. You know you're doing it because it must be done, because the nation needs it, or your friends need it. And... I knew that before, in my head, but I never really understood it, never... felt it. I do now."

I was a bit dumbfounded. "So, you'll be throwing yourself into battle from now on?"

She quirked a grin. "Once I'm healed, if I'm needed, I guess I will."

I shook my head. "Most people in your place would feel the exact opposite, I'm sure."

"Well, yes, the pain is bad, but knowing that I'm in pain because I helped the ones I loved and saved my nation... that makes it worth it."

"You're a strange little bird."

"And you wouldn't have me any other way."

"No, I wouldn't." I leaned in and kissed her gently. "Thank you."

She beamed. "You're welcome."

I sighed. "Sorry I haven't been to see you until now."

"That's understandable. You were hurt. And Ant and Alvere come to see me regularly to check in, then Silence started coming as well. He... seems different."

"Oh?" I hadn't seen him since the fight. "How?"

"More serious."

Silence had never really been a jovial fellow, always a bit somber. "*More* serious?"

"Yes. I think you need to talk to him."

"I was on my way there next."

"Then go. I'll be waiting, return when you can."

I nodded, kissed her again, squeezed her hand, then left.

In the next room I found Silence dressed all in black, standing with his back to me, gazing out the windows. He turned as I entered. Something about him, maybe the black suit, or how he stood with his arms clasped behind him, or his grim features, made him seem dangerous now, in a way he never had before. Certainly, the clothes looked exquisite on his slender form. Still, he smiled, if only slightly, when he saw me.

"Hello Legs."

I went to him, embraced him tightly. After a moment he held me too.

"I'm so glad you're alive and well!" I said into his shoulder.

I felt his head move next to mine, nodding. "As am I for you."

I released him after a long moment, standing back with my hands on his shoulders to peer into his face. "Sparrow said you were different, but this...?"

His smile appeared again, only for an instant. "Yes, dying will do that to you."

"Dying?" I furrowed my brow. "I heard Ant brought you back from the brink, but..."

Silence shook his head. "Perhaps that is the case, but that is not what I believe. I believe he reached into The Pits and pulled me from the grasp of death itself. I will forever be indebted to him. I believe it was bringing me back that burned him out." He shook his head. And with that one movement I understood the change which had come over him.

He wasn't more serious so much as in mourning. Mourning for his lost previous life, his youth, his innocence. Mourning for Ant's lost gift, which he believed to be his fault. He was a changed man indeed, and I had the feeling this sense of grief would linger with him.

"And what did you learn from death?" I asked. I wasn't sure where those words came from. They seemed to shock Silence as well.

"Learn?" He blinked. "Ah... well, I learned I didn't much like it and don't want to die any time soon."

I laughed a little at that. "And?"

"And..." He furrowed his brow in thought for a moment before he cocked his head to once side. "I learned that charging in against a foe with rage in your heart is a bad idea." He let out a self-deprecating laugh. "I honestly thought I could defeat her, myself alone, in that moment. I felt so powerful and purposeful and unstoppable. I thought I could get vengeance for what she'd done to Alvere." Silence grimaced, then shook his head. "But she... was so quick. Then I was choking on mists..."

I understood. I still shied away from the memories of when we'd found Alvere. They were too painful.

Silence let out a long sigh. "But now I know." Again, that fleeting smile surfaced and faded. "I'm not a front-line warrior, I'm... an assassin." He grew hard then, and I recalled the many guards he'd slaughtered in the tunnels. "I strike from the shadows, from... silence. I am cold, not hot with rage."

"I think you're hot," I said playfully.

The grin flashed again. Raising a hand to my cheek, he cupped it softly, and I leaned my face into his touch, closing my eyes. He drew me close, his lips to mine, soft and gentle. And despite what he had called himself, he was very hot with need soon after that.

What we shared then was a quick and impassioned lovemaking, a sating of hungers, not a tender moment. We didn't even fully undress.

"See," I said afterward, a little breathless. "You can still be hot and passionate."

"With you, yes, but not in battle."

I nodded, hoping I understood.

Crane found me in Silence's room. She knocked first and announced herself, so when she entered, it was to see us straightening our clothes.

She shook her head as she said: "Skyfire is ready for lunch in the atrium."

"I have no idea where that is."

"I'll take you there."

I kissed Silence good-bye. As I left, I looked back. Yes, he had changed. I'd never think of him as a boy again. He was a man now, and there was majesty in that, but also a touch of sadness.

CHAPTER 29

The Council of Nobles looked far different than it had the day Maverick had chosen me for his house. So many of the faces I'd known were gone, and one entire house was missing. Owl House had been removed from the lists. Perhaps it would be replaced with another in time, but for now, its members who had not been involved with Merlin — which were few — had been given the choice of losing their title or joining another house. A few had come to Spider House, penitent and wishing for a second chance. I had granted them that chance.

I sat as House Leader, with Crane standing at my side. Others from my house sat in the gallery around us. Members of the public crammed into the theatre where the Noble's Tests were held. They wished to see who would be crowned king or queen, which House would be elevated to Royal.

Silvermane no longer wished to be queen. She'd stepped down as leader of her House and gone into seclusion. That meant we needed to select a new monarch... again.

Skyfire, now the most senior House Leader, rose to open the ceremony.

"Today we crown a new monarch for Elista!" Her voice didn't carry well, harsh and raspy, but she'd insisted on doing this, and not having Drake do it for her. "This is a solemn yet joyous occasion. And though our nation has been through turbulent times, I am certain that whoever is chosen here today will usher us into a time of prosperity and peace!"

She looked around at the others. I did so as well.

Next to Skyfire sat the next most senior House Head, Grizzly. Ursa stood proud next to him.

Lady Tanuki and her second Red were the next most senior. Then Lord Spike and his second, Lord Quill of Porcupine House.

I was now the fifth most senior House Head on the Council, since I'd technically been appointed to my post before Lady Margay.

Margay had disavowed the behavior of her predecessors and vowed that her House would be a strong supporter of peace with Vauphan. Her second was Lord Serval, a serious looking fellow, tall and lean.

House Pterolycus had been renamed to House Kitsune for its new leader. Lady Kitsune had been my instructor at Silverveil, and I knew she'd do well as leader of her house. She hadn't been involved in Fang's support of Merlin, but she'd still have a lot of work to do — like Lady Margay and House Panther — to prove herself in the eyes of the public and the Nobility... and she knew it. Her second was Lord Husky, a jovial man with a ready grin.

Finally, and a thrill for me to see, Dove was head of House Pegasus. She was resplendent in her silver Fey armor, looking every inch the leader. She smiled at me when our eyes met. It wasn't unheard of for siblings to be Heads of Houses, but it certainly wasn't common. Her second was her long-time friend, Lady Willow. Lord Horn had resigned his Noble status and lived in seclusion. Lady Silvermane had done the same. She now lived with Skyfire, wishing only for a quiet life, out of the public eye. I'd spoken to her briefly while staying at Skyfire's estate and she seemed a reduced version of herself. I hoped someday, with Skyfire's love, she'd once again be the strong woman I'd known.

All attention was on Skyfire, which she drank in with a grin. She would give her vote for the next monarch first. The rumor was, she'd vote for herself, which was allowed.

"I Skyfire, of House Wyvern, select my candidate for monarch..." She knew everyone was hanging on her next words and drew out her pause. "Lady Legs of House Spider."

I sat a little straighter. "What?" I whispered to no one in particular.

Actually, that doesn't surprise me. Auwei said confidently.

Oh?

Yes, she didn't want to be queen when we selected last time, why would that change now?

I thought she voted for Silvermane because she loved her. But me? Why me?

I think we're about to find out.

Skyfire went on. "Lady Legs was of pivotal importance in defeating the tyrant Merlin and leading the Houses in defense of our proud nation. I believe she would make a great queen for us all!"

Oh.

See.

No, I didn't, not yet.

Skyfire sat and Grizzly stood. "I second Skyfire's nomination of Lady Legs. When we few Houses gathered to move against Merlin, it was she who led us, who guided us. She, though young, has all the experience and wisdom needed to lead our nation into peace... and Spirits-Forfend it should happen again... into war."

And now I was starting to see. I'd seen it then as well, when I'd been called to meet with Grizzly, Tanuki, and Spike to decide how to move against Merlin. They were all life-long political Nobles

and had little experience with what I'd been doing all of my —
admittedly short — time as a Noble: fighting to defend my nation.
They'd expected me to lead them and I had, with them as my
Council. And that's when it clicked for me. I wouldn't be leading
alone if chosen now. I'd have all of these Nobles to help me. I had
little experience with politics, but they did. They could guide me
through that, but it was clear to me now, as I looked around, that
none of them wanted to lead. They were happy to follow... me.

Lady Tanuki voted for me as well, as did Spike.

It didn't feel right to vote for myself, so I voted instead for Lady
Skyfire. She chuckled and shook her head. Clearly, she didn't want
to be queen.

But other than myself it was unanimous. I was voted the next
Queen of Elista. And when all the votes were in, everyone looked
at me. The crowd cheered in the gallery and chanted "Queen
Legs" and "Liberator of Elista!"

"Say something," Crane advised in a whisper. "Keep it short
and simple, be gracious."

Thank the Spirits for Crane. I'd have her to help me as well.

I rose and drew in a long breath. Everyone hushed.

You can do this, Auwei said, sounding so very proud.

"My dear people," I said, raising my voice and hoping it
carried. "I thank you for your confidence in me. As has been said, I
hope to bring only peace and prosperity to Elista. I am honored
and humbled to be chosen as your queen and see it as my duty to
serve you, the people of this great nation."

Another resounding cheer went up, and I sat slowly.

"Well done," Crane said, and I glanced over to see her smile of
motherly pride.

When the cheering died down, a single voice rose above the
rest. "Might I approach the esteemed Council of Nobles and Her
Majesty, Queen Legs of Elista?" The crowd below parted, and
there stood Alvere in full kingly regalia: crown, lush purple cape

edged with pure ermine, and his usual blue-trimmed-with-gold suit.

"Approach, King Alvere of Vauphan," I said.

He grinned at me and stepped forward before the Council of Nobles. He took a long moment to look at everyone, then spoke. "Not long ago, I promised my hand in marriage to whom-so-ever you chose as your queen."

Oh! Right!

His gaze landed upon me. "I would like to keep that promise now, if it is the will of the Council and The Queen?" He approached, mounting steps onto the stage, then knelt before me. "Will you bring our nations together, Queen Legs of Elista?"

Pits yeah I would!

Please don't say that out loud, Auwei giggled.

I looked to the other Nobles. "What say you?" I asked them.

"This would bring peace and expand our influence," Lady Tanuki said evenly. Then, she surprised me by winking at me.

"Oh... just marry him, we all know you love him," Dove said and everyone — after a moment of stunned silence — laughed.

I rose and went to Alvere. I gave him my hand and he kissed it, rising.

"Have you discussed this with the others?" I asked in a breath of a whisper.

"Yes, we've worked it out. Everyone's on board." He smiled.

Louder I said, "I accept your hand in marriage and bind our nations together in peace."

Another cheer rose up.

Alvere and I embraced in a sedate ceremonious way, exchanging a chaste kiss. And with that the ceremony ended...

... and so began the hard work of ruling not one, but two nations.

CHAPTER 30

That is my story.

If you're curious how I managed to keep everyone I loved close to me... well, it wasn't that hard. Lady Sparrow, once she'd recovered, became my lady in waiting, always at my side, so it was never awkward if she shared my suite of rooms. Silence and Ant became my — and Alvere's — permanent guards, so they were never far from our sides and were expected to be close to us when we retired for the evenings.

Silence eventually became the spy-master for our twin nations, and though he was often away, whenever he returned, he stayed with us. Luckily, being a master spy... very few people ever knew he was there.

Yet for all our secrecy, there were few who didn't know the truth of our little group relationship. In Elista, we were looked upon with joy, but in Vauphan, things were different. Alvere and I worked for a long time with the nobles to try to disband the hereditary inheritance of roles, but they fought us at every turn and didn't much like the uncertainty around the official heir to the throne.

My first child was Alvere's of course. She was born a little late, at mid-winter. Given the dark times, when we needed the light the most, we named her Dawn. She would not be an heir in Elista, but someday she might become a Noble and rise to the throne, if that was her destiny. Yet, she would be queen of Vauphan, no matter what. That much, at least, we were able to change. The Vauphani royal inheritance would go to the firstborn, not the first male child.

Dove married Fin and he joined her House. I was sad to see him go.

It was not always easy being the queen, especially during the war with Thraan. But that... is not my story to tell. That tale belongs to another, well... two others, actually. And when they are ready, I'm sure they will tell it, probably far more eloquently than I've told mine.

And so, I end my story, and wish you all the best in yours.

I remain your humble servant:

Queen Legs of Elista and Vauphan

Want another action-packed, sexy reverse harem epic fantasy?

Check out *Double Discovery*, the first book in my next epic fantasy reverse harem series.

All it takes is a single step to change your fate...

OTHER BOOKS BY CLARA WILS

THE GRECIAN GODDESS TRILOGY

written with Tessa Cole

Kiss of the Goddess, book 1

Power of the Goddess, book 2

Bonds of the Goddess, book 3

THE MISTS OF ELISTA

Bonds and Blood, book 1

Shape and Shadows, book 2

Form and Fury, book 3

SHADOWS OVER ELISTA

Double Discovery, book 1

Double Danger, book 2

Double Disaster, book 3

Double Doom, book 4

Double Destiny, book 5

SECRETS GODS KEEP

written with Tessa Cole

Craving Demons, book 1

Chaos Demons, book 2

Claiming Demons, book 3